SCHOOL OF REBIRTH AND REINCARNATION

FULL OCCULT TRILOGY

TOBIAS WADE

This is a work of fiction. Names, characters, organizations, businesses, places, events and incidents either are the product of the author's imagination or are used fictitiously. Any resemblance to actual persons, living or dead, or actual events is entirely coincidental.

First Edition: February 2020
School of Rebirth and Reincarnation
Full Occult Trilogy

PUBLISHING

Copyright © 2020
Tobias Wade

All rights reserved. This book or any portion thereof may not be reproduced or used in any manner whatsoever without the express written permission of the publisher except for the use of brief quotations in a book review.

WHAT ARE YOU AFRAID OF?

Join the Haunted House Book Club
For free books and stories.

TobiasWade.Com

CONTENTS

THE ROAD FROM DEATH

1. Mrs. Robinson's Adventure	3
2. Waking Up Again	24
3. Daymare 7	36
4. The Weighing Ceremony	48
5. The Mortuary	61
6. The Whispering Room	75
7. Transhumanism	84
8. Necromancy	97
9. Demonology	110
10. Halloween	122
11. Zombies	139
12. The Netherworld	151
13. Visoloth	164
14. The Matriarch's Wrath	175
15. Christmas	185
16. Spring Semester	194
17. The Contract Ends	204

THE SOUL NET

1. Soul Food	223
2. Back to School Shopping	235
3. Netherworld	247
4. Mirror of Ancestry	262
5. The Burning Altar	272
6. The Living Road	286
7. Demons of the Past	299
8. Halloween	317
9. Dweller Studies	332

10. Meep Warlington — 348
11. Trans Dimensional Department — 364
12. Christmas Break — 377
13. Hell on Earth — 389
14. Legacy — 404
15. The Soul Net — 418

NETHERWORLD

1. The Shallow End — 437
2. The Sylo — 450
3. Death of the Unliving — 466
4. Twisting Dimensions — 483
5. Bah-Rabba Kaba — 498
6. The Soul Net — 513
7. Demon Food — 530
8. The Summoning — 546
9. An Imp for Everyone — 562
10. The Living and the Damned — 577
11. Doors of Almorda — 593
12. Union of the Primes — 608

About the Author — 629

THE ROAD FROM DEATH

MRS. ROBINSON'S ADVENTURE

Mrs. Robinson wasn't in her room where she usually sat by the window. She wasn't on the sofa lording over the TV, nor in the kitchen supervising the cooking, nor anywhere else in her two-bedroom house. In fact, Mrs. Robinson has been missing for three days, and speculation has already begun on whether she would ever return.

"She could be dead," Samantha considered. The young girl spoke casually as if she was wondering whether it would rain tomorrow. "Dead in a ditch, I figure. Went and got smacked by a car on her way home, with little pieces of her raining down all over the neighborhood."

"Surely we would have seen the pieces?" Claire replied with undisguised horror. Claire was considerably smaller of the two girls, though they were both twelve years old, and she seemed even tinier now with thin arms tightly clutching her loose t-shirt against her body.

"Not necessarily," Samantha replied solemnly. "It could have happened at night. If I were the driver who hit her, I would have jumped out and gathered up all the pieces to hide the evidence of my crime."

"No!" Claire whined, shrinking farther into herself to form a sad little huddle which practically melted into her bed.

"Or maybe he didn't have to gather her up at all, see," Samantha continued, leaning forward to drive the words home. "Maybe birds picked up the little pieces, so that by morning there wasn't a single piece of Mrs. Robinson at all."

"I don't believe it!" Claire squealed.

Samantha shrugged, settling back into her seat, her long black skirt swishing over the rough carpet beneath her chair. She began to pick at her lavender fingernails, peeking at Claire from the corner of her eye as she continued.

"Well I'm not pretending to know for certain. I'm just trying to cheer you up by giving you the good scenario. It could be much, much worse after-all."

Claire bolted upright from where she lay on her bed. Her wide blue eyes quivered with apprehension, her skin so flushed that all her freckles seemed to dissolve.

"What could possibly be worse than being smashed into smithereens and eaten by birds?"

Samantha spent several exquisitely long seconds continuing to pick at her nail before looking up at Claire.

"Are we going to stay indoors all day? Aren't we going to play any games?"

"What else could have happened to Mrs. Robinson?" Claire shouted. "Tell me, or I'm going to tell your mother that you've been horrible to me!"

A sly grin flirted with the corner of Samantha's mouth. She narrowed her green eyes and leaned close to Claire so that the girls' faces were only inches apart.

"Well at least if she was hit by a car on her way home, then she would have still been trying to come home. There's always the chance that she doesn't much care for you and would rather not come home at all."

Claire jerked away from Samantha as though struck by an invisible slap, flinging herself face first against her pillow. Samantha had never heard a sound as pitiful as the sobbing howl which blasted from Claire's direction, the pillow only muffling it enough to provide a haunting echo to the cries. Samantha plugged her fingers into her ears and waited for Claire's outpouring to stop—she must draw breath eventually—but even when Claire paused to inhale, the ragged breath only transformed into two cement trucks making love.

The door flew open and in fluttered Claire's mother, Mrs. Thistle. She was a short, stout woman who appeared to possess a very soft hug, and she immediately demonstrated this upon her daughter. Unfortunately, the gesture only seemed to squeeze the remaining air from Claire, whose howl of anguish reached a truly piercing crescendo.

"Easy easy, there you go, I've got you," Mrs. Thistle said, rocking Claire gently back and forth.

"Mrs. Robinson doesn't love me anymore!" Claire cried, heaving for breath.

"Oh, darling, don't say such a thing. Of course she does!"

Samantha silently shrugged behind Mrs. Thistle's back, making a gesture with her hands that looked convincingly like an explosion, complete with the wiggly fingers which surely represented the pieces flying every which way.

"She's been smashed to bits then!" Claire continued to howl.

Mrs. Thistle glared over her shoulder at Samantha, who was now avoiding her gaze by engrossing herself once more in her lavender nails.

"Anyway, I think my mom is going to pick me up soon..." Samantha started to say. But she never got any further, because she made the mistake of looking up and catching a full dose of Mrs. Thistle's thundering glower.

"Well you can't blame me for being honest—" Samantha began again, having forgotten that she was still a twelve-year old girl, and that children could in fact be blamed for practically anything.

Ten minutes later, Samantha and Claire were both standing

outside in the warm August sun. Samantha was holding a stack of "Missing" posters with Mrs. Robinson's picture on it, although from the foul expression on Samantha's face, one might guess she was actually holding a heaping pile of someone else's soggy underwear.

"Can't you just buy a new cat?" Samantha whined. "Or adopt one from the shelter. It would think you're a hero for saving it."

Claire's glare was cold enough to make Samantha shiver despite the sun.

"Dogs are nice," Samantha mumbled, not meeting Claire's eyes.

There wasn't any fight left in her though. Samantha meekly followed her companion as they began their journey along Bentley Street where they both lived. Every time they reached a light or telephone pole, *slap* goes the picture of a very fat black cat stuffed into a very small glass bowl. *Squeee* goes the electric tape. *Crinkle crinkle* as it's fastened on. Then they're off again, no words exchanged as there was no need. Samantha was beginning to feel repressed and stodgy from holding so many sarcastic comments in for so long, and she was about to quip on how excellent dogs are at finding their way home when Claire spoke first.

"I found Mrs. Robinson three years ago before mom and I moved here. She was in a plastic grocery bag along with four other kittens who were all black like her, brothers and sisters probably. Someone had left them in the trash by the grocery store, right on top of a greasy old pizza box. The bag was tied at the top, and there wasn't even a way for them to breathe. I don't know how long they were in there, but none of them were moving when I found them, not even Mrs. Robinson."

Samantha didn't know what she was supposed to say about that, so she respected the wisdom of silence.

"We named her Mrs. Robinson after the song. There's a line that goes 'God bless you please, Mrs. Robinson', so I just thought that if there was anyone who needed to be blessed, it had to be her. And I guess God really did, because pretty soon she started moving again even though none of the others did. We gave her some milk, then Mom rushed off to the store to get some real cat food and medical supplies because it looked like Mrs. Robinson hadn't eaten in a really long while. And the whole-time mom was gone, I kept thinking that if Mrs. Robinson stops moving again that it would be my fault, because I was the only one in the world she had left to depend on. And every time she swallowed a mouthful of milk, or turned her head a little to look at me, well that was just a miracle that might be taken back any second. And now it has. Three years later, and I still wasn't ready."

Samantha silently thanked her mother for giving her sunglasses to wear outside, because at that moment she was very glad Claire couldn't see the moisture in her eyes.

"Nobody looks at posters," Samantha replied. "We should knock on doors instead. We can do the whole block in less than an hour, and then we'll know for sure if anyone saw her."

The girls left their posters and their tape at the end of Claire's driveway and began to knock on every door instead. There was no answer from the tall gray house with the carved lion head railings. There was an old woman named Warlinksi who lived in the next house with its forest of potted plants, but she hadn't seen Mrs. Robinson, and said she wouldn't tell them even if she did. Warlinski didn't understand why people don't just "mince cats up like any other critter". Claire thanked her anyway, for she was raised to thank people for giving you their time, even if they didn't spend it the way you hoped.

Samantha was making a real effort to be supportive now, but she still wanted to skip the next house. All the kids in town knew that a murderer lived there, even if the adults didn't want to admit it. The house even looked like the type of place a murderer would stay: perpetually dead trees rising like tombstones in the arid and withered garden, a deck that was rotten and fallen through in places, and a large collection of strange ornaments, wind chimes, and bead necklaces with funny stones which dangled from nails haphazardly hammered into the peeling plank walls.

"Mrs. Robinson wouldn't have come here," Samantha declared. "She had—has—better sense than that."

"Then we won't have to stay long," Claire replied as she picked her way between the brown and stringy bushes. She hopped over the first rotten step to alight on the next solid one above.

"It's just that my mom's going to be picking me up soon, and —"

"Not until dinner time. My mom called and said you were going to help me because you're a kind and gentle person. That is true, isn't it, Sam?"

"That's not fair." Samantha grimaced. "Your mother knows full well that I'd rather be a witch and put curses on people. I said as much in my Christmas card last year, and I know she saw it because she kept asking my mom whether I would like to join you all at church after that."

Claire wasn't paying attention. She was facing the house, calling, "Hello, anyone home?" She rapped on the door with her fist which caused it to rattle loosely in its frame. Samantha found sudden interest in peering through a hole in one of the dead trees, which was hollow and turned out to be filled with colorful stones and broken glass.

The muffled sound of a chair sliding against a padded floor came from inside the house. Claire looked over her shoulder and gestured emphatically for Samantha to join her on the old porch. Samantha pretended not to notice.

Standing alone in front of the dilapidated house, the idea that a murderer might really live inside didn't sound hard to believe after-all. And what would a murderer do if they opened the door to find two young girls, defenseless and alone? Claire's mother thought they were still putting up posters on the public street. No one knew where they were, and if they were to not come home again…

The door began to open, and all the worst parts of Claire's imagination came out at once. She forgot about the decaying step in her haste until her foot landed hard on the splintering wood. A shrill little scream preceded a thumping crash as she tumbled to sprawl on the dirt beyond. Claire scrambled to her feet and was about to launch herself away once more, but the moment she balanced her weight onto the offended ankle she felt it buckle in protest. A sharp, stinging pain devoured her senses.

Claire was on the ground again, staring at her scraped hands which had broken her fall. There were footsteps behind her now, and Claire was absolutely certain that the murderer stood only a foot away. Could she outrun him? Not likely. Fight? As if more capable victims hadn't tried before. His shadow was already looming over her, and Claire's lightning succession of thoughts only led to the inescapable conclusion of her impending demise. The sole reasonable course of action was to begin screaming again.

"Cut that out, won't you?" came the kindly old voice behind her.

Claire snapped her mouth shut for a moment before breathlessly demanding, "What did you say?"

"He means that if you don't stop screaming, he's going to cut your tongue out," Samantha volunteered cheerfully, still standing nonchalantly beside her dead tree.

Claire's eyes widened. She began to draw a great lungful of air to—

"That's not what I meant at all!" the voice behind Claire implored. "I just want you to stop screaming, if you please. You'll wake the little one, and Mandy just got him to sleep."

Claire didn't suppose a murderer would have cared about waking a baby, and he definitely wouldn't say please. If anything, he sounded like he was the one who was afraid. Claire wiped her eyes with the back of her hand before shuffling around on her knees.

"Of course a murderer would ask that," Samantha added, sagely stroking her chin. "He wouldn't want anyone to hear you screaming and come save you."

Claire could now see that the murderer in question was a pale-skinned elderly man with a long droopy nose like a sock half-filled with sand. He was tall and thin, very much like a spider which had learned to stand on its hind legs and dress itself in rather baggy and faded clothing. His wide deep-set eyes were as grey and calm as the sea before a storm. Claire felt immensely relieved, realizing that a strong tempered toddler would likely be sufficient to push this frail old thing around.

"I'm not a murderer!" the old man retorted, a faint flush rising on his cheeks. "That's Barnes' fault, my daughter's no-good boyfriend."

"Your daughter married a murderer?" Samantha asked, suddenly eager. "How many people has he killed? If it's at least three, then it counts as being a serial killer, but only if they weren't all done at the same time, otherwise he's a mass murderer instead."

The old man shook his head, "He hasn't killed anybody either. But he started telling stories about me and now everybody thinks..." his voice trailed off into indistinct muttering which might have been an attempt to disguise the type of language twelve-year old girls aren't supposed to hear, even if they secretly say those very same words in their head at every opportunity.

"You must be Noah then," Samantha declared. "I heard that people keep catching you with dead animals. They say that you kill them for fun. That's even worse than killing people you know, because animals never cheat on their taxes or lie to their mothers."

"I don't '*kill*' them, I put them to sleep," Noah replied indignantly, "and only if they're very sick and in pain. I do work at a veterinary clinic, after-all."

"I heard you like to watch them die," Samantha pressed.

"What's the crime in that?"

Claire and Samantha exchanged an unsettled glance.

"You *do* like to watch things die?" Samantha asked incredulously, her usual playful tone drenched in accusation.

Noah looked down at the peeling rubber sole of his sneakers. "It's not cruel or anything. I just... like watching what happens next." His eyes darted back to the girls suspiciously. "What are you doing here? Do your parents know where you are?"

"Did you kill Claire's cat?" Samantha demanded. Then, on a lighter note, she added, "Oh, this is Claire, and I'm Samantha, or Sam, but never Sammy."

"Hi," Claire mumbled, flourishing a half-hearted wave.

"Hello, Claire. Hello, never-Sammy," Noah replied, lighting up with good humor as Sam rolled her eyes. "Is the cat black with a white tuft on its chest like a general wearing a medal?"

"You've seen Mrs. Robinson?! Is she in the animal hospital?" Claire exploded, bouncing onto her feet. She had forgotten about her injured ankle in the excitement, so this action caused her to stagger dangerously. Samantha was there to catch her though, supporting her as they both turned on Noah ferociously.

"She's right there, isn't she?" Noah said, pointing behind Claire. The girls spun on the spot while still holding hands, almost knocking both of them to the ground in the process. They stared at the empty patch of dirt for a moment before rounding once more on the old man.

"Right where?" Claire asked.

"He's teasing you; there's nothing," Samantha said. "Don't you know it's not nice to play tricks on innocent little girls? Especially when they know how to trick you back."

"I'm not talking about her body," Noah said, sighing as though the words were weighing him down. He sat heavily on the creaking wooden steps and his remaining air all flooded out in a puff. "I'm talking about her spirit. She's chasing that butterfly, although she's never going to catch it because the butterfly is alive and well..."

The girls looked again, and sure enough they saw a butterfly dancing on the wind. Claire cast an uneasy glance at her friend, and she wasn't thrilled to see Samantha smiling. She always smiled when she wasn't supposed to, and that made Claire cross.

"This isn't a game, you know," Claire said. "Mrs. Robinson really is lost, and I'm worried about her. So if you aren't going to help us, then you might as well be a murderer because Mrs. Robinson needs us and—"

"I'm sorry," Noah cut her off, his voice gentle but sure. "If you don't see her now, then no amount of looking is going to help. But you should know that she is having a wonderful time, which means she didn't suffer much. When animals have a painful death, they tend to mope around and complain for a good deal afterward."

"Can you really see spirits?" Samantha inquired.

"It runs in the family," Noah replied, a bit defensively. He cast a wary glance around as though worried he would be overheard. "Cats can too, you know. Whenever they're fascinated by something you can't see, you can be pretty sure there's a spirit there. Dogs can't of course—too many distractions in this world, I suppose. Most people can't either, but people can't see their own nose and that's right in front of their face. Would either of you like a cup of hot cocoa?"

Claire seriously considered her nose, judging the merit of this explanation. She didn't seem satisfied.

"Yes, please," Samantha instantly replied. Standing, Noah offered a hand to help her over the rotten step. She chose to hop it on her own instead of accepting his assistance. "What does a spirit look like?" she pestered.

"It looks like how Christmas feels," Noah remarked instantly. "Would you take a cup as well, Claire? It's the least I can do."

Claire had absolutely no desire to enter the crumbling house of the strange old man whose denial of being a murderer was dubious at best. Her ankle was starting to feel much better, and she could turn around right now and be back on the street to resume her search. To continue a seemingly endless search, ignoring her best clue which was the first person to have accurately described Mrs. Robinson.

"It's only polite," Samantha said, her face refusing to match the gravity of the situation.

"Oh, very well, but only if Mrs. Robinson can come too," Claire relented.

Noah crossed the porch and opened the door, and the two girls followed him, completely oblivious to Mrs. Robinson's spirit which hopped up the stairs behind them. So too were they unaware of the gaunt stony creature sitting on the mailbox at the end of the driveway. They weren't aware of the long, hooked claws on the end of its wings or its yellow lidless eyes which watched them enter. Noah's gaze lingered on the creature for a moment, but he quickly averted his gaze as he smiled down at the girls who were walking past him into the house.

"I just want you to know," Samantha was saying to the old man, "that I will find out if you're trying to play a trick on Claire. Then you really *will be* seeing spirits, because you'll be one of them."

Noah chuckled and bowed low as he held the door open for the children. "I shall take your warning to heart and tread the line of truth with the utmost care."

That was good enough for Samantha, and so it was good enough for Claire as well.

The interior of the house was in no better repair than the run-down front. The carpet was patchy and threadbare, and only occasional tufts of color hinted that it might have been red in a previous life. Splotches on the ceiling marked where water had once dripped through, and the sofa and chairs had stains on them in enough colors that it was difficult to determine which were part of the actual design.

"We have visitors, Mandy," Noah called softly upon entering. He held the door open for considerably longer than necessary, his eyes presumably following an invisible cat which was taking time deciding whether to follow. The children sat carefully on the couch as though expecting it to collapse as soon as they rested.

"Hello, darlings."

The girls jumped, not having realized that Mandy had been sitting in the dark chair beside them this whole time. She looked to be in her thirties, wearing black all the way from her long brass-buttoned coat and her lacy blouse to her high leather boots. Her skin was as pale as a corpse, and the only color about her was the short golden hair which sprayed wildly from her head like a hose blocked by a thumb.

"Claire, Samantha, this is my daughter Mandy," Noah introduced the newcomers, a touch of pride in his voice. "She's such a devoted mother that it was like she was born to raise little Lewis. I swear she can be all the way across town and still hear him cry when he falls down."

"Oh please, you'll make me blush," Mandy said, her white skin showing no sign that this biologically was possible. "I suppose you're here about the kitten?" she added, looking at the same empty spot in the doorway.

"Mrs. Robinson is fully grown," Claire replied. "Perhaps you've got the wrong cat after all…"

"Not on that side she isn't," Mandy responded amiably. "They're always young again after they die. Didn't you know?"

"The cat doesn't want to come in," Noah grumbled, still holding the door. "Make up your mind, won't you?"

"Not so loud, he's still asleep," Mandy said. Then to the girls, "I'm so sorry about the mess in here. As soon as Lewis' father gets home we're going to move into a nicer place, so we haven't been worrying so much about keeping up with things."

"*When his father gets home,*" Noah mimicked. "Never mind that we haven't seen him since the baby was born, surely tomorrow is the day!"

"What's Mrs. Robinson doing?" Claire interrupted, trying to refocus the topic.

"She's walking away now," Noah sighed. "Just as well really. There's the spirit of a raccoon living upstairs, and they might not get along. He's been there ever since before the place was built, and he's never quite forgiven us for it."

"We have to follow her then!" Claire leapt to her feet, grateful for an excuse to leave.

"There's really no point," Noah replied. "Are you sure you wouldn't rather have some cocoa? We already have milk on the stove for Lewis."

"There's every point!" Claire insisted, hurrying back onto the front porch. "Where is she? Over here? Am I close? How about now?" Claire stretched her hands, feeling blindly through the air.

"Lower," Noah said. "Over there, rubbing against the railing."

Dusk was already gathering outside, and Claire had trouble following Noah's finger. She moved to where she thought he was pointing and reached out again. "How about now?"

"She's heading through the yard, toward the sidewalk."

"At least she doesn't have to worry about cars anymore," Samantha interjected. She'd just emerged from the house with a steaming cup in her hands. Mandy's pale face loomed behind her in the shadows.

"What are you waiting for then?" Claire asked, bounding down the steps, careful to skip the rotten one this time.

"I don't think that's a good idea," Noah cautioned. "Spirits can go places that people can't follow. What will you even do if you catch her?"

"She followed me here though, so she still sees me," Claire announced stubbornly. "I bet she's trying to send me a message or lead me somewhere."

"You have to come," Samantha said firmly to Noah. "We can't follow her without you."

"I've tried following spirits before," Noah despondently replied. "They always walk through a building or a highway or something. You can't keep up."

"The dead aren't nearly as stubborn as Claire," Samantha said, dragging the old man down the steps by one of his bony, wrinkled hands with their veins that could be felt through the skin. "Just point the way and we'll figure out how to get there."

"Oh go ahead, dad," Mandy bade them off from the door. "Lewis will have a chance to sleep, and then he'll be able to stay up late and watch your old movies with you by the time you get back."

"Dr. Strangelove is not an old movie!" Noah retorted. "I may be getting older, but movies aren't. Unlike me, they look exactly the same as the day they were made. Oh bother, this must be how dust-bunnies feel being swept from home against their will."

Despite his protests, the old man allowed Samantha to lead him to the sidewalk. Claire and Samantha didn't have any definite target to follow as they couldn't see Mrs. Robinson, so they kept their attention fixed on Noah as he loped in front of them. Noah often paused to wait for Mrs. Robinson to finish smelling a plant or rolling in the dirt, and he commented on this for the girls' benefit. Other times he declared that the cat had walked directly into a house, forcing all of them to race around to the other side. Noah was worried that the cat would then retrace its path, or exit the house from a side, or even stay in there, but so far Mrs. Robinson showed no inclination to deceive them.

Off they went between the houses, over the low brick wall, along the sidewalk and up to the intersection. The sun had now completely set, and the street was aglow with the racing blur of light. They were approaching midtown where the buildings soared imposingly and the lights glittered like a million unblinking eyes.

"Why doesn't Mrs. Robinson just come home?" Claire dreamily inquired, her unfocused gaze tracing the steel and concrete heights. Samantha grabbed her friend by the hand to prevent her from stepping off the sidewalk while their traffic light was still red.

"Keep walking during the red light and you'll find out," Samantha said. "Hey, Noah, did she cross here?"

Noah nodded and pointed toward the left side of a large apartment building ahead. The light turned green, but Noah hesitated to cross as the other people streamed past.

"Hurry up then!" Samantha insisted. She grabbed Noah's limp hand in the one not holding Claire and pulled them both forward. "She's getting away, isn't she? Come on!"

"It's not just her," Noah said, his sunken eyes blinking slowly. He followed Samantha's lead while panning his head to the left and right. "I've never seen so many in one place before."

"Why would so many animals want to hang around where it's so busy?" Claire puzzled.

"Not animals. People. Or... what's left of them anyway," Noah said. "There are three teenagers over there, sitting on the steps of the bank. Then a little girl sitting on the bus stop, and a bunch of old men gathered around the apartment. It's mostly children though—dozens of the recently dead all moving in the same direction as us. I think they know we're following Mrs. Robinson; they keep looking our way and whispering to each other."

Noah and the children stepped off the sidewalk on the far side of the street. Samantha dropped Noah's hand right away, but her grip tightened on Claire.

Claire was looking at the places Noah referred to, though in each case she couldn't see anyone there. She could tell out of the corner of her eye that Samantha was trying to get her attention, but she stubbornly avoided looking at her friend. Samantha would know that Claire was only pretending to be brave, and Claire refused to give her the satisfaction.

"Mrs. Robinson is inside that apartment complex now," Noah said. "I don't think we can go any farther."

"We've come this far," Claire said, trying to keep her voice casual. "Let's just see if it's locked."

Still clutching each other's hands, the girls walked briskly to the glass door leading into the apartment lobby. For a moment Claire thought she could smell an ancient leathery musk, but it was gone a second later. Had she just walked through the old men?

"They're still watching you, in case you were wondering," Noah said from where he'd remained on the sidewalk. "One of them has followed you to the door."

"So what do you want me to do about it?" Claire turned in exasperation.

"Nothing. Just thought you'd want to know."

"Well I don't!" Claire shot back. "They can't do anything to me, can they?"

"The people? No, I've never seen one of them interact with the living world. If I were you, I'd be more concerned about that stony creature with the claws on the end of its wings. It's been following us since we left the house, and it's got the nastiest upside-down smile I've ever seen."

"You must think you're pretty funny," Claire replied with dignity. She tried the door in vain. She peered through the glass, but she couldn't see anyone but potted plants in the lobby on the other side. She then began to study her reflection, searching for any sign of the stony thing or the dozens of invisible children or the stinking old men. She would have laughed at herself for being foolish enough to believe if she hadn't just taken another big lungful of that old musty smell.

"What's that supposed to mean?" Noah asked after a long silence.

"I didn't say anything!" Claire responded, still studying the glass. Samantha at her side was only looking at her own reflection. She settled the age-long debate whether sarcasm was limited to words by striking several sarcastic poses.

"I wasn't talking to you?" Noah huffed. "There's a fellow next to you who looks straight out an old-timey movie. He's got one of those striped hats, and a waistcoat with big gold buttons, and —"

Samantha fully turned around to face Noah, wriggling free of Claire's hand. "We don't care what he looks like. What did he say?"

"He said today is an excellent day to be dead, and asked if we wouldn't care to join him?" Noah coughed. "Now he's sniffing your hair. Seems to be rather enjoying himself at that."

"And that's how the party ended," Samantha declared emphatically. She swatted around her head as though pursuing a relentless fly. "Claire? Are you ready to go home?"

"Not without Mrs. Robinson!" Claire whined. "We've just got to wait until someone who lives here opens the door."

"Then what?" Samantha asked. "Search every floor for her? Maybe knock on all the doors too, asking if anyone's seen your dead cat?"

"She's not dead!" Claire grew increasingly red in the face. "If she was dead, then she wouldn't be walking around. She's just somewhere else, and I need to find her."

Samantha was still swatting around her head, dodging in anxious zigzagging lines as though that would lose her invisible pursuer. "Even if you do, you can't pet her. You can't pick her up or hold her or feel her next to you when you sleep. She's gone, Claire. And nothing this weirdo says is going to bring her back. Let's just go home."

Claire kept staring into the glass, watching her reflection as the tears started to swell in her eyes. Samantha made an exaggerated motion to block her ears, but Claire didn't scream this time. She only glared at her friend's reflection in silence with dark angry eyes, and that was a hundred times worse than the screaming.

"Let's go home, Claire," Samantha repeated more softly. "Our parents will be wondering where we are. You can still have your hot chocolate at your house, then you'll feel a lot better than if you were—"

"I don't want to feel better. I want Mrs. Robinson back."

The kids remained silent for a moment. Noah stared at his feet with his hands in his pockets. Claire and Samantha glared back and forth as though the other was personally responsible for everything that was wrong with the world.

"The old timer says he'd like to keep the cat then, if it's all the same to you," Noah's voice cracked slightly, like a Captain telling everyone the boat is sinking while trying not to cause too much fuss about it. "I think we should all be getting home."

Claire's lip began to shake, but she said nothing.

"You absolutely cannot," Samantha stepped up to argue into thin air where she assumed the spirit to be. "Mrs. Robinson isn't a possession to be traded about. Either she's coming with us or she's going where she decides."

Samantha searched for the invisible man around her with mounting frustration before turning on Noah to demand, "Well, what did he say?"

"He said 'Cats are the only thing more stubborn than the dead. You'd have better luck ordering the sun to set at noontime than telling a dead cat what to do.'"

"Obviously you've never met Claire then," Samantha replied, trying to focus on the same patch of empty air that Noah was. "She's twice as stubborn as the dead, and she doesn't rot and stink like old leather either!"

"He says 'I'm not the one you smell'. Samantha, stop looking there. It thinks you're staring at it."

"Tell him to look away first," Samantha retorted. "I'm not backing down."

"Samantha, look out!"

This would have been better advice if she could actually see the thing she was supposed to be looking out for. Samantha only managed to turn her face halfway toward Noah before her vision was replaced a line of searing agony. She felt like a bucketful of water that had been suddenly filled with hot steel. Her insides all wanted to be on the outside to cool off, and her outsides wanted to be safe inside for a change. It was the worst feeling she'd ever experienced in her life.

"Sam? What happened? Noah, did something hit her?"

Samantha was on her knees, although she couldn't remember how she got there. Her vision was starting to return in her left eye, but her right might as well be staring into the sun. The musty smell came back in an overpowering wave, and it was all she could do to keep breathing and not vomit from the shock.

"Get away from her!" she heard Noah shout. His voice sounded like it was coming through a hundred miles of tin cans. The musk lifted for a moment only to be replaced by a towering shadow.

"We've got to get her out of here," Noah urged.

"What happened to her? Why'd she fall?" Claire asked.

Samantha felt a hand under one arm, then two more hands on her other side. She lurched to her feet, staggering to keep up with Noah and Claire who dragged her along. They were almost at the sidewalk of the intersection, and again the light was red.

"We have to go back for Mrs. Robinson!" Claire cried.

"Not safe," Noah grunted, invisible on Samantha's blinded right side.

"That's why we can't leave her!" Claire insisted. "If that old man attacked Samantha, then we can't let him have Mrs. Robinson!"

"He's not the one who attacked her. It was the clawed thing. And I don't think you have to worry about Mrs. Robinson, because the thing is still following us."

The red streetlight glared malevolently overhead, as comforting as an umbrella full of holes in a storm.

"Where is it?" Samantha hissed.

"Behind us. No—don't turn around. They don't usually bother people unless they think they've been noticed. It must have thought Samantha could see it because she kept looking and speaking at it without noticing. Keep staring ahead. It will lose interest if we don't acknowledge it."

"So we're supposed to just stand here and pretend the thing that attacked me isn't right behind me?" Samantha questioned in disbelief.

"Uh huh," Noah mumbled, meeting her eyes. "How are you feeling? Your right eye is all…"

"Cloudy," Claire said from the other side. "It's going to be fine, really." She did not sound very confident.

The musty scent engulfed them once more like a heavy blanket, weighing them down. The streetlight seemed to burn redder out of pure spite. "Seriously," Noah warned. "Don't look back."

"Well, screw waiting here then," Samantha said defiantly. She looked both ways down the intersection before darting across the street toward the patch of grass and trees which separated the traffic lanes.

"Wait for us!" Claire called, breaking after her. Noah was close behind, muttering curses to himself as he hurried beneath the halo of red light. They caught up with Samantha where she crouched beside a bush, ready to sprint again. In the near-distance another traffic light turned green and headlights began to rush past. The party was tense and ready to run as soon when a space opened between the cars.

"Is it still there?" Samantha asked. She already knew the answer because the smell was as strong as ever, but any words were more reassuring than the oppressive silence.

"Don't look," Noah repeated softly. He seemed to be listening to something only he could hear.

"Is my eye going to be okay?" she continued.

"The old man is talking about it, but—"

"Tell me!"

Noah sighed sharply, looking hopelessly from side to side at the impenetrable wall of rush-hour traffic.

"He says your eye 'might shrivel up to a prune and drop out, or spring a leak that drains all the liquid out and leaves only a sad empty pouch.' I said don't look!"

Samantha's head was beginning to turn, but she quickly snapped it back.

"Will I go blind?" Samantha murmured.

"No. Samantha this really isn't the time—"

"Tell me exactly what he's saying!"

"He says 'If the eye stays in, it'll start to see again. But it won't be seeing what's in your world.' He says 'The things you'll see will take your *breath away.*'"

Just as Noah said *'breath away',* the words were accompanied by a hot, dry breath on the back of Samantha's neck. Something inside her became unhinged after feeling such a thing. It wasn't a physical pain: it was more of an intrusive thought which wormed its way into her head. It told her that she was a scared, helpless little girl in a great, big world that had no possible need for her. That no one would notice much less care whether she lived or died. It didn't feel like a passing opinion either, but rather a law of the universe that she had just stumbled upon, such as the law of gravity, that once noticed could not be overturned. Since she couldn't escape such a thought, she did the best she could using her legs instead.

Samantha was halfway into the oncoming traffic before anyone could stop her. A yellow jeep appeared suddenly, roaring across the asphalt directly toward her. The events of the next few moments couldn't agree on which would happen first, so they all crammed through the proverbial doorway and happened at exactly the same time.

Noah followed Samantha into the street. He didn't think of it as risking his life to save her. He only felt an instinctual responsibility for her, and he had to do something to quiet that voice in his head that said it was his fault for leading the children here at all.

Claire jumped up and waved her arms to get the driver's attention. It must have worked too, because the jeep slammed its breaks.

If he hadn't hit his breaks, then Noah wouldn't have had enough time to catch Samantha by the flying end of her long skirt and swing her back toward the island of grass.

The vehicle slammed to a stop exactly 1.2 seconds after the front bumper connected with Noah's right shoulder. The jarring impact buckled his neck and body, allowing the vehicle to make a second point of contact on his temple. His thin frame was lifted by the force and thrown carelessly into the air like a rag-doll.

Noah was aware of his flight, though he wasn't in any pain. He felt the massive wall of pressure from the collision, but this caused more numbness than discomfort. His whole body felt like static, all pins and needles, like a foot that had just taken its first step after being asleep. It didn't seem so bad, except for the inner voice which told him in no uncertain terms that he shouldn't be in the air this long. Either he would continue to float away indefinitely, which seemed unlikely, or he was about to make a close acquaintance with the hard, unsympathetic ground.

WAKING UP AGAIN

Noah must have landed on the asphalt eventually, but he was quite oblivious to the impact. He only knew he was on the ground because he found himself staring into the pool of blood spreading from his temple along the road. It seemed interesting that people in the reflection were running toward him with open mouths that weren't making any sounds. It was ridiculous that they would make such a fuss when he wasn't hurt at all. He looked forward to their excited relief when he stood up at any moment.

There was something about the puddle of blood that concerned Noah, although his thoughts weren't clear enough to understand what was wrong with this situation. He could see Claire and Samantha leaning over him: Claire with tears flowing down her face, while Samantha looked as though she'd been turned to stone except for her wide quivering eyes, one of which was now pure marble-white.

A bearded man had exited the jeep, yet he hadn't approached. His breathing was ragged as he held a cell phone to his ear, yet still there was no sound coming from him either. A thought floated through Noah's head that perhaps it shouldn't be so quiet if everything really was fine. He kept staring at the puddle of blood, trying to focus his fuzzy thoughts on exactly what was wrong with everyone.

"You noticed, didn't you?" uttered an aged voice, the first sound Noah heard since he'd been hit.

"We're on the wrong side of the reflection," Noah replied, not turning away from the puddle. Had his voice always sounded so thin and high?

"There isn't a wrong-side. No before-side, no after-side, no upside or downside. There's just the other side, the side you've entered."

Noah sat up at last. His body stubbornly refused to rise with him. He looked down to see himself still lying face down in the blood, which by now looked more like a lake than a puddle, complete with little streams that gushed through the cracks in the road to cascade down toward the gutter.

"That's disgusting," Noah remarked, scowling.

The old timer removed his striped hat and held it to his chest, closing his eyes in an apparent gesture of reverence. His head was bald underneath, and his thick wrinkled skin made him appear more turtle than man. "Beats going in your sleep. Dying is a once-in-a-lifetime opportunity that's not to be missed."

Noah began to stand to completely remove himself from his old body. He ceased abruptly when he realized his new body that was emerging was completely naked. Besides that, his skin was smooth and hairless. The scar on his chest from a heart surgery a few years ago was completely gone. He pulled himself entirely free from the carnage to stand over the pool of blood and saw himself as the child he could barely remember ever being, no older than the two girls who were still in shock about the mangled corpse he'd left behind.

Suddenly self-conscious, Noah sank back into the ground, blushing as the old man began to laugh.

"Shut up, will you? This is your fault," Noah huffed.

"If it's anyone's fault, blame the gargoyle. Anyway the girls can't see you, if that's what you're worried about. Here, try this on."

The man began to sketch in the air, and wherever one of his fingers went there remained a bit of soft fire which continued to smolder. The fire seemed to be spilling from a thick white ring that Noah hadn't noticed before. The old man was tracing the outline of a pair of trousers, fire spreading through the air as he went to knit sparks between the lines. The pants proceeded to burn in mid-air as a shirt was conjured beside them. The fires burned out into a bleak gray color before the clothing dropped to a heap on the ground.

Noah hastily scooped them up and self-consciously donned them while facing away from the old man. The clothes had fallen directly into the puddle of blood, but even so were soft and dry against Noah's new skin.

"Don't I get any shoes?" Noah inquired.

"Most spirit bodies don't bother with them. It's hard to find your balance walking up things like stairs when you can't feel them, but going barefoot helps grip the air better, if you know what I mean."

"No," Noah was now feeling flustered and obstinate. "I don't at all."

An ambulance had arrived on the scene. One of the paramedics was dragging Claire away from the body, and she kicked and swung her elbows at them as she was forcibly removed. Samantha walked willingly when she was asked, her face stiff and frozen. The silence of the scene made it even more unsettling.

"Isn't there some way for me to let them know I'm okay?" Noah asked.

"Sure there is. We'll need another jeep though."

Noah, now fully dressed, turned to scowl at him. The old timer grinned and placed his hat back on his head.

"Where's the thing that attacked Samantha?"

"The gargoyle didn't stick around. Took off when you got hit. Cowardly creatures, I'll never understand why the department puts so much faith in them. I've never seen one go after a human like that though, most curious indeed."

Noah watched as his body was covered in a white sheet and carried into the back of the ambulance. Part of him still hoped that it would stand up and shake it off, but that seemed to be growing less likely by the moment. He really was dead. Why did those words sound so strange to him?

"Mandy will still be able to see me though," Noah said. "I should go and tell her what's happened."

The old man shook his head. "Wouldn't recommend it. The T.D.D. is very particular about spirits communicating with unregistered mediums."

"The T.D.D.?" Noah asked, distracted by the progress of his body.

"The Trans Dimensional Department. You'll get that on your permanent record, then fat chance getting into a good school then."

"What would I want to go to school for?" Noah turned to face him. "It's not like I need to earn a living."

"You don't want to spend your next life sweeping graveyards, do you?"

"No, of course not. Why would I—"

"That's what will happen, you know. Or maybe haunting a teddy bear because that's all you'll manage, not having taken your possession work seriously. See all those children passing you by? They're headed for The Mortuary. Brilliant demonology course they've got, real cutting-edge summoning program. Not to mention one of the best necromancy curriculums you'll find this side of the ocean. They've got second year students already raising their own ghouls. Can you believe it?"

"Um, not entirely," Noah replied quite honestly. "Why did you say today was an excellent day to die? Are you the grim reaper or something?"

"George Hampton, a pleasure to meet you," the old man said, shaking Noah by the hand. Noah was surprised to feel how real and solid the other's hand felt. "And no, I'm not going to harvest you, whatever that means. You do have good timing though, because the bus leaves in…" he checked his watch, then the stars, then his watch once more, "about an hour. Little less."

"I don't want to go anywhere. I have to take care of my daughter and her son. Her husband isn't around anymore, and I know she tries her best, but she hasn't had a real job since the baby—what are you doing now?"

George Hampton's tongue was out of his mouth and he seemed to be tasting the air like a serpent. He turned suddenly upon being addressed as though he forgot Noah was even there.

"Your daughter and her son are already dead," George said. The words felt like a punch in the stomach.

"What?! How—"

"Well, not exactly, but they are to you," the old man corrected. "There isn't such a thing as dead really. There's either this side or the other side. When you aren't in one, you're in the other. Now if you do as you're supposed to, you study very hard in all of your classes, then in a few years you'll have graduated and will be ready to go back to the other side. In your words, pass the final test, and you'll be back alive again."

That didn't sound quite so bad anymore. Noah reflexively breathed a sigh of relief, surprised to find his lungs still making the motion out of habit despite not feeling any air enter his body. A siren illuminated the scene in flashes of harsh red and blue, and the sound was beginning to trickle back as though someone had turned the TV volume up from mute to low.

Noah watched as a policeman wrote down the statement of the bearded man in the jeep. Claire's mother was there, and Claire buried her face against her mother's side. Samantha was sitting on the sidewalk beside them, her arms clutched around her drawn knees.

"They don't seem dead. But I don't feel dead either, so I suppose it doesn't matter either way. How far is the bus?"

"That's the spirit!" the old man chuckled to himself. "Not far at all, we just need to follow all the other children."

George Hampton placed a gentle arm behind Noah's shoulders and steered him away from the bloody street. Away from his body that was already passing him in the ambulance. Away from every mistake he'd ever made, every place he'd ever been, and every person he'd ever loved. He wasn't sure whether to laugh or cry, or perhaps both at the same time.

The volume in the living world never turned all the way back on; all the rush and commotion of the street kept buzzing away barely above a whisper. Likewise, it all had a certain translucence to it in the same way that spirits had once appeared to him when he was alive. And while he had only ever seen the occasional spirit before, now they were everywhere, as real and solid and true as his brand-new body.

Owls—herds of deer—prowling wolves—all right in the middle of the city, in the middle of the street, heedless to the ceaseless traffic. Flights of birds swooped straight through the pellucid towers, and other strange creatures unseen in the living world strut their impossibility brazenly before all to see. One by one they came sparkling into existence before his eyes like the blossoming of a starry night. It immediately became very clear to Noah that all his life he had only seen the faintest edge of the other world which lay hidden over the one he knew.

George Hampton and Noah walked by buildings that couldn't possibly belong to this city. Tucked between a grocery store and a gas station rose a high tower which looked to be entirely built from jagged black glass, more real now than the familiar commercial buildings on either side. There on the other end of the street sat a fat round building whose brown walls rippled like a chocolate waterfall. A few hundred yards ahead, Noah could clearly see where part of the street was abruptly blocked by a marble mountain with a Grecian shrine like a miniature Pantheon carved directly into its mass.

"Some people of faith prefer to pursue resurrection at a temple rather than a school, but they aren't as popular on this side," George Hampton rambled, noticing Noah's fascination in the structure. "It's hard to convince people that you follow the one true God when he never shows his face, and right next door is another faith offering a different variety of resurrections at half the price. Of course none of them can guarantee it—all souls find their way back in their own ways —but The Mortuary will teach you all the essentials and give you your very best shot."

Noah suddenly became aware that humans have been dying for almost exactly as long as they'd been living. That he could run into Napoleon, or Caesar, or a Neanderthal which died before two sticks were rubbed to make fire. As long as their spirit didn't return to the other side, they must have stayed here.

"Why are you old?" Noah inquired.

The old man tapped the side of his nose and his eye twinkled. "Excellent question! Everyone who comes here begins their journey young. There is only one currency on this side: the years of your life. It's the only thing of value on the other side too, though you all hardly seem to notice it being spent. The more someone decides to spend here, the older they get, until one day they spend themselves completely and disappear, never to be seen again."

"You must have bought a lot of things," Noah said.

"They sneak up on you," the old man replied. "One day here, a week there—you don't even notice until they're gone, nor how precious they were until it's too late."

"That's rubbish. After you realized that you were getting older, you should have stopped spending right away."

"So you never wasted time again after realizing that it wouldn't come back?" George asked, rather smugly.

"But it does come back though, doesn't it? You can pass the test and come back to life as many times as you want?"

Noah stopped to watch a pair of horses pulling a carriage directly through oncoming traffic. Maybe it was just getting dark, but he kept counting the wrong number of legs on the beasts. His brain refused to believe half the things that his eyes were extremely confident about.

"As many times as you *can*," George Hampton corrected. "It's not easy to get back. Some never manage it, though they try for a thousand years. Others do it by accident, or maybe it won't happen until a conflict in their previous life was resolved or their soul mate has died and joined them. The way back is so different for everyone that it's quite impossible to have a reliable method."

"What good is trying to teach it then?" Noah asked.

"Schools aren't meant to teach you all the answers. How could they fit the whole world into such a small container? A good school should instead teach you to love the truth so you will search for it on your own."

"How come we could see stuff that was on the other side?" Noah asked. "My daughter Mandy too, and sometimes I thought even the baby was keen on them."

"You're Chainers, that's why." The old man grinned, evidently delighted by this. "Chainers keep repeating the cycle. You've been back and forth, dying and getting reborn again, over and over, until you've done it so much that you started holding onto something about the journey. Some people will come back still holding secrets from the other side. They might even remember spells or powers after learning them so many times. Of course the magic over there isn't nearly as strong as it is here, but every once in a while there goes a psychic with a neat trick or a man with a bit of old predators still in him. Or in your case, a family who can still see glimpses of the other side. Ah, but here we are with time to spare."

The bus stop ahead wasn't like any bus stop Noah had ever seen. It was closer to the size of an airport hanger with a single massive cavity. The building was entirely black, and inside loomed a towering bus, two lanes wide and at least five stories tall. Heavy clouds of purple-tinged steam flooded from somewhere underneath in regular pulses that looked almost like the bus was breathing.

"That's not a bus!" Noah exclaimed, feeling both deceived and delighted by the revelation.

A fresh gout of purple mist billowed from beneath the monstrosity. Noah covered his nose and mouth with his arm. In contrast, the old man spread his arms and inhaled deeply, wafting the mist up toward his face with both hands.

"It's grape flavored this time," George uttered with content. "Hurry up now, you've still got to buy your ticket."

The old man led Noah through the waiting area outside. Dozens of children filled the space, several sitting at each of the stone tables which were scattered beneath bright orange umbrellas. It wasn't just human children though—on one table a golden retriever puppy twirled in happy circles in the center of attention. There were all manner of domestic cats and other animals that were likely to be found in a city, including a very young hippo that must have come from the zoo. Noah paused in surprise to see Mrs. Robinson stalking along the top of the stone wall which surrounded the area.

"You weren't planning to leave me, were you?" Mrs. Robinson snapped, her voice sharp and accusing.

Noah opened his mouth to reply, but in his shock he couldn't find the words. Mrs. Robinson turned up her nose and strutted past, not showing the least concern that Noah had actually died in her pursuit. She cut the line in front of a pair of excitedly chatting girls and hopped directly onto the counter.

"One way ticket to Barbaros please." George Hampton was speaking to an adjacent attendant through the glass.

"Are you sure you've got enough time left?" the woman behind the counter answered. She was dressed in a smart business suit with an orange tie and white gloves.

"Maybe so, maybe not," he replied. "It's for the boy, not me."

Noah picked his way through the tables to reach the counter, and the saleswoman reached out a hand holding a neatly printed ticket. Noah reached out to take it, and white gloves seized his wrist.

"You'll be paying, correct? Can you confirm that your name and date of death is printed correctly on the ticket?"

Noah hadn't told her this information, but he could see that Noah Tellaver, August 22nd, 2018 was correct on all accounts. He nodded and tried to pull his hand away but was unable to break the woman's grip.

"If you'd died one day later then you'd have to wait a whole year," the attendant said, whistling low. "Someone out there is really watching out for you, eh? That will be two weeks."

"Two weeks? How far is this bus going?" Noah demanded.

The ticket woman smiled patiently as she rolled her eyes. "That's not the distance; it's the cost, silly. Two weeks for the fare with your luggage included."

"But I haven't got any luggage," Noah argued, quite confused.

"Your body. You *will* want to take it with you, I assume?"

"Yeah... Of course... I mean—am I supposed to?"

"Yes, dear," the woman replied kindly. "Deep breath now; this won't hurt a bit."

Still grasping his wrist tightly, the woman pressed a brilliant aquamarine stone into the back of Noah's hand. The stone turned on like a Christmas light, the aquatic glow bathing them through its numerous facets. Noah felt intensely groggy for a moment as though he'd just woken from an abrupt nap and was trying to decipher whether the clock read AM or PM. The white gloves released his wrist and allowed him to pull away with the ticket in his hand.

"I don't feel any different," Noah said.

"You won't until around forty," George Hampton responded. "Then it starts to sting a bit. No matter though, you're set to go. Remember not to talk to strangers, unless they have something worth saying, and all that sort of thing."

A loud whistle blew from the direction of the bus. There was a stout man with a mustache wearing an identical orange tie and white gloves standing in front. He was checking the tickets of the first children who were beginning to board. At his side was a similarly uniformed opossum standing on its hind legs, checking the tickets from the animals.

"Can you let them know I'm alright? My daughter, I mean. That it didn't hurt, and that they don't have to worry about me."

"I'll tell them you're going to the best place in the world," George Hampton assured him. "Besides, you can always check in on them from the Whispering Room when you arrive."

The whistle blew again, this time a tad more shrill and impatient.

"What about Samantha and Claire?" Noah pressed, not having time to ask all the questions he wanted. "We've only just met me, but I think they'd want to know since it must have been horrible for them to actually see me go. And oh, I can give you more names if we have the time—"

George tapped the side of his nose and smiled. "Find your way back and tell them yourself. That's how it's supposed to be done."

The third blast of the whistle sounded from directly behind Noah. He flinched and spun to find himself face-to-face with the bus attendant who promptly snatched the ticket from his hand.

"All aboard!" the Mustached Man bellowed. "Daymare 7 is departing, one way to The Mortuary on Barbaros Island. Last call!"

"Shut up, will you? If you tried to leave me, I can promise you'll be looking for a new job before sunrise," shouted a portly, red faced boy whose beady eyes were almost invisible in his pudgy face. "What ever happened to resting in peace?"

"Don't mind him, darling," cooed a tall, thin girl racing to catch up. "No-one would ever dream of leaving you behind."

"They'd better not. I'm not staying one more minute in this vile town. You told me Heaven was going to have everything I wanted in it, but nothing here is made of gold and I can't find a thing to eat."

The thin girl caught up and handed two tickets to the Mustached Man who nodded sharply. "Brandon and Teresa Hides, you're just in time. Get inside, three floors up, middle row."

"I don't think so," Teresa remarked curtly. "We'll be sitting on the top with the best view. We'd prefer a row to ourselves, but if we must share, we'll be taking those closest to the window."

The Mustached Man folded his hands behind his body and swayed back and forth on the balls of his feet. Noah keenly hoped that they wouldn't be allowed on at all, and he looked around for George to tell him so. The old man was gone without a trace though, and in his place sat only Mrs. Robinson who must have followed Noah from the station. She looked a little bigger than Noah had seen her last, and in her mouth she carried her own ticket.

"Very well, the top it is," the attendant conceded. "You'll have the whole place to yourself, if that's to your liking."

"If that's the best you can do, then we'll take it," Teresa said. "You'll like that, won't you Brandon? Not having to share with any of those dirty animals?"

Brandon screwed up his pudgy face as though trying to work out a particularly unpleasant math problem.

"The top is always the best," Teresa reasoned. "Come on, sugar, let's go check to be sure. If it isn't everything you could have ever dreamed of then I'll make sure they find you an even better spot."

"You'd better," Brandon snarled as he climbed aboard. "It's your fault I'm dead in the first place."

A few more stragglers came rushing from the station while they'd been talking. The attendant turned to take their tickets. Most of the human children were wearing plain white gowns made from a slightly shimmering material. Noah felt slightly out of place in his gray shirt and trousers, but no one seemed to be paying him much attention. Mrs. Robinson spat out her ticket distastefully and trotted at Noah's side as he stepped into the vehicle.

The inside of the Daymare 7 wasn't in the least recognizable as a bus. He used to ride the 247 city line when he'd had to let his car go. How was Mandy ever going to get by without him? Noah had been given his old job back at the veterinary clinic, despite being eight years into his retirement, and the daily commute had been the low part of his day. All the seats on the 247 were always mysteriously damp, and the windows were so filthy he could barely see out.

The city line would have been much more fun if it had a spiral staircase in the center with each step reminiscent of a coffin's lid, as was the case with the Daymare 7. The steps floated unassisted in the air, although they did have a shining brass railing and a fine brass mesh between the steps to prevent anyone from falling through. On each floor was a wooden walkway that extended to a floating platform which was filled with dozens of nervously chattering children and animals. More sets of stairs peeled away from these platforms, with steps going sideways or even upside-down to seat people in such ways as to make a physicist extremely uncomfortable. The people sitting upside-down on the underside of platforms didn't seem to mind, and their hair and clothing didn't hang downward but fell naturally upward as if the people were right-side up.

Noah had never felt further from home than he did staring at the mad scene before him. He'd never felt further from his daughter, who must have noticed he was gone by now and was going to pieces trying to find him. He'd never get to watch another movie with Lewis, or hear Mandy singing the songs his wife had once sang to her as a child. But how could he allow himself to stay morose with such a brilliant mystery unraveling itself before his eyes?

"I'm really dead," he told himself aloud, the fact fully sinking in at last, "and that's fine with me."

DAYMARE 7

"May I hold your kitty?" a ginger haired girl asked Noah. He blinked in surprise, realizing that he had been blocking the traffic by standing and staring. He quickly stepped aside to allow the other children to pass.

"Go ahead, ask him for permission. Why would you ask me?" Mrs. Robinson lamented. "Why should I have a say when some stranger decides to grab me for her enjoyment?"

"Oh, I'm so sorry," the girl mumbled in embarrassment. She knelt down to speak to the cat directly. "I'm so used to—may I pet you?"

Mrs. Robinson turned to allow the girl scratch her back, which she did with a practiced motion that seemed to hit all the right spots.

"I used to have one just like you named Sebastian," she told Mrs. Robinson. "Or is that rude? I don't mean 'have' like a possession; I mean 'have' like someone has a brother, or a sister."

"I shall choose not to be offended if you don't stop until you're told," Mrs. Robinson replied, flipping onto her back to expose her tuft of white fur.

"My son got Sebastian for me after my husband passed so I wouldn't be all alone. I hope someone is looking after the poor thing now."

Noah studied the girl's fair, smooth skin and tried to imagine her as a little old lady sitting alone with her cat. There was something wise and patient about her eyes that made the imagining easier, but the contrast still seemed too incredible to picture.

The formerly-old-lady made the bold move of picking Mrs. Robinson up, and after the initial suspicion the kitten settled quite comfortably in her arms. Noah was beginning to feel a little jealous that the cat preferred the newcomer to him after everything he'd gone through for her.

"Maybe Sebastian will find you again when it's his turn," Noah said.

"Do you really think so?" the girl asked hopefully. "My name is Jamie Poffin, by the way. I'd shake your hand, but I don't want to let go of…"

"Mrs. Robinson," Noah said. Then quickly added: "That's the cat's name, not mine. I'm Noah."

"You didn't strike me as a Mrs. Robinson," Jamie smirked. "Could I sit with you, Noah? I don't know anyone else here."

"Let me check my seat number…" Noah replied, but Jamie didn't wait. She was already leaping up the stairs, still cradling Mrs. Robinson.

"It doesn't matter, there are lots of empty seats," Jamie called back. "Oh, hello there. What are you supposed to be?"

Noah had to climb the stairs to see the thing Jamie was addressing. Only about a foot tall, it looked rather like a stuffed animal covered with soft red fur. Along its back was a line of hard ridges that looked like a series of shark fins, and its face was coarse and broad like an ugly little monkey. Mrs. Robinson was beginning to squirm, so Jamie set her down on the ground where she made a low growling sound at the furry red creature.

"Do you think it's a spirit?" Jamie asked. "Maybe an old one, something from an animal that doesn't exist anymore?"

"I don't think it wants you to pet it," Noah warned.

Jamie was already reaching for it though, her palms facing upward in a harmless display. The monkey-faced creature snarled and seized one of Jamie's hands with its stubby black fingers, biting viciously. Jamie howled as she jumped back. Mrs. Robinson hissed and all her fur stood on end, apparently scaring the creature which scampered down the wooden walkway. Mrs. Robinson sprang into action, chasing in hot pursuit.

"Don't touch the imps, please," shouted Mustached Man from below. He'd just closed the door behind the last children.

"Sorry!" Jamie shouted back. Her index finger had two prominent holes in it, but they weren't bleeding.

"Don't shout either!" roared the attendant.

"Sor—" Jamie began to yell, cutting herself off when she thought better of it. She gave the man a thumbs up with her free hand instead.

"No blood," she whispered enthusiastically. "We don't bleed anymore! That's fantastic, I always hated blood!"

The attendant moved toward the front of the bus where he seized a long brass tube, the other end of which connected with the brass railing around the stairs.

"Ladies and Gentlemen," he announced into the tube. The sound was amplified into a magnificent booming echo which radiated throughout the railing all the way to the top of the bus. "My name is Mr. Ludyard of the T.D.D., and welcome to Daymare 7, destination the island of Barbaros. We will be departing in a few minutes as soon as the last luggage has been stored."

"Were we supposed to pack luggage?" Jamie whispered, distraught.

"He means our bodies, I think," Noah whispered back.

"But I was cremated!" Jamie hissed. Noah shrugged.

"The Daymare 7 will depart at 10 PM and take approximately seven hours and twenty five minutes to arrive at its destination. To those of you who recently died in your previous life, congratulations for making it here in one piece. Please save any and all questions relating to the nature of death and the eternal secrets of the cosmos for your professors at school. Make yourself comfortable, and feel free to ask one of the imps for help if you need anything."

Mr. Ludyard dropped the brass tube and saluted to no-one in particular. He turned and made his way farther toward the front of the bus where a dark wooden door concealed the driver's compartment. Shortly after, the whole place began to rumble, and thick clouds of grape-flavored smoke began to flood past the windows outside. They were beginning to move.

Noah and Jamie climbed to the fourth level where there were more open seats. An imp dashed across the aisle in front of them, making odd panicked chittering noises with Mrs. Robinson in hot pursuit. There were more imps up here, grinning, and leering, and sticking out their tongues at the children as though daring them to do something they would regret.

"Do you want to sit in one of the upside-down ones?" Noah asked.

"No thanks," Jamie said. "I already get travel sick without hanging like a bat."

"Do we still get sick? Now that we're dead, I mean," he pondered.

"We're not really dead at all. We're just alive somewhere else. Didn't you read the pamphlets they have at the station?"

"No, I didn't have time," Noah said. "There was a man who helped me find the place though, and he explained some of it to me."

Noah paused; he watched a new boy sit down on his other side. The boy had dark skin and a cleanly shaven head, and he was nervously fidgeting and looking about all over the place.

"Hey, excuse me," the boy said. "Did you see where the imps went?"

Noah shrugged. They'd disappeared from the stairways, though he could still hear the scampering of their claws against the wooden flooring somewhere.

"Hey, imps!" the boy shouted. "Get your furry asses over here. I need something."

"No shouting!" boomed the echo which reverberated from the railing.

Claws immediately appeared to latch onto the platform, and two imps crawled over the edge to glare suspiciously at the boy. He glanced uncertainly at Jamie's wounded hand before clearing his throat.

"Yeah, hi, thanks," he said. "My name's Walter, my girlfriend's name is Natasha. We lived together at 423 E Ventmore Street, and I was hoping you could send her a message."

The imps looked at one another slyly. They started speaking an awful guttural, chirping sound rapidly back and forth. After a moment they faced Walter again with rather wicked grins spreading across their faces.

"So, um, you can do it?" Walter asked.

Both imps nodded enthusiastically, their grin spreading even wider to reveal at least two layers of razor sharp teeth.

"You're wasting your time," yipped a voice from behind. The golden retriever puppy was sitting there with a human girl on either side, both unable to keep their hands off him. "They don't understand a word you're saying."

"Didn't anyone read the pamphlet?" Jamie asked. "Demons are very intelligent and can understand every human language, even if they don't speak it themselves."

"What are you defending them for?" The dog asked. "You were the first one to be bitten."

"It doesn't hurt much, and it was my own fault for not asking first," Jamie huffed.

Walter cleared his throat again, embarrassed. "I just want you to tell her that I love her, and that she should wait for me. A few years at the most, tell her I'll be back as soon as I can."

The dog behind them snickered, and Walter looked even more embarrassed.

"Even if you do make it back, you're going to be a baby again. You won't remember a thing."

"You don't know anything, Bowser," Walter replied stubbornly. "I can possess someone else's body who is fully grown, now can't I? Or I can make myself remember a spell to grow up again real quick."

"Not unless you're a Chainer, and those are super rare." Bowser said. "Did you remember your other times?"

Walter's face soured. He shook his head.

"So what makes you think you'll remember next time?" Bowser asked. Walter turned back around in his chair to face the imps.

"Just tell her I love her then. That I didn't—that I won't ever forget her."

"You will," Bowser gloated. The two girls sitting beside him giggled, although Noah couldn't quite find the joke.

The imps didn't budge and only continued to stand there grinning.

"Go on then, you ugly little twerps," Walter said angrily, waving them away. "And don't let her see you. Just put it in a letter, or burn it in a piece of toast, I don't care. As long as she knows."

The imps darted along the wooden bridge and begun chasing one another in circles, chittering and laughing.

"They aren't going to do it, I can tell," Walter sighed.

"You didn't have to be so rude to them," Jamie said. "Not even a please or thank you…if I were them I'd never do it."

"You don't have to be nice to imps," Walter sounded doubtful. "They've got contracts to obey, they don't have a choice. I know the contract isn't with me, but I figured whoever did own it would have ordered them to serve the students."

The prospective students alternated between nervous chatter and reflective silence for some time before a sudden commotion on the stairs brought the next disruption. Noah and Jamie rushed to lean over the railing to see what was going on above. Brandon was bounding down the stairs after a pair of imps with Teresa chasing after him. The imps were cackling gleefully and seemed to be the only ones having a good time.

"Why are you so slow?" Brandon scolded Teresa. "Catch that little monster!"

"I'm trying!" Teresa whined. She lunged awkwardly at one of the creatures who dodged off the side of the stairs, scampering along the bottom with careless agility.

Brandon knelt to peer beneath the stairs. "I'll have your skin hanging in my room. Or are you too stupid to even understand? Get back here!"

One of the imps popped its head back above the stair to stick its tongue out at Brandon who was peeping over the opposite side.

Brandon didn't appear to notice and continued to shout underneath the stairs on the other side.

"I used to have a whole room just for the animals I've killed. I'm going to start a new one on this side just for you and your family. Assuming you even have one and didn't crawl out of a cesspool somewhere."

The imp grew emboldened and crawled right behind Brandon who remained oblivious to it. The little demon was silently dancing now, obscenely thrusting its hips in Brandon's direction much to the delight of the other imps. The distracted creature didn't notice Teresa charging from the side until she launched into a flying tackle which pinned it to the floor.

There was a chittering uproar as the onlooking imps gnashed their teeth in fury, but none of them came to the aid of the pinned creature. It buckled and thrashed on the floor and looked about to wriggle free until Brandon joined Teresa to help secure her hold.

"What's the meaning of this racket?"

The voice came from a tall thin man mounting the stairs who Noah hadn't noticed board the bus. The skin on his face seemed to be pulled much too tight and was discolored in places as though he'd found it and tried it on rather than having grown it himself. This had the side-effect of pulling his eyes into narrow slits, barely wide enough to see the red iris within. He was dressed in a perfectly fitted black suit with a black silk vest and tie which commanded a sense of power despite his sickly appearance. A long, thin dog trotted submissively at his heels, although instead of fur it only had black leathery skin which wrinkled up when it moved.

"They trapped us on the roof!" Brandon raged, his face twisting into the ugliest livid shade Noah had ever seen. "There isn't any top floor at all. As soon as we stepped up there, the beastly things locked the door and wouldn't let us down until..." He grimaced and turned away, too angry to even finish the thought. "They ought to be killed for this, or banished at the least."

"Until what?" the emaciated figure asked, apparently bemused. Nearly a dozen other imps had leapt and bound from the other floors to gather on the stairs behind him. They peered around him or through his legs, leering and giggling to each other in their strange tongue.

Brandon scowled and turned away. Teresa had to answer for him. "We had to do the apology dance," she sniffed indignantly. "Right on top of the bus for everyone below to see. I've never been so humiliated in my life."

The imps began to howl with laughter, even the one that was still pinned to the ground. Brandon's face contorted into a darker shade of purple. Without warning he rose and stomped on the imp that Teresa still held to the ground. There was a loud crack like snapping twigs when his foot impacted against it. The rest of the imps immediately stopped laughing in unnatural unison. The boisterous atmosphere was replaced with a sudden eerie silence.

Most of the children were on their feet now, peering over balconies several floors above and below to watch the drama. The imp on the ground gave a pitiful little moan.

"How could he!" Jamie hissed, outraged. "They're so small! And so what if they played a harmless trick? It served him right after how he's behaved."

"Apsolvo," the thin man said at once.

The imp on the ground began to dissolve into a thick black smoke. Its moan grew louder, turning into something like a shriek before it stopped abruptly. Brandon and Teresa gagged on the smoke and hurried up the stairs to get away from it. By the time the smoke had cleared, the imp was gone.

"Where did he go?" Brandon demanded of the thin man.

"The first lesson students in my class learn is that the demons we summon are our partners, not our servants," the man replied severely. "When one has been wounded in our service, it is our obligation to release them. To do anything other would be less than human. What is your name, boy?"

"Brandon Hides," he replied mistrustfully. "And I—"

"And you, girl?" the skeleton man interrupted.

"Teresa Hides," she replied, standing protectively in front of Brandon. "His mother."

"They look the same age though," Walter muttered. "I don't think I'll ever get used to that."

"You may call me Professor Salice," the man continued smoothly. "If I have the misfortune of meeting either you in my class, then a humiliating dance will be the least of your concerns. From what I've seen so far, I would not be surprised if you fail the weighing ceremony and are sent home at once though. You will behave yourself on the remainder of this trip."

The dog at his side opened its mouth, and instead of teeth a blossoming of cornflower blue tentacles emerged to spread impressively around its face. Brandon's mouth dropped open in dumb terror.

"How much longer is it, professor?" a brown haired, frightened looking girl on the opposite platform asked.

"We have two stops to make at Genesis General Hospital and the Rainbow Valley Vet," Professor Salice replied. "Make yourselves comfortable, and let us hope the freshly dead are more grateful for their second chance than you lot."

Professor Salice turned indignantly and swept down the stairs, his demonic dog and a small army of imps swirling around him and chattering amongst each other, some casting mistrustful glares back in Brandon's direction. The mood in the bus was more subdued after that, and Brandon and his mother Teresa found isolated seats in the back of a platform and showed no interest in talking to the others. Jamie, Walter, and Noah passed the time reviewing the pamphlet which Jamie had brought with her. Big purple letters at the top read: "The Road From Death."

The pamphlet folded out considerably like a road map with each square devoted to a different topic. "Cassandra's Corpse Comforting" offered counseling for traumatic deaths, and there was a special on "Wallace's Whimsical Windows" which promised such a "realistic view of home that you'd forget you were dead." There were magical stones that possessed various powers, including the "Eternal Spring

Aquamarine Line" which allowed the transference of life force such as what the woman selling bus tickets used.

"These are all advertisements!" Walter complained. "I don't want to waste my death on these things."

"That's because you're looking at the wrong part. All the stuff about the school is over here," Jamie pointed out patiently. "Look here's a bit about the professors. It says that Salice is the new demonology teacher this year. He's credited as the inventor of the modern contract which has revolutionized the whole demon industry. They used to be forced to trust the demons at their words, which it says here was about as 'smart as making an omelette with harpy eggs'. I'm not sure what that means, though."

"But look on the other page!" Noah said, flipping back. "They're actually selling Harpy eggs on the first page."

"Yeah, but they say 'for external use only'," Walter said. "Do we still need to eat over here? I haven't felt hungry since I… well, you know."

Noah suddenly regretted not taking a hot chocolate of his own. As it were, the last meal he'd eaten was just a boring ham sandwich at noon. Was that the last thing he'd ever eat? Perhaps the others were reflecting on similar things, because most fell into silent introspection after that. Walter kept bringing up his girlfriend without being prompted, but he didn't seem to be expecting an answer from anyone and seemed more intent on preserving every detail about her to make sure he wouldn't forget.

The Daymare 7 made two more stops as promised, several children or animals boarding each time. Some were laughing, others crying, others wide-eyed with speechless amazement. Ludyard bellowed his short welcome speech verbatim each time, and the empty seats filled up with the freshly dead. The newcomers gave Noah a sense of confidence as he realized that as little as he knew about this new world, at least there were others who knew even less.

The general chatter faded again as the road wound on. The city thinned into suburbs, then to isolated houses dotting the countryside. The bus barreled directly down the streets regardless of whatever traffic might be going in the opposite direction, sliding straight through the other cars more gently than a passing mist. The rest of the world was still going about its business, completely oblivious to the spirits going about their own.

The first shafts of morning light were amplifying into a bright, warm day when Ludyard blared his next announcement through the brass railing.

"Look ahead, and to your right. Behold the only known island entirely within the spirit world, completely imperceptible to the living. Welcome to Barbaros!"

All the children on the left side of the bus hustled toward the right or stood on their chairs to see out the porthole windows. The bus was driving along the beach, rumbling through families and their umbrellas and sunbathers stretched out on blankets. Noah was almost trampled to a second death as several people strained to look past him, and he only got the smallest glimpse out of the bottom of the window.

The bus hissed, releasing great gouts of purple steam which spread across the water before it. Collective gasps resounded as the bus turned from the beach to drive directly onto the water, apparently buoyed by the purple clouds which it continued to dispense.

"It looks like a tombstone," Walter remarked in a somber tone.

"Only because you're thinking about being dead," Jamie replied.

One side of the island was dominated by a sheer stone cliff which produced the effect. Lush grass and thickly wooded areas covered the top however, rolling down in gentle slopes along the other side of the island until it met with a black sand beach which glistened in the sun. Thatch roofed cottages and long wooden houses littered the grassy hills which grew more densely populated as they neared the cliff. There, at the edge, a single prominent stone building which resembled a cathedral loomed over the precipitous drop.

Noah would have liked to watch for longer, but there was too much bustling for the window and he soon grew tired of being pushed and stepped on. He pulled himself through the forest of legs until he emerged near the stairs, face-to-face with Mrs. Robinson again. Noah thought she looked rather forlorn and moved to pet her, but she dashed away again before he had the chance.

"Well don't just sit there counting your toes," Jamie said, pursuing Mrs. Robinson. "We have to make sure she gets off the bus."

"Why?" Noah asked, following her down the stairs. "She can follow the instructions as well as anyone else."

Jamie's expression over her shoulder clearly stated that Noah was speaking nonsense, but she answered anyway. "She's so frightened! She needs someone to look after her. This world must be even more confusing for an animal which hasn't learned to think like humans have."

Noah could have rightly pointed out that none of the other animals seemed to be having trouble adjusting, or that Mrs. Robinson clearly wanted nothing to do with them and would refuse their help even if she needed it. The bus would be arriving at the island soon and they'd need to be downstairs anyway though, so he kept those thoughts to himself and followed Jamie downward.

Mrs. Robinson paused at each landing as though to verify that her pursuers were keeping up before bounding off again whenever Jamie was almost within reach. Others noticed their movement and were quick to follow, so that by the time they reached the bottom of the stairs there was already a crowd of other children pressing for the doors.

Mrs. Robinson was the first out as soon as the doors were opened. She vanished into the final blast of purple steam which flooded around the bus as it reached a complete stop. Before Noah could even think of pursuing her, he collided with a wall of noise blasting from all directions through the open door. A pounding sound—roaring and shouting, then a scream. All his budding fantasies about the other side seemed to evaporate, replaced by the nameless dread of the macabre unknown.

THE WEIGHING CEREMONY

SCREAMING, STOMPING, POUNDING, AND... CHEERING? The scented smoke cleared to reveal a large crowd of howling and clapping people who formed a semi-circle around the bus. It hadn't looked like there were that many houses on the entire island from a distance, so the whole town must have turned out to welcome the new arrivals.

"Happy death day and welcome to The Mortuary!"

An elderly lady with the rigid posture of a drill sergeant stood at the front of the assembly to greet them. She was dressed all in red from her exaggerated high-heels to her black buttoned coat and wide-brimmed red hat which was tied with a black silk ribbon.

"Oh, I know that some of you aren't so fresh," she continued in a warm, velvet voice, "but even if you had to wait a whole year for the bus I promise you'll be glad you came. Don't be shy—and don't block the exit, please and thank you—come on out everyone. Feel the sun on your new skin and the grass between your toes. There's never been a better place to be dead."

The children were hesitant at first, but the lady's gracious smile and the cheering of the people behind her created an infectious, electric atmosphere. The bus quickly emptied onto the grass still heavy with the swirling vapors of grape flavored steam.

"Still in one piece, eh?" shouted a sturdy woman from the crowd. "Death wasn't so bad, now was it?"

"Good for you for making it," called a tall man with a silver buttoned vest. "Jolly worth the wait."

"Any nasty deaths? Remember Cassandra's Kill Counseling!" shouted a woman covered in jangling bracelets and ornaments. "It won't cost an arm and a leg this time!"

"Don't forget to call home with your spiritual operator!" a tall man in a yellow striped suit added, bobbing and nodding as he thoroughly agreed with his own proclamation.

The stately lady in red beamed as she raised her hands, slowly lowering them to still the crowd. It seemed to Noah that she was looking straight at him all the while, and his insides squirmed under her scrutiny. He ducked behind Bowser the golden retriever and his cluster of fawning girls who were now pushing towards the front, only to catch the Lady's eyes still tracking him when he emerged on the other side.

"And special welcome to our returning guests," the lady continued, turning away from Noah at last. "I am called The Matriarch, Headmistress of The Mortuary. Thank you Ludyard, your Daymare must be exhausted. Please relax, the both of you, and don't tarry on my account."

A last purple gust swept the ground, seeming to Noah like the bus was heaving a sigh of relief. Ludyard waved a smart salute with his gloved hand in the door of the bus before vanishing inside once more. The bus purred as it glided across its own steam to completely capsize onto its side on the grass. Noah couldn't help but stare at the thousands of legs like those of a centipede which wriggled and stretched luxuriously along the bottom.

The lean figure of Professor Salice cut through the assembly of children, which wasn't difficult considering how eager everyone was to get out of his way, to join the headmistress. She smiled and inclined her head toward him, allowing him to whisper something in her ear. Again she seemed to look in Noah's direction.

"If you have not already met Professor Salice, allow me to introduce this semester's new demonlogist," The Matriarch announced.

Professor Salice smiled as though the gesture physically hurt him—and considering how tight his skin stretched, maybe it really did. His leathery dog released its spread of tentacles in an arc that almost appeared to be a grin of its own.

"On my right, returning for his two hundred and twelfth year of distinguished service is Gregory Wilst. He will be overseeing your necromancy studies," The Matriarch said, gesturing to a figure that Noah hadn't even noticed a moment before. Perhaps that was because his bleached bones reflected the sunlight so strongly. Apart from a complete absence of skin, his most distinguishing features were the twisted metal staff he leaned upon, and the gold-trimmed, white linen wrapped around his bony waist. The skeleton nodded his head respectfully.

"A privilege, as always," the skeleton said dutifully in a voice like dry sand in the wind.

"On my left is Borris Humstrum. He will be instructing your transhumanism courses. This naturally includes reincarnation studies, morphology, and animal linguistics."

"An honor Matriarch. And I'm so glad to see so many new furry faces this year."

Borris' clear, high voice was audible before he was visible, which took a moment as he had to climb on top of tree-stump in order to be seen. It's not that he was small—he might have been as tall as The Matriarch if he stood upright and he surely weighed many times as much—but his characteristic slouch was understandable considering that he was an orangutan. His wild orange hair sprouted out of his forest-green robes, and he leaned upon a thick wooden staff with an antelope head on the top. The antelope head seemed quite happy for the attention and brayed loudly in response to the applause.

"But what are we waiting for?" The Matriarch asked, her voice taking on the hush of sharing a conspiratorial secret. The children were in thrall to her captivating presence and drew closer to hear what she was saying. "Wouldn't you rather skip right ahead to the main event?" Each word was softer than the last, so that the children were drawn inward with the nearest being almost within arm's reach before she stood rigidly upright and shouted, "To the Weighing Ceremony!"

The leading few children scrambled backward and fell into one another when she shouted. The Matriarch laughed and turned with a red swirl, marching toward the looming cathedral on the cliff side. Some of the town's inhabitants peeled off to return to their homes, but a good number continued to follow the children in an enclosed semi-circle as they approached the ledge. Professors Salice, Wilst, and Humstrum took up positions around the perimeter of the children as if herding sheep.

"Did they say anything about the weighing in the pamphlet?" Walter asked Noah. "I didn't see it."

Noah shrugged. "It sounds so arbitrary. All the different animals must weigh completely different"

Jamie began folding through the pamphlet to check as they walked. "Hold on, I'm sure I saw it," she said. "The Daymare 7... The Mortuary... Welcome to Barbaros... It says here that 'Everything you need will be provided for you on the island of Barbaros. There are shops in the town which will provide all of your school supplies, although no student is allowed to spend more than six months per semester to maintain uniform aging.' Here we go, the Weighing Ceremony. 'The Weighing Ceremony will precede your first classes at The Mortuary. Those who do not pass will be sent back on the Daymare, and will not attend during the current school year.'" Jamie's last words shook uncertainly as she read.

"Okay, how do you pass?" Walter asked.

"It doesn't say," Jamie groaned. "It just goes on to talk about the Bestiary, and the Coven, and the Graveyards, and all the other attractions on the island."

"I don't want to go home yet," Walter said in a small voice. "Natasha wouldn't be able to see or hear me, and I wouldn't know how to come back. I'd just be... lost."

Jamie's brow furrowed as she flipped the paper back and forth.

"That's not right of them to keep it a secret. Do you think we should ask someone to explain?"

"Shhh," Noah hissed. "It looks like she's about to tell us something."

The Matriarch had turned to face the children and was walking backward up the grassy slope now. Despite her apparent age, she moved with a sort of careless agility that turned the simplest gesture into the next component of a never-ending dance. Her rhythmic motions were soon joined by a sing-song honeyed voice.

> *My father was a soldier man*
> *Who served his nation proud.*
> *The battle lost, he turned and ran*
> *And was shot down to the ground.*
>
> *He's good and dead, the doctor said,*
> *Still and dead as he can be.*
> *He's got no head, his pillow red,*
> *He sleeps eternal as the sea.*
>
> *I'll never watch him growing old,*
> *Or catch him walking down the street.*
> *But I know if my heart is gold,*
> *Then he'll be watching me.*
>
> *Whether I go now or if I wait,*
> *Until I've passed ninety-three,*
> *I worry not, because it's our fate,*
> *To dream each other in sleep.*

The destination for the Weighing Ceremony was readily apparent from a fair distance away. A massive tree ruptured from the edge of the cliff with two ponderous limbs outstretched in either direction along the edge. From each limb hung a cage made of twisted black wires. As Noah drew nearer he noticed that one of the cages was already occupied by a solitary heart which must have belonged to a giant as the organ was several feet high and wide. The size wasn't nearly as troubling as the fact that it was beating on its own, pushing and pulling in wet gasps of air in place of blood.

"Don't be frightened, now," The Matriarch announced as she approached the base, still walking backwards to keep her eyes on the flock. "There's no beating around the bush with this one. The fact is that not all of you will find a path back to the other side. That not all of you *deserve* another life based on how you behaved in the last one. A simple calculation reveals there have been approximately 110 billion humans in the history of the world, whereas only about 7 and a half billion have currently found their way back. As a necessity, some of you will have to be turned away."

An uneasy hush fell over the assembly. The Matriarch's smile was inviting though, and her warm words continued to draw the students inward.

"One at a time—just like that, thank you. You there—with the ponytail, yes—step right up. You'll be the first."

The girl being referred to tried to melt back into the crowd, but the lady caught her by the wrist and dragged her forward. The girl looked at her feet and trembled from head to foot while the lady spoke.

"What's your name, dear?"

"Do-Dolly Miller," she stuttered.

"Well Do-Dolly Miller," The Matriarch mimicked with a reassuring smile, "why don't you tell the class a little about who you used to be?"

Dolly glanced at the cliff edge behind her as though seriously considering whether that might be the preferable route. Instead she swallowed hard and answered, "I was thirty two when I…"

"When you what?" The Matriarch prompted, leaning in with eager anticipation. "How did you die?"

Dolly looked down at her bare feet again and gripped the grass with her toes. "I did it myself," she said, barely above a whisper.

Almost as if by magic the words seemed to catch in the wind and blow across the assembly, clearly heard by Noah despite how far back he was.

"Shh... shh... that's all over now," The Matriarch cooed. "Please step into the open cage, Dolly."

She did as she was instructed, glancing at the heart opposite her with unease.

"Don't Dally Dolly," gurgled the air from the beating heart in short, rhythmic bursts. "You are safe." Needless to say this did little to comfort Dolly who was now shaking from head to foot. She clasped the bars of the cage with her hands and watched The Matriarch close the door behind her.

Over the next several seconds the girl's weight slowly lifted the heart off the ground as it began to level out. The heart huffed and puffed faster now, seeming to grow excited by the process.

"How heavy is your soul, Dolly?" The Matriarch asked eagerly, like a starving woman asking about the daily special.

"I d-don't know," Dolly stammered.

"There are many things that can add weight to a soul," The Matriarch said. "Great emotions are important. Happiness, grief, fear—it doesn't matter, so long as you've *really felt* something. Making hard decisions adds weight. Imagining interesting thoughts, telling funny jokes, perhaps a burning passion—anything that will make us look back at the end and say 'I lived because...' That *because* is what the scale is measuring. That *because* is the weight of your soul."

While she'd been talking, the scale had continued to shift in Dolly's favor until it reached a perfect level. Gradually Dolly continued to sink below that of the heart in the opposite cage.

"Dolly Miller!" the heart wheezed enthusiastically. "She lived to be loved. She is worthy to. Live again."

The townsfolk who had accompanied the children began to clap.

"Congratulations, my dear!" The Matriarch cheered with them and opened Dolly's cage, giving her a hand to help her back onto the grass. "You are most welcome among our company."

"I'm not going to move the scale an inch," Walter grumbled. "I never did a thing worth remembering."

"Don't say that," Jamie said. "Having a girlfriend will give you some points. You must have really loved her."

"I'm the one who hasn't done anything," Noah sighed, shuffling into his place in line. "I did get married, but it didn't last long. Always the same job, ever since I got out of school—seventy-five years of comfortable routines and daily habits and nothing to show for it."

"That's funny, I thought you were much younger," Jamie said. "You must get some credit for keeping a youthful spirit all the way to the end."

"What about you?" Noah asked. "Did you love your cat *passionately?*"

Jamie snorted in a not uncharming way. "Hardly. And I'm sure I miss Sebastian more than I do my husband. My son Erik might have noticed I'm gone by now, but then again he might not notice for a year on his annual visit. I've been to France though, do you think that counts for anything?"

Noah shrugged. "It can't hurt."

They waited in line while the students were weighed one by one—the first four all passing and being cheered by the crowd. Even the heart in the opposite cage seemed pleased, announcing each name with satisfaction. Noah didn't catch all the names, but he noticed Jason Parson was a human who lived to improve himself while Elizabeth Washent, the rabbit, lived to make the people around her happy.

There were a lot of students to weigh however, so whenever the beating heart wasn't making an announcement The Matriarch filled the time speaking about the school.

"The Weighing Tree was here even before The Mortuary was founded in 1647, although of course the living couldn't see it.

"The story begins with a ship named Alexandria which was carrying tobacco from America toward Europe. The ship was attacked by pirates, and every man and woman on board was slaughtered and burned aboard their looted vessel. Their spirits were not lost upon the ocean however, because on the other side they discovered the secret island of Barbaros. The men of Alexandria made an oath to one another that day, to never leave this place until they discovered a road back to life.

"In that pursuit they founded The Mortuary and began their studies. By the time one man had stumbled upon a way back to life, the whole community had become steeped in the knowledge of the spirit world. They decided that rather than let this knowledge disappear with them they would found a school so that each generation might pass on these secrets. Although each of the men has long since found their road from death, there remained one scullery maid who refused to abandon her school. Hundreds of years before women could even vote, yet since that day The Mortuary has been run by a Matriarch. *The Matriarch*, if you will."

At this she bowed low and flourished her red hat, leaving no doubt that she was claiming credit for this staggering act of good will. "Can you imagine?" she went on. "Giving up my own resurrection for the sake of forever leading others to that lofty goal? Of course I've already lived *so many* lives that I hardly need another. We should all be grateful that such a high-minded person as that has gathered you all here today."

Much of the assembled townsfolk moaned and shook their head at her boastfulness, but it was done so in good nature like someone pretending not to enjoy a good pun.

"Nigel Bronheart," the heart interrupted, "never understood. What he was living for."

The jovial atmosphere was replaced with many somber faces. Noah had been watching The Matriarch during her story and hadn't noticed the scale, but it was clear now that the heart sat considerably lower than the doughy boy dangling in the air. Nigel's eyes were wide with fear, and he began to jump up and down as though to force to scale lower. His efforts didn't move the metal cage in the slightest.

"Please step out," The Matriarch commanded, a sharp edge in her melodic voice. "It's time for you to go home, Nigel."

"That's not fair!" he protested, retreating to the opposite end of the cage. "I lived for plenty of things. I had a wife!"

"Did you love her?" The Matriarch asked patiently.

"The third one, sure I loved her," Nigel insisted. "At first anyway. And I had a steady job, and I never caused anyone any problems."

"Maybe you should have. Hush now," The Matriarch said. She opened the cage door and guided him out. "I can forgive mistakes, but I cannot forgive a blank page."

"I'm not blank!" Panic crept into Nigel's voice.

"*You* are not your experiences," The Matriarch explained patiently. "*You* are not your memories. *You* are not even your decisions, which many times are nothing but a spontaneous reaction. *You* are awareness itself, and if you failed to really feel the life you've lived, I don't see what good you'll do with another one. You have one year to revisit your old life and think about the person you used to be. If in that year you have learned what you must do differently next time, then you are welcome to come and try the scale again."

Nigel hid his face in his hands and refused to look at anyone. The Matriarch guided him gently by the shoulders to where Borris Humstrum stood leaning against his wooden staff. The orangutan nodded and wrapped a hairy arm around Nigel to lead him back the way they came. The surrounding townsfolk pushed each other out of the way to make room for them as though they were afraid of catching a disease.

"That must be so embarrassing," Jamie whispered. "If I were him I wouldn't ever come back."

"Bet he's going to go haunt somewhere now," Walter said. "Go haunt his ex-wife, throw some dishes around or something. That's what I'd do."

Noah didn't say anything though. His mouth felt like it was full of cotton, and his fingers wouldn't stop drumming against his thigh. He was next in line, and he could imagine the whole crowd sneering at him when the heart turned him away. How was he supposed to have truly experienced his own life when he'd always been focused on someone else? From his own sick mother whom he'd looked after until her passing, he'd barely had a moment to focus on his schooling before his daughter was born, and then everything he'd done was for her. Why hadn't it ever crossed his mind to spend more effort on himself? A sharp, loud sob broke the air from Nigel as he was led away, replaced by heavy silence.

"And you?" The Matriarch purred, appearing not to hear the crying boy at all. "What is your name, dear?"

"Noah Tellaver," he replied, keeping his voice as steady as he could.

"Go on then, Noah. Show us why you matter."

Noah swallowed hard, then nodded. He opened the wire cage, but hesitated before he stepped on. He glanced over his shoulder to see Jamie and Walter speaking in hushed tones. Jamie looked up and waved encouragingly, but Noah didn't feel the least relieved. At last he closed his eyes and stepped into the cage, jumping nervously as the door clanged shut behind him.

Noah couldn't feel the cage moving. There was no sound from the surrounding crowd to indicate his fate. They would have been cheering if he'd passed though, wouldn't they? There would only be silence if—but he couldn't open his eyes, because he was too afraid of seeing all those people looking down at him in disappointment.

"Noah Tellaver," the gurgling voice announced. "How many lives. Has he lived? Such a complex tapestry. I see a common thread. Runs through them all. From start to finish. With an unparalleled passion. He has lived each life. To kill. He is worthy to. Live again."

Noah opened his eyes to see a hundred eyes studying him with a range of curiosity and disgust. His cage was completely resting on the ground, the heart hoisted high above him. Hardest to bear was The Matriarch's deep brown gaze which felt like a spike impaling him against the wall. The fact that she was smiling did nothing to alleviate the pressure of her stare.

"Who did I kill?" Noah whispered to the heart in a gusty breath.

"Would you like. Their names?" the heart chortled. "It would take a while." Noah found small comfort in the fact that the heart didn't have a face, and therefore couldn't have been smiling as much as the voice suggested.

A murmur rose among the crowd of onlookers—first soft as the wind through reeds, yet steadily rising into a clamoring chorus. The Matriarch turned away from Noah to wave and smile, capturing their attention and urging them toward begrudging stillness.

"An unparalleled passion!" The Matriarch declared with excitement. "That's what I like in my students. Ladies and gentleman, please be at peace. So what if our young friend was a killer?"

"I wasn't, I swear!" Noah chimed, his voice seeming very small in the large open space. The Matriarch continued as though he hadn't spoken.

"There is no more evil in destroying life than there is in creating it. Who can say that it is worse to kill an evil man than to bring one into the world? Did the man being born have any more choice than the man who was killed? Both belong to the eternal cycle, and we do not condemn such expressions here. Welcome, Noah, to The Mortuary."

Noah glided back amongst the rest of the students, but there wasn't anyone to cheer for him as they did with the others. People stepped away from either side to make room, and even Brandon's lip was curled with disgust. Noah made his way toward Walter and Jamie again, but stopped when Walter turned suddenly to begin a conversation with a boy named Sandy behind. Jamie elbowed Walter fiercely in the ribs, prompting him to spin back once more.

"Play nice, will you?" Jamie scolded. "Does he look like a mass murderer to you?"

Walter grimaced and averted Noah's eyes. "It's none of my business," he grunted.

"I never killed anyone!" Noah insisted, hot in the face. "I sometimes had to put a dying animal to sleep at work, but I certainly never enjoyed it."

"It's not just your last life that counts," Sandy said, sweeping his shaggy blond hair out of his eyes. "It could have been your life before that.

"Or every life before that," Walter added ominously.

"I absolutely would not," Noah repeated stubbornly.

"You already did though," Walter said, still not quite meeting Noah's eyes. "You're still the same soul, don't you get it? We might not remember, but the soul we were then is the soul we are now, and it's the soul we're always going to be. You're a killer, man. I don't think that's ever going to go away."

THE MORTUARY

THE REST OF THE CEREMONY MUST HAVE COMPLETED, BUT NOAH WASN'T paying much attention. He sat away from the others on the grass with his eyes closed, wondering whether Mandy was able to look after Lewis, or whether she'd be too stricken by grief to even take care of herself. She'd always relied on him so much...

There was a thunderous round of applause, but Noah kept his eyes pressed tightly shut. Another person with a blessed life, how nice for them. Noah knotted the grass around his fingers and flung the loose blades into the air.

"Why didn't you tell me you'd found Mrs. Robinson?" Jamie asked.

Noah opened his eyes to find Jamie standing in front of him with her arms crossed. He hadn't noticed that Mrs. Robinson was stretched onto her back with curled front paws right beside him. Noah reached out to rub the cat's belly and was rewarded with a bear trap of claws.

"Ow, get it off me!"

"Ungrateful," Mrs. Robinson growled. "I came here to comfort you, and this is how you repay me."

"I was just going to pet you. Let go!"

"Hold on, you big wuss." Jamie unhooked the claws and pried the cat away to nestle it against her like a baby.

"Why are you okay when she does it?" Noah asked, nursing his hand.

"She's not a killer," Mrs. Robinson replied indignantly.

"You're one to talk," Noah grunted. "Bet you killed all sorts of mice and things."

"I even got a squirrel once," Mrs. Robinson boasted. "Took his head clean off and gave it to Claire. I think she liked it, because she ran to show it off to her mother right away."

"See? How's that any different?"

"It's not about what you do, it's about who you are," Mrs. Robinson lectured condescendingly. "When I was on the scale, the heart wouldn't shut up about how much Claire missed me. He said anyone who was loved so much must bring that love into the world again."

"Well you were both let in," Jamie said, "so you must both deserve another shot. Let's stop bickering and hurry up or everyone is going to leave us behind."

Mrs. Robinson allowed herself to be carried off by Jamie. Noah sat up to see everyone moving in the same direction.

"Where are we going?" Noah asked, hustling to catch up.

"The Mortuary! Come on!" Jamie called over her shoulder. "I can't wait to see our new home."

The Mortuary looked less like it was built and more like it was grown straight from the earth, as though it belonged as much as the forests or the cliff or the ocean itself beyond. The climbing ivy which engulfed the grave structure added to the effect, and thick moss upon every visible stone. Noah could only relate it to old gothic cathedrals he had seen in photographs, although it was impossible to compare those perfectly interlocking ancient stones with something as fragile and artificial as the buildings in his world appeared.

The far wall of the building was continuous with the cliff face as though the entire structure had been carved straight from the rock. There was a single round central tower which was composed of hundreds of smaller spires, as well as two smaller flanking towers. Each of the three towers was dominated by huge stained glass windows, and every inch of stone was intricately carved with miniature figurines, each nestled in their own alcove.

"They're gods!" one of the girls exclaimed, pointing at the closest figurines. "I never would have guessed there were so many religions. There must be thousands of them!"

"And look at the glass!" echoed another girl beside her. "What do you think the animals mean?"

From left to right, the three stained glass images were of heroically posed camel looking into the sunrise, a wide-eyed child beneath a blazing sun, and a snarling lion before a crimson sunset. There were words inscribed in the stone above the door in the central tower.

Life and death are each other's shadows,
Cast by the light of eternity.

The last of the curious townsfolk who had straggled along branched off here and returned to the cobblestone road, which in turn wound down through the grassy hills toward the town. The real sun was high overhead now, although Noah felt less tired and more like a deflated balloon. He shielded his face from the light, feeling as though he was fading beneath its relentless fire.

"Ah ah ah, not yet," The Matriarch said, calling back one of the boys who was already approaching the massive iron-studded double doors in the central tower. "It's so bright out, and you must all be so tired. Classes won't begin until tomorrow night. Mr. Wilst, would you be so kind as to show the students their resting place? When you're finished, you can join myself and the other staff in my chambers."

"Certainly, Matriarch," replied the dry, cracking voice. The Skeleton's metal staff clanked threateningly against the stone path as he turned away from the front doors. A few apprehensive glances were exchanged, but no one protested to following the morbid figure along the side of the building. He brought them around the building's flank to a tall black iron fence with severe spikes lining the top. Professor Wilst led them through the gate, and then waited there as the students filed in.

"We're going to sleep in a graveyard?" a blonde girl asked, her nose wrinkled in displeasure.

"There's something very comfortable about being with your own body that never goes away," Wilst replied.

"Ewww, they brought our bodies here?" she whined.

"Shhh Grace. Just let him talk," a taller girl beside her hissed.

Grace raised her hand instead, holding it excessively vertical.

Wilst stared at them expressionlessly for a moment before continuing. "The imps should have already stocked your bodies in the Mausoleums. There will be two names to a structure. Find the one where you belong and lie down. Professor Salice will retrieve you at sunset to collect your books and school supplies."

"How come we still need to sleep?" Grace asked, unable to contain herself any longer. "We don't need to eat, do we? I don't feel hungry anyway."

"Silly human," Wilst replied in a voice that implied he didn't have the first clue what silliness was, and only a faint recollection of being human. "Spirits don't need to eat or sleep, but even the dead must dream."

With that the Professor swept his white linen about him and exited the graveyard. Several other people were beginning to ask questions, but their voices were cut off by the loud grating sound of metal clanking against metal. Professor Wilst had fastened a chain around the gate and locked it with a heavy padlock.

The Professor turned stiffly on his heel bone and walked away, ignoring the mounting protest from the students locked inside. Within seconds there were students leaping onto the fence and clutching the bars. Others shouted after Wilst or rattled the chain around the gate, but none succeeded in turning the skeletal figure around.

"It's not so bad, look," Walter said, emerging from one of the stone mausoleums. He was holding a stuffed reindeer in his arms. "I don't see any bodies in there. I think he was just being dramatic to scare us."

"Did it work? Are you scared?" an older boy with a face that permanently appeared to be tasting something sour asked. He'd just emerged from another of the mausoleums.

"Oh boy, I love stuffed animals! Where's mine?" Bowser said. Then louder, the dog howled "Anyone see Bowser? Where's Bowser supposed to sleep?"

The hunt for their personal mausoleum quickly distracted the students who spread out through the graveyard. Walter had already found his place, but Noah didn't mind not sharing a place with his new friend after how he'd reacted at the weighing ceremony. Mrs. Robinson had wriggled free once more and Jamie was chasing her between the structures, so Noah didn't bother them either. He hunted on his own until he found his name, He ducked inside the low stone arch, grateful to finally have a chance to rest. He felt a lot less grateful when he saw who else was already inside.

"Why do I have to share with the murderer?" Brandon sneered. He was sitting cross-legged on the ground with his back against the coffin, holding a stuffed rhino on his lap. The inside of the mausoleum was small but clean with bare stone floors and a cushioned coffin against either wall. A burning lamp rested in the center, although the ball of fire which lit the enclosure floated unsupported in the glass. There was no curtain or barrier or any form of privacy between the two sides. On top of Noah's coffin sat a stuffed tiger waiting for him.

"I won't bother you if you don't bother me," Noah said, sitting down on his side of the room.

"Just looking at you bothers me," Brandon said. Noah was beginning to wonder whether he was really sneering at all, or whether that's simply how his face looked.

"I was expecting to find our real bodies in here," Noah said, trying to divert the subject.

"Look inside, idiot," Brandon said. He held up his rhino to reveal that he'd already ripped it open along the seam on its back. The skeletal remains of a hand clearly protruded from the white fluff, the curved forefinger making up the rhino's spine. Noah looked at the stuffed tiger and shuddered, preferring not to imagine what part of him might be inside.

Brandon waited for Noah to reply, but he didn't. Brandon sighed and climbed inside his coffin to lay down, still holding his stuffed rhino. "It's really not so bad," Brandon said, his voice seeming smaller and less hostile than it had a moment before. "If I close my eyes, it feels almost like I'm home."

"Why, did you sleep in a coffin at home too?" Noah replied sarcastically. He picked up his tiger and immediately understood what Brandon meant though. He felt a presence apart from the soft fur, a sort of harmony like an out of tune note that had just been adjusted to fit again. Noah climbed into the generous padding of his own coffin and held his tiger close. It was a perfect fit.

"Screw off, what would you know," Brandon replied. "Your home could have probably fit in my garage." He swung his lid shut to close himself inside.

Noah double checked to make sure there wasn't a lock on the coffin before carefully lowering his own lid. The darkness grew heavy, and this too felt nourishing somehow. The madness of the day faded into the comfortable buzz of voiceless thoughts, which in turn gave way to the haze of dreams. Violent dreams, bloody dreams, one after another, with Noah himself committing each atrocity he saw.

"Don't hit your head when you wake up!"

Noah jolted upright, trying to escape his dreams more than he was trying to lurch back into wakefulness. He immediately smacked against the lid of his coffin and flopped back onto the cushions.

"The moon won't wait. Come on now, you can rest when you're alive." It was Professor Salice, but the voice was muffled and moving away.

Noah opened his coffin with his hand this time. Brandon was already gone, and he'd taken his stuffed rhino with him. Noah couldn't imagine what he'd need it for, but the presence was so familiar that he couldn't resist taking his tiger along as well.

Professor Salice was standing near the open gate. He was scratching his demon dog behind the ears, which caused one of its tentacles to flop out of its mouth and twirl in sinuous spirals. A dozen imps had scattered through the graveyard to knock against the mausoleums and rouse those who resisted.

Noah moved to join the mass of students gathering around the gate, but most of them would take one look at him before quickly finding an excuse to stand anywhere else. Noah caught the eye of Walter, but he immediately looked away again without offering any sort of greeting.

"Noah! Over here!" Jamie called, waving and hopping up and down to be seen. "Look at this."

"Please do not touch the imps," Professor Salice drawled, looking in her direction. "I thought you would have learned your lesson on the bus already, Mrs. Poffin."

"He remembers me though," she insisted. "I think he's trying to say sorry for biting me earlier. Look he even let me pet—ow!" The imp bit her once more, and the students howled with laughter. Noah smiled and moved to join her, and, at least for the time being, everyone seemed to be too distracted to take any notice of him.

Professor Salice led the students through the gate and onto the cobblestone road. In the near distance, Noah could see open gates in other sections of the graveyard which allowed the free passage of older students. It appeared that only the youngest ones were locked in during the day.

"The sum of your supplies for the semester should cost no more than two months," the Professor said. "You should have all spent two weeks on your passage here, which leaves three and a half months available for discretionary spending. I strongly encourage you not to spend anything unnecessarily today, however. You are all without exception still very stupid and ignorant about matters of death, and the townsfolk with have no qualms about taking advantage of your unsuspecting wealth. While you may prevent yourself from aging by acquiring other people's life force later, you will never be able to reverse its process and become younger again while you remain a spirit."

The students pressed him with questions about what to expect, but he assured them that they would discover it for themselves soon enough.

"We will meet back here at the crossroads at midnight when I will escort you back to The Mortuary," Professor Salice instructed. He was passing out sheets of paper from a stack in his arms now. Some students were tentative to approach the professor and retreated the moment they received their note. "You will find the required items on the list along with a map of the town. Note the hourglass on the paper—when that is empty, it will be time for us to head back."

The words on the paper burned as though glowing hot, making them clearly visible even in the pale moonlit night. Grains of sands like sparks drifted down from the hourglass to fill the glowing base. Noah scanned the list of required items, which included three textbooks by the names of:

Understanding Undead: The Spirit's Guide to the Other Side
Twelve Signs Your Imp Might Be Plotting To Kill You: And Other Demonological Advice
Don't Be A Cow, Man: Reincarnation The Right Way

"What are we going to use Voodoo Dolls for?" Walter asked, reading the lower half of the sheet.

"Clearly to stick it to the man," Salice replied dryly. "Get going or you'll still be out when the ghouls wake up. Noah, you may stay with me."

Noah hadn't gone five steps before the note was whisked from his hands by two long and dexterous fingers. Salice handed the paper to one of his imps instead and shooed it away.

"See that it's filled," Salice said, dismissing the imp toward the village without taking his eyes off Noah. "We wouldn't want to burden our new Chainer with such trivialities, now would we?"

Noah wasn't sure who the 'we' being referred to was. He was acutely conscious that a disproportionate number of the students were staring at him. It made him immensely uncomfortable.

"I really don't mind getting my own books," Noah said quietly. He tried to surreptitiously retrieve his shopping list from the imp, but it growled as he reached for it and Noah backed off.

"Nonsense. Come. I have something else to show you that will be more worthy of your... lineage. Have you ever heard the story of the blind men and the elephant? Walk with me."

The sallow faced man pivoted sharply and reversed direction, making a direct route back toward The Mortuary. Noah shook his head, allowing himself to be led away. He felt as though he had no choice but to follow, although at that moment he would have rather done anything else even if it meant burying himself on the spot. It was bad enough everyone thinking him a murderer without being singled out again. He could already hear the word *'Chainer'* being whispered up and down the assembled students.

"One blind man stands at the elephant's tail, and he's asked by the others to describe what the elephant is like. The blind man grasps the tail and feels it up and down, confidently telling the others that the elephant is like a rope. Another blind man stands at the legs, and feeling these argues the elephant is a tree trunk. A third feels the tusk, saying the elephant is a sharp spear. Are any of these men wrong?"

"Couldn't they just keep walking around feeling the rest of the elephant?" Noah reasoned.

"Such is the life of a common soul," Salice said, ignoring the reply. "No matter how long they study what is within their grasp, they will only understand life through a single perspective, and thus they will not understand it at all. Only a Chainer may learn the truth of the elephant, and no secret of life may be hidden from one who experiences many lives. In the pursuit of truth and power, there is nothing more important than Chainers. How is it to be back?"

"I don't even remember being here before," Noah replied. "I don't remember any of my previous lives either. What good is it being a Chainer if I can't remember anything?"

Salice's tight skin seemed close to snapping as he grimaced. "Nothing? I wouldn't expect you to remember exactly how you made it back, but at least you must remember the other times you've died. Not every day that you die—very memorable, impossible to forget, I'd imagine."

"All I remember is being chased by something—A gargoyle, I heard it called—and then I was hit by a car while trying to get away. And that was only in my previous life."

"Mmm," Salice said through pursued lips. He appeared disappointed. "A gargoyle doesn't chase the living. Your mind must have already started to decay before you died. There are some things that can't be erased, even if they are forgotten. Experiences, people, even skills and powers—they become so ingrained in your being that they become inseparable from the soul. I've heard that Mozart was a pianist in every one of his lives, and that he would always master it again regardless of his opportunities to play."

If Professor Salice had been trying to make Noah feel better, then it wasn't working. It was impossible not to wonder for the hundredth time how many people he'd really killed. With an *unparalleled passion*, no less.

"No matter. I have no doubt that you'll find it all coming back to you sooner or later," Salice added languidly. "Perhaps the Whispering Room will jog your memory. It's typically reserved for staff and special guests, but I don't think anyone would protest to a Chainer making use. After-all, you're much older than even I."

The Mortuary doors ahead were open and a steady flow of older students were piling through. They all wore plain gray trousers and t-shirts, just like Noah had received from George Hampton what seemed like a lifetime ago. The Professor's imps were scurrying ahead as they walked to clutch and claw at the legs of students who were standing in the way. The demon dog never left its masters side though, not even by a few feet.

"Do you know how many lives I've lived before? Could you tell from the weighing ceremony?" Noah asked.

"More than ten—perhaps many more," Professor Salice answered.

He disdainfully swatted a boy on the back of the head who was taking too long to move aside. "Enough for there to be power in you, if one knows where to look."

Noah considered asking again whether he could have really murdered people in all of them, but there were so many other students about now and he didn't want to draw more attention than was necessary. Besides, he was entering the main doors and was distracted by his first look inside.

It was a rather imposing structure on the outside, but at least it still looked recognizable enough for him to think of it as a cathedral. Inside the whole central tower contained a single cavernous room which soared at least a dozen stories above his head. He stood upon a circular path which traced the perimeter of the tower with eight doors spaced evenly around.

The tower above him was only the tip of the iceberg though, for the center of the space was dominated by a massive pit which must have been carved directly into the cliff it rested upon. Within that pit a gargantuan tree soared up from unseen depths. Its highest boughs filled the central tower above ground, and its innumerable branches stretched out to the circular pathway to form natural bridges leading to the tree itself where doors were carved directly into the trunk. Noah rushed to the edge of the pathway and looked down over the brass railing to see another circular pathway on a floor below him, and another below that, and more beyond until they were lost in the inscrutable darkness below. The whole scene was illuminated in a red-tinged moonlight which poured through the stained glass window with the child and the blazing sun.

"Unless you plan to jump, I advise following me," Professor Salice said darkly. He was already striding across one of the thick branches which spanned the pit to the main trunk. "Contrary to the fondest wishes of many naive first years, the reckless dead can still die. It isn't easy to destroy a spirit, but once gone you are gone with it. We will be taking the stairs."

Noah hastened across the bridge after Salice who was opening the door within the tree trunk. The brass railings felt woefully inadequate over the abyss, and Noah made the mistake of looking down when he was about halfway across. The tree seemed to go on forever, and deep below two shades of darkness seemed to slide past each other as though some monstrous creature was stirring in the depths. It was fortunate that the space below the railings was too interwoven with branches to allow him to fall, because Noah wobbled dangerously before catching hold of the railing once more.

"Today, Noah," the Professor barked.

Noah tore his eyes away with difficulty and forced his weak knees to stumble along the remainder of the bridge. He was only too grateful to step through the door to enter the tree, which turned out to be filled with a two spiral staircases which wound around each other in a double-helix. These too seemed to wind down indefinitely, although at least it was well lit by an array of small burning orbs which floated randomly throughout the space. No—not orbs—he could clearly see the little winged bodies wreathed in flames. Noah reached a hand toward one, recoiling immediately after feeling its warmth.

"Will-o-wisps are for looking, not touching," Salice said without even glancing over his shoulder. "First floor is the living quarters for the teachers and staff. Do not disturb anyone unless you've been specifically invited." Noah was still transfixed by all the new sights so he did not answer. "Confirm that you understand me, Noah."

"Yes sir," he replied automatically.

"Second floor is dedicated to necromancy studies. You will find rooms for animation, possession, and other occult matters."

"Yes sir," Noah said again, immediately feeling foolish by the condescending look he received. They passed the second floor headed downward.

"Third floor is run by Professor Humstrum," Salice continued. "I wouldn't expect a Chainer to bother with something as lowly as reincarnation though. Why would someone who has already proven their ability to return on their own terms wish to waste their time as a rat or a cockroach? I've never understood it.

"On the fourth floor you will be receiving instruction from me. Do not dismiss demonology as the mere imps you see around you. This branch of science deals with much more profound and practical uses that can both aid your existence here as well as provide new routes back to the living world. There is nothing more powerful in this world or the next than the magic spun from the Nether."

Noah expected them to exit on this floor and even reached toward the door, but Professor Salice continued his descent. There was not a single student to be seen on the stairway below the fourth floor. Salice didn't stop until he reached the fifth floor where he held open the door for Noah. The stairway beyond this point was blocked by a metal gate which was fastened by many sets of heavy chains.

High overhead, Noah could see the students going to and fro across the bridges, but the circular floor on this level was completely deserted. The light from the stained-glass couldn't penetrate this far down, and everything was obscured in a thick layer of shadow.

"The fifth floor contains the Whispering Room, as well as the seven unspeakable words. Students are not permitted here without invitation. Come."

Noah couldn't help but look down once more while crossing the bridge, and this time he was sure he saw two great eyes blinking deep below in the darkness.

"Below this begins the Road From Death. A student may choose to walk it upon graduation, or more commonly, they continue their studies independently while finding work in the town below. Others will return to the living world as a spirit where they will watch over those they have left behind, although the T.D.D. has strict rules about permitted interactions. Don't be so slow—my students will be expecting me shortly."

Noah hurried across the remainder of the bridge to join Professor Salice on the circular floor. He was already unlocking and opening the first door to disappear inside. Noah hesitated before entering, noticing a wave of cool steel-blue mist pouring out of the room to stream about his feet and legs.

"Why do they call it the Whispering Room, Professor? What's it for?" Noah asked.

"In the Whispering Room, one might hear everything the living are still thinking and speaking of them. It is a valuable chance to connect with your previous lives, even more so for a Chainer who might possess an enduring legacy. Aren't you curious what they have to say?"

THE WHISPERING ROOM

THE WHISPERING ROOM WAS SMALL AND ROUND, LOOKING TO BE designed for no more than one or two occupants. Most of the space was filled by an elevated marble dais on which a large mystical circle was carved into the stone. Its outline was filled with occult writing and strangely interlocking geometrical shapes. The pale blue mist was bleeding from the carved lines.

"I don't think I want to hear," Noah said, reluctant to enter. "Mandy will be in pain, and there won't be anything I can do for her. Can we try again another time when it isn't all so… fresh?"

Professor Salice watched Noah in silence, the colored mist casting odd shadows across his angular face.

"Do you know what I hear when I stand in circle?" Professor Salice asked.

Noah shook his head. Salice pursed his lips, for the first time appearing vulnerable.

"When I first died," Salice continued, "it used to be almost deafening in here. I had a big family—three sons, two daughters, brothers and sisters. I owned my own business and a hundred people owed their jobs to me. I had two homes, and four cars, and a boat that I would take out on the lake during the summer. And that's what everybody was talking about. All I ever heard in here was people trying to figure out which of my things they would get to keep. And now..." the Professor cleared his throat. "I haven't heard so much as a peep for a long time now. Listening to the Whispering Room is rarely easy, even for the purest souls. But the earlier you listen the truer it will be, and such insight will aid you in preparing for the next time round."

Noah nodded as he cautiously mounted the marble dais. The Professor slid along the wall behind him to shut the door. The mist began to pool on the ground and fill the room now that it wasn't leaking out, and in that mist Noah could hear a soft murmuring. Noah stepped inside the circle and the sound immediately became clear.

"I don't know if you can hear me, Noah, but I know you aren't gone." It was Samantha with her white eye, her face briefly flickering within the shades of blue mist. "I've been starting to see things ever since my eye was hurt. Spirits—dead things, I guess, and other creatures I've got no name for. One that looks like its made of stone except for its yellow eyes is prowling my street every night, rummaging through the trash cans, searching for something. I don't know if it's the same one that attacked me, but I keep pretending that I don't see it and it hasn't bothered me yet. Am I safe? Please—if you can hear me—please help me understand."

"What a pretty eye you have, girl," Professor Salice said softly.

Samantha's whisper was already growing fainter as another one rose to drown it out. Claire's face was in the mist now. She seemed to be praying. "Dear Noah, please take care of Mrs. Robinson for me. It was hard at first thinking she wandered off and didn't want to stay with me, but now I'm glad that she has a friend over there. Don't forget about us—Samantha talks about you all the time, and I know she won't forget about you..."

Next a three year old child—it was Lewis, but only for a moment, his image distorted and blurry. "Noah..." he said. "I'm hungry, where are you?" Then he too was gone.

There were other whispers—fainter ones from the man driving the jeep, or the people in the ambulance who took him away. There was the echo of phone calls made between relatives, and the gossip between neighbors. These too gradually faded into silence though, and the mist was beginning to dissipate. Just when he thought it was over, his daughter's face finally appeared within the mist.

Mandy's hair was messier than ever, and her face was red and puffy with tears. "Not dead..." she mumbled. "He's with Lewis and they're playing a game. They're playing a trick on me, but I'm not going to be fooled. Oh no, not me. I'm the one who invented fooling people, don't you know?"

Mandy pinched the bridge of her nose and closed her eyes as though trying to concentrate.

Noah's fingers tingled. He looked down to see his hands clenched so tightly that they trembled. He took a deep breath and forced himself to relax.

"I don't want to hear anymore," Noah said. "Make them go away."

Mandy opened her eyes, her gaze darting this way and that—searching for something.

"She can't see me, can she?"

"Of course not," Professor Salice said. "Not unless—"

His words cut short as Mandy's gaze focused deliberately on Noah's face. "I knew it! Noah, I knew—but you're just a boy. Where did my father go? I want my father back! Those horrid girls lied about him. The police—the hospital—they were all part of the game. My father is still here though, isn't he? Tell me he's still here!"

"Oh Mandy, I'll always be there with you," Noah spoke with difficulty, forcing the air out of his throat which seemed to have closed to a pinhole. "I'm not the same as I used to be, but I still remember everything. I need you not to look at the spirits you see though. There's a stony thing with yellow eyes that is looking—"

"Dispersus!" Professor Salice commanded. The word had an unnatural metallic echo to it, and the echo grew louder with each iteration instead of softer as it ought to. Within a few seconds the word 'dispersus' pummeled Noah with a physical force, assaulting him from all directions as it ricocheted off the walls. Noah stumbled out of the circle with his hands clutched over his ears. The mist around him evaporated as the last echos blasted through the room, now at last growing softer until the last reverberation had disappeared completely.

Noah rushed back to the circle and stepped inside, but the mist was no longer bleeding from the cracks and his daughter was gone.

"What did you do?" Noah shouted, scraping the marble floor with a furious swipe of his hand.

"Why didn't you tell me your daughter was a Chainer too?" Salice hissed. Noah felt his own bluster vanish as that tight skin contorted into a snarl overhead.

"I didn't know—" Noah stammered impulsively, bewildered.

"Liar! You knew how important Chainers were, and still you hid her from me. What were you going to tell her, hm? Come on now, out with it."

The professor's black dog leapt to its feet from where it had been been silently sitting at Salice's side. The flare of tentacles flew from its mouth and a low growl rose in its throat.

"Nothing! I was only warning her—" Noah began, backing away from the creature.

"The gargoyle. Which she could only see if she was a Chainer too. Which means you knew she could see spirits—of course, how could you not, your own daughter. But to have her detect your presence through the Whispering Room—a rare prize indeed."

The dog's growl turned into a wet, squelching howl. It began to advance on Noah with its head low as though stalking its prey. Noah pressed himself against the wall to get as far away from it as he could.

"Visoloth, down," Salice commanded.

The dog sat instantly as though its rear end was magnetized to the floor. The swiping tentacles slowly receded back into its mouth, though they still occasionally snapped through the air like a shadow-boxer.

Salice began to strum his fingers upon his cheek, pinning Noah with his gaze. Then he took a long breath and Noah could see the individual muscles in his face relaxing one by one. "Your grandson. Does he see spirits as well?"

Noah hesitated. "I don't know. He's only three and wouldn't know a spirit if he saw one."

Professor Salice finally succeeded in relaxing his face, except for a single muscle at the corner of his eye which continued to twitch. "Allow me to apologize. I have been rude to you." To Noah's shock, the Professor swept into a low bow at Noah's feet. "I allowed the excitement of my discovery to overpower my manners. Chainers are just so useful and I... but no, I was rash and unpleasant. Please take this key as a token of my apology. You are welcome to use the Whispering Room whenever you'd like."

Noah accepted the metal key in silence, suspicious of the sudden change in behavior.

"Of course, you might still have trouble getting a message across if she isn't thinking about you while you're in the room," Salice continued, his words slow and measured as though he was dictating something to an unseen scribe. "I would be better service to you if I arrange to have your message personally delivered."

"Very well..." Noah said, guarded. "You will have to give me time to write something though."

Salice nodded rapidly—almost eagerly. "Of course, of course—as long as you need. And where will I be sending it?"

Noah felt more unsure than ever. It seemed that Salice wanted to know where his daughter lived for a reason completely apart from delivering a message. Refusing him outright seemed like a mistake though, and Noah didn't want to enrage the man again.

"I'll write the address on the letter when it's done," Noah said. "Thank you."

The muscle just above Salice's top lip curled independent of the rest of his face, then released. The Professor then smiled broadly, although the smile never made it as far up as his eyes. "That will do nicely. Well I can't keep you all day, as much as I would like to. Your imp should be waiting for you on the ground floor with your books and school supplies. Don't wait for me; I plan to remain here a little while."

"I thought you couldn't hear anything anymore?" Noah asked, scolding himself for being nosy.

Professor Salice wasn't angry though. He smiled a sad little smile and said, "Silence sometimes has more to say than words, if you know how to listen. Go along, I will be seeing you again Wednesday for our first class. Do bring the letter you've written then."

Noah was only too happy to exit the room. He wasted no time darting back across the bridge and didn't even look down until he'd gotten to the other side. Then up the stairs, taking them three at a time all the way back to the ground floor.

All the students he passed were now wearing the same gray t-shirt and pants that he was wearing, which apparently was some sort of uniform. None of them were wearing shoes though, which by now had ceased to seem nearly so odd.

Noah found the imp immediately upon exiting the tree. It was on the other side of the bridge sitting atop a pile of books within a cheerfully bright red wooden cart, snarling and baring its teeth at anyone who got too close. This seemed to have unfortunately encouraged some of the students to make a game out of trying to steal its treasure without being bitten.

"You sneak around on the left," Brandon instructed Teresa. "Try and pull its tail, and then when it looks away I can grab the stuff."

"You awful brat!" Jamie scolded. "What could you possibly do with two sets of books?"

"I'd like to see how long it takes for them to hit the bottom of the pit," he replied casually. Several on-looking students snickered at this.

"Watch who you call brat," Teresa huffed, "unless you'd rather be tossed over instead. It might be easier to tell how deep the pit is by listening to you scream all the way down."

"Leave off!" Noah shouted as he began racing across the bridge. "I need those!"

"Go!" Brandon hissed. Teresa dove for the imp and snatched its tail. The creature wailed pitifully but refused to turn away from Brandon. The boy shied away, pacing the perimeter of its reach. As soon as it became clear that he was hesitating, the imp spun around and took a bite out of Teresa's hand. She let go and stumbled backward, swearing bitterly which sounded all the worse coming from a child. Brandon dove forward and managed to knock over the cart and scatter the books to the ground. He then retreated as soon as the imp refocused its attention on him.

Noah burst through the circle of gawking students to arrive beside the imp. He snatched the fallen books and things indiscriminately, dropping some again in the process as he tried to keep one eye on Brandon.

"First day and you already can't keep up." Brandon scoffed. "Better hurry before the Daymare leaves. I don't think they allow murderers to resurrect anyway."

"Leave him alone." It was Walter, blocking Brandon's route to the imp. "He's not the one you should feel sorry for."

"What's that supposed to mean?" Brandon demanded. Despite the bluster, he seemed less sure of himself now that he was outnumbered.

"It's bad enough having a clingy child without it following you after death," Walter said. "I bet your mom can't wait to start over without you."

Brandon made a lunge toward the imp as though he was going to smash it straight into the wall behind. Walter dove between them and pushed Brandon back. The imp clutched its claws together and gazed up with wonder at Walter as though he was its salvation.

Noah took the opportunity to hurriedly stack his books back in the cart. Teresa hadn't taken Walter's comment well though, and she was scowling wickedly, about to reply when—*SCREECH*—an earsplitting scream exploded overhead. Great gray feathered wings wider across than Noah was tall beat the air, prompting students to hurl themselves to the ground left and right. Talons like scimitars curled around the brass railing, and brilliant green eyes skewered each student in turn with their baleful glare.

"Professor Humstrum. First year class. Fifteen minutes. Third floor!" screeched the creature in short bursts with a voice that sounded like fingernails on a chalkboard. Her face was remarkably smooth and feminine apart from the blazing eyes, although the rest of her torso was covered in a sporadic layer of feathers that looked more like they had been stabbed into her skin than naturally grown.

A hushed whisper passed up and down the gawking students. Noah clearly heard the word 'Harpy'. This distraction gave Noah ample time to right his cart. The imp was reluctant to give up the: *Twelve Signs Your Imp Might Be Plotting To Kill You* book, but Noah managed to wrestle it away without Brandon or Teresa interfering.

"I never noticed—there must be dozens of them," Dolly Miller breathed nearby. "Look up at the tree top!"

More gray shapes were swirling through the boughs of the massive tree. They must be just waking up though, because Noah was sure he would have noticed their screeching the first time he passed through. Noah squinted and thought that he could even make out a number of small ramshackle houses balanced among the higher branches.

The Harpy continued to glare at the students who wasted no time in hustling across the bridge to the central stairway.

"Thanks for that," Noah said to Walter.

Walter grunted in reply, focused on trying to keep his own cart upright with all the other students jostling against it. "Don't get used to it," he said. "I just hate seeing someone teamed up on, that's all."

"Aren't you still worried that I'm going to murder you?" Noah asked, keeping his voice light.

Walter looked him up and down and shrugged. "Just remember I stuck up for you next time you start killing."

"Deal. I'll get you last, and if I'm feeling tired then I'll skip you completely," Noah said, relieved to see Walter grin in reply.

The carts didn't bump down the stairs like Noah expected. In fact they were surprisingly light from the start, but as soon as they were pushed down the first step they continued to glide as though rolling down an invisible ramp. This was especially convenient for the animals who couldn't hope to carry their own books. Elizabeth Washent, the rabbit, had already figured out how to steer her cart and make it propel itself while she sat inside.

There was a commotion as they went down the stairs however.

Bowser the dog had pushed his cart ahead only for it to sail off through the air without him. The cart kept going straight ahead until it smashed into one of the curved walls of the tree. Despite this example, several others were beginning to experiment with gliding their own carts, causing even more collisions and accidents and blocking up the stairway terribly. Some of the older students howled with laughter at the fumbling first years, but they were all having such a good time learning to drive their books around that they hardly minded.

The students exited onto the third floor and marveled at the stunning vegetation which existed there. Long tendrils like vines grew from the tree to wrap around the brass railings, and from them bloomed magnificent and alien flowers. The vines spread out along the entirety of the floor, dividing over and over into entirely new plants. Tall ferns, thick bushes, even complete trees were growing straight up from the floor with their long roots interweaving with the branches of the tree.

"Transhumanism and reincarnation studies!" boomed an unseen orator. "Welcome to your first class at The Mortuary."

TRANSHUMANISM

"Drat, now how many were there supposed to be again? It seems like there are more every year."

The fair, high voice sounded like it was coming from a student at first, but it was Professor Humstrum himself. The ape was scratching its back with the tip of its staff as it leaned against the wall, almost invisible beneath the broad leafed ivy hanging around the door frame. The students were still chattering loudly to one another, and it seemed that most didn't notice him at all until the antelope head on his staff began to bray.

"Shh, shh, don't startle them Hazel," the Professor said, stroking the side of its head. "Just because you haven't met them yet doesn't mean they aren't your friends."

The students quieted down immediately to watch this odd spectacle. Professor Humstrum continued to pet his staff, mumbling soft words of reassurance to it that Noah couldn't hear. The orangutan waited until the last of the students had exited the stairway onto the bridge before setting his staff aside and rearing to its full height which appeared to be about five feet, only slightly taller than the students.

"Welcome, young Transhumanists!" Professor Humstrum announced. He grinned broadly revealing a pair of deadly sharp fangs, and a small bird stuck its head out of its shoulder fur to see what was going on. "Don't give me those faces. No tests—no essays—I'm not here to try to trick you into learning anything. If your heart has a true fondness for what lies ahead then you will remember my lessons, and if your heart lets go then you will find something else to love. I do hope you all brought your copy of *Don't Be A Cow, Man...* Oh no, you won't be needing your stuffed animal quite yet. Right then, follow me."

Noah counted eight rooms around the circular floor, each numbered with the appropriate number of brilliant red flowers. As he was turning he caught the eye of Jamie who had found her way behind him in the crowd. Her gray t-shirt was bulging, and there was a black tail sticking out below the bottom, swishing with distemper. Jamie's face was almost glowing from the sheer force of how hard she was smiling. Noah grinned and turned back to the front to see the students following the Professor into the first room.

The classroom was entirely organic, from the chairs and desks which grew from the floor to the florescent mushrooms dangling from the ceiling like a chandelier. The Professor nodded and bobbed merrily like an enthusiastic waiter ushering diners to their table.

"I know a lot of you must feel pretty overwhelmed by this point in your death, so let's get the basics out of the way first," the Professor spoke as he waddled toward his wooden pedestal with branches shaped like cupholders. "Our modern understanding of the spirit world is really quite simple. You are a soul, here and there, now and always. If you're a soul with a corporal body, then you're considered 'alive'. If you have no physical body, then your soul projects a spiritual body until you can find a new one. Which body you'll be able to pick will be largely determined by how much you learn in this class. I, myself, spent a life as a lion before giving orangutan a try."

Professor Humstrum puffed out his hairy chest in pride at this declaration as he beamed around the classroom. Hazel, the antelope head, snorted derisively.

"A lion in a zoo. Don't forget to tell them you lived in a zoo," it said.

Professor Humstrum deflated a bit, but he rallied immediately. "I would have told them if it mattered. It's not like that made me any less of a lion."

"'Course not," Hazel said. "Just like I don't need legs to be just as fast as the other antelope."

"Any questions so far? I know it can all be rather overwhelming at first," the Professor asked suddenly, prompting giggles from the class at his overt attempt at changing the subject. "Yes, you, the little blonde dog. Did you have something to ask?"

Bowser put his front paw back down on his desk. "What happens if your spirit body is killed?"

"First you must remember that a spirit body is more than arms and legs," the Professor answered. "You've got a spirit brain too, with memories and thoughts and habits and personality, and all those things about you make you feel like you," Humstrum replied, his voice kind and patient. "If that is destroyed, you will lose all that, but that doesn't mean everything is gone. Your soul is a hard seed at the center that can never be harmed. In time it will grow a new body and a new mind, and although you won't remember the person you used to be, the cycle of life will begin again."

Bowser' paw went up again, and he continued before the Professor had a chance to call on him. "But what if you get really old and you keep spending your last months? Or you get ripped to little pieces and scattered over the oceans? Will you still come back?"

"Every thinking being that has ever lived is either on this side or the other, in one form or another. Does anyone else have questions?"

"Ouch, let go!" squealed Jamie abruptly. Mrs. Robinson dropped from beneath her shirt and made a mad dash for the door. The kitten clawed desperately at the wood, lifting itself off the ground before collapsing in sullen defeat.

"How'd she get in there?" Jamie asked, her voice very small and self-conscious. The class seemed uncertain how to react until Professor Humstrum burst out laughing, and guttural oohs were so warm and heartfelt that the students couldn't help but to follow suit. Humstrum knelt down beside the kitten and whispered something inaudible, and Mrs. Robinson's raised fur and tail settled at once. The Professor cupped his hands to carry the kitten back to his pedestal.

"What is your name, child?" Professor Humstrum asked. There was a brief confusion before it became apparent that he was speaking to Mrs. Robinson.

"I don't have a name," she replied. "I don't want to be here anymore. I want to go home."

"But you *are* home," the Professor said soothingly. "Haven't you gotten your books or anything yet?"

"No," Mrs. Robinson said stubbornly, "and I don't want to read or do human things. I want to be a cat forever."

"Her name is Mrs. Robinson," Jamie peeped up. She immediately slapped her hands over her mouth, apparently startled by her own words.

"Wouldn't you prefer to be a living cat though?"

"No, I don't care," Mrs. Robinson replied. "I miss my Claire. She'll be all grown up by the time I finish school and get back."

Professor Humstrum closed his eyes and ran his hand down Mrs. Robinson's back. A zigzagging sapphire-blue spark raced up his staff, through his body, around his cumbersome knuckles, and in an instant danced across the cat to burst into the air like a tiny firework.

"You used to be a human. Did you know that, Mrs. Robinson?"

The cat looked distrustfully at the staff and didn't say anything.

"It's quite natural for souls to have an affinity toward things they used to be. As for you..." Professor Humstrum strode across the room and placed his hand on Jamie's forehead. "What is your name, girl?"

Jamie told him, and as she did a similar blue spark raced up the staff again and danced through her hair.

"You were once a cat," the Professor said confidently. Then returning to his podium where Mrs. Robinson still sat, he continued. "As I have already said, I have no intention to force anyone to learn against his will. I simply wish that all who attend my class are aware that life is so much bigger than the taste they've had, no matter how rich that experience was," he nodded at Mrs. Robinson, "or how many lives they have already led," and another nod toward Noah, who pretended not to notice.

"It is natural for the freshly dead to obsess over the life they've already lived, because that life and life itself are synonymous to them. Some are never able to let go of that life, and they spend the rest of time dreaming about how it used to be. I would be failing as an instructor if I did not acknowledge this possibility, but so too would I be failing if I did not encourage you to see what *could be* as well as what *was*. Will you consider staying with us, Mrs. Robinson, at least until you better understand what your options really are?"

Mrs. Robinson looked so tiny and alone sitting there on the podium with the whole class staring at her. In the big scheme of things though, Noah decided they were all in the same boat.

"For a little while," Mrs. Robinson conceded. "I'll share a book with Jamie until I get my own."

"Is that alright with you, Jamie?" Professor Humstrum asked. He puffed out his chest and beaming with pride as the cat hopped onto the ground and made her way to Jamie's desk.

"Of course she can. I love her." Jamie said shyly, clearly embarrassed by all the attention. More giggling erupted around her.

"Ah, love," Humstrum said, stroking his orange beard. "A passenger of the soul, so closely entwined that it gets carried along from one world to the next. No doubt you have all experienced an inexplicable attraction or fascination in your life. The glimpse of a stranger with the familiar eyes—kindred spirits—yes, I'm talking about soul mates. When you have loved another soul in a previous life, you can't help but love them again, sometimes without knowing why. Some famous lovers in history—Paris and Helen of Troy, Cleopatra of Egypt and Mark Antony, Amal and George Clooney—have loved one another for a thousand years. Such feelings should always be trusted, because you would have never loved them so long without them being worthy of it. Yes, in the back?"

"Teresa Hides," the girl stated her name in clear, clipped tones as though terrified someone would misspell it. "I noticed everyone has started over as a child here, but not as a baby. What happens when a baby dies?"

"The souls of young children haven't finished crossing from the spiritual world to the corporal world," Humstrum replied. "That is to say, they are still a lot of who they were and very little of who they will be, and the whole process leaves them very confused. An early death will send them back to the spirit world where they will be ready to try again in the form of their previous life. Now please take out you textbooks, and let us begin with *Chapter 1: The First Soul.*"

The remainder of the class was spent learning about the tree of life with its great bloom from which new souls grew like seeds. Such a bloom was theorized to occur every few millennia, but there was a prominent disclaimer that read that seed theory was merely a mathematical proof consistent with the findings of modern spiritology. The fact that no one has yet found this legendary tree does not, however, mean that there isn't strong evidence that it exists.

"Before our next class, you will visit the bestiary, marked by the stained-glass lion, where you will try to determine which animal you have an affinity toward. You are also welcome to use the library, marked by the camel, at any time, although you will only be permitted up to the floor equivalent with your grade level. You may now stash your books in the mausoleum except for *Understanding Undead: The Spirit's Guide to the Other Side.* You will need that for Professor Wilst when the harpy announces it's time. Class dismissed."

Most of the students hadn't gotten the hang of their self-propelling carts yet, and there were multiple collisions as the students pressed for the exit. Noah waited until the traffic jam had subsided, causing him to be near the back of the crowd as they made their way toward the central stairs.

Walter too was straggling behind the others, because every few steps he would turn around and swear at something. Noah had to get closer to reveal the offending pursuer to be an imp trotting along at his heels.

"Get the hell away from me," Walter said, "or get to hell—whatever you do. I've got no business with you."

"Not afraid of an imp, are you? He looks like he only wants to play," Bowser said, surfing by gracefully in his cart.

"He won't leave me alone," Walter whined, "and look, he's holding something. I think he's trying to stick me."

"I don't think so," Noah said. "Isn't that the imp you defended before?"

"I was defending your books, not him. And how am I supposed to know—they all look the same, don't they?"

"This one's got kind of a long nose," Noah said.

The imp made a little charge toward Walter who dodged out of the way and let it tumble past.

"I think he's trying to give you a present," Jamie said, hurrying to catch up. Mrs. Robinson lazed comfortably in her arms, apparently accepting her fate. "I bet he wants to thank you."

"I don't want anything he's got, thanks anyway," Walter said. He shirked around his cart as the imp came round the other way. The imp leapt from the ground onto the rim of the cart, then set a small black stone on top of Walter's books. The imp grinned with all its sharp little teeth, nudging the stone closer. Walter picked up the stone and inspected it distastefully before chucking it across the ground. The imp chittered crossly before scampering after it as it clattered across the floor.

"He doesn't mean it!" Jamie called after the imp. Then, to Walter, "There's no reason to be so rude. You know they're intelligent, so they must have feelings."

Mrs. Robinson failed the temptation and bounded away to chase after the imp. The pair darted through the legs of one student after another, causing a ripple of confusion and counterbalance to spread throughout the whole group. This led to even more collisions from the already unstable drivers, some of which veered dangerously close to the edge of the pit.

"Now look what you've done!" Jamie scolded.

"That's all Mrs. Robinson!" Walter protested. "It's not my fault I don't want to be friends with those nasty little things. If it wants to thank me, it can deliver a message back home. Otherwise it's no good to me." He slid his cart angrily through the air and started climbing the stairs.

"The people you left are going to be okay," Jamie said, keeping up. "Your girlfriend will know you love her without you having to say it—"

"No she won't! Not after how we left things..." He pushed his cart ahead, not looking at her. He seemed like he was about to say more, but his jaw tightened and he shook his head.

"This isn't quite a message, but I know how you can hear what she's thinking about you," Noah said. Walter stopped abruptly and turned around. Several other students glanced at them too. Noah wasn't sure how Professor Salice would react to him making this public knowledge, so he leaned in closer to continue in a hushed voice.

"The Whispering Room, fifth floor. Professor Salice gave me a key."

Relieved to have a chance to talk about it and try to figure out what happened, Noah told Walter and Jamie about his experience with Salice. Walter became excited as soon as Noah explained what the Whispering Room could do, and he turned around to cross the nearest junction of the double-helix stairway to head in the descending direction instead.

"Why do you think he was so interested in Chainers?" Jamie asked.

"I don't know, but it made me uncomfortable just to be near him," Noah said.

"I wouldn't worry about your daughter," Walter said. "They're in a completely different world now."

"That's what I'm worried about though," Noah said. "If he's so enthusiastic about having Chainers around, don't you think he'd be happy if Mandy died?"

"So what if she does?" Walter asked. "She'll just show up here, right? Then you could go to school together."

"That's just callous." Jammie sniffed indignantly. "Who would look after the baby then? And anyway, life is precious even if you do have a chance to do it again. You never know which one will be your last."

"Exactly," Noah said, "and Salice could send a demon or something there. Or maybe he already has—there was a gargoyle that got me killed."

"I think demons are only in this world," Jamie said. "Otherwise people would know about them, don't you think?"

Noah explained the monstrous thing that had attacked Samantha before chasing them to his death.

"He's a *Professor* though, Noah," Jamie insisted. "He's already delaying his own rebirth to pass on his knowledge, which seems like a pretty noble thing to me. I think you're worrying over nothing."

"I don't know, that guy gave me the creeps on the Daymare," Walter said. "If I were you, I wouldn't tell him where you lived. Give him a wrong address on the letter."

"Yeah? Then what if some other innocent person gets killed?" Noah countered. After checking to make sure the fifth floor was empty, Noah unlocked the Whispering Room. "I think I'll just keep stalling."

Jamie hesitated outside the room. "I'll just wait out here then. Let him have a private moment."

"Actually, if it doesn't bother you… I wouldn't mind the company," Walter said, sounding embarrassed.

"Well, I should be there to show you how it works," Noah mused.

"Yeah, that's the reason," Walter agreed readily.

"And I should be there to see, in case I want to use it!" Jamie volunteered.

Walter grinned in appreciation and they all went inside. The mist bleeding through the circle was definitely more of a pale green than the blue Noah remembered last time. Noah didn't see that it mattered though, and he instructed Walter to stand in the circle, describing his first experience with seeing the faces appear in the mist. Almost immediately upon entering the circle, tears begun to swell in Walter's eyes.

"Is she saying anything?" Jamie asked. "I can't hear it."

"Neither can I," Noah said. "Salice saw and heard my daughter when they were talking though, so we should be able to."

"I'm sorry," Water mumbled as he turned in slow circles. "Baby, I'm so sorry."

"Well he's clearly talking to her," Jamie said. "You know what that means, don't you?"

"Yeah... No. Actually no."

"It means Salice was doing something special to listen in!" Jamie said. "He brought you here for a reason, then he eavesdropped to learn something from it."

"Last time the mist was more blue than green," Noah conceded. "So you're saying my theory about him wanting to get my daughter isn't so far off after-all?"

"I wouldn't go that far," Jamie said, "but it is suspicious. I guess I'm just saying it wouldn't hurt to be careful."

Walter staggered out of the circle, breathing heavily. His brow was damp, either with perspiration or from the mist, and he wiped it with the bottom of his t-shirt.

"Are you okay?" Jamie asked. "Was she—"

Walter closed his eyes and took a deep breath. Then nodded. "Yeah. She'll be okay. With or without me."

"Oh, that's a relief—" she started.

"We can't just focus on our previous lives, right?" he blurted out, the words all competing to be the first out of his mouth. "I mean we've got to look forward too, right? No point dwelling on—" he took another deep breath, then weakly added, "aren't you going to listen too?"

Jamie shook her head slowly. "I don't know if we'll hear the harpy down here, so we should probably go now."

"It only takes a minute," Noah said. "You shouldn't feel like you have to though. I know it can be hard."

Jamie shook her head, resolutely this time. "I've lived my life, and I don't have any regrets to linger on."

"I want to try again then," Noah said, mounting the dais, "This time without Salice interrupting."

Noah stood in the circle once more and saw his daughter's image appear in the mist. She noticed him immediately this time, but she closed her eyes and slapped her hands across her ears.

"He's not real," Mandy said before Noah could speak. She prattled in a sing-song voice which sounded like it had been repeated so many times as to become a practiced mantra. "I know he's not real. I see things that aren't real all the time. Barnes told me so, and he's real. I'm real, but they're not real. And if a real thing thinks too much about not-real things, then the real thing becomes not so real herself. We can't have that, now can we? Stupid, horrible woman. Who will ever love you if they find out you're crazy?"

"Mandy I am real…" Noah said, but he could tell she couldn't hear.

"Sad? Why should I be sad?" Mandy asked herself, clenching her eyes more tightly shut than ever. "I shouldn't feel sad about something that isn't real. I *mustn't* feel sad."

Noah couldn't bear to watch anymore. He leapt down from the dais and waved his hands through the mist to clear her face away.

"Did you hear what she said?" Noah asked the others, perhaps more sharply than he'd intended.

Walter and Jamie shook their heads. Jamie was about to speak, but Noah cut her off.

"Jamie is right! We won't hear the harpy down here. We should be upstairs now." Noah was halfway out the door before either of them could say a word. They took the hint and did not press him for an answer. That was fortunate because Noah had no answer to give, not even to himself.

There weren't any students left in the stairway, but Noah remembered that necromancy studies were on the second floor. If he could get there fast enough, then he wouldn't have to think about what Mandy was going through. How could she tell herself he wasn't real? She'd been seeing spirits her whole life, although perhaps not as vividly as he did. Of course it might be more convenient to pretend, but why did she have to erase him to do it?

Noah found the distraction he was looking for when he emerged onto the second floor, although the atmosphere here was considerably less inviting than the jungles on the third. As soon as Noah opened the door from the tree, his nostrils were assaulted by a powerfully sterile smell like an insecure hospital.

"Beats the smell of rot, I guess," Walter said, covering his nose.

"Can you not smell the rot?" Jamie whined. "It's definitely under there."

The vertical safeguards on this bridge were primarily composed of rib bones. Long femurs on top formed the railing, some of which were much too large to be human.

"Feels just like home," Noah said, pushing his cart across the bridge.

"What, seriously?!" Walter asked.

"Yeah, whenever I murdered people I'd bring them back to the cave I lived in," Noah said conversationally. "This is how I decorated."

"He's *obviously* pulling your leg-bone," Jamie said.

Walter didn't look so sure, but at least the conversation kept them busy long enough to cross the unwholesome bridge.

"Which room do you think they're in?" Walter asked.

Jamie moved ahead to listen at the first of the eight doors which was identified by a skull mounted overhead with a single remaining tooth. Jamie shrugged, apparently unable to hear anything inside.

"It has to be number one, doesn't it?" Noah asked. "We're first years, it's our first class."

"Yeah but what if it's not?" Walter asked. "It could be a changing room for ghouls for all we know. There could be a vampire just waking up from its nap."

"What exactly would a vampire do to you?" Noah asked. "You haven't got any blood."

Jamie opened the door, revealing little as it was so dim inside. "Hello?" she called. "Is this Professor Wilst's class?"

Walter and Noah huddled behind her to peer down the long, round hallway. The rays of will-o-wisp light reflected from a thousand glinting diamonds embedded every few inches along the wall and ceiling like so many stars. It might have been beautiful apart from the oppressively hot and humid air. Jamie took another step inside.

"He wouldn't be teaching a class in the dark," Noah said. "Let's try another one."

"How do you know?" Walter asked. "Maybe Necromancy only works when it's dark. Hello, is there anyone here?" Jamie stopped suddenly a few feet ahead, her stance rigid.

"Let's get out of here," Jamie said carefully. "Slowly—well not that slowly—go!"

Without seeing what she had seen, both boys beat a hasty retreat. Jamie backed out right behind them, not taking her eyes off what she had seen until the door slammed shut.

"What was it?" Walter asked. "The room looked empty to me."

"It was empty," Jamie said, heaving a sigh of relief. "It wasn't a room though. Didn't you see the walls? They were *breathing*."

"No they weren't," Walter said, unconvinced.

"Go ahead. Open it and look," Jamie replied.

Walter didn't think much of that suggestion. The door in the tree stairway presently flew open though, and a mass of first year students came pouring through. Most of the human children weren't pushing their carts anymore and were instead carrying a single book in their arms. At their lead strode Professor Wilst who looked quite at home with his own foot bones clattering along the skeletal bridge.

"Are they in trouble for sneaking down here early?" Brandon asked hopefully. "They probably stole something. You should—"

Professor Wilst pivoted without a word and moved to the door marked by the skull with two teeth. He opened it and vanished inside, prompting the perplexed students to hurry and catch up. Brandon gave Noah and Walter a wicked grin as he passed, shortly followed up by Teresa's signature stink eye.

"Necromancy," the dry voice from the darkness within said. "Your one true path to resurrection begins now."

NECROMANCY

"What is an animal to man? Limited, weak, stupid, unable to recall yesterday or ponder tomorrow with more than a dim glimmer. So is man to the undead, lost and isolated in his single life without memory or foreshadowing of who he was before or what he will return to after."

The powerfully sterile and pickled stench was coming from this classroom, although a morgue might be a more fitting name for the space. There were no desks or chairs, but rather evenly spaced metal slabs each occupied by a naked human body. Their eyes were closed and they drew no breath, yet they were so immaculately preserved that they looked more asleep than dead. The walls were lined with jars on shelves containing hands, eyeballs, brains, and other assorted body parts preserved in a syrupy liquid.

The students filed uneasily into the room. "You could have at least put a sheet over them," Dolly Miller said, averting her eyes from the naked bodies.

"Or some underwear," Elizabeth Washent mumbled, crinkling her rabbit nose.

"Why?" Professor Wilst asked. "You are not your organic body, and need feel no shame. You are not bound by death, and need feel no fear. One student per body, spread out."

Noah chose the body of a very fat man with a long drooping mustache to stand beside. He seemed comical enough to rob some of the unpleasantness from the situation. Jamie took an old woman nearby with skin that sagged so much it looked like it might drip right off the table, and Walter stood by what once might have been an attractive woman, if you could get by the bullet hole in the side of her head. Mrs. Robinson never showed up at all.

All the students kept a healthy distance from their bodies except for the blonde boy, Sandy, who found it enormously entertaining trying to open and close the mouth of his corpse as if it were speaking. He quickly gave up though when his hands kept passing through the body as if it was just an illusion.

"These are corporal bodies, and you have no physical force with which to move them," the Professor said. Then in a commanding voice, he added, "Excieo."

Bright yellow light ran up his metal staff, running through his hand and radiating out through his body before bursting into the air. Radiant yellow sparks rained down softly like rain throughout the whole classroom. Students either dove to get out of the way or actively reached out to try and grab them. As the sparks settled amongst the bodies, they all opened their eyes simultaneously to stare vacantly at the ceiling. There was a loud scuffle as curious students quickly backpedaled away from their tables, bumping into one another as they did.

"Consurgo," the Professor commanded. The bodies all sat fluidly upright, their arms hanging limply at their sides. "By the end of the semester, I'll expect all of you to be able to awaken and command your own zombie. Incapable of independent thoughts or feelings, these spiritual puppets grant us a corporal servant to influence the living world. While a living person is a single spirit within a single body, the animation of objects or corpses is the process of dividing the necromancer's spirit amongst the things he wishes to control. This can leave the necromancer weak and vulnerable. When you are ready to return your spirit, you must put the objects under your control to sleep with the spell: Somnus."

At this command the bodies uniformly collapsed back to the table, their eyes closed once more.

"Notebooks out," the Professor commanded in the same authoritative tone he used to animate the bodies. The bones of his toes clattered with each step as he paced between the dormant corpses. "Zombies are the simplest form of undead. Some, such as myself, have chosen to escape the endless cycle of rebirth by choosing to permanently inhabit a corpse. My own corpse, in fact. This is known as a lich. All spirits can focus their power using a bit of their corporal remains, which is what you will be using your stuffed animals for.

"Other notable undead you will become familiar with include the poltergeist, spirits which can interact with the corporal world, vampires, whose corporal bodies use living blood to strengthen their connection to the other side, and the dwellers, which overpower the spirit of living beings to control them. The process of becoming a dweller will not be taught in this class, and they are not welcome in polite society."

"Why does it feel like we're getting career counseling?" Walter whispered.

"Is that what this is?" Noah whispered back. "I thought it sounded more like a retirement plan."

"Textbooks out," barked Professor Wilst. "You should all have a copy of *Understanding Undead: The Spirit's Guide to the Other Side* by Salvadore Frann. Please open to *Chapter 1: You're Only As Dead As You Act*."

Noah was surprised to find himself disappointed that they did not get to use the bodies for anything yet, but he still quite enjoyed the rest of the lesson which elaborated on the four types of undead creatures. He felt somehow uncomfortable reading the definition of life though, which read only, '*Life: The short duration in which a spirit borrows a biological body and fights everybody and everything to avoid returning it to the biological system it was taken from.*'

"I don't think necromancy is for me," Jamie said as they were leaving the class. "I'd much rather be a rabbit or a bird than any of those grizzly things."

"I would have thought you'd want to be a cat again," Noah said.

"Maybe," Jamie replied in contemplation, "but oh, there are so many more things to try. And what if I can't keep finding my way back to life? We can't all be Chainers."

"We could though, couldn't we?" Noah asked as they ascended the stairs. "Didn't the book on Transhumanism say that souls were only created every few millennia? So the rest of you must have been doing something this whole time."

"I wish we could find out what," Jamie said. "I'd rather be learning about that than all these supernatural encounters we have to read. What do I care whether it was a vampire or a ghoul that bit her? She's just as dead either way, isn't she?"

There was a hub of activity on the ground floor of The Mortuary. An energetic fiddle was accompanied by a lively drumbeat. Colorful pamphlets were exchanging hands, and students were chatting with excitement as they rushed to exit the front doors. A line of large tree stumps were arranged outside, each decorated with posters and stacks of cards, as well as the occasional dismembered hand, crystal ball, tarot deck, and doll. Noah recognized some of the same villagers who had greeted them now sitting behind the stumps.

"They can bury you, but they can't keep you down," shouted an olive-skinned woman with long, curly, black hair and fingers so filled with rings that it was a wonder she could still bend them. "Two apprenticeships remaining. Get Cassandra's Kill Counseling Certificate here and start helping people cope with the rope."

Dolly Miller slipped past Noah and approached the stump to speak with Cassandra.

"Help the right spirits reach the right mediums," announced a tall thin man with yellow vertical stripes along his suit. "Single apprenticeship available, easy to fit in after class. First years welcome." His sign read: 'Spiritual Operator'.

"You there—girl with the ginger head," an ample woman wearing a bright orange dress and a large black belt called to Jamie. Jamie pointed at herself in surprise, and the large woman nodded enthusiastically. "Yes you, darling. You remind me of the babe."

"What babe?" Jamie asked, allowing herself to be drawn in.

"The babe with the power," the woman replied in the hushed tone of a conspiracy.

"What power?" Jamie asked again, quite mystified.

"The power of voodoo!" the woman shouted, barely able to contain herself. "Don't tell me you've never wanted to pay somebody back for the horrible things they've done. A pretty girl like you must have broken some hearts and made some enemies in her life."

"I should hope not!" Jamie said. "No thank you, I don't want to hurt anyone."

"How about doll stitching?" the woman called. "They won't feel the needle yet, what do you say?"

Jamie hurried away, but Teresa swooped into her place to take one of the pamphlets. The sign read 'Ungela Granka's Voodoo. A nearby sign read 'Miss Thatchers Witchery: Curses and Broom Delivery.'

"What's going on?" Noah asked, turning in wonder.

"Oh that's right, you weren't in the village so you must have missed it," Jamie replied. "We all have to work an apprenticeship alongside our classwork. That way we'll have career options if we aren't able to resurrect right away, plus the work covers the tuition of the school. Any idea what you're going to do?"

Noah spotted Walter speaking with the Spiritual Operator.

"Hey—Chainer kid," Bowser barked, wagging ferociously. He was sitting by a sign which read, 'Supernautical Activity'.

"It's Noah," he replied, approaching.

"Okay Noah. This guy is looking for a Chainer to help power his underwater expedition. They're researching sea spirits—want in?"

The grizzled seaman tipped an end of his white captain's hat toward Noah. There was a lull in the general conversation as multiple villagers turned their attention on the Chainer in their midst. The ensuing wave of noise assaulted Noah from every direction.

"Don't settle for him, I've got—"

"A Chainer would be wasted on—"

"Why don't you give back and do some good—"

And a dozen other calls which jumbled over one another. As soon as they'd begun, the calls all cut short as the attention was diverted directly behind Noah. He felt a very human chill run down his spine as a hard, cold hand closed around his shoulder, one curling finger at a time.

"There is no need for such commotion," Professor Salice said from behind Noah's ear. "The Chainer boy will already be working as my apprentice this semester. Isn't that right, Noah Tellaver?"

Noah thought quickly whether he'd told Professor Salice his last name before deciding that he definitely had not. Did he already know something about Mandy? If so, then Salice's words sounded like a threat.

"Yeah," Noah mumbled. "Yeah I said I'd..." and his voice trailed off. He turned around to look at Professor Salice whose tight smile was putting unnatural stress upon his face which peeled back around the ears.

"Tuesday at nightfall then, before our first class on Wednesday," Salice said. "Don't forget to bring your letter." With that he turned to go back inside The Mortuary, not giving Noah the least chance to respond or change his mind.

"Demons are my favorite thing, Professor," Brandon called, hurrying to intercept Salice. "I'd make a much better apprentice than him—"

"Absolutely he would," Noah agreed readily. "I'd probably summon a fairy by mistake, klutz that I am."

Professor Salice didn't slow his pace or turn his head in the least. "You disgraced yourself on the bus already," he replied. "Don't waste my time."

Brandon was at his ugliest wearing the mean, spiteful look he now possessed upon his face. It was almost as if he had wanted to be rejected just so he could have something to be angry about. Noah had never seen someone look so pleased to be furious.

"What's your problem? I agreed with you," Noah said.

"Of course. After-all, you're so much better than me," Brandon said.

Noah wouldn't have minded if Brandon had yelled at him. This clearly fake, goading voice was far more sinister. Noah said nothing and turned to look for his friends. Jamie was speaking to Professor Humstrum, although the ape didn't have any kind of booth or table.

"You're better than everyone here, aren't you?" Brandon pressed, stepping closer. "You don't need us. You already know how to go back to life, don't you? So what are you doing?"

"I don't remember how I did it before," Noah replied. "I'm not any better than anyone."

"Yes you are," Brandon said, his voice lowering to a hiss as he got nearer. "But when I was alive, I was twice the man you ever were. People worshiped the ground I walked on, and I'm going to get that power again. And when I do—"

Brandon lurched toward Noah, forcing him to flinch and stumble backward. Brandon caught himself halfway and laughed at Noah for retreating. Noah was ready to throw the first real punch when Professor Humstrum passed by with Jamie tagging along at his heels.

"Hey, Noah!" she called. "I'm going to help Professor Humstrum take care of the bestiary this semester. Do you want to come with us to do your tranhumanism assignment?"

Noah readily agreed, grateful for a chance to slip away from Brandon. He followed the Professor along the stone path which was flanked by rows of tall juniper trees toward The Mortuary tower with the lion on it. Before the door had even opened, he could hear the stirrings of massive feet and a graveled roar which shook the dust from stones.

"Go ahead and put out your hand then—palm facing down, just let him sniff you," Professor Humstrum said. "That's right, he's not going to hurt you. Everything needs a reason to fight, but getting along is its own reason."

Jamie closed her eyes and stuck out her hand a little farther. A black tongue half the length of her arm curled over her wrist, slithering its way up round and round as if tasting her.

"This doesn't feel like sniffing!" Jamie said, still clenching her eyes shut.

"Hold very still now. If you squirm too much he's going to feel threatened," the Professor said.

"He's going to feel threatened!" Jamie exclaimed. "I'm the one being eaten by a —"

"A baku," Professor said cheerfully. "The dream eater. Cassandra has several of them working in her counseling facility. Some spirits will keep having nightmares about their death, but a baku doesn't mind the taste."

The tongue slackened in pressure enough for Jamie to politely disentangle herself. The baku—which could have almost passed for a dog until it turned around to reveal its elephantine tusks and trunk—fell back onto its haunches and blinked its vacant white eyes. Jamie discreetly turned around before furiously wiping her arm on her t-shirt.

"This place is wonderful," Jamie sighed, turning in a slow circle to take in the tower.

The entire building was a single massive room which was flooded with the light of thousands of will-o-wisps which flew together in a massed swarm, giving the appearance of a fiery sun which floated throughout the space. Trees and plants were growing everywhere like a greenhouse, although the room was divided into distinct biospheres. Snow fell softly from the arched ceiling, icing the tops of the trees where furry animals slid and chased one another. An open stream gurgled from a hole in one of the walls, creating a waterfall which fed into a pristine tundra formed entirely on another layer of branches.

From there the water drained down through the leaves as a heavy rain, creating a tropical rainforest a little further down. There was hardly a dribble of water left by the time it made it all the way to the ground, where stretches of sandy desert and grassy savanna gave ample space to walk around.

"The baku is not the only myth based on reality," the Professor said, turning to stroll through the desert sand. "You'd be amazed at how often a Chainer or a psychic of some sort sees a spiritual creature and then tells everybody who will listen, whether they can see it or not. You'll be looking after the baku's schedule now, making sure he's gotten a walk through the graveyard every morning before people wake up so he can get a nice breakfast in. Oh, and when it comes to cleaning up after him, I should warn you that sometimes when he eats an especially foul nightmare he can leave a rather unpleasant… oh, well, you'll figure it out, don't you worry."

Jamie gave Noah a beseeching 'help me', sort of look.

"You'll be fine," Noah replied, grinning. The prospect of being Salice's assistant didn't seem half as bad anymore, at least assuming imps could clean up after themselves.

There must have been a lot of creatures living here because the odor was thick enough to taste. It wasn't a necessarily a bad odor—something like sweet curry—but the prevalence and potency would have surely been sickening if Noah's digestive system still whirred.

Noah and Jamie followed the Professor toward the back of the room, pointing out key aspects of the facility such as feed cabinets, medical supplies, and a dauntingly large shovel caked with something pink that smelled like frosting.

"Don't let the smell fool you," the Professor said, gesturing at the shovel. "You don't want to touch anything that comes out of the jinn."

An angular green face with long, pointed, overlapping teeth leered out of a hole in the sand. Noah recognized a few of the animals, such as the restlessly pacing manticore with its scorpion tail flicking over its back, as well as the cyclops at least twice his height who was shaking a fig tree to knock all the fruits onto the ground.

The vast majority were like nothing Noah had ever seen before though. Many looked like conventional wild animals until they turned to reveal part of them as something else entirely, and those with human faces were especially disconcerting as they turned and watched them pass. There were small scaly creatures and giant eyeballs with a dozen irises, and even two-dimensional things which disappeared at the wrong angle. Despite this maddening variety, it was apparent that most of the life was still hidden and rustling through the higher biospheres in the trees.

"The harpys do most of the work mind you, although they spend a disproportionate amount of time with the birds in the upper floors," the Professor said. "If any of the critters ever give you trouble, a harpy is always only a screech away." Then turning back to Noah, he added, "Find any affinitys yet? A Chainer is likely to have been all sorts of creatures before."

Noah was staring at an iridescent turtle shell which not only reflected Noah's image, but actually morphed into a replica of his face to stare back at him until he turned away. "I don't think so," Noah said.

"Ah, well, no need to bother yourself then," the Professor sighed. "I always hope we'll get a real animal Chainer one day, but maybe you were just human all the way back. Nothing wrong with humans, not most of them anyway. Nothing to feel ashamed about."

"Thanks," Noah said. "I'll try not to let it bother me."

In fact he was doing a very good job of not minding in the least, but the Professor still circled back to clap a sympathetic hand against the middle of Noah's back. The antelope staff stuck out its tongue at Noah in what he could only assume to be an insult.

"If you aren't sure you can always touch one of them," the Professor said. "I've left a spell in here to help the students. An affinity will be clearly seen by the scarlet sparks—"

"Sorry, no need," Noah said firmly. "I'm pretty sure about this one."

"So be it, so be it. How about you, Jamie? Maybe there's a little fire in you from an efreet that never went out?" he asked, hopeful.

"Just the cat, I think," she replied. "They are happy here, aren't they? Wouldn't they prefer to be taking classes too?"

"An excellent question! Just what I'd expect from my apprentice. Spiritual creatures who have no counterpart in the corporal world are not the same as spiritual animals who do. The beings who exist entirely in the spirit world often do not speak our language, although some like the harpy are sharp enough to learn a few words and phrases. Bestiary's like this may be thought of like a conservatory. They exist all over the world to protect and study these marvelous creatures, as well as utilize their fantastic properties. Not to mention keeping them out of trouble, as many can interact directly with the corporal world."

"Do you have any gargoyles?" Noah asked.

Humstrum's face crinkled like he'd just witnessed clumps pour out of his milk carton. "You won't find any of those in a bestiary. The T.D.D. has them all employed."

"But there must be wild ones. Or some that have gone rogue and attack people."

The Professor shrugged and his antelope head Hazel snorted loudly. "I wouldn't think so, but anything is possible. You see gargoyles aren't natural like the other animals are—the T.D.D. makes them from scratch. No one outside of the department knows exactly how it's done, but I can't imagine there's anything wholesome about it."

A chittering snicker sounded from one of the jinn, which was swiftly followed by a series of protesting honks, growls, barks, hisses, and all manner of other sounds from the agitated spirits.

An imp who had been stealthily clinging to the back of a tree dropped to the ground, likely realizing its cover had been blown. It looked around in a wild panic at all the protesting spirits.

"What is a demon doing here?" Professor Humstrum asked sternly, his voice boiling with a barely contained rage that Noah had never heard from him before. "Unnatural creature—you do not belong in this sacred space!"

The imp cast a quick glance at Noah before attempting to creep back toward the door, crouching and slinking despite being in plain sight. Noah scanned the surrounding trees, trying to spot if there were any more. He had the unnerving feeling that the imp had been sent to spy on him.

"Did someone send you?" Noah asked, hurrying after the demon. "Was it Professor Salice?"

The imp left all covert pretensions and leaped wildly for the door.

Crawling up the wood to pull on the heavy metal handle, it struggled and gasped as it heaved against the indomitable door.

"Hey—I'm asking you a question!" Noah demanded. He flung out a hand to seize the imp by its shoulder. A jolt of electricity shot through Noah's hand, and scarlet sparks hissed and smoldered into the air. He withdrew his hand at once, and that was all the time the imp needed. With a last surge of strength the demon yanked the door open a crack—just enough for it to slip through and disappear. Noah was left nursing his scalded hand, staring at the smoldering sparks which continued to burn sporadically in the air like tiny fireworks.

"You've found your affinity after all," Professor Humstrum said with a tense, hushed voice. "You used to be a demon, boy."

"I didn't know demons could even become human," Noah said. The severity of Humstrum's tone made him feel that he had done something wrong, although he couldn't see what.

"No," Humstrum said after a pause. "Neither did I. Nor anyone else I've ever taught, and believe you me there's enough of them to sink the island if they ever had a reunion."

"I bet that imp is going to run straight back to Professor Salice," Jamie said. "He's going to know too."

"Is that okay?" Noah asked. "I mean, does it matter? People have been loads of stuff."

"Elizabeth told me she used to be a slug before she was a rabbit," Jamie said cheerfully. "She says now she finally knows why her nose is always runny, although I don't think that's really how it works, is it Professor—"

But the Professor wasn't listening. He was having a hurried and whispered conversation with the antelope head on his staff. The antelope kept glancing at Noah every few seconds.

"Please excuse me," Professor Humstrum said. "I've just forgotten that I was supposed to have tea with—never mind with whom, I'm already late. Jamie, please join me tomorrow evening for the rest of your bestiary instructions. Noah…" The Professor paused, chewing on his lip. The orangutang reached out a hesitant hand and patted Noah on his back, rather tentatively as though he was afraid the contact would burn him. Humstrum then turned suddenly and made for the door.

"Professor?" Noah asked, his voice higher pitched and more strained than he'd intended. "Please don't tell anyone."

Professor Humstrum forced a shallow smile over his shoulder, although the bird did not emerge from his beard as usual. "You're human now, eh? Just the same as the rest of us. Our past is only our own burden to bear, and I won't breathe a word."

Neither the Professor's farewell nor his speedy departure did anything to reassure Noah, who was by now feeling a little nauseous. He meekly followed the Professor back toward the courtyard and the rest of the students who were still milling about the remainder of the apprenticeship stalls.

"So nothing to worry about," Jamie said meekly. "There's nothing wrong with imps, and nothing for you to be ashamed of. Anyway, you got over the murderer thing pretty quickly, and I think that would have been much harder for me—"

"You don't think they're related?" Noah asked glumly. "What if I was a rampaging, murderous demon?"

"Oh," Jamie said. "I hadn't thought about that. Well even if you were, you aren't now, right? Have you had any urges or anything… you haven't, have you?"

The more Noah heard about it, the more murder sounded like a perfectly practical solution to get everybody to shut up. Even his thoughts were only joking though, something to try to lighten the pit he felt in his stomach. He never would have…

Couldn't have…

Could he?

DEMONOLOGY

Noah took his next chance to visit the library to search for more information about his affinity. The third tower marked by the camel reminded Noah of the Daymare because of all the floating platforms which contained reading tables both above and below. A spidery web of stairs branched haphazardly from one platform to the next, but none of the platforms were devoted to the actual bookshelves, which didn't exist.

The books themselves were spread open and glided through the air like flocks of fat, lazy birds. Whenever a book was needed, a student would simply announce what he was looking for and the book would sail over to land on his table. There was a rumor going around that one of the students made the mistake of simply asking for 'books about reincarnation', and his failure to be specific caused multiple flocks of books to swarm him from every direction and bury him completely.

The librarian, a bespectacled vampire named Mrs. Vanderlooth, vehemently denied such a rumor. Her denial was hardly credible though, as she insisted that it's best to be as specific as possible and warned that students should hide underneath the table when a vague statement was unavoidable. Mrs. Vanderlooth was an elegant creature with long purple robes and a prominent beauty mark at the corner of each of her voluptuous red lips.

Noah vastly preferred spending time in the library to studying in the tight mausoleum quarters with Brandon. This suited Brandon just fine, who had responded by scattering his clothes and books across both sides of the room. Noah's coffin now served as storage for Brandon's maps, rope, life vest (the name stamped across the breast without the slightest sense of irony), and other equipment that Brandon had received from the supernautical man.

None of the books Noah could find about affinity gave him the least resolution to his quandary. Some books didn't even consider demons to have souls, while others spoke of them as having their own, distinct type of soul that allowed them to be reborn as another demon, but not as anything else. Noah couldn't even ask Mrs. Vanderlooth for help, considering Humstrum's reaction. He felt it was best to keep his affinity a secret, and her ability to amplify a rumor while pretending to deny it would only make matters worse.

"It's time to earn your keep," Professor Salice's voice spoke directly into Noah's ear. Noah nearly fell backward from his chair, only catching himself just in time before he tumbled off the platform altogether.

"Fourth floor, second room, ten minutes. Don't be late."

Noah spun in circles trying to find the orator. It quickly became apparent that he was alone. He briefly considered ignoring the request and pretending he hadn't heard, or perhaps even hiding here to avoid the meeting. There still existed the possibility that Salice had some leverage over his family though, and in any case even normal teachers couldn't be disobeyed without repercussions. There's no telling what kind of foul thing Salice could do to him, or how powerless Noah was to resist. Shivering involuntarily, Noah climbed down from the spidery stairway and headed for the main tower.

Noah expected the demonology floor to be the most unpleasant of them all, and he felt somewhat dissatisfied in discovering he was incorrect. The railings on the bridge and around the pit were composed of thick red lines that looked more like beams of light than any solid material. They were arranged artfully into perfectly interlocking geometrical shapes and patterns. The floor itself was clean white tile, and the doors were iron portals engraved with the same dizzying array of patterns. Some of the shapes glowed with a soft red light, while others blinked or lit sporadically as though they were having a conversation with each other.

Noah knocked upon the second room, which was distinguished by Roman numerals prominently embedded within the designs. Several of the other symbols flashed in silent unison as soon as his fist touched the iron, although there was no other discernible effect.

Professor Salice opened the door to loom over Noah. If the imp really had told Professor Salice about Noah's affinity, then the Professor showed no immediate sign of it.

"The letter?" Salice asked immediately, his hand outstretched.

"You said I had until our class," Noah protested.

"Ah. I would have thought you'd be eager to contact your relatives," Salice replied, disappointed. "Or have you already found another way?"

"I don't know, Professor. Is there another way?" Noah asked.

Salice gave a thin, lipless smile, then stepped aside to allow Noah to enter. "Do not touch anything that you have not been invited to touch. Do not say anything unless you are invited to speak. And if you are invited to speak," Salice paused to glance pointedly at Noah, "you shall speak to me no lies. Do you understand?"

"Yes, Professor," Noah replied.

The room they were in looked a bit like a police lineup: a large transparent, frosted plane divided two spaces. The walls and ceiling of this side were tiled, while those of the other were overlapping slabs of corrugated iron. The side of the room Noah had entered contained half-a-dozen plain wooden chairs, as well as a filing cabinet and a desk. The other side was completely empty except for a large pentagram within a circle drawn onto the ground. The design seemed to radiate the same beams of light that comprised the railings. Salice's demon, Visoloth, was lying on its back on a dog bed in the corner, revealing its strange, scaly underbelly.

"The cost of your attendance is being covered by the labor of your work as my apprentice this semester," Salice said. "Do you know what that means?"

"No," Noah replied, as much to be difficult as he was confused about the direction this was going.

"Of course not," Salice said. "It means that your presence at The Mortuary is conditional on my approval of your work. It means I have the power to dismiss you from this school if I ever find reason to do so."

"I could always get another apprenticeship," Noah said. "The supernautical man offered—"

"Did I ask you a question?" Salice snapped.

"No, Professor," Noah replied.

"And yet you spoke," he drawled.

Noah bit his tongue to avoid agreeing with Salice out of pure stubbornness.

"That's better. I would like us to be friends, and that can only happen so long as you don't fight me. I will have different tasks for you on different occasions, but you will be spending the majority of your time in my service in this room. Please stand against the glass."

Noah did as he was instructed.

"Closer," Salice prompted. "All the way. Feet against the glass, forehead against the glass."

As soon as Noah had done so, Professor Salice placed one hand against the back of Noah's head and pressed him against the barrier. The cold flat surface immediately gave way to a freezing mist. Noah tumbled directly through the glass, barely catching himself on the other side. He spun around and tried to regain his previous position, only to smack head-first against the pane which had grown solid once more.

"Demonic summoning requires at least two demonologists," Professor Salice said, his voice distant and muffled from the other side. "One to sign the contract, and a second to serve as the vessel for the demon. Today I will be bringing…" the Professor produced a black leather notebook from his pocket and began to flip through it.

"...two imps for The Matriarch, replacing gardeners who have expired. One Peruvian Blue Scale for cleaning the Daymare, one Lava Salamander to stoke the fires of Mrs. Thatcher's witchery, and three Gobbler's to polish Francisco Pintilo's gemstones. That's seven total, so you will be out of here before midnight."

Noah raised his hand to ask a question, feeling silly as he did so. The humiliation increased as Salice glanced up, then looked back to his notebook as though he'd seen nothing.

"Sit in the center of the pentagram with your legs crossed and your eyes closed. All extremities should be within the innermost lines. Once you are seated, you are not to move until the ceremony is complete, or risk part of your body being banished to the netherworld during the exchange. That happened to one of my apprentices once— it only took him a few minutes to find his hand in the nether, but by then the demons had already stripped it to the bone."

The beams of light marking the pentagram were warm as Noah passed through them. The sensation might have been pleasant if it weren't for the looming dread for what was about to occur. Surely it couldn't be worse than risking his chance to come back to life though... could it?

Professor Salice described the summoning process as three distinct steps. First Salice would read aloud one of the contracts which he had already prepared. That would bridge the connection between Noah, the "host", and the demon in the netherworld. The second step was for the demon to be summoned here, and the third step was for the demon to be bound by the contract.

The words Salice read were meaningless to Noah; they sounded more like the chittering, cackling sounds the imps made than any human tongue. As Salice read the image of the demon grew gradually clearer in Noah's mind.

The long snout appeared in his thoughts first, just as though he'd consciously conjured the image. Then two beady black eyes, then a lithe, thin body like a snake. Four legs ending in sharp claws gradually resolved themselves from the darkness, and then all at once the skin turned deep blue and cracked like dry mud under a blazing sun.

Noah found it deeply unsettling that he was imagining this creature against his will, and that try as he might he could not force himself to stop thinking about it as the image continued to become more vivid and focused. The cracked skin continued hardening into distinct scales, and quite soon he was picturing what he could only assume to be the Peruvian Bluescale.

"Genitus," Professor Salice said at last. "Hold very still now. Take care not to cross any of the lines on the ground."

The image in Noah's mind vanished, and at the same instant he felt sharp claws sinking into his shoulder. A high pitched screech blasted directly in his ear. Every instinct demanded that he flee. He opened his eyes to stare directly into the long blue snout and beady black eyes he'd imagined a moment before. It would have been bad enough for the demon to simply materialize on top of him, but it was far worse seeing that the full demon hadn't arrived yet. The claws dug more deeply into Noah shoulder for support as the Peruvian Bluescale dragged itself directly out of Noah's forehead.

It didn't feel like his head was being split in two, although he did feel an immense amount of pressure which didn't relieve until the demon had completely pulled itself out of his body. It was only the size of a medium dog, and it didn't take long before the demon had completely tumbled free to land in Noah's lap. The demon tried to flee, but as soon as it began to cross the first beam of light in the pentagram, the light flared and red sparks flew into the air. The demon recoiled as though burned, prompting more high pitched, whistling screeches.

Professor Salice slapped the contract he'd written against the glass and answered the demon with a similar screech, sounding all the more unnatural coming from his human lips. His other hand held a black stone which he also pressed against the glass. The whole pentagram flared once more, this time burning green. The colorful sparks bled from the air and drifted into the black stone which absorbed the light.

"Sit," Professor Salice ordered, and the demon did so at once, its long body curling several times beneath it.

"Rise," Salice said. The demon stood on its hind legs, lifting its head high into the air. "Dance; on my beat." Salice began a rhythmic clap and the demon swayed, bouncing and hopping about on its hind legs in time with the clapping. After a few moments Professor Salice nodded, content.

"Wait in the corner," he commanded. The demon seemed hesitant to cross the pentagram lines. When it did work up the courage it crossed all at once in a terrified dash without meeting any resistance this time. Noah began to rise as well, but Salice's words were sharp enough to make him drop back at once. "Sit down, boy. We have six more to go before you're finished."

The imps came easily enough, as did the Gobblers who were little more than giant, toothless mouths embedded in a misshapen fleshy lump like melted candle wax. The Lava Salamander was much less pleasant, its purple rubbery skin scalding Noah all the way out. Despite being vaguely shaped like a salamander, the creature moved as though it had no bones in its entire body and propelled itself by stretching parts of itself until they were almost transparently thin before snapping the rest of its body into the new location.

"You must remember that a contract with a demon is one of partnership, not servitude," Professor Salice proclaimed after a particularly nervous gobbler seemed reluctant to exit the circle. "The netherworld is a terrifying place, even for those that call it their home. Most demons are eager to work for a chance of freedom in one of the other planes, though it is up to the summoner to help them fulfill that dream once their contract is complete. To abuse their trust or attempt to cheat them would be... unforgivable."

Noah's forehead was burning when Salice invited him to lean against the cool glass once more, thus allowing him to pass. The Professor became preoccupied with instructing the newly summoned demons on their duties and paid little attention to Noah, who was only too relieved to escape.

Despite being told he'd be out by midnight, it must be almost morning by now. Noah was filled with restless energy after sitting for so long though, and he didn't take the stairs up toward his mausoleum to rest. Instead he turned downward, slipping down through the emptiness toward the Whispering Room. He stood and stared at the greenish stone circle for a long time, unable to bring himself to step inside.

Instead he sat with his back against the marble dais and closed his eyes—near enough to hear the whispers, but not so close as to make out exactly what they were saying. He shivered as the cool mist drifted over him, but he didn't suppose it could do any harm now. In that weary state he dreamed of home, so close that he might really be there and dreaming of here, and yet so far that he may never see it again. He dreamed of his daughter, and his grandson, and the taste of hot chocolate fresh from the stove, and softly he cried himself to sleep.

"THE KNOWN universe is divided into three distinct worlds," Professor Salice said in the first demonology class the next day. "The living world, also known as the corporal world, the spirit world, and the netherworld."

This room was much less interesting than the others had been, with nothing but plain white tiles, rigid metal desks and chairs, and a dusty chalkboard at the front.

"Pssst," Jamie leaned over to Noah. "Did you finish the letter to Mandy yet?"

"Yeah," Noah whispered back. "A fake one anyway. It's just addressed to a random government building in a different city."

"The term for a soul passing from the living world to the spirit world is called death, or resurrection in reverse," Salice droned on, sounding so uninterested in his own words that the students were obviously struggling to do otherwise. "A soul going from the spirit world to the netherworld is a banishment, and one going the other way is called a summoning. There is anecdotal evidence of souls transferring directly between the living and nether worlds, although there has yet to be a controlled experiment to replicate those results."

"Aren't you worried that he'll find out?" Jamie whispered.

Noah shrugged. "It'll buy me some time at least."

"I think you should tell The Matriarch," Jamie said. "She defended you during the weighing ceremony, so I think she's taken a special liking to you."

"Tell her what? I don't have any proof that he's up to something. I don't even know what he could possibly want another Chainer for. He's already got me hosting his summonings."

"The diagram on page seven details this process," Professor Salice said, turning the page. "Demonic servants can be useful for all sorts of things because they are comprised of both matter and energy, allowing them to operate equally in all worlds. From protection, to cleaning houses, or even transportation, such as the Daymare… The Mortuary itself was constructed by the demon Morogoth, who planted the great tree from a seed it brought with it from the netherworld. The ceremonies to summon such powerful demons are extremely complicated and require the minds of many dozens of souls to conceive and host them."

"I've got an idea," Jamie whispered, raising her hand. Noah tried to kick her under the table, but she swung her legs away and stretched her hand even higher. "Excuse me, Professor?" she asked.

Professor Salice looked up from *Twelve Signs Your Imp Might Be Plotting To Kill You*. The sour look on his face would have been extremely appropriate on the cover. "What is it, Mrs. Poffin? I presume you do not need to use the bathroom."

"Could a Chainer be used to host more powerful demons than a non-chainer?" she asked. "Even if it's only one soul, it's heavier than normal souls because of how many lives it lived, right? We saw that at the weighing ceremony. Does that mean it's also bigger?"

Noah felt the eyes of the whole classroom fall upon him. He wanted to try and kick Jamie again, but he couldn't manage it now without being seen. Instead, he pretended to be extremely interested in the soul transfer diagram in his textbook.

"Yes," Professor Salice said, his voice barely above a whisper but clearly audible in the suddenly still room. Even the two imps who had been wrestling in the back stopped to listen, their squabble forgotten. Noah looked up and met Salice's gaze for an instant before turning back to his book, a feeling like ice in his veins.

"Professor Humstrum might have told you that all souls are created equal, and perhaps they were, but that should not be confused to mean that all souls *are* equal," the Professor continued, his voice still low and hushed. He began to pace between the rows of chairs, but Noah kept his eyes firmly on the book in front of him. "An animal that lives its life in a cage before being slaughtered has had little chance to expand its soul. It has little experience of new things, new feelings, or new thoughts. And if it were to never live again, its soul would remain small and cheap, disposable and useless for any greater purpose. But one who has lived many lives, who has learned and grown from each, and loved and lost so many times…"

His voice trailed off as he stood directly over Noah, who stubbornly refused to look up.

"Pain," the Professor said, almost purring the word. "Suffering, loss. Like the accumulation of scar tissue, it may harden the soul against future injury. Such a soul can endure and be used for many useful things."

"You're bonkers," Walter whispered, perhaps louder than he'd intended in the quiet room. He winced immediately as other students suppressed quiet laughter around him. To their surprise, Professor Salice only smiled and returned to the front of the class.

"If death has taught you anything, it should be this," Salice replied, "that sanity, morality, and our fragile cultural beliefs are nothing but the current whims of those who happen to be alive at the same time and place. Reality does not care whether or not it is popular. Page eight, you will find descriptions of the different stones used for sealing contracts. The unique attributes of each stone will determine whether it is best suited to add duration, fine control, or protection in case the demon rebels, etc. You will each be required to memorize the twenty four most common forms of opal and be able to recite their strengths and weaknesses."

The lecturing drone continued through the rest of the period, although there was an interruption near the end that jolted Noah back to alertness.

"Professor?" Brandon asked, his voice high and ingratiating with artificial respect. "Can we come back as demons next time?"

Noah watched Brandon out of the corner of his eye. Was he asking out of curiosity, or did he know something about his demonic affinity? Brandon didn't seem to notice Noah and gave no hint as to what he was thinking.

Professor Salice closed the book on his podium with exquisite delicacy. "Some consider such a transformation to be the highest obtainment possible for a soul, something which bridges them with the divine. Would you choose such a path?"

"Of course, Professor!" Brandon said in his whining voice. "I think demons are amazing. I can't think of anything I'd rather be."

"Is that allowed though?"

It was the first time Noah heard that girl speak. He'd always assumed she'd been a boy because of her closely shaved hair, but hearing her voice it was undeniable.

"Hand, Rachelle," the Professor barked.

Rachelle raised her hand and continued, not waiting to be called. "In Chapter 16: Demonic Stigma, it says that human transformation into demons was banned in 1940 by Theodore Oswald, then Magistrate of the Trans Dimensional Department. It says—"

"I do not need to be lectured on the contents of my own textbook, Mrs. Devon," Salice said with a sneer. "If you were listening earlier instead of reading ahead, you would remember that public opinion is as arbitrary as it is inane."

"But didn't that happen right after the purges?" Rachelle persisted. "A lot of people were being killed by—"

"Do not mislead this class with such idle propaganda. We can discuss it after class, if you wish," Salice cut her off. "Noah, perhaps you will stay as well? I believe you have something for me."

The harpies had begun to screech outside, and the students were gathering their things to leave. Noah crumpled his note tightly in his hand while waiting behind Rachelle.

"You are correct that demons perpetrated a good deal of slaughter during the purges," Professor Salice was saying to her, "but your presumption of guilt is unfounded. Magistrate Oswald of the T.D.D. began the conflict by persecuting the large population of liberated demons. They were on the verge of earning voting rights from his progressive rivals, the Elmond twins, when Oswald vilified the movement as nothing short of a demonic uprising in order to stay in power. The escalating tensions led to the mass banishment of free demons at a political rally, which in turn sparked actual demonic attacks. Oswald used these as justification to begin the mass banishment of demons, an unforgivable act known as the purges. You must understand that these are demons who had served their contract faithfully for years on end, only to finally earn their freedom and be banished before they could make use of it."

Professor Salice was powerfully animated by the conversation, the topic obviously close to his heart. He seemed to have forgotten Noah was even there.

"But I heard that the demons attacked first. Did Oswald get rid of all the free demons then?" Rachelle pressed.

"Most of them," Salice said, his eyes wandering over the girl's shoulder to Noah. "It was rumored that the Elmond Twins helped a few of them transform into humans to escape the purges, but again this is the type of political fear mongering that has never been proven. His ban on human transformation was not meant as an actual policy, rather a mean-spirited attempt at convincing his followers that former demons could be hiding anywhere. If you really want to learn more, I recommend the book *Those Teeth Are For Smiling: The Misunderstood Demon*. Now Noah—where was that letter?"

Noah wordlessly handed over his note and turned sharply from the room.

"Not even a thank you?" Salice called after him in a sardonic tone. "I am doing you a favor, boy. Best remember that."

Noah couldn't get away fast enough. Demons... who killed people... who became human to escape punishment. If only he could outrun the implications of that thought as well.

HALLOWEEN

THE THRILL OF NEW DISCOVERIES DID NOT COME WITHOUT THE BURDEN of learning, and Noah had hardly any free time. Besides the main subjects of Necromancy, Demonology, and Transhumanism, there was a never-ending stream of guest lectures that Noah was forced to attend. These were intended to broaden the student's perspective on life and death.

Noah had never stopped to consider what it must be like to live a hundred generations as a turtle before spending one as a bird, but Ikella, the finch, explained at length. On a different occasion, an old man named Barosca who wore his beard like a belt said that he spent all his years gambling five hundred years ago. Fearing he would disappear completely, he swore a death of austerity. After that he hasn't spent a day since, and he swears he couldn't be happier, although admittedly he'd wished he wouldn't have minded being twenty five again.

The Necromancy class consisted of a lot more anatomy than Noah expected, and they were required to learn the names of every bone and muscle fiber for them to weave magic into. Noah would have expected his medical knowledge from his previous life to serve him well here, but despite his proficiency in naming the muscles he always had trouble getting them to respond.

Professor Wilst said that lurching zombies were an unfortunate stereotype caused by amateur Necromancers who made sweeping commands like 'Kill them all' without telling the poor confused zombies how to do it. The studying was exhausting, but it was all worth it when Noah was able to get his corpse to raise its hand and wave for the rest of the class. That was at least as well as Jamie or Walter could do, and considerably better than Mrs. Robinson who hardly ever bothered to show up for class at all.

Despite the experience of his previous life not helping much, there were bits and pieces which did come to him as sudden revelations. The more he read, the more it felt like he was reviewing long forgotten information rather than learning something new. When Professor Humstrum asked the class whether plants had souls, Noah knew at once that they possessed something similar but distinct which spiritologists have named the life-force, which instead of having a unique soul meant that their essence was returned to fuel the cosmic tree and its millennial bloom.

When Noah was asked how he knew since it was not in the required reading, he made up an excuse about Professor Salice mentioning it during his apprenticeship to hide the fact that he didn't know how he knew. Noah could only assume that one of his previous selves knew the fact, and that somehow all those experiences were still buried inside him somehow.

Despite Noah's aversion toward Salice, he confided in Jamie and Walter that Denomology was actually his favorite class. He still hadn't told Walter about his demonic affinity—being a murderer seemed like more than enough to test their friendship—but it was demonology more than anything that caused these feelings of deja vu. As soon as Professor Salice mentioned that the full moon can make it easier for the host to find demons in the netherworld, Noah not only remembered that different phases of the moon can help find different demons, but he also remembered that the Boarheaded Thimbler could only be found during a solar eclipse.

If Professor Salice had realized that Noah gave him the wrong address yet, then he didn't mention it. Their relationship had even improved on account of how much additional time Noah spent with the Professor as his apprentice. Salice responded to Noah's interest with encouragement, and he spent as much time receiving private guidance and tutoring as he did actually working on Salice's behalf.

There were only two things about this period at the school that Noah did not enjoy. He didn't like how Brandon and Teresa treated the imps, which was almost as bad as how they treated him whenever he tried to defend them. And he didn't like that he couldn't stop thinking about the Whispering Room.

Noah couldn't bear to enter again after the morning he'd fallen asleep there, and for several nights afterward all he could dream about was his daughter's tormented whispering. At the same time he blamed himself for allowing that fear to prevent him from checking on them. Not to mention poor Samantha who must be so frightened by the spirits she sees, and Claire who would have loved to know how well Jamie was taking care of Mrs. Robinson.

Their first real opportunity to interact with the living world came sooner than anyone was expecting though. Noah was playing a game of knucklebones on the grass with Walter and Dolly Miller when Elizabeth Washent came bounding through the high grass in the graveyard.

"We're going to have a Halloween surprise!" she exclaimed, bouncing vertically on the spot, "and I'm going to spoil it! Who wants to know what it is? I heard it straight from The Matriarch's own mouth."

Elizabeth was quickly surrounded by students who came scrambling out of their mausoleums from all around to hear. Everybody knew that The Matriarch had taken Elizabeth as a personal apprentice because Elizabeth had made sure to tell everyone that very same day. She had never been very clear how exactly a rabbit was able to fulfill that duty, or what the duty even consisted of, but it was hard not to be swept up in her contagious enthusiasm.

"We're each going to have our own imp for the day!" she squealed, unable to contain her excitement.

"What would we want an imp for?" Walter asked in disappointment. "The ones we have don't do anyone any good."

"Well that's because they're stuck here on the island," Elizabeth said smugly. "We're going with our imps to the mainland to make mischief in the living world!"

"Why would we want to cause mischief?" Jamie asked, appearing from the graveyard gate with Mrs. Robinson on her shoulder.

"That's what's expected on Halloween!" Elizabeth said in exasperation. "*The Matriarch* said people would be disappointed if they *didn't* have their laundry all died pink or have toilet paper thrown over their house."

The more they thought about it, the more sensible Elizabeth's excitement became. Walter's apprenticeship with the Spiritual Operator hadn't given him the chance to make any calls, so he decided this would be his chance to finally send his girlfriend a letter. Bowser also wanted to check in on his family, although he was only planning to use the imp to terrify the superstitious father of his household who had never once given him a treat or called him a good boy. Noah overheard Brandon making a list of all the people he wanted to get revenge on, but he'd be hard pressed getting to every name in that notebook in a single day.

By the time The Matriarch arrived at the graveyard gate everyone was already massed about the entrance in anticipation. She stood in her customary red hat and coat with her hands on her hips, wearing a coy smile which suggested she knew perfectly well that the news of her 'surprise' had already spread.

"How are we all this fine autumn night?" The Matriarch asked, taking her time to draw out each syllable. "If I didn't know that this was a perfectly ordinary Tuesday, I would have thought you were all expecting something."

"Does it have to be an imp?" Jason Parson shouted, breaking his poorly concealed mask of ignorance. "I think gobblers would be much more fun for stealing candy."

And then everyone was talking at once, about where they were going and how long they'd be and whether the imps were allowed to bring anything back with them, and a hundred other questions which washed over The Matriarch like waves breaking against the implacable cliffs below.

"I don't suppose there is any use pretending then," she said, pouting her bottom lip. "But it *does* seem that one part of the surprise has been exaggerated. The imps will be going to where they're directed in the living world, but our class will not be leaving the island. We will all be going down to Montgomery Wolf, the Spiritual Operator who lives in Teraville, where we will be monitoring our imps through scrying crystals."

There was a collective wave of small disappointed groans, but The Matriarch waved it into silence with a flick of her wrist. "And yes, your imps *will* be able to bring you back a souvenir. Although I wouldn't recommend candy because you won't be able to eat it. If anyone has a problem with that, then they can sit in their coffins all day for all I care. Who is with me?"

This time the response sounded with unabated enthusiasm. The Matriarch waited at the gate while the students streamed out onto the grassy hillside. The moment Noah had passed her however, The Matriarch left her position and merged with the crowd by his side.

"How is our little Chainer doing?" she asked him. "I imagine you'll be excited to send the imp to visit your family."

Noah had already dismissed the possibility. The imp might be obeying him for the day, but it was Salice they had the contract with and he had no doubt that they would report where his family lived directly back to him. For all he knew this entire holiday could have been planned around that fact.

"I don't want to scare them," Noah replied. "I'd rather just have it go trick-or-treating in a friendly neighborhood."

"Very sensible, you never know when demons will try to pull something horrible," she said, looking about her in a conspiratorial fashion. The surrounding students were gradually spreading over the grassy hillside. "You know, if it were up to me, I wouldn't let the little beasties anywhere near my school. We've got the T.D.D. to blame for that—requiring a 'full curriculum' to qualify for department funding. It's a disgrace if you ask me. I've had more than my share of problems with them in the past, and even when they aren't fighting each other or playing tricks on people, they're still the ugliest little monsters I've ever seen."

Noah said nothing, wondering whether Professor Humstrum really had rushed off to tell The Matriarch about his affinity. Noah glanced behind him and met Brandon's beady eyes for an instant. He'd been whispering with Teresa, and both of them were staring at him with undisguised loathing. Noah wasn't sure whether they could overhear him, but this wasn't a conversation he wanted to be having regardless.

"I'm going to catch up with my friends now, hope you have a happy Halloween, Mrs. Matriarch."

"Elanore Barrow," The Matriarch said. "You may call me Elanore, and if you ever want to discuss anything that has been troubling you, my office is the first door on the first floor. I think you'll find me a very attentive listener."

Noah thanked her and hurried forward, making a show of joining Walter and Jamie as though they had been expecting him. To The Matriarch's credit—Noah didn't think he'd ever be able to call her Elanore—she hadn't pushed him on visiting Mandy or sharing more than he was comfortable with. It was a welcome contrast with the constant pressure he'd grown accustomed to from Salice, and it was almost enough for him to want to tell her everything and ask for her help. On the other hand, she clearly saw the same significance in being a Chainer that Salice did, and Noah didn't want to expose his family to a whole new avenue of risk.

"I think you can trust her," Jamie said once Noah had explained his doubts. "She's been teaching at the school for so long that I'm sure she's come across loads of Chainers before. Someone like that wouldn't think of interfering with the living."

"I'm not so sure," Walter said, "You were all for trusting Salice too, and one look at him will tell you he's up to no good."

"We still don't know he's not!" Jamie said. "You'd think someone who just shed their body and is on the way to find a new one would know not to judge someone on their appearances."

"How about their personality? That whole 'I'm better than you just because I can summon a demon that can melt your face' attitude? Is that fair game?"

Noah was eager to drop the subject and instead asked Walter about the Spiritual Operator they were approaching. Walter pointed out Montgomery Wolf's house, a stone tower that was so twisted it looked like someone trying to wring out a wet towel. The whole tower was completely engulfed in climbing ivy, and there was a large glass room on the top which glowed beneath the moon like a lighthouse.

"That's where Mr. Wolf—and you have to call him that or he gets really mad—that's where he keeps the Netherball which he uses to look into the demon world. I'm not allowed to touch that one," Walter said. "Mostly, the place is just filled with crystal balls for spying on living people. They're enchanted so people who can see and hear spirits like mediums light up. Once he's found one, he can send messages to them and ask for them to relay that onto the nearby people. Some of the stronger psychics learn how to call him back, and then he's the one who is supposed to go find the spirit."

"That's really good of him, helping people find their families again," Jamie said.

"Not really," Walter sighed. "He charges six months to find the right person, and he won't even give me a discount for being his apprentice. I'd still have done it if it weren't for The Matriarch's stupid restriction per semester."

"I might be able to buy it," Noah said. "Professor Salice had an imp pick up my school supplies, and I never had to pay for any of them."

"Would you really?" Walter asked. "I've still got two months left this semester, and I'll pay you the rest back after Christmas."

"You shouldn't take his time. I thought the imp was going to deliver it," Jamie said reproachfully.

"Well I've thought about it, but any message I wrote down would be on spiritual paper. I'd have to get the imp to write down the message on material paper, but I don't think they can even write."

"How do you know they can't write?" Jamie said, frowning. "They're very—"

"Not this again. Did you know that imp Brandon has it out for won't leave me alone? I think it's trying to haunt me."

"Aha!" she exclaimed. "So you *can* tell them apart now. And don't think I don't recognize the necklace you've started wearing. That's the rock the imp gave you," she added triumphantly.

Walter clutched at the string around his neck self-consciously. "I didn't want it," he mumbled. "He just seemed so hurt and I thought it would shut him up..."

Soon the entire class was gathered outside Mr. Wolf's tower where he stood waiting to greet them. He pulled the knees of his long striped legs past his waist as he stepped through the children, walking with a haughty disdain as though he was afraid of getting one of them on his feet.

"Are there supposed to be so many, Matriarch?" Mr. Wolf asked in a long-suffering voice. "Might as well open the bestiary and let them all run amok inside. Scrying crystals are very fragile, you know, and if anything breaks—"

"Nothing is going to break, my dear, silly man," The Matriarch replied. "I know how much the T.D.D. is paying you for the day, so do play nice. If it's really too much of a burden on you, then I'm sure the students will have just as much fun spending the holiday turning into frogs and riding broomsticks at Miss Thatcher's Witchery."

"Miss Thatcher? She has a broomstick so far up her backside that she —"

"Mr. Wolf!" The Matriarch interrupted sternly.

"—lifts off every time she farts. There, you made me say it. Come along then children, one at a time. Yes, yes the crystal balls are very pretty, but they aren't for touching. Or licking, Mrs. Horlow! Why on Earth—"

The inside of the tower was dazzlingly bright. Hundreds of thin silver chains suspended from perfectly smooth crystal balls of every imaginable color, as well as at least two colors that Noah had never seen before and couldn't even imagine when he wasn't looking directly at them. Some crystal balls were barely the size of marbles, while others must have weighed a ton and required four supporting chains securely anchored to the walls and ceiling.

"It's all very simple really—not the business, that's more complicated than any of you could manage—but what you'll be doing today," Mr. Wolf said. "Two people per ball, it doesn't really matter which, they've all been configured for you already. All you must do is look into your reflection and tell it where you'd like to see. Once the scene has resolved itself, look around until you find your imp—you do not need to touch the crystal to do this, Mr. Parson—simply walk around to view the scene from another angle. Do look where you're going though—it's as crowded as a mass grave in here."

Noah found a pale creamy crystal a little smaller than a globe, and Walter spoke the name and neighborhood of an unfamiliar city. Tall dark buildings huddled together deep within the glass as though it was a snow globe.

"Your imp will automatically travel through the nether to the chosen location," Mr. Wolf continued, prowling incessantly through the room. "Look for him now. He'll be easy to recognize because he lights up."

Walter raised his hand which prompted Mr. Wolf to strut over to them. They explained that they would rather find a medium, which Mr. Wolf was happy to oblige as soon as he realized he would be paid in full.

"You won't tell The Matriarch, will you?" Mr. Wolf asked, bending low. "I won't be giving any refunds for the simple scrying she's already ordered."

"Not a word," Walter agreed. "There is a medium who is close by then?"

Mr. Wolf reached inside his mouth as though he was fishing for something. Noah winced as the man plucked one of his own teeth out, which was actually an aquamarine stone shaped like a tooth. He grinned to reveal the gaping hole which remained.

"Can never be too safe with these," Mr. Wolf said. "Go on then, grab hold. Six months it is, that's the deal, take it or leave it. No discounts, no bartering, and definitely no backsies."

"I'll be giving two months, he's got the rest," Walter said. "Thanks again, Noah. You don't know how much this means to me."

They both paid the transaction, and Noah was surprised to realize he didn't even mind holding the tooth when it was his turn. This whole place was so macabre that nothing that used to bother him had any real horror left. The groggy, dizzying feeling was more pronounced this time, and he was sure he could distinctly feel his hair and fingernails growing. His shins suddenly became extremely sore and tender. He was sure Walter had been taller than him a moment ago, but now they were the same size.

Mr. Wolf meanwhile grabbed the crystal between his hands and began dancing a complex pattern with his fingers. The image spun smoothly in response, the viewpoint soaring upward before swooping between the tall dark buildings like a bird. The view whirled straight through walls, catching one man on a toilet and others sitting in their living rooms or eating dinner at the table. The only indication that they were noticed was that people tended to shiver briefly as the viewpoint passed through them.

"Margret Vintilo?" Mr. Wolf mused, his brow furrowed with concentration. "No, she stopped doing business after that gobbler got her fluffy little dog. Pedflam Grasowitch? Now I'm sure nothing would have stopped old Pedflam."

The viewpoint in the crystal shifted sharply to the right, breaking free of the apartment buildings and speeding down the street.

"Although he did have that run in with the police when he started selling amulets," Mr. Wolf continued thoughtfully. "'Course, it was the boy's own fault when he thought it would stop a bullet, but that's what you get when you think you're too good for disclaimers. Are you in there, Pedflam? Come out come out, or I'm coming in."

The scene in the crystal paused briefly before a crumbling stone cottage. It looked like it had been built a hundred years ago and had only been maintained by dry wind and the occasional tornado. A moment later and they were through the door within a living room that was stacked from floor to ceiling with old magazines, newspapers, and casually discarded books.

A fat middle-aged man with thick glasses, greasy hair, and an uneven beard sat in an armchair which was the only furniture in the room. He grunted in surprise and swiftly shut his bathrobe, or at least closed the part that wasn't being obstructed by his low-hanging stomach.

"Get off then!" he shouted. "No spooks allowed, not in here. Out, out, or I'll—"

"You'll what, Pedflam?" Mr. Wolf asked. "Who you gonna call?"

Pedflam was still glowering, but his face softened with recognition. "I'll call your daughter, if she's still alive. What is it this time, Montgomery?"

"A message for Mrs. Natasha Cortico of 324 Browsly Street. It shouldn't take you more than an hour, a little more if you'd like to make yourself presentable."

"Make myself present—hmph," Pedflam said. "That's what I've got a lock on the door for. What's in it for me then?"

"A week. An hour for a week, you can't say no to that."

"A week?" Walter asked incredulously. "You charged us six months."

"Shh, quiet," Mr. Wolf hissed. "There are conversion rates to account for... it's not easy sending time over, you know. It gets all compressed and... it doesn't matter, just stay out of this."

"Who is there?" Pedflam asked suspiciously. He stood up and waddled over to open the curtains, although the window was so dirty that this did little to bring in more light.

"Just the client, a poor lost soul missing his love. Ten days, that's my best offer."

"Get off then, I'll take it," Pedflam grumbled, "but only because it's in the name of love. Give me a few minutes and I'll meet you there." He began stomping across the room toward an adjoining bathroom which looked dirty enough as to instantly negate the effect of a shower as soon as he got out. "And don't follow me in here!" he bellowed, snapping the door shut behind him.

"As if," Walter said. "Is he really the best we can do? I think Natasha would laugh him straight out the door."

"It's hard finding a reliable medium, especially this far south," Mr. Wolf replied indignantly. "Something about warm weather makes it harder to concentrate. Besides, you should have learned by now not to judge a soul by its shell. Mr. Grasowitch is doing very well for being over eighty years old. He's been officially licensed by the T.D.D., and he's been paid handsomely by the looks of it."

The crystal view whirled out of the house and began meandering down the moonlit street.

"Do you recognize the area?" Noah asked.

"Yeah, sure," Walter said, barely glancing at the crystal before averting his eyes to gaze around at the other students.

"Aren't you excited to be seeing her again?" Noah pressed. "What are you going to say?"

"I don't... It doesn't matter," Walter said. Noah had the impression that Walter wasn't really seeing anything, least of all the crystal which he was purposely avoiding. "I don't think she'll want to hear from me," he added quietly.

"Of course she will," Noah said reassuringly. "And it won't be any pressure, because Pedflam will be doing all the talking."

Walter was fidgeting so bad that he couldn't stand still. He darted outside for a bit of fresh air while waiting for the medium to be ready, and Noah could see him out the window pacing in agitation. Noah took the chance to track down his imp and had just begun having it howl below people's windows when Walter returned, as pale as Noah had ever seen him.

"Ready then? Pedflam should be there soon," Mr. Wolf said,

swiping the crystal ball so that the image spun. "324 Browsly Street? Could that be her?"

The crystal viewpoint zoomed in on an elegant dark skinned lady with a soft, curly afro. There wasn't a straight line in her entire body, as was abundantly evident from her red dress which flowed along her curves as tightly and smoothly as a second skin. She sat on the front steps of a clean white house with a leather purse between her legs, her attention focused on her phone.

"Walter?" Mr. Wolf asked. "I've spent quite enough time on you two already, and The Matriarch would complain mightily if I didn't make sure the imps weren't getting into too much trouble."

"Yeah," Walter breathed, his eyes fixed on the woman. "It's her alright."

"She's quite charming," Mr. Wolf said rather nasally. "I'm glad that I was able to give you this opportunity. Just wait here until Pedflam catches up. I'll check in with you again before—hey! Little fat boy! What's going on over there?"

Mr. Wolf hurried away to where Brandon had begun to shout into his orb. Noah caught a glimpse of an imp chasing a group of costumed trick-or-treaters, its sharp teeth flashing in the crystal. Despite the commotion, Walter didn't turn to look or even blink.

Noah couldn't help but think back to his own wife, a cheery English woman named Olivia Wells. They'd had a brief but fulfilling affair, but it was undeniable that his awareness of spirits had put a strain on the relationship. They were fighting all the time by the point of Mandy being born, and when the child began seeing spirits as well it was too much for Olivia to bear and she was never to be seen again. This sent his thoughts spiraling back to Mandy once more, and what she must be going through trying to raise Lewis on her own. It was no wonder that she'd prefer not to see the things she did, but denying them didn't seem like any solution at all…

Had Noah ever truly fallen in love? He'd loved the idea of love, from books and movies and all the ways it could have been if life hadn't gotten in the way. He had no doubt that he loved his parents, and his daughter, and his grandson, but that wasn't the same as falling in love with a stranger. There had been a few times in his life when he thought he'd found the one, but it always seemed like the more he got to know her, the less he knew himself, and in the end he'd be alone again. Perhaps he'd been too selfish to ever lose himself in someone else.

Noah studied Walter's face, how he had barely moved a muscle this whole time. It hardly seemed worthwhile to fall in love if it hurt so badly when it was over. Even now that Walter had found her again, it didn't seem to make him happy. If anything he looked like he was about to cry. Slowly, tenderly, with trembling hand, Walter reached out to touch the crystal ball. At almost the same instant Natasha looked up from her phone, her deep, brown eyes lighting up the stone.

"Oh, there you are, I've been waiting almost an hour," she said, her voice low and smooth.

"I'm sorry, baby," a husky voice replied. "Next time you can take two hours getting ready and we'll call it even."

She laughed and smiled, allowing herself to be swept into the arms of a man in a suit that looked so new that it bent rather than folded. Noah thought it was only decent to turn away when they kissed, but Walter still didn't blink.

"We should hurry though," Natasha said, nestling against the man. "The curtain is going to open before we even get there."

"Fine with me," he replied. "The only show I'm interested in will be going on in the back of the theatre."

Natasha laughed again and drew away teasingly, leading the man away from the house. They were approaching a sleek black town car parked on the street when another car driving much too fast swerved to drift into an uneven park nearby.

Pedflam squeezed himself out at once, and Noah would have laughed to see him if it weren't for the severity of Walter's stare. The medium had dressed in flowing robes of red satin, his ample neck almost invisible beneath a mass of silver and gold chains attached to amulets, mystic symbols, and what appeared to be the lower jaw of a human skull whose teeth were entirely gold.

"324 Browsly Street? Natasha?" he shouted before Natasha had a chance to enter her car.

"Who wants to know?" she asked uneasily.

The man in the suit looked highly amused. "A friend of yours?" he asked.

"No," Walter said. "It's not her. Get back in the car."

"What do you mean it's not her?" Pedflam asked, turning to meet Walter's gaze in a huff. "Of course it's her. You think this is my first transmittance?"

"Who are you talking to?" Natasha asked. "I'm sorry but we really have to go—"

"Just a moment," Pedflam told her, turning his attention back on Walter, which to her must appear that he was speaking into the empty air. "Montgomery doesn't offer refunds, and you're not going to get another chance at this. If you have something to say, then say it. If not, then I'm going home. It's all the same to me."

The man in the suit opened the passenger side door of the town car and gestured for Natasha to get in. Then to Pedflam, he said, "Whatever you're selling, we aren't buying. Happy Halloween man... whatever you're dressed as."

"This," Pedflam replied magnanimously, sweeping his hands down the length of his satin robes, "This is no costume, sir. This robe represents the highest trust and honor that the Trans Dimensional Department may bestow upon a living mortal. And the only thing I'm selling you is the truth, unless of course you were interested in a protection amulet…"

"It wasn't supposed to go like this," Walter moaned. "Just tell her—tell her to be happy, okay?"

Natasha's door was already swinging shut when Pedflam spluttered, "Walter wants you to be happy."

The door halted so suddenly that time might as well have stopped. Walter was speaking quickly now, and Pedflam hurried to repeat every word.

"He says he's sorry he didn't show you how important you are when he still had the chance, but he wants to say it now. He wants you to not take any of it too seriously, because it'll all be over too soon and none of it can follow you where you're going. That it doesn't have to all be done right the first time round, because you'll get to try again and everything will be easier next time. He wants you to know that there's no feeling so heavy that your soul can't carry, and whether it's good or bad it doesn't matter so long as you can feel something that makes you feel alive. Walter wants you to know that he loved you while he was alive, that he still loves you now that he's gone, and that he'll continue loving you in the next life too. Even if you're a hawk and he's a rabbit, because it's your soul that he loves, and you don't have to belong to him for him to see its light."

Natasha didn't have words to respond with, but her mouth parted and her eyes glistened, and to Walter that must have been enough. Not even waiting for a reply, Walter turned away from the crystal globe and stumbled blindly through the room, nearly tripping over Elizabeth and pushing past Rachelle on his way out. They giggled at him as he passed, but he didn't seem to hear. It's probably best he left when he did, because Pedflam had appended the speech with a well rehearsed sales pitch for his amulets.

"… and I'm sure he would have wanted you to stay safe with one of these harpy claws, hand-calcified to be in the physical world, of course."

Noah turned away from the crystal as well. Everyone else was still playing with their imps, but such games lost their appeal in the face of the heavy wistfulness filling his heart. Love didn't seem quite as silly to Noah as it had a moment before, although he still had a hard time believing that it was worth it.

"Is Walter okay?" Jamie asked from a nearby orb which she shared with a tall, thin girl named Jennifer Alaski. Jamie's imp was in a kitchen washing dishes, looking glum.

"Go and find out, why don't you," Jennifer snapped. "You're not using your imp right anyway."

"They needed the help!" Jamie insisted. "All those kids running around and making a mess already, it's the least I could do."

"He'll be okay," Noah said, watching Walter exit the building. "I think he just wants to be alone."

"I understand," Jamie said. "It's funny, but for years and years I was afraid of dying alone, but now that I'm dead I have more friends than I ever did alive. Do you feel that way too, Noah?"

Noah wasn't listening anymore though. He'd gone to the window to watch Walter walking a few unsteady steps outside, then tipping over to land on his back in the grass and stare up at the moon. How odd that it was the same moon that stirred such feelings in the living. Would they look at it any differently if they knew the dead were watching too?

ZOMBIES

There must have been a secret pact among the professors to all begin increasing the workload at the same time. Demonology remained Noah's easiest subject as he kept remembering things he never thought he knew, but even so there were long histories to learn that he knew nothing about. Professor Salice had an extremely sympathetic view of demons and lectured at length about how they were persecuted throughout the ages. He seemed to think they were a universal scapegoat for everything that went wrong, and tended to gloss over the 'historically insignificant' massacres which they caused every few decades.

Professor Humstrum's class had moved onto communicating with living animals. He'd setup a scrying crystal in the middle of the class which went on a tour from house to house looking for cats to speak with. Noah could never seem to get the cat's attention, although the Professor admitted that sometimes cats prefer to feign disinterest even when they're perfectly aware of the spirit's presence. Mrs. Robinson was a regular feature of the class now, although her attendance for the other classes was sporadic at best. She never attended necromancy at all, saying she couldn't stand their smell.

Humstrum did seem to act more cooly toward Noah since the

incident in the Bestiary, however. The ape maintained a constant air of being politely unimpressed by Noah's work, saying that Chainers are often weak at transhumanism because they're 'so busy with the cycle that they don't stop to appreciate the beauty of individual lives'. Noah thought that sounded made up.

Necromancy was even worse though. Despite zombies not having spirits of their own, Noah was convinced that his was being deliberately obstinate as it never seemed to do what it was told. Brandon was the star pupil in this class, which only served to frustrate Noah more. His zombie was practically tap-dancing while Noah struggled to get his own to stop chewing on its arm long enough to listen.

While Professor Humstrum never gave tests, Professor Wilst was an endless source of pop-quizzes, chapter evaluations, and a looming final exam. Wilst threatened that the worst performing student would have their body exhumed, while the best performer would be allowed to use it for the next semester. It was almost impossible to tell whether the dry, skeletal voice was speaking sarcastically, but the thought of Brandon being able to use his body like a puppet would have been nauseating if Noah still felt that sort of thing.

Help came from the most unlikely place one November afternoon class where Noah was performing abysmally. The students had taken their zombies out to practice walking up the stairs, but Noah's zombie had somehow gotten scared of the pit and refused to cross the bridge. Noah grew so frustrated that he shouted at it, causing it to collapse and flop violently on the ground like a fish out of water.

"You're going to fail, you know," Teresa told Noah conversationally. She stayed back with him while the other students went ahead to cross. "I wouldn't be surprised if you've already lived your last life."

Noah ignored her and began reciting commands from the textbook once more. The zombie flopped onto its back and rocked from side to side, unable to stand up.

"Do you want to know how Brandon does it?" she asked coyly.

"No, I don't," Noah replied sharply. "Of course he gets along with zombies. They're both braindead."

Noah expected her to become outraged at any slight against her precious son, but to his surprise she only giggled.

"He's got a mermaid skull from Nepon Vasolich, the supernautical sailor. It translates his commands into a smooth music that only the dead can hear, and it helps them understand."

"So he's cheating," Noah said bluntly.

Teresa's face crinkled into a sneer, but an instant later it was gone. She was smiling now. "No more cheating than being a Chainer. Anyway, it's not even cheating, because Professor Wilst never said it wasn't allowed. Would you like to use it?"

Noah hated the idea of needing help at all, but as things were he was at risk of being the very bottom of the class. Noah kicked his zombie, his foot making contact as its animation imbued it with spiritual energy.

"Why do you care?" he asked at last.

"I don't," she said curtly, spreading her fingers to look at her glistening white nails. "It's all the same to me if you never get to the advanced classes or come back to life at all. Rumor has it that you have a key to the Whispering Room though…"

"Says who?" Noah asked, as stubborn as his useless zombie.

"I want it," Teresa said. "I know you don't use it. The mermaid skull would do you more good."

"How do you know I don't use it? Who has been talking about me?"

"Words have wings of their own," Teresa replied cryptically. "I want to use it tonight. You'll take me there and show me how it works, okay?"

"Let me see the skull then," Noah said.

Teresa only smirked. "I'll give it to you in the Whispering Room." She turned to her zombie which had been standing motionless behind her the whole while. "Consurgo!" she barked. The zombie lurched forward to follow her across the bridge.

Noah spent the rest of the class trying and failing to get his fat zombie to even stand up again. It rolled back and forth and moaned most piteously, and at one point it began humming loudly to itself to prevent any commands from being heard. Noah hadn't made any conscious decision yet, but part of him already knew that he wanted to make the deal.

Noah asked Walter afterward whether he was the one who told Teresa about the whispering room, but he denied it vehemently. Walter called her a snake and said not to trust her, but Jamie was quick to disagree.

"Do you know how she died?" Jamie asked.

"No, but I can guess," Walter said. "My money is on being shot by the police after trying to kick a puppy."

"I bet Brandon killed her," Noah said. "Spoiled brat didn't want to die alone, so he took her with him."

"Close, but no," Jamie said. "She did die trying to save Brandon though. They were on a boat when he went over, and she went after him. They both drowned in each other's arms."

"How do you know?" Noah asked suspiciously. "Were you the one to tell her about the Whispering Room?"

"So what if I did?" Jamie asked, turning up her nose. "She's got loved ones like anyone else. Doesn't she deserve to hear them too?"

"No," Walter and Noah said in unison.

"You murdered people," Jamie reminded Noah sharply. "So what if she hasn't always been the most pleasant person? We've all got a chance to leave ourselves behind and start again. If she wants to say goodbye before she can have a fresh start, then she deserves that."

After some bickering, Noah decided that he would meet Teresa for the exchange, although Walter insisted he and Jamie accompany as backup to make sure she wasn't trying to play a trick on him.

The fifth floor which contained the Whispering Room was empty as usual when the three arrived. Noah could still hear the speech and laughter of jostling students above, but it was muffled and tinny like they were only hearing an echo. It might have been his imagination, but even the will-o-wisps seemed to be burning lower than usual, their normally warm red light muted into pale orange.

"I was wondering when you'd show up," Teresa said. She was standing outside the Whispering Room with her arms crossed. She didn't seem surprised to see Walter and Jamie, giving them no more attention than a swift, contemptuous glance.

"Let's get this over with then," Noah said. "Do you have the skull?"

Teresa nodded and produced a round object covered in a piece of lavender cloth. The air seemed to grow colder and more brittle for an instant, and Noah shivered involuntarily. Mrs. Robinson, who had taken to sitting on Jamie's shoulder, hissed softly at the bundle and flattened her ears against her head.

"Disgusting creature," Teresa said, stepping back from the cat. "I don't know why anyone would choose that over being human."

"How do we know the skull works?" Walter asked. "You could be trying to cheat us with a piece of rubbish."

"How do I know the key works?" she countered. "Show me how to use the Whispering Room, and I'll show you how to use the skull."

Walter looked like he was ready to argue again, but he held himself back when Noah approached the door. Noah slid the key inside and pushed it open, not taking his eyes off Teresa the whole time. She smirked, her dark eyes twinkling in anticipation.

"After you, murderer," she quipped sweetly.

Noah rolled his eyes and pushed open the door. The room was deserted with pools of green mist floating along the floor, just as Noah had seen it last.

"Where are they?" Teresa asked.

"Where are who?" Noah said.

"All the people. Everyone I used to know."

"That's not how it works," Noah said. "You've got to stand in the circle and listen. Sometimes you can see them if the connection is strong enough, but mostly it's just whispers like the room says."

Teresa looked suspiciously at Noah for a moment before mounting the raised dais. She was still clutching the bundle in her arms, and Mrs. Robinson's attention was still fixed on it. The cat had crept along behind her, stopping a few feet away, still crouched and ready to spring.

"Gentle now, Mrs. Robinson," Jamie said. "We're all on the same team, okay?"

"Can I talk to them?" Teresa asked.

"Not unless they're a psychic or a Chainer," Noah said. "Then it's more like a two-way window."

Mist was beginning to billow upward and swirl around Teresa's feet.

"There's nothing to be frightened of," Jamie said, prompting a sharp glance from Teresa.

"I'm not frightened," Teresa snapped. "I just don't like being watched."

"Don't worry about us," Jamie said reassuringly. "I was in the room when the others used it and I couldn't hear anything the living said."

Teresa took a deep breath and nodded rigidly. "Thank you," she said, her faint smile seeming more genuine this time. "I needed this. Did you look inside too?"

Jamie shook her head. "I think we often need something until we get it," Jamie said, "but some things are better not to have."

Teresa's top lip pulled tight into the beginning of her customary sneer, but her face relaxed quickly. She nodded and, taking a final deep breath, plunged her face into the swelling green mist. "Now what do I—" she began, the words strangled in her throat as the mist began to flow around her and obscure her face.

Teresa's face was invisible for several minutes before she jolted out of the circle and gasped for air. Her hair was damp from the mist and her eyes glistened with tears.

"I hate it!" she screamed, the sound painfully sharp and piercing in the silence. "It's a lie, and I hate it!"

"Your own fault I bet," Walter said. "Did you think people would miss someone who treated them so nastily?"

"Deal is off," Teresa said, wiping her face with the back of her sleeve. "I don't want your stupid key anymore."

"You can't do that!" Noah protested. "I did my part, now let's see the skull."

"Not happening," she spat, shoving past Noah to make her way toward the door.

Walter leapt in front of her to block the way. "I knew you were going to try and cheat," he said. "You're not leaving with the skull."

"Brandon!" Teresa screamed in her piercing voice. "They're attacking me, Brandon! Help your mother!"

"I didn't touch you, you horrible hag," Walter shouted back. "Now give us the skull or—" he snatched at the lavender bundle in her arms, but whisking away the cover revealed only her stuffed Whale underneath.

Something slammed violently against the outside of the door, powerful enough to shake it in its frame. It sounded like claws were dragging along the wood, then another shuddering boom as the force drove in again. A shower of dust and splinters rained upon them, but the door remained standing.

"There's no way Brandon is doing that," Jamie said.

"His zombie wouldn't have claws either," Walter said. "Maybe a demon?"

"Get out of my way," Teresa screamed, diving for the door.

Walter tried to snatch away her stuffed Whale, but at the same instant the door behind him was assaulted again. The jolt knocked Walter off balance, giving Teresa the chance to evade his sweeping arms. She pushed the door from the inside and the lock clicked open. By then Walter had regained his balance and grabbed Teresa by the shoulders.

Noah meanwhile tried to scramble past both of them to close the door again. He drove his weight against it to slam it shut, but it didn't close all the way. A long bony foot was wedged into the crack, each nail a deadly curved point like the talons on a bird of prey.

As they stared, more curved claws slipped through the crack and folded around the door. Walter shoved Teresa out of the way so he could join Noah in trying to press the door shut again. An irresistible pressure swelled from the other side however—it felt like bracing against a car to prevent it from starting. There was nothing they could do but leap out of the way as the door swung outward.

"He's got a ghoul!" Jamie shouted, identifying the lithe corpse which loomed in the doorway. Its tongue lolled all the way past its chin, and a sloppy grin bristled with teeth which overlapped and forced each other to jut out at odd angles.

Jamie snatched up Mrs. Robinson who was cowering against the dais, and all three friends retreated onto the raised ground. The ghoul fell onto all fours and sauntered into the room, its movements so fluid that it almost seemed to be dancing, completely unlike the rigid zombies they'd grown accustomed to.

"Do you like it?" Brandon asked, now entering the room. Both of his hands were clutched around an elongated but almost-human looking skull whose eyes glowed with soft yellow light. "I picked it up loping around the graveyard last night. Puts those zombies to shame, doesn't it?"

"I told you not to wait so far back," Teresa scolded her son. "Let's get out of here."

"Already?" Brandon said, his grin vanishing. "We haven't even had any fun yet." The ghoul matched its master's agitation and began shuffling back and forth along the floor, its gruesome face locked on Noah and the others.

"Ghouls are corporal, right?" Walter whispered hurriedly. "It can't really attack us, can it?"

"It absolutely can," Jamie said, "don't you ever pay attention?"

"We can try to control it then," Walter said nervously. "There's three of us and only two of them."

"Yeah, but we don't have a mermaid skull," Noah countered. "And I'm no good at undead anyway, so they'd win for sure."

"That's enough," Teresa said. "The deal is off, so we're leaving. As much as they deserve to be punished for trying to cheat me, it's not worth getting kicked out of school."

"Just the cat then?" Brandon asked. The ghoul turned its head toward Mrs. Robinson so sharply that it looked like something snapped inside its neck. Mrs. Robinson spat and hissed, all hair raised. "Cats disappear all the time, and no-one could prove anything."

Teresa sighed, giving into her petulant child. "Very well, just the cat. But leave the rest alone."

"Thank you, mother," Brandon said in a breathy gush.

"I won't let you have her!" Jamie shouted. She grabbed Mrs. Robinson just as the ghoul lunged up the dais toward them. Long claws shredded the air where the cat had been an instant before. Mrs. Robinson made a long, low growl of warning, now from within the circle etched into the stone. Fresh mist was bleeding from the circle—blue again this time. It quickly reduced the ghoul to a silhouette, which only made it even more frightening as it was difficult to tell when it was preparing to lunge.

"Mrs. Robinson?" a faint voice called, as light as wind with the cool of mist. "Is that you?"

"Who said that? Who is here?" Brandon snarled, drawing back upon the skull and causing the ghoul to stumble. The ghoul jerked unevenly backward as though a rope around its waist had snapped taunt. It turned without apparent instruction to glare at Brandon, annoyed at being deprived of its prey.

Inspired by Brandon's hesitation, Noah grabbed Walter and Jamie by the arms and dragged them to cluster inside the circle as well.

The blue light was becoming more intense around the lines, even more than when Noah had entered the first time with Professor Salice. The stone carving was beginning to move, the lines snaking and twisting and scribbling themselves into new patterns. The mist was flooding more powerfully than ever, growing deeper and darker until it was almost purple. The whole room swam with ghastly shadows as the lines altered and the new light shined upon the ghoul.

"Mrs. Robinson?" the voice said again, louder this time and almost as clear as if it were spoken from within the room.

"That's Claire's voice," Noah said. "It was her cat, and she must have been thinking of her, but I don't know why we can hear too."

"What's the light? What's going on?" Brandon demanded.

Noah shrugged helplessly, but Jamie was quick to interject. "He's casting a spell, that's what. He's going to melt your faces off if you don't get out of here."

"Yeah?" Brandon asked, stepping back uneasily. "How's he going to do that?"

"She's lying!" Teresa said, trepidatious. "Where would he learn to do something like that?"

"He's a Chainer, stupid," Jamie replied. "He learned it in another life—I've seen him do it. Just you watch."

The mist was so thick that they could barely see the silhouettes anymore, but they could tell from their shadows that they were hesitating.

"There's something else out here," Walter said. "Something in the mist that wasn't there a second ago."

"He's still got the key!" Teresa insisted. "Take it from him!" Her voice was fainter now, little more than a shouted whisper.

"I'll leave the window open, okay?" Claire's voice came again, so close and real it made them all jump. "Just in case."

The purple light at their feet vanished, as did the circle. They were left blind in the mist which had begun to whip around them as if they stood in the eye of a hurricane. It was dissipating though, blowing off in every direction as it went.

"...and don't worry, because I won't be mad that you've been gone all this time," Claire said. "I won't even ask where you've been. I'll just be happy to see you again, okay? So please, if you can hear me... Please, come home."

Noah, Walter, Jamie, and Mrs. Robinson were now standing in a tight huddle in the center of a bedroom. The last of the mist vanished to reveal yellow sheets, curtains, and a bright blue carpet. Claire, dressed in a white night gown was staring out the open window, apparently oblivious to the whole scene which was unfolding right behind her.

"Claire?" Noah asked in disbelief.

She turned from the window and seemed to look straight at him for a moment. The instant was insubstantial though, and a moment later she'd climbed back into her bed. She didn't see them after-all. Neither did she notice Mrs. Robinson who had leapt onto her bed and curled on the pillow beside her. The cat's fur had settled along its back, and a contented purr was rising from deep within it.

THE ROAD FROM DEATH

"Where are we?" Walter asked, stepping away from the others to explore the surroundings.

"A long way from The Mortuary," Noah said. "The Daymare departed not far from here."

"That was over a seven hour drive!" Jamie protested. "Or walk, or scuttle, or whatever the Daymare did. But that's a long way!"

"How do we get back?" Walter asked, sounding so disheartened that it was hard to believe he'd just escaped a ravenous ghoul.

"Look, the circle is still there!" Jamie said, pointing at the faint outline indented within the carpet. "You never told us the Whispering Room could send us to where people were thinking about us too."

"I had no idea," Noah said. "Professor Salice! What if he cursed the room to transport me so he can find my family?" Noah spun in rapid circles, checking for imps in all the dark corners of the room. "The blue mist was something he did before—I'm sure of it. What if he's here too?"

"Calm down, Noah" Jamie said. "Professor Salice didn't even know we were in the room."

"Unless Brandon told him," Walter said, inspecting the board games stacked on a chair beside Claire's bed.

"It's not going to work," Noah said, pacing in agitation. "I'm not going to visit them. I'm not even going to look at them. He's never going to know which ones are Chainers."

Noah stopped suddenly mid-stride, then turned to walk straight through the bedroom door.

"Where are you going?" Walter called. "We need to figure out how to use this circle to get back."

Even as he spoke though, the circle had continued to fade. The subtle imprint was almost completely gone.

"I know someone who we can talk to, and she might be able to help," Noah said. "Her name is Samantha. She's not a Chainer, but she got attacked by a gargoyle and now she can see spirits."

"What about Mrs. Robinson?" Jamie asked in dismay. The cat was nestled against Claire and showed no inclination to follow.

"What about Claire?" Mrs. Robinson asked. "She's been looking for me this whole time. I'm not going to leave her again."

"You have too," Jamie said. "You need to go to school."

"I don't *have to* do anything. It never felt right, being in school. Everything I want is already here."

"But she can't see you! Please come with us," Jamie insisted, distraught. "She won't even know you're there."

"I'll know," Mrs. Robinson said matter-of-factly.

As if in response, Claire cuddled closer to the cat, her arms passing straight through it without seeming to notice.

"I'll make sure Samantha tells Claire that you're back," Noah said.

"We can't just leave her though!" Jamie pouted. "I'll miss her so much."

Mrs. Robinson didn't reply though. She was only purring.

"It's where she belongs," Noah said reassuringly. "I understand because part of me doesn't want to go back either. Sometimes it's hard to tell the difference between what is familiar and where we belong though, and I don't think the rest of us will find that until we're alive again."

THE NETHERWORLD

"I THOUGHT I MIGHT SEE YOU AGAIN," SAMANTHA SAID, "THOUGH I liked you better as an old man. You're too skinny and weird looking now."

Noah jumped. He thought he was going to be the one to surprise her, but he hadn't seen her standing outside her house in the darkness. She was dressed in pajama bottoms and a purple sweatshirt which was drawn tight against the sharp night air.

"What are you doing out here? It must be past midnight!" Noah exclaimed.

"Does it matter? Were you worried about me?" she asked innocently.

"Why would I be worried about you?" he asked. "I'm the one who is dead. I just mean that most little girls wouldn't be standing alone on the street after midnight."

"Thank you," she replied, even though Noah hadn't intended it as a compliment. Her milky white eye almost glowed in the moonlight as though drawing focus to the fact that she was not a typical girl afterall. "You're being rude though. I know you aren't used to having any friends so you might not know how it goes. You're supposed to introduce me."

"Right, sorry," Noah said. "This is Walter and Jamie, and we've all gotten sent back here by accident and —"

"Oh, I know," Samantha interrupted. "That's why I was waiting here for you."

"Hello, Samantha," Jamie waved.

"What happened to your eye?" Walter asked. Jamie elbowed him in the ribs and he muttered something indistinct under his breath.

"What happened to your body?" Samantha shot back without losing a beat. "Hello, Jamie. Hello, Walter. Let's all go inside, or else someone will drive by and try to kidnap me."

She turned smartly and opened her door, leading them in.

"But how did you know we would be here? We didn't even know we'd be here," Noah said, hurrying to keep up.

"Mr. Hampton told me," Samantha said. "We've become good friends, although my parents don't like it when I talk to the spirits. They think I'm going crazy. I tried to reassure them by telling them I was crazy long before the incident with my eye, but that only seemed to make matters worse."

"Hello Noah! How has your death been treating you?" George Hampton was sitting at the kitchen table with a cup of deliciously steaming cocoa in his hands, although closer inspection revealed that his fingers were overlapping with the corporal cup. He wore the same waistcoat and pinstriped hat as Noah had seen him last, although that was hardly a surprise as laundry was one of the burdens that spirits have left behind.

"Fine, thank you," Noah said guardedly. "How did you know I was coming tonight?"

"A little bird told me," George said, trying to lift his cocoa mug, then scowling as it remained on the table. "Well, not exactly a bird. Quite a lot uglier, in fact."

Something bumped under the table. The scratching of little claws along the edge, followed by an imp's leering face poking into view.

"He's been keeping an eye on you for me," George added.

"I told you not to let those in the house!" Samantha scolded. "The last one tore up my mother's under clothes and she blamed me for it. If she catches that thing in here I'm going to—"

"You'll what, exactly?" George asked mildly. "Make me wish I was deader?"

"I'll catch a thousand spirit spiders and drop them down your back," Samantha declared ferociously.

"Oh dear," George sighed. "We do need him though. He'll be leading our friends back to school through the netherworld. Better be quick about it too."

The imp disappeared beneath the table once more, and Walter squatted down to watch it chew on the base of the wooden table.

"Salice really did send us here then?" Walter asked. "And you knew?"

"Clever lad," George said, a touch of pride in his voice. "The Whispering Room is a nexus where the three worlds meet. It's typically restricted to verbal communication, but it would seem your Professor altered it to allow travel as well. Do you have any of his possessions with you?"

"I don't think so…" Noah began.

"The key!" Jamie said. "You never gave it to Teresa, did you?"

"Quickly now, let me have it," George said, extending his hand. Noah obliged. "Dissipati," George declared, causing the key to glow red hot. The metal bubbled and ran into a silvery liquid which trickled through George's fingers. Just before it vanished completely, a small puff of blue smoke separated itself to dissipate into the air.

"Hey! I might have wanted to use that," Walter protested.

"As I thought, the blue you just witnessed was a tracking charm. Destroying it is necessary to prevent him from tracking you further, although we were too late to stop him from knowing where you are now. There won't be any living people here thinking of Salice, so he won't be able to establish a link through the Whispering Room either. That means he will be making his own journey through the netherworld to join you here. If he left shortly after you, then he should be here…" George casually checked his golden wristwatch, "in about ten minutes."

"But but—" Noah spluttered, unable to decide which of his thousand questions to ask first. "How do *you* know that Salice is trying to find my family? How do you know any of this?"

"Ca'akan here," George gestured to the imp. "Your professor isn't the only one who can summon them. He's been looking after you for a while.

The imp bowed sheepishly, his tiny claws interlocking behind his back. He garbled something in his own language.

"He'd also like Walter to know that he's glad he started wearing the stone he gave him. He says he was scared going undercover with the rest of the school imps, but Walter made him feel welcomed."

The imp covered its face with its claws and ran around behind the table to hide.

"I've been suspicious ever since the gargoyle attack, and Ca'akan has been helping me to understand," George Hampton continued, tapping his nose. "I nose all sorts of things, and my gut guesses many more. I found it interesting that the gargoyle went after Samantha rather than you, although it makes sense when you consider that she was the one looking at it while Noah purposefully averted his gaze. That makes me think that the gargoyles are hunting psychics and Chainers and only got Samantha by mistake."

"Is the gargoyle still looking for them?" Noah asked.

"Your daughter was smart enough not to stare at spirits, and the gargoyle never figured out that she was a Chainer. I haven't seen it in some time so I presume it has continued its search elsewhere. Did you ever tell Salice when or how you died though?"

"No, I don't think so…" Noah said.

"Good," George continued rapidly, his fingers dancing a silent but erratic rhythm on the table. "In that case he only knows that someone was thinking about you somewhere around here. That's plenty of obscurity to shield them. Enough dawdling, you must be off."

George stood and vanished straight through the wall. The imp followed at his heels, running face-first into the kitchen cabinets. George leapt back through the wall and turned for the door instead.

"Enough to shield them?" Noah asked. "Do you mean—"

"Quite so," George replied, vanishing through the door. Samantha opened it and they all chased him back onto the lawn. "If he is the one sending the gargoyles, then the reasonable thing for him to do is kill your daughter and her son. Well, maybe not the *reasonable* thing, but certainly the likely thing."

"But why?" Noah demanded. "What does he need Chainers for?"

George stopped suddenly to consider this, and the imp following him rammed against his legs. "An excellent question. Rest assured I will be investigating. Oh, and one more thing…"

George's hands were rhythmically weaving through the air as he spoke, leaving soft trails of light wherever they went. Noah recognized his white ring which radiated the light, now understanding it to be the bone of George's physical remains.

"My imp told me about the affinity," George said quietly out of the corner of his mouth. "I'd keep that a secret if I were you."

"That was your imp too!" Noah exclaimed. "So, Professor Salice doesn't know."

"He might," George conceded. "Professor Humstrum may have told The Matriarch, and she might have discussed the matter with him. But it's more important that the other students don't know. I daresay you already have enough trouble fitting in being a Chainer."

"And a murderer," Walter added.

"I knew it!" Samantha declared happily. "Well I didn't *know* know, but that's pretty cool all the same."

"You think so?" Noah asked.

"As long it's a people murderer," Samantha said. "I wouldn't even mind being friends when you come back to life. Of course, you'll be a baby though, but I can be your teacher or something. Won't that be fun?"

"How come you can hear us?" Walter asked, looking as confused and flustered as the rest of them. "If it was just your eye—"

"You notice all kinds of things when you start paying attention," Samantha cut him off. "Do you want to know how spirits smell?"

"Now, if you please," George Hampton said. The light from his hands blew outward into a nova to suspend an erratic circle in the air.

The space surrounding the circle seemed to shimmer and melt, while the area within had darkened to black. Walter walked around the floating circle suspiciously, peering at it from every side.

"Follow the imp back to the school," George said, "and make sure it's the same imp, mind you. Ca'akan is missing one of the ridges on his back just below his head. Follow the wrong imp and you could very well end up all sorts of nasty places. Oh! and one more thing," he added, blocking the hole with his arm as Ca'akan tried to crawl inside. "Try not to touch anything in the netherworld. Even if it touches you first."

George removed his arm to open the way. The imp chittered something which sounded like it would have been mortally insulting if Noah could have understood, The imp crawled inside and continued crawling as though it had entered a tunnel, not emerging on the other side of the hole.

"What do you mean 'even if it touches you first'?" Walter grumbled, although no-one paid him much mind.

"Can I come too?" Samantha asked.

"The netherworld is dangerous enough for spirits, but a living body would be killed almost immediately," George Hampton dismissed.

Samantha shrugged. "That's okay. I don't mind."

"Well, your parents would," George said.

"They'd get over it," she quipped.

Noah put his hand through the hole and recoiled immediately. It felt like he'd just stuck his hand into a pool of cold jello, and his fingers still tingled after he'd removed them.

"Well, come and visit again soon then," Samantha said. "George and I will keep an eye on your daughter for you, so you've got nothing to worry about."

"Thanks," Noah said. "Tell Claire that Mrs. Robinson is back with us. We left her sleeping on her pillow."

"Do we really have to leave Mrs. Robinson here?" Jamie asked. "Claire won't even be able to pet her!"

"You don't really have to do anything, because it's not really your choice," Samantha replied. "Mrs. Robinson has made her own decision."

Noah took a deep breath, closed his eyes, and plunged headfirst into the cool abyss, leaving the two girls glaring at each other behind. There was an initial shock as he slid into the gelatinous space, but almost immediately it became an incredibly comfortable feeling. Every movement felt controlled and deliberate, and the soft pressure around him seemed to mold around his body like a perfectly fitted wet suit. It was completely dark with his eyes closed, and Noah spent several lazy seconds floating through the timeless space before he heard the first sounds.

Chittering, slurping, smacking lips. It was the same type of sound he'd grown accustomed to from the imps, but it was greatly magnified as it traveled through the gelatinous space. The sound reminded Noah of a time he went snorkeling and heard the echo of dolphins communicating through the water, only this was much more powerful and emanated from every direction at once. The next shock was realizing that even though his eyes were closed, he could still see Ca'akan waiting just ahead, as well as Walter and Jamie crawling along behind.

Noah's first impression of the netherworld was that it wasn't his first impression at all. His second impression was that it was the most magnificent sight he'd ever not seen.

What at first appeared as empty darkness now resolved itself into an infinitely textured space filled with overlapping layers and shades. He felt like he was on the inside of a giant paper origami that was folded and twisted upon itself into maddening abstraction, yet he also had the sense that if he could only see the place from the right angle it would be clear that it wasn't abstract at all and that every line and crease was exactly where it needed to be.

"Where's the light coming from?" Jamie asked, close behind. "One second it feels like it's pitch black, and the next it's all lit up, and then it's black again without anything even changing."

Jamie's voice sounded thick and slow and incredibly low pitched here. No wonder the imps chittered, Noah thought, as those sounds seemed to carry more easily.

"There is no light," Noah replied, unsure of his words until he said them, "but you don't need light to see here. The part of your brain that processes the seeing is interacting directly with the environment. Try and 'see' something behind you and you'll understand what I mean."

"That doesn't make any sense," Walter complained, his voice even more thick and syrupy.

"It does to me," Noah said, effortlessly turning and flipping while the others struggled to swim and catchup. It was difficult to distinguish directions in this vacuous world, but Noah had the distinct feeling that they were going upward.

"I hate it," Walter moaned. "I feel like a soggy vegetable floating in soup."

"The soup isn't so bad," Jamie said, turning in a slow circle. "It's the noises that bother me. I can't tell how close they are or what's making them."

Noah concentrated on the sounds, and gradually he became aware of dark shapes slipping through the nether around them. None came close enough to be clearly distinguished from the textured background, and he decided his friends would be happier if he never mentioned them at all. He contented himself to study his surroundings in silence.

Flocks of small shapes that could be imps pulsed in rhythmic motion to an unfelt beat like schools of fish riding the tides. Other serpentine things circled around them, so long that they completely encircled the travelers despite seeming a long way off. There were other solitary creatures that followed them curiously for a while, but most soon lost interest and swam away.

Walking, crawling, and swimming all seemed to have a similar effect in the netherworld. The three students alternated between different forms of movements as they struggled to follow Ca'akan. Progress was slow and the imp often looked back impatiently at them, but at least it provided ample time to get used to the new environment and the altered sense of blind perception.

Most interesting of all were the subtle shifts in the textured background at the edge of awareness, like distant mountains which briefly reared or sighed, changing the landscape with the slightest change of position. Noah tried to imagine something like that in the living world, but it was difficult to guess their true scale in this place where perspective and distance were so hard to judge.

A much closer chittering caused Walter to make a little gurgling yelp, but it was only Ca'akan who had paused to wait for them.

"Hold still," Noah said automatically.

"Not happening," Walter said. "I'm not spending a minute longer here than I have to."

Ca'akan made a short, sharp squeak.

"Don't talk either," Noah said softly. "Not until it passes."

The nether had gone silent. The demons had stopped chittering, the flocks of imps dispersed, the long serpentine shapes breaking their circles to flee. The silence had a force of its own, uninterrupted even by the draw of breath or a beating heart that would accompany any such living encounter. Embedded in that silence was the unmistakable sense that they were not alone.

It was difficult to understand what was approaching because there was nothing to see and nothing to hear. If Noah's mind really was interacting directly with the environment, then it wouldn't have been any of his known senses which tracked the being. It was a deeper part of his mind, the activation of an animalistic impulse that he'd forgotten was even there. This feeling was not an interpretation of a sensation, nor a conscious realization of danger, nor even a reaction to an imagined outcome—this was the raw fear of a screaming mind, and here in the netherworld it had a life of its own.

Walter opened his mouth, but Jamie slapped a hand across his face. A moment later something like a shadow passed over the group. Noah could only associate the feeling with swimming with a sea monster slowly rising from the depths.

Noah's body prickled with a thousand freezing needles. It felt like his brain was replaced by a block of ice, and his thoughts felt rigid and immovable. He had the most unnerving instinct that if he tried to force himself to think in that moment then his entire mind would shatter into a thousand pieces and trickle out through his ears.

Noah was vaguely aware that Walter and Jamie were shivering uncontrollably behind him. He had to reassure them that everything was going to be okay, but he couldn't make sense of the words in his head, let alone work his locked and rigid mouth.

The feeling continued to grow more intense for the next few seconds, until Noah was so numb that he couldn't tell whether he was awake or asleep. The pressure of a suppressed scream was building in his chest, but he couldn't let it out even if he wanted to. The pressure became so great that he felt he would be ripped apart if he had to hold it any longer, but a moment later it began to subside once more.

The shadow was lifting, slowly swimming away from them. Already Noah's mind was beginning to sluggishly stir back to life. Jamie had calmed considerably—she might even be unconscious as she floated peacefully with her eyes closed. Walter did not share the same tranquility, and even though the chill was fading he was trembling worse than ever. Walter's head was flopping back and forth as though his neck had no bones in it at all, and his fingers were convulsing as though his life depended on clutching onto something that wasn't there.

"It's almost over. It won't hurt you," Noah said quietly as soon as he was able. At least, that's what his mind had instructed his mouth to say. Somehow the message was scrambled in transit though, and what he actually said was a burst of short, harsh, grating syllables that sounded like metal saw blades clashing against one another.

Jamie jolted suddenly as though just waking. "You can speak demon?" she asked.

"Of course not, it's gibberish," Noah tried to say. The sound that came out was comparable to a brick in a clothes dryer. He clamped his mouth shut and covered it with his hands.

Jamie wasn't the only one to notice either. The shadow which had almost completely passed was now stopped, and the icy needles were beginning to intensify once more. It was aware of them for the first time.

Ca'akan squealed in the universal language of terror and hurled itself through the nether. Jamie needed no translation. Walter had gone completely limp however, except for his head which continued to thrash from side to side. Noah surged back through the nether to grab a dangling arm, and Jamie snatched the other to drag him along.

"Wait for us, Ca'akan!" Jamie gurgled with as much strength as she could muster. The imp was barely more than a silhouette scrambling away from them as fast as it could.

The nether parted smoothly before Noah as he bent his entire body into pursuing the imp. Jamie was struggling mightily to match his pace, and it didn't take long before Noah had to drag both her and Walter behind him. All the while the icy feeling was growing once more, threatening to sap what remained of his strength, his will, and the very instinct which begged him haste.

"Where's he gone?" Jamie slurred, her pace slackening once more.

"This way," Noah said. "Ca'akan is just ahead, don't stop now."

The truth was that Noah couldn't sense Ca'akan either though. The imp had completely vanished, and it was all he could do to follow where it had been and not allow Jamie to give in to despair. If they stopped for even a moment, that would be enough to realize they were lost in an alien world with no way of finding their way out again. Just a moment, and the shadow would pass over them and freeze their bodies and minds into surrender. Already these thoughts were beginning to slow as Noah's brain stiffened with cold, when—

A short squeal, just on the other side of a great gray wall which loomed ahead. Noah shot forward dragging Walter and Jamie behind, prepared to slam straight into the barricade if there was no other way to escape their silent pursuer. The distant chirping and chittering from the demons rose in a feverish pitch as Noah sped forward, each sound closer with more intent than the last. Straight into the gray mass, and then through as if it were no more than a soap bubble.

Noah tumbled straight onto a stone floor and sprawled out on the raised dais inside the Whispering Room. One of his hands was still firmly clutched around Walter's limp wrist, and he had to laboriously drag his friend up through the stone floor with Jamie scrambling after him. The circle below their feet was blazing with light, its interior a dark tunnel like the one they'd entered from the living world.

Ca'akan shrieked like mad, flinging itself around the empty room like a child having a tantrum. The hole in the ground was constricting rapidly after they had all exited, but Noah couldn't resist dropping to his hands and knees to peer back inside one last time. That was the first time he got a good look at the shadow.

He was surprised to see that it was not much larger than himself, since its presence had seemed like a looming leviathan beside them in the nether. It bore a generally humanoid shape, although the gray rubbery skin looked like it would be more at home on a seal than a person. The most striking feature was its face though, which was long and sharply angled. There were no eyes or nose, only a single fleshy toothless mouth which the chill seemed to be emanating from.

Noah braced, half-expecting it to make a final lunge and drag its way into this world before the hole had closed. The creature drew itself all the way up the ground, but it never went any farther. The mouth made a few wet smacks, then gave Noah a wide and sloppy grin. Next Noah knew, he was staring into the hard stone floor and the light from the circle had faded.

"Shut up, you little monster," Walter growled at Ca'akan who was still throwing itself around the room. "You tried to leave us behind!"

Jamie began to scold him, insisting that he be grateful to the imp who had, in her opinion, saved their lives.

Noah shivered involuntarily and pulled himself off the floor.

"Are you okay, Noah?" Jamie asked, eyeing him critically.

"Yeah," he said, relieved to hear human words coming from his mouth once more. "Just rattled, that's all."

"Did it say anything to you?" Walter asked. "Right before the hole closed up, it sounded like it was talking."

Noah furrowed his brow, unable to get the wet smacking out of his head even if he wanted to. "Yes," he said at last, forming the word deliberately with his mouth.

Jamie and Walter looked at one another, then back at Noah. They waited several seconds, but he didn't say anything more.

"Noah?" Jamie asked, tentatively. "You understood Ca'akan when he was warning us. You never told us you could speak demon. What did it say?"

But Noah shook his head, unsure himself. "I couldn't speak demon. I still can't, I only understood Ca'akan while I was in the netherworld. I'd already exited by the time that cold thing spoke though, and it didn't make any sense to me either. Probably just an idle threat or something though."

Noah didn't believe that though, even as he was saying it. He felt that the creature had been trying to say something specific, and that it had been directed at him. The thought alone was enough to make him start shivering again.

VISOLOTH

Professor Salice was not pleased with Noah the next time they met. He wouldn't allow him to ask questions anymore during his time as his apprentice, and he kept Noah in that small glass summoning room for hours. There were so many more demons that needed summoning than usual, but Salice was never willing to explain what they were being summoned for. The ones who appeared rarely satisfied him, and he always blamed Noah for catching such weak, scrawny demons.

Noah now realized that his mind was floating in the netherworld when he played host for the new demons. Sometimes when he sat in the circle and the demonic images flooded his mind he would hear them chittering and understood isolated words and phrases, but the moment they were summoned away from the nether he was unable to comprehend anything but the vaguest intention. Despite searching his textbook thoroughly for an explanation, he couldn't find any mention of anyone understanding demons at all, and Salice refused to comment on his own ability.

Professor Humstrum's class became considerably more enjoyable as it neared the end of the semester as he held true to his promise not to test the students. While necromancy and demonology were filled with tables to memorize and cram sessions for the finals, transhumanism had moved to the bestiary where the students were allowed to directly interact with the spiritual creatures.

The whole class was jealous of Jamie who was the only one allowed to ride the temperamental manticore. She stroked its mane tenderly and attributed their bond to her affinity for cats, although Walter thought it was more likely that she was only tolerated because she fed it and cleaned up the environmental disasters it left in the sane. None of the spiritual creatures consumed corporal bodies, but that didn't stop it from draining a small bucket of aquamarine stones every night. Professor Humstrum proudly declared that it ate almost an entire month every single day, but the trans-dimensional department gladly paid its salary in case they ever needed it in war.

More than any class or test, what was first in everyone's mind was the upcoming Christmas break. The Matriarch had announced that the Daymare would be back to bring everyone to the living world so they could spend the holiday with their families. She warned that it wasn't easy to celebrate Christmas with a family that was still mourning their loss, but most of the students were excited all the same.

Walter decided that he would rather not go back to watch Natasha and her new boyfriend, although he was still looking forward to seeing his parents and his two brothers once more. Jamie remained adamant that there was nothing left for her to return to though, and Noah was glad to have the company as he had no intention to give Professor Salice another chance to follow him anywhere.

"You think you're being a hero or something?" Jamie asked when Noah told her his intentions to stay.

"What's that supposed to mean?" Noah asked, ripping up a fistful of fresh grass to scatter to the wind. They were sitting together on one of the hillocks overlooking the other students who boarded the Daymare below. It would have been a dark, moonless night but for the whirling will-o-wisps. The Daymare lazily swatted at them with its numerous legs.

"By staying away from Mandy," Jamie continued. "You think

they're really better off if they never see you again? If your daughter can see spirits, then she's going to wonder why she can see all of them except you. She's going think you don't love her."

"You're one to talk," Noah grunted. "I don't see you making much effort."

"I'm not a Chainer," she countered, leaning back onto her elbows to look up at the sky.

"What's that supposed to mean?"

"I mean my family and I had just met," Jamie said. "We were a couple of random souls who found each other then went our separate ways. If Chainers are so rare, do you really think it's a coincidence that there could be two or three in one family?"

"I hadn't really thought about that," Noah said, shrugging. He wanted to change the subject, but he couldn't find the words. Talking about his family just left him with a great, empty pit inside.

"Well, I have," Jamie said matter-of-factly. "I think you've been helping each other come back to life through the years. When one of you is dead, you protect the other ones. Then the dead one comes back as a child, and it's the other one's turn to protect them."

"I'm not coming back as my daughter's son," Noah said decisively. "That would be too weird."

"How so? When did your mother die?"

Noah fell back onto the grass as well. The way the dark clouds were layered reminded him of the netherworld, which was never far from his thoughts anymore.

"Before your daughter was born, I bet," Jamie continued, "about six years before."

"Six and a half," Noah said after a moment to do the math. "How'd you know?"

"It takes six years to graduate from The Mortuary," Jamie said. "Did she die around March?"

Noah sat rigidly upright, looking down at Jamie suspiciously. "March 10th."

"There you go then," Jamie said, as though that proved everything.

"There I go what?"

"It took six months to wait for a new semester in August, then six years in school before she graduated. Mandy isn't just your daughter, she's your mother too. And what about her son, Lewis?"

"Lewis isn't a Chainer," Noah said cautiously, his mind spinning as he double-checked the numbers.

"As far as you know," Jamie said. "When did your father die?"

"About ten years ago," Noah said. "A little less."

"Six years for school, plus… how old is the boy now?"

"I haven't always been human," Noah replied, feeling flustered. "Whatever family line you're imagining isn't real. If you're trying to convince me to go visit them, then it's not going to work. Even if we did share multiple lives together, then that's even more reason not to put them in danger now."

"They're already in danger," Jamie said gravely. "How long do you think it will really take Salice to figure it out? There will have only been so many people who have died in your area within the last year. He can do the math, same as me, and sooner or later he's going to narrow it down. If you really want to protect them, you're going to need to do more than pretend they don't exist."

"I'm not going back," Noah repeated stubbornly. "I can't do anything for them there."

"Then do something for them here," Jamie insisted. "We can tell The Matriarch —"

"That her star teacher who revolutionized demonology is secretly plotting to kill my family? Fat chance she'll believe me."

Jamie leapt to her feet and began rapidly brushing the loose grass from her clothes. "If not, then we need to *make her* believe you. We need to find out what Salice wants more Chainers for so we can have proof, and I know how to get it."

Noah was on his feet too—Jamie's excitement was contagious.

"The only question is, how are we going to get Visoloth alone in the nether where you can understand him?"

"That was a stupid thing to do," Professor Salice said with a crisp voice like thin ice. "I wish I could say that I was surprised." He leaned back in his leather chair (which was stitched together from at least a dozen different kinds of skin), and steepled his thin fingers together in contemplation.

This was the first time Noah had been in Salice's office, and the demonology professor seemed even more menacing in his own element. The will-o-wisp here was locked in a small wire bird cage where it darted back and forth in restless agitation, causing the thick shadows of the room to constantly shift. Noah tried not to look at the cruel array of nameless bladed devices lining his shelves, or listen to the ceaseless whispering which emanated from stacks of hefty books. Visoloth was curled in apparent sleep beneath Salice's desk, looking almost like a normal dog now that its mouth was closed.

"You're right, I'm sorry," Noah said, forcing a tremor into his voice. "I thought visiting my daughter would only be hard on us both, but this will be her first Christmas alone and..." he allowed his voice to trail off, half-surprised to feel how naturally his voice cracked. Was he really doing this for Mandy? Or was he putting her in even greater danger to satisfy his own suspicions?

"The Daymare won't be coming back," Salice said, studying Noah's face intently. "You're sure the Whispering Room is quiet?"

Noah hoped his face was inscrutable as he replied, "Yeah, it's been quiet for a while. That's part of why I'm so worried. There was only a connection last time because Claire was calling for Mrs. Robinson, but Mrs. Robinson didn't come back with us after we fell through. So I was hoping Visoloth would take me through the nether to let me visit my family that way."

Professor Salice's already tight face strained further in a motion Noah had come to recognize as a smile. "Passages through the nether are not pleasant affairs, even for seasoned demonologists. You may have traveled that way in ignorance before, but you must be desperate to attempt it again."

"Please, sir," Noah said. "I'll do anything to spend Christmas with my little girl again. I thought that maybe because I was your apprentice, and you've been kind enough to help me before that…"

Salice's face slackened. The will-o-wisp darted backward once more, casting him into deeper shadow so that only the slits of his red eyes colored the darkness. Had Noah gone too far? Salice wasn't known for his kindness anywhere in the school, and their tense relationship in the past would only heighten his suspicions. The wisp was back to the front of the cage though, and Salice was smiling once more.

"Today is your lucky day," Professor Salice replied. "It has always been my intention that you should see your family again, and I'm not disappointed even though it has taken you so long to come to your senses. Visoloth!"

The demon dog opened one eye which focused laser-like on Noah. He had the unnerving feeling that it had only been pretending to be asleep this whole time. A single inquisitive tentacle poked from its mouth to taste the air.

"You know the way, don't you Visoloth?" Salice asked, stroking the dog's rough hide with his foot.

Of course, he does, Noah thought. *You were tracking me the whole way there, weren't you?*

Visoloth made a wet, slurping sound as the tentacle retracted into its mouth. Salice nodded, finding this satisfactory. "Very good. You will take him through the nether to see his family for Christmas. You will then wait until he's ready to return, no later than the resumption of the new term, and then you will lead him back again."

Visoloth cocked its head to the side, listening intently. Then it looked at Noah, letting its mouth hang loose to let its full dozen tentacles slide out and twist through the air. It let out a long, gurgling howl.

"Those are your instructions," Salice said cooly. "If I need them to be altered, I will tell you as such. Now stand."

Noah was only too happy to slide his chair back, eager to be away from his professor. He knew that Visoloth could not break its contract and disobey a direct order, but that wouldn't be a problem. Even if he had to travel all the way back to his hometown, he could still say he was ready to return immediately without interfering with the directive.

Salice was already drawing a circle of light into the air, opening the way into the nether. Noah couldn't help but notice that the lines Salice conjured were considerably cleaner than George's had been, and that the circle was large enough that Noah wouldn't have to crawl this time. The light seemed to be focusing on his professor's cufflinks—small bones that must have once been part of his long-discarded corpse.

Visoloth sat upright to attention, its eyes still fixed on Noah while the circle was being drawn.

"You're doing the right thing, you know," Professor Salice said as the interior of the circle darkened to black. "Actions have reactions which have their own reactions, and even the wisest have trouble understanding where the final piece will fall. Although today it seems that you are only facing your past, you are facing your future as well, setting a course of history whose ramifications will far outweigh these small steps today. I am pleased that my apprentice has begun the path of his own mastery."

Those words sounded genuine, but they were poison to Noah. Salice was already gloating about his perceived victory. Even now he might have been imagining Visoloth attacking Mandy and ripping her son from her arms. Noah swallowed hard, refusing to allow himself to react to the image. "Thank you, sir," he replied stiffly. "May I go now?"

Salice waved his hand dismissively and made his way back around his desk to sit down. He looked strangely small and tired as he slumped over the wood. Visoloth paced around the floating circle twice before bounding inside. Noah paused only a moment to consider the weary figure before stepping into the circle to return to the netherworld.

The cool welcome of the nether slid around his body in an encompassing embrace. The dull, chittering echos filtered through his consciousness once more, and as the circle closed behind him he became suspended in the vast nothingness that felt like home.

Visoloth made a gurgling sound which Noah understood to mean "Follow me".

"Not yet," Noah replied. "I didn't come here because of a deal with Salice. I came to make a deal with you, Visoloth."

The dog paused and sat down, despite there being nothing definite to sit on. It twisted its head from side to side. "I already have a contract," Visoloth replied. "Come."

"I'm not talking about a contract. I need to know something about your master."

Visoloth stood and began to pace a circle around Noah, its mouthful of tentacles stopping just short of brushing against him. Noah remained still and fought against his instincts to draw away. It was impossible to read the demon's monstrous face. Was it curious that he could understand it? Would it attack him for his impudence? Was Salice listening through its ears somehow even now?

"I do not make deals with students," Visoloth said slowly.

"I wasn't always a student," Noah replied with more confidence than he felt. "I can understand you, can't I?"

Visoloth was behind Noah now, but he could perceive it as clearly as if it stood in front of him. He felt one of the tentacles slide along the back of his knee and then slither down his leg, leaving his skin tingling as though charged by electricity.

"Does Salice know that you once lived as a demon?" Visoloth asked. "I'm sure he would be interested to know."

Was it a threat? There didn't seem to be any malice in Visoloth's tone. While a human voice might disguise itself with many subtleties, the speech of a demon felt more like a bond between the minds. Noah could only hope that Visoloth felt the same connection and allowed itself to trust him.

"Not unless you tell him," Noah said. "One secret deserves another though, don't you think?"

"What do you want to know?" Visoloth asked.

"He needs hosts to summon something," Noah guessed. "Regular students don't have heavy enough souls though. He needs Chainers, more than one of them. He needs me and my daughter."

"That wasn't a question," Visoloth replied languidly. It began to groom itself with its tentacles.

"That wasn't a denial," Noah shot back. "What does he want to use us for?"

"It wasn't a denial," Visoloth consented. "You mentioned a deal. I'm still listening."

"I can help you become human too," Noah said. "I've done it before; I know how it's done."

There was a long silence between them where only the distant echoes of the nether floated past. Visoloth had stopped grooming itself and was staring at Noah once more.

"You're lying," Visoloth replied.

"I'm not," Noah insisted. "It might still take some time before I've figured it all out, but I used to know, and I'm remembering more all the time. If anyone can do it, it's me."

"Why would I want to bother with being human?" Visoloth asked, turning a lazy backflip through the nether as though to prove how content he was. Noah understood its voice as implicitly as he did his own thoughts though, and he could feel the strain behind the calm it sought to portray.

"Because even when you're set free, you'll never be treated like the other spirits," Noah said. "People don't trust demons. Even if you go back to the nether, there will always be a bigger fish in the pond. You'll always be living scared of whatever else is out there. But once you're human, you can come back as anything. You can be free."

Visoloth didn't reply. Its face was inscrutable, seeming to have already figured out how well Noah could read its speech. The longer the silence stretched on, the more aware Noah was of the magnitude of the gamble he was taking.

If the demon decided not to take his deal, then it could immediately report to Salice and tell him everything it had learned. Salice would know that his game was up, and he'd have to resort to force to learn where Mandy and Lewis were. Noah's mind went unbidden to the many bladed instruments lining Salice's shelves and he tried not to imagine what creative and deranged uses they might have.

"You're cheeky," Visoloth replied at last. "Arrogant, even. You should have stayed a demon. No more sure than Salice though; there is nothing in our contract to forbid me from telling his secrets because it never occurred to him that someone could understand them."

"It's a deal then?" Noah said hopefully. He inwardly cursed himself for sounding so eager, but he was also keenly aware of the vastness of nether around them and didn't want to delay in this place any longer than was necessary.

Visoloth had completely circled Noah several times, but now he had stopped directly in front of him. "What's it like, being human?" he asked. "Is it worth it?"

Of course it is, Noah thought. But the thought of trying to explain exactly how was more daunting than he expected. To explain what it was like to be alive—to feel yourself grow and learn—the warmth of falling in love—the pride of helping someone achieve something they never thought was possible. And yet reconciling that with all the doubt, and regret, and grief of loss that all sounded unpleasant until you lived it, before you realized life wouldn't have been worth living without these things giving life meaning.

"What is so great about being alive?" Visoloth hissed, its words trailing away at the end to leave the heavy thought floating beside them in the nether.

"Do you remember the first time you were summoned into the spirit world?" Noah asked. Visoloth said nothing, so Noah continued. "I guess you were so used to being in the netherworld that you thought that's all there was. Then you set foot in the spirit world and suddenly reality got bigger than you could have ever guessed. There were more things to see, and more to discover, and more spirits and histories and cultures—more than you could have ever guessed existed when you only lived here."

Visoloth cocked his head to the side, silent.

"But you were still a demon—an outsider—and seeing it wasn't good enough, was it?" Noah continued. "No-one could understand you, and you weren't allowed to do all the things that the other spirits were doing. It won't be like that when you're human. When you're human you aren't just watching the show—you are the show. You can do everything that can be done, and learn everything that can be learned—you can spend your whole life finding out more about life, or you can find one thing you love more than anything, or one person you love more than anything, and spend all your days with them. And once you're done you'll get to live again as something else and everything will be new again. Being alive is the best thing there is, because the world is only as big or as small as what we think is possible. And everything is possible only when you're alive."

"I want that…" Visoloth growled. "Very well, I will hold you to our deal. You are correct in your assumption that Salice needs at least two Chainers to host the demon he wishes to summon. The Rasmacht would destroy any single mind which tried to contain it. Even Salice cannot claim to control such a creature."

"The Rasmacht?" Noah prompted hesitantly.

"You've met it once before, on your way back from the living world," Visoloth said. "I watched it chase you back to the Whispering Room. Professor Salice wants to summon it into the spirit world. We best keep moving though, unless you'd like to risk meeting it again. I still received a direct order to take you to the living world, and that's what I intend to do."

"That cold thing?" Noah said, swimming hastily through the nether after Visoloth. "What could Salice possibly want with that?"

"The Rasmacht is only ever summoned for one reason," Visoloth said, "which is why it is better known as 'The Soul Eater'. Those consumed by it are gone forever, not leaving even so much as a shade behind. Every life they've ever lived, every life they ever will live, all erased so that no one will remember they've ever been. The Matriarch will be devoured and all her teachings will be undone. She who has claimed to have lived a thousand lives will cease to exist, and every soul she has ever painted will shed her colors. Now, where was that exit to where your family lives?"

THE MATRIARCH'S WRATH

When Noah was a child, he used to believe that good and evil existed. There were noble knights and champions of justice who fought the brigands and cheats, always conquering the wicked. Not one of his favorite stories contained a darkness so dark that it could continue to exist when the light was shone through it.

As he grew older, he wasn't so sure anymore. Even good people did things out of pure self-interest, and even evil men had their own principles and people that they loved. He figured that everyone was doing the best that they could in a mixed-up world, and that even when they were cruel to each other, they were only doing so as reflections of their own pain.

Now more than ever he decided that evil must exist, and that its name was Zandu Salice. The Matriarch had devoted her entire existence to helping souls come back to life, yet Salice was planning to destroy her and steal her teachings from the myriad of souls she had touched.

Visoloth didn't know exactly why Salice was set upon this path, but Noah didn't think such heinous act could ever be justified. Perhaps he was jealous of her power, perhaps he wanted to run the school himself, or even preferred that demonology was the only lesson to be taught. Salice made no effort to hide his disdain for the *'lesser domains'*, especially reincarnation, and it was no great leap of faith to assume he'd abolish them altogether if he was in charge.

"You know he's watching you, right?" Visoloth asked, rousing Noah from his thoughts. They had arrived at a folded corner of nether, a pocket of space that Noah had come to recognize as an opening into the living world.

"Yeah, I figured," Noah said. "You've brought me here, that was your job. You were also ordered to bring me back when I was ready."

"Not even a step into the living world? Not even going to say hello?"

"It's too much of a risk to bring him that close," Noah said. I want to go back now."

"He won't be happy to see that," Visoloth said. "He'll know something is up."

"He'll know anyway. We need to hurry," Noah said. "You're not afraid of him, are you?"

"I'm not afraid," Visoloth said, pacing restlessly before the folded nether pocket. "Fear is just the anticipation of danger. I have been in danger since I spoke to you, and it is no greater now. We will run together, on my count. We must be well on our way before he realizes what has happened if you ever want to make it back."

"I'm ready," Noah replied, grinning despite himself. It felt good to have his suspicions proven, even though it was to his detriment. A known enemy was so much more reliable than a suspected one.

"Three, two, one," Visoloth said, coiling its body in preparation to spring. "Let the fire in your soul give wings to your flight."

And they were away, the nether flowing against them without dampening their speed. The omnipresent chittering seemed to grow louder, and dark shapes began to curiously orbit their race. It felt so liberating to hasten through this void, and Noah couldn't help but swerve and soar for the pure joy of the infinite feeling.

Visoloth kept a direct course as straight as an arrow. His legs sprang ceaselessly forward as though he ran on solid ground. Watching him, Noah realized that with concentration he too could harden the nether around his feet and thus launch himself more effectively forward. He still preferred a swimming motion though, as that made him feel like he was flying.

"Stay straight," Visoloth called.

"I am! Basically. I'm keeping up with you."

"Our destination is directly ahead. If you are facing even a few degrees off, then you won't find it."

"I've got you to follow," Noah replied stubbornly, twirling dexterously as the nether rushed over him.

"Seven minutes, directly this way," Visoloth said. "The pocket you're looking for will have three folds in a triangular shape, each lighter than the last. That will take you directly to The Matriarch's chambers."

The severity of Visoloth's tone gave Noah pause. "You're coming with me all the way, aren't you? Everything looks the same here, and I don't think I'll find it —"

"He's here," Visoloth interrupted. "I'll take you as far as I can, but I cannot overpower my contract. As soon as he catches up with us you must not trust me anymore."

As if in answer, a booming crack rippled through the space. The nether stirred chaotically, rising up into waves which beat against Noah and disrupted his flight.

Visoloth stopped dead as though rooted in place. Noah slowed too, but Visoloth roared with a ferocity quite unlike his usual calm tone. "Get away from me! As much distance as you can!"

Noah oriented himself against the turbulent waves of nether and pushed onward, aware once more at the enormity of the space around him. If he wasn't going exactly the right way, then it would be only too easy to get lost forever in these endless folds.

"Visoloth!" boomed Salice, his voice deeper and more powerful than it had ever sounded in the spirit world. "The boy is escaping! Hunt him down."

Visoloth's effortless grace which Noah had admired before transformed into a predatory and lethal blur. The demon was lunging and bounding through the nether behind, his tentacles flailing from his mouth in ravenous anticipation. Noah hadn't realized that Visoloth was moving slowly before in order for Noah to keep up, but now the demon was gaining swiftly.

"Three folds, triangle," Visoloth panted. "Don't stop. Don't watch me. You'll never escape if I catch you."

Noah had never gone faster in his life, but it wasn't fast enough. He couldn't help but watch Visoloth closing in as his awareness extended even behind him. Every passing second brought those grasping tentacles closer. Soon one was already brushing against his ankle. Noah surged away from it, snarling in pain as a ragged patch of his skin tore free to remain attached to the suction cup.

"Faster!" Visoloth howled. "I'll have you next time."

"Stop him!" roared Salice. "Rabie!" Again the nether bucked and heaved in response—an underwater storm in an alien sea. The ripples were spreading throughout the nether, smothering the chittering sounds which encompassed them. A moment of terrible silence, then all the sounds came back at once, this time with a screeching intensity that sounded like the whole world had turned against him.

The dark shapes at the periphery of Noah's awareness were now swooping in from every side. Flocks of imps, rubbery Lava Salamanders, fleshy Gobblers, and others of more hideous deformation which Noah couldn't recognize. Serpentine creatures slipped smoothly through the nether, open mouths lined with razor teeth which gnashed their way toward him. All the while screaming, gurgling, bellowing, frothing with frenzy born of the impetus of Salice's command.

Three folds, a triangle, that must be it ahead. But the escape seemed so far that Noah would never reach it in time. Already he could feel the tentacles snaking their way around his ankle once more, this time securing a stronger hold with dozens of suction cups latching against his skin. If he pulled free this time he might have to rip his entire foot off.

He wouldn't stop though. Couldn't. He strained against the implacable grasp, dragging Visoloth's whole body along as he staggered onward. Another tentacle latched hold onto his other calf, dragging him to an almost complete stop. The demons swooped and shrieked in from every direction. Three folds in a triangle—unobtainable far —now blocked from view completely by a thick mass of imps which swarmed over one another and bit each other to be the first to descend upon him.

The sight was too horrendous to bear, but even closing his eyes did nothing to shield him from the churning madness around him. He was forcibly aware of each grasping claw, each slimy tooth, each razor spine, all converging on him from every direction. Helpless, terrified, and utterly alone, Noah called out for the last thin hope which he could conjure.

"Rasmacht!" Noah called, funneling all the power he had into one desperate shout.

He might as well beg a wild lion to help him against a pack of wolves, but there was no denying that the name had power over these teeming creatures. "Rasmacht, Rasmacht, Rasmacht!" His shouts were obdurate, the word cutting through the frenzy and giving pause to even the most ferocious of the flock. Even Visoloth's vise grip seemed to have slackened for a moment. What was this thing that could inspire such fear with the first mention of its name?

"Seize him!" Salice commanded. "There is no Rasmacht."

The demons shook themselves as though breaking from a spell and began to converge once more. They had barely begun to move again before a familiar numbing chill stole over Noah's senses. Whether summoned by his call or simply curious to the commotion, the Rasmacht was here. No command could overcome the blind panic which set into the teeming masses at the arrival of the soul eater.

The imps broke first, shrieking and scattering in every direction like a flight of startled birds. Demons tore at one another as they crawled over each other to escape, and Noah braced as the swarming things dug into his body to push away. Salice was shouting something, but Noah couldn't make out the words over the commotion. A shock of pressure released as Visoloth relinquished his grip to bound howling back the way he'd come.

In a matter of seconds Professor Salice was clearly visible turning in an angry circle in the nether, his strained face contorted in anger as he shouted at each fleeing demon. He completed the circle to face Noah once more, his red eyes boring into the boy.

"You don't understand," Salice growled. "Your daughter isn't doing any good in the living world. You must let me kill her."

Three folds, in a triangular shape. Noah had to focus. His mind was already so cold that his thoughts moved as ponderously as a glacier. The Rasmacht had idly floated into view, its toothless mouth gaping like a whale filtering the ocean. Webbed fingers and toes spread luxuriously through the nether to propel its sleekly closer. Noah pushed away and drove his body toward the exit.

"I won't let you!" Salice bellowed. "You are my apprentice, and you will do as I say. I order you not to—"

Noah flew headfirst through the pocket and tumbled onto something hard. A stone floor. His skin prickled with the shock of exiting the nether, and his body wouldn't stop trembling.

"Goodness me," The Matriarch said, quite bewildered. She was sitting on the other side of the room in a generously cushioned armchair with an open book on her desk. Will-o-wisps floated idly around her to illuminate dark wooden bookshelves stuffed with dusty leather volumes, each shelf rising so tall that it curved at the top to meet in an arch without spilling the books. There was a real fireplace in the corner, although it was only inhabited by another pair of wisps which lazily chased each other in slow circles.

Noah jolted upright and turned to see the hole into the nether closing swiftly behind. He barely had time to rise to his feet and leap out of the way before Professor Salice came tumbling after him.

Noah pointed a trembling finger at the Professor. "He's trying to kill my family!" Noah shouted as soon as he could fill his chilled lungs.

"Calm down, you look like you've seen a ghost," The Matriarch replied, her voice warm and patient. "Professor Salice would never—"

"He needs more Chainers to summon the Rasmacht. He wants it to eat *you*!" Noah spluttered, diving away as Salice snatched at his leg from where he lay sprawled on the ground. A moment later and

Visoloth bounded through the hole and fell into an immediate crouch, ready to spring.

The Matriarch snapped her mouth shut and narrowed her eyes. She lifted the book from her lap and set it calmly on the desk in front of her. "Is this true, Zandu?"

"Preposterous…" Salice moaned, lifting himself unsteadily to his feet. "Who would believe such a thing—"

His words were interrupted by a loud smacking sound. Just as the hole to the nether was closing, a blank rubbery face rose into view. It continued floating past through the nether, giving everyone a clear look into its toothless mouth before the hole completely closed with a pop.

"Thank you, Noah Tellaver," The Matriarch said softly, not taking her eyes from Salice as she spoke. "I see that you have gone through considerable personal risk to warn me. You will find that I do not forget those who have been loyal to me. *Nor forgive those who have not.*" Her voice completely changed when speaking this last line, twisting into something cold and biting.

Salice scowled ferociously. His fingers began to dance through the air, a new glowing circle stitching itself into existence.

"I wouldn't do that if I were you," The Matriarch said with iron in her voice. "The Rasmacht will be waiting for you."

Salice's fingers fumbled for a moment, and his circle of light dissipated into a sparkling nova. His eyes darted to The Matriarch before beginning again with redoubled focus. The old woman rose from her chair.

"I'm speaking to you, Zandu," The Matriarch said. A casual flick of her wrist prompted hurricane force wind to lift Salice straight off the floor and slam him into the stone wall behind. He crumpled to the ground like a marionette doll with severed strings. The circle of light he'd been spinning flared briefly with defiance before being extinguished by the torrent.

"Visoloth! Attack her!" Salice demanded, prompting the dog to release its tension and lunge through the air. As soon as his feet left the ground that same wind flared to life and knocked him spinning.

Both dog and master collided violently by the force they were helpless to resist.

"You cannot silence us," Salice hissed. "You will not survive another purge." Then to Noah, his stretched eyes wild and pleading. "Don't walk the road from death while that woman is—"

The Matriarch was smiling a thin, shallow smile while he spoke, but she didn't let him finish. She blinked twice, and when she opened her eyes the second time Noah could clearly see the glowing skull beneath her flesh. Dazzling white diamonds rested in place of where her eyes had been. The stones seemed to gather all the light in the room until nothing was visible except their piercing brilliance. Noah heard Salice scream powerfully for a second, but he couldn't see what was happening and the sound cut short a moment later.

One of the diamond eyes flared even more brightly. It flashed blood red in stark contrast to the other shining as a star. Light was returning to the room once more, but Noah still had to blink away the spots as though he'd just been staring into the sun. The Matriarch stuck one of her fingers behind the red diamond and popped it out of her eye socket. She blinked twice more rapidly, this time revealing her old eyes back in place once more as the glowing skull faded from view. When Noah's vision fully returned, he stared in disbelief at the empty stone floor where Salice had lain a moment before.

The Matriarch rolled the red diamond in the palm of her hand and smiled down at it. "There we are," she said with satisfaction. "He won't cause any more trouble in there, now will he?"

"What did you do to him?" Noah asked.

"What *didn't* he do to Mandy and little Lewis?" The Matriarch asked sweetly. "That's the only question that matters, don't you think?"

There was something about the way she asked the question that made Noah think she didn't really require an answer. The Matriarch opened a drawer in her table and dropped the red diamond inside. It might have been Noah's imagination, but he thought he heard the faint echo of Salice's scream as she did so.

"Heel, Visoloth," The Matriarch said without glancing. The demon had just been regaining its feet and a low growl began to rise in its throat. "Heel!"

The wind stirred again and the dog was flattened to the floor. It pulled itself painfully upright once more, but did not rising beyond a sitting position.

"Better. You will be taking orders from me now, do you understand?" The Matriarch told it. "Salice served at my pleasure, and by extension you and all the other demons will think of me as master. I will not release you from your contracts early."

Visoloth looked expressionless at Noah for a moment before bowing its head. Noah couldn't help but feel as though he'd betrayed it somehow, but shouldn't it be happy that Salice was gone? Being free from his power hungry dominance should be a victory for all of them.

"I suppose I'll be needing a new demonologist," The Matriarch reflected, sighing. "Halfway through the year with no notice, what a shame. I might have to even teach the class myself. Would you like that, Noah?"

"Yes ma'am," Noah said automatically. He gauged that to be the correct answer by The Matriarch's enduring smile.

"Yes indeed," she said, "but then is only a poor man's now. Have you been staying here over Christmas just because you were trying to protect your family?"

"Yes, ma'am," Noah repeated, eyeing the writing desk where Salice's soul was bound.

"You dear suffering soul," The Matriarch sighed again. "Well, you did the right thing, and now you have nothing to worry about. There's no reason for you not to spend Christmas with them anymore, is there?"

"No, ma'am."

But Noah couldn't meet those eyes which had been diamonds a moment before. His gaze found excuses to look everywhere else: the towering books, the drawer with a soul inside, the stained-glass windows now dark without the faintest glimmer of moonlight to give them life. And finally, to the stone gargoyle with the upside-down smile sitting motionless in the corner of the room...

He supposed he should feel like a hero, but heroes must be surer of themselves than Noah felt now.

"You must be worn thin, you poor thing. Why don't you go rest in the graveyard? First thing tomorrow evening, I'll collect you for the journey home. You'll be spending Christmas Eve with your family again, isn't that marvelous? It will be a happy reunion all around."

"Yes ma'am," Noah said, bowing his head and feeling like Visoloth as he did so. He caught the writing desk again out of the corner of his eye—had it just rattled? Or was that only his imagination?

He didn't just feel worn thin. He felt worn away completely, with nothing left inside.

CHRISTMAS

NOAH DIDN'T SEE JAMIE IN THE GRAVEYARD THAT NIGHT. THE BURDEN of all he'd seen weighed heavily upon him and he couldn't wait to tell her everything. She must have an opinion about what the gargoyle in The Matriarch's office meant, and why Salice had used his last words to try and warn Noah about the road from death.

Without an easy answer, he forced himself to refocus his thoughts on Mandy and Lewis and how good it would be to see them again. Would his grandson have grown in the months since Noah had last walked the earth? Would his daughter recognize him this time, even though she now appeared old enough to be his mother?

Fortunately, Brandon had left with his mother to check on how their money was being spent so Noah didn't have to worry about another run in with him. The graveyard was almost entirely empty, although he did see Bowser and Elizabeth Washent sitting close in private conversation as he made his way to his mausoleum. It was strange to think that a dog and a rabbit had enough in common to forge a friendship, but it's not like she would have much in the way of family to go home to. Bowser might have visited the family who had owned him, but Noah could only imagine how hard it would have to watch them getting a new puppy on Christmas morning.

Noah climbed on top of his mausoleum where he'd grown used to sleeping to avoid Brandon. It seemed that Noah had barely closed his eyes before the red glow of the setting sun pierced his eyelids.

"Don't you use your coffin?" The Matriarch asked, immediately rousing Noah. It took Noah a few tense seconds before he could locate the origin of her voice as she had been sitting completely still on the moldy gravestone of an alumni. She was wearing a long dress the color of the night speckled with real twinkling stars which looked exactly like someone had taken a cookie-cutter to the sky. How long had she been sitting there watching him?

"I hope you at least use your stuffed tiger," she added. "I make those myself, did you know? Not all the stitching, mind you, but I *did* cut out your jaw and put it inside. It's always tricky figuring out which part of the body to hold onto, but I just had a feeling that you'd feel more comfortable with it. There's nothing like a bit of body for the soul to feel at home, don't you think?"

Noah was very fond of his tiger, but The Matriarch didn't stop talking long enough for him to say so.

"No home like home either though. You are ready, aren't you? Of course, you are, why wouldn't you be? It must be a relief not having to worry about Salice anymore. You'll never understand how sorry I am for bringing him to this school, but I suppose that's what I get for trusting someone who consorts with demons. Shall we be off then?"

"Will we be going through the nether again?" Noah asked with trepidation. The Rasmacht had come so quickly last time that Noah had the unnerving feeling it had been waiting for him. He couldn't even think of the place without remembering what it felt like to be engulfed in all the grasping, clawing, biting…

"Of course not," The Matriarch said disdainfully. She rose from the gravestone and dusted off her already pristine dress. "It is nothing short of abdication of duty to allow a student to travel somewhere so dangerous. No, we will be traveling by Whispering Room, as is the only T.D.D. approved method for teleportation."

Noah expected The Matriarch to explain how the Whispering Room functioned as she led him through The Mortuary, but she either didn't think he needed to know or took it for granted that he already did know. Considering that Professor Salice had been operating behind her back, it was unlikely that he had told her about his previous visits. Considering that Brandon had been terrorizing him with a ghoul at the time, he probably hadn't recounted the expedition either.

"Is it unusual for there to be a whole family of Chainers?" Noah asked as they walked.

The Matriarch didn't turn to look at him as she continued her brisk pace. "Chainers themselves are unusual. However when they are found, it isn't uncommon for them to be found together. It's no easy feat finding your way back so many times without losing yourself in the process, and we all need a little help sometimes."

The cathedral was still dark as most of the wisps were still asleep, but The Matriarch snapped her fingers to prompt a pair of them to leap into the air and begin to orbit her. She held the door to the stairway open for Noah and smiled at him as he passed.

"It's convenient of course for humans to pretend all souls are the same size, but they don't really believe it. Insects are killed without hesitation, chickens and fish are slaughtered in mass, but try and do the same with a dog or a horse and you'll have people up in arms about the sanctity of life. They find it quite acceptable to eat intelligent animals like pigs, but teach that same pig how to paint, how to perform tricks, how to dance—they can learn, you know—and suddenly its soul becomes a little too big to destroy. A genius composer weeping over his music has a doubtlessly heavy soul, but who can even compare that to the drug-addled youth whose mind can barely grasp his own name?

"Mind you, I'm not saying that humans are correct in their imagined hierarchy of souls, merely that they believe it whether they like to admit it or not. The fact is that your average sea sponge can lead a more fulfilling life than a human who is always bitter about one thing or another. You have no idea how many complaints I've received about using the weighing ceremony to turn students away, but even the smallest souls have a chance to grow during their lives. Those which do nothing to add to their weight can hardly justify being alive at all. I'm sure a Chainer such as yourself can appreciate that."

"I haven't really thought about it," Noah replied honestly. "I've never thought of myself as any more important than anyone else."

"But you do still surround yourself with other Chainers," The Matriarch said, opening the door onto the fifth floor.

"Maybe it's just because I love them."

"Ah ah ah, but would you still love them if they had shallow souls?"

"Id love them anyway, all the more because I only had one life with them instead of many," Noah replied defiantly.

The Matriarch looked at him with either pity or disappointment, perhaps both. "This iteration of you is still young. You'll know better when you get back to your old self. Come though, no matter. Let's find out if your daughter is still thinking about you."

Noah followed The Matriarch into the Whispering Room, his brow furrowed in thought. He didn't like the way she had said that, as if there really was a chance that Mandy had forgotten him already.

The sight of the glowing blue circle chased away these bitter thoughts though, and bounding onto the dais he could hardly wait for the whispering to begin. The instant both his feet had crossed the line in the stone he was met by a wave of blue mist and those sweet words.

"My little boy looks so handsome in his new coat. Dad would have been so proud to see him now."

And a moment later, Noah really did. The mist grew thicker and deepened to purple. It twisted sinuously in the air until two little hands were clearly visible. A moment later and Lewis' face resolved from the air, scowling fiercely down at his generously padded winter jacket. Larger hands appeared, a woman—Mandy, it had to be Mandy —stuffing a warm red and black trooper hat lined with thick brown fur onto the boy's head.

"Don't like it," Lewis muttered. "Wanna be cold."

The red light of the circle was pulsing, growing brighter with each cycle. Lewis and the rest of the mist began swirling around Noah, distorting his image. The Matriarch stepped into the circle and laid her hand on Noah's shoulder.

"You're coming with me?" Noah asked, momentarily setback.

"Of course, I am. How else did you plan to get home, my silly bumpkin?" she replied patiently.

Noah had no time to protest. The swirling mist had turned to a storm, flashing around them so wildly that each image was torn apart the moment it had formed. The Matriarch clutched tightly to Noah's shoulder, her long nails digging slightly through his t-shirt into his skin.

"Is Papa coming too?" Lewis asked. There he was in the flesh with bright red pudgy cheeks, right in front of Noah. The rest of the room spun into place as the mist dissipated in every direction.

"Papa isn't…" Mandy began, her voice vaguely trailing off. She had her own winter coat on, caramel colored and padded with large black buttons down the front. A black cap was pressed onto her head that did little to hide her wispy golden hair sprouting out at all angles. She stared vacantly at Noah, her eyes not quite focusing, her brow lightly drawn.

They were standing in an unfamiliar modern house with great glass windows. Shining steel shone with harsh white light in the kitchen behind them, everything looking new and sterile and cold. Mandy turned away from Noah and refocused her attention on putting Lewis' boots on.

"Your father is going to be home any minute, and he'll expect you to be ready," she said. "He doesn't have much time tonight, so we mustn't keep him waiting."

"Mandy?" Noah asked, the word coming out as little more than a breath.

"Papa!" Lewis declared excitedly, seemingly oblivious to the fact that Noah only appeared to be a boy himself and looked almost nothing like the grandfather the boy once knew. Lewis rushed to Noah and tried to hug his legs, but he sailed straight through and tumbled to the ground.

"Enough with this silliness," Mandy said sternly. She passed through Noah to force the second boot onto Lewis' foot. "Papa is in the happy place, remember? He isn't coming tonight."

The Matriarch meanwhile had peeled off to snoop through the kitchen. Noah caught her eye for a moment, but she quickly looked away as though fascinated by the double oven.

"You can see me, can't you Mandy?" Noah asked, louder this time. "I'm right here. I'm sorry that it's taken me so long to visit and I know I don't look like you remember, but just wait until you hear about…"

Mandy passed straight through Noah a second time on her way to the kitchen counter. She retrieved a sleek black purse with a golden buckle, her hands trembling slightly as she did so. She paused, looking lost as though she'd forgotten what she was doing. Then nodding to herself, she passed through Noah again and joined Lewis by the door.

"He should be here any minute," Mandy said, her voice thin and strained. "Please stop wandering off."

Lewis had been walking toward Noah once more, but Mandy had seized him by the shoulders and turned him back toward the door.

"Papa's coming?" he repeated.

"No, baby," Mandy said. "I want you to stop asking that."

Noah squatted down to Lewis' level and looked him in the eye. "I want you to tell your mother that my spirit is here, alright? I've come to spend Christmas with you both."

"Mommy—" Lewis began.

"I heard him," Mandy said sharply, her attention focused on the door. "He isn't your Papa. Remember what your father said: only crazy people talk to spirits. We aren't crazy, Lewis, and we won't let anyone think that we are. Your father takes such good care of us, but he wouldn't love crazy people. We aren't crazy. We're normal. Perfectly. Perfectly normal."

The door opened and Barnes Horton stepped through smiling. His thick black beard made him look much older than when Noah had seen him last before Lewis was born. His dark hair was short and cleanly cut, and he wore a well fitted dark suit with a deep burgundy tie. Noah had seen zombies with more life in their eyes than his cold grey stare which didn't alter in the least when his mouth smiled.

"Not waiting too long, I hope?" Barnes asked, swooping in to kiss

Mandy. He then hoisted Lewis into the air, prompting the boy to giggle madly at his flight.

"We'd wait for you forever, dear," Mandy replied smoothly. "Do lets hurry though. I feel like I've been cooped up in the house all week."

"Forever isn't nearly long enough," Barnes said through his perfect teeth. "I would wait forever and a day."

"Forever and two days!" Lewis squealed.

"I can wait here too," Noah said from behind her. "I won't touch anything—I can't, obviously, but I won't cause any problems. Then when he's not around we can—"

"Enough waiting! Let's all *leave*," Mandy said, putting particular emphasis on the last word. "Please," she added, casting Noah a glance for a fraction of a second.

"But Papa—" Lewis started to whine, barely getting the word out before Mandy gave his arm a tight squeeze. Barnes looked instantly suspicious as his mouth pressed into a hard, thin line.

"Peppa Pig and all your other cartoons can wait until you get home," Mandy interrupted at once. "We're going to enjoy Christmas Dinner with your other grandparents." She avoided Barnes' probing eyes and exited immediately, holding Lewis by the hand. Barnes swept the house with his grey eyes before turning to follow them out the door.

Noah felt like he was watching a dream, powerless to interact or even wake from the sight before him. He wanted to say something more, but by the time his wits had returned the door had already closed. He rushed toward it, but a hand on his shoulder caused him to lurch to a halt.

"Easy there," The Matriarch said, her voice sweet and soothing. "It isn't uncommon for the dead to carry the living longer than the living carry the dead. It isn't your place to force a burden onto those who cannot bear the weight."

"I'm not a weight," Noah said, pulling away from her. "She's still my daughter and—"

"—and her life is with him now—"

"Not by choice," Noah interrupted back. "He left her. She's just afraid, but she doesn't have to be because I'm here and..." his voice trailed into silence.

"...and you're going to take care of her?" The Matriarch prompted. "You're going to build her a house that she can live in? You're going to hold her when she's sick and help her down the stairs when she's old? There's a reason not many of the dead continue dwelling amongst the living."

"She can see me," Noah said, the words sounding flat and useless even as he said them.

"She can see a boy she's never known," The Matriarch replied. "She can see lots of spirits every day. Some of them talk to her, others torment her, others just watch and say nothing. And none of them help her in the least. You must remember what that's like."

"I'm not going back," Noah said. "Even if she doesn't want to talk to me, I can still be here with her. I can get to know her all over again. And I can talk to Lewis when he gets older, and we'll be friends and he'll think we're the same age."

"Do you really think that would make his life easier than if he had living friends? Or is that just something you want for yourself?" The Matriarch asked.

Noah didn't answer. He didn't trust himself to open his mouth without screaming in frustration.

"You're a Chainer, Noah," The Matriarch said gently. "You are destined to live again, but you can't do that here. You must be diligent in your classes and find your way back the right way. By then maybe Lewis will be all grown up, and he'll have a son of his own. You can be part of his life forever and ever, but you must know deep down that it is not yet time."

"I hate Barnes," Noah said. "I can curse him, can't I? Or get that witch to make him into a voodoo doll."

"If that would make you happy," The Matriarch said. "I can't imagine that it would be what's best for Lewis or Mandy though, do you?"

Noah said nothing again, finding more validation from nursing the seething fire within him than anything that could be said.

"Let's go home," The Matriarch said, already drawing a circle of dull yellow light on the ground around them with her cane. "Your new home, for as long as I am the headmistress and you are my student. The past cannot be made more beautiful by the present, but the future can be."

Noah kept his silence as the circle flared into life. Mist was beginning to come from somewhere again, and Noah didn't do anything to resist as The Matriarch laid her hand on his shoulder once more. The mist became a hurricane, and he was swept away back into the Whispering Room. The room of false hope and lies, that Noah swore he would never enter again.

SPRING SEMESTER

Noah was far from the only one to be disappointed with his Christmas break. It was with considerable satisfaction that Noah witnessed Brandon's despondent return, as it turned out a large portion of his fortune was "wasted" on charitable donations. Grace Horlow wouldn't stop blubbering about how few people attended her funeral, and Jason Parson lamented to everyone who would listen that his lazy son had immediately dropped out of medical school which he'd apparently only attended to please his father.

The only one who seemed to be in really good spirits was Walter who had been to visit his brothers. They had held a Christmas Eve candlelight vigil in his honor, and he was downright boastful about seeing his normally stoic family still in tears over his untimely demise. Jamie, on the other hand, was unusually quiet and self-reflective, although she was briefly animated by Noah's description of how Professor Salice had vanished into a diamond.

On the positive side, the results of last semester's examinations were completely discounted. The Matriarch announced that Professor Salice had chosen to resurrect over the holidays before he'd even graded his tests and that she'd decided to start over with a fresh start.

Likewise, Professor Wilst's exam, for which Noah had been unable to even get his zombie to walk in a straight line without staggering drunkenly into a wall, had been invalidated upon the discovery of contraband in the classroom. An anonymous tipster had disclosed the unfair use of mermaid skulls, and as the Professor could not decipher who was thus aided, had decided to grant everyone a pass. No one's body was to be used for the class' entertainment this time, although Wilst declared earnestly that the same leniency would not be granted next semester.

The next section fortunately required considerably less anatomical precision as it dealt with poltergeists. These beings consisted of a spiritual body that was devoid of a soul and were formed by a deep emotional imprint upon the world.

"Anger is the most common," Professor Wilst told them. The corpses that had once been distributed on the metal tables had been replaced with ceramic urns which had to be tied down to keep them from rattling off the table. "Poltergeists can be formed by any strong emotion though, like an echo which lingers after the soul has departed. In fact, I once met an especially ardent poltergeist which continued making love to the deceased's living wife every night after his death. I was working as an exorcist for the the T.D.D at the time and was dispatched to assist her, but she turned me away insisting things were fine the way they were."

Despite the students being primarily composed of the middle aged and elderly, that didn't stop them from giggling in response like the children they appeared to be. Noah was especially surprised to see Teresa stifling back laughter, although she stopped and coughed as soon as she met Brandon's glare. It seems that she had been in a considerably better mood than her son ever since his return from Christmas.

Professor Humstrum's class had become more enjoyable as well, as it had moved past the theoretical aspect of affinities and moved to the practical implementation of test-driving animals.

"Before you decide which animal you'd like to return as, I highly recommend spending as much time as possible viewing the world through its eyes," Professor Humstrum said, gesturing to the rather confused great horned owl perched on his wooden podium. It kept swiveling its head and staring at each student in turn as though trying to decide whether or not they were real.

"Each week the class will have the company of a different animal," Professor Humstrum continued, occasionally adjusting his orange beard to ensure the finch that lived there remained hidden from the owl. "While it is extremely advanced magic to dominate the mind of an animal as a Dweller might, it is rather simple to enjoy a ride as a passenger. While inside the animal's mind you will not be able to dictate any actions or even read the animal's thoughts and feelings, but you will be able to experience its senses. Only one student will be able to do this at a time to avoid giving the poor creatures headaches, however, so the rest of the class will be continuing from the textbook while waiting their turn."

Noah didn't even have to turn to recognize the squeal of excitement coming from Jamie.

The most expansive change of curriculum doubtlessly came from demonology. The Matriarch made good on her threat to teach the class herself, and waiting beside her were a towering stack of new textbooks which she distributed to the class as they arrived.

"I must say I was most disappointed upon a closer review of Professor Salice's previous lesson plans," The Matriarch said, sighing mightily to reinforce the fact. "I would have thought that a book titled *'Twelve Signs Your Imp Might Be Plotting To Kill You'* would have more appropriately warned of the *dangers* of demonology, but it turns out that the book was as deceptive as he was. I read it cover to cover over break, and there's hardly anything in here about the righteous purges or forced demonic mutations at all!"

The new book was considerably thicker despite its smaller print. The title read: *'The Forbidden Fruit: Demon Do's And Don'ts'*. As soon as Noah sat down and flipped it open to the table of contents it was clear that the *Don'ts* category comprised the much larger portion.

"Let me begin by correcting his teaching as clearly as I can," The Matriarch said. "Demons are not your friends. They are not your pets.

They do not have souls. They may seem to have individual personalities, but they are no more their own entities than your arms and your legs are independent creatures. All demons are made from the nether, and to the nether alone they belong. We may borrow them for a time and bend them to our will, but they are all threads from the same fabric. They are not owed any more consideration than a shovel, or a teapot, or any other tools we use for our convenience."

Noah had to bite his tongue to keep from protesting. Of course they had souls—otherwise where was he supposed to have come from? And the way the other demons had scattered when the Rasmacht appeared—they wouldn't have done that if they weren't afraid of their soul being eaten. The Matriarch was looking directly at Noah now, but he turned his eyes away to pretend to study the textbook.

"Yes? The boy with the shaved head?" The Matriarch asked sweetly.

"It's Rachelle," Rachelle Devon responded, unfazed. "Professor Salice said we were going to be taking turns as hosts to summon imps this semester. Is that still going to happen?"

"Goodness, no," The Matriarch said. "We already have more demons than we know what to do with. The late professor seems to have been summoning far more than were required for service in the last stages of his term. Besides, Zandu was the only one here who knew how to write the contracts in demonic. By next semester we might get another so versed in the *profane* art, but contracts typically last for ten years so it's not exactly essential. A much more useful understanding of demons can be derived from a *historical perspective*."

Several more hands appeared in the air, but The Matriarch had already begun reading from the textbook, showing no signs of stopping. One by one the hands dropped, and she spent the rest of the class reading about the purge of 1940. Her account was considerably different than that of Professor Salice, who had said the purge was a politically motivated persecution.

This textbook described the purge as a necessary emergency response to a demonic uprising. The consensus of cited scholars was that this was proof that demons cannot be trusted to ever be free. The innocent victims were certainly in the thousands—tens of thousands by some accounts—and this number only increased as the T.D.D begin to fight back. The whole incident was later disguised as a genocide instigated by humans, and the offending demons were permanently banished so that no summoner could ever bring them out of the nether again.

The effect of The Matriarch's lessons were not limited to the classroom. The imps working at The Mortuary quickly became a favorite scapegoat for every unfinished assignment or lost item. Of course, it didn't help that the naturally mischievous imps really had stolen their fair share of personal effects over the course of the previous semester, and all sorts of things were turning up now that they were being actively pursued.

With each passing class, the harmless pranks the imps once played were seen with more vitriol and the students were beginning to respond in kind. Brandon, who was once scorned for his abusive behavior, had begun to gather a small following of his own. Dolly Miller, the girl who had killed herself, as well as Jennifer Alaska and a tall boy with a Jack'o lantern grin named Kyle Thrope were often seen together now, jeering and laughing as Brandon hurled stones and clods of dirt at the scampering imps.

Noah did his best to stand up for them, but as the weeks wound on he found himself spending more time alone and trying not to get involved. When he'd first attended the school, his mind was scattered with worries about his family and the distractions of this new world, but now more than ever he had a clear goal in mind: to return to life whatever way he could. He studied in the library late into the morning when the rest of the graveyard was heavy with the dreaming dead, resolving not to get distracted in the social dramas and intrigue that kept so many others away from their work.

While the necromancy class advanced with poltergeists, Noah asked for and received special permission to return to his zombie after class. He practiced until he could animate it fluidly enough to pass the physical portion of the field sobriety test administered to drunken drivers. He devoted the time once spent on being Salice's apprentice to studying some of the professor's old contracts, trying to decipher the meaning of the arcane symbols.

Even his transhumanist studies received extra attention. He had no intention to return as an animal, but there was no telling where a hidden insight might be that would aid in his rebirth. Professor Humstrum said that a comprehensive understanding in all fields would provide the very best chance at another life.

The heavy snow of winter had given into the reluctant thaw of spring by the time Noah made his next great breakthrough. He had been sitting in the empty demonology classroom copying one of Salice's contracts when he realized one of the symbols was familiar to him. This wasn't unusual in itself, as he had continued to slowly recall bits and pieces here and there from his previous life, but this particular symbol of the bottom quarter of a sun with a small door inside had appeared on every contract he'd encountered so far.

He flipped through the pile of papers on his desk and located the symbol on each, always on a line of its own. Closer inspection revealed that these were always drawn in a slightly different shade of red than the rest of the contract, indicating to Noah that they were either written at a different time or with a different type of blood entirely.

The Matriarch's new textbook had no translations for demonic, so he brought out Salice's old one and flipped through it for the hundredth time. Even here translations were limited, and no amount of scanning or restless pacing gave him the least satisfaction. The meaning was floating at the back of his brain somewhere, but the more he thought about it the more elusive it seemed. He was sure that it meant something crucial, but additional effort only translated into additional frustration at its secret.

Head in both hands, Noah would still his mind in quiet meditation hoping the answer would shout itself from up high, or down low, or somewhere deep within, but such a shout never came. On one such occasion his concentration was disrupted by a shrill screech. The harpies were going off again, but unlike their usual alarm there were two distinct words clearly audible amidst the noise.

"Noah Tellaver. Noah Tellaver!" they screeched.

Disconcerted, Noah abandoned his work and made his way to the demonology door. He had only just touched the handle when the screech sounded again.

"Matriarch's office. Bring the contracts." *Screech.* "The contracts!"

Noah scanned the room, searching for a sign that he was being watched. The light of the overhead will-o-wisp glittered against something high on the upper reaches of a bookshelf against the wall. Standing on a chair to inspect more closely, it looked like a white diamond, very much like the one The Matriarch had plucked from her eye. The light dimmed for a second as he stared at it—no not dimmed. *It blinked.*

"Noah Tellaver! Noah Tellaver!" the screech began again. Noah hastened to scoop the pile of papers under his arm and ascend the helical staircase toward The Matriarch's office on the first floor.

"Wonderful, just the boy I'd like to see," The Matriarch said from her reading chair. "Be a dear and shut the door behind you." The door had already been standing open as Noah had approached it leaving no doubt that he was expected. He did as he was asked and moved to stand before the old woman.

"Yeah, I heard," Noah said. "Have you been watching me?"

The Matriarch swatted the question out of the air with her hand as though driving away a fly. "How nice, you brought the contracts with you. I'm so glad to see you taking such a keen focus on your studies. Oh, but I'm being rude. Sit, won't you?"

The room contained only a single chair, that which The Matriarch herself occupied. She gestured toward the circular rug at her feet though, and Noah hesitated only briefly before sitting cross legged before her.

There was a slight pause while The Matriarch regarded him critically. Noah opened his mouth to reply, but she immediately cut him off.

"I imagine you're learning a lot. About the contracts, that is. You've been reading them, haven't you?"

"I've been trying," Noah admitted, "but I still don't know what most of the symbols mean."

The Matriarch stood abruptly and puttered over to one of the bookshelves looming over her chair. She ran her fingers across the spines, and in the silence the murmuring from the books was more pronounced than ever. Noah thought he could even make out a few of the words like "secret", "blasphemy", and "death", as well as a good deal of barely audible hissing and other demonic utterings. She selected one, a thick leather volume with golden demonic symbols along the spine.

"I have something that may assist you. A curious Chainer like yourself may unveil many hidden truths that are beyond the most arduous study of a common soul."

She thinks I'm learning demonic because I'm a Chainer, Noah thought. *Does she still not know I have an affinity?* Noah kept his face as uninterested and expressionless as he could to not betray his thoughts. He stretched out his hands to receive the book which The Matriarch was carrying in his direction. At the last second before his fingers closed around the spine, she withdrew it from him and flipped it open.

"Of course, I wouldn't normally encourage an interest in the profane arts—especially not in a first-year student—but I do see a certain benefit from our partnership of minds. You would like to help me, wouldn't you Noah?"

"Help you with what?" Noah asked, weighing his words carefully.

"Wrong answer," she replied curtly, snapping the book shut. "You are a student at my school, of course you will do as you're told. More than a student in fact—now that Professor Salice is no longer here, you will be needing a new apprenticeship to earn your keep, and I can think of no higher honor for a Chainer than to serve the headmistress herself."

"Don't you already have an apprentice, ma'am?" Noah asked. "Elizabeth Washent—"

"Useless," The Matriarch dismissed. "And so nosy! Always going through my personal things, although I suppose that's what I should have expected from an animal soul. All this talk of infinite potential and they tend to forget their place. You will be my new apprentice, do you understand?"

"Yes, ma'am," Noah replied uneasily. The book she was holding continued to murmur, and now that it was close, Noah was sure that it was speaking in demonic. If nothing else it would be worth it to learn from her personal library.

"Better," The Matriarch said, smiling as sweet as artificial sugar. She extended the book once more. Noah grasped it quickly before she could remove it again. The Matriarch allowed him to take it and turned to pace the room. "Your first assignment is to continue your study of demonic from this book. You will do so in my office every other night from civil twilight until dawn. And when does civil twilight begin?"

"When the sun is six degrees below the horizon," Noah replied quickly, a fact he knew from his necromancy class as the prime hours for awakening the undead.

"Very good," she said. "Once you are able to read the contracts fluently, you will be assisting me in making some small… alterations. It would be irresponsible to permit any lingering loyalty to that disgraced man who sought to kill your family, wouldn't you agree?"

"Yes, ma'am," Noah said, already flipping open the book. Each page was intricately illustrated in rich crimson reds, azure blues, and glimmering gold like a medieval manuscript, while all the text was in demonic. The murmurings from the open book were even louder, and Noah had the unnerving sensation that they were less of a dumb recording and more like a living entity trying fervently to speak to him.

"They must answer only to me," The Matriarch said, tracing idle patterns of light in the air as she paced. "The expiration dates must be adjusted too. A free demon is just a disaster waiting to happen. Speaking of, those mischievous harassments they do will have to stop. You will need to add a clause punishing such behavior. How am I to expect the students to behave if I can't even get my minions to obey the rules?"

"They already had a contract when they agreed to be summoned," Noah said. "Changing everything now doesn't seem very fair—"

"Fairness is only relevant between equals," The Matriarch interrupted, pivoting on the spot. "It isn't fair to the tree to cut it down, nor to the animal that is eaten, but it's done without hesitation because they serve a higher being."

"How would you like it if a higher being came along and did the same to you?" Noah asked.

The Matriarch snorted and chuckled. "My dear boy, we have both worked very hard through many lives to be where we are now. A heavy soul is earned, not given. We are *entitled* to our place at the top. Let's not get ahead of ourselves though, speculating about hypotheticals. It is time for you to learn the symbols. Right where you are is fine, thank you."

Noah had begun to stand, but she gestured him back down upon the carpet. The open book in his lap, he stared down at the illustrations and tried to connect them with the rapid mumbling which rose to greet him. The Matriarch didn't understand Noah any better than Noah understood these books, but at least Noah could learn.

THE CONTRACT ENDS

Every other night in the hours before morning, Noah returned to The Matriarch's office to study. At first she would hover over his shoulder with anticipation, constantly needling him with questions he had no answer to. She swiftly grew bored with his rate of progress however and returned to her own readings, which suited Noah just fine.

There was another book or two waiting for him on the carpet every day he returned, each mumbling or hissing or chittering in its own way. Some contained dense paragraphs of symbols, while others were nothing but pictures and geometric patterns that wouldn't have looked out of place in the netherworld. Some of the pictures moved on their own, the color bleeding through the page and running down only to reform into another shape.

Noah considered asking to take the books into the netherworld to see if he could make more sense of them there, but the image of all those demons closing in on him still burned fresh in his mind, often sneaking their way into his dreams at day. Besides, he'd seen many of these patterns in the nether and they hadn't made any more sense to him there, so it stood to reason that he would not find it any harder to learn the symbols here.

Visoloth never left The Matriarch's side now. The demon dog made no attempt to speak to Noah, and its tentacled face was perfectly inscrutable as to how it viewed its change of master. Perhaps he could have helped Noah read the symbols, but again he would have to travel to the netherworld to understand it and Noah had no inclination or opportunity for that.

Noah had grown accustomed to being singled out for being a Chainer, but now that he was The Matriarch's apprentice the effect had only grown more pronounced. To make matters worse, a side-effect of Noah spending so much time studying demonic was that he'd occasionally slip those horrible, guttural words into his regular conversation without notice. This combined with the growing negative opinion of demons to prompt looks of disdain or even revulsion from his peers.

Jamie and Walter didn't seem to mind, but Brandon in particular would loudly call the slips to everyone's attention. The rumor had begun to spread that Noah's mother had been a demon, and the malicious glee which Brandon repeated it made Noah sure it had originated with him. Noah did his best not to engage or retaliate though, hoping that it would just blow over as these things typically did. Walter wanted Noah to try and get the imps to gang up on Brandon, but Noah figured that would only draw even more attention. If everyone really did find out that he had a demonic affinity, then he'd probably never hear the end of it.

The end result of these interactions was for Noah to enjoy his time alone studying the demonic books more than ever. He began going to The Matriarch's office early, and when he found that she invited him in, he began going on his off nights as well until he spent nearly every twilight there. He still didn't understand much, but just like the complex patterns in the nether, he felt that he was perpetually on the edge of some keen insight that would magically click if he could only view it from the proper angle. Even when he couldn't comprehend the words, listening to the book's murmurings made him feel connected to something more profound and important than himself.

On one such session sitting cross legged on The Matriarch's rug,

Noah encountered what he'd forgotten he'd even been seeking in the first place. The quarter sun with the door in it: not on a contract, but part of an intricate clock displayed on a double-paged illustration. The clock was rotating before his eyes, and as it did, the forest in the background was cycling through the seasons. Magnificent summer greens gave way to bright, bloody leaves, which in turn withered to skeletal trees which bloomed to life again, all in the span of about fifteen seconds. Entranced by the image, his mouth formed words with minimal input from his conscious mind.

"The contracts won't last ten years," he mumbled.

"Why do you say that?" The Matriarch asked, her voice low and musical, almost hypnotic.

"Because they're already over. They ended at the beginning of spring. Every one of them."

"You must not be reading it right," The Matriarch said curtly. "That's been weeks now, and the demons still do exactly as they're told. The contracts were written to be ten years each."

"Did Salice tell you that?" Noah asked.

A deep, warning growl rose in Visoloth's throat.

The Matriarch narrowed her eyes. "You're an obedient little slave, aren't you, Visoloth?"

The growl faded. Its yellow eyes blinked, and a single tentacle flicked the air. Visoloth rose slowly to its feet as though unsure of his own weight.

"Sit down, Visoloth," The Matriarch commanded. "I am still your master."

Visoloth flinched back toward the ground before reversing direction. It stretched its legs luxuriously, rising to its full height.

"The demons didn't know either," Noah said carefully. "They were afraid of being punished."

"I can still punish them," The Matriarch replied with a harsh edge. "Heel!"

The demon dog flinched again, but it was less discernible than the previous time and it recovered more quickly.

"It is no loss being rid of you," The Matriarch said, rising warily to her own feet. "You can join the traitor in the stone for all I care. Sit. DOWN!"

Visoloth lowered itself once more, but it wasn't cringing this time. Its body was tensed, preparing to spring. The full bloom of tentacles flared from its mouth in defiance.

"Visoloth, don't!" Noah shouted. "You need to tell the other demons in the school!"

The Matriarch rounded ferociously on Noah, brilliant diamonds now in place of where her eyes had been. "What did you tell him?"

Noah hadn't even realized that he'd spoken in demonic. He picked through his limited vocabulary to say something to the effect of: "Tell them all they're free! Then down to the village, and tell all the ones there too."

Visoloth replied something in demonic, but it was too fast and complicated for Noah to follow. The dog's tension was apparent from his frozen stance and stiff tone however.

"Stop using those filthy words," The Matriarch demanded, turning rapidly between the two. "What are you saying?"

"I'm not giving you an order," Noah added to Visoloth in plain speech. "It's advice from a friend."

"Enough!" The Matriarch bellowed. "Traitors, both of you! To think I welcomed you to my school. You didn't deserve the lives you had, and now you've lived your last."

Visoloth began to lunge toward the old woman, tentacles springing in a wide sweep through the air. She defensively crossed her forearms, prompting twin beams of light to spring into the air which rotated to form a searing shield. Visoloth never followed through with his attack however, and instead turned away at the last second to bound toward the door.

The Matriarch dropped her shield the moment she realized the deception. She pointed an index finger, trembling with rage. If Noah was going to resist her, it was now or never. He flung the demonic tome at the woman which opened in the air and began to shriek. The

Matriarch reacted at once, blasting it from the air with a torrent of wind which dismantled the book into an explosion of loose pages. The room was momentarily obscured in a blizzard of flying sheets, each screaming and cursing in a maddening chorus of rage.

The Matriarch was shouting something, but Noah couldn't hear her over the cacophony. A booming crash resonated an instant later, but this too was instantly swallowed by the screaming paper. Another gusty nova spread from The Matriarch to flatten the pages against the walls where they slid to the ground in rumbled heaps.

When visibility returned, the door stood thrown wide and the demon dog was gone. The Matriarch lifted the ends of her long dress and dashed after it with a supernatural blur of speed which made mockery of her apparent age.

"Harpies!" she shouted as she ran. "Catch that dog! Bring him to me!" Then pausing for a moment at the doorway, The Matriarch turned to glare through Noah with her diamond eyes. He was trapped with nowhere to run. All it would take was a blink, and his soul would be sealed within one of the stones.

"Don't leave this room," she snarled, "or it won't just be your soul that pays the price."

The door slammed behind her, but that was hardly the end of the chaos. The door then flipped around in its frame, so that the outside face was now pointed inward and the lock was on the other side. Hundreds of moaning pages from the ground flooded the room with a wave of despair, and outside the screech of harpies mingled with the confused shouting of students.

"Out of my way, imp!" The Matriarch's muffled voice howled. "I'll skin the lot of you, don't touch me!"

Noah didn't need a beating heart to feel terror, and his heaving lungs didn't need to move the air to feel flustered. He moved instinctively toward the door, grasping the handle only for a seething jade arc of lightning to leap across his hand. He jolted backward and clutched his injury, cursing, only realizing after he did so that he'd done so in demonic once more.

"The top drawer of her desk. Quickly, child."

Noah jumped in surprise. It took him a moment to realize that a page from the shattered book was speaking to him.

"It isn't locked. She was in too much of a hurry," another page chimed in. Then a dozen voices in susurration around him: "Open it—open the drawer—look inside!"

Noah cast a nervous glance at the gargoyle in the corner of the room which had remained as still as stone. He then did as the pages instructed, bracing himself for another shock that never came. A small stack of parchments, a jewelry case, a bag of gemstones, quills, sets of keys, satin gloves, Brandon's confiscated mermaid skull, and other personal effects—as well as a blood red diamond. Noah had no doubt that Professor Salice's soul was still bound inside.

He looked questioningly at the pages around him, but their incessant voices were growing weaker. He thought he could distinguish the demonic words for "your friend", but it was almost too faint to hear. Then a whispered shout said "look inside," and this too was gone, replaced by the softest of tremulous moans.

Noah carefully lifted the red diamond to the light of a will-o-wisp and tracked it across the air. The stone glittered as the light pierced it, and Noah could faintly see something moving inside. He glanced around at the scattered pages again, but they were too faint to hear now. Back to the diamond, he lifted it to his eye and peered inside the stone.

Noah had the sensation of looking into a telescope revealing something very far away. A hexagonal room built entirely from the blood-red diamond mirrored the external facets. Professor Salice was sitting cross-legged on the ground with his back against one of the walls, his hands folded in his lap. His eyes were open and he immediately met Noah's gaze, apparently aware of his presence.

"Are you angry?" Salice asked. The voice sprang up in Noah's mind, only distinguishable from his own thoughts by the barest intonation. "It's alright if you are. I'd be angry if I were you."

"She's not very nice, is she?" Noah asked.

Salice chuckled dryly. "You don't know the half of it. I heard some of what is going on though, so I know her mask must be starting to slip. Is Visoloth alright?"

"You really care about a lowly demon?" Noah asked.

The light of the blood diamond caught in the Professor's eyes. "I care about all souls, but him more than most. I know he was the one to betray my plans, but I know he was only following his own conscience. I have no one but myself to blame for not being open with him about the full extent of my charge."

"You lied to me too," Noah was quick to add. "I was your apprentice, and you used me. And if you think I'm going to help you now just because I don't like The Matriarch either—well you can rot in there for all I care."

The Professor's head hung limply and he sighed. "I don't expect to be rescued. For any of us to be rescued—because I am far from the only one she has sealed broken from the cycle of life and death." He lifted himself wearily to his feet, then straightened himself rigidly with his old look of haughty arrogance returning. "I do, however, expect you to be taking up the fight in my place."

The horrible cackling screech of the harpies interrupted them. It was answered by a squeal, agonized and terrified. Noah imagined an imp being hoisted into the air by those long, curved talons and perhaps hurled down the pit as well.

"We don't have time to waste," Salice said. "We cannot let their suffering be in vain. Take the keys in the desk and my diamond and be prepared to run. I will show you why The Matriarch must be destroyed."

"I can't open the door. It shocks me when I touch it—"

"Only from the inside. Someone is approaching to open it soon. Be ready."

Noah took the set of keys, barely turning toward the door before it had already begun to open. His relief was immediately cut short as the face he least wanted to see in the world peered through.

"Brandon?" Noah hissed in shock.

Brandon's beady eyes quickly scanned the room. He opened the door the minimal amount to slip his pudgy body inside, and Teresa slid in behind him.

"Don't close the door!" Noah warned. "You won't be able to open it again."

"Teacher's pet hiding from the demons?" Brandon leered.

"What are you doing here?" Noah demanded. "Doesn't matter, get out of my way."

Noah darted toward the door but Brandon shoved him roughly back. "Not so fast. Where's my skull?"

"Your what?"

"My mermaid skull!" he demanded. "The Matriarch had it confiscated. It's your fault, and I want it back. Now while everyone's busy."

"Give it to him," Salice said, "we have no time for this foolishness."

"I won't," Noah protested. "Let me through!"

"Professor Salice?" Teresa asked uncertainly, looking everywhere around the room. "I thought you already came back to life. Where are you?"

Brandon looked suddenly fearful as well. His greedy eyes fell upon the skull in the open desk drawer though, and he lunged to seize it. This time it was Noah blocking his way, the two boys pushed and wrested to keep the other from moving around.

"Stop it, both of you!" Professor Salice shouted. "Noah, let him have the skull. Brandon, let him pass!"

Noah reluctantly broke away and stepped aside. Brandon gleefully snatched his skull, although the instant he picked it up he already seemed to be losing interest in it. "Where are you going that's more important?" Brandon asked suspiciously. His eyes fell upon the keys clutched in Noah's other hand. "You're going to steal something too, aren't you? Something better."

"I am not," Noah said. He didn't waste his chance and was already almost out the door. He didn't know where he was actually being led though, and the lack of conviction in his voice seemed to fuel Brandon's suspicions further.

"You're not taking anything without sharing it with my boy," Teresa said.

As soon as Noah made it outside the office, he tried to shut the door to lock the pair of them inside. Teresa had gotten in the way however, so instead Noah turned and sprinted toward the stairs as Professor Salice was instructing.

"You'll understand when you get there," the professor promised. "These keys will open the final door leading to the road from death."

The Mortuary was in chaos. Noah had never realized how many demons operated the school until this moment when they were all running wild. Imps were swarming along the ground, biting and scratching at the legs of panicked students. A Lava Salamander had climbed onto the central tree and was spitting sticky molten gobs at the harpies, and those that missed were starting fires all over the place. The harpies in turn were trying their best to lift demons and hurl them outside the school. The entranceway was dominated by the roaring Manticore whose barbed tail was being pinned down by a pair of Gobblers, their fleshy bodies melting into puddles like glue to hold the enraged beast down.

Noah was vaguely aware of Brandon and Teresa closely pursuing him, but there was so much going on that they were the least of his worries. He made it a few steps down the first helical stairway, but swiftly had to retreat and choose the other one as a patrol of zombies came marching up from the lower floors with Professor Wilst at the lead. This reversal allowed Brandon to close the distance on Noah even more tightly, so that he was only barely out of arms reach as Noah raced down the second flight of stairs.

Undead moans echoed through the stairway, and it quickly became apparent that Brandon had used his skull to peel off a pair of the zombies from the troop to join in his pursuit. His ability had advanced considerably throughout the semester, and the corpses were bounding down the stairs with a ravenous impetus that put the class' initial shambling to shame. Professor Salice was urging Noah on with every step though, and Noah had no time to question anything about this mad dash.

Past the second floor and its marching zombies, past the screeching owl and the frightened animals on the third, through the demonic fourth floor echoing with Visoloth's word of freedom. Onward to the fifth floor and its whispering room, all the way to the iron doors crossed with chains. At Salice's instruction, Noah plunged the largest key, ornate and gilded with gold, into the ponderous padlock and heaved to turn it. The chains slithered sinuously back like snakes, and just as Brandon and his zombies came thundering down the last stairs, the iron door swung open which led to the road from death.

The zombies staggered to a halt, throwing up their arms to shield their eyes against the searing light. A dozen or more bright beams crossed the path horizontally, with another dozen vertical beams criss-crossing in a regular pattern. Noah squinted to peer through them and could just barely make out the descending stairway vanish into the darkness beyond.

"Is it another door?" Noah asked. "I don't understand."

Before Salice could answer, more footsteps sounded pounding down the stairs above them. A moment later and Walter and Jamie had appeared, stopping short a little higher up the tree. Brandon raised his skull prompting the zombies to shuffle into position to defend him as the corpses braced for impact.

"Aha!" Jamie shouted. "I knew something was up when I saw you chasing Noah. Why can't you leave him alone?"

"Where's the treasure?" Brandon demanded. "Is it on the other side of the light?"

"Life is the only treasure!" Professor Salice cut through the tense standoff. "And there's no life to be had, so everyone needs to calm down. Not for you, not for the graduating students, not for the other schools or the furthest monasteries and temples in the highest mountains of the spirit world. The Matriarch has lied to you. Everyone has lied to you. There is no going back."

"Professor?" Jamie asked, mystified.

"Every way has been blocked," Salice continued. "The Matriarch doesn't serve her students, she serves the Trans Dimensional Department. Together they have created the Soul Net you see before you now."

"I don't understand," Noah said. "Why would she bother teaching people how to come back to life if it's impossible?"

"She's a peddler of false hope," Professor Salice said. "Six years of education, all to give students a sense of false confidence that they are ready for the journey home. The moment a soul passes into the net however, they belong to her. Trapped forever between life and death. In this way does the department seek to control both worlds, allowing only those they choose to return to life while filtering out all who would resist them. That's why I made it my mission to summon the Rasmacht and destroy The Matriarch, so that I could be rid of her net and free the souls she has been keeping from their fate."

"But what makes you so sure?" Teresa pressed. "How did you know about all this?"

"Because this is not the first time I've tried to be rid of her," Professor Salice said. "The Purges all those years ago were not a response to the evil of demons, as the T.D.D. would have you believe. They were a demonstration of the good that resides within all souls. The demons rose up to destroy the first soul net, giving up their freedom in mass to accomplish their task. I myself was killed during that violent time, and it has taken me a lifetime to relearn everything that I once knew. The net is back though, and there aren't enough free demons left in the world to destroy it again.

"I'm sorry, Noah," Salice continued, his voice heavy with weariness. "I thought that I could use you and your family to be rid of her, but in doing so I resorted to the same lies and secrecy that have plagued her tormented reign. I should have trusted you and been honest from the beginning, but I feared that my plan would be discovered before it was ready and I would lose my chance to be rid of the witch. I have no power in here, so you must be the one to summon the Rasmacht and destroy The Matriarch now."

Echos of the conflict above filtered through the stairway in the silence after his words. Noah could never remember feeling so small and helpless, even when he was surrounded by demons in the heart of the nether.

"I can't possibly," Noah said. "I don't even know how to start."

"You've already started," Professor Salice said, "and you won't be alone. Your friends here all carry the same secret, and now it is their charge to bear as well."

"I'm not his friend," Brandon said, sneering.

"You have a soul, don't you?" Professor Salice snapped. "In the face of such evil, all souls must be united. I fear that the demons alone will not be able to tear this school down, but at the very least they will be able to disrupt the resurrection ceremony that was planned for the end of the year. You will have time to prepare yourselves for what must be done, but know that the longer you wait, the more helpless souls will be ensnared as they cross the path nature intended.

"Now I must swear you all to secrecy, for the moment The Matriarch discovers what you have learned she will doubtlessly trap you as she has done with me. Noah, it would be best if you locked yourself back into her office and return me to her drawer before she realizes you escaped. She will not dispose of you as long as she thinks she can benefit from your Chainer soul. Brandon, you must return the skull as well. It is not worth risking her suspicion until you are ready to be rid of her completely."

"Do you think I'm an idiot?" Brandon asked. "It sounds like she's won and you've lost, and I'm not going to be on the side of a loser. And I'm definitely not giving up my skull."

"You will do as you're told," Teresa scolded him, much to Noah's satisfaction. He'd never heard her use such a tone with him, and Brandon seemed as shocked as he was.

"But mother—" he protested, his voice taking on a particularly obnoxious, nasal whine.

"No excuses. This is far more important than anything you can do with your toys. I'll make sure Nepon Vasolich gets you a new skull, or something even better. We're all going to work together to stop The Matriarch though, and I'm not going to hear another word about it."

At least as shocking as anything else Noah had seen today was Brandon's slump capitulation. "Yes, mother," he consented, shuffling his feet.

"Go now, before she returns," Professor Salice said. "A darkness will befall this school after the demons are driven out, and you will all be told many lies about them. You must remember that a soul burns in the heart of all beings, great and small, but no matter how clouded the mind or the spirit may become, no falsehood can ever tarnish the divine in you. The Matriarch is not the first to try and poison the well of life, nor will she be the last, but though individual leaves may wither and die, the eternal vine will always remain. Not always in the same shape, not always as we wish it to be, but this too shall be endured."

There was no victory or cherished treasure in the heavy hearts which ascended the stairs once more. The upper levels were as wild as ever and the tree itself burned in many places, but Brandon's zombies helped to push through all the way back to The Matriarch's office. Through the stained glass they saw the mighty bulk of the Daymare rearing into the air with its hundreds of flailing legs, battling against a seething host of undead specters. The Matriarch was nowhere to be seen, and it was likely she was part of this battle. This gave Noah ample chance to slip back inside her office without being seen.

Brandon seemed more upset to give up his skull than at any revelation, and he fled the moment he relinquished his prize. Jamie hugged Teresa and thanked her for helping. Teresa seemed so taken aback by this that she was at a complete loss for words, but after a few seconds she relaxed and loosely held Jamie back. Teresa quickly excused herself to dart after her son with a thousand apologies and promises on her lips.

"I'm closing you in now," Jamie said to Noah after she'd gone. "Just play along with what The Matriarch wants and please don't do anything stupid to make us worry."

"Yeah, leave that for us," Walter added, grinning. "I'm more worried about Brandon than you though. I don't trust him for a second."

"I'll be okay. It's getting quieter out there. You need to go."

Noah waited until after the office door was closed before he said to Salice, "I know what you said, but I want to take the blood diamond with me. The Matriarch might think it was only lost in the confusion."

THE ROAD FROM DEATH

"It is not a sacrifice for me to remain," Professor Salice said. "Stopping The Matriarch is more important to me than my freedom, and I will not jeopardize you again."

"I'm frightened." Noah hadn't wanted to say it in front of his friends, but now that he was alone it came rushing out unbidden. "I don't understand any of it, not really. I don't understand anything more about death than when I was alive. Every time I think I'm starting to, it all gets mixed up again. I can't summon the Rasmacht without your help."

"When you say 'I', who are you referring to?" the Professor asked.

"I'm me. I'm Noah," he replied, confused.

"Noah. The name of the seventy-five year old man who died last year. That Noah? Or what about the one who lived before that? Or the hundred other lives before? Are they not also you? And how many times do you think they all were afraid? How many times do you think they could not possibly go further than they were?

"It is a common mistake to think our current perspective is who we are. We think ourselves limited by the tiniest sliver of what our recent memory has done. You are not this thin slice of life, this forced perspective of reality that you are familiar with. You are not your mind, or the habits it has acquired, or the things it's done. I believe that you will access those other lives just as you learned to speak demonic, and I believe you will find a way for everyone to live again. You are life itself, Noah, and through you all things are possible."

The next half hour waiting for The Matriarch to return was agony for Noah. He was forced to listen to the roiling chaos and battle outside his door while being helpless to aid the wounded or block the aggressor. Even more difficult were the words he forced himself to say when the door finally opened and The Matriarch reappeared at last.

"I'm so sorry," Noah blurted out at once. "I never should have gotten in the way of you chasing Visoloth. It was those demon books telling me what to do, and I was listening to them for so long and I got so confused—"

"Hush, child, all is forgiven" The Matriarch replied, the sweetness in her voice turned poison. Her star-lit robes were immaculate despite the battle she'd returned from, and every curl on her head was exactly in its place. Noah stiffened as she crossed the room toward him, but he did nothing to resist as she put her arms around him and drew him close.

"The demons are all gone now, and there's nothing left to be afraid of. Of course, it would have been better to dispose of them before they learned of their freedom, but perhaps this way is for the best. The people of Teraville would have given me quite a fuss if I'd tried to force away their precious servants, but at least now everyone realized that those nasty things cannot be trusted."

Noah cursed himself silently, realizing for the first time the full extent of the damage he'd done. The Matriarch drew away from him but left her hands on his shoulders, her smile fixed upon her face. "If you truly repent for what you've done, then I will not send you away from The Mortuary. This is your home, and you are my apprentice. Someday you will have learned everything I have to teach, and perhaps you will be the one to run this school. Would you like that? To help all those lost souls find their way back to life?"

"Yes ma'am," Noah said, doing everything within his power to keep the anger from his face and voice. "There's nothing I'd like more."

The Matriarch stared deeply into Noah's eyes. For a moment he thought he saw the diamonds in her eyes flash once more, their gaze penetrating the deepest parts of him. Her eyes darted to her desk, then back at Noah, her smile cracking at the edges. Casually, she released him and strolled to her desk, looking inside the top drawer. She stared down for a long moment before withdrawing her satin gloves and putting them on, one meticulous finger at a time.

"The school is a mess, and we don't have any more demons to clean it up," she sighed. "Let's hope a good war brings in enough souls to do the job for us, eh?"

Noah wasn't sure whether he was supposed to agree with her, or whether she was joking. She held her fixed smile a few moments longer before chuckling to herself, and Noah forced a similar sound to come from somewhere inside him.

"Ah well, at least we have the whole summer to clean it up," The Matriarch added. She mimed filling an invisible glass and raised it as if toasting. "To a demon free school, and a new semester."

Noah mimed his own glass and clinked with her in the air. "To eternal life," he replied.

THE SOUL NET

SOUL FOOD

THERE AREN'T ANY BREAKS FROM BEING DEAD. NO WEEKENDS OFF, NO after-hours, and certainly no summer vacations where a lost soul can dip their toe back into the well of life. Once a soul has moved onto the spirit world, they're stuck there until they either find a way back, or give up and get a real job. And at a place like the Mortuary, with the smoldering mess left by rebellious demons, discontent zombies, and runaway ghouls—with spiritual creatures to look after and a whole lifeless ecosystem to maintain, there is always work to be done.

"… and to make matters worse, he expects me to do even more now than during the winter," Walter Edmond complained. "So what if I don't have classwork? The nights are half as long, and there's never enough time. I was still working last morning when the sun came up, and all the light reflecting off the crystal balls made me straight dizzy. I had half a mind to start *smashing* the crystals that the imps hadn't already gotten to before they were banished."

Walter broke a stick over his knee as he said *smashing*, as if to prove he was serious before tossing the two ends into the campfire. The flames greedily accepted his offering and flared into the night sky, their flickering light casting long shadows along the black sand beach.

"Consurgo," Noah Tellaver ordered at once, prompting his fat, mustached zombie to scramble back from the flames. "The fire is big enough already. You've got to be more careful."

"We told you not to bring him," Jamie Poffin chided. "Zombies and campfires don't mix. He's so stupid, he wouldn't even notice lighting up like a torch."

"I need the practice," Noah countered. A pale purple light danced around his stuffed tiger which radiated out toward his zombie, prompting it to scoot a little farther back up the sandy bank. He always tried and failed to stop himself from wondering which of his old bones was inside, but of course the act of deliberately not-thinking about something was the same as thinking about it. "And anyway, I'd trade jobs with you in a heartbeat. Spiritual operator sounds a lot more fun than being The Matriarch's footstool."

"What's she have you doing now?" Walter asked. "There aren't any demons left to talk to."

"Well that's the problem, isn't it? She's got zombies trying to do all the chores the imps used to do, but they're so big and clumsy they end up making more of a mess than they pick up. So I'm left directing them, even though by the time one crew finishes they've dropped so many body parts that I practically need to start all over again."

"Neither of you know how easy you have it," Jamie sighed, prodding the fire with a long stick. "The bestiary has been a disaster. Before they got all the demons out, some of them managed to break the snow generator. It's been a nonstop blizzard in there. The rainforests have practically frozen solid, and we haven't even found all the desert animals yet. If it wasn't for Haxafla the manticore sticking up for me, I don't know what I'd do. Which reminds me, Professor Humstrum said that if anyone comes across a jinn they're supposed to get help right away and not to try to catch it on their own. One of them has already bitten a girl—Amelia Wexington I think—and she was two years older by the time she got it to let go."

"I wouldn't mind being a few years older…" Walter mused. "I don't want to still look like a little boy if I ever find a way for Natasha to see me."

"I thought you'd given up on her now that she's with someone new," Noah said, not realizing how thoughtless it sounded until Walter screwed up his face into a bitter scowl.

"Just because she can't be with me anymore doesn't mean she has to be with *him*. I check on her whenever Mr. Wolf lets me use the scry ball, and I can tell she's not happy."

"I told you to stop putting things in the fire!" Noah grumbled as the flames soared once more.

"I didn't do anything," Walter protested. "Must have been your zombie sticking his leg in again—"

"Don't blame it on him, he's all the way up on the bank—"

"I'm not blaming him, I'm blaming you for bringing him—"

"Shut up, both of you," Jamie broke in. "It's obvious neither of you are doing it. Can't you tell there's something weird going on inside the fire?"

As if growing larger and hotter on its own wasn't enough, now that they were paying attention it was clear that images were flickering through the flames. There one second, gone the next, all manner of peeping eyes and long snouts and scaly backs flashed into and out of view.

"They look like demons," Noah said, transfixed. "Can fire be used to host demons too? I thought it had to be a spirit."

"No one would be stupid enough to summon a demon now that they're been banned," Jamie said. "The Matriarch would kick them out of school without a second thought."

The images were solidifying before their eyes though, enduring for several seconds now and maintaining their shape even when the flames danced in another direction. A long branch stirred, and a forked tongue darted out of its front, tasting the air a good distance outside of the fire. The three children were on their feet at once, backing slowly away from the animating flames. The branch was looking more serpentine by the moment, and a dozen yellow eyes were beginning to open along its length.

"We should find a teacher and let them know," Jamie said anxiously. "It could be dangerous…"

"Someone has to be summoning it," Noah replied, turning in a slow circle to scan the empty banks of black sand. He then squinted into the dark waters of the ocean, and the thick white spray of foam...

"Noah look out!" Walter shouted, but by the time the words left his mouth the creature had already sprang from the fire. Scalding coils wrapped their way around Noah—two times around, then three—pinning his arms to his sides and filling his nostrils with thick, acrid smoke which rose from his burning t-shirt.

"Don't move! I'll get help!" Jamie shouted, turning to hurry toward the Mortuary which loomed high above them on the clifftop.

"Don't *not* move!" Walter said, running to Noah's assistance. "Get out of there!"

"I'm... trying..."

But there was very little Noah could do without the aide of his arms. He glared furiously at his zombie, which was lying nonchalantly on its back, moving its arms and legs to create a sand-angel. "Consurgo!" Noah tried, but the purple light scattered, unable to focus. Noah had dropped his stuffed tiger, and he hadn't learned to concentrate his power without it.

The serpentine creature continued to grow since it left the fire, and had by now almost completely wrapped Noah up from head to foot. His body was so restrained that he couldn't even kneel to try to retrieve his tiger. "Let go of me!" he said, this time in the demonic language. The heat was becoming unbearable, and the serpentine head was rearing back as though preparing to strike when—

"Dissipati," a confident voice clearly articulated.

The serpent hissed violently before dissolving into black smoke which stung Noah's eyes. It didn't hurt nearly as much as the howling laughter which swiftly followed though. As the smoke cleared, Noah saw a pair of older teenage boys clamoring over a sand dune toward them.

"I'm... trying... " mocked one of them, black haired and muscular with an uneven patchy beard. A finger-bone necklace hung from around his neck, still softly glowing from the energy which coursed through it a moment ago.

"...but I'm too weak... teacher help me..." mimicked the other, a tall blond haired boy. His right arm wore a stretch of dead skin like a sleeve, thickly covered with softly glowing white tattoos which looked almost like scars on his pale skin. "Oh come on now, don't give me that look. You'd be laughing too if you could have seen your face."

"What was that for?" Jamie scolded, quickly returning down the rocky slope as soon as she'd seen what had happened. "Noah, are you okay?"

"Fine," he grunted, not wanting to give the older boys the satisfaction of knowing how badly his burns still radiated heat.

"You don't look fine," the black haired boy said, bounding up to stand next to him. "You do look medium though. Maybe medium-rare."

"Seriously though, you good?" said the blond one. "I was just trying to give you guys a scare. I didn't think it would jump on you."

"What did you expect, trying to summon a demon without a contract?" Noah lashed out. "Where'd you learn to do that with the fire, anyway?"

"Wouldn't you like to know?" scoffed the black haired boy. "Come on Elijah, let's do those other kids who are still swimming next. We can make something grab their foot in the water."

"Hold on a second," Elijah said. He leaned down to rest his hands on his knees to bring him to eye level with Noah. "You said something to the Borovian Worm, didn't you?"

"No. It was just a grunt—it hurt, okay? Are you happy? Leave us alone."

Noah purposefully avoided Elijah's eyes, determined not to give him any reason to press the issue. He focused on his tattoos instead: interlocking geometrical patterns not unlike a summoning circle. Pieces protruding from around his collar and from under his short-sleeved shirt indicated that much of his torso was also covered in them.

"You're the new chainer, aren't you?" Elijah asked, unrelenting in his scrutiny. "I knew there was one who showed up last year, but I never knew who it was."

"That's right," Walter chimed from behind Noah's shoulder, causing Noah to flinch. "He has all sorts of powers that you don't even know about. You better clear out before he blows your head off, or turns you inside out. Who knows, it might improve your looks though."

"Thanks, Walter," Noah said dryly.

"Shut up, nobody is impressed," said the dark haired boy. "Elijah is a chainer too, and he could wipe the floor with you kids. And he already graduated, so—"

"Thanks, Olly," Elijah said, mimicking Noah's tone. "You go on ahead, I'll meet you at the cave before everyone gets started. I want to meet the chainer kid."

"Thanks, but no thanks," Noah said. He turned around and retrieved his stuffed tiger from the sand. He brushed it off while glaring accusingly at his useless zombie, which had now flipped onto its front to dig into the sand like it was dog-paddling.

"Don't be late," Olly said, casually waving as he strolled down the beach. "I don't want to have some rando' for a twin."

"You two are twins?" Walter asked Elijah. "You look nothing alike."

"He's talking about next time," Jamie said, elbowing him. "You're planning your own resurrection, aren't you? Is that why you aren't worried about getting expelled?"

"No harm in having some fun before we go, eh? Are you sure she's not the chainer?" Elijah asked. "She's a lot quicker than you two. Elijah Carlton here, what's your name?"

"But you can't!" Jamie said, distressed. "The Trans Dimensional Department said resurrections have been canceled until next year! People need demons to help them resurrect, and the road goes through the Netherworld where it's too dangerous right now. The Mortuary is still such a mess, and the door is locked, and if you try—"

"Don't say it, Jamie," Noah interrupted. "Let him go, it's his own business."

"Jamie, is it?" Elijah asked. "And it's not just my business, it's *our* business. The whole graduating class is going, except for a few—Angela and Ruma, who are staying to work in Miss Thatcher's Witchery. They would have gone too, but Miss Thatcher promised to help make sure their new bodies would be beautiful if they helped her open a new location in—"

"You have to stay too! All of you, just a little longer," Jamie insisted.

"Come on Jamie, you have to drop it," Noah said. The Matriarch's Soul Net which let her pick and choose who came back to life was supposed to be a secret. And why would Elijah even believe him anyway?

"We have to tell him. You can't just let the whole class walk into—"

"And then what? Once the word gets out, it would be chaos."

"Yeah, The Matriarch is scary enough while she's pretending to be nice," Walter agreed. "Brandon or Teresa are going to spill it sooner or later anyway."

"Don't be like that, Walter. Why do you always have to go back to blaming him?" Jamie asked. "He's got no reason to—"

"Like assholes need a reason to—"

"We're all in the same boat—"

"Then we're all screwed, because he's going to leak."

Elijah's head silently went back and forth between the children like he was watching a tennis match. "Is there something I should know?" he asked at last, cautiously weighing out each word.

"Yes," Jamie said.

"No," Noah and Walter said at almost the same time.

"Why do we need The Matriarch's permission to resurrect?" Elijah asked slowly.

"We can't tell you," Noah said, crossing his arms. Behind him his zombie did likewise, sticking his chin up in defiance.

"Please trust us though," Jamie chimed. "Tell the others to wait and we *promise* we'll let you know when it's safe."

"You can't be serious," Elijah replied. "It took months to setup our own road, and everyone is really excited. You aren't going to convince anyone without being more specific."

Jamie filled her cheeks, appearing as though she might explode if she wasn't able to say. Just as she opened her mouth to release the air, another sound from high on the stony cliff cut in line. The type of sound that slices through time like a picture being torn in half, forever separating the world which heard it from the world which existed in peaceful ignorance of what was yet to come.

It wasn't the volume that was so distressing, although it must have been deafening at the Mortuary for it to sound like a gunshot all the way down here at the beach. Rather it was the texture, so raw and grating that it continued to echo inside the listener after it faded, like a nightmare which refused to relinquish its victim upon waking. And in that rich texture a thousand flavors could be tasted: the impression of an infant's pain as only a mother would hear, the anger of a lifetime's innocence lost in a single moment, the regret of the dying who knew they were leaving before they'd ever learned to live. It was impossible to tell whether that sound lasted a second or several minutes, because it was impossible to be conscious of anything besides the sound to measure the time against.

"What was that?" gasped Elijah, his calm confidence replaced by a sheet of terror.

"A soul being destroyed," Noah replied before his mind had a chance to catch up with his mouth.

No one asked him how he knew, and no one could doubt his words after what they'd just heard.

"Forever?" Walter asked, the word dry and flat, a statement more than a question. "Wait, where are you going?"

Elijah was already scrambling up the stony slope, using his hands as much as his feet to propel his loping climb. Noah was right behind him, leaving his zombie whose response had been to stuff his head into the sand.

"Why would you go toward it?" Walter asked in disbelief. "Let's stay here until—"

The sound rang out again, no less potent for its second iteration. Noah slipped on the rock to send him skidding down the slope, the rough stones cutting into his bare feet and flailing hands. He was moving again before the sound had even faded. Clumsy, shaking, but still climbing, now passing Elijah who had cowered against the stone until the blaring breaking sound had subsided.

"Race you there," Elijah panted breathlessly. A keener yellow light radiated from his network of tattoos.

Noah only looked away for a moment to secure a handhold, but by the time he looked back he found himself staring at a large black crow where Elijah had been a moment before. His wings spread and launched him into the air, quickly ascending the treacherous climb.

Noah braced himself for another shattering sound as he followed, but a third blast never came. The silence was short lived, however, and soon the air was filled by the screech of disturbed harpies.

"All students—to the Mortuary! Teraville residents—to the Mortuary! All souls—calling all souls."

More harpies were soaring into the air from the top of the Mortuary's central spire. They repeated the scream, flying in an expanding spiral which radiated over the island. One of them, a particularly buxom harpy with a warbling throaty voice, swooped so low over Noah's head that he could feel the wind of its wings.

"Inside—inside—you're not safe," she demanded, before gliding down the rocky slope toward Jamie and Walter. "Demons—demons—demons were here."

By the time Noah reached the top, Elijah was nowhere to be seen. There were a stream of people surging up the road from the village, variously brandishing staves, rings, amulets, hats, or whatever else had been furnished with a bit of their corporal remains. A number of tramping zombies made up the rear, with lithe loping ghouls defensively roving the perimeter. Shocked, scared, and rattled, the air was filled with nervous chatter.

"No no no, the zombies stay outside," The Matriarch was saying.

She was standing beside the open main doors of the cathedral-like structure, dressed in her customary red coat with big black buttons. Professor Humstrum was hurrying toward her from the bestiary, while his antelope headed staff named Amber brayed in distress. Noah spotted Professor Wilst ushering the frightened students from the graveyard. The Vampire Mrs. Vanderlooth stood outside her library tower, trying to swat the frightened books which fluttered madly in their attempt to escape. She kept trying to close the door, but there was always one fat tome which took one for the team by jamming itself in the crack.

There was also a new figure standing protectively in front of the school that Noah didn't recognize. It's not like he could have seen him once and then forgotten him either, because as a rule it's very difficult to forget someone without a head. The jack'o lantern mounted on his shoulders served as a reasonable replacement, however, complete with such a wide grin that it reached half way around the pumpkin. The figure was dressed in an iron-gray suit and was erratically waving a sickle with a bone handle in the air. Noah didn't realize what exactly bothered him so much about this person until he realized the face was on the wrong side of the pumpkin. This was quickly remedied when he turned around to reveal a second face on its front side, this one snarling and angry. Noah was now close enough to see through the slots in the pumpkin, and could tell that it was completely hollow inside except for a single burning candle.

"Come on, not all at once," The Matriarch was saying, gesturing people in. "Women and children first—quickly now."

"Well excuse you, I was a woman the time before last, so let me in," Montgomery Wolf said, stepping over the heads of a pair of children with his long striped legs.

The Matriarch gave him a withering glare that stopped him in his tracks, prompting him to bow and step to the side as the rush of students from the graveyard began to pour through. Walter and Jamie joined Noah a moment later, and together they were swept up in the wave which pushed them inside. The crowd within filled swiftly with several hundred frightened faces, their anxious whispers sounding like the spray of a troubled sea. Dogs, cats, lizards, birds of all sorts, and other animals spread throughout, all disheartened in their own way. There soon became so many that they were forced to spread out around the entirety of the circular platform, around the central tree filling the room.

"Well don't just stand there, make room—and close the door behind you, for goodness sake," The Matriarch said. She was now standing on top of an overturned school cart, although this still only barely raised her head above the swirling crowd. The old woman took her time adjusting her red hat and smoothing out the gray curls which snuck out around the brim, making sure that the crowd's attention was firmly on her before she continued.

"There's no use obfuscating or equivocating. Those of us who are old enough to remember the purges know the sound well. We know the terror of waking up in the middle of the day to hear that terrible blast echoing through our ears. We know the frantic panic of searching for our loved ones to make sure they're alright, and we know the gnawing emptiness of realizing they are forever beyond our reach. I'm speaking of course, of the attack of the soul eaters."

The wash of whispers sharpened violently, rearing as a crashing wave. Exclamations of anger and fear resounded throughout the room, punctuated cleanly by the long, anguished howl which came from Amber the antelope. The Matriarch bobbed and nodded solemnly, raising her hands to calm the assembly. Noah couldn't help but notice the twinkling light in her eyes—the faintest glimmer of diamonds hidden between each blink.

"Long have I warned of the danger of allowing these soulless monsters to dwell amongst us, and I regret that it has taken an event of this magnitude to make the situation clear. Two students will not be attending their classes this year. They will not be graduating, nor returning to the life which fate promises all souls who seek it.

"A soul once eaten might as well have never existed at all. I cannot tell you their names, nor recognize them in photographs, though I may have seen them walk these hallowed halls for years. Those who cared for them will feel the loss without understanding why, and those lives they have touched with light will find only darkness where it had once shown. Yet I mourn their loss, because they are us, and their souls are as sacred as our own. And with the same breath do I condemn the beasts who did this. There is no us without a them, and only by being united will we endure these trying times."

Jamie leaned in to Noah to whisper, "How does she know they were students, if she admits she doesn't know who they were?"

"How's she even know a demon did it?" Noah replied. "The hateful old bat just wants everyone else to hate them as much as she does."

"Are we safe now?" Mrs. Vanderlooth voiced hesitantly. "They wouldn't attack us inside the Mortuary, would they?"

"What about Teraville?" prompted Ungela, the large woman bedecked in charms who ran the Voodoo shop. "We can still go home, can't we?"

"Of course, my dear. You have my word as the caretaker of this school and the warden of this island that there will not be another attack while I am in charge. I have already sent word to the Trans Dimensional Department, which will be providing immediate assistance. Within the day, there will be gargoyles perched on every rooftop. I must ask all of you to maintain your own vigilance however: to report any demon sighting or suspicion that one of our own may still be participating in the profane art. It is important to remember that demons cannot leave the Netherworld without being summoned. Students, please repeat after me: A friend of a demon is no friend of ours."

"A friend of a demon is no friend of ours." The chorus of voices sounded, almost robotic in its unison. There was that twinkle in The Matriarch's eye again. Diamond or no diamond, Noah was sure she was enjoying this.

BACK TO SCHOOL SHOPPING

THE MATRIARCH WAS RIGHT ABOUT ONE THING: IT WAS TERRIBLE NOT knowing whose souls had been destroyed. Nearly everyone was sure that they had been friends with them, although the incessant buzz of conversation made it clear no one knew for certain. There were so many speculations flying around that it was impossible to tell who really had an empty place inside, or even how to tell if they did.

In the days leading up to the first classes of the semester, Noah made an effort to seek out everyone he knew to make sure they hadn't disappeared. Logically it was a hopeless pursuit, because he reasoned that he wouldn't remember to search for them in the first place if they really were gone. If nothing else, it was still a reassurance to see so many familiar faces though.

There was Jamie and Walter of course, along with Brandon who Noah wouldn't have minded if he had disappeared. Bowser the golden lab was here—still a puppy, but considerably larger with darker fur than he had been last year. Sandy with the shaggy hair had taken up apprenticeship with Francisco Pintilo the jeweler, and none of the other students mentioned showing up to work without a master, so all of the shopkeepers Noah knew must still be around. Dolly Miller and Grace Horlow were both still working at Cassandra's Corpse

Comforting, and Elizabeth the rabbit had gone to Miss Thatcher's Witchery after Noah had replaced her as The Matriarch's apprentice.

There were others too, but no matter how many people Noah checked off, he couldn't shake the feeling that someone he'd known really had disappeared. Part of what made it so horrible was that any experiences or interactions he'd had with those people must be gone too: a hole in his life that could never be remembered or filled.

Last semester when Professor Salice had shown Noah the Soul Net, he'd told him that the only way to destroy it was to summon a soul eater to destroy The Matriarch's soul. According to her, she'd been at the school since it had been founded in 1647. There were about fifty new students who came every year, which a quick calculation revealed to be almost twenty thousand whose lives she must have touched. And that didn't even include all of the people she'd known over her long death besides, or the potential for untold thousands of others who she'd once known in a previous life.

To destroy her soul meant to destroy a part of all those countless people. To leave each of them with a little bit of emptiness inside, a part of their life which no longer made sense. It was a terrible thought, but perhaps not as terrible as the idea that some distant bureaucrat making the final decision on who would be born again, and who would be forever trapped between life and death.

These were only some of the thoughts which troubled Noah as he made his way toward Teraville on the last day before the new semester. There was also the mix of shame and defiant anger at his own demonic heritage, a secret only Walter and Jamie knew. Then there was the worry that last year's class had already become trapped in the net from their unauthorized ceremony, and the ever persistent dread about how his daughter was being treated by that dreadful Barnes who had discarded her so coldly in the past.

All the students of all ages were required to make the trip to Teraville as a single group, and they were escorted by the professors for their protection. The pumpkin-headed man was revealed to be their new demonology teacher Alf Yobbler, although Noah had yet to hear him speak, or learn how a pumpkin could even speak in the first place. He supposed that it was no harder to believe than the skeletal Professor Wilst pushing air through his ribcage without lungs though, or the orangutang Humstrum with his decapitated antelope head.

"Did you hear what happened at the weighing ceremony?" Dolly Miller's voice surprised Noah, causing him to lose his place in his internal book of thoughts. The girl was mounding her curly brown hair on top of her head while trying to strangle it with an elastic tie. Noah had only ever seen her with long bangs covering most of her face, which was likely the better look for someone who had so much face to show. Noah scolded himself for the thought, reminding himself that the poor girl was only here because she'd taken her own life just last year.

"There was more of them this time, right?" Jamie replied. "I feel sorry for the ones who were turned away."

"Not just that. A lot of them came from the same airplane crash, and there were even several chainers on board. That must have been really traumatizing," Dolly replied, beaming. "Cassandra's Corpse Comforting is going to do great business this year. Have you ever thought about stopping by?"

"Oh no, thank you," Jamie said. "I went in my sleep. It was really no trouble."

"That's a pity. Once in a lifetime opportunity, dying is. Shame to waste it on something so bland."

"Airplane crashes are really rare, aren't they?" Jason Parson asked. "I bet there was a demon attack in the living world too."

"Why would they do that?" Noah asked.

"Demons don't need a reason. They're just nasty, that's all."

"I wouldn't be surprised," Dolly said. "There could have been a Gobbler that got all gunked up in the engine, or an invisible snoot that snuck into the pilot's chamber."

"Or a mechanic that didn't know what he was doing," Noah countered.

"That reminds me, how is your mother doing, Noah?" Dolly asked caustically.

"You know that was nothing but a vicious rumor," Jamie cut in.

"You should apologize, Dolly. Someone in the counseling business should be more sensitive."

"How am I not being sensitive?" Dolly sniffed. "He's the one defending those creatures. Or did you already forget the two students whose souls were eaten?"

"Of course I forgot them—everyone did," Jamie replied hotly. "That's the whole point of having your soul destroyed, isn't it?"

"Everyone knows Noah is a demon lover," Jason said, and somehow it sounded so much worse that he said it conversationally rather than as an accusation. "I never believed that rumor about his mother, but he still became Salice's apprentice, and he's the only one I know who managed to learn demonic."

"See, that's all I was saying," Dolly said. "I just wish you'd have the courage to admit it."

Noah was suddenly aware of how close all the students were walking together, and how many of the surrounding conversations had fallen silent.

"Say it," Jason goaded. "Say that you're a demon lover, and we'll leave you alone."

"Noah, you really don't have to—" Jamie began.

"You've got it all wrong," Noah said deliberately. He didn't look around, but he knew that if he did he would meet more than a few eyes turned in his direction. "I was only studying them to learn how to fight them. I hate demons more than anybody."

Gradually the conversations around them resumed. Jamie puffed out her cheeks and turned away.

"Well, that's alright then," Jason said slowly. "I still think it was a demon that took down the airplane though. Ever since the demons here went wild, there have been movements to banish them all over the country. It's only a matter of time before they attack again."

Noah didn't speak for the remainder of the walk, and soon all the students were distracted by the prospect of buying their school supplies. Everyone had spent most of their allotted age in the first year on getting the basic class necessities, but this was the first time they would have more discretionary budget to buy whatever they liked. Walter had been good on his word to repay Noah the four months he'd advanced him last year in the form of a dull aquamarine stone. There was only two months payment for the required material, which left him a total of eight months available to spend freely this semester. Noah intended to spend every day of it too, because he was already feeling singled out more than enough without appearing smaller and younger than everyone else too.

Noah didn't want to talk to Jamie about the conversation that had transpired. He waited to make his escape until she was engaged in another conversation with Grace Harlow about polishing teeth into jewelry—Jamie could quite happily talk to anyone about anything—before he pushed ahead toward the front. This was easier than expected, as there seemed to be a deliberate effort from the students not to stand directly behind the pumpkin-headed Professor Yobbler. His grinning face was pointed forward at the moment, which meant that anyone behind was forced to stare into the second snarling visage. It was more than a little unsettling to watch the pumpkin carvings subtly change shape as the eyes scanned back and forth across the procession of students.

Noah averted his gaze to the cobblestone road, then to the first houses they were beginning to pass. Some of the buildings were practical affairs, built in a variety of architectural styles ranging from modern glass and concrete, to victorian era mansions, to rough stone covered by a thatched roof. Noah supposed that many of the residents must be most comfortable dwelling in the style they were accustomed to while they were still alive.

Other buildings were like nothing that could have existed in the living world. Miss Thatcher's Witchery was easily identifiable as the house high in the air, resting on a pair of spindly chicken legs which supported the structure in clear defiance of all natural laws. Another tower looked to be made of solid ice which continually melted and reformed elsewhere, so that the layout of the building was continuously changing. There were houses made from jagged black glass, or living planted trees interwoven together, or even puffy white marshmallow with a door that looked suspiciously like graham cracker.

Stranger still was the long low house with walls of skin stretched between supports like bones, complete with blinking eyes in place of where the windows should be.

The only unifying aspect of this motley assortment was the stone gargoyle perched on top of each and every house. The gargoyles leered down with wicked and sinister faces at the students as they passed. Their shoulders were so hunched that they extended well past their faces on either side, and two chiseled and clawed wings were frozen stiffly in a position which made them continuously look as though they were about to take flight.

"Woah now, that's far enough for me," spoke the grinning side of the pumpkin-headed professor. His voice was surprisingly light and musical, almost as though he was struggling to prevent himself from bursting into laughter. "You will all be perfectly safe collecting your school supplies on your own from here. We will return to the Mortuary together in two hours, so please be mindful of the hourglass on your shopping lists."

"If a building doesn't have a gargoyle on top, do not enter." This voice was spoken from the back-side of the pumpkin. The tone was much deeper, with an unmistakable twinge of condescension. "Do not engage with the gargoyles, or look them in the eye."

"Why not?" Bowser the lab asked. "Are they dangerous?"

"Nothing instructs as much as a good demonstration," the scowling face replied. "Go ahead and see for yourself if you want the rest of the students to understand."

Bowser's tail sank between his legs. He decided not to take Professor Yobbler up on his offer, and neither did any of the other students.

"Come now, there's no need to be so grim about it," Professor Humstrum said, loping up from the back. "Each new year is bringing you closer to a new life, and each new class completes you as you complete it. There's always more to look forward to than there is to worry about, and today is no exception. Who else needs to stock up on parchment and pens with me? Come along, or I'll know which of you hasn't been taking notes! Professor Wilst?"

"I will be getting my bones waxed, thank you all the same," the skeletal professor replied, gliding past the students on the other side. "These old joints just don't slide like they used to."

The momentary spell of foreboding was lifted, and the street bubbled with animated conversation on all sides. The students scattered throughout the town, each pushing or riding in their self-propelling red carts while studying their lists of required materials. Noah spotted Walter waving and jogging up to meet him as the crowd began to clear.

"Hey Noah," he called. "Have you thought about what you're going to spend my months on?"

"I figured I'd just look around see what popped out at me."

"Let's hit Ungela's Voodoo shop then. We need a lot of stuff from there this semester, and I bet she has all kinds of wicked toys."

"You're not still on about your ex's new man, are you?" Noah asked as they walked.

"Don't say ex. That makes it sounds like we broke up. I just died, that's all. And if Darius happens to get a sharp pain in his back whenever he's around her, then maybe he'll get the hint and move along."

"Or maybe he'll go to the doctor and not assume his girlfriend's dead boyfriend is trying to punish him. You know, like a sane person would."

The two boys walked down the street toward Ungela's Voodoo shop, which needed no sign to make clear who lived there. The entire house looked like a giant stuffed toy. From its stitched fabric walls, to its zipper windows, all the way up to the chimney from which puffs of cotton gently floated free into the wind. A gargoyle was perched nearby, peering down the chimney and snapping at the puffs as they passed. If that wasn't enough of a clue, then one must look no further than the garden of shrunken heads which appeared to be growing from the soil like so many cabbages.

"I thought Yobbler was supposed to be the new demonology professor, but they don't even have demonology on our lists anymore," Walter commented as they entered. "It says he's going to be teaching us 'exorcism and banishment.'"

"I'm not surprised, considering how everybody's been talking about demons lately."

There was barely any room to walk inside Ungela's place, so they left their carts outside. Hanging low from the ceiling were a wide variety of embroidered baskets, beaded gourds, and strange feathered instruments of indiscernible purpose. Cramped shelves were overflowing with potions of various color, many of which containing shrunken heads, eyeballs, and other various body parts best left unmentioned. More than anything were the dolls though, rows and rows lined upon every flat surface. Blank white ones, red ones covered in targets and scribbles, and realistic human ones with tiny delicate features. The dolls weren't limited to humans either: little houses, churches, cars and trains, and every animal that Noah could imagine cluttered every nook and cranny.

"Hello pretties," a voice cooed from behind them, causing both boys to jump. Ungela squeezed out from between two shelves, her bone charms and golden bracelets rattling as she moved. "School things for second years in aisle two. You might want to get a few extra Loa dolls—you don't want to get one bloody and soggy and be stuck with it forever."

"What are we going to use the eyeballs for?" Walter asked, looking at his list.

"Don't think eyeballs are useful?" Ungela asked incredulously. "Fine then, sell me yours, you see how much you miss them when they're gone."

Noah busied himself about collecting the required items first, by which point the already tight shop became so crowded that Noah was grateful he no longer had to breathe. Walter was getting much too interested in an enchanted knife which was advertised as being able to cut out parts of a living person's memory, and Noah decided it would be best for them to move on.

If it were up to Walter, Noah's extra eight months would have been spent ten times over within the next hour. He couldn't understand why Noah wasn't interested in a pair of dentures which would allow the user to taste food again. He was baffled that Noah wouldn't want a calcified harpy claw which shielded against demons, nor the mysterious golden egg which Francisco Pintilo the jeweler swore would hatch into a pocket-sized version of the owner.

Gnawing at the back of Noah's mind, however, was the knowledge that returning to life might not happen for a very, very long time. He might regret spending any more time than he had to. After-all, he didn't want to spend the rest of time as an old man, no matter how many interesting items and doodads he'd picked up along the way. He was even beginning to feel quite proud of himself for his restraint as he climbed the rope ladder which dangled from Miss Thatcher's Witchery, the last shop from which he needed supplies.

The Witchery was a perfectly ordinary looking stone cottage once you got past the chicken legs. Miss Thatcher was relaxing in a purple gown which pooled in her rocking chair on the porch, and Noah was astounded to see an elderly imp with long drooping ridges dozing on her lap.

"Are you allowed to still have those?" Noah asked.

"A witch doesn't need to be allowed, she just does," Miss Thatcher replied, gingerly stroking the imp along its side.

"There isn't a gargoyle on your house either," Walter said, craning his neck. "Aren't you worried about being safe?"

"A witch doesn't worry, she just is." There was a bit more snap to her voice this time. "Lot of good those clumsy statues are. When a coven wants to ward off demons, you better believe they're using dwellers. Demons might not mind possessing someone else, but nothing scares them like sharing their own head. What am I saying though—inside, the both of you. All the potion ingredients you'll need for your classes are already sorted by the door. If you need anything else, ask Angela. If you need it done right, ask Ruma instead. Either way, you won't need to bother us with your nonsense."

Walter and Noah entered the house. Both of them stumbled over themselves the moment they stepped inside. While the wooden floor had looked perfectly normal from the outside, the moment their feet landed they found themselves tethered upside-down from the ceiling, which was in fact still the floor. The wooden rafters were now far below them, although all the things on the shelves stayed put despite clinging to the bottom of the shelves.

"Mind your step!" A pretty girl a few years older than them with long brown hair and a red apron whisked past. She wore a prominent name tag which clearly displayed 'Angela'. "The switch surprised me the first time too, but you'll get used to it."

"Why does it do that?" Walter gasped, taking a tentative step forward as though afraid he would fall the moment he lifted his foot.

"Keeps the spiders out," grunted a dark storm cloud possessing the vague shape of another girl. Jet-black hair, black nails, thick black lipstick and mascara—she would have been hard to spot at all if it weren't for her considerable weight. Noah supposed she had to be Ruma. "The flipping around makes them uncomfortable, and they always skip right out again. I keep telling Miss Thatcher that it doesn't make any sense not to like spiders, and that she of all people should know what it's like to be persecuted without a good reason. You try conniving a witch of anything though, and see how that goes for you."

"Yeah, I got that impression too," Walter groaned.

"It's no worse than sitting on the underside of the library floors," Noah said.

"You're the new chainer, aren't you?" Angela asked. "Noah, yes?"

"That's right."

"Not so new anymore, I suppose. There are quite a few more chainers this year, you know. I'm sure you're the one Elijah was talking about, though. He said to save the mirror for you. Just a second, I've got it over here." Angela hustled behind a wooden counter and bent below to rummage around.

"He's still here then?" Noah asked. "He hasn't... gone anywhere, or anything, has he?"

Ruma raised her eyebrows—or lowered them if you consider they were upside-down—and gave a knowing smile. "Shhh, we don't talk about that. None of them have gone yet, though. Elijah said there was something he had to find out first. I told them to just wait for the Mortuary's road to be fixed, but nobody ever listens to me."

"I don't see what the big rush is either," Angela added. She had returned with a flat round object the size of a large picture frame covered in a velvet sheet. "What's another year compared with infinity?"

"Or two years. Or ten," Ruma declared. "I'm having a perfectly nice time being dead. Shall I ring you up for the class bundle?"

"Plus six months for the mirror," Angela added.

"Six months?! What's the mirror for?" Noah asked. "Why does Elijah want me to get it?"

"The Mirror of Ancestry is to help you get to know your previous lives, of course," Angela said. "Why that was so important to him is a matter for the two of you, but he was adamant there was something you needed to learn from it."

"Not adamant enough to pay for it himself," Walter grumbled. "I bet he's just playing another trick on you."

"He trusted us enough to put off his… trip, didn't he? I might as well repay the favor."

"Would you like me to wrap it for you? It's quite fragile."

"Seven years bad luck for breaking a regular mirror," Ruma added. "I can only imagine what you'll get for a magic one."

"What do you mean 'getting to know my previous lives'?" Noah asked. "I just look inside and…"

"And they look back, that's right," Angela replied. "Of course there's a bit more to it, I don't claim to really understand it myself. You can ask Miss Thatcher, but I know she has plenty of things squirreled away back here she doesn't really understand. She hates to sound like she doesn't know what she's talking about though, so she'll probably just make up an elaborate lie that will lead you farther from the truth than if you knew nothing at all."

"Can I ask them questions too?" Noah pressed. "Can they… talk?"

"Who knows? Maybe they'll reach right through the mirror and grab you by the throat!" Ruma said, delighted by the idea. "Murderers, isn't that right? What they said at your weighing ceremony?"

"Ooh, I don't think they would do that…" Angela said, although, she didn't sound the least convinced. "They wouldn't want to murder their own future."

"Says who?" Ruma asked. "They're gone and you're still here. You don't think they'd be a little jealous of that?"

Ruma snatched the covered mirror from Angela and advanced on Noah, causing him to involuntarily stagger backward across the upside-down floor. It was disorienting enough to make him stumble, and for a second he thought he'd plummet straight down before landing on his butt. "You're no afraid are you?" Ruma pressed, looming over him. A corner of the fabric had folded back to reveal the edge of the glittering mirror. Noah immediately averted his gaze, pretending to be focused on slowly picking himself up—or down—from the floor.

"Of course not. Don't be mean, Ruma," Angela said. "How can anyone be afraid of themselves?"

NETHERWORLD

"A BANISHMENT IS NOT THE SAME AS THE OTHER FIELDS OF STUDY YOU have addressed so far," spoke the grinning pumpkin. "To summon a demon is to reach an agreement with it. Zombies and ghouls have no say in their animation, and animal links can be done without their knowledge or permission."

Professor Yobbler paced as he spoke, and upon reaching the edge of his classroom he turned sharply back toward his chalkboard. This allowed the snarling face on the back of his head to slip in a few words in a deeper voice as he returned:

"A banishment, however, is a battle against the unwilling. Done carelessly, and the only victim will be you."

The demonology class had undergone considerable renovation since Professor Salice had taught there. The once plain white-tiled floor was flooded with a thick layer of sticky brown goop. This forced the students to clamor from one metal desk to the next in order to be seated. From the ceiling draped hundreds of unfurled scrolls which created an almost jungle-like atmosphere to navigate through.

Bowser hadn't understood what all the fuss was about and had plowed straight through the goop to get to his chair. The sticky stuff seemed to have some sort of magnetic property which caused more of the viscous liquid to become attracted to him as he went. By the time he reached his desk, he had puffed out to double his size as though he was engulfed in a giant frizzy coat.

Noah caught Brandon's eye from across the room as they both stared at the dog between them. The boy hadn't grown much taller after his latest expenditure of time, but he had grown considerably fatter with a poorer complexion. Noah looked away at once, pretending not to have seen him.

Brandon had even left their shared mausoleum in favor of sleeping at the supernautical docks. Noah assumed this to be for the best. He couldn't imagine an interaction between them that didn't escalate the tension, thus prompting the brat to spoil their secret out of sheer spite. He didn't know how Jamie managed to stay friendly with him, but then again, she seemed to be everyone's friend.

A squeal from several girls interrupted Professor Yobbler, who had just finished wading back to his chalkboard. Bowser looked considerably smaller than he had a moment before. His tongue was hanging out, apparently immensely satisfied with himself after he had just vigorously shaken much of the goop from his fur—and onto Dolly Miller and Grace Harlow who sat on either side of him.

"What is this horrible stuff?" Dolly moaned. "You can't just jump straight into a lecture and pretend that you haven't made us all sit in this vile swamp."

The interruption suspended the spell of wary silence, and all at once a rapid succession of voices broke out.

"Yeah, and what happened to demonology?" Jason Parson asked. "Are we just not going to learn about it anymore?"

"Why do you have a pumpkin for a head?" Rachelle Devon demanded.

"Why are you teaching us something that's not safe? Isn't keeping us safe, like, part of your job?" Kyle Thrope added.

The voices cut short almost as soon as they began. Professor Yobbler used his hands to lift his pumpkin straight from his body to reveal the empty space directly above his shoulders. He slowly turned the pumpkin in the air so that the angry face was on pointed forward before setting it back down. While the pumpkin was in the air, the face appeared perfectly static as it might on a real jack'o lantern, but the moment he put it down on his shoulders the fearful visage animated.

"Silence!" howled the angry face into the already quiet room. "Impudence! Disrespect!"

Yobbler turned abruptly to face the chalkboard and began to write out his name, which fortunately caused the grinning side to face the class once more.

"Please forgive us for any confusion, we shall start again. My name is Professor Yobbler, and of course I want to keep you all safe. That's the primary reason why I'm here, in fact, as a specialist in the art of demon repulsion. I will not be teaching demonology though, as it appears some of you were expecting. As of 4:30 AM last night, the Trans Dimensional Department has suspended the practice and teaching of demonology anywhere in the world. At least until they work out their current tensions with the demon community."

Professor Yobbler was sketching out a globe to illustrate his statement while he spoke. Each of his hands held a separate piece of chalk, and together they danced in mesmerizing harmony to sketch out a precisely accurate map which miraculously traced the subtlest contours of each coast and island.

"England, two weeks ago, a family of five," Professor Yobbler said, marking the location. "Flight 747 before that with a good number of our freshman class, crashing right about here. Seventeen in the Ukraine when a train went off the rails. Another twelve in India—pulled underwater while swimming."

Yobbler turned away from the chalkboard, turning his pumpkin around in the same fluid motion to continue from his grinning face without missing a beat. "It is the duty of everyone at the Mortuary to keep you safe, but shielding you from the truth is one thing I will not do. Beginning with the insurrection in the Mortuary last year, a ripple has spread from one community to the next causing demons to rebel against their masters. We wish there were a kinder explanation for the amplifying attacks we have witnessed over the summer, but the conclusion is inescapable. The demons have declared war against the spirits and the living alike. If this situation is not brought to a swift conclusion, I fear the risk is high that a second purge will begin."

The Professor turned back to his board and began a new drawing, neglecting to turn the pumpkin as he did so. The deeper voice resonated in the quiet chamber.

"By department regulation, all roads from death are currently closed. The only living births will be from those who have flouted precaution to attempt to find their way back alone. We can protect you as long as you remain at the Mortuary, but in order to be reborn, a spirit must pass through the Netherworld. Doing so without the aid or permission of the demons adds an unacceptable level of risk. The Trans Dimensional Department expects to come to a peaceful resolution soon though, and there is no reason to think that this will not all be history before the next graduation ceremony."

Yobbler stepped away from the board to reveal two more globes beside his original drawing. The second one was a complex network of fine lines, while the third looked more similar to the original, familiar Earth. A series of dashed lines connected the three drawings.

"This horrible stuff, as you call it," the grinning face said as Yobbler gestured toward the goop, "is a rough replica of nether. We will be training in it to become more familiar with its properties and reactivities. In addition, I am using this pumpkin because I have misplaced my original head, and I believe that should address all your questions. Now if we may continue—"

Rachelle Devon's hand sprung back into the air, and the pumpkin nodded. Noah noticed her shaved head had grown out somewhat since last year, although this only made her look even more boyish than before.

"If the road from death is closed, then what happens if a baby is born and there aren't any spirits that have crossed over to be reborn?"

"Impossible. Nature has always sorted itself out in the past. Besides, there are still those spirits which have already crossed and are waiting their turn to be born. The roads from death would have to be closed for years before the birthrates began to drop. More importantly, I presume everyone has their new books: *Essential Exercises in Exorcism?* Careful not to get any nether on it—it's so hard to get the stains out."

As was typical with Professors everywhere, the remainder of the first class had very little to do with learning practical knowledge and quite a lot to do with the type of factoids better suited to the back of a juice-box. Instead of teaching the children about banishments, or defensive spells, or any really useful things, he deviated into musings about the three Prime Demons, the original demons who supposedly gave rise to all the rest.

The first was Borowrath the Unsplendid, a confusing beast which began with a thought which then speculated its body into existence, rather than the usual opposite way. Momslavi Lapis was apparently once an ocean whose mind was the sum of all the creatures who lived in it, and the mysterious Zee Zee Balloo, who may or may not even exist yet, and is rather the last demon at the end of time who won't stop meddling in things before he was born.

No one had the least idea what any of these beings looked like, if they were real at all, and the maddeningly abstract artistic renditions of them in the textbook only confused matters further. The only thing anyone seemed to know for certain was that each was to blame for unimaginable suffering and catastrophes, from natural disasters to plagues to one madman in a desert beating another madman over the head with a stick. By the time Noah was packing up his things at the end of the class, he'd already forgotten all of their names, a fact he was almost proud of. In his mind, that decreased the likelihood that he had anything to do with these monsters in one of his previous lives.

This thought circled insidiously back to the magical mirror which he had not uncovered once since its purchase. He had convinced himself at least a dozen times already that he would be happier not seeing whatever foul face looked back at him from the glass. Then again, he also convinced himself just as many times that it was selfish and cowardly to think that way. The knowledge he could gain may well assist him with returning to life, or even summoning the rasmacht which he still believed must be done.

The internal debate went unresolved yet again, however. Upon exiting the classroom and collecting his cart, his thoughts were interrupted by the clamoring of harpies.

"I've never heard them so loud all the way from the fourth floor," Jamie commented, emerging from the classroom alongside Grace Harlow.

"I can't believe we're going to have to walk through this every class," Grace sniffed with disinterest, kicking the last slimy nether from her bare feet.

"I bet there's been another attack," Brandon said from farther behind. "I bet someone's been all sliced up, and the harpies are fighting over the scraps."

"Don't be so gruesome," Grace huffed. "There are any number of perfectly clean ways to destroy a spirit."

"They don't sound frightened or angry," Jamie replied, "just excited. I still believe Professor Salice who said demons are persecuted through no fault of their own. Don't you, Noah?"

She locked gaze with him with her chin held high in a challenging gesture. Of course he agreed with her, but while she could remain popular through sheer will of personality, it was unfair to expect him to say the same without repercussion. Her continual efforts to get him to acknowledge his sympathy for demons publicly was really getting on his nerves. He was considering replying with something truly derogatory about demons just for spite, but fortunately they were interrupted by the growing commotion upstairs.

"They have no place in the bestiary!" Professor Humstrum's high voice wailed. "Do you have any idea how bad it is for a Bakku's health if they go in for a snack, only to inhale sand and stone? The poor thing has been coughing up dust for a week. Not to mention that hairline motion trigger which has the gargoyles mistaking every creature they don't recognize for a demon and having a go at them."

"Nor the library," Mrs. Vanderlooth's voice added severely. "I've already had to clean up the tattered remains of Rawlan Boofafa's Alchemy series, which was guilty of nothing but flying too high in the spire—besides a propensity for pedantic verse that is, which I highly doubt is what offended the nasty thing."

The class emerged onto the first floor to find a heavy scattering of feathers on the bridge. Overhead whirled a half-dozen harpies in tight, angry circles; conspicuous bald patches were evidence of their foul-temper. The space was considerably darker than usual, as most of the will o' wisps had fled to the higher branches of the central tree. The illumination granted an eerie radiance to the leaves which swayed and splashed the shadows back and forth across the scene.

The Matriarch stood with her back toward the students in haughty defiance with her arms crossed. Beside her stood a gangly man wearing white gloves and an orange tie, an outfit Noah had come to associate with the Trans Dimensional Department. He had long stringy green hair which looked like vegetarian noodles, and when he opened his mouth, he displayed a smile that could make a dentist rich. A stone gargoyle sat on either side of him, their open-mouthed faces frozen in perfect stasis.

"The gargoyles are strictly instructed to protect each and every soul. If there are technical difficulties, then you'll just have to wait for the latest model from the manufacturer—" The green-haired man was cut short as The Matriarch raised her hand.

"While we are on the subject of school security—a topic I am *entirely responsible* for as headmistress—might I ask where the two of you were on that preeminent August the 22nd?"

"In the library—where I always am, of course. You can't possibly be suggesting—" Mrs. Vanderlooth baulked.

"Come now Matriarch, you're going much too far—" the orang-utan spluttered.

The Matriarch raised her hand again, and they both fell silent. The green haired man chuckled to himself, glancing down to adjust his gloves by pulling on the fingers. Each motion caused an unsettling cracking sound which was more indicative of pulling the bones cleanly out of the joints rather than the regular popping.

"Don't be absurd," The Matriarch replied. "All I mean is that *wherever you were*, it was definitely somewhere. As much confidence as I have in both of you to keep one somewhere safe at a time, it would be preposterous to suggest that either of you can be everywhere. And that's exactly the kind of vigilance we need in such troubling times. Meep Warlington has been building and training gargoyles since they were first installed in the Notre Dame in the 13th century. It would be absurd to presume any of our malcontent would supersede the safety of our students, and I will hear no more on the topic."

The harpies began to squawk again. Noah couldn't make out any words, but it seemed to have something to do with one of the gargoyles sticking out its tongue. The Matriarch glanced behind her, appearing to notice the students for the first time. She turned back sharply to Mrs. Vanderlooth and Professor Humstrum, and in a considerably warmer tone, she added, "I do so appreciate how busy this time of year is for you both, what with the new semester and all the repairs still to be done. I am glad that we've all agreed to this elegant solution to keep yet another burden from your shoulders, so that you may both focus all your energy on the spryness of your student's minds and not the security of their souls."

Professor Humstrum was looking over her shoulder to the students when he bowed his head. "Thank you for listening to our concerns, Matriarch. I trust you know what is best."

Mrs. Vanderlooth stuck her nose into the air and turned in an elegant wave of her black cloak. She said nothing as she exited through the front doors, not even bothering to close them behind her as she disappeared.

"You have been most accommodating," Meep Warlington drawled, glancing back at the students which had begun to hesitantly cross the bridge. "I promise this will only be a temporary matter until the other matter we discussed has matured. Perhaps we should continue this conversation in a more private setting?"

"Noah Tellaver," The Matriarch barked without looking. "My office." She strode with purpose toward the first of the eight doors around the floor perimeter.

Meep Warlington's eyes glazed across the assembled students as though trying to give all of them the stink eye simultaneously before hustling after the old woman. "Don't you think the two of us might be better served by a more intimate conversation…?"

"My apprentice will be able to contribute," The Matriarch said, holding the door open.

Meep Warlington glared back again until Noah reluctantly separated himself from the crowd. His distinction caused the full weight of Meep's glower to fall upon him, although the messy grin of uneven teeth which followed was even more uncomfortable to bear.

"The madam knows best," Meep said, bowing and entering The Matriarch's office.

She continued to hold the door until Noah had arrived with his cart. He kept his head down and didn't look at her as he passed, but that didn't stop her from whispering to him.

"Do not mention your family in his presence."

By the time Noah looked up, The Matriarch was already inside and drawing a chair into existence for her guest. The comment struck him so much by surprise that he half wondered whether he'd heard it at all. Noah parked his cart and waited for a second chair to be drawn for him. The Matriarch did no such thing and immediately sat behind her desk once Meep Warlington was seated. Noah felt a sudden sympathy for unwanted dogs as he sat down on the rug, and the feeling intensified by the look of disdain the green-haired man cast in his direction.

"I'm so glad that you two have a chance to be acquainted," The Matriarch said. "Meep Warlington is the newly promoted Minister of Energy at the department. My condolences again for the old minister… whatever his name was. The school has also suffered the bite of the soul eater, so we know the weight of that emptiness well. Mr. Warlington is doing an excellent job in making sure it does not happen again though. He's a very important person to know in the best of times—and one who might save your soul in those we now occupy."

"Nice to meet you, sir," Noah said, automatically sticking out his hand.

Meep lifted his arm to scratch his nose and inspected what came off under his nail. Whatever came off apparently wasn't supposed to, so he stuck it back on his face.

"You may know my apprentice by reputation, if not by name," The Matriarch continued smoothly. "He is responsible for alerting me to the premature termination of Professor Salice's contracts. His fluency in demonic is rare asset, even within the department, if my memory serves me." Her tone of voice indicated that her memory had no other option, and would regret trying to do otherwise.

Meep swiveled in his chair to size up Noah again. His uneven teeth made another showing in something that he must have thought was a smile. Noah remained tense, wondering if The Matriarch would also mention that Noah had instigated the rebellion in the first place by telling Visoloth to spread the word to the other demons. It seems The Matriarch had forgiven that fact, however, as it had given her an excuse to banish the lot of them.

"Is he now?" words as smooth as oil seeped between those uneven teeth. "However did he learn to do that?"

"I'm a chainer. I know all sorts of things," Noah said, annoyed that Meep was continuing to address The Matriarch as though he wasn't there.

"And I am the headmistress, and I teach all sorts of things," The Matriarch interjected. "I believe his talent will be singularly useful to remedy your concern about the nearby folds. I know it has been a great concern of yours ever since Mr. Wolf's netherball was broken during the attack."

"Instrumental," Meep agreed. The way his eyes roamed up and down Noah's body reminded Noah of a particularly intrusive airport security probing. "Will we be able to send him more than once, or will he be used up the first time?"

"Um, excuse me…" Noah started.

"He has traveled safely to the Netherworld and back before, although that was before the open insurrection we see now. I do, however, have a safety precaution which should negate any cause for concern." The Matriarch rummaged in her desk as she spoke, procuring a spool of glimmering silver thread. "One little yank at the first sign of danger and he'll be back immediately, whether or not he has access to a fold."

"Is there something going on I should know about?" Noah tried again.

"What if there is already a Borovian Worm wrapped around his neck?" Meep Warlington asked, leaning onto the desk with both of his elbows. "Or a Gobbler chewing on his foot, or something like that? They wouldn't be dragged back with him, would they?"

"I don't want to go," Noah said, as loud and clear as he dared. "Not unless you tell me what's going on."

"Do you always permit such rudeness from your students?" Meep Warlington asked scathingly.

The Matriarch smiled a patient, long-suffering smile at Noah as though he was a misbehaving baby who could not be held accountable for his actions. "Isn't it obvious? You're going to be our spy. Making sure the demons aren't plotting anything, or trying to get in around the school."

"Last semester you told me it was too dangerous for students to enter the Netherworld. That's why you had to go with me to—"

Noah shut his mouth suddenly, remembering that he wasn't supposed to mention his family. It made him even more frustrated that he was following her orders in this regard, but at least he had a sense that it was for their own safety. Meep Warlington raised a solitary and artful eyebrow as he granted Noah a rare moment of his attention.

"Too dangerous for first years, but you have some experience now, and you'll have the silver thread, so there is nothing to fret over. Do be a dear and tie this around your waist." The Matriarch offered Noah one end of the glimmering thread. "Nice and tight, the more knots the better. It would be a shame for your tug to unravel and leave you floating… best not to think about, really."

Noah hesitated only briefly before accepting the offer. He considered leaving it loose on purpose and staying in the demon world for good, although the echo of that soul-crushing sound was still fresh enough in his mind to make that an unappealing option. Reluctantly, he tied the string around his waist, not seeing what choice he had in the matter as long as he wished to stay at the school. The Matriarch smiled broadly as though she had reached the same conclusion. She was already drawing her precise circle of light into the air, the faintest outline of her skull visible through her skin as she released the energy.

"Make sure to check all four folds around the school," Meep Warlington said. The sparkling light in the air reflected in his eyes to produce a maniacally eager effect. "They will look a bit like paper pockets to you, all fairly close together. One will lead to The Matriarch's office, and another to the demon summoning chamber in the fourth floor. A third will be an exit somewhere in the village—I believe that is a yellowish fold with a floral imprint—and the fourth is a rough blueish one that exits near the water at the base of the cliff."

"Won't you be the popular one when you get to boast about how you're protecting the school?" The Matriarch said, adding a final jab with her finger like an exclamation mark. The interior of the circle fell away into nothingness: a cookie-cutter bite out of reality. "Feel free to go as far as the thread will allow, and remember you're only a tug away."

"Gee thanks, I feel as safe as bait on a fishing hook," Noah replied, climbing inside the hole.

"Do you have any backup students that speak demonic?" Meep asked The Matriarch conversationally just before Noah plunged into the cool gel.

The tingling sensation enveloped his fingers, up his arms, around his body, welcoming him into the alien world. All the light and sound behind him extinguished in an instant, and Noah reflexively closed his eyes in vain attempt to ground himself during the sharp transition. This did nothing to block out the world around him which imprinted itself upon his mind from all directions.

The first intrusion to his thoughts was the last time he had been in the Netherworld. Professor Salice had given call to the sentient ocean, and swarms of demons had converged on him from every direction. Noah tensed now as though tooth and claw and gaping mouth were all descending upon him once more, a monstrous army that cursed his existence and readied to extract its price. It was hard to imagine finding anything that would be worse than that, but there it was waiting for him as soon as his body was fully immersed in the cool nether.

Silence. As loud as any sound he'd ever heard. There were no chirping from distant imps, no *woosh* from passing beings in the nether. No demonic words, no ethereal wind, not even his own breath or beating heart that he'd long since left behind. It felt so wrong—like he was the last being at the end of the universe waiting for nothing and no one forever more. And as far as he could see through the endless paper folds, there was nothing to hinder that thought.

Until all of a sudden a voice rippled through the nether at his side.

"Noah Tellaver?" it asked.

And then it seemed so silly that he could have been more afraid of the silence than he was now.

"Noah Tellaver?" the voice repeated. "What in this world or the next are you doing here? And why did it take you so long?"

It took a moment for Noah to process that the words weren't demonic at all. They sounded a bit garbled and odd as they came through the nether, but at the same time they were familiar enough to banish his budding fear.

"George Hampton?" Noah asked incredulously.

"One and the same," he replied, floating into the open from behind a tumbling gray hexagon, previously unremarkable from all the other shapes littering the geometrical landscape.

"You haven't been spying on me, have you?"

George folded his hands comfortably behind his head and stretched out as though laying on an invisible hammock.

"Spying? Do you mean that as praising or pejorative? Tell me so I know whether to be flattered or offended at such an accusation. Regardless, you must respect the fact that I asked you first."

"I'm on the lookout for demons around the school." Noah gestured to the silver thread, which scrutiny revealed it to be attached to a patch of empty space wherein it simply vanished. He wondered whether Matriarch would ever check on him and see George, or even if his old friend could come back with him along the same silver thread.

"What an extravagant punishment. I hope you got away with something excessively fun before you were caught."

"It's not because of something I did," Noah said. "This is how The Matriarch treats everyone: like tools only as good as what they can do for her. Now it's your turn to tell. What are you doing here?"

"Oh you know. Same as you, only the opposite," George replied with a tap of his nose.

"Where are all the demons?"

The old man shrugged, making his wrinkled neck disappear and then reappear like a turtle coming out of its shell. "I was wondering the same thing. How have your classes been though? Samantha talks about you all the time. She told me once she'd like to be your mother when she grows up, although don't mention that to her because she'll get embarrassed and try to hit you, and she really might. She doesn't just see and hear spirits anymore—she's learning all sorts of things," he said, a touch of pride in his voice.

"What about Mandy and Lewis?"

George floated past and turned away from Noah who had to paddle through the nether to keep up.

"You said you'd keep an eye on them," Noah pressed. "Has Barnes been good to her? Is she still afraid to be honest about the things she sees?"

"Don't look down on her for being afraid. You would do better to be a little more fearful yourself." George peered briefly into a blue-tinged paper fold, the one that must have exited near the base of the cliff, before hurriedly closing it and moving on again.

"I'm not scared of demons. They've got a perfectly good reason to be fighting the department."

"The Soul Net is back, yes I heard," George replied in an off-handed way. "All the existing roads are entangled, so we'd best hope some new ones come along soon. Visoloth has told all the demons by now too, which of course is the real reason they're so angry. There is a lesson you should have learned by now in the course of those many lives though: the only thing more dangerous than an evil purpose is a good one. The nobler the cause, the more pain and destruction can be used to justify its pursuit."

George floated behind the paper fold, and Noah swam around the other way to anxiously wait his reappearance. Several seconds passed by, and he did not emerge from the other side. Noah was beginning to wonder whether he had slipped inside when George's voice rang out in his mind.

"Go back to school, Noah. There are forces at work writing history, but your only job is to study it. You won't be any help to anyone until you've relearned who you are."

Noah finished circling around the blue fold to where he started, but the old man had vanished entirely. All at once the silence returned along with an awareness of the enormity of empty space encompassing him on every side. Noah tested the length of his string, reaching its outermost limit as he checked the other folds which represented the thin spaces between the spirit world and the nether around the school. He saw no point in swimming around here any longer than was necessary. It was obvious there were no demons about, so he pulled sharply on the silver chord and waited to be returned.

George had never answered why he was there after-all. What other forces was referring to? How did he even know Visoloth, and what did he have to do with the demons? And why was Mandy right to be afraid? The more Noah thought about it, the less satisfied he was with any of the answers the old man had given.

MIRROR OF ANCESTRY

"BEING HUMAN IS OVERRATED, BECAUSE THE ONLY ONES TO RATE THEM are other humans," Professor Humstrum said. "If you ask the trees, they will tell you that squirrels have a much better time."

The first transhumanist class of the semester was held in the second room of the third level. The thick brown furs which carpeted the spherical space stood in stark contrast to the overgrown vegetation of the first room, but the more significant difference were the two giant eyes which were embedded into the far wall. Each of them spanned several feet across, although thankfully they didn't seem to notice the students and only stared vacantly outward, their iris barely visible behind the semi-opaque mass. On either side of the glass, the backside of two ponderous cat ears were stretched and embedded into the wall. Overall this gave the effect of sitting inside someone else's head.

Professor Humstrum was standing directly between the eyes with his back turned to them, evidently not bothered in the least. "I myself would have remained in my lion body if it weren't so hard to turn the pages of my books," the orangutang said. "My paws were always too big and made me lose my place, and when I tried to use my tongue the book would be an absolute sticky mess by the end. Come along come along, don't block up the doorway. I'm not going to start until everyone has taken their seat."

The giant eyes swiveled to peer inside the room, crossing as they tried to focus on Humstrum between them. This seemed to make them confused, and they kept blinking as they tried to sort out what was going on.

"Psst, Noah look," Jamie whispered, kicking Noah beneath the desk. "Between the rugs."

Following her gaze, he found a small, bare patch where the furs did not overlap. The underlying floor was made of glass. Through it he glimpsed a gray and wrinkled surface which he stared at without recognizing for several seconds before replying with blank incredulity: "A brain. The room's got a brain."

"And why shouldn't it?" Professor Humstrum asked as he strode between the aisles. "Can't see much with eyes alone, now can you? Yes, this semester we will be getting a feel for different lives by living vicariously through them, and nothing gives you as genuine a feeling as the living room. Unless of course you're a dweller actually taking a real body for a spin, but what do we think about dwellers?"

"Not allowed in polite society," chorused a few voices, causing the Professor to bob and nod in approval. Hazel snorted derisively to emphasize the point.

"As well they shouldn't. Taking the free will away from a sentient being is one of the most loathsome acts known in this world or the next. This room is a purely artificial construction like the gargoyles, and will not resent our intrusions in the least. The living room will be able to simulate life experiences without becoming mired in such a moral quandary. When you reach the fifth year you will learn to transform your spiritual body into animal shapes for a more immersive experience, but until then this is the next best thing. Let me begin with a demonstration."

Professor Humstrum returned through the aisles from the far wall from which he'd collected a glass cylinder half the length of his arm. A blue frothing liquid churned inside the glass as he carried it to an appropriately sized hole in the floor between the eyeballs. Inserting the cylinder caused a satisfying *wooosh* sound, followed by a gurgling as the liquid presumably drained down to the brain below the floor. The eyes swiveled frontward facing and began to rapidly blink before closing for an extended period. Upon reopening, the eyeball was no longer visible, and in its place two windows looked out onto soaring green trees, green all the way through.

No, not trees at all—they were stems of grass, some of which bearing yellow wildflowers the size of cars. The colors were so real and vibrant as to make everything in this world seem to be painted in shades of gray. Instead of bland and uniform surfaces, everything was composed of intricate detail and patterns and textures that turned the simplest blade of grass into a work of art. Through the ears poured an array of sounds: a torrent of whistling wind, the rumble of stirring earth, the symphony of bird song, and beneath it a vast assembly of subtler vibrations that Noah could not have even conceived of before.

"When humans think of life as a mouse, they invariably scoff. How could such a small, pitiful creature enjoy the full richness of the world? But the smaller you are, the grander the world becomes, and a whole new world of subtler things reveals itself that a human could never have appreciated. A more complex creature might better ponder high thoughts, but it will never hear the plants growing, or feel the fluctuations of little breezes write a story across one's whiskers. Every living thing will experience something utterly unique and wonderful, and it's not hard to see how much happier a simple life can be."

EVERYTHING inside the Mortuary looked unbearably dull after the transhumanist class. The flicker of passing wisps that had once seemed so warm and bright glowed feebly compared to the expansive iridescence which lit the world of the mouse. Even visiting the living world as a human would have been a considerable improvement to this dreary place though. Noah couldn't help but regret losing his key to the whispering room last year as he glided up the stairs in his self-propelling cart. It would have been nice to spend more time watching his grandson Lewis discovering the world for the first time, or at least the first time he could remember. He must be starting kindergarten about now. Would Mandy miss him when she dropped him off? Would Barnes share in those simple joys, or listen to the stories he brought home with him each day?

"Have you looked inside yet?" Walter asked, breaking Noah away from his ruminations. Walter sat within his own cart which bumped roughly up and down as it ascended the steps. He still hadn't gotten the hang of a smooth trajectory, but part of him was stubborn enough that maybe he'd rather always bump than admit he was doing it wrong.

"Huh?"

"Why didn't you tell me you bought a magic mirror?" Jamie asked from the other side. "You didn't have to feel pressured into it if you didn't want to look. Elijah is a bully, and you don't need his approval just because he's another chainer."

"He wasn't pressured, I was there," Walter said. "If he doesn't find out about his other lives, then how's he supposed to learn how to summon the rasm—"

"Shhh! Don't be an idiot," Jamie cut in. "You can't talk about that here. Let's meet by the cliffside. Make sure to bring the mirror, Noah, and we can discuss it there."

"Now who is being an idiot?" Walter retorted. "The gargoyles won't let us leave. I tried earlier, and the one over the door almost bit me. They won't even let us into the graveyard alone until the whole class is together. We can use the library though."

"Don't use that language with me. The library isn't private enough, and you know Mrs. Vanderlooth gets offended by mirrors. She thinks they discriminate against vampires. It'll have to be the bestiary then—I know where to find a quiet spot."

Noah, who hadn't managed to get a word in between them, nodded reluctantly. He didn't want to admit that he'd regretted purchasing the mirror, or that even now he had no desire to look inside. He didn't know how to try and explain that some things were better off unknown without sounding afraid though, although perhaps that was simply because he was too afraid to even admit to himself how afraid he was. What an unsettling thought. Everyone at the school seemed to think being a chainer was the most wonderful thing in the world, but Noah would have been much more comfortable knowing that who he was now was who he'd always been.

"Are you okay, Noah?" Jamie prompted. "You've been as quiet as a corpse. You do *want* to learn about your past lives, don't you?"

"Yeah, I think I have to," Noah replied with heavy words. The three of them glided toward the second door on the first floor which led to the bestiary. "It's just weird though, isn't it? I feel a bit like a criminal with a head injury who has forgotten all the bad things he's ever done."

"Or all the good things," Jamie insisted. "If you're already assuming the worst, then finding out its not so could make you feel a good deal better. Besides, even if some of them did do something bad, well that's not exactly your fault…"

"Isn't it though?" Noah asked. "I'm still the same soul. Anything they were capable of, the same goes for me now."

The hierarchal biosphere of the bestiary had been almost entirely repaired since the demons went wild last semester. The only thing that was still not working properly was the snow generator at the very top, although this caused additional problems down the line as the melting runoff never formed the waterfalls or streams in the lower habitats. A temporary fix consisted of a collection of inflatable pools spread sporadically throughout the zones. A glum mermaid hanging over the side of a kiddie-pool glanced up as they entered before allowing herself to slip with, slow, dejected increments back into the water.

"You've got a mermaid in the bestiary?" Noah asked. "Aren't they too intelligent for that sort of thing?"

"Everything in the bestiary is intelligent, whether it talks or not. She's just resting a broken tail until she's well enough to swim in the ocean again. Over here, in the manticore nest. We won't be bothered in there. Haxafla has been going on missions for the department to fight off demons. He won't be back until after Christmas."

"The Manticore is named Haxafla?" Walter asked.

"That's right. And he wasn't very happy about the arrangement either, but that creepy department man wouldn't take no for an answer. They had to put shackles on Haxafla before Warlington led him away. Professor Humstrum practically had a fit, but The Matriarch said it had to be done."

'Nest' isn't the word Noah would have used to describe the thick mound of thorny brambles which Jamie led them toward. There was a gaping hole plenty large enough for them to crawl into, but it was unfortunately placed about five feet off the ground. The three children had to leave their carts at the bottom and climb carefully through the brambles. There was just enough space between the thorns to find safe footholds for their bare feet. Only once Noah had climbed ahead was Walter able to lift the covered mirror up to him.

"It's much nicer inside," Jamie reassured them as she picked her way through. "Professor Humstrum filled it with rugs so Haxafla has a comfortable place to lay down, although the manticore's skin is so tough that I'm not sure he would have really minded the thorns. It goes to show how caring Humstrum is though. You know, I've often thought that if there is anyone we should tell about the net, then he would be the best one to trust. He kept Noah's secret about his affinity, after-all."

"Noah's affinity was only about him. The Soul Net is about everybody," Walter said. "Besides, he'd never believe The Matriarch was behind it. He'd trust her over us any day."

"Exactly," Noah agreed. "We can't give The Matriarch any warning that we're onto her. It's not just about preventing people from getting stuck. It's about saving all the ones who are already tangled up. Even if the whole world knew about it and turned on The Matriarch, she could just whisk off with all those souls and they might never get out. We've got to do it once and do it right."

Noah laid the covered object on the floor. A corner of the velvet cover slipped from the edge as he did so. His eyes helplessly locked on the patch of uncovered glass, and he caught a glimpse of a formless dark shape like rolling smoke trapped within a bottle. He immediately readjusted the cover to block it from view. Every half-examined thought and buried instinct was rearing inside him, shouting a uniform command that he turn away before it was too late. He was proceeding into a forbidden knowledge, and that always came with consequences. *Your friends will find out what a monster you really are. Your secret will spread until no door is open to you. You will wander as an outcast to spirits and demons and living alike, unable to return to life. Lost... and alone... and hated until the end of time.*

"I can look first, if you want," Walter said.

Noah jolted, his fingers trembling where they still clung to the edge of fabric which he had moved back into place. The inside of the manticore nest was dark except for a single wisp which snuck in after them to watch curiously overhead, bathing them in a cool, pale light.

"I should warn you that I was having a rough patch before I went. I let myself go a bit before the end," Walter rambled. "I wasn't always that heavy. I'd started following a real plan to eat right and get myself back into shape, and Natasha was helping me..." his voiced trailed off into silence. "You're going to look too, aren't you Jamie?"

"We're here for Noah. He's the only one who needs help understanding the summoning. I'm just here to be supportive."

"What is it with you?" Walter asked. "You never used the whispering room. You didn't visit home last Christmas. And now you don't want to look into the mirror. How can you have lived a whole life, and still have nothing to look back on?"

"I told you already. I was just a little old lady with nothing worth revisiting," she said testily.

"I don't buy it. You're hiding something."

"I'm not. And even if I was, it wouldn't be any of your business. You can look in the mirror if you want, and I'll respect your privacy enough not to peek."

"What are you afraid of? It can't be worse than being a murderous demon like Noah."

"Thanks, Walter. Real helpful."

"I'm not afraid. You're just feeling insecure about us seeing what you used to look like, and you're trying to project it onto me."

Noah meanwhile was steadying himself with several deep breaths. He didn't need the air, but the familiar motion was still calming somehow. It wasn't going to get any easier, and if his friends started fighting then it could get a good deal harder. Walter and Jamie were on either side of him, but they were both far enough that neither of their reflections should be caught in the mirror. There wouldn't be any doubt—whatever was staring back at him would be him. Ripping off a bandaid, all at once he pulled back the cloth and looked into the magical glass.

There was definitely a face looking back at him, and it definitely wasn't his own. More than that was hard to say, because the surface of the mirror was molten black like a slab of melting obsidian. Even with the wisp looking over his shoulder and shining its light directly onto the surface, all the light could reveal was the rough outline of a face drawn in a subtly lighter shade of black, almost invisible.

Noah had to focus hard on a single feature to make it out, and as soon as he'd done so, the feature had already shifted into something else in a smooth and endless transition. The skin aged as he stared, the nose drooped, then grew longer, then stretched into a snout before morphing back. The ears curled in on themselves and disappeared, only to regrow again higher up the head in a different shape. Long teeth snaked out of a twisting upper lip, seamlessly transforming into the flicker of a gleaming smile before being obscured by a heavy beard which dissipated with inexorable change. Some of the forms were handsome, others cruel and clearly inhuman, others mismatched as though part of the face belonged to one creature while the rest had already moved on.

The only aspect which endured were the two eyes: not quite black, but a deep shade of midnight blue which stared into his own. No matter what form the rest of the face was taking, those unblinking orbs remained fixed on Noah. They tracked his slightest movement without judgement or expression, moving independently of Noah's own. They were the most terrifying part of the experience, at least until the face spoke. A thousand voices from a thousand different throats all rushed out at once. Each was no louder than a gentle whisper, as if a mighty crowd was murmuring a synchronized prayer. There were so many different textures, and inflections, and languages whispered in unison that it was again impossible to decipher. Noah couldn't shake the feeling that the whole assembly was uttering the same statement though, and that it was directed to him.

Walter drifted closer to stare into the mirror as well. Noah couldn't take his eyes off his own reflection to even notice. The whole experience was so uncomfortable, and it was obvious he wouldn't learn anything. Noah pulled away to let the other two have a turn. Walter angled the mirror away from the others in an obvious protest to Jamie, and they couldn't see anything besides him sticking his tongue out and making funny expressions.

When he finished, Jamie stoically took his spot in the corner where the others couldn't see, glaring daggers at Walter as she did so. Her lips immediately pressed together so tightly that they both trembled. She fumbled for the cloth on the ground without taking her eyes from the mirror, then clutched and kneaded the fabric with blind, groping fingers. No more than ten seconds could have passed before a high-pitched squeal escaped her. She flung the cloth over the mirror once more and clutched her knees to her chest, rocking back and forth as the pitch in her throat continued to mount.

Noah hastened to fully cover the mirror and turn it away from her. There was nothing else he could think to do as her distressed sound reached a piercing apex. Her outpouring cut off a moment later to be replaced by a heaving gasp. She rolled onto her side, still clutching her knees, and began panting heavily. Walter kneeled beside her casting, an anxious look to Noah.

"I don't like it!" Jamie said with more ferocity than Noah had ever heard from her. "I don't like her, or them, or me, or whatever it was. The mirror must be cursed. Elijah was playing another prank on us, and I'm never going to look inside again."

"What did you see?" Walter asked, leaning over her. "I didn't think it was so—"

"And it's your fault for making me!" Jamie interrupted, pushing him back and pulling herself to her feet in a sudden, jerking motion. Her hands flew to obscure her face, and before Walter or Noah could fully process whether or not she was being serious, Jamie had fled from the manticore nest and disappeared.

"Girls," Walter muttered, avoiding Noah's confused look.

"She isn't really though, is she? She was an old woman by the time she died. I don't know why she's acting like that."

"What's growing older have to do with it? We are who we are for as long as we are. I would have thought you'd got that by now. Besides, we only think she was a little old woman because that's what she told us. Who is to say that any of us are who we pretended to be when we were still alive?"

Noah nodded as he reflected upon his own vision and climbed out of the nest behind Walter. He certainly felt like an imposter compared to that kaleidoscope of forgotten lives. Whatever he was supposed to learn from that experience was lost on him though, and he couldn't shake the feeling that all his other lives would have been ashamed to see their lineage culminate in someone like him.

THE BURNING ALTAR

Noah didn't see Jamie again until he'd returned to the graveyard close to dawn. Upon exiting the bestiary, he'd been intercepted by The Matriarch who had swept him off to her office to stitch the pages back into some of her ruined books. The demonic tomes had fallen silent, their once active imagery static upon the parchment. Each finished volume was now fastened with a thin silver chain, although the effort seemed redundant now that all the fight in them had fled.

Jamie briefly apologized for her outburst when Noah entered the cemetery gates, but she never elaborated on what she saw. That was just as well though, because if she had then Noah would have felt obliged to describe his own maddening sight, something he felt unprepared to do even within the privacy of his own mind. Jamie did tell Noah that Elijah had been looking for him though.

"I'm not saying you should speak to him, just that you could. If you wanted to. It's up to you, but if it were up to me, which it isn't, then I'd have nothing to do with him," she told him. "…which I'm not."

By the time Noah got back to his mausoleum, he had an enormous sympathy for the heavy fog which had begun to disperse into the wind. He didn't feel weariness in his muscles like he used to when he was alive, but there was a certain *thinness* about him that longed for a quiet day's sleep. He wasn't thinking about anything other than his stuffed tiger and his padded coffin when he entered the low stone dwelling. He certainly wasn't expecting to see Brandon sitting on his own coffin, his pudgy legs swinging in idle wait.

Noah froze, unsure whether to address the sudden reappearance of his roommate, or simply go to sleep and pretend he wasn't there. They hadn't even spoken since Professor Salice had shown them the Soul Net.

"Have you told anyone?" Brandon asked after a pause. Noah was surprised to hear how soft and uncombative his voice was.

"No. Just you, me, Walter, and Jamie know. Unless you told?" Noah asked, his words sharpening at the question. That doesn't mean no one else knows though, he thought, thinking of his conversation with George Hampton. That didn't seem like a necessary detail for Brandon to know. He already knew too much for how trustworthy he seemed to be.

"No. I promised—Not even Nepon Vasolich, and I trust him more than anyone in this wretched place."

Another pause. Thump, thump of swinging legs against the wooden coffin. Noah moved to his own side of the room and sat down.

"The Matriarch won't let me be outside the school grounds during the day anymore, so I'm going to be sleeping here again," Brandon said. "She said that if the demons attacked me out by the docks, then no one would be able to get to me in time before… you know…"

"They eat your soul?" Noah asked, relishing a certain satisfaction in the words. "You'd be the first to deserve it, the way you've treated them. You know people are still teasing me about that stupid rumor you made up about me last year?"

Brandon's fat face scrunched up in a way that caused his beady eyes to disappear into two angry sparks. He looked more familiar that way, and Noah braced for the explosive insults that were sure to come.

"I'm sorry. I didn't know. I'll tell everyone that I made it up first thing tomorrow night," he said in a voice that sounded like it should have come from a much younger boy. He slid off his coffin and opened it to climb inside, but not before Noah caught a glimpse of what could have been tears in his eyes. Brandon didn't close the lid once inside. He just lay on his back and stared at the ceiling while Noah climbed into his own coffin.

"I think I knew her," Brandon said to the ceiling.

It didn't seem like he was talking to Noah, so Noah didn't say anything in reply.

"One of the girls who disappeared," Brandon continued more rapidly, as though he was afraid of the quiet.

"How do you know one of them was a girl?" Noah asked. "You can't remember someone after their soul has been eaten."

"I don't remember. I just know," Brandon said. "I can feel it by the shape of the hole she left behind."

"Stop being a baby," Noah said. "You can't be hurt by something you forgot. Half the school thinks they knew who it was, but none of them have any idea either."

"You're right," Brandon said, surprising Noah yet again. "It doesn't hurt. But I wish it did, because then I'd know that she really meant something, you know? I could punch something and start to feel better. But feeling like it should hurt when it doesn't, that's a whole different kind of pain, and I don't know how to make it stop. You still want to make that happen to The Matriarch?"

"Yeah. I do."

"You must really hate her," Brandon said.

"I don't. I just want to be alive again. And for everyone else she's trapped to get that chance too."

"I hate her. And I hate the demons, and I hate this place. I want to start over and forget that there was ever anything to forget in the first place. I want to help you destroy her."

"Thanks. Just don't do anything stupid yet, because we're still working out how to do the summoning. We'll let you know how to help once we've got a plan."

"Not good enough. I want to be part of your group. I want to help make the plan, not just wait and follow orders. And Master Vasolich can help too—I know he will. But only if you trust him. Trust us, I mean."

"I don't trust anyone, not even myself. Don't tell anyone anything if you want to join our group."

"Okay. Deal," Brandon replied before Noah even finished what he was saying. "And you don't tell anyone either. About the girl I forgot, or anything else I told you."

"As quiet as the dead," Noah promised, closing his coffin lid to blanket him in the comfort of the dark.

"Keep moving fat boy, these benches can't handle you," Walter said, jerking a thumb over his shoulder.

"I invited him. Brandon is going to sit with us now," Noah said, scooting over to make room.

"Spirits don't weigh anything, dumbass," Brandon said as he sat down.

"Seriously? I thought he liked sitting all by himself. More room to spread out," Walter grumbled.

Jamie leaned behind Walter's back to wave at Brandon. She was grinning from ear to ear. "That was so nice of you, Noah! I knew we'd all find a way to get along."

"Yeah, whatever," Brandon said, unable to completely conceal his own grin. "I feel like someone needs to supervise you lot anyway, running wild like you are."

They sat on a circular bench before a circular table which dominated the third room of the necromancy floor. The ground was decorated in an exquisite mosaic of colored tiles. The design was reminiscent of forest ground littered with holes, from which crackling waves of purple tiles spilled forth. This all converged on the ball of pure purple energy in the center of the room where Professor Wilst was counting out glass jars.

"Good to see that everyone has brought an eyeball with them. We were one short last glass, and two children had to share one—very uncomfortable for both of them, I can tell you."

The Professor nodded in satisfaction and clapped his hands together violently. A nova rippled through the air like a heatwave which spread the jars throughout the room to evenly disperse them on the table. Within each jar was one of the human eyeballs they had acquired from Ungela's shop, now floating in syrupy fluid.

"When I heard Professor Humstrum was taking you into the living room, I couldn't resist moving around our schedule so we can use our own eyes. I think you'll all agree that seeing through these will be a much more *visceral* experience." The way he said *visceral* made Noah imagine well-cooked meat sliding off its bone.

A second nova of glass jars exploded from the center of the room once more to slide into place beside the first. This one was empty apart from the same thick liquid.

"Hey, there's nothing in mine!" Elizabeth Washent complained from across the room. "Can I have another?"

"The second jar, my small furry friend, is for you to fill. Bowser—please do not drink from the jar, it is not water. It will keep your old eye perfectly safe while you are using the new one."

These words caused an uproar of whispering and a forest of raised hands to all grow at once. The professor waved the hands down and tried to resume silence. "Hush hush, don't tell me you are still so anxious about your bodies. I would have thought you'd be over such childish delusions by now. That's only part of what's good about being a litch—finally no more squishy tissues, spiritual or otherwise. Taking out your eye won't hurt in the least though, and the optical nerve will reconnect itself to the new one once you've popped it in.

"Now, you'll want to split into pairs for this. Otherwise it can be a tad difficult to force out your own eye… You'll only be replacing one of them, so you don't make a mess here. It isn't uncommon for necromancers to replace both eyes when they need perfect transference, but one will be sufficient so long as you close your original. It can be quite confusing when each eye has a different perspective into a different world, so please stay seated for the duration to avoid falling over.

"Today we're going to be getting a first-person view of being a zombie. As you can imagine, this will be giving you far more precise control than you'd be able to achieve otherwise. As a bonus it might even give you a bit of insight to help you better take care of those under your dominion. It's always good to remember that someone once lived in these bodies, and the least we can do is show some respect."

Noah glanced around the room, relieved to see that everyone else seemed just as hesitant to pop each other's eyes out. Another shockwave rippled the air as a third item clattered onto their desks: one spoon per person.

"I guess you're with me," Brandon said, grabbing his spoon with a bit too much eagerness.

"Yeah, okay, let's get it over with."

"Mind which direction the eyeball is facing when it's inserted!" Professor Wilst rattled on in his dry voice. "Zombies are confused enough without being operated by the blind. Here Elizabeth, let me help you with that. Those paws are just going to get in the way."

Getting your eyes gouged out is exactly the sort of thing you'd want to keep your eyes closed for, but unfortunately that wasn't an option. Noah clenched his teeth as the spoon grew larger and larger in his field of vision, and it took a few tries before he could hold still without flinching away at the last second. It was as if time slowed down the closer it got, until that terrible moment when it seemed frozen forever and that waiting was worse than what was yet to come. Then all at once it was through without the least sensation. Time raced on to full speed and more, and within a few seconds, and a few unwholesome squelching noises, Brandon was able to cleanly remove Noah's left eye and drop it into the open jar.

"Stop smiling already," Noah said. "I liked you better as a bully. Let's see how you like it when its your turn."

"Do it wussy. I'm not even going to flinch."

The deliberate act of sliding the spoon behind Brandon's eye was likely more difficult than having his own eye removed. Brandon didn't flinch, but he did squirm quite a bit in his seat, and Noah was able to blame the delay on that. Soon enough they both worked up the courage to get it over with though, and with a satisfying plop the eye was dropped into the open glass.

The click of Professor Wilst's heel bones could be clearly heard over the buzz of uncomfortable students as he paced back and forth across the floor. Noah fumbled in the first jar and felt inside to grasp the squishy, slippery new eyeball. He carefully oriented it so that the iris was facing outward before placing it in his empty socket. The eyeball slurped into place as though it were magnetized, although it still felt a little out of place until Noah rubbed it to readjust.

"Professor?" Noah asked, straining against the darkness with his new eye. "I still can't see anything. Do I need to turn it on somehow?"

"I can't either…"

"Did I put it in wrong?"

"I think I see a little bit of light… oh wait that's coming from my old eye."

And other such exclamations rang out across the room.

"Ah yes, I almost forgot," the professor said, strumming his bony fingers along his chin. "You won't be able to see anything until you do a little digging. The bodies you are occupying are currently underground. Not to worry, I was careful to pick a graveyard that didn't use caskets, so you aren't going to have to break out of anything. From here you will be operating your zombie just like you learned last year. The body will already be awakened by your link the moment you inserted the eye, so please animate them now by taking hold of your stuffed animals and repeating after me: *Consurgo*."

"*Consurgo!*" from the class in unison.

"Now, mentally instruct them to dig upward by imagining you were doing so yourself, just as if you were controlling a zombie right in front of you."

Noah did so, although it took nearly a minute before there were any signs that his zombie was making progress. Then a shaft of light broke through the darkness on his left side, and he knew he must be close to emerging. He closed his right eye to keep from getting distracted, and watched the light growing until all at once his perspective broke free of the earth to stare across moonlit grass studded with gravestones. The earth was churning all around him as hands and elbows and heads began poking up through the soil.

"These bodies are all in the living world, right?" Jamie asked. "What happens if someone sees us?"

"All the better!" Professor Wilst declared. "These eyes tend to get worn out quickly, and I could use some extra bodies for my next class."

"I couldn't!" Jamie protested. "Can't we just chase them away?"

"Oh, I suppose. But if they leave any body parts while they're running, please don't let them go to waste."

"People don't just leave body parts," Jason Parson piped up in that know-it-all voice which might have seemed wise when he was a doctor, but now sounded quite condescending coming from the body of a thirteen year old. "How long has it been since you've been alive anyway?"

Noah's zombie had completely emerged from the ground and was shaking itself off like a dog. Looking down, he could see that he was using an elderly woman dressed in a filthy white dress. By the state of her hands, which were more bone than flesh, she must have been down there for a very, very long time.

"Look! There's a light on in the church," Brandon said out of the corner of his mouth. "Let's go inside and freak someone out."

"I think the class is supposed to stick together," Noah said. "Look, they're all gathering together by that old oak tree."

"If you're ever going to learn how to use undead properly then you have to actually *do stuff* with them."

"Says the guy who used a mermaid skull to cheat last year."

"Says the only first year to use a ghoul at all," Brandon shot back. "Besides, if we don't get any closer to the church, we're going to miss finding out what *that* thing is."

Brandon's zombie—a thin elderly man whose shock of white hair had slipped along with his decaying scalp to the back of his head—was already moving in that direction. Noah couldn't see what Brandon was talking about, so he urged his zombie to move just far enough to circumvent a few trees and get a clearer view of the church.

"Is everyone at the tree yet?" Professor Wilst was saying. "Please look for the woman in pink without a face and follow her lead. She will be running through some basic yoga moves that will help you become more comfortable in your new body."

Noah wasn't looking at the rest of the class anymore though. He was looking at the yellow eyes which glowed like embers all along a lithe, serpentine back. It must have been a Borovian Worm like the one he'd seen Elijah summon, but it was so much larger that it was difficult to associate them under the same name. Its body circled the entire base of the stone church, and as it made its way around the building it was steadily climbing toward one of the windows. The stone it had already passed over was scorched and blackened from the molten heat of its body.

"Professor?" Noah asked. He closed his borrowed left eye to open his right. The skeletal form of Wilst was bent in a low lunge on the opposite end of the room.

"Is calling the teacher all you ever do?" Brandon asked. "You're going to get us stuck in an hour of undead aerobics. Look at the roof—there's at least four gargoyles up there to protect people. Stop worrying and let's have some fun with it."

Noah closed his right eye and peered back into the dark night. The stone gargoyles had shifted from the four corners of the building and were now lined up along the edge of the roof directly above the demon's fiery head. The worm didn't appear to notice, and was instead focused on its task of licking the glass window. A trickle of smoke sizzled from where its tongue made contact with the wooden frame. The glass was warping and melting to run down the wall where it re-fused into dribbled icicles.

"The gargoyles aren't doing anything," Noah protested. "If there's a light on, there's likely people inside. We need to warn them."

"Yeah, great idea. Because nothing reassures someone like seeing their dead granny drop in for a visit."

The head of the Borovian Worm disappeared inside the church

window. Long stretches of its body spread and condensed to propel it inward, moving more like a massive slug than the winding fashion of a snake.

"I bet the gargoyles are going to attack any minute," Brandon continued. "If I were them, I'd wait until it was halfway inside so it couldn't turn around and bite them."

Noah glanced back into the classroom and nudged Walter on his other side. "Where are you and Jamie? Can you get to the church?"

"Not really," Walter whispered back. "I tried to get my zombie to do the splits, but one of its legs fell off. Why, what's up?"

An elbow from Brandon on the other side. "You're going to want to see this."

Back to the church, and the smoke that had begun to billow from the window. Nearly half of the Borovian Worm had to be inside by now, but the gargoyles still hadn't budged from their ledge. They were leering over so far that their claws clamping down on the gutter were the only thing keeping them from falling off. They must be seeing what was going on.

"Professor Wilst, there's smoke!" Jamie cried. "The church is on fire!"

The class erupted in commotion. "Not to worry, that sort of thing happens all the time in the living world."

"Aren't we going to help put it out?"

"With Zombies? Nonsense. All that dry skin and bones, you might as well be a walking torch. More than that though, fire is the quintessential tool for breaking the link between the undead and its master. If your zombie begins to burn you will feel it immediately and burn right along with it until you remove the eye. Living humans will do a much better job of it than we will."

"A demon started it though, and there are people inside," Noah said. "We can't just watch."

"I quite agree. Watching will only be a distraction from your lesson. Please remain focused on maintaining your warrior pose. We will all be quite safe this far away from the conflagration."

"I don't believe it. He just doesn't care," Noah hissed.

"Why should he? You can hardly expect a walking skeleton to be concerned about people dying."

"How about people being burned alive?" Noah asked. He couldn't wait any longer—his zombie was loping toward the window which the worm's long body continued to occupy. "I'm going to try and slow the worm down. You get to the front and try to help the people out."

"This is stupid," Brandon whined. "If they saw a zombie, they would run right back into the fire. And you heard what Wilst said about feeling the flames…"

"Now who is the wuss? Hey Walter—Jamie—you're sure there's nothing you can do?"

"I can crawl, but not fast enough to make a difference," Walter said.

"The Professor won't let us leave the tree!" Jamie whispered. "A few people tried to go look, and he's stopping everyone. Please be careful, Noah. I don't think he would be making such a fuss if it weren't really dangerous."

Fire emerged from the window alongside the smoke now. A dozen red tongues of flame licked up the side of the building, each stretching farther than the last. It wouldn't be long until they were tasting the overhanging roof, and from there the whole building would go up in flame.

All four gargoyles took flight simultaneously. Finally, they were going to help! Or so the hope of a fragile second promised. It looked like they were rising in preparation to dive, but as they continued to climb into the air it swiftly became apparent that they weren't coming back. Their hard faces with their upside-down smiles were lit briefly from below by the rising flames. Within moments, all four had disappeared into the night sky.

Noah's zombie recoiled from the heat—a blast of hot dry air that he could feel as clearly as though it were in the classroom. He tried to force his zombie to advance regardless, but the old woman he was operating instead dropped to her knees and let out a long, thin, piercing cry.

"Where did that come from?" Professor Wilst asked. "Are we missing anyone?"

By the time Noah was able to force his zombie back to its feet, the worm's tail had already completely vanished inside the building. There was no point trying to follow. The fire was at its hottest billowing out the window. Noah turned instead for the front entrance, quickly passing Brandon's zombie which had continued to stand motionless.

"Well? Aren't you going to do anything?"

"But the Professor said…"

Noah growled and Brandon fell silent. Waiting for help was a waste of time. Each step was a mental battle as he strove to overcome the zombie's natural aversion and inch ever closer to the burning building. The front door was still closed, and the metal handle was glowing hot. Noah didn't spend long enough thinking to let that stop him. The heat seared his hand as his zombie heaved the door open. It might as well have been an oven door for blast of heat which washed over his body.

Wooden pews to either side, smoldering and crackling. Alternating white and gray floor tiles as hot as coals. Long blue curtains engulfed in fire. Three figures dressed in monastic habits hustling away from the wooden altar at the end of the long chamber. Thankfully, the way before them was clear, and it looked like they would be able to safely escape. Noah allowed his zombie to lurch back and conceal itself in the darkness amid thick rose bushes nearby.

A window smashed outward, and the head of the Borovian Worm emerged. It swept the darkness with its gaze, the multitude of yellow eyes on its back staring in different directions as more of its body spilled from the window. Noah pushed his zombie onto its stomach and inched it farther through the thorny bushes, which fortunately he could not feel the same way he did the heat.

Enough of the worm's body was outside the window now for it to reach across to the front entrance. It pressed the length of its body against the wood and forced the doors closed again. This was no haphazard movement—it was holding the coil in place to pin the door shut and trap the three women inside.

Muffled screams began to rise from inside the building, along with the desperate flailing of fists against the opposite side of the door.

"Brandon?" Noah tried, but the other zombie was nowhere to be seen. The only way the people were going to escape was if the demon was moved, and the only way for that to happen was if Noah moved it.

Demons weren't stupid like so many people seemed to think. They didn't do things without a reason. From the helpful demons he summoned, to George's imp who lead him back to school, or Visoloth who freed the others of his kind. Their persecutions always seemed unjust, and even when Noah heard about the attacks, there was always a voice in the back of his mind that justified it as righteous or defensive somehow. But now there was the ugly, naked truth of the Borovian Worm's intent, and it was clear that evil was the only reason to explain this senseless execution. This had nothing to do with whose side you were on. Evil must be resisted, whether it's from your own kind or not.

The worm's head was beginning to circle back toward the window to watch its victims burn when Noah took his chance to charge. His zombie offered a flair of resistance to the heat, but it could not overcome Noah's focused anger. Perhaps the worm was distracted by his victims, perhaps its night vision was blinded by its own fires, but either way it didn't see him coming. Noah didn't slow down as he hurled himself forward and wrapped his arms around its neck just below its head.

It felt like being pressed against a stove top, but Noah didn't back down. The juncture buckled under the weight of Noah's flying zombie. The creature began retracting back into the window as it tried to shake Noah off. That forced him to cling on even tighter to prevent it from turning its head on him, turning up the heat up to eleven.

An inadvertent side-effect of the shock was for Noah to open his right eye. While the left eye observed his zombie catching fire from its embrace, his right watched his spirit body turn red and blister. Gritting his teeth, he suppressed the zombie's shriek and held on. He forced it farther away from the church door, which flew open as soon as the obstruction was removed.

The three women inside froze in the doorway, the church wreathed in fire behind them. Noah could only imagine what must be going through their heads to see a zombie wrestling against a burning snake. Noah's body was an inferno, and he knew he couldn't hold on long though—he couldn't even keep the building pressure in his chest from escaping. The anguished wail tore free from the zombie's withered throat. That seemed to shake the women awake, and all three of them dashed free into the night.

Not a second too soon. Noah dug his finger behind his left eyeball and gouged it free. The screaming didn't stop. It was just then that he realized his zombie hadn't been the only one making that noise. The heat had vanished along with his vision of the burning church though, and Noah collapsed back into his chair, gasping breathlessly. He didn't want to look up and see the class or the professor staring at him. Noah fumbled around his table until he found his original left eye. He stuck it inside the socket. Nothing—he'd put it in the wrong way round. He popped it out and put it in again and turned it around, the room silent the entire time.

"Noah Tellaver, you'll be staying after class," Professor Wilst said.

"Yes sir," Noah replied, not looking up from his lap.

"I hope it was worth it," the professor said.

"Saving a life is always worth it, sir."

"You'll lose points putting an answer like that on one of my tests. You can't save a life from death any more than you can save the day from night. You'll understand that by the time I'm done with you."

THE LIVING ROAD

NOTHING NOAH EXPERIENCED IN LIFE COULD HAVE PREPARED HIM FOR one of Professor Wilst's detentions. He had never been alone with the Professor before. Being part of the class with many other human children and animals made the skeleton seem almost comical and out of place. The last student had already left the room though, and the full intensity of that expressionless skull was bearing down on him. Noah shifted uncomfortably in his seat, noticing the skull track his movements perfectly with incremental adjustments almost like a machine might. Did the professor even remember what it was like to be alive?

"How are your burns?" the skeleton asked.

"Um, a lot better, thanks." Noah was surprised to have even forgotten about them for a moment. The pain had faded quickly after the link with the burning zombie was broken.

"One hour will be plenty to set you straight," Professor Wilst said stiffly. He broke the connection and strode to the back of the classroom where he began to rummage through a cupboard.

"Yes sir," Noah said, imagining all sorts of nasty things the professor might have him do to pass the time. Cleaning the eyeballs, maybe. Or stitching up wounds and reattaching legs on broken undead. Maybe he'd even have to 'reskin' one of them, a gruesome process that had been described in his textbook as necessary for long-term undead maintenance. Whatever it was surely couldn't be as bad as what Professor Salice could have come up with though. The professor returned with only a large jar filled to the brim with black liquid, giving no hint as to what was within except for the single copper wire which extended from its surface.

"You are hardly the first to maintain your obsession with life, even after it is gone," the skeleton said. "Rest assured, I have just the trick to cure such delusions." The professor set the jar on the desk in front of Noah, which caused the object within to slosh against the side. Something distinctly wrinkled like a brain pressed against the glass for a moment before becoming encompassed in the dark liquid once more.

"I don't think I need to be cured. It's not like I'm the only one obsessed with life—isn't the whole point of this place to teach people how to get back?"

Professor Wilst waved his hand dismissively. "Misguided, frivolous. Life is nothing but suffering and loss, and you will be much happier remaining undead as I have done. You're about to learn that for yourself though. Please insert the copper wire into your nose."

"What? Seriously?"

Nothing about the impassive skull gave confidence that Wilst even knew what a joke was. The empty sockets continued to fixate on Noah as he slowly did as he was told, resting the wire gingerly inside his left nostril.

"Am I supposed to smell something? I don't understand—"

The professor slapped Noah across the back of his head without warning so hard that he thought he felt his own skull rattle. His head jolted downward and drove the copper wire deep into his nasal cavity. Noah tried to pull back, but Wilst kept a hand on the back of his head and forced it to stay in place. All the colors in the room seemed to bleed and run together, swirling, morphing, and separating again into new shapes.

Noah wasn't in the classroom anymore. He wasn't even Noah. He was a child sitting on the ground and playing with blocks. But the blocks didn't stay put, and the colors didn't stop running. He was in his bed with cartoon sheets—in school laughing over a messy lunch—at home doing homework— climbing a tree in the yard, years older than what he had been only a moment before.

It was like moving through life on fast forward with one key distinction. When he saw his mother flash before his eyes, she wasn't just the blur of a stranger. This woman whom he had never seen before *was* his mother, and all the emotions associated with a mother couldn't have been stronger if he had been seeing his real mother. All the stress of school—the excitement of his first kiss—the agony of his dog being hit by a car—all experienced as powerfully and truly as though it were real, all happening almost simultaneously as one scene sped and morphed into the next.

Noah caught a glimpses of reflections from time to time, and watched this stranger's body growing older. He fell in love and had his heart broken, and fell in love again so quickly that the glow and the ache overlapped each other, mixing together into one powerful throb that threatened to tear him apart and promised to make him whole at the same time. He was graduating college and his parents were getting older—he was changing jobs, changing cities, changing houses—all the excitement, the hope, the fear, all running together into a single maddening noise.

All too soon his body slid toward the decay of old age, complete with all the pain and discomfort of each medical failing. Everyone he had ever loved was drifting away or dying one after the next, and each death caused the specter of his own demise to rear greater in his realization.

None of his understanding of the spirit world or logical rationalizations that this wasn't his real life made the least impact on the emotions he was experiencing. No thought in his head could allay the mounting dread of death, years worth of anxiety and doubt condensed into mere moments. Until the day finally came when the running colors faded to black, and a piercing anguish flooded his body, carrying with him all the regrets and sorrows and nostalgias with him into the dark. He hadn't even felt his own death as vividly as this.

"Is it over?" Noah gasped, back in his own body once more. He struggled to pull the copper wire out of his nose, but the pressure on the back of his head intensified and he was forced to remain in place.

"I have you for an hour," Professor Wilst said. "Your first time round took about three minutes. Are you ready to go again?"

It was impossible not to think ahead with apprehension. Noah was emotionally exhausted. Even the idea of feeling more happiness and love in the next life felt daunting and frustrating, because the feelings were so intertwined with grief and loss. Admitting that to the professor seemed like the profoundest betrayal of his defense for life, however, and Noah refused to give in that easily.

"Yeah, that was pretty fun," he said, grimacing as he heard how weak his wheezing voice sounded.

It might have been his imagination, but it seemed like Wilst's smile had a few more teeth than it had a moment ago. "There are twenty lives loaded into this brain. Let's see if we can go through all of them by the end of the hour, and see if you still feel the same by the end."

Noah's heart sank. He closed his eyes and went through the motion of a steadying breath, another lingering attachment to life that had never felt so shallow and meaningless. What if he really did hate the very idea of life by the end of this? Would he stop trying to return at all? Maybe he'd even join the Trans Dimensional Department and prevent other people from resurrecting just to spare them from that endless wearisome cycle. It was one thing to resist an unpleasant experience by staying true to your core, but three minutes in, and already this was threatening to change who Noah was at his deepest level. It was a terrifying thought.

"Excuse me, Professor?"

"Ah Elijah, how nice to see you again. You aren't still taking classes, are you?"

Noah opened his eyes just in time to catch Elijah winking from where he stood by the door. "No more classes, but I've been helping around the school until the road from death is open again. I came to let you know that The Matriarch wishes to speak with you in her office." Elijah glanced at Noah, then back to the professor to say, "It's urgent. Can't wait—not even for an hour."

"Of course she can't. If everything is urgent then nothing is," Wilst grumbled. "I'm sorry Noah, but we'll have to reschedule for another night."

"I can make sure he finishes the hour if you like," Elijah said. "God knows I've done enough of these myself to know how it works."

"Not enough apparently, if you're still talking about the road back. If you wouldn't mind though—it's already setup so all you have to do is hold his head down. He still has nineteen lives to go—don't let him get off with less just because we're getting distracted now."

"I know how valuable your lessons are, and wouldn't dream of it." Elijah moved to sit beside Noah who struggled to keep himself from celebrating too obviously. He mouthed the words 'thank you'.

The professor snorted with a sound like a vacuum inhaling sawdust. "Don't think your flattery will make me forget why you needed all those extra lessons in the first place!" He then shuffled out the door, muttering to himself something about how The Matriarch herself would benefit from a few lessons in patience.

"You're not going to seriously make me keep going, right?" Noah asked as soon as the door had closed.

"I could care less. I always thought it was pretty fun, but it's definitely an acquired taste," Elijah replied. He kicked his feet up on the table and leaned back on the legs of his chair in a game of chicken against gravity. "You'll probably have to do at least one more round when Wilst comes back though, depending on how long The Matriarch takes."

Noah winced as he slid the copper wire out of his nose. "Why are you really here? What are you trying to use me for?"

"What, no 'thank you'? No 'how have you been'?" Elijah's chair slapped back onto all four legs, and he began to rebalance once more. "I've been twice as good to you as I have been bad, so save your suspicion for when I've really earned it."

"Okay, you're right, sorry," Noah fumbled. "It's just this place.

These people. This stupid wire. It's hard to keep track of what's right and wrong when death is behind us instead of ahead."

"Speak for yourself. You might be staying dead, but I'm not."

Noah struggled against the little voice in his head that said how satisfying it would be to bump the bottom of Elijah's chair and tip him onto the floor.

"Why did you want me to have the mirror?" Noah asked. "I tried to look inside, but I couldn't make any sense out of what I was seeing or hearing."

"Keep trying. You will. You'll have to."

"Why?"

Thump go the four chair legs crashing down again. Elijah looked over his shoulder to make sure the room was empty. "Because I don't want my secret path to end with me. I want a chainer I can trust to keep it open and make sure there's always a place for spirits to make the journey without needing anyone's permission. I want that chainer who can speak to demons to help ferry people to the other side. And I want to make sure I know who you really are before I give you that power. Can you keep a secret?"

"You don't know any of my secrets, so I must."

Elijah laughed. "I wouldn't be so sure about that if I were you. I've been snooping around this place for a lot longer than you have. But I understand that prying isn't going to earn your trust. The only way to do that is for me to trust you first, so here goes. How would you like to visit the secret road that Olly and I have built?"

Noah felt the protective shield of his suspicion begin to relax. Maybe it was the fact that Elijah intervened in his detention, or even the simple earnestness which characterized his manner. It was common for older students to treat the younger ones with condescension at their unsophisticated understanding of life and death. Elijah didn't make demands like The Matriarch though, or threats like Professor Salice. Why should Noah rely more on someone like Brandon who had run at the first sign of danger than someone who actually had a chance of helping?

"Where is it?" Noah asked cautiously. "We aren't allowed outside school grounds alone."

"You won't be alone, you'll be with me," Elijah replied with a disarming smile. "I'll meet you at the graveyard gate tomorrow morning at dawn. Make sure to bring the mirror in your cart while you're at it. It takes more energy to work on chainers, but I know just the trick to get you started."

NOAH MADE a point to spend as little time in his mausoleum as possible. He parked his cart beside his coffin, and swapped out his books for the mirror. The world was already growing light outside, and the weariness of a long day would only be made worse when the sun began shining through him. If he couldn't get back before noon, then he'd have a hard time feeling whole again for his next classes. To make matters worse, The Matriarch had hinted that he would be playing sentry in the Netherworld again, and the thought of dozing off there was a terrifying prospect.

"Where are you going?"

Brandon's voice behind him made him flinch. He hadn't even noticed him lying on his back in his own coffin with the lid open. Noah pushed his cart another step toward the door. If he could get out fast enough then he could pretend he didn't hear. The *thump* of Brandon clamoring out of his coffin made Noah look around though, and once they'd locked eyes the option of a silent retreat seemed impossible.

"I'm coming with you," Brandon said. "I want to help."

"It's got nothing to do with you, and I've already seen how helpful you can be at the church."

The heavy boy's face darkened into a scowl. "That wasn't my fault. The professor told us not to—"

"Well now I'm telling you not to. I don't need you. Nobody does."

It was harsher than Noah had been planning to say, but it was too late now. Brandon opened his mouth as though about to cite evidence to refute him, but his mouth didn't close and no words came out. Noah took advantage of the opportunity and bounded out the door. Once outside, he turned briefly to say, "Sorry, I didn't mean it. I'm just in a hurry. Don't tell anyone I've been out, okay?"

Noah couldn't hear any reply. Fine, let him sulk. The graveyard in the early morning was such a peaceful place that it seemed almost sacrilegious to contemplate negative feelings here. Cool mist pooled around the mausoleums, almost completely concealing the gravestones of previous classes. It was odd to think that the same soul could have multiple graves in the living world and the other side. At least one of these stones could have even been for Noah, if he'd studied here in a previous death.

Then again, some of the 'graduates' could have also begun the road back only to fall into The Matriarch's Soul Net, never to return. What kind of person would build a place to glorify those it destroyed in the first place? The thought dispelled the tranquility and hastened his progress toward the metal gates. A heavy chain was wrapped between them, with a thick metal padlock fastening them shut. Noah squinted through the growing light. Where was he?

"Elijah?" Noah whispered as loud as he dared.

"Quiet."

Noah strained his eyes against the brilliant sunrise which streamed through the bars. There wasn't anyone on the other side, he was sure of it. But that had definitely been Elijah's voice. Noah began to pace along the fence, looking every which way for—

"And stop moving! How is running around like a chicken without its head discreet?"

The voice was coming from his feet. More specifically, Elijah's voice was coming from a ferret standing on its hind-legs on the other side of the fence. The ferret was dragging a stuffed elephant by the trunk, although it was so patched and worn that were it not for the trunk, Noah would have guessed it was the last dog at a shelter. The ferret stepped through the bars, one hand still holding onto the elephant while the other grasped Noah by the foot. The only warning of what was about to happen next was that the elephant was beginning to glow.

And grow, and grow, and then grow some more. Noah was transfixed on the stuffed animal as his mind struggled to comprehend its actual size. It looked exactly the same from one moment to the next, yet at the same time it always appeared to be bigger than it had a moment before. Then Noah noticed that it wasn't only the elephant: the ferret was growing to be tall as a man, the grass was soaring into trees, and the trees were vanishing into the unfathomable depths of the sky. The only thing that didn't seem to grow was Noah's cart and mirror at his side.

By the time the elephant stopped growing, it really was the size of its namesake. Slow came the realization that nothing had grown at all, and it was in fact Noah and his cart that had shrunk. No less shocking was the sensation of looking down to see a furry brown mouse body where his own arms and legs should have been.

"What's the matter? Haven't gotten to this in your transhumanism classes yet?" Elijah asked. The ferret busily parted some of the thick grass which rose like a forest around them to burry his elephant into concealment. "I'm going to leave my human remains here. I've got the feeling that The Matriarch has been trying to use them to track me. I like being able to wear my old skin, but there's something about that elephant that I just can't let go of. And who knows, maybe I'll see an elephant in my next life and it will be a trigger, and some of this will start coming back to me."

"Why do you get to be a ferret, and I have to be a mouse?" Noah asked.

"Because ferrets are cooler," Elijah replied, as though it was obvious. They were now easily able to navigate between bars of the fence with the cart and the mirror. "You want to be something cooler, learn how to do it yourself."

They both climbed inside the cart on the other side, which was still large enough to comfortably seat the two rodents with the mirror propped against one of the walls. Elijah sat in front where he was able to steer, which is a generous description for the type of erratic swerving that 'made the journey more interesting.' Soon it became apparent that they were headed toward the rocky slope toward the beach, which now looked like a titanic cliff with boulders the size of houses.

"How are we going to get down?" Noah asked.

"You have so much to learn, young one. We can leap through nether portals, or summon the wind to carry us, or ride on a broomstick. The advanced classes will teach you that there's a thousand ways to do it, but none of them are as powerful or effective as using the oldest magic there is."

They were picking up speed as the slope increased. Gargantuan boulders soared into the sky on all sides around them, and every narrow miss brought another monolith rearing into view.

"What's the oldest magic? Does it have something to do with demons?"

"Older." Elijah leaned hard against the side. The mirror rattled free from where it was wedged, and Noah had to dive across the cart to save it before it slipped out. There were no remaining obstacles before the sheer edge of the cliff ahead.

"What could be older than demons? Maybe the tree of life? How is that going to help?"

"Older, before life even began. I mean the oldest power in the universe. Are you ready?"

"You better not be talking about—"

"Gravity. I'm talking about gravity. Here we go!"

Three seconds. That's how long Noah had to consider his options. He contemplated leaping out to smash into the rocky ground, but he didn't want to break the mirror. He would have considered a second option, but he was already out of time. Elijah deliberately aimed the cart for a triangular stone that hung over the edge of the cliff. One moment the wind was whistling beside them, the next it was whistling below.

Noah kept expecting some magic to kick in at the last second, but the last second was several seconds ago and they were now plummeting through the air. He clutched the mirror with his mousey arms while his feet clung onto the side of the cart. His tail lashed out to wrap around Elijah. The black sand beach glittered below them in the morning light as the sunrise seared over the horizon. It would have been beautiful if it weren't for the implicit promise of mutilation which they were rushing to meet.

"Let… go… of… me!" Elijah shouted against the wind.

"I can't! I'll fall out!"

"Just do it!"

If Noah wasn't sure whether or not to trust Elijah, then he should have thought about that before now. There was nothing left to do but unravel his tail from around the ferret's waist and hope for the best. Elijah made a sharp salute, then raising his paws above his head like a diver, he stepped onto the edge of the cart. The rush of wind was flapping his fur in every direction as he dove. The sleek animal angled itself downward to minimize air resistance and disappeared. Noah spent his next solitary moment regretting everything he'd ever done since his death that lead to this very moment. It took all his courage just to look over the side to see what had happened to Elijah.

The ferret was nowhere to be seen. It was extremely hard to focus on anything that wasn't the wall of black sand which stretched as far as he could see. So what if his soul survived the crash if his spirit body was destroyed? He'd forget everything, and everyone. Noah, whoever that was, would cease to exist the moment his spirit brain was dashed into a million unthinking pieces.

But suddenly the ground wasn't getting closer, and that moment never came. Giant talons encompassed the cart and snatched it from the air. Noah didn't slow down in the least, but all his downward momentum shifted toward the horizontal—a lurching acceleration that slammed him into the back corner of the cart. Great black wings flared up on either side of him. The world was no longer a deadly blur, but Noah didn't relinquish his terrified grip on the mirror or the cart in the least.

Up to this point, Noah would have never guessed that birds could grin. A wrinkled, naked, pink head the size of a small car was bent around to stare at him though. Now it was laughing—a hacking cawing sound which sent fresh waves of terror ricocheting through Noah's mousey mind. The bird swerved into a lazy spiral before touching down at last on the sand. Noah tumbled out to press his entire body thankfully against the sand. To his surprise, he felt his human fingers and toes digging into the receptive beach.

"Didn't drop the mirror, I hope."

Elijah was standing over him in his human body once more, wearing his same uniform of grey pants and a short sleeved shirt. Noah sat up rigidly, a flare of panic surging to be felt amidst the rest of his overtaxed senses. Elijah bent over the cart to withdraw the mirror, still wrapped in its velvet cloth. He whisked back the covering and ran his hands over the smooth surface. Light from the morning sun caught the mirror to illuminate Elijah's face.

"Why didn't you do that from the beginning?" Noah demanded, spitting sand and wiping his face. "Your stupid bird could have just flown over the graveyard fence."

"It's an andean condor, and it's not stupid. If we flew the whole way, then one of the gargoyles would have tried to stop us. Besides, if I did that, then I couldn't have saved you and made you eternally grateful." Eliah tucked the mirror under his arm and turned to walk along the beach.

"It doesn't count as saving if you're the one who put me in danger in the first place!"

"Does too. Don't worry, I'll let you make it up to me."

Noah charged after Elijah and hurled a clod of sand at the back of his head. The older boy hunched and flinched from the impact.

"Now we're even," Noah said. "I could have thrown a rock and murdered you, but I saved your life by throwing sand instead."

"That's not the same. If you really want to save my life, and the rest of last year's class, then this is how it's really done. Make a note of this spot—directly below the third spire of the Mortuary, exactly between that rock that looks sort of like a mushroom and those leaning trees that make a big V."

Elijah turned to hand Noah the mirror before dropping onto his hands and knees in the sand. He began to dig with his hands, and

Noah had to scamper out of the way to avoid being hit by the scattering debris. It only took a moment to uncover what he was looking for: an otherwise ordinary stone with a keyhole in it.

"Remember these words too: *Voya Tomba*."

The sand around their feet began to stir. It circled them like water circling a drain, but it wasn't exactly disappearing. Instead the sand was fusing together, growing brighter and hotter as it did so until it seemed like they were standing in the middle of a circle of fire. Just as quickly it began to cool, not as sand but a black glass tunnel which led directly into the cliff.

"I call it the living road," he said with pride. "Much cooler than the road from death."

"Does this lead back toward the school?" Noah asked. "Aren't you afraid that it's going to be found since it's so close?"

"It has to be close. It connects with the other road, after-all. It just circumvents The Matriarch's lock on the door. What's the matter? You didn't think I built a new way back from scratch, did you?"

Noah swallowed hard. All this work, and they were going to end up in the same road with the same net as everyone else. There really was no escape from The Matriarch.

DEMONS OF THE PAST

"You were supposed to build a new road."

Elijah had already vanished inside the glass tunnel before Noah managed to get the words out.

"We were. We did."

The reply reverberated hauntingly in the confined space. Elijah looked different without the skin bearing his glowing tattoos. It wasn't just the lack of light, which surely would have helped in the dark tunnel. He seemed less confident, weaker posture, more vulnerable. He even looked a little shorter. Perhaps the transformations without the aid of his corporal remains had taken more out of him than he was letting on.

"No you didn't. Not unless it goes all the way back to life," Noah said, cautiously entering the tunnel. The glass was hard and cold under his bare feet. He had to move slowly with his right hand on the smooth glass wall as he followed Elijah's voice through the darkness. He carried the covered mirror tucked under his left arm.

"What's the difference? It'll get you there all the same. We got around the locked door which she was using to keep us out. There aren't any other obstacles, are there?"

The tunnel behind them rumbled briefly before giving off a long sigh like someone setting down a heavy load. A wave of sand began to pour across the entrance, swiftly extinguishing the sunlight as it concealed the secret way once more.

"Isai."

The word prompted a soft white light to radiate around Elijah's outline. It wasn't even bright enough for Noah to see his own feet, but at least it would be something to follow.

"What are you afraid of?" Elijah asked.

It would be wrong to tell an outright lie after the trust the older boy had already put in him. "There is something, but I promised not to tell anyone," Noah admitted instead. He hadn't planned to even say that much, but in the heavy silence he couldn't help but blurt out, "Something secret that The Matriarch doesn't know anyone knows, but if she did, then it would end badly for a lot of innocent spirits."

"You don't seriously think I'd tell her, do you?"

'*Do you, do you,*' repeated the echo, each time sounding more accusing than the last.

"I don't know if you know this," Elijah continued, "but even if she unlocked the road from death, I still wouldn't be allowed to go. Failed my final examinations—at least that's what she claims. I knew everything on there, and twice as much as Olly, and he passed just fine. Point is, I'm not exactly a fan."

"I know you appear to be a good and honest person who is only trying to help people," Noah replied, still weighing each word carefully. "I also know that ever since I've died, what appears to be has very little to do with what it is."

One of the outlined arms lifted as though to reach for Noah, but it stopped part way and pulled back. "Good. I like that," Elijah said, his voice subdued and distant. The light turned abruptly, and he started moving down the tunnel once more.

"You're not offended, are you?" Noah asked, hastening to keep up.

"Anyone who is offended by the truth doesn't deserve it. This way, don't fall behind."

Elijah's light was progressing to the left, but with Noah's hand on the right wall he could feel the tunnel curving toward the right.

The way must have split into two distinct paths. How many other invisible branches might he have already passed without noticing? And how could he ever find his way back out again if Elijah weren't there to lead? Noah released the wall and followed the light, stumbling until he found a new wall to balance himself against.

"Where does the other path go?"

"That's the one that connects with the road from death. We're not going to use it until I get a clear answer out of you about what's going on. The road won't help you understand the mirror, though. What you need is over here."

A sharp turn in the tunnel revealed a dull light which grew stronger as they continued. Shadows walking back and forth were visible on the other side of the black glass, and muffled voices were gradually becoming more distinct.

"… just checked in on Mrs. Reed. She's still having trouble breathing. The antibiotics aren't helping," a woman's voice said.

Noah paused to watch her shadow bend over something like a desk and set some papers down. There was another silhouette seated on the other side.

"Do you think we should call her emergency contact yet?" a male voice replied.

"Maybe. Soon. I don't know. Let's give her another hour, and see how she's doing."

"Over here, Noah," Elijah called. "Take a seat, we might have to wait a while."

More voices spoke as Noah continued down the tunnel, growing clearer as he went. More shadows, each slowly resolving themselves into nurses and doctors bustling back and forth, or patients in wheelchairs being pushed alongside him. The black glass was growing less opaque, and gradually it seemed to dissolve completely as it transitioned into a hallway.

"Where are we?"

The light was strong enough to reveal Elijah's features once more. He lifted an eyebrow and said nothing. His hands were in his pockets, but he gestured vaguely at their surroundings with an expansive shrug of his shoulders.

"I get that it's a hospital, and that this is part of the living world, right? But what are we doing here?"

Elijah sat down in an empty chair and crossed his legs, patting the chair beside him. "When a chainer looks into the Mirror of Ancestry, the mirror isn't powerful enough to bring back so many different faces from so many distant times. It needs a little energy boost—like the kind that's released when someone passes over from the other side."

"You mean we're waiting for somebody to die?" Noah tried to sit down next to Elijah, but he sailed right through the chair and fell onto the ground. Elijah grabbed him by the arm and hoisted him back up. Trying to sit on a corporal chair felt like trying to balance on a cloud: too much pressure and he'd sail straight through.

"There's a lot of energy that gets released when someone dies. We built this offshoot with a portal to a hospital to provide energy for the rest of the construction and resurrection ceremony. It's not like we're stealing it or anything either, because that stuff just gets wasted if nobody collects it. Have your mirror ready for when the next burst comes."

"Exploiting someone's death as a fuel source seems pretty messed up. What's to stop a spirit from getting people killed just because they need a boost?"

"The T.D.D. investigates that sort of thing. It's called the Department of Energy."

"I know about that!" Noah exclaimed, pleased to finally have some exclusive knowledge of his own to share. "I heard The Matriarch talking with the department head, Meep Warlington. The old minster of energy had his soul eaten too, so Meep got the job. So what's to stop *him* from killing people for energy?"

Elijah gave Noah a blank expression of dumb shock. "That's like asking why the police don't murder people. They just don't."

"But who would stop them if they did?"

"The people, I guess. They'd force the Prime Minister to replace him, or elect a new Prime Minister next time round. You seriously don't trust anyone, do you?"

Noah pursed his lips and said nothing.

"Anyway, it's got nothing to do with us, because we aren't killing anyone. We're just waiting for it to happen the old fashioned way. I don't think it's going to be long either."

One of the machines from the nearby room #204 had started beeping urgently. A nurse dropped an empty bed that she'd been rolling and hustled inside. A moment later the nurse stuck her head back out the doorway, a wild look in her eyes.

"She's not breathing! Get the tracheotomy kit, fast!"

Elijah stretched and yawned. Noah began to stand to go see what was going on, but he was pushed back into his spot. "Got your mirror ready?"

"We don't know she's going to die. They could still save her. You've got all kinds of powers—isn't there anything you can do to help?"

The waiting room was suddenly abuzz with commotion. The beeping machine increased in pitch and frequency, and people were rushing back and forth.

"That defeats the whole purpose of bringing you here today. I've been keeping an eye on Mrs. Reed for a while. It's her time."

Noah remained helplessly frozen as the activity whirled around them. Elijah pulled the mirror from under Noah's arm and pulled the cover off, placing it firmly in his lap.

"You've got to focus. You're not going to get another chance anytime soon. What do you see?"

Noah took a deep breath and closed his eyes, but he couldn't block out the sound of distress all around him. When his eyes opened he was looking at the same shifting form he'd been confronted with before. Nose, mouth, face, all in a continuous state of seamless morphing except for the eyes—midnight blue and curious.

"I still can't make any sense of it," Noah said, furrowing his brow. "It won't stop moving."

"She's not dead yet. Keep looking."

The eyes finally shifted. Now red, serpentine eyes with a long black slit down the middle persisted for several seconds while the rest of the face continued to change around them. Some of the features lingered for a moment: a hard jaw, cracked and ashen skin, thin bloodless lips, then they too were gone. Noah focused on the mouth and watched it moving. Whatever it was saying was louder than it had been last time, but the voices still clashed so discordantly with each other that it was impossible to decipher. The urgent beeping had meanwhile changed in tone to a long, uninterrupted ring.

"What's the reflection saying?" Elijah asked eagerly, leaning in close to hover at Noah's shoulder. Fiery sparks were catching in the air around them, lingering and crackling like the afterglow of fireworks.

"I can't tell. There are too many voices."

"Concentrate."

"I am concentrating!"

Even the red eyes weren't staying put any more. The pace of change accelerated rapidly, and everything was a nonsensical blur again. Whatever had been starting to form was gone, and it wasn't coming back.

"Time of death: 10:42 AM," spoke a loud, clear voice. The room was much quieter than it had been a moment before.

"Nothing?" Elijah asked, disappointed.

"Not really. For a moment I thought—" Noah cut himself off. There had to be some clue. All he could think was that whatever he'd seen wasn't human. Noah shook his head. "It did slow down while she was dying, and I saw some new forms that I hadn't seen before, but it was still going too fast."

Elijah sighed. "Ah well. There's always next time."

"Did it make sense to you the first time?"

Elijah nodded. "Maybe I've lived less lives than you though, or they were more recent and easier to reach. It doesn't matter. At least now you know how to practice. The more of them you see and the slower they change, the better you're doing. Don't worry, you'll get there sooner or later."

Elijah clapped Noah on the back and stood. His hands were

moving through the air, and a trail of burning light was stitching something into existence. He gave a little gasp as a bit of the fire caught on the skin of his arm where he had been accustomed to wearing his second skin. The fire burned itself out into a simple white gown. He took it to walk through the doctors and nurses who were exiting room #204.

"Cheer up, love. The worst part is over. You're going to want to put this on, and go to this address. The Trans Dimensional Department is going to explain everything once you get there."

Elijah emerged from the room again and gave Noah a helpless shrug. "Next time, eh? People are dying everywhere, all the time. Come on, let's get back to the school and hope no one noticed you slipped out."

"Did I screw up?" Noah asked, following Elijah back through the tunnel of black glass.

"You getting to know yourself wasn't the only reason I brought you here. I wanted a chance for us to get to know each other too, so no, it hasn't been a waste. When I'm headed back to life, I'll be glad to know that someone I can trust is out there helping everyone else get their shot."

"Elijah, before we go, I've made up my mind. It isn't fair of me to hold back something that could prevent you making it back to life. I need to tell you about the Soul Net we found…"

"Let's talk about Voodoo," Professor Yobbler said from the grinning side of his pumpkin. The forced nonchalance with which he spoke reminded Noah of an uncomfortable teacher broaching the subject of sex-education to a class full of sniggering teenagers.

Walter leaned back and sighed in anticipation. There was a particular eagerness in him that Noah hadn't recognized with any of the other classes. An intrigued hush fell over the class as similar excitement rebounded though the room.

"Just as the physical body can be identified by unique sequences of

DNA, each spiritual body has a singular energy signature which can distinguish it. The voodoo effect is established by the Loa demon, which has the marvelous ability to mirror its sensations and project them. This can be used to target either a biological or energy signature. Common applications include instantaneous communication, and creative curses. Please produce your dolls and form groups of three for us to practice."

"Do you mean we're going to practice on real people?" Jamie asked. Professor Yobbler began turning his head toward her, but it didn't stop until it had turned all the way around to show its displeasure. Jamie quickly raised her hand after that. Shifting uncomfortably in her seat, Jamie languished for several seconds under that silent snarl before she added, "I just mean to say that it wouldn't be very nice, and I don't want to hurt anyone, whether they deserve it or not."

"You don't want to?" the second face sneered.

Jamie looked helplessly around her, but everyone seemed to be staring down at their textbooks. "I won't," she said, a bit more decisively.

"Then it is your lucky day, because it sounds to me like you've just volunteered to be the victim instead. Twenty-one strands of hair, Mrs. Poffin. Provide one to every student. And one to me." Professor Yobbler's head rotated back to a smile as he turned to pace the room. "Everyone else, please produce your dolls and tie the hair you receive around its neck. Not too tight—neither the hair nor the neck will appreciate it."

Jamie looked especially pale, even for a spirit, as she moved around to let the class pluck strands from her head.

"Don't worry, he's not going to let anyone hurt you for real," Noah said as she passed.

"*He's* not," she said nervously, wincing as she pulled the hair free, "but what about the other one?"

"We'll be extra careful not to bother him so his head doesn't turn around," Walter reassured her. Both Noah and Walter glanced back at Brandon sitting alone near the back of the class, the same unspoken doubt nagging in their heads. He may not be acting out as much this year, at least not to them, but the cruelty of a bully sleeps lightly.

"Bowser, the doll is not a chew toy. Take that out of your mouth right now," Professor Yobbler said.

"Ysh Prfssr."

Jamie shuddered as she moved on. The Professor meanwhile began to follow Jamie around the class to distribute a small vial of blood to each student.

"On pages 47 and 48, you will find the designs for summoning circles appropriate for the Loa," the Professor was saying. "I've had to get special permission for this lesson, so please take extra care to read the instructions carefully to ensure none of the Loa escape. Once trapped inside their doll, these demons are practically powerless on their own and pose no threat. You may use a quill to duplicate their circles onto your desk with the blood. Today we will be using goat's blood, which is particularly adept at conferring thermal sensations. On pages 49 and 50, you will find a table detailing other common blood types and their specialities."

When Jamie had finished distributing she came back to sit beside Noah and Walter, who were almost finished drawing their circles. Noah recognized some of the patterns from Professor Salice's contracts, and he was excited to finally be learning a real summoning technique that might help when it came time for the rasmacht. It was a delicate act to moderate his enthusiasm in the face of Jamie's obvious dread.

"The doll will be placed in the center of the circle where a demon's host normally sits. Once the summoning is initiated, the Loa will try to escape from the doll. At this point you must take the silver needle in your voodoo kit and poke whatever part of the demon is sticking out of the doll until it goes completely inside. Only then will it be safe to remove the doll from the summoning circle. From that point on, the doll can be viewed as a miniature replica of the person who has been copied. We will banish the demons again at the end of class, so no contracts will be necessary."

To Jamie's relief, it took most of the class just to get the Loa to stay in the doll. They never got a good look at the demon, but after the summoning there always seemed to be little blue fingers poking out here or there, interspersed with the occasional top of a bald blue head or a spotted blue rear which stuck out of the most unlikely places. A swift jab of the silver needle always sent it back, but like a game of whack-a-mole there was always another target. Professor Yobbler was a flurry of motion with a needle in each hand. Even he seemed frustrated though, as evidenced by his slowly rotating head.

"They aren't usually this troublesome," Professor Yobbler huffed. "Something is getting even these minor demons all stirred up. There's no helping it—we're going to have to try again next class. I'll bring some extra-strength mule blood next time to make sure they stay put. In the meantime, continue practicing on your own until you're able to trap the Loa in a minute or less."

"Do you want to practice with us?" Walter asked Jamie as they were packing up their things. "You're going to have to learn sooner or later."

"Depends. Are you still trying to put a curse on Natasha's new boyfriend?" Jamie asked.

Walter blushed and scowled, but said nothing.

"Hrmm," Jamie grunted through pursed lips. "Maybe another time. I've already promised to help out Sandy O'Nell to repay him for helping me catch that runaway jinn."

"Sandy? That kid who looks like his past life was a llama in need of a haircut? Is there anyone you aren't friends with? Come on, Natasha needs us way more than he does."

"I wish you'd leave them alone. It's not his fault you're dead, and nobody should be punished for trying to live their life and be happy."

"I'm not punishing him for trying to be happy. I'm punishing him for not making Natasha happy. He's been seeing other women behind her back, didn't you know? I caught him with the scry ball."

"It's none of your business either way," Jamie said. "You can't put a curse on everybody who does something you don't like."

"Why not? Wouldn't the world be a better place if, whenever someone did something bad, they felt a red-hot needle up their ass?"

Jamie crinkled her nose and shook her head. "Noah—make sure Walter doesn't misbehave, will you?"

"Yeah, I'll help," Noah said, mounting the helical staircase. "I still need all the summoning practice I can get. How are you getting to your apprenticeship with Mr. Wolf anyway? Aren't we not allowed to go down to the village?"

"They've got a gargoyle on patrol now. He makes the trip every hour on the hour, and you're allowed to go with him," Walter replied, stubbornly bumping his way up the steps in his not-quite levitating cart.

"Lot of help that will be. I saw how useless those things are when the demons attacked the church. It'll probably just fly away at the first sign of danger."

"Have you thought about why they attacked though?" Jamie asked. "About all the attacks, I mean."

Noah frowned. "Visoloth told them about the... you know. They're all furious about it."

"They aren't attacking that though, are they? They're attacking people. I'm not saying that all demons are bad or anything," Jamie added quickly, "I know you wouldn't have—I'm sure *most of them* wouldn't attack—but innocent people really are getting killed. They have to have a reason... don't they?"

"I've got a theory..." Noah said. "There's a lot of energy that's released when someone dies. What if they're killing people for that? Although that still doesn't explain why the gargoyles wouldn't have tried to stop them. If they really were building up energy to attack the school, or the T.D.D., or something, then there's no reason the department's own gargoyles wouldn't interfere."

"All the more reason to practice your summoning," Walter said. "If we can get rid of The Matriarch, then they'll stop attacking and it's going to be better for everybody."

"We shouldn't talk about this here," Noah muttered. He glanced back across the bridge they were crossing on the first floor, although no one seemed to be close enough to hear. "Let's wait until we're farther from the school."

Jamie waved goodbye, promising to still meet them with the next gargoyle if she and Sandy finished early. Walter and Noah didn't have to wait long before the gargoyle arrived at the central tower to escort them down to the village. Dolly Miller and Rachelle Devon were already waiting there to travel to their own apprenticeships at Cassandra's Kill Counseling and Rogden's Exorcisms. Noah didn't know much about what went on at either of those places, but he'd often overhear the girls discussing it during class. Dolly stopped talking abruptly as they approached and cast a suspicious glance from under her dark bangs.

"...anyway, it can't be that dangerous," Rachelle said to Dolly, jerking a thumb toward Noah. "He snuck out of the graveyard yesterday, and he never got attacked by a demon."

Noah pretended that he hadn't heard. He focused on the gargoyle which had taken flight and was weaving slow loops around the students as they walked away from the school.

"No he didn't," Dolly replied. "The gargoyles wouldn't have let him."

"Did too," Rachelle said. "Rogden didn't let me out until late, and when I got back I saw one of the older boys sneaking him out through the fence."

"Do you think he was running around with his demon friends?" Dolly made the pretense of whispering, but it was clearly loud enough that she was trying to get a reaction from him. Their eyes met and she gave a sly grin. "Oh don't make such a face. Brandon told me there really wasn't anything to the rumor about your mother, and since he was the one I heard it from I suppose he could be telling the truth. Nowadays everyone is much more interested in figuring out where Mrs. Vanderlooth is getting her blood from."

"Don't get the wrong idea anyway," Noah said. "I was just doing a job for The Matriarch. I've got nothing to do with demons."

"Then how come you can speak demonic?" Dolly asked sharply. *"Everyone knows* that you're the one who freed the demons last year."

"Lots of chainers can probably speak demonic, and he didn't free them. He just read that their contract was up," Walter jumped in.

"Besides, the only reason everyone would think that is because you can't keep your mouth shut about things you don't understand."

"Well, I wish you did have demon friends," Rachelle said. "Then you could ask them what's going on with these new possessions." There wasn't the least trace of accusation or vitriol in her voice. She seemed genuinely interested, as though she were posing a purely academic question in class.

"What do you mean?" Noah asked. "What's changed?"

"Well there's more of them, for starters," Rachelle said. "They aren't acting like normal demon possessions, or even like a dweller has taken up residence. There's all these people becoming secretive and cold and cutting themselves off from everybody else though, and none of Rogden's exorcist techniques are making the least difference. The whole exorcism community is extremely concerned about it."

"How do they know they're possessed if they can't be exorcised?" Walter asked.

Rachelle couldn't have looked more bewildered if Walter had confidently declared that 2+2=5. "*Everything* that goes wrong is because of the demons. Didn't you know?"

"Most things anyway," Dolly added. "You can't exactly blame a demon if you stub your toe on a chair."

"Oh but you can!" Rachelle insisted. "You wouldn't have been distracted in the first place if there wasn't a demon playing with your thoughts. Or maybe the demon put the chair there in the first place. It's not always obvious, but if you follow any chain of causation back far enough, it's going to lead you straight back to a demon doing something he wasn't supposed to."

"That's ridiculous," Noah said. "People have to take responsibility for their own mistakes. It's not like everyone would be perfect all the time without demons."

"Why not?" Rachelle asked, mystified that this was even a point of contention. "All souls are created perfect. I always try to do the right thing, and I always would do the right thing if something else didn't stop me."

"What if a mugger beats someone up and takes their wallet?" Walter asked.

"Demon cursed them with anger and greed," Rachelle replied instantly.

"What if an animal gets sick?" Noah asked.

Rachelle rolled her eyes. "Please. Why else would people get sick? A perfect soul wouldn't create a spirit body that wasn't perfect. And a perfect spirit body would only inhabit a perfect physical body. It doesn't matter how you look at it: there can't be any imperfection unless it comes from something imperfect without a soul, and the only thing like that is a demon."

Walter and Noah looked at each other with consternation, neither sure how to refute her claim.

"If I keep it secret that you snuck out, will you promise to tell me if you figure out what the demons are up to this time?"

"You'll be the first to know," Noah said, allowing his voice to drip with sarcasm as it seemed Rachelle didn't register that sort of thing anyway. He was relieved when the cobblestone road branched off toward Montgomery's tower and they parted way with the girls who continued on to the village.

"It's all nonsense," Noah said when he and Walter were on their own.

"Yeah, I guess… maybe. If demons really don't have souls, I mean, then maybe there's something to it. And we don't know for sure that they do. They certainly seem different than everything else, don't they?"

Noah didn't reply. All he could think about was how disappointed Elijah seemed when he couldn't make sense of anything in the Mirror of Ancestry. If it was supposed to show the history of one's soul, then what if he couldn't make sense of it because the demons he came from really didn't have a soul at all? And what did that mean about who he was now?

Walter meanwhile checked in upstairs with Montgomery Wolf. He returned swiftly and pointed to a large amber colored orb in the corner that he said they were allowed to use. Walter unpacked his voodoo doll and a vial of mule blood from his cart and set them upon the floor. Noah opened their textbook to the pages with the diagrams began to copy the design onto a clean piece of parchment.

"What are you using for the physical connection?" Noah asked.

"Protection amulet." Walter produced a curved harpy claw on a string and set it on the ground beside them. "Darius—she calls him 'Dari dear', isn't that disgusting? Anyway, it turns out he bought an amulet from Pedflam last year and I've caught him still wearing it. So I bought the sister amulet, and he told me I could make a connection through that."

"Tormenting someone through a protection amulet? That seems a little…"

"Devious? I know, isn't it great?"

Noah wasn't so sure, but Walter seemed so pleased with himself and Noah felt isolated enough without alienating the few friends he had. If nothing else, then it was good Noah was here to make sure Walter's tricks didn't go overboard and really hurt the man. Noah lifted himself onto his knees to produce the Mirror of Ancestry and lean it against his red book-cart.

"It's going to watch us," Noah explained. "I figure if my other lives see me summoning the Loa, they might figure out that's what I'm trying to do and help me with my summoning."

Walter shrugged. "Couldn't hurt. You ready?"

The summoning came swifter this time, likely aided by the mules blood which seemed to slow the demon's movement from inside the doll. An extra pair of hands with probing silver needles did even more to keep the demon from escaping. Several tense seconds passed without a sign of the blue skin, then the doll's eyes opened and two fierce yellow orbs glared out.

"And let that be a lesson to you!" Walter shouted at the doll. "Hold him still—I'm going to put the necklace on now."

"Walter wait. Something's happening in the mirror."

"Yeah, but it's too dark to really see anything. Check out the doll though—it's perking up."

The yellow eyes of the cloth doll were staring directly into the mirror. The longer it looked, the lighter the image in the mirror became. A pale face was gradually becoming visible.

"What are we looking at?" Walter asked. "Do you think it's who the Loa used to be?"

"Remember what Professor Yobbler said: the doll becomes a copy of someone."

"But I haven't even put the necklace on yet…"

Pale skin. Curly ginger hair. Warm brown eyes. Interlocked fingers knotted on top of her head. The image was gradually becoming clearer.

"Did you remember to take Jamie's hair off?" Noah asked.

Now that the thought had been voiced aloud, there was no denying the resemblance. The woman in the mirror looked much older though—perhaps in her thirties—and her face was twisted into a mean scowl that was hard to imagine ever crossing the girl's fair face. She was gently rocking back and forth, her interlocking fingers continually rearranging themselves into new configurations.

"I don't like it," the reflection spoke. The timber of Jamie's voice was again familiar, but there was a terrible strain underlying the words that sounded wholly unfamiliar. "Don't ignore me. I'm nice." Rough, halting syllables, barely articulated as though there was too much tongue in her mouth.

"Something's wrong with her…" Walter said in a hushed voice.

"It's not," Jamie's reflection replied. "It's not. It's not. Don't say that. I don't like it."

Without provocation, the girl in the mirror stopped rocking. Her hands dropped from the top of her head and interlocked under her chin instead. The scowl melted into a giant beaming grin: childlike in its intensity despite her age.

"It's nice here," she said, looking around the confines of her mirror. "Really quiet. Not as nice as my home. There are flowers there. Blue and red and purple and…. and yellow—there aren't any flowers here. Where did the flowers go?"

The smile vanished, and she began to rock back and forth again. Her fingers were rearranging position once more, but it didn't look like an intentional movement. They never stopped moving for long. From her voice, to her features, to her ceaseless fidgeting, it was clear that this wasn't the same Jamie they knew.

"We shouldn't be watching this," Noah said. He reached for the velvet cover, but stopped when the reflection said:

"Stay with me. Don't leave me alone again. They always leave me alone."

Walter and Noah exchanged uneasy glances. Walter cleared his throat with difficulty before asking, "What's your name?"

"Jamie. And you're Walter."

"Yeah, how'd you know?"

The rocking stopped. Her face contorted in confusion.

"Did you have an accident or something?" Walter asked.

Noah shoved him and mouthed the word 'special'. Walter shrugged and threw up his hands as if to say 'that could mean anything'. Jamie didn't seem offended. She was smiling again.

"I hit my knee on the bed this morning. I don't break easy. When are we going home to see the flowers? I need a friend to show me the way."

"It's going to get easier," Walter suggested. "You're going to get really smart and have lots of friends when you're dead."

Walter knew it was the wrong thing to say as soon as it escaped his mouth. Jamie's eyes grew wide and startled, and her fingers pressed so hard against each other that they all turned white.

"Is a tree going to fall on me?"

"I don't think so—"

"Am I going to be hit by lightning?"

"Probably not—"

"How am I going to die? I don't want to die. Don't make me die—I don't like it!" Her voice kept rising in pitch and intensity. She was breathing fast. She might have still been talking after that, but it was more like a shriek than actual words.

"Make her stop!" Walter howled.

"Calm down Jamie. You're not going to die!" Noah said, unable to break through her misery. The reflection was shaking all over, and she seemed to be in enormous pain. Desperate, he seized the textbook and began to read from the incantation to banish the Loa, ending the incantation by shouting 'Dissipati' to be heard over her awful wailing.

The voodoo doll heaved a mighty sigh and black smoke poured from its eyes. The cloth figure slumped forward onto the circle of blood. Rolling gray clouds boiled across the mirror, and the scream was no more. It wasn't quite silence that replaced it though—underneath the scream was a tiny sniffle, and that was just as hard to hear.

The real Jamie—or at least the dead one they were familiar with—was standing across the room with her demonology book clutched to her chest. They must not have heard her quietly climbing toward them with all the noise coming from the mirror. She turned now without a word and raced back down the stairs.

Walter ran to the balcony and leaned over. "Jamie wait—"

"I don't like it!" she interrupted. The raw emotion in her voice was a perfect match to what they'd heard from the mirror. "And I don't like you."

The door slammed behind her. Hard enough to make all the crystal orbs tremble in their mounts and sockets. Hard enough to stop Noah and Walter from chasing after her. And the silence which followed still ached with the anguish she'd left in the air.

"Let's go back," Walter said, slamming the book shut. "I don't feel like practicing anymore."

HALLOWEEN

"As I'm sure many of you have already guessed, we will not be celebrating Halloween with imps this year," Professor Humstrum said.

It was already Halloween evening, but this was the first time it had been mentioned by any of the faculty. An excited murmur raced up and down the class, amplified by the intrigue from the actual classroom. The room was currently dressed like a colossal elephant, complete with a grumbling mouth and tusks embedded on one side, thick gray leathery floor and walls, and a trunk exiting through the ceiling. The two great peaceful eyes which took the place of windows were focused inwards on the orangutang between them.

"No—no—that wouldn't be safe. I was surprised enough to hear that Professor Yobbler was permitted to summon the Loa, but at least they're small enough to be stepped on if required. Having *even more* demons running around the living world is the last thing we need."

"Even more?" Noah whispered to Walter. There hadn't been any more news of attacks since the new batch of students had arrived, but none of the teachers had been keen to talk about it either. If Wilst's reaction to the demons at the church was any indication though, the students weren't likely to hear about it even if the professors knew.

Walter shrugged despondently and glanced back at Jamie and

Brandon who were sitting at the back of the room. She'd been aloof and distant ever since the confrontation in Mr. Wolf's tower. She hadn't wanted to talk about what they'd seen. If Walter had just apologized for talking to her reflection without permission, then she might have gotten over it on her own. He'd gotten defensive though, and accused her of lying about who she used to be. That type of reaction turned out to be just as disastrous a move after death as it always was before.

"We will, however, still be influencing the living world, as is a firm Halloween tradition. This year we're going to bring a little much needed joy back into the world instead. It will be your assignment to choose a human in need of help, and to guide an animal to their rescue. We won't actually be *forcing* the animal to go against their nature, but rather instilling a compassion in them which will inspire it to help someone on their own. We will be splitting into groups of three this time, and in the spirit of learning to work together, I would like you to only partner with students you have yet to collaborate with this year."

A dash of grumble was added to the murmuring soup, but it didn't ruin the flavor. People began to wave at each other across the room as chairs shuffled across the floor.

"Hey chainer—do you want to work with us?" called a sleek brown squirrel named Pepper. Noah didn't know anything about her, besides the fact that she'd made it through her whole life without being officially named, and that spirits had started calling her Pepper because she sneezed when she got nervous.

"Only if you can remember my name," Noah said, dragging his chair with difficulty over the rough elephant hide.

"Let's see who else wants to join first," Elizabeth Washent said, wrinkling her nose.

"Don't mind her, Noah," Pepper said. "Lizzy is still jealous that The Matriarch picked you to be her apprentice instead of her."

"Well you shouldn't be. It's the worst job in the world," Noah told the rabbit. "She's got me doing nothing but float around in the nether three times a week being a lookout for demons."

Elizabeth seemed pleased by that fact, as evidenced by her relaxed nose, and she didn't have any further objection to Noah joining their group. She insisted Noah go to lengths on exactly how miserable The Matriarch was making him until the rest of the class got organized.

"Once your group has decided which human you will be assisting, please raise your hands to let me know," Professor Humstrum said as he paced between the students."

"I don't know any humans I like," Elizabeth said. "Why does it have to be a human?"

"They're the only ones... well you know..."

"Being attacked by demons," Brandon voiced loudly.

The orangutang stroked his orange beard and nodded solemnly, passing by without a word.

"Well, I don't know any humans either," Pepper said, "so you're going to have to choose someone, Noah."

The subject could not be considered without his thoughts returning to his family. He had been tempted many times over the last few months to ask The Matriarch to use the whispering room, but something clenched inside of him every time he thought about their most recent interaction last Christmas. Mandy had made the decision not to have him in their life, and he'd respected that. Then again, if an animal were to drop by and help her, then she'd be able to accept the gesture without ever knowing it came from him.

"My daughter, if you don't mind," Noah said. Then considering a moment, he altered his choice. "My grandson, actually. He's only four, and he'll appreciate an animal friend more than anyone."

While the rest of the class was deciding, Professor Humstrum approached a tusk and stroked it, whispering something as he did. He then moved to the back of the class to retrieve a bundle of large incense sticks, each at least two feet long. Each group received two sticks, which the orangutang thrust directly into the wooden desks where they took root at once.

"Let the person who has chosen a human fix a mental picture of their subject while holding one of the emotive sticks. They will recite the incantation from the beginning of chapter 4. This will ignite the sticks, and cause a colored smoke to arise. Each color will represent the amount of each type of emotion the subject is currently experiencing. The second partner will hold the second stick, whose incantation will seek out a nearby animal and burn with their emotive spectrum. The third partner shall be reciting the third incarnation, and meditating upon compassion, which will be transmitted to the animal. If we are successful, the animal will then assist the chosen human as seen by a decrease in the red and orange colors, which represent anger, fear, and anxiety. You will notice that just as some hues blend together, so too emotions are often intermingled to create something new."

The students did as they were instructed, with Pepper holding onto the second stick while Elizabeth meditated upon her compassion. Noah read the first incantation, which caused a blue spark to race its way from his stuffed tiger into the incense. The colored smoke cycled through a few colors, but nothing flowed as powerfully as the orange and yellow which ensued. Noah felt the same fear flare within him as he focused his thoughts on his grandson.

"Hurry up," Noah told Pepper. She was still flipping for the right page in the textbook. "I think Lewis is in trouble."

Soon Pepper's stick was streaming its own smoke, with other multicolored columns rising from all over the classroom. Fortunately the elephant's trunk served as a chimney from which the smoke escaped, and the rest of the air remained surprisingly clear.

"Look inside the smoke," Pepper said. "There's kind of a black shadow over the color—do you see? It sorta looks like a snake. Do you think that's what we're connected to?"

"I think so," Elizabeth replied. "It says purple relates to compassion, but Mr. Snake doesn't seem very inclined to that. He's all green and proud at the moment."

"Well tell him to get over himself!" Noah said with exasperation. "Look, the orange in Lewis is getting brighter."

"I'm trying! He's not listening," Elizabeth complained.

"What is pride?" Professor Humstrum asked as strutted behind Elizabeth's chair. "Nothing but a celebration of life, focused narrowly on a personal experience. A creature will resist any attack against their celebration, but they will be open to expanding the celebration so that it encompasses all living things. Do not fight with the snake. Pride in oneself—the declaration that oneself deserves to be loved—is the first step on the journey toward realizing others deserve love as well."

The rabbit took a deep breath and expelled it forcefully. She closed her eyes and furrowed her little brow.

"It's working, keep it up," Pepper said. "It's getting more yellow than green now, which the book says indicates hope and excitement. No—pull back a little. I'm starting to see some anxious oranges in there too. There we go—we've got some nurturing and secure blues, just like we're supposed to."

"It's moving." Noah pointed at the shadow of the snake. "It looks like it's going upward—maybe coming out of the ground. I can see Lewis's shadow faintly in my smoke too. He's sitting with his hands over his head. I think he's trying to hide."

Noah's mouth snapped shut as he stared into the smoke. There were two other shadows on either side of his grandson's silhouette. They were only barely taller than him and looked like children at first, but as one of them turned it revealed the jutting ridges along its back. Then Noah noticed the long, thin claws. A pair of imps had found his boy.

"I think we've got a rattlesnake," Pepper said. "Doesn't the end of his tail look a bit thicker than the rest? It's so hard to tell inside all this smoke."

The imps were moving too. They were prowling on their hands and knees, their faces pressed to the ground. Sniffing. Lewis was trembling now, and his hands pulled at something over his head.

"Wait, I think he's in his bed," Noah said. "He's pulling the covers over his head."

"Well duh, it's like one in the morning," Elizabeth said. "What kind of party life were you expecting a four year old to have?"

A flash of orange flickered through the snake's emotions.

"Don't talk. Just concentrate!"

"Sheesh, okay."

"I think we're close," Pepper added encouragingly.

Noah couldn't understand why she thought that, but it was reassuring all the same. He briefly considered how absurd it was to be relieved at a rattlesnake entering the child's room at all. If something went wrong and it became agitated, then it was only too easy to imagine how badly things could turn out. Noah tried to concentrate on his own smoke and the silhouettes of the imps instead. Last year he would have had more faith in their decency, but all the attacks and relentless fear of demons was wearing him down. If Noah was being honest with himself, he really was beginning to mistrust them too.

The imps were beginning to climb up the bed. Noah wished he could see their emotive colors too, but it was hard to imagine a good intention for terrorizing a little boy. Noah flinched as he felt a hand on his shoulder, his whole body coiled tightly as a spring.

"Relax," cooed Professor Humstrum's soothing voice. "You and your human subject are linked now. Your fear is his, but so is your courage."

Noah nodded and willed himself the confidence of belief. After-all, Lewis was a chainer too. He'd lived many lives, and overcome many obstacles, and nothing had stopped him yet. A flicker of yellow daring spluttered up through the orange fear. And he'd need it too, because the silhouette of the snake had just slipped under the door and entered the room. The imps didn't notice until the snake's tail began to vibrate at the tip—definitely a rattlesnake. The sound startled the imps, who both tumbled off the bed, bounding around like distressed frogs. The two imps crawled over each other as they both lunged in the same direction at once, disappearing through what might have been an open window.

"They're gone," Noah said. "Can you stop the snake now? Maybe scare it off?"

"That's missing the point. We're supposed to inspire compassion," Elizabeth said. "Don't worry—look how blue the snake's smoke is now. He's quite calm."

"Yeah, but my grandson isn't. He's more orange than ever."

Noah felt his own tension rising again as the snake began to work its way around the bed post. It took all his concentration to push those fearful thoughts from his head and replace them with ones of gratitude and security. The effect was immediate: blue smoke began to compete against the orange, and Lewis wasn't shaking any more. The incense sticks had burned a little more than half-way through, which meant there was plenty more time to maintain the connection. Noah allowed himself to relax further, marveling as his grandson mirrored the feeling.

The rattlesnake slipped under the blanket and slithered its way around Lewis's leg. Watching their intertwined shadows was making Noah too anxious again, so instead he focused on the stick that Pepper was holding between her paws. He concentrated on how peaceful the snake was feeling, and he knew Lewis must understand that too.

The snake spent a full minute playfully coiling around the boy and allowing itself to be pet before an invasive strand of purple smoke entered its awareness.

"Don't worry, that's just sleepy and bored, as long as it's still mixed with blue," Elizabeth said, checking the chart.

The serpent slid gracefully away from Lewis in the direction the imps disappeared. Soon it too had vanished out the window completely. The remainder of the two incense sticks burned down, both blue and purple now as Lewis settled down to sleep and the snake returned to its hole to rest. Noah looked around to see the same colors reflected through most of the classroom. Even Brandon had managed to get a strong blue flow from his raccoon, although Noah figured that was mostly thanks to Jamie who was the one meditating on compassion.

Noah turned back to watch Lewis's silhouette gradually grow fainter as the last of the incense smoldered away. He couldn't always be there to watch over the boy. Wasn't George Hampton supposed to be keeping an eye on him? Or Samantha, how could he get in contact with her again? There had to be more he could do to keep his family safe against the demons. He hated them for—

There was that thought again. How subtly it had appeared. The thought of demons as the other, as the enemy. How could he think like that, when he knew full well where his own soul came from. If he'd seen a rattlesnake when he was alive, he would have made the same mistake of trying to conquer fear with hatred, reds and oranges which would only feed into each other and create something horrible. If he could accept that a soul dwelled within the snake, and that it was capable of compassion, why should he accept any less for the demons?

Noah didn't need to talk to a spirit to solve his problem. He needed to have the courage to follow the problem to its source and address the demons directly. The first thing Noah did after class was climb the stairs straight to the first floor and march directly up to The Matriarch's door. He was scheduled to perform his sentry in the nether tonight anyway, and even though he was over an hour early he couldn't wait to knock upon her door.

Several seconds of silence answered him. Then quite clearly, Professor Yobbler's voice said, "Ignore it."

"Who is it?" called The Matriarch in honey-sweet tones.

"I'm ready to begin sentry duty, ma'am," Noah replied through the door.

"Come back in an hour. Half-hour at least." That was Meep Warlington, Noah was sure of it. What could those three have to talk about?

"No, that won't be necessary, we were just finishing. Do come in," The Matriarch cooed.

Noah opened the door to reveal the three sitting around the desk, with Professor Yobbler's angry side directed toward The Matriarch. The old woman stood, brushing down her galaxy dress with real twinkling stars. The other two recognized the signal and stood as well, with Warlington bowing low over the desk to take The Matriarch's hand.

"Thank you again for being so accommodating." Meep tried to kiss one of her rings, but failed when she pulled away.

The pumpkin slowly turned to present the pleasant face toward The Matriarch. Both faces spoke the same words simultaneously, with the angry backside addressing Noah. "Sacrifice is the privilege the best of us are honored with."

Though the words were identical, the variation of tone and expression was so pronounced that Noah couldn't help but feel The Matriarch had been praised while he had been threatened. Did the students being trapped in her net count as sacrifices, even though they never volunteered? Noah imagined blue smoke pouring from his head as he nodded and smiled, pretending to only interpret Yobbler's best intentions.

The door closed behind them, and Noah was left alone with The Matriarch. She pressed her lips into a thin smile. Without a word, she began weaving the light into the Netherworld portal that Noah was becoming so familiar with.

"Could you teach me how to do that?" Noah asked.

"Yes. But I won't, because that would be irresponsible."

Noah bit his tongue to avoid pointing out how equally irresponsible it was to send him there in the first place. "Is it like summoning in reverse?" he asked instead.

"Don't be silly. Only demons can be summoned. How would you like being whisked away to a foreign world without your permission? Only something without a soul to ground it could tolerate such a thing."

Noah watched the circle of light coalescing into a portal and thought about his own death. Hadn't that taken him to another world without his position? Or when Professor Salice turned the whispering room into a portal that brought him back to the living world. It seemed like every time someone thought demons behaved by different rules than everyone else, they were wrong. The Matriarch was no exception. Noah put his hands through the portal and felt the cool gel of the nether slurping through his fingers. Hoisting himself up and fastening the silver thread around his waist, he began to climb inside.

"Do take care now," The Matriarch said. "No being eaten, and all that. See you again in a couple of hours."

Noah plunged into the blackness without looking back. Even if it took more than a few hours, he had no intention of coming back until he found out what the demons were really up to. Floating in the vast nothingness of the nether, he would have immensely preferred to have Jamie or Walter with him now. They would have only tried to stop him if he'd told them his intentions though, and there is no way The Matriarch would have let them through. At least it was peaceful here, and he wouldn't have to listen to their bickering.

Nevertheless, Noah felt less sure of himself now than he had in The Matriarch's office beneath the warm light of the playful wisps. It was hard to even imagine how endless the Netherworld was when you weren't floating in its emptiness, seeing nothing forever in every direction at once. If only there were more reliable landmarks…

"You're early! I wasn't expecting you for another hour," George Hampton said. He was stretched out in his old-fashioned formal clothing and suspenders, peeking over the top of a book he was reading titled: *The Inside-Out Head*.

"I wasn't expecting you at all," Noah said. "I'd ask what you're doing here, but I don't suppose you'd tell me."

George lifted the back of his pin-striped hat and scratched his bald head, grinning. His eyes twinkled with their own luminescence despite the lightless world. "Your studies are going well, I presume? Keeping up with your work?"

"Yeah, what about you? You can't be watching over my family if you're floating around here. I just caught a pair of imps trying to crawl into my grandson's bed!"

"You contradict yourself. It sounds like the imps were keeping a very close eye on him."

"But he was frightened, and they could have hurt him! You must know about all the attacks going on. I'd ask why they were happening, but I've given up expecting to ever get a straight answer out of you."

"A straight answer misses all the nuance of a circular one. I'm sorry my boy, I don't mean to play games with you. It's just my nature to want to know the essence of things without settling for superficial speculations. The fact that I keep returning here means that I'm still looking though, listening on The Matriarch's doorstep just as you listen on the demon's. I'll happily tell you what I find, if I find it, and hope there is generosity in your heart to do the same."

"I'm not staying on the doorstep anymore. I'm going to look for answers in the nether."

"What, at random?" George asked, fluttering a hand to his breast in exaggerated shock. "I can already tell you what answer you'll find: only silence. And she is more mysterious than anything you'll get out of me. If it's a demon you want to talk to though, I know a place nearby that's always inhabited these days."

George Hampton tucked his book under one arm and propelled himself through the nether by paddling his feet. Noah began to swim after him on instinct, but paused a moment later to reflect on the limited length of silver thread around his waist. He couldn't follow George far without untying it, and then there's no knowing how he'd ever get out of this place.

"You're not going to disappear again, are you?"

"If not in space, then surely in time. The best intentions can hardly avoid it."

Noah had come prepared to take such a risk. He untied his silver lifeline and let it hang in the nether so he could accompany his friend. No flocks of drifting imps, no twisting serpentine bodies, not even the faintest echo of demonic chittering from some distant source. But there could hardly be said to be nothing at all, not when the space within the Netherworld was so intricately folded around itself. The stillness gave Noah more chance to appreciate the hyper-dimensional geometries which caused parallel lines to pass through each other without intersecting, and produced shapes where the insides and the outsides flowed through each other in ways his mind could not understand. He couldn't have been more confused if he'd lived his whole life on the page of a book only to step out one day into the real world.

"Whose side are you on, anyway?" Noah asked his companion.

"I didn't know there were sides," George replied coyly. "If it's a game, I'd very much like to know who is winning before I choose."

"You weren't on Salice's side," Noah said, thinking aloud to himself as much as he was talking to George. "Otherwise you would have told him where my family was. And you aren't with The Matriarch, or the trans-dimensional department, because I know you think the Soul Net is wrong. You won't interfere to help the living, otherwise you wouldn't have let me die right in front of you in the first place. But you also can't be like the spirits in Teraville, because they're all afraid of demons. That only leaves…"

"Shhh…" George said. "Pay attention. What do you see?"

The problem wasn't that Noah couldn't see. The problem was that he could see too much. It took a moment of shifting his awareness from one piece of the surreal architecture to the next before he focused on a multitude of flickering lights ahead. The light they cast was so warm and familiar, but that made them seem more out of place than anything in this absurd world.

"Who put all these candles here?"

"Haven't you ever seen a vigil before?" George Hampton asked.

"There must be thousands of them though," Noah replied, transfixed. The burning candles were spaced a few feet apart and were suspended in the open nether. It didn't seem like the wax was melting, but around the perimeter of the collection were still numerous waxen puddles which had burned out and extinguished.

"Hundreds of thousands," George Hampton said in a hushed voice. With his spare hand not holding the book, he withdrew his pinstriped hat and held it to his chest in reverence.

"Have that many people died? Why haven't we heard about it at the school?"

"Oh that's right, humans light candles for the dead. No, that's not how it's done here. When the demons light candles, it's to pay respects for the ones they have yet to kill. The candles won't melt until the job is done."

They were completely encompassed in the floating candles now. The light which had seemed so warm a moment ago suddenly felt tainted: a thousand evil eyes all boring into them from every direction at once.

"If you had finished your earlier thought, then it might have gone like this," George added. "If I'm not with the spirits, or the TDD, or the living, then that only leaves the demons. And it's lucky for you that I am, because most spirits wouldn't have been nearly so tolerant if they knew that's where you came from too. Oh don't give me that face—I really have very little to do with what's going on here. I'm not the one who set history in motion, I'm just hoping for a nice mention in a footnote somewhere. The keeper of the vigil is the one you really should be talking to."

George Hampton pointed through the floating candles with his hat. Noah was sure there hadn't been anyone there a moment ago, but now the glimmering light was reflecting off a black, leathery hide. From the razor claws on its four feet all the way up to the tentacles swirling the nether into little eddies, the newcomer was unmistakable.

"I'd been hoping to find you again, Visoloth," Noah said. "I was worried you hadn't made it out safely when you were setting all the demons free."

"Likewise," the demon dog replied. The demonic language was as clear and expressive as always, and Noah could distinguish the cold suspicion in Visoloth's intonation despite his short response. Noah looked pleadingly to George for help, but the old man's face was carved in stone.

"Do you have something to do with all these candles?" Noah asked.

Silence. Visoloth must know how accurately Noah could comprehend demonic in the nether, and he didn't seem to want to give anything away.

"You haven't been part of the attacks, have you?"

One by one the tentacles retracted into Visoloth's mouth with a slow, slurping sound.

"What about the souls that were destroyed at the beginning of the semester?" Noah pressed. "Do you know why? Or who they were? Or when all of this is going to stop?"

The silence was becoming harder to bear, and Noah felt compelled to keep speaking faster and faster as he filled the space before Visoloth replied. "There isn't any reason to bother the living. They don't even know you exist. The T.D.D. and The Matriarch are the only ones to blame for the Soul Net—the other spirits don't even—"

"Are you any closer to completing your goal?" Visoloth interrupted. There was no missing the accusation in his voice.

"I'm trying. It's just that summoning isn't being taught much, and a rasmacht is—"

"We had a deal." The tentacles dribbled free of his mouth once more. He began to weave his way through the candles and circle Noah as he spoke, causing the shadows to dance over his skin like stripes. "You were going to show me how to become human. Or had you forgotten once I already followed through on my end? After I betrayed my master's plan?"

"I hadn't forgotten." Noah turned to keep his eyes on Visoloth as he circled, even though he could see him perfectly well without being pointed in his direction. There was something low and dangerous in the demon's voice, and letting it get behind him left Noah feeling too vulnerable.

"I've been looking for answers in my past lives, but I haven't been able to understand them yet. As soon as I learn something, I'm going to tell you. We're on the same side—you have to trust me."

"I do not."

Noah turned desperately to George Hampton. The old man remained motionless at the edge of the field of burning candles with his hands behind his back. His cold, hard gaze was barely visible beneath his pin-striped hat. Noah looked away and held himself still, allowing Visoloth to finish circling around behind him.

"I trust you though," Noah said. He was aware of the demon stalking toward him from behind, and his whole body ached from the tension of forcing himself not to react.

"You do not."

"You're wrong." Noah had to work his way slowly through the heavy guttural syllables of the demonic tongue. "I only want everyone to stop fighting. I'm hiding nothing from you."

"How many candles do you count?" Visoloth asked, an amused intrigue interwoven with his words.

Noah shifted his awareness throughout the field, but he couldn't even begin to count. "Too many."

"New Years Day. The demons will attack the city of your birth, and a thousand candles will go out. You will not interfere. You will not warn anyone. You will not save a single soul. This is how trust shall be tested, and this is the test you must pass to receive my help again."

"You can't…"

Whatever plea was forming died on Noah's lips. He could understand the implacable intention those words were laden with. No protest was possible, but he knew he wouldn't forgive himself if he didn't at least try. "Don't give them a reason to hate you, or it will never stop."

"They don't need a reason to hate us."

Visoloth was close enough to Noah that he could feel the tip of a tentacle tracing down the back of his calf. He couldn't get his body to relax, but he still he refused to turn around and show his fear. Noah concentrated on George Hampton's emotionless visage, but he couldn't distract himself from those terrible thoughts.

"Trust me, trust us," Visoloth said. "Trust who you used to be, and do not fight against your nature. The purges must begin again. You have my word that no blood shall be spilled, save that which the balance of the universe demands. Speak of this to no one, and together we will have the resolve to accomplish where Salice fell short. Let me trust you, and we will destroy the Soul Net once and for all."

DWELLER STUDIES

THE IMPENETRABLE WALLS OF CLOUDS THAT ROLLED OVER THE ISLAND of Barbaros seemed to muffle all sounds, and an unusually heavy chill frosted the air without the satisfaction of snow. Professor Humstrum had taken a break from his usual curriculum to instruct the students how to disassociate their spiritual bodies from the cold, although it wasn't unusual to still see first years huddled inside their carts with a thick blanket thrown over the top. Professor Wilst admonished this and frequently pointed out that bundling up was worthless now that their bodies no longer generated heat. Some familiar habits were hard to break, however, and Noah could only feel sorry for those who couldn't get over the fact that they were dead.

It wasn't the weather that was making Noah feel deflated and alone though. Jamie had sworn she didn't want to talk about what they'd seen in the mirror, but she was spending a lot of time working with Brandon now and Noah didn't want to deal with him. Walter and Jamie still weren't speaking, however. His residual bitterness seemed to overflow onto Noah, and he'd often complain how unfair it was that Jamie had forgiven Noah but not him. Their relationship was further strained as Noah had put his foot down about not helping

Walter with his voodoo revenge, and the two of them could barely spend time together without snapping at one another.

It was all so stupid, but when Noah was being honest with himself, he knew that it was as much his own fault for not getting along with his friends. He was keeping his precognition of the demon attack secret from everyone, and it was eating him up inside. There was nothing he could do that wouldn't result in him blaming himself for how it turned out. Noah desperately wanted to confide in his friends, but every time it felt like he had the chance to bring it up, he'd fumble the words and the opportunity would be lost. Part of him was even bitter that his friends didn't try harder to get him to open up, although of course that was ridiculous because he was often the one being distant and cold.

The only person Noah was really getting along with was Elijah. He visited Noah frequently in the library to check on his progress with the mirror, and he was the only one who remained relentlessly positive about the future.

"Just think how marvelous it will be to have our very own shortcut to life," Elijah said one day. He was lounging on top of one of the library tables beside Noah while he studied. Or rather on bottom, as they were hanging upside-down on the underside of a platform. All the right-side up tables were now occupied by students preparing for their midterm exams though, and upside-down was still better than the dark and frosty graveyard.

"No tests to pass, no fees to pay, no rules or schedules or dogmas to adhere to," Elijah sighed, quite content to talk to himself. "And most importantly no net—"

Noah slammed his demonology book shut and glared at Elijah. "You promised me you wouldn't talk about it."

"I just wanted to see if you were listening," Elijah replied with a wolfish grin. "You really are afraid of The Matriarch, aren't you? Think she's hiding behind every bookshelf?"

"Two chainers plotting together, one of which doesn't even attend classes anymore? Yeah, what's suspicious about that?" Noah asked.

"Not much, honestly," Elijah said, stretching languidly. "There were almost a dozen of them in the new first year class."

"I've heard there were a few on an airplane, but not that many. That's pretty unusual, isn't it?"

"Not if someone is killing them on purpose." Elijah slipped effortlessly from the table, unconcerned by the treacherous drop from the underside of the platform.

Demons? Noah's mind raced to his family, then to Professor Salice who'd wanted to kill them last semester. But he said he'd only needed two to summon the rasmacht, and besides, he was still locked away in one of The Matriarch's soul stones. If he wasn't the one killing them…

"Oh don't give me that face—you're still my favorite young 'un," Elijah said, apparently misinterpreting Noah's distress. "I've been keeping tabs on them though. You'll never guess how the rest all met their end."

"Gargoyles," Noah said at once.

"You too, huh? One of them even spotted a gargoyle outside the plane before it began to dive. What are the odds…"

Their conversation was interrupted by a large harpy—it might have been Ikella, but it was so hard to tell them apart—fluttering through the rafters.

"Second years. Fourth floor demonology. Room change." *Indistinguishable shriek.* "Third room. Fourth floor. Room change—time is now."

"No harpies in the library!" Mrs. Vanderlooth scolded from somewhere below. "Out—out—you're worse than the pigeons."

"Bloody lady hungry?" *Indistinguishable shriek.* "Bloody lady angry!"

"I've got to go to class," Noah said, gathering up his parchment and books. "Just don't go around blabbing all your secrets, okay? It doesn't make you cool, and it doesn't help anybody."

Elijah slapped both hands around his face in mock astonishment. "But *dahhhling* don't get jealous. You know you're the only chainer for me!"

Noah hurried away without dignifying that with a response. He didn't know how Elijah could be so blasé about such serious matters.

Wasn't he even curious what the T.D.D. was really up to? He had to be if he was going through so much trouble to investigate matters, not to mention all the work that went into his secret path to circumvent the department's closure altogether.

Noah worked through the problem as he descended the helical stairway toward the second floor. If the department was just trying to capture as many chainer souls as they could in the Soul Net, then The Matriarch wouldn't have failed Elijah when he was taking his final examinations. As much as he might goof around, he certainly wasn't lacking in magical ability. So why else would someone want to start moving chainers from the living world?

Moving them. Noah reprimanded himself for the thought. They weren't being moved, they were being killed. Their lives had meaning. They had people who loved them, and mourned for their loss. It didn't matter if the rest of this place seemed to forget that; Noah couldn't let himself become one of them.

The new demonology room was clearly marked with the burning Roman numerals. Even without the marking, it was obvious where to go because of the press of students piling in around the door. It wasn't until Noah had crossed the geometric light bridge that he saw what was really drawing all the attention though.

"Is it alive?" Jason Parson asked, invisible near the front.

"Quit shoving!" from Grace Harlow, whose thin body bent and twisted like a reed as she tried to get a better view.

"Can someone lift me up?" Elizabeth Washent's voice came from somewhere amidst the legs. "I can't see a thing!"

"I can't imagine why The Matriarch thought this was a good idea," Professor Wilst snapped from somewhere in the middle. "If the students can't even watch respectfully, then they simply aren't mature enough to handle it."

"You don't need to be so rough," a man's voice grunted. "I don't even care for children all that much. Haven't had more than a handful my whole life."

"There will be no children today, Billibus. We have something else planned for you."

Noah was surprised to hear Professor Yobbler's voice without seeing him. He was certainly tall enough that he should have been visible no matter how many students were pushing their way in front. The curiosity was in no way lessened when Professor Wilst stood to his full height while hoisting Yobbler's detached head in his arms to give it a better view.

"What's going on?" Noah asked Jamie, who was standing at the back of the group, likely too polite to push her way in.

"It's a human—a living one. He's real, with flesh and blood and everything," she said. "I got a glimpse of him before everyone started getting in the way."

"He must be terrified," Noah said. "Even if he can't see us, he should at least be able to see Professor Wilst. What's he doing here?"

"He's definitely not human. A human wouldn't be this big a deal." It was Walter who had just ducked his way out of the crowd.

"I know a human when I see one," Jamie interrupted. "I'm not stupid."

"I never said you were—"

"He's got a big red beard, and a big belly, and you can tell he's got blood by the way he was all flushed. He's absolutely human."

"Well duh, the outside is human. But he's got a dweller in his head. That's the only thing people are interested in."

"That's enough!" Yobbler roared. "Let's make some space and get him inside."

The crowd parted sufficiently for Professor Wilst to make it to the classroom door. He continued to carry Yobbler's head, which looked so ludicrous now that it didn't have a body. Wilst carried the head in one hand by the green stem on top while the other hand held a leather corda which was attached to the human's neck like a leash. Noah finally caught a glimpse the large man, dressed in jeans and a red and black flannel shirt, as he was pulled to his feet to stagger along behind the professor.

"Did you see his eyes?" Brandon asked, pushing free from the dispersing students. He noticed Noah and Walter for the first time, but quickly turned his attention back to Jamie. "They're all black. No iris or sclera or anything—just black."

"The sclera is the white part—" Walter began.

"I know what a sclera is," Jamie said testily. "I got a hundred percent on Wilst's last quiz, you know."

Walter gave Noah a helpless pleading look, but Noah just shrugged. The students began filing into the room after the two professors. "I thought dwellers were illegal. Where did it come from?"

"Do you ever think before you talk?" Brandon asked. "They can't make an entire species illegal. That's like making it illegal to be a cat."

"No it's not," Walter argued. "Dweller's aren't a species. Anyone can choose to be a dweller if they figure out how. It's more like making it illegal to be an asshole, which it's lucky for you that it's not."

Noah wasn't sure what he was expecting upon entering the room, but it certainly wasn't a vegetable garden. Freshly plowed soil formed rows along the ground, and thick leafy vines sprung up everywhere to grow in an ordered and deliberate fashion. Bright orange pumpkins, brown ripe squashes, and bulbous colored gourds of all shapes and sizes grew abundantly without any apparent source of sun. The room was garnished with a thick cloud of will o' wisps, however, and these floated diligently through the garden to groom and brighten the healthy plants.

"Are you considering an upgrade, Mr. Yobbler?" Wilst asked the pumpkin he was carrying. It was impossible for sarcasm to infiltrate the excessively dry rasping voice, but Noah was sure there was an underlying hint of condescension in the skeleton's tone.

"Ah ah ah, someone is getting jealous," the pleasant side of Yobbler replied. "A fat, juicy pumpkin must be a much more satisfying host than that old bag of bones. Yes yes, get Billibus down on his knees over here. Don't worry—the plants will hold him still."

It was unclear how much the human understood, but the wild-eyed terror on Billibus' face was universally recognized. He staggered backward toward the door, shoving Rachelle and Dolly Miller backward as he did so. The wild-eyes never strayed from Professor Wilst even as he tripped over one of the long vines. At first it looked like an accident, but before he could rise the vine had snaked its way around his ankles to hold him firmly in place. The man scrambled on his hands and knees, attempting to free himself. More vines seized his wrists, then around his neck, quickly immobilizing him as they tightened their hold.

"I don't like it!" Jamie protested loudly. She seemed momentarily surprised by her own exclamation, but even as both professors looked in her direction, she continued steadfast. "You're hurting him. I don't care what we're supposed to learn from this, I'm not going to listen until you let him go."

Jamie was visibly wilting beneath the collective scrutiny. She looked like she was about to turn around and run straight from the room when Brandon stepped up by her side.

"I'm with her," Brandon said. "This is the type of thing a demon would do."

"It's the type of thing you'd do, you pretentious brat," Walter muttered under his breath.

"Sit down, Mrs. Poffin," Wilst replied cooly. "Sit down, Mr. Hides. Do not let the dweller fool you. There is no harm being done."

Jamie tucked her skirt between her legs and sat down heavily on a pumpkin, looking rather deflated. Brandon continued to stand for a minute with a vacuous expression as though he'd forgotten his own name. He snapped to, looking rather embarrassed, and swiftly sat on a thick green gourd nearby.

"Please be patient," Wilst continued. "What you're about to witness may be distressing for you, but education so very often is until the lesson has sunk in."

"Help… me…" choked the man. He was staring right at Jamie now. His mouth continued to work as though he wanted to say more, but the vine was so tight around his throat that nothing but a thin wheeze escaped his lips. A bright red flush crept around the edges of his beard, quickly progressing to the livid purple of suffocation.

"I'm going to scream!" Jamie shot back.

"Go ahead. I doubt you'll be the only one," Yobbler's grinning face replied.

The pumpkin vine flexed and snapped taunt. The human's head flashed an even ghastlier shade before popping off completely and flying into the air. Yobbler was right—Jamie wasn't the only one screaming. Sudden cries from all around the room competed to reach the most piercing crescendo, punctuated only by Yobbler's deep guffawing laugh.

There wasn't any blood. The first screams cut short as they realized this. The headless body slumped motionless against the ground, and the severed head was beginning to swear from where it rested atop a wide green leaf. One by one, the students fell silent until it became easier to understand what the head was saying.

"... you could have just asked. I would have taken it off myself if you'd just asked, but NOOO... I didn't even have to be here, you know. I could have stayed where I was in the woods and been perfectly happy with my old head for years to come. I had a house. A perfectly nice one, built it myself from interlocking logs. Any vagabond is going to move in now, and there's nothing I can do. I don't suppose you care about any of that though, do you?"

The students began to push one another as they crowded in to get a better look. The headless body remained suspended upright by the vines, and the neck already had a fresh pink layer of skin sealing the top without any messy bits like a spine to be seen. The stump of the decapitated head wasn't visible where it sat on some vegetation, but something under there seemed to be moving.

"Would one of you mind giving me a lift?" Professor Yobbler asked from where his pumpkin sat on the ground.

No one made the least move to go to his aid. If anything, the space around Yobbler grew as the students shuffled backward, each determined not to meet his gaze.

"It was a good, strong body," the decapitated head sighed. "It could carry a goat for miles and miles without getting tired. My new ones had better be at least as good. Don't think I'm going to go along with an old woman with a bad back—I'll file a complaint with The Matriarch, that's what I'll do. Then we'll see who gets the cushy professorship, and who has to live in exile."

Professor Wilst obliged in lifting Yobbler's pumpkin from the ground and setting it upon the neck of the headless body. The skeletal hands moved deftly as they spun the pumpkin several times around as though screwing on a bottle-top. The last revolution brought Yobbler's angry side around to the front once more. A shiver ran through the body, and the first thing he did once he was in control was slap Wilst's hand away. The vines redoubled their effort to pin the body once more.

"Don't you recognize your master?" Yobbler spat several pumpkin seeds and a little blood from his fearsome mouth. "Be off with you."

The vines relinquished their hold on Yobbler's new body and slithered back amidst the vegetables. He stood and brushed himself down, scowling at everyone who had the misfortune of standing in his line of sight.

"Eww look at the head!" Jennifer Alaski squealed, gripping her friend Dolly by the arms as she hid behind her.

The collective attention shifted back toward the decapitated head on the ground. Toward the shifting, squirming movement that was coming from underneath the stump. It was now apparent that hundreds of little worms were wiggling free and spreading across the vegetable garden. It wasn't just the neck either: worm-shaped strips of skin were peeling away from the face, thick wild hair was knotting together and crawling away, and more worms which appeared to be made of brain matter dribbled out of the nose like a faucet. In seconds the entire head had deconstructed into a multitude wiggling worms which frantically burrowed into the soil.

It took a long time for the class to settle down after that. Bowser was howling and running around in circles, Elizabeth was bouncing off the walls trying not to touch the ground, and all the other students were madly climbing over each other in an impossible pursuit to get out of the way of the manifold worms. It wasn't until the creatures had largely dispersed and disappeared from view that it got quiet enough for Professor Yobbler's booming voice to reclaim the floor.

"The next person to make a sound will have their head removed next!" he bellowed.

Professor Wilst placidly spun the pumpkin with a flick of his wrist so that the friendly face returned to the front. "I think we've had quite enough disturbance without such idle threats, don't you, professor?"

Neatly folding one arm behind his back, Wilst began to strut up and down the garden rows while addressing the students. "The spectacle you have just witnessed is the natural reproduction process of a dweller. As you may remember from last semester, a dweller does not possess a physical body of its own, but rather inhabits a host body.

"The dweller begins its life cycle as a single worm which infiltrates its host, gradually taking over its mind and converting the victim's head into more dwellers. While undetectable from the outside, the host experiences a fractalization of its mind which is almost impossible to resist. He will begin to hear voices, and develop multiple distinct personalities, until at last he and the dwellers reach a peaceful cohabitation or the host is killed and completely replaced. Upon the removal of the head, the dweller will divide and seek out new hosts—" Jennifer began to squeal again, but Wilst placed a hand on top of her head and she quieted down —"new *vegetable* hosts, in this case. We have provided this garden for them to inhabit, so no mind-control or killing will be necessary today."

One by one, all eyes began to turn on Professor Yobbler, who was currently readjusting his pumpkin head so that it fit more naturally onto his new body.

"Yes," Professor Yobbler said, shifting uncomfortably from one foot to the other. "Yes, I am."

The buzz of whispers cut abruptly short as he continued.

"The fact of the matter is that we dwellers haven't always been on the best of terms with the rest of the spiritual community. We can thank your gracious Matriarch for standing up to the T.D.D. guidelines and fighting for our acceptance, and it is to her I am grateful for being allowed to teach here. If it weren't for the rising threat of demon incursion, my people might have continued being seen as the *other*. In these trying times, it is imperative that all spirits learn to co-exist. To have a soul at all means that we have more in common than we are different, and we must all stand together in the face of the demonic *abominations*. As we will soon learn, there is nothing quite as effective as dwellers at repelling demons. They won't come within a mile of one of us when they can help it, contract or no. It's a pity the department doesn't trust us more, or we could do away with those silly gargoyles for good."

Professor Yobbler proceeded to unearth the various bulbous vegetables and show where the dwellers were burrowing in from the bottom. He explained how it would take about a week for them to make their home inside, thus turning the gourds into their new heads. Professor Wilst meanwhile spent most of the class with his back against the wall, his passive skull tilted back to survey the whole scene with polite disapproval. He only stepped forward once more when Yobbler was content that every gourd in the room had become occupied.

"Aren't you forgetting something, professor?" Wilst asked. It was the type of question that would reduce a student into shivering stammers, but Yobbler remained unimpressed.

"How could I remember if I was?" the pumpkin-headed professor replied peevishly from the back of his head. Then from the front, he continued to address the class with, "Next week we will return to this room to carve faces for our new friends. Ultimately the face will not determine the personality any more than it does with a human, but it will be the dweller's first impression of themselves, so we must all take extra effort to give them something they'll be proud of."

Professor Wilst coughed into his closed fist with a sound like dry sticks rattling down a chimney. "The sealing, professor?"

Yobbler's grinning face fell. He nodded his ponderous head reluctantly and swatted roughly at a will o' wisp that had the misfortune of floating too near. "Rules are rules, I suppose. Yes, the T.D.D. does have their way with regulations. It's unavoidable that this current crop will have to be sealed to prevent their continued replication."

Professor Wilst was already distributing long, thin white candles throughout the class. As Noah took one, he couldn't help but think back to the candles in the Netherworld and the lives that would be extinguished with them.

"Insert the candle through the base of the vegetables, right where the dweller crawled through," Professor Wilst instructed. "Professor Yobbler, I trust you will be gathering all the excess dwellers who have not found a new head today?"

Professor Yobbler said nothing, seemingly distracted as he assisted Elizabeth Washent with inserting her candle.

"Mmm," Wilst said. "I will be stopping by your office after class to be sure. There were thirty four vegetables available, and fifty dwellers are produced per division. I will be counting."

"I'll collect them in a jar and have it on my desk. You can look, but you can't have them." Yobbler sighed. "Poor little squirmy babies—life can be crueler than death, sometimes, but I'll watch after them."

Wilst continued to monitor in silence as the final candles were inserted into the gourds. The sealing process was quick—just an incantation from Wilst and a soft glowing light through the flesh of the gourds.

"As the candle burns out, the wax will coat the interior and prevent its deconstruction. You will find details of the incantation in tonight's reading, along with instructions you will need to be familiar with before we perform the carvings. Class dismissed."

∽

"You didn't tell me she was going to be here," Walter said, crossing his arms defiantly. "Doesn't she usually have something better to do? Like Brandon's homework?"

"Maybe I do," Jamie replied testily. "Shouldn't you be putting curses on someone who doesn't even know you exist?"

The cold wind blew through them without stirring Walter's t-shirt, or shifting the smallest hair on Jamie's unruly head. A sliver of moonlight snuck through the clouds overhead, but it was still a few hours from dawn. It would have been almost completely black if it weren't for the solitary wisp which had followed them around the side of the bestiary tower. Noah was glad that his friends had met him here when he'd asked, but it was clear that ignoring the bitterness between them and waiting for it to blow over had only made things more tense.

"We're on a team, aren't we?" Noah broke the icy silence. "Ever since Professor Salice showed us what The Matriarch was really up to, we've had a special responsibility. I need both of your help if we're going to keep going."

"Brandon knows the secret too," Jamie said. "Why didn't you invite him?"

"So does Elijah, and I didn't invite him either," Noah said. "I need to make sure we can still work together."

"You told Elijah?!" Jamie stamped her foot on the frosty ground. "Noah, you promised!"

"Yeah, not cool," Walter grunted. "And who knows who he could have told, probably that bully Olly he's always hanging around with. You had no right to do that."

"I know. I'm sorry," Noah said. "But he was working on something real to help, and lately I didn't feel like I could count on you. On either of you. You're both so focused on your old lives that you've lost sight of how much more important this is. Walter—you need to get over who you used to be and who you used to be with. Jamie—I get that you had trouble before, and you want to make friends now, but nobody cares that you used to be different. This isn't about us anymore. It's about everybody else who deserves to have another life, and won't have a chance unless we stand up and do something."

"You're one to talk," Walter said. "The only reason we're in this mess is because you had to get involved with your family last semester. If you took your own advice, then Salice would have gotten rid of The Matriarch and destroyed the Soul Net and it wouldn't be up to us at all."

"Seriously," Jamie chirped in. "The only reason we got tangled up in this is because we were trying to help you when you were being chased by zombies."

"By Brandon's zombies," Walter emphasized.

"Fine, whatever," she said. "But the point is, neither of us ever asked to be involved. We aren't chainers, and we don't speak demonic, and we don't know the first thing about summoning a soul eating demon in the first place. I don't even know why I came out here to meet you tonight—we could all get in trouble if they caught us out here alone."

"It's not like I asked for this anymore than you did," Noah snapped. "Fine, be angry at me if you want. Just stop fighting with each other, okay? Walter—apologize to her for talking to her past life without her permission."

"But so did you—"

"I already told her I was sorry. And she knows I don't think any less of her for it. Now it's your turn."

Walter looked down at his feet, his face disappearing into shadow in the faint red light. "Yeah. You're right. I've been an ass, sorry Jamie."

"Mmhmm," she replied through pursed lips.

"And Jamie, you stop ignoring us and our mission. You're twice as smart as either of us, and we can't do this without you."

"Only if you let Brandon back on the team," she replied stubbornly. "He isn't the same person he was last year. I think he was really close to one of the souls that was destroyed at the beginning of the semester, because something hurt him deep and it changed him. You say you need help, but he only wants to be part of the group and you're always turning him away."

"Fine. Deal." Noah said. "Walter?"

Walter mumbled something incomprehensible.

"Walter?" Jamie pressed. "I know it was wrong to lie to you about who I used to be, and I'm sorry for that too. But I'm not just pretending to have friends now to compensate for how lonely I used to be. I really do think Brandon is a good person, and I want all of us to get along."

"Okay, okay," Walter said. "So is that it? We're here sneaking around just so everyone can apologize and feel bad about themselves?"

"No, that's just something that had to happen first. I needed your help because I met Visoloth again in the Netherworld. And the attacks we've seen so far from the demons… they're nothing compared to what's still to come."

Noah proceeded to unburden himself of the secret he'd been holding onto. He told them about Visoloth, and the purges which were about to start in earnest when they attacked the city. The chilled wind blew through them unfelt as the silence settled once more around the children.

"You shouldn't have told us," Walter said at last.

"You shouldn't have waited so long." Jamie said, anxiously wringing her hands in front of her in a way that reminded Noah of what he'd seen in her mirror. "We can't let them do it, right? You weren't planning to…"

"If anything is going to end this, it's getting rid of The Matriarch," Walter interrupted. "Visoloth was Professor Salice's servant while he was preparing to summon the rasmacht. If anyone can help you do it, it's him."

"You think it will just end there if all those people die?" Jamie replied. "I know a lot of spirits are scared right now, but they've all been summoning demons for years. It's not too late to remind them that they can work together again, but once the purges begin, there won't be any going back."

"It might be too late already," Noah said. "Everyone I talk to seems to hate demons so much. I can't even defend them without being singled out too."

"People say hateful things when they're afraid," Jamie said. "They don't mean it…"

"They do too. And I'm not even sure if they're wrong," Walter said. "Demons have caused nothing but trouble since we got here. If they're planning to kill all those people, then I don't see how they're anything but evil. Maybe we should just let them all have a go at each other and try to keep out of the way. Maybe that's the way things are supposed to be. None of us have exactly been here long enough to know otherwise."

"Just because things are a certain way, doesn't mean they should be," Noah replied. "I've got a plan, but I'm not sure how to do it so I need your help. If we can steal the jar of dwellers from Professor Yobbler's office, I can bring them with me when I'm visiting my family for Christmas. If I plant them around the city, they might be able to ward off the demons and prevent the attack. It should at least buy us a little more time to figure out how to summon the rasmacht on our own."

"And if we can't?" Walter asked.

The sharp, stinging light of morning began to breach the horizon. Noah instinctively flinched and shielded his eyes. It was hard to believe he ever found sunrises to be beautiful, ruining a perfectly peaceful night with that awful, burning glare. Jamie and Walter both had their backs to it, but even they seemed diminished under the harsh rays. It had never been so obvious how small, how frail, how helpless this band of children was.

"We live again or stay dead trying," Noah replied, shrugging. "What more can anyone do?"

MEEP WARLINGTON

THE PLAN BECAME MORE FLUSHED OUT IN THE FOLLOWING WEEKS before Christmas break. There were about two hundred thousand people in the city they had to protect, but Noah was able to find a map in the library and calculated that they all lived within about ten square miles. Their textbook said that one dweller strategically placed per square mile should be an effective ward, although Noah still wasn't sure how a demon could sense, let alone fear such a tiny worm. There should be plenty of time to plant and seal them too, since they had over a week from the winter solstice when their break began to the new year attack.

Noah worried that the dwellers might not stay put once they were placed, but Jamie had an idea for that. She would stay at the school over break again, and Humstrum had no problem with his apprentice using the empty classroom during this time. That would give her the opportunity to burn the incense and form an emphatic connection with the dwellers, thus allowing her to instill greater compassion in them and ensure they played their role correctly. She insisted on telling Brandon about the plan, and he offered to stay and help her as the ritual required at least two people.

Walter volunteered to accompany Noah to help seal the worms in their new homes. If he was disappointed about not getting the chance to visit Natasha or his brothers, then he did an admirable job concealing it. If anything, he seemed excited by the prospect of accompanying Noah, although perhaps he was just relieved to discover that he wouldn't have to be working directly with Brandon. The two were able to sit civilly enough together when Jamie sat between them, but they hardly spoke to one another besides the occasional snide remark. It was obvious that Walter still thought Brandon was a sniveling, cowardly, jerk, while Brandon maintained an air of superiority that seemed offensive to everyone but Jamie.

As for the actual breaking into Yobbler's office, that prospect remained daunting. Noah reasoned that it would be much easier for a mouse to do the job than someone his size, and to wait until Elijah dropped by again to help. The days were stretching into weeks though, and there was still no sign of the older chainer. Besides, it was nearing the end of the semester and work was beginning to pile up, and Noah found one excuse after the next to put off the dweller heist.

Professor Wilst said he could tell who was going to fail his exam simply by looking into their eyes. The cryptic words were less metaphorical than Noah initially suspected, as many of his fellow students were wearing one of the zombified eyes at all times. This made the stairways extra chaotic as students bumbled and bumped into things while struggling to coordinate their movement with their unseen zombie.

Yobbler had become no gentler now that his pumpkin had been moved onto a new body. He often made allusions to the jar of dwellers in his office, casually mentioning to struggling students that 'two brains were better than one', and that they 'wouldn't even feel the worm slipping into their ear'. It was enough to turn the seemingly pleasant activity of carving faces into their new crop of dwellers into a nerve-wracking experience. The fact that the faces moved and leered at them even as they were being carved only exaggerated the unease.

Even Professor Humstrum was becoming uncustomarily strict. At one point Bowser was struggling to form a connection with a rather testy warthog when Humstrum snapped: "If you can't get him to care about you now, then I don't know how you can expect anyone to care when the demons get their claws on you." To his credit, Professor Humstrum immediately apologized when Hazel bleated disapprovingly at him, but everyone could still feel the tension mounting in the air.

Like electricity in the atmosphere before the first lightning strike, everyone could feel that something was going to happen. There hadn't been any more demon attacks or even sightings reported. Even the demons who hadn't been explicitly banished had fled back into the nether, and those few brave or foolish enough to venture after them through a portal reported finding nothing on the other side. No one could agree on what was going to come next, but everyone agreed they must be scheming together on an unprecedented scale.

"Safety can only be paid for with vigilance," The Matriarch announced once to an assembly on the first floor of the cathedral. "Just because you don't see the maggots, doesn't mean they aren't hiding beneath the flesh. All you have to do is make a cut to see them squirm. The demons will not catch us with our guard down again!"

The deadline for action came sooner than anticipated in the last week of November. Noah, Walter, Jamie, and Brandon were all sitting together in the library when a harpy announced: "Second years. Fourth floor demonology. First room."

"What are we doing back there again?" Walter wondered aloud. "I thought the rest of the semester was going to be all about dwellers."

"Do you think we've waited too long to—"

Noah was interrupted by an equally loud screech from the ground floor. "I'll turn your feathers into drinking straws, you overgrown, scavengers. Out—out! I said. No. Harpies!"

If the students had stayed a little longer, they could have enjoyed the spectacle of a flight of books swooping through the air to chase the squawking harpies through the upper echelons of the library. The creeping doubt was already taking hold and propelling them onward though, and by the time Noah reached the fourth floor he was practically running. His fears were realized by the procession he encountered on the bridge moving in the opposite direction.

A long train of self-propelling red carts were streaming out of the third room, each heavily laden with the new crop of freshly carved dwellers. Meep Warlington stood to the side with Professor Yobbler, their heads bent low together in quiet conversation.

"I thought the dwellers were going to stay here," Noah blurted out. He'd stopped so abruptly that his friends piled into him as they hustled down the stairway. The door was momentarily blocked as they sorted themselves out again, and the procession of dwellers came to a halt.

"Thanks to our new crop, the T.D.D. will be able to provide demon-free safety to a good deal of vulnerable zones," Meep Warlington replied cheerfully.

"What about the dwellers in your office, professor?" Brandon chirped from behind. "Are they going to—er—stay and protect the school?"

"The department will be using those as well. Nothing to worry about," Professor Yobbler's pleasant side replied. "The demons won't bother the school again—not as long as I'm here. Do make room now—you're blocking up the stairs."

"I never got to meet them," Jamie tried. "Couldn't we at least say hello and thank them for keeping us safe?"

The pumpkin turned. For a moment it looked like the angry face was about to resurface, but it seemed that Yobbler was only looking at Meep. The green-haired man shrugged, and Yobbler grinned.

"It brings warmth to my still heart to see dwellers being accepted among the spirits," Yobbler replied. "Our persecution has endured for too long, and though I'm sorry to see a common enemy rise its ugly head, I'm glad that this threat has brought us all together again. Of course you can say goodbye to the other babies."

"Yeah, why wouldn't anyone like a bucket of mind-stealing worms?" Walter grumbled under his breath. "Crazy world."

"I do have a schedule to keep," Meep Warlington added stiffly. "I'm afraid I can't tally around until your class is over."

Professor Yobbler waved his hand dismissively. "A good education cannot be constrained within the classroom. You children may accompany Mr. Warlington to my office and assist him with anything he needs. Do be gentle with my darlings—they are so sensitive before they've found a nice secure head to bore into."

Noah and the others made room for Meep Warlington to march by with his procession of red carts. An unpleasant greasy odor pervaded the air in his wake as the children fell into line behind him. Meep showed no inclination to talk to the students who quickly fell to the end of the cart train to formulate an impromptu plan.

"I could just grab the jar and run," Walter offered at once. "He doesn't look that fast."

"The Minister of Energy at the department is very high rank," Jamie said. "There's no way he wouldn't have some trick up his sleeves to stop you."

"Well obviously the others would have to distract him," Walter said. "Brandon can do that thing where he sucks up to the teachers and try to get his autograph or something."

"He'd still notice. You're about as sneaky as a manticore in the grocery store," Brandon shot back.

"What do you know about groceries? I thought you were too rich to ever—"

"We could swap them out," Noah interrupted. "Dump the jar, fill it with string or something."

"I've got some sinews that might work," Jamie said, rummaging in her own cart which had fallen in with the procession. "I was going to save them for animation practice, but they look a little wormy."

"There's no way he wouldn't notice," Brandon said. "If we'd done this ahead of time, we could have sent in a zombie, or charmed an animal into doing it for us. I could have done it no problem if you'd told me the plan sooner."

"Well go ahead and sulk about it, see if that makes us want to include you next time," Walter snapped.

They still didn't have a plan by the time they made it to the first floor where Yobbler's office was. Meep Warlington didn't hesitate as he marched around the circle to the fifth door. His white-gloved hands inserted his own key which had little tentacles writhing around the base. Noah caught a glimpse of slightly rotten, somewhat pickled looking skin between the glove and his coat jacket as Meep unlocked the door and pushed inside.

The room hadn't changed much since Noah had seen it last semester. All of the cruel bladed devices that Salice had displayed were still on the shelves, and the meagre light still emanated from a solitary wisp locked within its wire cage.

Meep Warlington went straight to one of the shelves and pressed the back with two fingers. A small stretch of the wall behind swiveled around to reveal a secret compartment, and a moment later a glass jar appeared clasped in his gloved hand. It was hard to tell how many of the squirmy things slid past each other inside, but Noah remembered that there should be fourteen total: enough to protect Noah's home town against the demonic incursion.

"Ah, there we are. See them? All done? Ready to go?"

The glass jar was only visible for a second or two before Meep whisked it into the inside pocket of his coat.

"How come you know Professor Yobbler's office so well?" Noah asked, drawing out the words to buy for time as his brain strained for a solution.

Meep wrinkled his face. "The department seeks to maintain superb relations and intimate knowledge of all things relating to the Mortuary. Given that Yobbler is a dweller who relies upon the approval of the department to teach here, he appreciates the necessity of this alliance to an even higher degree."

"Can we see them again?" Jamie asked sweetly. "What are their names? Do they talk yet, or do they need to—"

"I'm sorry, but these are really questions your professor should be answering. I've got important business—inter-dimensional treaties—people relying on this protection—matters of life and death, all that rot. Everything that happens at the department is far too significant to be kept waiting."

"Oh, I'm sorry. I didn't understand how important you are," Jamie replied, her voice melodic and calm. "Now that you've explained everything so nicely, it's clear that we should be doing more to help the department."

Warlington was momentarily taken aback. He scratched his chin, and the skin remained indented where his finger had been without reforming. "Um, quite so, yes. Well I'm glad you understand anyway, so I'd best be off…"

"Which is exactly why we should come with you," Jamie pronounced emphatically.

"Come again?"

"The trouble with relying on an alliance with the professors, is that they're all loyal to The Matriarch," Jamie said, casually striding closer to Meep. "And maybe they are telling you the truth—or the parts she wants you to know at least—but an important person like you knows that people have to look out for their own job first. Now, I don't know how long it will take me to come back to life with all these demons interfering, so the best thing I can do for my future is to learn about working for the department like you. And since it's my future job at stake to tell you the truth, and the professors job at stake to keep the truth from you, I think it's clear where your most beneficial alliance really stands."

"The parts… she wants me to know?"

"Mhmm," Jamie said. "Like, I bet they told you the Manticore was their only fighting creature here, because that's the only one you took away. I bet Professor Humstrum never told you what a jinn can do, but he's told me because I'm his apprentice."

"Your Professor will be wondering where you are…"

"But education can't be confined within a classroom," Noah cut in, catching on. "He said so himself. And I can't think of anyone in the world who we could learn more from than an important person in the department such as yourself."

"You don't know the half of it," Meep Warlington said, standing a little taller than he had a moment before. "You know, I could have taught my own Necromancy class if I'd wanted to, but I turned it down. Didn't pay half as well."

"Well now is your chance," Jamie said. "And if anyone else at the department asks us who our best teacher is, we'll have to say it was you for giving us this opportunity. Won't they be impressed to know that you're better respected than any of the professors? Not to mention crawling over themselves to find out all the secrets we can tell you that *only you will know*."

Meep Warlington's yellow teeth popped into display one by one as his smile steadily grew. "Yes, yes, they'd have to listen to me then, wouldn't they? No more of that 'he only got the job because the last Minister of Energy disappeared' nonsense. Oh why not, if spirits can't stick together and help each other out, what hope do we have against the demons? Very well, you can all come for a field trip. Just so long as you remember that you're working for me and not the school, and that anything you see or hear while you're at the department stays a secret."

"Thank you, Mr. Warlington!" Noah said, elbowing Walter and Brandon as he did. They both reluctantly mumbled the same thing, but Meep didn't seem to notice. He was already half-way out the door with an extra bounce in his step that hadn't been there on the way in.

Meep briefly voiced an intent to let The Matriarch know before they left, but Jamie was quick to reassure him that Professor Yobbler had already given them permission just a moment ago. And besides— doesn't she already have *enough control* over the Mortuary without needing to know exactly how the T.D.D. gets its information? In fact, perhaps there wouldn't be any harm if the students hid amongst the pumpkins and gourds with a blanket thrown over the top: an invention suggested by Noah which Meep greeted with delight.

"She is nosy, isn't she? Knows too much for her own good." Meep Warlington said as he spun light from the air into the shape of a few blankets. His entire skull was glowing from the resonating light, which might indicate that he was inhabiting his real corporal body as a lich like Professor Wilst, albeit with a good deal more skin attached. "It's those damned eyes," he continued as he tucked the blankets over the heads of the children. "I can never tell when they're really in her head, and when she's popped them out and hidden them around the school. Not to mention the harpies—very keen sight, mind you. They can read over your shoulder from the top of the highest spire. Getting away from all that scrutiny is such a relief that I'll almost breathe again."

There was only enough room for one of the children in each cart amidst the dweller heads. The candles were still burning inside them, so it wasn't dark under the blankets. Noah moved to one end and made a small opening under the blanket so he could peek out. A moment later, a rustle in the adjacent cart revealed a flash of curly orange hair as Jamie peeked out from her end.

"Ow, watch where you're stepping!" a large yellow squash lamented. "Half-pulled my stem out, bloody spirit."

"Sorry," Noah whispered. "Please don't make a fuss. We're all friends here."

"Hmph. dwellers don't have friends. We have another word for them: future hosts."

The carts began to move again in a circular path. They must be going around the central tree now. Noah peered back out at the passing stone slabs, and spoke softly across the gap between the carts. "That was a brilliant job, Jamie. How did you know he didn't trust The Matriarch?"

"He's a man and she's a powerful woman. Of course he'd be insecure about it: those are laws of nature. If I ever wrote a textbook, I'd put that in chapter one."

"Do you have any idea how we're going to get the jar of dwellers from him though?"

"Not yet. At least we'll have more time to figure it—shhh, get down!" Jamie vanished back underneath her blanket. Noah ducked deeper within his own cart. There were voices outside now—laughing, shouting, talking. The closely fitted stones underneath shifted to a rougher cobblestone path. They must be exiting the Mortuary.

"Nobody ever told me about a jar of dwellers."

Noah jolted. He'd almost forgotten about the squash-head sharing his cart. "Ummm, yeah. You all came from a dweller named Billibus, but there were some others who haven't been given heads yet."

"What are you going to do with the children?" the squash asked suspiciously.

Noah looked about the cramped cart uneasily, but there was no getting out of answering. Besides, he couldn't risk angering the dweller lest it set off the alarm and expose him.

"We're going to plant them in the living world and let them be free. I think they'd be happier with heads, like you."

"Bah, this vegetable? It doesn't even come with a body. Not half as good as a human head."

"Well, most humans wouldn't want to share a head with a dweller. I promise if we find any heads that aren't being used, we'll plant them in there instead. Would you like to help us?"

The boy stared at the squash. The squash stared at the boy. Neither had to speak for the absurdity of the request to be fully realized, although that didn't stop the dweller from pointing this out, presumably for the sole purpose of making sure Noah understood how ridiculous he was.

"I haven't got a body, stupid. I can't help anybody with anything."

"That's not true. Even without a body you can still scare off demons, although I'll admit that I'm not quite sure how."

A slow smile spread across the squash's face which flickered with the candle inside. "There are demons? They're my favorite. I'd much rather be a demon than a squash."

Noah was able to resume whispering with Jamie once they'd gotten a little distance from the Mortuary. Within half an hour of bumping along, Meep Warlington tossed back their blankets to reveal the great expanse of open night sky. The Mortuary on the cliffside was still visible in the distance, but they hadn't taken the familiar route which lead down to the village of Teraville. The cobblestone road gave way to a smaller gravel track which wound its way steeply through the hills toward the water.

"We're going to Nepon Vasolitch?" Brandon asked, climbing out of his own cart which he'd shared with an extremely bad-tempered looking melon.

"He's the boatman, yes," Meep Warlington replied. "It's not like we can use the daymare anymore with demons being as troublesome they are."

"Can't we use a portal or something?" Walter asked. "How far away is the department, anyway?"

"You might as well ask how deep the ocean is. It won't take us much more than an hour though."

Brandon was the only one who seemed excited by this prospect. He puffed out his chubby chest with pride and extolled the grandeur of the open ocean as though none of the others had even seen it before. Nothing they had done in life or death, Brandon said, could compare with drifting through the specter filled abyss on one of Nepon Vasolich's expeditions.

Noah doubted it could compare with the exhilaration of floating through the Netherworld besought by demons, but he held his tongue. As tempting as it was to put the pompous boy in his place, it was a relief to see all four of them putting on a united front in the face of a common goal.

The morning sun had yet to spoil the tranquility of the frozen night when the descent began to level out. The grassy slopes were deeply penetrated by the zigzagging path, which caused the sheer stone to rise ever higher around them on either side. The rocks parted quite suddenly as the way emerged onto a narrow strip of wooden dock that stretched into the water. There were no black sand beaches on this side of the island, and the frothing waters which lashed against the stone seemed like the least hospitable place imaginable to shelter a vessel.

The boat that was tethered here looked nothing like the mighty ship Brandon had conjured images of with his praise. The tattered gray sails looked as though they'd forgotten their original color in their youth and seemed hopelessly inept to capture the wind. A thick layer of barnacles smothered the moldy planks even above the water-line, and the railings were intertwined with sea-weed that looked stronger than the coils of frayed ropes that were haphazardly piled on deck. The only extraordinary thing to note was the wooden mermaid figurehead whose orange eyes glowed like the headlights on a car. The way the light shifted as they approached unmistakably proved that the wooden eyes were tracking their progress.

"Wake up Nepon, you old bastard. Where's my welcome?" Meep Warlington bellowed.

"The ocean never sleeps, and neither do I."

The grating words rolled rhythmically in pitch like a chain smoker trying to perform slam poetry. It seemed to be coming from on board, but the orator was unseen. The train of carts containing the dwellers continued to roll past them and onto the wooden dock. The candles burning within the vegetables paled before the baleful glare of the wooden mermaid.

"Why don't you and the ocean both take the night off and let me take it from here?" Meep called. "I've never been much for sailing, but I shouldn't have any trouble finding my way to the department."

"Aye, but can you find your way back again?"

A coil of rope was beginning to unwind itself and crawl toward the mast. There was still no visible sign of Nepon Vasolitch, which was disconcerting considering how close his grating voice sounded. Noah had to use his hands to block out the light from the mermaid eyes before finally spotting Nepon leaning against the wooden railing.

The mottled, bearded face wearing a white captain's hat rose as the seaman climbed onto the railing, He teetered for a moment before tumbling overboard into the water with a resonate *plop*. The procession of candles within the vegetables boarding the ship illuminated the surface and revealed the head dissolving before their eyes. What once was Nepon's beard now appeared as a dozen white fish swimming in close formation. Other spotted fish parted from the flesh of his face, and a great jellyfish pushed off from his hairline to float free in the water. His body seemed to belong to a much larger shark-like creature which swam in a different direction altogether.

"Her name is Alexandria, and she deserves to be treated with respect," Brandon interjected, running his hands reverently over the barnacled planks. "She's the same ship The Matriarch was on when they first went down in 1647—Alexandria is even older than the Mortuary."

"A pleasant surprise to see my favorite apprentice tonight. Nothing round here stays down, not even the ships," Nepon's voice rippled up from the water. It sounded just as it had before, despite it no longer being clear which of the fish was talking, or whether it was all of them together.

"Maybe, maybe, but the T.D.D. is even older than her," Meep Warlington replied sagely. "We've been monitoring everything and processing the souls for as long as war was war and man was man. If anything deserves loyalty in this world or the next, it's the department which protects us all."

Once they were all loaded, the vessel moved smoothly through the water without the least wind through its tattered sails. Nepon Vasolitch remained in the water alongside them to guide the mermaid figurehead, who seemed to be doing her own steering. Meep didn't broach the subject of his original interest until the island of Barbaros had completely vanished on the horizon. Perhaps he was still afraid of The Matriarch's long reach all this time, and needed the open ocean before he felt secure enough to pry.

"I'll tell you the truth. I don't trust her. She's too smart by half, and too cold by three-quarters. A plotter, a schemer, that's what she is. And worst of all, I don't think she's even scheming for us anymore."

"You're both on the same side though, aren't you?" Noah asked cautiously. "You're all trying to protect the spirits from the demons."

"I hate them," Brandon grunted. He'd turned away from the others to lean on the railing and look out over the black waters. "Banishing them isn't good enough if they can just come back again. I don't know why the department doesn't try to kill them for good."

"It's not the department's job to pick one side or the other," Meep replied. "The cycle of life needs demons to be part of the balance, or none of it works. The living must die to become spirits. The spirits need demons to help them return to life through the Netherworld. Ever since the demons of Barbaros were freed though, there's more human deaths than ever and fewer spirits coming back to life. If this keeps up, it will get to the point where there's no one left alive, and nothing but spirits roaming an empty world. Installing these dwellers around will slow down the attacks, but it won't stop the underlying problem.

"The Matriarch has always hated demons. Wonderful headmistress with the other subjects, but she puts up a fight whenever the department makes her hire a new demonologist. I think she'd rather have a full-blown war with the demons than ever work with them again. That's why it's so important for you to tell me if there's something she's doing to antagonize them."

"She won't let any of last year's graduates walk the road from death," Walter volunteered.

"The roads everywhere are closed, department decree. Too dangerous for spirits to be in the nether."

"There are more chainers than ever too," Noah said. "There's about a dozen of them in the new first year class."

Meep nodded absentmindedly, his green hair spilling forward to conceal his face. "Yes, yes, anything else?"

The children exchanged uncertain glances, all except Brandon who was continuing to stare out to sea. Salice had said that the department was already involved with the Soul Net, so telling him about that would do nothing but put themselves at risk. Noah was pretty sure that Meep didn't know about Elijah's secret pathway, but there wasn't any point to betraying his friend. It did seem that Meep was sincere about his efforts to protect the living from the demons though. Noah's thoughts returned to his daughter and his grandson, and a wave of guilt seized his still heart. He had an obligation to use anything that might save them, no matter where that help came from.

"I know where the demons are going to attack. I know when they're going to attack. Please don't let them hurt my family."

Jamie made a small gasp, but Noah didn't look at her. He kept his eyes locked on Meep Warlington while he rapidly explained what he had learned from Visoloth. Meep listened intently and did not interrupt. The initial surprise softened his rough pock-marked features, although swiftly his face furrowed into revulsion and anger. Noah's hope that it was directed at the demons gave him the strength to finish.

"A demon lacks the imagination to break their word, so I believe what you've told me. Does The Matriarch know?" Meep asked when he was done.

"No. Not yet. I didn't think she'd really help."

"Not yet, not ever. Not only do I not trust her to help, I don't even trust her not to make matters worse. You did the right thing by telling me. The Prime Minister Theodore Oswald will need to know, of course, and together we will make sure that this evil you spoke of will not come to pass."

"The dwellers in the jar would be enough. If you could just give me those, then I could plant them myself and The Matriarch would never need to know."

Noah felt a pressure on his hand. He looked down to see Jamie giving it a squeeze of reassurance. Walter shifted uncomfortably from one foot to the other, and Brandon continued to look out over the water without reacting to Noah's account.

"Something to be considered. You all knew about this, didn't you?" Meep scanned the others through the slits of his eyes.

"So what if we did?" Brandon asked, his voice blunt and hard. "We trust each other not to snitch."

"Well, thank you for trusting me too," Meep replied. "Brandon Hides, is that right? I know this semester must have been especially hard on you, what with your mother and all. I appreciate what you're doing though, and I won't let you down."

"I don't know what you're talking about," Brandon replied, misty eyed. "My mother died when I was born—I never knew her."

"Oh, that's right, you don't know. I wouldn't expect anyone outside of the department to be able to keep track of the space left by eaten souls. I suppose one secret deserves another though, so here goes. Do you remember the souls that were destroyed at the beginning of the semester?"

Brandon turned sharply to face Meep, his eyes fierce and wide.

"Not an isolated incident, mind you," Meep continued, seemingly oblivious to Brandon's rigid intensity. "We had a pair of attacks at the department on the same day. Two of our best souls, vital officers that we're sorely worse off for, or so I've been told. Of course I can't remember them, but you know how that goes considering it was your mother who was destroyed. You must have been rather close, to together and attended the Mortuary at the same time."

There is no sound so horrendous as the breaking of a soul, and this was no exception. The sound that came out of Brandon's throat wasn't piercing, and it didn't shatter the air into a thousand pieces. It didn't echo across the wide ocean with anguish, or drip through the other senses and taint them with its grief. The sound Brandon made was small, and muffled, and strained, like someone who had just stubbed their toe in the night and trying not to wake anyone up. The pain wasn't in the sound as much as it was underneath it though, and like spotting the tip of an iceberg, Noah could sense the unseen immensity of the damage those words had caused.

"What you can't remember can't hurt you though, eh?" Meep continued with a yellow grin. The ship lurched downward, and his grin widened. "Is that you Nepon? Are we here?"

The boat lurched again. Walter leapt into the air and gesticulated wildly toward the back of the boat. "Water is getting in! We're sinking!"

"How else would we get to the bottom of the ocean?" Meep replied, chuckling at his distress. "You can't drown if you don't breathe."

The boat swayed treacherously from side-to-side, almost tipping over. Water was flooding onboard through a large hole. Floating beside them was an unplugged cork on a string. A couple of fish peered through the hole that looked like they might have been Nepon Vasolitch, but it was so hard to tell with fish.

"Double-check to make sure all the carts are securely tied down," Meep Warlington called as the gushing water rose around their legs. "Next stop: the Trans Dimensional Department."

TRANS DIMENSIONAL DEPARTMENT

IT TOOK LESS THAN A MINUTE FOR THE DARK WATER TO CLOSE OVER their heads. There was an initial shock from the cold, but it wasn't hard for Noah to dissociate the feeling just as he'd learned to do with the winter weather. The carts carrying the dwellers remained tightly held down by the rope, but Meep and the children had to hold onto the railings to ensure they sank alongside the ship.

It was completely black below the surface, except for the radiant headlights beaming from the mermaid which nosed the boat downward. Everyone pulled themselves hand-over-hand until they reached the front of the vessel where they could catch a glimpse of the underwater world that opened up before their eyes.

The experience reminded Noah of his first venture into the Netherworld, in that the ocean stretched endlessly in all directions. The comparison ended there. Unlike the nether, the only visible space was directly in front of the boat, and instead of vast emptiness, the ocean was teaming with movement. Schools of spectral fish drifted silently through the water alongside a massive skeletal whale which turned to watch them pass. A pair of mermaids with flowing seaweed hair paused in their pursuit of a runaway seahorse the size of an actual horse, and other strange and multifarious creatures flirted past at the edge of the light.

"One of the best things about being dead is being able to dwell underwater," Meep Warlington declared emphatically, wafting in a great lungful of water which permeated his body. "No blood to boil from the pressure, no lungs to struggle for air, and no pesky humans getting in the way. It's like the bottom of the ocean was made for the department."

There was no need for Meep to point out the sight as they approached. The narrow illuminated strip seemed to create a road of light which cut through the abyss all the way to the ocean floor to where the spiraling towers rose up to greet them. Orange banners with a blue diagonal cross unfurled in the current, and the white sand sparkled beneath the headlights. Terrace upon terrace, with crisscrossing walkways between them and high arches under which the teaming sea-creatures swam. Great garden beds of coral were illuminated by fountains which circulated light instead of water, and marble statues in glorious poses held aloft glass objects inhabited by glowing red wisps. The trans dimensional department was housed inside a white sandcastle stretched for miles in every direction, and it was the most beautiful thing Noah had ever seen.

Alexandria continued her descent until the front of the vessel became ensnared in a nearly invisible net which spanned between two towers. Four mermen with glistening emerald-green tails exited the towers to surround the boat. Their white-gloved hands brandished golden tridents, their muscular chests bare except for the customary orange ties that signified their employment in the department. The school of fish and the jellyfish that represented Nepon Vasolitch returned onboard to greet them, merging together so tightly that the man's familiar form appeared once more.

"A pleasant voyage I hope—" Nepon began.

"Minster of Energy, Meep Warlington," Meep bellowed, ignoring Nepon to instead address the guards. "No time to waste, I must see Theodore this instant."

As one, the four mermen bowed low over their tridents, their posture then rigidly returning to attention. One of them who was distinguished by the string of pearls interwoven between the trident points moved forward to address the newcomers while the others turned back toward the towers.

"The Prime Minister has been expecting you, Mr. Warlington. I take it the dwellers are fully grown?"

"Grown and ready to be deployed, Lieutenant Greigex. And not a moment too soon. The attack is more imminent than we anticipated, please do not delay."

The Lieutenant signaled to the other three over his shoulder, and they proceeded to unhook the net from one of the towers.

"You haven't been very nice to me ever since your promotion," Nepon lamented in his graveled tone. The fish that was serving as his nose began to swim away, but he gently prodded it back into place. "When I was a Vice-Admiral of the Royal Navy, I vividly recall the day when I ordered my fleet into Boston harbor, and—"

"It must be embarrassing to have to think so far back to the last time you were respected," Meep cut him off. "Why don't you make yourself useful and show the children around while I meet with the Prime Minister? They have all become special friends of mine."

"Hrmph. Very well. Just so long as you know that were it not for the regal flag that I have sworn my death to..." Nepon's voice trailed off as Meep Warlington turned away to instruct the mermen on untying the dweller carts.

"Hmph indeed," Nepon repeated, turning to the children. "Don't mistake his incivility for wickedness though. Mr. Warlington has always had the highest reverence for his service to the department. I do hope that at least my apprentice will show proper deference to an old admiral though."

Brandon swept into a bow which seemed passably sincere, and Nepon was contented to turn and drift between the two glittering towers. His component fish separated as they swam, though they still remained close enough to give the semblance of his body.

"The Trans Dimensional Department has been the brunt of many unfounded jokes and sneers, but that's just because most people look down on the idea of death being regulated. It's necessary work, to be sure. Can you imagine what a mess the world would be in without laws? Vampires in the hospitals, ghosts in the pipes, demons in the—well you can just see what happens when they get out of control. Dreadful, dreadful business."

Nepon Vasolitch led them all the way to the ocean floor where a broad stone walkway wandered through the castle. Crabs half as tall as they were scuttled back and forth carrying baskets woven from sea-weed, but the mer-people and human spirits appeared to be the primary denizens of the place. That is, so long as you didn't count the gargoyles which seemed almost as common as people down here. There was one of them in every nook and cranny, every balcony railing, every rooftop and statue perch. Always leering, but never moving except for an occasional adjustment of their head to watch the newcomers pass.

"Take that tower for instance, the Department of Childbirth. Very important department—I was so sorry to hear that their minister's soul was destroyed at the beginning of the semester alongside the Minister of Energy. Can you imagine what would happen if two spirits tried to push their way into the same child at the same time though? One person per soul, that's their job. Or over there at the Portal Department—yes that long building with the statue that's split into a torso and its legs. It's bad enough that these demons keep sneaking in without some half-wit forgetting to close a portal in the kitchen and waking up with a house full of the critters."

"Have they figured out how the demons are getting in in the first place?" Jamie asked. "I always thought someone had to summon them."

"True, true. Even decent sized portals are still extremely unstable, and require vast amounts of energy to maintain. Never underestimate the bestial cunning possessed by a demon though, or the weakness in the heart of a man who dreams of power. While a demon may not lie, they certainly have no qualms about manipulating those foolish enough to try and use them for their own gain. Now if you'll follow me, I'll be happy to show you the beautiful palaces where the higher society resides…"

Nepon might have continued to say something else, but Noah's attention had been diverted by an unexpected sight. Emerging from a doorway halfway up a set of four circular, interconnected towers came The Matriarch herself. She was wearing her distinctive bright red coat and wide brimmed hat. She carried a gray purse bulging with something—something squirmy based on how the bag contorted and deformed in her arms.

"What are those towers for?" Noah pointed, pretending not to notice The Matriarch as she turned to speak with someone still inside.

"Department of Energy, where Meep works," Nepon replied automatically, hardly looking. "Can't say I stayed in school long enough to make sense of what goes on in there. All very technical stuff having to do with currencies and life-forces and spectral-physics mumbo jumbo. Once you've tasted the exhilaration at the helm of a fleet of warships, it's hard to settle for anything a book and a desk can offer. I imagine studying is so much better suited to people with boring lives and nothing to compare it to. Oh, what am I saying though—of course you should be taking your classes seriously. Now about the palaces…"

Nepon Vasolitch was floating off in the direction of the admittedly exquisite architecture, but Noah couldn't turn away from The Matriarch.

"You see her?" Noah whispered to Jamie who was also staring in the same direction.

"Sure do. What do you think she's doing here?"

"Don't know, but I'd love to find out. If Nepon notices I'm gone, just say Meep needed me for his report. If he doesn't buy it, remind him that I'm The Matriarch's apprentice, and she's been using me to keep watch in the nether."

"Oh, but you shouldn't go off alone. What if someone catches you?"

"I'll only be a moment. I'll meet you back at the ship—don't leave without me!"

Noah was already half-way around the circular tower so he could avoid being spotted. Walter noticed a moment later, but Jamie put a finger to her lips and waved him onward. If Brandon saw, he made no sign. The same glassy indifference was on his face that he'd worn ever since he'd learned about his mother's soul.

When Noah reached the tower, he swam upward along the opposite side from where The Matriarch had emerged. He stopped once he heard her voice and pressed himself against the wall, straining to listen to what was being said. The tower was too broad to hear properly though, and he didn't dare inch closer around the side without risking being seen. There were only two words that he could make out clearly from the conversation: *chainer battery*.

It sounded like she was departing shortly after. He silently counted to ten before inching along the side—just far enough to see The Matriarch's back as she kicked her way through the water, her arms still encumbered by the bag. Then the sound of a door slamming shut, and a gray haired spirit in loose blue robes came hurrying after her.

"Mrs. Barrow!" he called loudly. "They really mustn't be removed from the tower. If you would only reconsider…"

"You wouldn't have them at all if it weren't for me," The Matriarch said over her shoulder, not slowing down in the least. "Unless of course, if you'd like to explain to Theodore that you're the reason he's not going to get his hands on any new chainers…"

"Elanore, please, not so loud," the gray haired man hissed. He was gaining on The Matriarch as his hands weren't encumbered. He might have said something else, but they were too far away to hear properly.

They were both turned away from Noah now, which allowed him to circle all the way around to their side of the tower. While they were both distracted, he tried the door that they had emerged from—a giant spiraling pink shell which swung inward at once. Noah pulled his way inside hand-over-hand, and shut the door behind him as quickly as he could. It was all done in such a rush that he hadn't stopped to consider what he would do if there were more people inside.

"Excuse m-me?" stuttered a voice. "Do you have an ap-p-ointment?"

White gloves, orange tie, blue robes, and thin wire glasses with lenses so thick that his eyes were magnified and distorted. There was only one spirit in the room, and he looked barely older than Noah. The boy ran a thin hand nervously through his wild tufted brown hair, acting more like he'd been the one caught out of place than Noah was.

"Yeah. I'm The Matriarch's apprentice," Noah said, surveying the interior of the tower with an artificial air of confidence. The walls were lined with spiral shelves containing hundreds of life-sized, semi-opaque pink crystal sculptures. About a dozen of them were slowly pulsing with alternating yellow and red light, while the majority remained dark. The pulsing ones were engulfed in a tangle of metal wires which connected them to the wall, and each time the crystals pulsed with yellow light, the energy seemed to be siphoned off through the wires.

"She already left. If you hurry, you can cat-tch her."

"Actually, she just sent me back because she forgot something," Noah bluffed, feeling more sure of himself as he appraised how timid the other spirit appeared. "Her hands were already full, so she asked me to carry another one for her."

"Another chainer batt-ttery?"

"Yes please."

"She shouldn't have have t-taken one at all!" the spirit declared emphatically. "You t-tell her: absolut-tely no!"

"Okay, okay. No reason to get worked up. I'm just doing what I'm told," Noah said, shrugging. "What are those things, anyway?"

"Oh they're marvelous. Perpet-tual energy machines, used t-to gather and st-tore the great-test power in the universe."

"What's that?" Noah asked, swimming up to inspect one of the pulsing statues. The stone became slightly more translucent when the light was flashing through it. There seemed to be a large mass where the sculpture's heart should be, with more wires coming out of that. These interior wires squirmed every time the light passed through them, reminding Noah of how The Matriarch's bag had moved.

"Do you really not-t know? Nothing gives more energy than a

death. Mast-ter Noozwink invent-ted them himself, won all kinds of awards, he did. He discovered how a chainer soul can ut-tilize the second principle of life force dynamics to cycle bet-tween life and death, collecting 1.5 t-times the energy from the cycle as it does to kill and rebirth the soul. They can lit-terally run forever."

"There's a soul in there?" Noah asked, horrified. "Dying over and over and over again?"

"And being brought-t back, with a net positive release of energy!" the spirit declared cheerfully. "Pure genius how—"

"Mundy! Who are you talking to?"

Noah spun to see the gray-haired spirit enter through the shell door behind him. His arms were crossed, and a nasty scowl soured his face.

"He's the lady's apprent-tice, sir. He came back for another—"

"Out!" Noozwink shouted. "Out before I call the Department of Security. One is already more than she could possibly need. You surface dwellers have no respect for the institutions you rely upon. Outrageous."

"Yes sir, I will let her know," Noah said, tumbling over himself in his haste to exit the door.

"And tell her I'm still waiting on last year's chainer!" Noozwink called after him.

"Last year's? Do you mean Elijah?" Noah asked.

"I only care about whether they're on schedule. Their name makes no difference to me."

Out in the open water, the shell door slammed shut behind him. Noah spun in a quick circle to scan the sand-city for any sign of The Matriarch, but she was gone.

The Soul Net was capturing souls. The department was killing chainer souls over and over again to generate power. The department gargoyle caused Noah's death, and there were more freshly dead chainers in the first year class than ever before. It all fit together, all except for the mistrust which seemed to linger between The Matriarch and the department. Was she trying to keep Elijah safe by failing him? And what were any of them planning to use the energy for?

Noah returned towards the net which had stopped the ship Alexandria. He felt relieved to have gotten out of there as innocuously as he did, but he felt like any more scrutiny would be enough for his story to collapse. Nepon and his friends hadn't returned yet, but Meep Warlington had. Noah was just beginning to wonder whether he should try to rejoin the others before Meep saw him, and by then it was already too late.

"All alone, are we?" Meep called.

Noah hurried his pace back toward the boat, trying to appear relieved. "I made a wrong turn and got lost. Did you tell the Prime Minister about the attack?"

"Matters of state are confidential," Meep said with an upturned nose. "It is enough to know that we were both grateful for your assistance, and that your town will be well protected from the demons."

"Did you ask Theodore about the jar of dwellers?"

"Don't call him that. Just because I used his name doesn't mean just anybody—he's the Prime Minister. And yes, we both decided that the most discreet way to handle the situation was for you to plant the dwellers yourself. You may have the jar, so long as you make sure every dweller is sealed the moment it has been installed."

They didn't have to wait long before the various components of Nepon Vasolitch came swimming around the corner with Noah's friends trailing along behind.

"Ah good, you're both already finished," Nepon said. "It's so gratifying to know that the Prime Minister has time to see you right away, even though he makes me wait weeks for an appointment and then forgets to show up when it's finally time…"

Noah was silently thankful that Meep never seemed to listen to Nepon too closely. It seemed that none of his bluffs had been revealed, and they were going to make it safely back to the Mortuary. Noah gripped the sealed jar of dwellers a little tighter against his body and smiled to himself. No more secrets—he couldn't wait to tell the others what he'd learned.

THE APPROACH of Christmas was a time of high hopes at the Mortuary. There had been a rumor going around, propagated mostly by the librarian Mrs. Vanderlooth, that students wouldn't be allowed to return home because of the danger. This was thankfully dispelled by The Matriarch shortly later when she announced that the T.D.D. was making progress with demon relations and that there might soon be a peaceful resolution. Mrs. Vanderlooth was the only one who seemed disappointed by this news, and by the next nightfall she was already spreading whispers about a batch of escaped dwellers who were infiltrating the minds of hapless students.

The fact remained, however, that there hadn't been any additional demon attacks reported since Halloween. Professor Yobbler even announced the possibility of returning to a more summoning oriented curriculum next semester if everything continued to go well. The general mistrust of the denizens of the Netherworld wouldn't evaporate overnight, but the fields of pure snow which sparkled beneath the dancing wisps at night painted a scene where anything was possible.

The only one who didn't seem optimistic was Elijah. He caught Noah outside the library just once, and then only for a few minutes. Withdrawn and concealed within a large hoodie, his usual carefree demeanor was as dark as the circles under his eyes. He didn't elaborate on his whereabouts beside a brief allusion to his secret road. He instead pressed Noah about the pending demon attack, the chainer batteries, and everything he'd seen and heard at the department. The screeching harpies made Elijah flinch and press himself to the wall, despite never having been bothered by them in the past. He mentioned several times that he didn't want to be seen, and he was gone before Noah could discern what had been troubling him.

Noah felt that he had accomplished what he set out to do though, and for the most part he was left to focus on his studies. Despite everything going on, he never remained focused for long without his mind returning to his daughter and grandson. Lewis didn't have any trouble recognizing him last year, and now that he was four, he'd be old enough to have real conversations with. Noah had spent a long time wrestling with his daughter's aversion toward him, but he couldn't shake the hope that Lewis's own vision into the spirit world would help convince her that she wasn't crazy. If that wasn't enough, then perhaps Samantha would serve as a medium to let Mandy know that Noah wanted to be a force for good in her life.

It is exactly such thoughts that made what The Matriarch told him one evening so hard to bear. He was in her office, preparing to perform his sentry duty in the Netherworld, while she conjured the portal into existence. He was about to crawl inside when she casually mentioned, "You might only have to do this for another few weeks, you know. If all goes well with the demons, then I'll have new uses for you next semester."

"A few weeks?" Noah asked, hesitating before the sparkling circle. "Christmas break starts this weekend."

"And I'm sure everyone without responsibilities will have a lovely time," she said sweetly. "As for you and I however, now more than ever it is important for us not to let our guard down. Any demonic incident that occurs during the T.D.D.'s negotiations will ruin everything for everyone."

"Do you mean that everyone else gets to visit home except me?"

"Don't act so surprised, my dear. You'll break my old heart. The price of power has always been responsibility, just as the reward for responsibility is more power. People can't take vacations from who they are, and chainers like you and I are born to rule. Chin up now, off you go."

Born to rule? Noah thought back to the chainer souls trapped within the crystal hearts. That certainly didn't seem like ruling to him. Nobody is born to do anything—things just happen to them whether they like it or not. He couldn't bear to look at the flash of diamond behind The Matriarch's eyes, and there was nothing he could think to say to change his fate. Weeks of fantasies evaporated before his eyes as Noah nodded glumly and climbed into the portal.

"Always vigilant!" The Matriarch called after him. "It is when you feel most safe that the greatest danger is near."

How fortunate it must be then that Noah hadn't felt safe in a long, long while. Slipping into the cool embrace of the nether was no exception. The first second always made him flinch no matter how many times he did it. That moment where his senses adjusted to the new environment and everything was dark and overwhelming. The sensation of some invisible hand reaching out to seize him before he had a chance to orient himself or react, or some disembodied voice whispering at his ear.

"Hello, Noah. Are you ready?"

Noah lurched backward from the sound. It would have been enough to send him tumbling back through the portal if it hadn't already closed behind him in a shower of sparks.

"Elijah?" Noah asked, dumbfounded. "What are you doing here? Where have you been?"

"Come on. I don't want to spend any more time here than I have to. I've already got your mirror and your stuffed tiger—there's nothing else you need, is there? Then let's get you home."

The older boy wasted no time in slipping off through the nether, dragging a red cart with Noah's things behind him. Noah even spotted the jar of dweller worms nestled within the grasp of the stuffed tiger. Noah took a moment to take in the immensity of the abstract geometry around him to make sure it was still empty before hurrying after Elijah.

"The Matriarch will be furious," Noah said. "How did you know she wouldn't let me go? Hey—slow down! I can't leave yet anyway—I still haven't taken my exams."

"You still think exams matter? When your soul can be trapped in a net, or bound up in a machine for all eternity whether you fail or not? I didn't know she wasn't going to let you go, but I'm not surprised she wouldn't want you to interfere. I'm just here because we don't have much time."

"Are you talking about the demon attack?" Noah asked. "That's not going to be until the new year, and the department already knows—"

"We can't rely on them. We need to plant your dwellers and give them a chance to grow, and not count on the department for anything."

"They aren't going to let people die now that they know. I think Meep Warlington really cared about keeping people safe—he's not like The Matriarch."

"I don't trust him. I don't trust her. I don't trust any of them. And you shouldn't either. How can you even defend them after finding out about the batteries? Letting a thousand people in a city die is no worse than killing the same soul a thousand times. Every one of those could have been an animal, a person, a distinct life from beginning to end."

Elijah didn't turn to face Noah while he spoke, and his pace never slowed. It was impossible to tell how he was navigating through the empty nether, and every moment brought Noah farther away from figuring out the route back. He was putting his faith in Elijah now, and trusted his friend not to lead him astray.

"So let me get this straight. You don't think the living are helpless and stupid. You hate the demons, and you hate The Matriarch, and you don't think the department is any better. Is there anything you do believe in?"

"I trust myself. And I want to trust you, but I'm not there yet. It's nothing personal, but you of all people must understand from the deceit and lies all around us. That's the other reason I came to collect you from the Mortuary though. I'm going to work with you on the mirror. Before Christmas break is over, before the demon attack, we're both going to know who you really are. Then I'll finally know if trust is more than a vulnerability in this place."

"You'll only find out who I used to be," Noah said, but there wasn't any fight left in his words. How could Elijah not realize that he was already telling him all his secrets? How could he not see that he was always trying as hard as he could to do the right thing, in a world where good and evil were as colorless as the long-forgotten dead?

CHRISTMAS BREAK

NONE OF THE FEARS IN NOAH'S HEAD COULD SURVIVE SEEING HIS daughter again. That was small consolation, however, and his head was soon occupied by an entirely new set of gnawing doubts. He'd planned to present himself to Lewis, and then have his grandson reintroduce Noah to his daughter. She might turn him away at first, but he'd keep coming back. Every day, every hour, helping them in any way that he could, until eventually his presence became impossible to ignore.

That plan lasted a good minute before he wondered how that would go for his grandson. If Lewis spoke openly about what he saw in front of Mandy's new husband, would the man take out his anger on the child? Or even Mandy for that matter—how far would she go to discourage Lewis from talking about his vision into the spirit world? No matter how much it hurt her—or him—she might think it was for the boy's own good to prevent him from growing up as different and damaged as she felt herself to be.

By the time Elijah found and exit to the Netherworld and Noah was standing outside of Mandy's house, all the courage and hope that had endured within him was burning as low as a guttering candle within a dweller. The sun was hanging low in the sky, reminding him how out of place he was as it cast long shadows on everything except him. He stared at the door for a long while, then circled round the house at a distance to look at the closed curtains all the way around. Noah heard Elijah say something about meeting him tomorrow to begin their work, but the words passed through Noah as insubstantial as the breeze.

There was one window on the second floor that was open. A pair of long and slender hands were sticking out, cradling an open book. Would her golden head appear if he called to her right now? Would she take one look at him before closing the window, never to return? The thought was too painful to bear. Noah kept himself hidden, discreetly crawling up a telephone pole a fair distance back to sit upon the wire which had no trouble bearing his spectral weight. The silver Lexus in the driveway looked like a toy from up here. Then he caught his first glimpse of his daughter: of her face, warmer and more vital than he'd remembered her in the dark rooms of his house. Of her hair, longer now, brushed and glossy and styled in a fashionable sweep. She was even wearing lipstick—something he'd never known her to do.

There was only so much that he could read from a surface glance alone, but it was enough to know that she was still there. That she was healthy, maybe even happy. Who was he to come to her with all of his troubles and burden her with the dread of demonic attacks and the world yet to come? Who was he to furrow her smooth brow with worry and spoil her peace, just so he could grasp at something he'd already lost so long ago?

Noah wasn't the only one watching Mandy. Below him on the opposite side of the street from her house was a line of purple hibiscus flowers, and one of the shrubs had just rustled. There it went again—whatever it was couldn't be too large to conceal itself so completely. Noah remembered the imps creeping into Lewis's bedroom as he slid down the telephone pole. If he was careful not to scare it off, he might be able to learn something.

If only he wasn't still a second year student. If only he could transform into animals like Elijah, or draw his own portals in the air, or control the winds like The Matriarch. For all the magic and wonders he'd seen since his death, he felt so helpless and clumsy as he snuck across the ground toward the bushes. He hadn't even thought to hold onto his stuffed animal with his physical remains—where had Elijah gone with the cart, anyway?

The closer Noah got, the more wicked creatures and unfamiliar demons his imagination conjured. He didn't have to think any farther than the inconspicuously toothless rasmacht to know the most dangerous creatures weren't necessarily the largest. It was therefore with great relief that he spotted the young dark-haired girl kneeling on the ground with her long black skirt tucked under her legs. She turned to see him at almost exactly the same time, and the immediate delight on her face was everything he could have dreamed to see on his own daughter.

"Hello corpsey. Still dead, are you?"

"Samantha! What are you doing here?"

"Your job, you lazy old man. You told me to keep an eye on them, so every day after school I've been stopping by to check. I'm on break now though, so I've been able to come twice a day. Mandy called the cops on me once."

Samantha couldn't stop grinning, evidently enormously proud of this last fact. She looked utterly maniacal between her milky white eye and all those little teeth, but it suited her all the same.

"I'm sorry—I mean thank you. I never thought that after all this time—"

"Damn right, all this time. I haven't seen or heard from you for a whole year. You could have at least written a thank-you note in blood on my mirror. But I kept coming back, because I knew you'd show up again one day, and when you did, which you have, I knew you were going to owe me, which you do."

"You're right. I'm sorry, you've been wonderful for watching over them, and I've been selfish. But if you only knew everything I'd been going through on the other side, you'd understand."

"Deal," Samantha replied without missing a beat.

"Deal... what?"

"Deal you telling me everything is the *first* thing you can do to make it up to me. And don't leave out any of the gorey details—you can even throw in some extra ones that never happened if you want. I won't mind."

The meagre winter light was fading fast, and while Noah didn't feel the chill, it was evident that Samantha was beginning to shiver. It was equally evident that she'd stay out here all night listening to Noah without a word of complaint if someone didn't force her not to. After some coaxing, and a little threatening, Samantha retrieved her skateboard which was hidden in another bush. Noah walked by her side while she coasted slow beside him down the residential streets, and Noah told her everything as they went.

He'd only intended to tell her the light-hearted parts. About the animals in Humstrum's class, and the goofy antics of their zombies, and all the mischievous pranks the imps had played. But then out slipped the fact that Noah was once a demon in a previous life, then all the events with the banishments, and the attacks, and the war that was looming within the spirit world.

Samantha was such an eager and encouraging listener that she even dropped her customary snark. She never judged Noah for the choices he made or the situations he got himself into, even when he talked about wanting to summon the rasmacht to eat The Matriarch's soul. She was fascinated by the Soul Net and the chainer batteries, and she didn't interrupt even when he talked about demons planning an attack on the very city she lived in.

By the time they arrived at Samantha's home, Noah had told her everything worth knowing about the past year and a half since he'd died. They stood together in silence in the dark outside her backdoor, and Noah paused to reflect upon what he'd just done.

He'd become so accustomed to being in a school full of spirits who looked like children, despite possessing the minds of full grown adults. And yet now he'd just told a thirteen year old girl things that would have terrified old men with a lifetime of experience and resolve. She might be interested in morbid topics, but the types of inescapable horrors he described waiting for her after death might well be the stuff of nightmares which would haunt her for years to come.

Samantha pulled away from him to lean her skateboard against the house. Every second of silence between them magnified Noah's dread that once again he'd been selfish to burden his troubles upon another. She never would have been attacked in the first place if it weren't for him, she'd been watching over his family all this time, yet still he'd betrayed her trust again.

"Ooh boy," Samantha said with a long breath. "Thanks, that's good to know. Follow me—it's my turn now."

Samantha led Noah inside and briefly greeted her parents who were sitting in the living room. Mr. and Mrs. Bailey appeared to be intelligent, stern people who dressed like they believed casual day only goes as far as untucking the shirt. Mr. Bailey buried his ample mustache on top of Samantha's head for a kiss, while Mrs. Bailey only looked up from her book long enough to tell Samantha dinner was in the fridge. Neither asked her where she'd been, and Samantha volunteered no answer as she bustled up the wooden staircase. Noah drifted through the house unseen, feeling entirely out of place as he glided after her.

Stepping into Samantha's room felt like being swallowed by a fabric monster. Gypsy curtains covered the doorway and draped everywhere in the small space, with additional colored cloth pinned across the ceiling, and thick embroidered rugs covering the floor. She sat down on the center of a round one with a spiral design and patted the ground in front of her to indicate Noah should sit as well.

She began with the gargoyles. The one that attacked her last year only stayed in her neighborhood for about a week, although it hadn't bothered her as she pretended not to see it. The week after she'd spotted it a few blocks down, with several more sightings across the last year. She'd also witnessed two attacks where they'd caught hold of someone by the neck and clenched their claws until they'd stopped moving and the spirit came out. Both the victims could see the gargoyles before they were attacked. Noah didn't need to voice his own opinion for her to guess that it was the T.D.D. going out of their way to collect chainer souls to turn into batteries.

Then there were the demon attacks. She'd seen half-a-dozen since the beginning of the summer. Four of them resulted in deaths—more than deaths. Samantha guessed that their souls were eaten, because she didn't see any spirit emerge like they had with the gargoyles. Noah asked her about the horrendous noise of a breaking soul, but she said she didn't hear anything. Then again, it was only her eye that was cut by the gargoyle, so maybe it was too much to expect to hear everything going on in the spirit world as well.

Samantha had also caught a pair of imps sneaking into Mandy's house on one occasion last month, some time after Noah had caught them on Halloween. She'd gone through the window after them, but they bolted as soon as she got them cornered. That was also the time Mandy called the cops. Lewis hadn't been afraid of the imps though—in fact he seemed familiar with them as though he'd grown accustomed to their visits.

There was one more visitor that Noah should know about, a spirit who had come to visit more than once. Perfectly curled grey hair, a midnight dress filled with stars, and a face like she'd just been served spoiled food, but was trying to be polite about it. Samantha hadn't been able to determine what she was doing inside the house, and Noah confirmed that it sounded like The Matriarch.

"I can't explain it either," Noah said. "She brought me to visit them through the Whispering Room last year, so of course she knows where they live. She must not be on the same team as the department at all, otherwise she would have turned them over to the gargoyles that were hunting the other chainers. She also wouldn't let Elijah—another chainer who helped me get back here—get caught in the Soul Net. Maybe she's trying to protect my family too? I can't imagine why the imps are meeting with my grandson though, or what she might be doing here."

Samantha shrugged and yawned. "You're going to let me help you plant the dwellers around town, right?"

"Yeah, we could use the help." Noah stood from the rug. "I'll come get you first thing in the morning."

"You're not going anywhere. You can sleep on the rug, right where I can see you."

"I don't usually sleep at night. Spirits just get tired during the day when the light is going through us."

"Well you're in the living world now, so you're going to have to adjust. My parents have given me a curfew, and I'm not allowed out at night anymore. You should also get your friend and invite him too—don't think I didn't see him lurking around. I'm not going to let you sneak away again and leave on an adventure while I miss out on all the fun."

The following days leading up to Christmas were divided between three tasks. First and foremost, Noah was determined to distribute his entire jar of dwellers to help ward off demons. Despite Elijah's deep mistrust of the department, they spotted several of their white-gloved agents methodically placing some of the pumpkins and gourds around the city. These were garnished with a Santa hat or Christmas lights so as not to look too out of place, and they were invariably installed around malls, the business district, and other densely populated areas which they must have deemed most vulnerable to attack.

This left Noah and Elijah to cover as many of the suburban neighborhoods as they could with their supply. Noah would ride in the cart while Samantha rode her skateboard ahead to scout out good locations to plant the dwellers. Suitable heads included artificial Santas, reindeer, and other such decorations. Elijah cautioned that the dwellers would likely crawl away unless they were happy with their new home, and he'd often make them pass several likely locations until he was satisfied.

Noah made a special point of installing a dweller into the head of the lumpy snowman in his daughter's yard. Noah was confident he must be the best in the class at the sealing spell by now, despite missing his semester examinations. After the spell, he took a few minutes to thank the dweller for keeping his family safe. It wasn't clear whether the freshly planted phantom worm understood him, but it felt good to say nonetheless.

The second task which occupied his time was practicing with the Mirror of Ancestry. Samantha wouldn't leave his side during these sessions either. She would remain cross-legged and silent for hours at a time, endlessly fascinated by Noah's frustrated attempts to make sense of his image. Noah warned her not to mention to Elijah that he used to be a demon, advice which seemed especially prudent as they prepared for a possible attack.

Elijah assisted by bringing Noah around several more hospitals, but all of the attempts proved fruitless as even the occasional death failed to generate enough energy for the mirror. Samantha helpfully volunteered to write a list of people who totally deserved to be knocked off, but Noah laughed the suggestion off in the hopes that she was joking. Noah idly mentioned that they'd have plenty of energy if they could get their hands on a chainer battery, but just the thought of it put Elijah into such a bad mood that they had to cancel practice for the rest of the day.

The third and most pleasant occupation was for Noah to keep watch on his family. Elijah was instrumental in this field, as he would transform Noah into a mouse and allow him to enter the house undetected. He still didn't dare approach them directly, but he was able to pass through the walls unhindered and enter any room at will. There weren't any strange visitors or imps dropping by, and Noah was able to spend many pleasurable afternoons watching Lewis haphazardly building with his favorite LEGO space-station set.

Despite his caution, these visits did not come without their cost. It was Christmas Eve, and Lewis was putting together the puzzle of an old-fashioned train on his own. It was a huge puzzle for his age, at least a hundred pieces, and he must have been working on it for quite a long time. He'd already jammed in a couple of the wheel pieces where they didn't belong though, and now he was growing visibly frustrated as none of the last pieces would fit in the remaining spots.

He looked like he was getting close to tears, and Noah couldn't bear to watch.

"Look at the chimney where it's crooked," Noah whispered in his little mousey voice. "Those aren't part of the boiler, they're wheels!"

Lewis did as he was told and switched the pieces around without looking up. The giggle and smile that lit up the child's face was a moment of magic that none of his classes could ever hope to teach. The purity of this innocent bliss was surely a light Noah could carry with him on all his journeys ahead, no matter how dark and gruesome they might be.

"Papa?"

It seemed impossible for the boy to recognize Noah, a year later and in the form of a mouse, but Lewis was looking right at him now. Noah hadn't realized how close he'd crept, and now under the full intensity of attention that only a child can give, Noah was helpless to run away.

"Always," Noah replied, his voice breaking with emotion.

"Papa's back!" Lewis squealed—too loudly.

Lewis was on his feet and rushing toward Noah, who remained frozen on the carpeted floor. Then another sound finally got Noah moving—the opening door. Mandy would still be able to see him. If she caught him there—

"Wait come back!" Lewis shouted. "Papa!"

"What is this foolishness?"

It wasn't Mandy though—Barnes was standing in the doorway. Everything about the man bothered Noah. From the polish on his black shoes, to his smooth-pressed khakis, to his perfectly shaved face and cold, passionless eyes.

Noah paused to watch, realizing he couldn't be seen. That was a mistake. Lewis launched himself across the floor and tried to seize Noah, although his hands passed smoothly through him with barely a tingle. Lewis began to giggle, swiping his hands through Noah again and again.

"He's right there. I can see him!" Lewis declared resolutely.

"Who was?"

"Don't say it. Don't—" Noah began.

"Papa. Papa's here. He's helping me puzzle."

"He helped you with your puzzle?" Barnes asked in his bland voice. He stooped down to inspect the train, running his fingers along the nearly-finished picture. Noah took the opportunity to creep back through the wall, letting no more than the front of his face push through the barrier to watch what was going on.

"You did this all by yourself?" Barnes asked. "It's quite good."

"No, I told you—"

"Wrong answer," Barnes interrupted. He brought his other hand down, and slowly, deliberately, crushed the puzzle together. The pieces bent and sprayed past each other as they crumpled into a heap.

Lewis howled and rushed to stop him. He flung himself on the man's hands and tried to hold him back. Barnes shoved the child roughly back to the ground and finished scrambling the pieces, looking directly at Lewis the whole while.

"No, you did it by yourself. There's no one else here, do you understand?"

Lewis was breathing too heavily to reply. He was still trying to collect the pieces with trembling hands.

"Don't look at the puzzle. Look at me. Did anyone help you with the puzzle?"

It would have been bad enough if he was speaking in anger, but that cold, almost bemused voice was even more repulsive. Barnes ripped the remaining pieces from the boy's hands and scattered them across the room. Lewis had tears in his eyes when he was finally able to look up.

"No dad," Lewis mumbled. "I did it myself."

Barnes clapped him on the back and grinned. "That's right. And you can do it again. Now go brush your teeth and get ready for bed. Tomorrow's going to be a big day."

Noah didn't stay long after that. He only left for long enough to retrieve his stuffed tiger from the cart he'd kept with Elijah. He'd grown quite attached to the thing over the last year and a half, but it was too large to carry with him as a mouse. He was going to miss it now that he was using a claw to rip the seam and tear it end to end. He still burned with anger while he pulled out the stuffing until he found the magical core: the clean, white, polished lower jar from his old corpse. A bit of string wound through the teeth, and he'd have a necklace he could carry with him even as a mouse.

Before Noah began on his quest to make things right, he stopped by Claire's house and collected Mrs. Robinson, who had remained with her girl. He discussed his plan with her, and she readily agreed to help. Noah remembered that when the cat was still alive, she often killed small animals and brought them to Claire as a present. The girl didn't much care for these gifts, however, and she'd made her mother Mrs. Thistle throw them away. Mrs. Robinson had gone back into the trash later to bring them out again, where she kept her trophies safe in the attic where Mrs. Thistle wouldn't find them.

Noah found them with Mrs. Robinson's help, and he was going to put them to good use. Noah thought back on his necromancy lessons and used his jaw bone to channel the spell. It only took two attempts before he got one of Mrs. Robinson's old squirrels to sit up on its own, and from there he began his Christmas miracle.

The squirrel zombie was clumsy and slow. Its little hands weren't very good at picking up the puzzle pieces strewn across Lewis's bedroom floor, but Noah had all night to direct the work, and he was determined not to leave until he was finished.

The next morning Lewis would wake up to see his puzzle finished again. And whether or not he ever said it out loud, he'd know in his heart that it was his grandfather who had put it back together again. After-all, what good was all the magic in the world, if it couldn't be used to bring a little joy to a child on Christmas Day?

THAT EVENT WAS NOT the last run-in with Barnes this Christmas vacation. The next was far more sinister. It was December 31st, the last day of the year. The last day before Visoloth warned the demons would descend upon the town, and tensions were high.

It was late in the afternoon, and Noah was back in his human body. He thought it best to keep a little distance from his family's activities, but he couldn't resist stopping by just to check on them. That's when he saw that the snowman in the yard had been decapitated and smashed into pieces. Every clump of snow was finely strewn across the icy ground. The dweller was gone.

It was Barnes. Lewis must have bragged about the puzzle being finished, and he'd decided to ruin something else out of spite. Noah had to go collect one of the nearby dwellers and bring it back here, and he cursed Barnes the whole way. He was just beginning to fantasize about fashioning a voodoo doll out of him when he turned the corner and saw the plastic Santa head he'd installed the next dweller in: smashed to pieces. Pummeled, splintered, and spread across the sidewalk. It was the only ornament that was destroyed in the yard, and the dweller was gone.

This wasn't just an accident, or a reckless lash of anger. These were deliberately destroyed, and the only explanation was that someone wanted to make it easier for the demons to attack.

Noah rushed to get Elijah right away. He was upstairs in Samantha's room while she was downstairs celebrating her own New Years eve with her family. The pair of boys didn't disturb her as they rushed out to scout the third location for where they stored the dwellers: a festive gourd that someone had placed on their porch. Pulverized, with the juices still fresh and sticky as they ran down the rocking chair it had been placed on. The dweller was gone. The demons were attacking tomorrow, and there was nothing left to keep them safe.

HELL ON EARTH

"There he is. Come on, he's getting away!" Elijah shouted.

Noah tore his eyes away from the dismembered gourd, just in time to see a sleek grey Lexus turning at the end of the street. A few staggered steps quickly brought him to a halt again—there was no way he was going to catch the car on foot. Elijah sat down on the deck and was already mumbling something under his breath as the faded markings on his skin glowed with the spell.

"How do you know it was him?" Noah asked. "How would a living person even know the dwellers were there?"

Elijah's tattoos pulsed twice, then went dull again. His eyes were closed. All his urgency seemed to be gone. He couldn't have fallen asleep, could he? Noah paced back and forth across the deck several times in rapid, agitated succession before Elijah finally reacted.

Elijah's hand lashed out and seized Noah by the arm. His eyes snapped open, and there was something almost like a grin on his thin lips. A glint in his eye reminded Noah of a feral animal about to leap into the hunt.

"I don't think a mouse is going to cut it this time. You ready to fly?"

Noah would have said no if he could figure out how to speak through his beak. It felt like he was falling as the ground rushed up to meet him. Everything was getting bigger at the same time—a dizzying sensation of contradictory perspective, made more so as his instinctual response was to explode back upward as he launched involuntarily into the air. The jawbone necklace was cumbersome around his neck now, but it was more familiar than his new body and reassured him against whatever lay in store.

First came the bliss of the wind beneath his wings, followed by the realization that he was already as high as the rooftops, leading to the helpless terror of the distant drop below him. Long black feathers beat the air in frantic disarray on either side. An ugly, strangled squawk rumbled up his throat. He swerved sharply to the right, fluttering madly to stay aloft like a dog paddling water.

"Stop thinking about it so much," a second raven cawed as it soared past him. "Flying is all about letting go. Ride the current like you're surfing."

Elijah was already far above by the time Noah managed to steady his flight. The wings took over and ruffled into place on their own, adjusting single feathers with the unconscious ease of someone putting one foot in front of the other to walk. The trick was getting his conscious mind to relax and not interfere in a mad panic. Fear and exhilaration can start to taste the same with enough exposure though, and it didn't take long before the true extent of his freedom in the open sky dawned on him.

The alien atmosphere in the Netherworld was too oppressive to give a sensation like this. Swimming in the ocean had been fun, but again the force of the water was too limiting to go anywhere quickly. Flying was another world altogether, one where anything was possible and nothing but lightning could rival the mastery of these skies. His wings powerfully captured the air now as he mounted into the heavens, and then turning to angle himself back to the earth, he sliced through the sky with deadly accuracy, a comet hurled by God.

Noah repeated the dive two more times, only pulling up from the ground at the last possible second. His mind was flooded with the thrill which engulfed him like electricity. He didn't remember what he was supposed to be doing until he heard Elijah's discordant caw overhead.

"I see him. He's a living man, and he's driving straight toward the next closest dweller. There's someone else in the car with him too. I can't tell who the other is, but I don't think it's alive. I'm pretty sure that's what is giving him directions."

"Oh right, yeah. Don't leave me, I'm coming," Noah replied, working his way awkwardly around his new beak. He scrambled for a moment in the air as he tried to take conscious control again, but a moment later he was swooping gracefully after Elijah. It would have been hard to keep up with the car on the open road, but they were cutting diagonally through the winding neighborhood, and it didn't take long before Noah caught sight.

Looking down on the Lexus jogged his memory in a way seeing it at the end of the street hadn't. It reminded him of the angle when he was sitting on the telephone wire, looking down at the car in Mandy's driveway. It didn't seem possible, didn't make sense, but the closer he got, the more absurd it was to deny.

"Barnes is driving," Noah declared. "My daughter's husband."

"He's not a chainer, is he? I didn't think he could see spirits."

"He couldn't. He can't. I've been right next to him without him noticing before."

The car below slid to a smooth stop at a red light. Noah glided past to perch on a street sign, overshooting slightly and fumbling to clamor back on. He was able to look through the front windshield this time, and the shock of what he saw almost made him fall off again.

There was a corpse sitting beside Barnes in the passenger seat. Its skin sagged so much that it drooped off the face entirely, frayed and ashen pale. Its once thick white beard now barely clung on in matted uneven clumps, vanishing completely where its lower jaw was missing. The eye sockets were so deeply set that they were nothing but gaping holes, fully concealed beneath a baseball cap. Noah was glad he couldn't see them though, because he knew they'd lack the keen light he'd grown accustomed to looking back at him over the years.

"He doesn't have a spirit with him. He's got a body. *My* body."

The zombie lifted a ragged hand and pointed toward the right. The car signaled to turn, then it was off again. The traffic was becoming substantial as they approached downtown where they slowed to a crawl. The corpse looked down into his lap and pulled the hat low to conceal its rotting features from idle eyes. Its movements were as controlled and smooth as a living person—whoever was animating it must really know what they're doing.

"They aren't getting anywhere fast. New Years Eve, no surprise there. It looks like they're heading to the dweller in the mall though. I'll meet you there."

"How... why... what?" Noah stumbled, his beak feeling clumsier than ever as he recovered from the shock. "Where are you going?"

"Gotta check the other dwellers, see how many of them are still left and which can still be saved. Don't lose him—and hey, try not to take any of it personally, you know? That body has nothing to do with you anymore. It's just loose skin and bones, the same as everyone else's got. You're so much more than that. Don't worry, we're going to figure this out together."

"Yeah, right, sure. My son-in-law and my dead body are just teaming up to invite demons in to slaughter people. What's to worry about?"

Noah was only talking to himself though. Elijah was already a black speck in the distance, soon lost above the sea of lights which were sparkling to life amid the growing dusk. His mind raced through his studies, searching for something he could use to stop Barnes. Raising his own zombie? Where was he going to find a body in the city? Summoning a demon? They were already trying to get in for the attack, bringing more would only make things worse. A voodoo doll? He'd need to find the ingredients for the summoning. There was a butcher's shop in town he could probably get some blood from, and if he flew ahead to the mall...

The silver Lexus made another turn. It was getting onto a freeway, not headed downtown at all. Noah scanned the sky in frantic panic— no sign of Elijah. He was on his own, trapped in an alien body that he didn't even know how to get out of by himself. The irony wasn't lost on him that his real body was below... no, not his real body. There was no such thing as his real body. There was just his mind, his soul, and the choices he made when fate called upon him to act.

Noah turned away from the glimmering city lights, and plunged into the gathering night after the silver car. The traffic wasn't as bad in this direction, and without the city intersections, he didn't know how he was going to keep up. It wasn't enough to just relax and let the animal instincts fly anymore—he had to push himself harder and faster with every fiber of his being. Intrusive images of demons crawling over Mandy's house and slithering around his grandson while the boy slept lent power to his every beating wing. The sky didn't feel like freedom anymore. It felt like a prison, and the only way to escape was to keep diving deeper into its embrace.

A physical body would have tired long before Noah's spirit gave up. There was, however, a mental cost to his toil as he fought to maintain coordination over his unfamiliar form. Pursuing the speeding car felt more like fighting to understand what he was reading after long hours of weariness took hold and numbed his mind. His wings slipped again and again, pitching him into an ungainly dive, but each time he righted himself and redoubled his effort to not let the car disappear.

The city gave way to the surrounding suburbs. The houses interspersed more with wild vegetation as the car sped along the dark road. Noah had to fly lower to the road as the airspace became tangled with the grasping branches of sycamore and maple trees. It wasn't until they were traveling five minutes or more between houses when the car began to slow on an uninhabited portion of the road. The headlights became brighter, and it continued along at a crawl until they found what they were looking for: a dirt track ambling off into the thickest part of the woods.

The Lexus edged off the paved road and rumbled over the increasingly treacherous ground. Several loud *cracks* and *scrapes* resounded from the underbelly of the car as it dragged itself over hidden rocks. On one hand this helped, as it forced them to drive slow enough that it became much easier to keep up. On the other, the recklessness worried Noah. Barnes always fretted over cleanliness and perfection. He should have been more concerned about the damage to his car. Unless of course, he wasn't planning on returning alive at all. Or could Barnes be a helpless hostage, forced on this course against his will?

Noah received no answers until the car pulled to a complete stop beside an especially mighty sycamore tree, broad of branch with bark so white it seemed to glow as it reflected the headlights. Noah concealed himself amidst the branches of a nearby tree, and watched as Barnes stooped unsteadily to inspect the scratches along the bottom of his car. The zombie exited the other side, its fluid movements making it appear even more alive than its companion. The corpse removed its baseball cap and threw it on the ground before approaching the pale tree. It was carrying something in its arms, but its body was blocking Noah's line of sight.

Noah fluttered to the next tree to get a better angle. His movement caused the zombie to react, turning its head in a viciously sharp twist as it peered over its back shoulder. There was no mistaking those eyes which pierced the darkness scanning for him: two diamonds glittering in the depths of its sockets. He also caught sight of what the zombie was carrying: a grey purse that bulged and squirmed from what must be the chainer battery inside. It was sickening to watch his own corpse moving on its own accord, made worse for knowing The Matriarch was pulling its strings.

"You could have told me we were going off-road," Barnes grumbled. "It was bad enough getting that pumpkin juice on my suit, but—"

"Forget the car," the zombie ordered, its voice a macabre, rasping parody of Noah's own. The head swiveled away from the branches where the spectral raven was concealed. "Get the dwellers. Bring them here."

Barnes continued, mumbling something under his breath as he circled around to the trunk. The zombie meanwhile approached the tree, running one hand down the trunk almost reverently. A dirty finger cut into the white bark and began drawing a circle. It then cut a variety of symbols that reminded Noah of geometric summoning components.

"Put them down," the zombie rasped as Barnes approached. "No, over there where it's flatter. Careful not to spill!"

The man handed off a flower vase—one taken from Mandy's dining room table—now filled with the struggling, naked worms that were the captured dwellers. Noah couldn't count them exactly, but there seemed enough that it was likely they had collected all of them. Slowly, deliberately, with relish, the zombie stuffed its dirty hand into the vase and crushed the worms against the glass. Each of them made a small, sad, squeaking noise as they popped. The zombie then smashed the glass against the tree trunk in a savage display of power. Elijah should have realized what had happened by now. Would he be able to find them here?

"Stand against the tree. Back against the bark, where I've drawn the circle," the zombie demanded. Barnes did as he was told, folding his hands peacefully in front of him.

"Are you going to kill me now?" Barnes asked. He might as well have been asking what time it was for how calm he was.

"Are you afraid?"

Barnes snorted derisively, but said nothing.

"Oh my dear, sweet Barnes. If only the world had more people like you in it. There's nothing quite so admirable as knowing your place."

"It's all the same to me, my Matriarch—"

But he never got any further than that. The next thing to come out of his mouth was a bubble of blood. In one brutal movement, the zombie had thrust pointed fingers deep into the man's belly. Now up to the wrist, now up to the elbow, and deeper still until the hand must be penetrating straight into the tree behind him. The wound wasn't bleeding, however, and the blood seemed to be running inward directly into the tree. A rusty, red color was spreading across the white bark around him. It wasn't exactly staining the tree though—it looked more like it was going underneath the bark, like blood flushed beneath the skin.

Noah couldn't believe his eyes. Being impaled like that should have been excruciatingly painful for Barnes, but he didn't struggle and hardly seemed concerned as his face turned waxen white. Vasculature like a network of arteries were branching out beneath the bark to send the blood coursing through the tree. Small holes like cigarette burns began to open in the bark. They smoldered from the inside-out, growing hotter and brighter as small tongues of flame began to lick out of the internally burning trunk.

The zombie withdrew its hand from Barnes' belly with a awful, squelching sound. It opened the grey purse to remove a beating crystal heart, just like the ones Noah had seen inside the statues at the Department of Energy. The hand plunged back in to implant the heart deep into Barnes' open wound—then deeper, all the way into the tree. The zombie's arm was stained red past the elbow when it pulled free once more, and it used the excess fluid to continue painting the circle on the bark with spiral patterns. The multitude of burning holes in the tree were glowing hotter more numerous by the second.

Noah watched, transfixed, finding the whole thing almost beautiful in a dreamlike way he couldn't verbalize in thought. He had the oddest sensation of watching two halves of the same whole coming together again, lost soul mates finding each other after eons apart. His helpless captivation endured until words spoken in his old voice from his old throat shook him back into the present.

"Remember the name of the one who welcomed you back. All demons should be grateful to their brother, the chainer Noah Tellaver. Through his flesh you will enter this world and wage war against the department which has betrayed you."

The zombie hurled itself into the growing spouts of flame emanating from the tree. The dead, dry skin took like kindling and was swiftly engulfed. It wasn't just a matter of being flammable though—it looked more as if all the fire that had been raging inside the tree was pouring into the two bodies. The thousand smoldering holes were no longer spitting fire—they were blinking. A thousand glinting eyes blossoming from the flame which brought them into the world.

"Get out of there. Noah, can you hear me? Go!"

"Jamie?" Noah asked, mystified. He still couldn't tear his eyes away from the baleful conflagration.

"Walter and Brandon are here too," Jamie's voice continued. "Well not here, here, but that doesn't matter—"

"We're scrying on you from Wolf's place," Walter's voice cut in. "I can't believe you didn't take me with you. Never mind, doesn't matter, you seriously have to run. Or fly, I guess, whatever."

"How slow can he be?" Brandon's voice chimed in. "Doesn't he realize he's at ground zero of the nether portal?"

"Are you sure that's even him?" Walter asked. "What if we're just talking to a crow? Noah, can you hear us? We've got our textbooks open and some banishment spells ready if you want to try and—"

The tree exploded outward with the brilliance of the sun. Shards of splintered wood formed a circular nova which tore through the surrounding forest like shrapnel. If Noah had been corporal, the pieces which flew through him would have torn him to shreds. Nearby trees were ripped from the earth and hurled outward. The parked Lexus was overturned end over end as the ground below it heaved like an ocean storm.

Out from the center of the wreckage they came, crawling, slithering, flying, oozing—dozens, hundreds, countless twisted and gruesome forms pouring free from the Netherworld. Scampering imps, Peruvian Bluescales, Borovian Worms, Lava Salamanders, Gobblers and so many others that Noah couldn't recognize, all flooding free from the gash in reality which existed where the tree had once been.

The tide of demons flowed unevenly from the rift. Even in their wild charge, they were taking care to avoid the patch of ground where the glass of dwellers had been smashed. Then Noah spotted the tiniest movement on the ground, what surely would have been invisible if not for his keen avian eyes. He made a swift dive and plucked a solitary surviving dweller which was struggling to bury itself inside the earth. He could feel the heat emanating from the surrounding demons as he did, but they never got close enough to impede his rescue. A moment later and he was back in the air, struggling to gain altitude.

The solitary worm wrapped around his talons, squealing and clinging on in terror.

"What are you doing? Fly the hell out of there!"

Noah beat the air madly to rise above the maelstrom below him. It was difficult to distinguish all the churning bodies below, but one thing was clear: they were all headed straight for the city. All those people—Mandy and Lewis—preparing their celebrations. They had no idea what the new year had in store for them.

"Walter, get Mr. Wolf now," Jamie's voice ordered. "Tell him to scry Meep at the department and get help. Brandon, you get back to the school. I want you to get as many people as you can to follow you. Meet me in Professor Humstrum's room—I'll be setting up the empathy spell to try and mediate the attack."

"Someone has to stay and help Noah," Walter protested.

"Elijah is looking for you, Noah," Jamie said. "He wanted you to meet him at your daughter's house. He knows more advanced stuff than we do, so I'm sure he'll be able to help. I don't know what the zombie was talking about, but none of this is your fault. We have to go—just be careful, okay? Everything is going to be fine. And don't try to fight the demons on your own!"

There was no point in replying. Their presence was already gone. Wasn't his fault though? Everything was going to be fine? How could she possibly say that? Why did The Matriarch have to use his body, anyway? It occurred to him that she must have realized he'd told the department about the demon's plans while he'd concealed them from her. How could she not, if she was in on the attack the whole time? Using his body must have been some sort of petty revenge. And trying to keep him from going home over Christmas—that was more than just a personal slight. She hadn't wanted him to try and prevent the attack. But how could The Matriarch possibly benefit from having the demons here? So many people would be killed… and so many spirits would be sent to the spirit world. And so many more souls would become caught in her net. She really didn't care how much suffering and death she caused, as long as it put more power into her hands.

Noah kept an eye on the demons for a little while, but he was able to quickly outpace them in his flight. Most seemed inexperienced with the living world and were taking some time to acclimate to the atmosphere here. Some of the imps kept hopping into the air and trying to swim like they would through the Netherworld, only to fall back onto their faces in the earth. Others pushed and shoved each other in a playful way, chasing and hopping over one another.

The demons didn't seem evil. They did have souls, no matter what the other spirits thought. They weren't stupid either—they must understand that their quarrel was with the Trans Dimensional Department, and that the living had never done anything to them. The living couldn't even agree on whether demons existed! It didn't make sense for the demons to just indiscriminately slaughter people. They'd achieve nothing but justify the prejudices against them. Was there a chance Noah had misunderstood Visoloth completely? Could the demons have some other prize in mind? Perhaps they were only seeking to destroy the Soul Net. That's what made them so angry in the first place, wasn't it? Sure, there was that business with The Matriarch trying to cheat at a few contracts, but surely that was insignificant compared to the abomination of trapping souls all around the world.

Noah had just about convinced himself that the demons weren't going to attack at all when he heard the first screams filter through the trees. Those living in the isolated houses in the woods must be the first victims. Again Noah allowed himself a flutter of hope—it's only natural for people to scream when they see a demon for the first time. It doesn't mean that—

But then the screams cut short, even quicker than they started. It was hard to imagine more than one reason why someone would stop screaming after they saw the demons. There was nothing Noah could do but push himself ever harder back toward his daughter's house and try not to listen as each fresh scream began and ended below. Soon the demons would be reaching the more densely populated areas, and Noah could think of nothing that could hope to stem the wave of anguish from the winds.

Noah felt worn thin by the time he reached the house. He'd

managed to outpace the demons, but already the panic was swelling through the streets as and endless procession of sirens created their own artificial shrieks. Elijah was already there back in his human body, the tattoos on his arm glowing fiercely as he mumbled a rapid succession of incantations. He lashed out a hand to seize Noah as soon as he landed, prompting the ground to rush away from him as he too returned to human form.

"I managed to save one of the dwellers," Noah gasped as soon as he had lips again.

"That's more than I could find. Get it into the snow, quickly now," Elijah said.

Samantha was there putting the finishing touches on a new snowman to house it. She took off her own blue woolen cap to place on its head as Noah slipped the worm inside. Elijah already had a candle and the sealing spell prepared. He laid his hands upon the snow to bind it with a flash of light.

"I can't believe we've been so careless. I never would have thought someone could find them all so quickly."

"My parents are here too," Samantha said. "So is Claire and her family, and Mrs. Robinson, and a few others inside they were able to convince. They don't understand what's going on, but Mandy seems to understand more than the others, and she's trying to encourage them to stay."

"Is she alright? And Lewis? I have to see them!" Noah began moving for the house, but Elijah caught him by the arm.

"The lone dweller might be enough to keep them away from the house, and it might not. I know some banishments, but even the advanced classes won't prepare you for anything like this. We're going to need help from someone with a little more experience."

Elijah turned to race over by the snowman where Noah's red cart was parked. "Who else is there? What are you talking about?" Noah called after him.

The older boy returned a moment later, his face plastered with an almost maniacal grin. In his arms he carried an object concealed in velvet—the Mirror of Ancestry. Noah furrowed his brow in confusion. "You can't be serious. We don't have time to practice—"

"This isn't practice. This is the real thing," Elijah cut him off. He planted the mirror in the snow and whipped the covering from it. "We may not be able to save everyone, but at least we can make sure their deaths aren't in vain. The energy released from one death was almost enough for you to make contact with your previous lives. Just imagine when the air is charged by the slaughter of a whole city."

Noticing the look of disgust on Noah's face, Elijah hastened to add, "Well, we won't let them *all* die, that's the point. I've only ever been able to contact a few of my previous lives too. But they'll be able to help us, don't you see? We're both chainers, and between the two of us we must have lived so many lives that surely one of them will know what to do."

"How many will have to die before there's enough energy in the air?" Noah asked, uncertain. He glanced around to see Samantha kneeling in the snow in silence, her green and white eyes stretched wide and quivering. Flashes of movement behind the windows of the house as someone pulled the curtains shut. The chorus of distant emergency sirens were unending, and splashes of red and blue sparkled across the snow whenever the police or an ambulance raced past their street.

"That will depend on us," Elijah replied in a hushed voice. "On who we are, and who we were, and depending on how this night ends, who we will be going forward."

Noah nodded and moved to stand with Elijah in front of the glass. Two distinct faces appeared side-by-side in the reflection, both morphing and changing so quickly as to leave no distinct features.

"Concentrate," Eljiah murmured. "You're going to hear things around you that you've never heard in the living world before. There will be spirits coming out of the dead. They will be confused, and scared, still traumatized by their death and the deaths of those around them. And even then they will not be safe, because demons can attack the spirits as easily as they can attack the living. But if you really want to help them, you have to block all of that out and put everything you are into the mirror. It's the only thing that exists in the world right now. Do you understand?"

Noah nodded again, not turning away from the glass or even speaking lest the words disrupt him. The dance of shifting images was mesmerizing, and his mind was clear and focused. He was ready.

"I can help though," Samantha said, her voice seeming so small beside the wall of panicked noise that was rising all around them. "I can go where the people are dying and lead the spirits back near our dweller where it's safe."

"No. The demons will—" Noah began. A firm hand on the back of his neck turned his head back toward the mirror.

"Focus," Elijah repeated. "We can stop this."

"I'll be back before you know it," Samantha said more firmly. "Just don't go anywhere leaving me behind again. And if something does happen, you'll find a way to tell my mom, okay?"

"Samantha wait—ah…" The grip on the back of Noah's neck tightened. He couldn't look away, but he could hear the crunching snow and knew Samantha was running in the direction of the advancing demons. He was more aware than ever how loud it was getting. How many scared and helpless victims still stood between him and the creatures from the rift. The texture of the shouting was beginning to shift though, magnified in intensity as fear and disbelief turned to the pain of the dying.

Noah didn't have to turn away from the mirror to see the rising energy in the reflection. Bursts of blue and red and green like fireworks whose radiant sparks drifted upwards instead of down. Why did death have to be so beautiful?

"Concentrate…" Elijah hissed low. "Ancestors, can you hear us? Please give us a sign…"

The two faces in the mirror both split down the middle, shifting away from each other until four distinct morphing forms appeared. Then there was eight, sixteen, thirty-two, crowding the other side of the glass until it looked like the entire street was filled with people.

As the noise grew louder and more energy poured into the air, it became increasingly clear which images belonged to Elijah's past and which belonged to Noah. The more they split, the slower the faces morphed. There must be hundreds of people on the other side now, each real and solid and unchanging. Elijah's half of the mirror was dominated by a crowd of mostly animals, including multiple crows and ferrets similar to the shapes Elijah had borrowed. There were also people: men, women, children who must have died young, and aged scholars still clutching their favorite book.

On Noah's side of the mirror, however, there was only a single human face: the man he had been most recently, whose body was so casually used and destroyed by The Matriarch. Beside him stood rank upon rank of monstrous forms. Hunched backs, inverted exoskeletons, spines in place of hair, eyes of fire—each demon fouler and more deformed than the last. And right at the front, unconcealed by its monstrous brethren, leered the terribly blank gray face of a rasmacht itself, the soul eater. No features at all except for its grinning gummy mouth, and yet there was no doubt it was self-aware with all its attention bearing down on the two boys.

More terrifying than any form was the familiar chill which emanated from its image. The air seemed to crystallize as if they were suddenly trapped beneath a frozen lake, and even the act of thinking seemed so daunting as to be hardly worth the effort. The rubbery face pressed itself against its side of the glass, growing larger and larger until it dominated the entire mirror. Time seemed to be slowing down, and all the noise behind them grew muffled and indistinct. It was impossible to tell how long this state persisted before cold, gray, rubbery fingers suddenly gripped Noah by the front of his shirt.

The rasmacht's upper body had moved through the glass and into the living world, and Noah was helpless to evade its clutches.

LEGACY

Elijah didn't say a word. He looked like he'd forgotten how. His ancestors might have been saying something, but if so their voices simply joined the rest of the unintelligible static which hung in the frozen air.

"You aren't afraid, are you? That I would eat my *own* soul? Preposterous pickle that you've gotten yourself into, but don't worry, I'm here to help," the demon said. Even through the piercing cold, there penetrated the glimmer of shock through Noah's crystalized thoughts. He hadn't expected the rasmacht to have an English accent. It ran the back of one of its rubbery hands along the side of Noah's face, and he was helpless to even shudder at its touch.

"So this is who I became. Will become. Had been. Not disappointed, mind you, just… well I'd always imagined that if I ever became human I would have a little more gravitas. Oh true, true, you're just a boy so perhaps it is to be excused. I know you've been looking forward to me telling you how to summon a rasmacht and gobble up The Matriarch's soul, but I'm sorry to say that it can't be done. And even if it could, would you really be willing to sacrifice a second soul for the summoning? A soul for a soul, everything has its price.

"Ah, but how it would put your mind at ease to send all these other demons scampering home. Is that what you were hoping I'd do? Well I don't mind one bit telling you that they're exactly where they need to be. Let the demons kill as many as they like. It's important work, and there's no point putting up a fuss. I've heard that humans are such sentimental creatures that they can feel sorry for a lamp that has been treated unjustly. Whatever nonsense you think is important about saving lives has no importance next to something as sacred as the laws of reality. Life ends, spirits carry the soul after death, and demons help spirits get back to the other side. If I will be you, which I must be for you to have been me, I'd worry more about helping the demons restore order to the universe than I do about any broken lamps along the way.

"You're never going to get the right answers until you stop asking the wrong questions. Once you do, I suggest having a chat with my old friends, the primes Borowrath and Momslavi Lapis. And don't forget to invite me when you do—I'd hate not to collect on the bet we have running as to which of us will bring the end of all things. Chin up until then—death isn't so bad. We're already written into the final act, and won't miss it for anything. Zee Zee Balloo… bids you adieu."

The prickles of a thawing mind are at least as bad as the freezing itself. It was difficult to discern exactly when time started again, but when it had, there was no sign of the rasmacht named Zee Zee Balloo. The volume of the ambient noise turned back up, and the flavor of the anguish in the air had shifted subtly from the bleating of terror to the wailing of grief.

A tight formation of a dozen or more gargoyles swooped through the air overhead. The demons must have begun to withdraw while Noah had been lost in his reflection. There weren't any more explosions of colorful energy to mark each spot where a life had ended. There was only the mirror and its two inscrutably shifting forms. Only two frightened boys who had waded too far into the depths of the unknown, and were now mentally struggling to swim back to safety.

It wasn't just fear or confusion on Elijah's face though. Suspicion, anger, even hatred was twisting his features into a cruel caricature of the companion Noah had come to rely upon.

"You're a demon." It wasn't a question. It was an accusation.

"Yeah. I mean I was, but I'm not now. Obviously…"

"And you knew."

"Okay. So what?"

Elijah's face relaxed, but now it seemed so passive as to be concealing something even worse. Noah spotted Samantha standing nearby. She hadn't managed to bring any spirits back with her, but at least she appeared unharmed.

"You didn't tell me," Elijah continued, his voice cold and inflectionless. "You'd think it would have come up after the souls were destroyed. Or when I was asking you about who you were. Or when we were talking about the demon war. No wonder you didn't stop the portal when it was opening."

"What's that supposed to mean? You think I wanted this?" Noah threw up his arms in a wild gesture to encompass the surrounding city. "I just wanted to protect—"

"Zee Zee Balloo," Elijah interrupted.

"Huh? It sounds familiar…"

"Zee Zee Balloo," Elijah repeated, practically spitting the words. "A rasmacht. A soul eater. One of the three prime demons, asking you to meet the other two. I don't know whose side you're on or what you're after, but it isn't my side."

"There aren't any sides!" Noah said in exasperation. He glanced to Samantha for help, but she was silent. "There's just the cycle of life and death, and it's out of balance because of the Soul Net—"

"You even sound like him. Of course you do—he *is* you. I don't know why I was so stupid to think we were the same just because we were both chainers. I can't believe I delayed coming back to life just because I believed your ridiculous story about that net. You were just making excuses for the demon attacks this whole time."

"That's not true! Elijah, I know what I saw!"

"And I know what I saw," Elijah said, roughly shoving the mirror to topple over backwards. The glass shattered against the frozen ground to scatter shards of searing light. The whisper of a thousand voices rose and vanished from every broken corner. "You can find your own way back to school, if you're even going back. Maybe you'd rather go find your friends Borowrath and Momslavi Lapis and laugh about all the people you've killed."

"I hope you do come back to life," Samantha piped up, causing Elijah to jerk back in surprise. "And when you do, you become a human again and not a crow, because crows are loyal and clever and you're just a brat. I hope you come back as a fat, depressed, office worker with bad skin and more back hair than head hair, because that's all you deserve with your attitude. If it wasn't for Noah saving at least one of the dwellers, then the demons would have gotten us too. He doesn't even know half as many tricks as you do, and he was still the only one to help. You're the one who ought to be ashamed of himself."

Elijah's mouth churned for several seconds without any words coming out. He then turned sharply and leapt into the air, transforming in mid jump into a crow—just for spite, most likely. Within seconds, he was gone. The wail of sirens seemed to increase in the space of his absence.

"Thanks," Noah said, the word swallowed up by the heavy air.

"You aren't really going back, are you?" Samantha asked, her voice quivering slightly. Again Noah had to remind himself how much harder this must all be for someone as young as her. If she was holding it together, then how could he not do the same?

Noah shrugged in defeat and sat down in the snow. "It's not like I could even if I wanted to. George Hampton helped me the first time, but he's with the demons now and I don't want anything to do with them. And The Matriarch brought me here and back once, but there's no chance of that again. I really am stuck here."

"Oh poor you. A man who escaped death so he can continue living as a ghost with magical powers like some sort of super hero. Who can float around doing whatever they damn well please without having to go to school, or pay rent, or work. Who could ever wish for such a terrible existence?"

"It could be worse." Noah smiled. "I could be a sarcastic little girl whose only friends are dead people and a dead cat."

"Claire is my friend too. And there's a boy who sits with me at lunch sometimes, but I think he's doing it on a dare because all the other boys are scared of me."

"You're wrong about not having any work to do though. As long as I'm here, I might as well make myself useful. I know we can't bring all the dead people back to life, but there's a lot I can do to help repair the damage the demons have caused. Will you help me, never-Sammy?"

"What do you think I've been doing this whole time, dummy? You're absolutely helpless without me."

The damage caused to the Mortuary after the first demonic rebellion seemed extensive, but it was nothing compared to the ruinous destruction this time around. Though the demons had departed as mysteriously as they appeared, the fires they left behind were still sweeping the city. Smashed windows, broken doors, and the scars of grief and fear in the survivors would take a long time to heal. But so long as this darkness had to be endured, at least there was the blessing of being able to do it with a true friend.

OFFICIAL REPORTS in the news put the death toll from the initial attack at almost exactly one thousand, although that number continued to rise in the following days as a result of the fires and the wild panic which persisted for almost a week. Federal aid descended upon the city from all directions to treat it like a natural disaster, but all who survived that terrible night knew there was nothing natural about the monstrous denizens of the Netherworld.

The demonic attack on the living was an act of heinous cruelty. Their attack on the spirits was nothing short of blasphemy. Noah had expected the spiritual refugees of the dead to be overwhelming, and he was shocked to find that no spirits had escaped the demons at all. Investigators from the Trans Dimensional Department scoured the city without finding any trace of the victim's souls. Whether they were eaten, or destroyed, or perhaps stolen for something even fouler remained an unsolved mystery.

Stranger still was the manner in which the demons attacked. They didn't sweep through the city like a pillaging horde of vikings, launching themselves at everyone who got in their way. They picked and chose, killing all who lived in one house while skipping by their neighbors. Even within families, they would exterminate one son and leave the other, or kill only the wife and leave the husband. The only justification Noah could think of was that they were trying to spread as much fear and trauma as possible, leaving some survivors to spread the horror.

Those who were passed over in this way were initially sympathized with, but there was no denying the suspicion which quickly descended upon these orphans and widows. What darkness must reside in them for the demons to find compassion? Did they truly escape unharmed, or was there something planted in them, an unseen possession or infection that would rear its head the moment the others let down their guard? This mistrust combined with the trauma and survivor's guilt to make these lingering souls the most unfortunate of them all.

Many people left the city in the immediate aftermath, believing on good grounds the place was cursed. Some of these left their homes empty, which were quickly discovered and broken into by those left homeless by the fires. The police department was so overburdened by unrest that they soon stopped responding to these vacancy quarrels, leaving locations to be squabbled and fought over until one group evicted the other inhabitants. It soon became common knowledge that all the best places in town were occupied by violent gangs, which in turn drove out more people from the neighborhoods until even those places untouched by the demons decayed into shoddiness and crime.

It is from this disorder that allowed Noah to operate undisturbed at night. There were no shortage of bodies to choose from lined up beside the city center waiting to be identified, and no one noticed if a few slipped out so long as they were returned by sunrise. Noah and his zombies would work all night: clearing debris, cleaning trash, and doing their best to mend the communities they had once been part of.

After the easier clearing and scrubbing was done, more dextrous work such as carving, painting, plumbing, and electrical wiring took long hours of excruciating practice on Noah's part. There was more than a handful of lost fingers, as well as one incident where a zombie got a screwdriver permanently stuck in its forehead. The practice was rewarding, however, and within a few weeks he was able to control several zombies at once, each independently going about their specified task without requiring direct supervision.

Noah did his best to convince himself that it was just as well that he was missing class because of how much he was learning on his own. The truth was that he missed school more than he had expected to. He missed watching Jamie feed strange animals in the bestiary, or listening to Professor Humstrum speak dreamily about bringing out the best in a soul and sharing that feeling with the rest of the world. He missed Professor Wilst's macabre ideas, and if he was being honest, he even missed the connection he felt with demons and the Netherworld.

No matter how busy Noah kept himself all night long, he couldn't lie down to sleep in the morning without thinking about his encounter with his ancestor Zee Zee Balloo. If only he had access to the library to look up this infamous demon and understand what historical role he had played in previous lives. It was disgusting to think of himself as one of the same creatures to have perpetrated this atrocity, but at the same time, he felt like there must somehow be a justification for their actions.

How could such evil ever be used for a righteous cause though? Perhaps Elijah and the other students were right all along—that demons really were the source of evil in this world, and that he deserved to be alone. After-all, if it wasn't for him, Professor Salice never would have known to go after his family. If the price for summoning a soul eater really was a second soul, then Noah had unwittingly put those he loved in the gravest of danger. If Noah hadn't made a deal with Visoloth, maybe Salice never would have been caught, and the demons never would have gone free, and the rebellion never would have happened in the first place. The whole demon war and all the suffering around him really might be his fault. Too often such thoughts would accompany him into sleep, taunting him that it was his fate to be the bringer of evil no matter how hard he tried.

The silver lining to all of this was that he at least got to spend more time with his family. Barnes was the one person he wasn't feeling sorry for. To Noah, this seemed like the best thing that could have happened for his daughter. The deceased had amassed a sizable fortune, while neglecting his family no-doubt, and Mandy's house was unharmed as the demons had avoided the dweller in her yard. She was able to live quite comfortably without working, and she made up for her grief by lavishing all her devotion onto little Lewis.

The problem, however, was that she still stubbornly refused to acknowledge his existence. Was it possible that she had smothered her power for so long that it had ceased to exist? She'd walk straight through him if he tried to block her path, and not turn her head in the slightest no matter how much noise he made. She became more adamant than ever that Lewis not react to spirits in her presence, and she even brought the boy to sleep in her bed to keep an eye on him.

Noah was afraid that Lewis would begin to lose his power as well if it was continually suppressed. His only opportunity to speak with Lewis was at his kindergarten, which was no good without all the other kids thinking he was crazy. Noah's only recourse was to wait for Lewis before and after school. The boy only had a short solitary walk from the curb where he was dropped off to the front door, but Noah never missed a chance to catch his grandson and remind him that he was loved. It couldn't have been easy to lose a father, even one so cruel and distant as Barnes had been.

This wasn't how life was supposed to go in the city Noah once lived. And it wasn't how death was supposed to go now. Noah fought these thoughts the best he could, however, and as the weeks stretched into months he found pride in the help he was able to offer. The city had yet to heal, but he was beginning to forgive himself for any inadvertent role he had played in the disaster. He began counting on his blessings: on his opportunity to watch over his family, his companionship with Samantha, and always looking forward to the rare opportunities for Walter to scry on him and tell him about the school.

Mr. Wolf never gave Walter long with a crystal ball, but his friend made the most of it by filling Noah in as quickly as he could. Demon attacks had become regular occurrences now, although none had come close to the scale Noah had witnessed. Professor Yobbler was forming a voluntary school militia with instructions to banish all demons on sight. Wilst was developing the art of growing bone shields, and even Humstrum had turned his mind to the growing threat of all-out war by training the spirits in the bestiary how to fight.

These visits were always all too brief, however, and Noah grew steadily more frustrated by how little he was able to help. It didn't matter how good his zombies were getting at building houses, he was missing all the important stuff and would never be able to catch up with his friends. That's assuming there even was still a Mortuary to get back to, and that the demons didn't get to it first. Haunting thoughts of that beautiful tree burning and all the mysteries of those locked rooms vanishing forever was too much for him to bear. If he had to pick a side, he had to be with the spirits.

There were no excuses left—it didn't matter who he used to be or who they still thought he was. Noah hated the demons. It felt good to finally mean it when he said it. He hated them, as only one can hate that which gleefully seeks the destruction of all he loves. He hated them, he hated them, he hated them. And he was going to do everything within his power keep them banished for good.

The last snow had melted and given way to the chilly invigoration of spring before Noah decided what he was going to do. He fastened on his jaw-bone necklace with a fresh cord of cloth he'd cut from his shirt hem, packed his mirror back into his little red cart, and said his last goodbye to Lewis on his way home from school that evening. The sun was just beginning to set, and the long shadows made good company as they replaced the wearisome intensity of the insufferable daylight.

"Where are we going?" Samantha asked cheerfully.

Noah hadn't noticed her as he was sneaking out of the house, and it now became clear that this was because she'd been sitting on the fence outside waiting for him. She swung her legs beneath her long purple skirt, looking a bit like a ship's sail trying to catch the wind.

"Nowhere," Noah replied, dragging his cart conspicuously behind him.

"How far is nowhere?" She hopped down from the fence and began walking beside him. "Is it far from somewhere? Because I've been there and wasn't much impressed, but nowhere sounds much more fun."

Noah sighed. It was clear she wasn't going to make this easy, so there was no point beating around the bush. "I'm going to look for the rift in the woods that the demons entered through. See if I can't get back to the Netherworld that way. Remember what George Hampton said last year though—it isn't safe for the living to go there. So I'm sorry, but—"

"When the demons attacked, there weren't any spirits that escaped either," Samantha interrupted.

"Yeah, so?"

"So it isn't safe for spirits either. So I've got just as much right to be there as you. And I'm faster than you, and I'm cleverer than you, so don't even think about trying to slip away."

It was impossible to stare down that great milky eye of hers. As much as Noah would have liked the company, he had to put his foot down.

"Sam, this isn't a game—"

"Then stop playing around," she cut him off again, swelling exasperation straining her voice. Despite her nonchalant facade, it was clear how much she meant what she was saying. "It was one thing when you were just going to school, and I didn't want to miss out on the fun. Do you think I didn't see what happened here? Do you think I didn't know some of those people who died? I'm not stupid, and I'm not a child. I know what we're up against, and I know the price of doing nothing to stop it. I can stay home and hide and wait and still die, all alone, cursing you with my last breath. Same as you. Or I can fight and put my fate into my own hands, knowing that even if everything I feared came to pass, at least I would be facing it head on. So for the last time: how far away is the rift, and should I pack any sandwiches?"

"Don't you think your parents have been through enough already? Are you going to be the one to explain to them where you've gone? Or would you rather they just wake up tomorrow morning to find their only daughter missing?"

"I don't care!" Samantha shouted fiercely. A curtain on the other side of the street closed sharply. It occurred to Noah how strange it must look for Samantha to be yelling at herself.

"At least be a little quieter—"

"I won't! So what if people think I'm crazy? Or maybe they'll think I'm talking to the demons and will burn me at the stake, is that what you'd prefer? I'm coming with you, and that's the end of it. I'll fit in better there than here, I *promise*. You of all people must know what it's like to see things others don't. You know what it feels like to know you don't belong, but unlike you, I'm not going to go through my whole life faking it."

"Don't make me get a zombie to chase you around until I'm gone..."

It wasn't Samantha that interrupted him that time though. Noah's voice trailed off as his eyes slowly focused on something behind her shoulder.

"Hah, pathetic attempt. I'm not going to look and let you run away."

A low growl proved sufficiently convincing to change her mind. There's nothing that makes an animal snarl more terrifying than when it comes from the face of a man, except when that man also happens to have the body of a lion. Wide leathery bat wings, bristling ridges down its back, and a long scorpion tail soared high above its ferociously bearded head as though poised to strike.

For all Samantha's talk, she couldn't conceal her spastic leap of terror. To her credit she rallied impressively though, even raising her little fists in an impotent gesture that looked all the more absurd as the massive beast stalked closer to them along the street.

"Don't worry, it isn't a demon," Samantha said. "Other people can see demons, and look—Mrs. Warlinski is looking right at us and doesn't notice."

"His name is Haxafla, and he's a manticore." It was Jamie, sitting between its shoulder blades, suddenly revealed as one of the massive wings unfolded. The manticore made another low growl, and Jamie buffeted it playfully on the ear. "Hush now, you know Noah. And this is Samantha: she's still alive, but there's nothing else wrong with her."

"Is this your new pet after you had to let go of Mrs. Robinson?" Samantha asked breathlessly.

"Jamie!" Noah spluttered, at last overcoming his shock. "What are you doing here? How did you get Humstrum to let you borrow the manticore?"

"He isn't 'the manticore'. His name is *Haxafla*," Jamie repeated firmly. "And Professor Humstrum doesn't technically know, so do let's hurry."

"Hurry? You mean you came to give me a ride?"

"*Us* a ride!" Samantha declared emphatically. She was already racing up to the beast, which stepped back from her uncertainly. "Can I just climb up? Oh wait, here, I'll use the tail."

"Sam be careful!" Noah hissed.

"It's alright, he's very good with the living," Jamie said. "He's already protected a number of them from demons. We're only here to pick up Noah though…"

"It's alright, he said I could come," Samantha replied hurriedly. "Is there something I should be holding onto? Drat, I really wish I had packed some sandwiches now."

"It's not like you to go behind Humstrum's back like that." Noah hesitantly approached Haxafla, who had lain down to make it easier for Samantha to climb on top. "There's something you're not telling me."

"Well, erm, yes, but I'd planned to tell you in confidence..." Jamie said, eyeing Samantha uncertainly.

"It's okay, I know all about everything," the other girl replied, distracted by running her hands through the manticore's thick fur. "The demons, the school, the Soul Net. *Everything.*"

Jamie scowled at Noah, then nodded. "There is a bit of an emergency, and I didn't think it could wait any longer. It's about Elijah. He wouldn't talk to any of us since he got back, and he called us nasty names like demon-lovers, never mind that we were doing our best to stop the attack too. The T.D.D. has still banned using the road from death because of the demons though, and Elijah has made up his mind that you were lying about the net. He's already begun the resurrection ceremony for the last two graduating classes, and they're going to get trapped if somebody doesn't stop them. You're the only one who knows how to get into the living road though, so we need your help!"

"Do you mean you're only getting me now that you need me?" Noah asked stubbornly. "You could have picked me up at the beginning of the semester and I wouldn't have missed so much class!"

"I wish I could have come sooner, but Haxafla only just came back to the Mortuary last week. And I can't just steal a manticore—" a growl from Haxafla forced a quick correction—"can't just borrow a friend without permission when it isn't an emergency. This is serious though, Noah. I wish we had been able to get you earlier, but Elijah is a chainer, and you know what that means."

"He's going to be turned into a battery!" Samantha chimed, a bit too enthusiastically. "Sorry, yeah, it sounds awful. I'm just saying I know about that stuff too."

Samantha reached a hand down to Noah to help him up.

"I'm returning you to your parents as soon as we're finished," Noah grumbled. He took her hand and clamored onto the beast's back to settle precariously between the razor spikes along its spine. "How do you get him to—" Noah began, lurching into silence as the manticore sprang into the air as nimbly as a cat. The leathery wings stretched out to catch the wind, and after a few brief plummets, they were all soaring into the sky.

A thousand worries fell away with the earth, and no fear or foreboding could keep pace with their tremendous ascension. All the troubles of the city seemed so insignificant from this height, and all the green open world bursting into spring seemed endless in its natural power. Samantha squealed with glee and tried to stand before Noah forced her back into her seat. They were flying again. If only being dead was like this all the time.

THE SOUL NET

One may trick themselves into forgetting fear for a short duration. They might pretend the tingle in their nerves is a pleasurable thrill, and that existing without the exhilaration of danger is no existence at all. There will be doubt creeping from the dark, subconscious places where the mind's eye forces itself not to look, but that can be drowned out with a repeated mantra.

I will be strong. I will be brave. I will be strong. I will be brave.

Or some other such self-reassurance, repeated ad nauseam, until bit by bit each word begins to grow fuzzy and lose its meaning. And bit by bit, the whisperings of doubt will swell until they're too loud to be ignored. Neither the beauty of the passing landscape, nor these futile self-assurances could endure the long hours of the manticore's flight. Even Samantha—once flushed with anticipation and the midnight chill—seemed to have shrunk into herself with wide, fearful eyes.

The black sand beach was desolate under a stark and cloudless sky. The soaring cathedral on the cliff-side was a distant streak of warmth, too distant to offer any familiarity or comfort. The cold ocean waves broke unforgiving against the stone to send sprays of angry foam lashing through the air. It was nights like this whose shadows could not be cast out by morning light.

"Go on Haxafla," Jamie whispered, her voice subdued despite their apparent isolation. "Get back into the bestiary and please don't mention any of this to Professor Humstrum. You've been a good and loyal friend, and I hope the jinn see that and stop picking on you."

The feral face of the man tossed his beard back and forth, a graveled rumble of acknowledgement in his throat.

"Can't he come with us?" Samantha asked, watching the manticore flinging itself back into the air.

"We can't draw too much attention. I'd hate to think what would happen to all the older students if The Matriarch caught them trying to sneak into the road from death without permission."

"Elijah's living road is too narrow for a manticore anyway," Noah added. "Are Walter and Brandon here too?"

"Yeah, they should be waiting for us somewhere around..." Jamie scanned the dark cliffside. "They said they were going to try and find their own way in—just in case we couldn't find you in time."

"It must be nice having friends," Samantha said wistfully. "I think it's the eye people have trouble with. Someone told me that once. I offered to poke out one of theirs so they don't feel weird about it, but they weren't interested."

"You'd be right at home in our necromancy class," Jamie replied, distracted as she continued to search for the others. "Maybe they're on another part of the beach. It's already past midnight when the resurrection was supposed to begin. I don't think we have time to go looking for them. Noah, do you still remember how to get inside?"

Noah nodded and oriented himself in the correct position. He had been quietly rehearsing the incantation in his head since they landed, and repeated it now to open the secret way.

"*Voya Tomba.*"

A moment of terrible silence stretched past his final syllables, unbroken until the sand beneath their feet began to swirl.

"Get out of the way, it's opening!" Noah spread his arms wide and pushed the two girls back beyond the perimeter of the tunnel. The sand circled and condensed before their eyes, swiftly fusing into a tight tunnel of black glass.

"Elijah lit the way last time I was here though. I don't know how we're going to find our way without a spell to create light."

"Abra-ka-duh." A brilliant white light appeared, much brighter than the one from Elijah's outline. Samantha marched ahead fearlessly with her cell-phone brandished high.

The glass tunnel reflected the harsh light and scattered it across the many facets. Samantha used a bit of her shirt to dampen the beam so they wouldn't make themselves too visible.

"That's the branch that goes to the hospital through a portal," Noah explained, pointing in the direction he traveled before. "We were using the energy of the dying to help make sense of the Mirror of Ancestry."

"Did you ever get it to work properly?" Jamie asked.

"It was broken during the attack…"

"He used to be a demon named Zee Zee Balloo," Samantha cut in.

"Sam—"

"—and it wanted him to go to the Netherworld and find the other prime demons. I told you I didn't need to be dead to know all sorts of things."

"Noah, is that true?" Jamie asked in an inadvertently loud voice.

"Please be quieter. Let's talk about it later, okay? We've got to focus on stopping the resurrection first."

"Noah, this is really important. You do remember the lesson about the primes, right? No wonder the demons are taking such an interest in you and your family."

"No. Don't do that. Don't try to empathize with them as if they think like we do. You weren't there. You didn't hear the screams, or see the bodies, or see the lost look on the survivors who were wondering why they were spared. The demons aren't our friends."

"I'm sorry. You're right, it must have been awful," Jamie looked to Sam, but the other girl said nothing, her brow furrowed by the weight of the things she'd seen.

"When I was alive, I didn't…" Jamie began. She cleared her throat, and started again, "I wasn't like other people. They didn't understand how deeply I felt everything, and I couldn't even fathom what was going through their heads most of the time. I always thought they were angry at me, even when they were smiling. And if that life was all there was, I never would have understood how hard they were trying to make me feel like I belonged, or how much it meant to me now that I'm gone."

"What are you trying to say?" Noah asked, not taking his eyes from the wall of black glass that he ran his fingers along.

"There's good in everyone, even the demons. Even if we're too short-sighted to see it from the perspective of a single life. And there's good in you too, and nothing you ever did, and nothing you ever were is ever going to change that."

Red light. Reflecting from the walls and ceiling on all sides, coming toward them from down the tunnel. Noah made a frantic gesture with his hand to shut off Samantha's light, but she pulled her phone away from him.

"So what? It's a tunnel," she whispered. "There's nowhere for us to hide anyway."

"Then why are you whispering?" Noah hissed back, making another grab for the phone and swishing through the air.

"Hello? Is someone there?" The light grew brighter. It was coming from a wisp, orbiting around...

"Brandon!" Jamie called with relief. "How did you get inside? Where's Walter?"

"I managed to slip in after one of the graduating kids, but Walter is still stuck outside. There's no time—hurry and follow me!" Brandon waved them on the way he came. "The resurrection ceremony has already begun. Wait—who is that?"

"Yo, Sam here." She waved. "How are you fat? I didn't think spirits ate anything."

Brandon scowled and turned away to hustle down the tunnel, his wisp in hot pursuit.

"Wait for us!" Noah called. "What's going on, Brandon? What's the ceremony?"

"It's the final spell spirits have to learn before they graduate. Something to do with weaving the living world, the spirit world, and the netherworld together in one place. It's a really complicated spell and it uses a lot of ingredients and takes a lot of time though, and they aren't finished yet."

Around the next bend, and the jagged glass tunnel began to diverge into other paths. Brandon didn't even slow down as he veered off decisively down a side-passage. The walls and ceiling were constricting around them. Soon they were hurrying at a stoop, or forced to slide horizontally through a particularly tight spot. Then they were on their hands and knees, crawling along the faceted glass which pressed in on them from every side.

"This is dreadful," Jamie said, wincing as a jagged bit cut into her arm. "Is it going to open up soon?"

"Yeah, this is the worst part. We're almost there, keep going," Brandon said. He'd fallen to the back of the line, as it took him longer to work through some of the tighter locations.

"How'd the bigger kids get through here?" Noah asked, second to the front behind Samantha who held her phone in her mouth to light the way. "Some of them were over a foot taller than me."

"This is the last tight spot, don't stop now," Brandon called. His voice was fainter, and had an echoed quality. He was falling more behind.

"Thrsh ish fnn!" Samantha grunted around her phone. She was the smallest of any of them, and had no hesitation to drop flat onto her belly to crawl through the final stricture.

"I hate it," Noah grumbled. "I feel like toothpaste being squeezed out."

"It must seem pretty claustrophobic after the open nether," Brandon's voice echoed. "Bet you wish you were home right now, don't you... demon spawn?"

Noah froze. There was too much malice in those words to be a playful jab. It was too confined to even turn around, and he couldn't see the other's faces to see whether they reacted. There was no choice but to keep going forward.

"Don't talk that way," Jamie said softly from behind Noah, a subdued strain in her voice.

"Why not? Should my mother have taught me better?" Brandon's voice sounded farther away than ever. "Well I don't remember if she did, and we all know whose fault that was. The soul eaters got her, but that didn't stop the rest of you from wanting to summon one, did it? And I went along with it... like an idiot. I thought we were going to stop the attacks."

"What are you talking about, Brandon? Of course we're trying to stop—" Jamie began.

"You lied to me. I thought he was a demon when he started talking in their filthy language. I thought you were my friends, but every one of you lied to me. Elijah was right about you—you're only trying to help the demons win."

"Get out. Get out—it's a trap!" Noah hissed.

"Brandon, you don't understand," Jamie said, struggling to reverse her crawl and scoot backward along her stomach. "Just because he used to be a demon doesn't mean—"

"You admit it, and you're still defending him. I thought you were different than the others, Jamie. I thought you cared. Unbelievable."

"We had nothing to do with what happened to your mother," Noah shouted back. "A soul for a soul—I found out that's the price for summoning a rasmacht. I think The Matriarch sacrificed your mother's soul to destroy the people in the department who were getting in her way. I'm not planning to summon one anymore, and I couldn't have known before I learned about the cost from the mirror."

"You learned from a demon, you mean."

"Brandon you're sounding crazy. You saw the Soul Net yourself, you know we aren't lying!" Jamie said. She was making no progress in reversing through the confined space. Something was stopping her from getting out.

"I only know what demon lovers like you and Professor Salice have told me. Hey Olly! I've got them over here!" Brandon shouted, causing the echoes to redouble in intensity and assault them from every direction. "They're all stuck. Your ghouls can do whatever they want with them. I don't care anymore."

Samantha made a terrified gasp and jolted backward. The sound was especially startling because, until now, Noah had forgotten that she still had to breathe. Being trapped might be an inconvenience for him, but it could be fatal for her. The phone dropped from her mouth and rattled face-down on the ground, casting them all into utter darkness.

"There's something on the other end ahead. It's trying to get in!"

"There is another one back here!" Jamie shouted. "I can't turn around. I can't get out!"

The tunnel walls suddenly felt like the confines of a tomb. The grating of claws dragging along the glass sent shivers down Noah's spine. Samantha fumbled with the phone, and a flash of light gouged through the dark. There was just enough space over her back for Noah to see the gruesome skull of a ghoul with its long tongue lashing the air. Its lower jaw was disconnected at one end, flopping grotesquely and bristling with overlapping teeth as it inched itself toward them on its belly. Jamie began to scream—shrill and piercing, and mingling with the other echoes until it felt like they were not merely hearing it but were inside the sound entirely. So too did their nerves sing in tune, an electrical saturation so intense that it threatened to catch fire from the inside out, burning, burning, until nothing more could be felt again.

"I don't like it. I don't like it. I don't like it!" Jamie's voice, over and over, repeated until each word began to lose its meaning.

There was only one meaning that could come from such a dire situation, and that had to come from within. Noah had just enough room to retract his arms and latch both hands around his old jawbone which still hung around his neck. He never controlled a ghoul before, but he'd spent the last several months moving whole crews of zombies at a time. If Noah couldn't save his friends after leading them to danger yet again, then how was he better than the demons and the destruction they caused?

"Consurgo," Noah bellowed, the sound a shockwave in the enclosed space.

A growl caught in the throats of both ghouls. They shook their heads viciously from side-to-side as though trying to free themselves from an invisible leash tightening around their necks.

"Jamie, you have to calm down and help," Noah pleaded. "I can't do this on my own."

"Idon'tlikeit. Idon'tlikeit." Blurred together now.

The ghoul on Samantha's side made a lunge forward. She shielded her head with her hands. The undead face got close enough to nick the skin of her finger with a long yellow tooth before snapping backward by the neck.

"Idon'tlikeit!"

"Jamie, please. You aren't that girl anymore. That was never who you were."

She quieted a bit, but that may have just been a reaction to her ghoul. She'd be even more helpless than Samantha, as it would be attacking from her feet. Noah could feel the relentless pulse of Olly's will through the creatures though, and there was no doubt the advanced student was far more potent at this skill. Trying to hold the ghouls back felt like holding onto two steel cables that were ripping him apart, but it was all he could do to buy time until Jamie recovered.

"You have to pull back the curtain, Jamie. Just like the fear you're feeling now, it was only a shade to darken the light of your soul. It doesn't matter if a whole mountain is piled on top though, with not a speck of light shining through. Your soul is still just as bright and clean as it ever was at the center, so once you get back there, none of the rest will matter. Not the ghouls, not the school, not the worst day of your life. Find your center, Jamie. That's all you've got to do."

"I-don't-like-them!" Jamie gasped defiantly. "Consurgo!"

A second shockwave resonated through their bodies and around the chamber. The ghouls reeled and clutched at their throats, their own long nails digging into themselves. Samantha took the opportunity to risk scrambling after it, punching the undead monster squarely in the face so that it tumbled backward and into a wider tunnel beyond.

"Hurry, it opens up just ahead!" Samantha shouted. The others scrambled after her, and within seconds all three had pulled themselves free into a cavernous black space.

Olly was standing there, staring in shock at Samantha. "How did a living human girl—"

His shock persisted, seeming to indicate he was learning for the first time that a corporal girl with a magical eye really could punch a spirit in the face. And kick him on the side, and twice more in the legs, and once very hard between them.

"You can do that?" Noah asked.

"I can do all sorts of things." She snatched the finger-bone from around Olly's neck and stomped on it, grinding her heel until it was dust.

Jamie and Noah took advantage of the ghoul's vulnerability—they were always weakest right after losing connection with their master. Together they commanded the two ghouls to turn and scamper back the other way. It was hard to monitor them crawling back down the tight tunnel, but they must be doing what they were told because Brandon's fleeing scream could be heard reverberating through the tunnel for a good time to come.

"I hope he's alright. It wasn't all his fault... after losing his mother..."

"You're still making excuses for that brat?" Samantha asked incredulously. "Sometimes people are just assholes. It doesn't always have to be more complicated than that."

"I just hope we didn't wait too long," Noah said. "Hurry, before they finish their ceremony."

"Are we sure this is the right way?" Samantha asked, flipping her flashlight onto her hand to focus on peeling back the frayed purple paint from her nail.

"Why else would Olly be standing guard?"

Noah's intuition proved correct. They were passing through a large stone chamber, and it didn't take more than a minute before they spotted signs of the ceremony. The ground was stained deeply red, and there were dozens of bare footprints which looked as though they had been dancing in a circle. Hot embers and charred wood marked the remains of a once mighty fire. There were empty bottles, vials, and baskets, some with a few herbs and flowers still sticking to the fibers.

"Look over here!" Jamie was near the back of where the circle of people had danced. "More footprints. Another circle. They must have been down here for a long time"

"We're… too late?"

"It can't be," Samantha said. "They wouldn't have left that other oaf behind."

"… unless of course Olly *decided* to stay behind," Noah replied. "Elijah said he'd wanted me to stay behind and keep his living road running after he was gone. That obviously didn't happen, so Olly might have volunteered instead. We've got to search this whole room. Check for any other outgoing passageways."

"What about a circle of sparks? That's kind of like a passageway."

Samantha had wandered a bit in the other direction. It took Noah a moment to figure out what she was talking about, but that was because it was getting easier to notice with every moment that passed. The circle was growing from nothing in the air. It looked like being on the other side of someone cutting through steel in expanding circles, except without the someone or the steel.

"That's not an outgoing passage. That's an incoming portal!" Jamie said. "Someone is coming. We should hide!"

The circle had grown to about four feet. If someone was going to come out of it, they would have to be very tall indeed for it not to be soon. There were no shortage of hiding places in the landscape of jagged glass. They had to be careful and pick the thickest slab that could be found though, so that the light would not pierce through. Backs against the glass, a short tense silence, and the spray of sparks sizzled to a stop.

A new light appeared in the cave. Warm, splashing wisp-light, growing as though more and more of them were flooding out. And voices, one of which was as distinctively familiar as it was reviled.

"I do apologize for the delay, Mr. Oswald. There were a few protection charms to work through before I could open the portal." The sugar tones of The Matriarch floated through the open space.

"An inconvenience, but well worth the prize. And you're sure they're all finished?" A second voice—confident and gruff.

"Of course, just look at the mess. Watch your step, sir."

Samantha started inching her way around the glass to peek, but Noah pulled her away and shook his head. He held a finger to his lips.

"Don't keep me waiting. You're sure one of them was a chainer?"

"I wouldn't have brought you out for a common soul," The Matriarch cooed.

"You would have been a cheat if you had, after taking a battery from my energy department without warning like that."

"Really now. Without me, you wouldn't have a renewable source of spiritual energy at all. You'd be back to old fashioned plagues, and wars, and all that. Just like the dark ages. And we both know how hard it was to store that kind of energy—there had to be a new one every few months."

"Hmmph. Well no argument here. It always was nice to talk to you, Elanore. You don't waste a pretty word when an honest one will do."

The Matriarch laughed—a flat, tinny sound.

"We have to try and stop them," Jamie whispered.

Noah shook his head. "Too powerful. Even Professor Salice couldn't do anything against her, and with the Prime Minister here too? We have to stay hidden."

"This one. It's this one, isn't it?" The Prime Minister's voice.

"The others really do look pale in comparison."

Samantha was peeking again, and the voices seemed to be far enough off that Noah couldn't resist to look as well. A small cloud of wisps were orbiting the pair, illuminating what at first appeared to be a large round table between them. Longer inspection revealed that it was in fact another portal, this one horizontally stretched through the air about three feet from the ground. The Prime Minister was a tall, broad-shouldered man, almost twice the height of The Matriarch beside him. He wore a ceremonial, militant looking blue suit, and he had sleek, salt and pepper hair. His back was facing them, and they couldn't make out his face from their vantage point.

From the portal between them, they had pulled out a stretch of net like fishermen inspecting their catch from the sea. Thick black chords radiated a soft white light, and diamonds like gleaming stars were embedded into the lattice. Theodore Oswald reached down to pluck the brightest diamond of the group to cup in his hands. There was a distant scream that never quite started and never quite stopped, was never quite heard but was never quite imagined either. Noah thought it sounded like Elijah.

"Very well, let the other fishies swim away then. He's the only one I need from this batch," the Prime Minister said. "It's going to be something else in five years when all those fresh chainers graduate, eh? How many did you say there were?"

"Eleven."

"Not a bad job, these kids did with the place. And doing their own resurrection ceremony and everything." Theodore looked down at the diamond cupped in his hand and sighed. "Ah well. Better to be made useful than be eaten by a demon, eh? Let me know when you catch another one, and carry on. Those soulless monsters aren't going to know what hit 'em."

The Matriarch smiled broadly and curtsied in response. "Good evening, Prime Minister."

A shower of sparks, then he was gone. The Matriarch continued to stand there alone, staring down at the horizontal portal which continued to persist. She waited a good five seconds before reaching back into the portal and pulling out the net once more. She continued unraveling a large expanse of it into the room, carefully inspecting every inch of it. The more of the net they were able to see, the better they were able to see the larger pattern. It looked more like a spider's web than a net.

"Ah ah ah, my pretties. And where did you think you were going?" One by one, she carefully plucked out every single remaining diamond from the net. A few dozen tiny screams broke the air and dissolved into the never-were.

Jamie grabbed Noah by the arm, beseeching him with wild, fearful eyes. Noah shook his head and put his finger to his lips again. He peered around the stone to see The Matriarch returning the net into the horizontal portal, which was now closing down to a pinhole. She then moved to the far wall of the glass cavern and laid her hand against the smooth surface. Light flowed from her fingertips and into the glass, pooling idly there like colored ink in water. Gradually the light began to take form.

Infants in a nursery. There must be a dozen of them, with pink and blue blankets. Medical charts hung at the side of their transparent cribs. They were looking into a hospital, but what did it mean?

"Their eyes!" Samantha said, barely breathing the words.

White. Pure white, just like Samantha's was. None of them were closed either, which looked odd considering they were all newborn. They were awake, but not one of them were making a sound.

"Conceal," The Matriarch said, the word hard and flat.

The children all blinked as one. When they opened their eyes again, the iris and pupil were clearly visible, appearing as normal. As one they all begun to cry, the rise and fall of their breath in perfect unison.

The Matriarch tapped the glass again and the image dissolved back into ink, then into nothing at all. A spray of sparks and a circle flashed into existence. All of the wisps poured after, causing a torrent of flashing light and shadows to converge on her. And then they were gone, the last smoldering bits of light raining down to extinguish against the hard glass floor.

"She took every single soul," Noah said aloud into the quiet room.

"Children are still being born." Jamie said, her voice dull and lifeless. "They're still being born without souls."

"What does that mean?" Samantha asked. "Oh! When the demons attacked, there weren't any spirits coming out. Could all of those people not had souls either?"

Neither Noah nor Jamie found the strength to answer. It was such a horrible thought... or was it? If there hadn't been any spirits at all, could the demons have only attacked people without a soul? It would even explain why the gargoyles weren't helping some people—they were only designed to protect souls.

"Did aunt Wilmington not have a soul?" Samantha kept speaking, her voice so small in the quiet. "I knew her my whole life, and she always seemed nice to me. She gave me a chemistry set for my birthday one year. She had a husband, and two children who were grown up and had moved away. She was killed during the attack. Did she not have a soul? What could that even mean?"

"A soul is like consciousness, I think," Noah replied at last. "I don't know about your aunt, or any of the others. But if any of them didn't have a soul, then they must have been sort of like robots. They could react to everything they sense. Their body would still undergo emotions. They would learn and remember things. They would have all the feelings without the thing to feel them. It must seem to everyone else as if there's a person in there, but there isn't."

"Aunt Wilmington was over sixty years old, Noah," Samantha said. "How long has the Soul Net been going? How many people in the world still have a soul at all?"

"I want to get out of here," Jamie said. "I don't want to think about this. This must be what it's like having a dweller in your head —and intrusive thought that won't go away. I don't want this in my head."

The three of them were silent, lost in their own thoughts as they passed through the tunnels back to the surface. How could that have been anything but a bad dream? Now they were standing under the purple night sky, with the infinite reassurance of the ocean lapping against the sand, and all of those existential terrors felt so far left behind. But even here, there was no way to escape that lingering thought: what would a world be like, full of people living their lives, none of them conscious at all?

"We should get back to the school..." Jamie began.

"No. I don't think I can go back there. Not after what we've learned."

"You and Sam stay here then. I'll get Haxafla, and I'll take you both back."

"Thanks, Jamie. Keep an eye out for Walter. I hope Brandon didn't do anything to him when he turned on us."

"Yeah, okay." Then after a pause. "Is that it, then? Will you really not come back to the school? Where will you go?"

"We're going to look for the rift back to the Netherworld," Samantha answered for him. "We're going to find the other prime demons and find out the truth about what's going on."

Noah nodded, surprised to hear her voice his own thoughts. "Whatever a demon is, they don't lie. It's the only way. This isn't goodbye for us though. You and Walter have to keep studying. We're going to need you inside the school to keep an eye on The Matriarch. As soon as I find out what I can from the demons, I'm going to find you again, and we're going to put a stop to her for good."

"It's not just her though, is it?" Jamie replied. "The Trans Dimensional Department are involved somehow, and then what are you going to do? Run for the next Prime Minster? It's not fair to expect us to do it all alone."

"We won't be alone though, will we? It's not just us, it's everyone we ever used to be, and everyone we ever will be. It's all the souls we can trust who know the universe isn't meant to be that way, all empty and unaware. We have to believe there are enough of us left to save the rest. If we can't believe in something as essential as that, then what is belief even for?"

"You'll be careful in the Netherworld? And not let them turn you into demons—although there's nothing wrong with it if they do, but please don't. You'll come back and visit when you can?"

"Don't worry about me," Noah replied. "I'm already written into the final act, and wouldn't miss it for anything."

SAMANTHA AND NOAH were standing in front of the nether rift less than twenty four hours later. Jamie had given her final goodbye before departing with Haxafla, and she had flown back to the Mortuary though the sun had already risen in the sky. Samantha spent the New Years day with her family, quietly loving them harder than she ever had without speaking a word about what was yet to come. Noah spent the day watching his grandson play at his kindergarten, and when he and Samantha met they both pretended not to notice the tears glistening in the other's eye.

"You never told me it was going to be cold in here," Samantha said, slipping into the emptiness of the nether.

"Sounds like you'll be looking for a Lava Salamander to warm you up," Noah replied, stepping after her.

They both jolted when a third voice on the other side resonated between them.

"Welcome to the Netherworld," Visoloth the demon dog said. "Your true education begins now."

NETHERWORLD

THE SHALLOW END

THE SUN IS GLORIOUS TO THE LIVING. THE SPREADING LEAF AND THE growing stem are helpless but to worship the celestial fire, and so too must all the animals be thankful for consuming such bounty. Even the creatures who dwell in the dark and quiet places below the sea must pay their respects for belonging to the same web of life.

The undead do not go to the same parties. It isn't the heat—although it's no secret that zombies are quick to burn and slow to forgive—but the light which wearies the spirit thin. Perhaps it is the brilliance, perhaps because it dries the bones, or perhaps it is the burden of remembering the dear life they've left behind. With this curse they must endure, until the day they are ready to walk the road from death. They must pass through this place without sun or moon or stars, their empty presence replaced by the looming shades of demonic horrors which fill the sky like constellations.

There is no light in the Netherworld. Contrary to popular belief, neither is there darkness. It's difficult to say which is up and which is down, or whether there is any difference at all. There are no clear boundaries between the thoughts in one's mind and the world outside. Anything which can be conceived can be perceived, as can many things beyond one's wildest imagination. No mortal in their right mind would dare leave the world which gave them life to step through the ring of fire into the sticky nebula of the unknown.

"I am still alive, aren't I?" Samantha asked. The girl's dark hair billowed in all directions: a storm cloud with a life of its own. The large backpack she wore seemed to be steering her more than she was carrying it. "I don't feel very alive. There's supposed to be me, and then everything else, with a line drawn in-between. I can't tell where the line is anymore though—there's just everything everywhere and I'm part of it. Do you feel it too, Noah?"

"Hush. We don't know what could be listening," the boy replied. He floated naturally here, his thin body slipping through the nether like a spoon through custard. He was quick and alert, with such smooth turns and pivots that it wasn't hard to believe the soul of a Netherworld demon had found a new home in him.

"Did you complain when the dog was making that awful howling sound? No. You didn't. You made those nasty noises right back. Well I'm sorry I don't speak demonic, but I'll never learn if I can't ask questions."

"Make her be quiet." Visoloth's words lashed through Noah's mind. The demon's black and leathery skin was taunt and quivering with tension. The demon was sniffing—tasting the nether which drifted through its twisted tentacles.

"I can't. You make her."

"You're the one who brought her. Take responsibility."

"I did not. She brought herself," Noah replied with frustration, this time in plain English. "Sam wait—where are you going?"

The girl continued to drift while Noah and Visoloth spoke. She backflipped slowly through the nether to look at Noah upside-down. Her green eye seemed to be roving independently of the marble-white one which had been cut by the gargoyle. The old wound looked worse here than it had in the living world, and the marbled texture was clear on the skin above her eye all the way up to her eyebrow. Her living eye was no less ferocious. Noah melted beneath the scrutiny until they shifted to focus on Visoloth once more.

"You're sure he won't attack us, right?" she asked. "He can smell our souls… or something? Do different souls smell different? Does mine have a flavor? I'd like to know if it's different from all the other souls."

"Tell her she is not safe from me," Visoloth growled. "I need to focus, or we're never going to find our way."

"He says you're—"

"What about the folds? All those lines like crumpled paper in the distance. Why do some of them go through each other like they aren't even there? Why does the world look so different when one eye is open versus the other? Why can't I see any other demons if they keep getting out into the real world? How come—"

"What's the point of asking questions if you won't even stop long enough to hear the answer?" Noah blurted, finally finding an opening as Samantha paused to draw breath.

"I didn't think you were going to answer anyway, so I was asking myself. Oh, and what about those candles? I wonder what the point of them is, if we can see perfectly well without light."

"She can see the candles from here?" Visoloth asked. His tentacles began to curl back into his mouth. He wasn't searching anymore. "Ask her if she can see something that looks like a wall made of doors."

Noah translated the message from demonic. Samantha remained quiet and suspended upside-down as she listened. She then twirled in a circle, kicking her legs to propel herself along the way. "Sure I can. They're over this way. It's kind of shimmery and glossy, but I wouldn't call it a wall. They're all piled on top of one another in a big ol' jumble."

Visoloth nodded and pushed himself to a loping run in the direction she indicated. Samantha didn't need to understand demonic to realize what had happened. Her face lit up with a wide grin. "Be quiet, he says. She brought herself, did she? Well good thing she did, because it looks like I've been helpful already."

"You're right, I'm sorry," Noah replied, hurrying to keep up with Visoloth. "I guess I'm just on edge being here. It must have been hours since we entered the rift, and I've never gone this deep into the nether before. I don't know how you're so calm when you saw exactly what the demons can do back at home."

"I guess I just don't see how being a whiny little twerp will help us find... what did you say it was called?"

"The Sylo. Visoloth told me that George Hampton is waiting there for us."

"Then what? Is he going to take us to the Prime Demons?"

Noah shrugged. "I don't know. I hope so. Visoloth just said that he was going to give us what we were looking for." Noah paddled closer to Samantha, before adding in a softer voice: "Just be careful not to mention anything about the dwellers you helped us plant. I was afraid that Visoloth would be angry that we tried to ward off the demons, but it seems like he doesn't know. He might even think we helped them attack the living by opening the rift, because The Matriarch used my old body when she opened it. We don't want any trouble with the demons while we're here though."

"I can play nice. I really did quite like George's imp Ca'akan, even though I always got in trouble when he made a mess inside. It's not like they're all monsters or anything. Just don't ask me to forget what I saw, or forgive their attack. Even if they were only after the soulless, it doesn't excuse all the hurt they caused everyone else to make it happen."

"I understand. When we find the Primes, I hope we'll be able to convince them there's a better way. Until then we'll just try to keep our heads down not to make too much noise—"

"WHAT ARE THOSE?"

Noah winced as the shout bounced around the inside of his head like an angry hornet that couldn't find its way out.

"Yeah, fine, I get it. They're imps though," Samantha clarified more softly. "I'd guess there are hundreds of them, all moving together like a school of fish. Can you really not see that?"

Noah closed his eyes and concentrated. He always felt like he could see better with his eyes closed here. It was liberating to look in every direction at once, but the endless shifting sea of nether seemed empty all around him. The distant folds which wrinkled the space gave the impression they were within some gargantuan structure too massive to visualize or comprehend. He shook his head.

"Your stone eye must see things I can't. Where are they going?"

"Same direction as us, but I can't tell how far away they are. Do you think George has a whole flock of imps?"

"That's the wrong way to think about it. Imps might seem like pets when they're summoned into another world, but we're in their world now. I don't think George has imps any more than the imps have George."

Samantha turned in slow circles, apparently marveling at a sight only she could see. "Do you think they're going to the Sylo too? What is that, anyway?"

Visoloth slowed his place and craned his head from side to side, searching for something Noah couldn't see. The dog spoke to Noah in the harsh demonic syllables, leaving him to translate for Samantha.

"George promised to continue our education here. He said we won't be any good to anyone as long as we're as… erm… stupid and reckless as we are now. And that if we really want to work with the demons, we're going to need to learn to—"

"Wait, what is THAT?" Samantha interrupted, pointing wildly into the empty Nether. "That enormous, hideous, bloated, prize-winning entry for the disgusting blob contest?"

Visoloth responded, and Noah hurried to translate.

"That sounds like Mr. Mufflafo. He's—what, really? You don't mean for us, do you?"

"What? What is it? What did he say?" Samantha said, bouncing up and down with excitement and apprehension.

"Did he have a bow-tie?" Noah asked uncertainly.

"Does he even have a neck?" Samantha asked. "Look, he's getting closer. Right there where all those crinkles are focused. No wait, the crinkles are unfolding and folding to move with him. It's almost like he's in a house that keeps taking itself apart and building itself back up wherever he goes."

Noah still couldn't see the demon she was describing, but he could just make out the crinkling and un-crinkling of space.

"Visoloth seems to think it's sort of like... you know... that he's going to be our..."

"He ate an imp! A tongue just shot out and snapped it out of the air!"

"... going to be our teacher at the Sylo," Noah finished through a knot in his throat.

The enormity of the silence finally pressed in around them. For once Samantha didn't have anything to say. Then the distant chittering began to filter in, distant but omnipresent, slowly mounting in volume as it closed in around them.

"Cool," Samantha said at last. "You better keep translating for me, Noah. I'm not going to want to miss any of this."

Visoloth meanwhile had discovered something like a stairway made of large round platforms suspended in the open nether. The steps were black and glossy, and so far apart that it would be impossible to stretch between them. Besides, they were angled inward in such a way that each step faced the next one, although Noah didn't suppose that mattered much in the Netherworld without discernible gravity. The demon dog sat down upon the first step and waited for the two children to join him.

"Demons go to school?" Noah asked, still not quite believing what was going on. Everything here was so strange that it was hard not to think of it as a dream, where any moment he would wake up again and find himself... where, exactly? It had been so long since anything made sense that if he was dreaming, he must have been asleep for years.

"Where else would they learn to grow and mutate into the myriad of forms you see around you?" Visoloth replied. "Come now, stand right beside me. We're almost there."

The flock of imps was finally coming into vision. Hundreds—perhaps thousands of the red-furred beasties soared through the nether in perfect formation. Noah was accustomed to seeing the multifarious diversity of demonic ranks and was momentarily surprised to see only imps. It took him a moment to fully process what Visoloth had said.

"Do you mean the imps are just children? And they grow up to be different kinds of demons? Did you used to be an imp too?"

Visoloth made a solid effort at a smile, but the parting of his mouth only let the tentacles slip out in a disgustingly fearsome display. As Noah joined him on the platform, he momentarily recoiled to feel the warmth emanating from the step. The material also yielded to his pressure, molding around his feet as though grasping them.

"Let that be your first lesson," Visoloth said. "As much as the spirits pretend to study us, all they're really doing is studying themselves and how they can make use of us."

Samantha gingerly stepped onto the platform beside them, kneeling to run her hands along the strange pliant material.

"Let the second lesson be this: demons do not use tools. They do not build buildings, or wear clothing, or use any other material that is common to spirits and the living. That means anything you find in the Netherworld is, more likely than not, a demon in one form or another."

As he was speaking, Visoloth made a sharp kick into the platform. Samantha scrambled to the corner as a large purple eye opened beneath her feet in the middle of the black material. The iris was so incandescently bright that the light began to radiate outward. The eye shifted, focusing the light until it was a solid purple beam which lanced through the nether toward the next platform. The second step reacted, opening its eye to let out a second purple beam which bridged the gap to the third step, and so on until a zig-zagging chain of light had materialized before them.

"The classes for demons begin the same time those for the spirits end," Visoloth explained. "There used to be a time when the students who failed to come back to life came to the Netherworld to study next, but of course the Department doesn't trust us and The Matriarch has other plans for them now."

The imps were still flooding in from every side, now close enough for Noah to make out their broad ugly faces and the sharp ridges along their backs. They were all converging on the first platform without any signs of slowing down. They were so densely packed together in their tight formation that the imps threatened to bury them as soon as they began to land. Visoloth didn't wait for that to happen.

The demon dog stepped into the beam of purple light and launched outward as though shot by a cannon. In less than a second he had already reached the second step, whereupon his trajectory was altered by the second beam to send him flying once more. Noah and Samantha both leapt into the beam as he did, not having any choice in the matter before the teaming imps descended upon them. The light was a lot hotter than Noah expected, and he had just enough time to wonder if he'd made a terrible mistake before he too was launched.

Everything was a blur. Flying through the nether wasn't like flying through the air, a sensation Noah had sincerely missed ever since his brief time as a crow. The thick, cool gel which washed over them suddenly transformed into a flooding torrent. The powerful beam of light which propelled him was enough to overcome the resistance, but being blasted between the opposing pressures and temperatures was an overwhelming experience. He couldn't decide whether he was about to freeze from the rushing nether or catch fire from the searing light.

Back and forth. Back and forth. Ricocheting from one platform to the next until they lost count of how many they had passed. Counting wasn't the only thing lost in the tumultuous journey—a sense of time, sense of direction, sense of distance or temperature—all muddled up together in the break-neck pace of travel. At last they slammed into a final platform which did not have a beam to send them onward. The yielding skin which caught them stretched and stretched, threatening to snap and send them slingshotting back the other direction. Thankfully it held firm, however, gently relaxing itself back into its flat state with a long sigh.

Samantha's already wild hair turned absolutely feral from the experience. She sat there dazed for several seconds, stretching her fingers and groping the empty nether uselessly as though surprised to discover she still had fingers at all.

"Look out!" Noah shouted. The imps had boarded the beam

behind them, and even now a steady stream of them were bouncing between the platforms in their direction. Noah snatched Samantha by the wrist and heaved her off the platform, diving off himself just in time before the first imps began barreling in.

The imps were squealing and roaring with delight as they came tumbling in one by one. They seemed more experienced with this sort of travel, and they knew to bound out of the way as soon as the final platform returned to a relaxed state. Even so, sometimes they wouldn't be fast enough and the next imp flying along the beam crashed into them. This caused the pair to become entangled with one another, which invariably started a fight as they bit and scratched and rolled around long after they had escaped the platform.

When Noah and Samantha were a safe distance from the landing terminal they were better able to appreciate their surroundings. The object Samantha had described as a 'pile of doors' soared above them: a teetering tower which bent and swayed with the invisible current of the nether. Doors isn't the word Noah would have used to describe the hundreds of opening and closing flaps though.

Heavy, glossy sheets rolled up and down over the entranceways, reminding Noah of multi-colored eyelids more than anything else. Puffs of colored gases and trickles of mysterious liquid drained from a few of the openings. The bottom of the tower was anchored in a network of lines from the folded space which converged from all sides. This produced an effect similar to a tree with massive roots, assuming those roots were powerful enough to warp the earth around its bulk. The highest part of the structure tapered off into a network of progressively thinner branches which stirred the nether as they swayed.

"When you say everything in the Netherworld is a demon..." Noah's words trailed off as the tower bent toward them. The thin upper branches brushed through the massing imps, stroking dozens at once in an almost affectionate way.

"Correct," Visoloth replied.

"You don't mean that thing—" Samantha gasped.

"Correct," Visoloth repeated, prompting Noah to hastily translate:

"The Sylo began its life as an imp, just as all other demons before. Obviously it has been growing for a very long time, being one of the oldest demons in the shallow end of the Netherworld. When smaller demons exit through a rift from the netherworld, that rift connects to a creature like this."

The Sylo reared back to its full vertical height, shaking free from the imps which had begun to clamor through its branches. It let off a long, low moaning sound, so deep that Noah felt it as a vibration of the nether around his entire body. His body tingled and prickled with static, an all-encompassing sensation not unlike the mental freeze which accompanied the presence of a rasmacht. An overwhelming impulse told Noah that the sound was laden with wisdom and intent, and he couldn't shake the feeling that the gigantic being had just addressed him directly.

"The Sylo is so old, in fact, that it doesn't even speak the unified demonic language which is commonly spoken today. I don't know if there's anyone still here who understands him, but fortunately it is not the being that will be instructing you."

Visoloth's words were drowned out by the terrified squeals coming from imps at the landing terminal. A giant spinning ball came hurtling along the purple light like an incoming meteor. Imps scattered as it slammed into the platform with enough force to flatten the ball into a pancake. The black receiving terminal stretched twice as far as its width, straining so far and thin that it was practically invisible before it began to relax.

The fleshy ball which emerged was the most repulsive thing Noah could imagine. It looked like a tumor that had learned to walk. Dozens of eyes and as many noses were embedded in the fat, fleshy folds of overhanging skin, rows of teeth jutted out at odd angles without any mouths, and thick matted hair sprouted at odd angles. There wasn't an inch of skin that wasn't somehow mottled with bulbous swellings or misplaced facial features. And yes, it did have a single red and yellow bow-tie, neatly displayed beneath a small wispy beard that Noah could only assume was at its front.

"Mr. Mufflafo, punctual as always," Visoloth said to the disgusting ball. "You do remember the spirit that I spoke of? He and his pet human are honored to be included in your upcoming curriculum."

Noah left out the line about his 'pet human' when translating for Samantha. She didn't seem any less horrified for the exclusion.

"I thought we were just here to meet George. You never said anything about a class."

"We don't have time for that anyway," Noah added. "We need to find the Primes, so…"

"You? See the Primes? Like that?" Mr. Mufflafo burbled. It was unclear where the sound was coming from, but it had the unmistakable wheezing quality of escaping gas.

"Forgive his ignorance," Visoloth said. "It only goes to show you the importance of their education."

The imps had begun to crowd around on all sides to listen to the conversation. They kept a cautious distance from Mr. Mufflafo, which displayed impressive restraint considering their typical irreverence.

"I don't understand what anyone is saying!" Samantha said with exasperation. "Why is everything about this world so confusing?"

"Ah, yes, English, very good," Mr. Mufflafo said, his enunciation of the familiar words impeccable despite their wheezing utterance. "Is this better, human girl? How nice for me to have a human and a spirit to broaden the education of our little ones."

"But we can't go to school," Noah insisted. "I don't want to learn how to become a demon, or transform myself into anything like… no offense meant, sir."

"None taken," Mr. Mufflafo replied amiably. "You misunderstand though, my dear boy. Visoloth has told me of your quest, and it is not a lack of permission which prevents you from finding what you seek. The Primes do not live near here. Not in a year, not in ten thousand years could you reach them through the shallow end of the Netherworld. They exist in higher dimensional space than this, and if you are committed to your quest, you will need to learn to see the world a little differently than you do now."

Then turning from them, the great ball of flesh rolled past, leaving them wondering if they had even been addressing the front of the creature at all.

"There, you see?" Visoloth replied. "I've helped you out, just like I said I would. And if in the course of your education you happen to learn about how a demon becomes human... well you know I'll be anxious to learn as well."

"You're not staying with us here?" Noah asked.

"There are more things stirring than your aspirations, no matter how well intentioned they may be," the demon dog replied. "The Trans Dimensional Department is mobilizing in ways I have never seen in this lifetime, and the soulless who dwell in silence among the living may have plans of their own. You will have George Hampton and Mr. Mufflafo to guide you though. I know things here may seem a little strange to you, but no one ever grows from more of the same."

"Thank you for bringing us this far," Noah replied. "I know it must be difficult to trust spirits and humans in a time like this, but I'm glad we all want the same thing and are working together."

"Never assume you know what a demon wants. Let that be your third lesson, and the last you will learn from me. I do hope you find your way to the Primes and rouse them to action though. They have been so far removed from the affairs of the living and the dead for so long that I fear they do not understand the urgency the Soul Net represents. Good luck upon your journey and may we meet again, in this life or the next."

"Come little ones, come along. Into the Sylo," Mr. Mufflafo wheezed in English. "Any door will do, they all lead to the same place."

"We're going inside a demon then. Lovely, just lovely," Samantha said, her hands on her hips as she gazed at the tower from top to bottom.

"You're sure you want to do this? It's not too late to go home. We don't even know if a living human can go through the higher dimensional space to where the Primes are."

"Summer vacation is about to start," Samantha replied wistfully. "If I'd planned this better, I really should have left during the school year. I could have gone to the beach next week."

"Is that what you'd rather do?"

She didn't say anything. She just stared at the revolting fleshy ball that was Mr. Mufflafo as he squeezed his way through one of the holes in the Sylo. It seemed like he couldn't make it at first, until a long tongue slid underneath him from within the tower to slurp him inside.

"Yes," Samantha replied with quiet determination. "I'd rather be home right now, but I'm not going back. Because one day I'm going to be a witch, and a witch knows that all the most interesting parts of life happen when you think you'd rather be doing something else. Besides, I always thought the sun was overrated anyway."

THE SYLO

THE BUS WHICH BROUGHT STUDENTS FROM THE LIVING WORLD TO THE mortuary was named the Daymare. It was a demon which had been working under contract for the Trans Dimensional Department, until the day when Visoloth and the other demons in the school had rebelled against The Matriarch. Noah hadn't known the Daymare was a demon when he first rode it though, as the interior was so well furnished with platforms, seats, and even a massive spiraling staircase.

That's what Noah anticipated when he and Samantha entered the Sylo alongside the jostling imps. He was expecting to see a fully furnished facility, perhaps decorated with summoning circles, demonic runes, and towering bookshelves filled with muttering pages whispering forbidden knowledge. He expected chairs, and desks, and perhaps the occasional portal where the folded space came together to send the class off to exotic field trips and great adventure. He expected any number of things, except for what was really here.

"Noah?" Samantha piped up, her familiar voice a great reassurance in the alien landscape.

"Yeah?"

"Do demons eat? I know they aren't exactly alive, but they aren't dead either."

"You know, I've never thought about it before now. But they must, considering…"

"Noah?"

"Yeah, I'm here." There was no light within the Sylo, but that was no barrier to sight in the Netherworld.

"Have we been eaten?"

"I think that's probably a good guess."

They stood in place together, overwhelmed by the sight of what lay before them while the imps streamed past on either side. The inside of the Sylo very much resembled what Noah imagined the inside of any other creature to look like. Bulbous, twitching organs the size of cars were tethered to the walls by stringy networks of fatty tissue. Networks of arteries and veins formed walkways and bridges between the organs, with swarms of imps crawling over them or leaping between them with gleeful shrieks. An especially large internal structure the color of strained peas had a gaping mouth with razor teeth. It continually gnashed at a steady stream of glittering stones which poured from an opening in a pulsing vein.

"Black opals," Noah said. "Those are used to seal contracts when a demon is summoned from the Netherworld."

"Very good. And once those contracts are up?"

Noah jumped at the sound. He'd been so distracted by the strange landscape that he hadn't noticed the enormous Mr. Mufflafo waiting against the wall where he'd entered behind them.

"The demons go back to the Netherworld," Noah replied.

"With the opals. And what's inside the stone?" Mufflafo said, his voice encouraging like a math teacher guiding a student through a problem.

"The time he spent on the other side," Samantha cut in. "Demons are eating time to grow."

"How did you know that?" Noah asked.

She shrugged. "It just sort of makes sense, doesn't it?" Then to Noah's bewildered shrug, she added, "Well it makes sense to me."

"The human girl is full of surprises," Mufflafo burbled, "but you aren't a typical human, now are you? Tell me where you have found such an unusual eye."

"I didn't find it. A gargoyle attacked me, and then it started changing. Pretty soon I was able to see things in the spirit world, and then I started hearing stuff from the other side too. I don't think it's done yet either, because the area around my eye is getting stiffer, like it's made of stone too."

"It does look like you're losing some color on that side of your face," Noah agreed. "I still don't understand how demons are eating time though."

"Even experienced spiritologists have a hard time understanding that time does not exist in the Netherworld. It has to be brought in from somewhere else in order for demons to grow and change. It sounds to me like that eye of yours has begun to notice something deeply hidden about the world though. I would pay attention to what it tells me, if I were you."

Mr. Mufflafo began rolling toward one of the tangled bridges, but Noah called after him. "Of course there's time here! How could we all be moving around if there wasn't time?"

The corpulent demon seemed to ignore the question, not slowing down as it sailed across the bridge. "Sssalama, how nice to see you again," he called. "You'll be gathering the imps in the liver, won't you? You and Trebedara will be meeting me after the orientation, yes?"

"George Hampton will be using the liver, I'll be in the flubber-stoo. He said he doesn't mind the bile, but I think he's just being polite," a smooth, rolling voice replied in English. Noah hadn't noticed the bat-like creature hanging from one of the higher bridges. Its leathery wings almost entirely concealed its body, except for a single gigantic red eye peering over the top.

"Excuse me, but where's the liver?" Noah called up to the demon called Sssalama.

"The yellow and green one, that way." Sssalama pointed with one wing, unfurling it as he did so to reveal dozens of toothy mouths on the inside flap.

"Thank you!" Samantha called. "I like your big eye! Very cool!"

"Thank you, I grew it last week. I like your purple skirt. Who did you kill for it?"

"Nobody. It was second-hand, on sale," Samantha replied with pride.

"It has the rich color of a greater demon's blood," Sssalama added amiably. The demon refolded its wings into a shape like a megaphone, switching to demonic as it shrieked: "No stealing the opals! Next imp I catch playing around the stomach will be going inside."

Samantha began to swim upward toward the yellow and green organ in the distance, but another shriek from Sssalama encouraged her to remain on the networked walkways. It seemed unnecessary at first, but the reason became abundantly clear when a flap in a nearby organ opened to pour gouts of steaming liquid through the space between the walkways. The liquid flowed to where it was received by another organ, where a tongued mouth would slurp it out of the nether. It wasn't obvious what would happen to them if they were caught by such an unwholesome blast, but both were positive that this was one lesson they were happier not to learn.

The spotted liver was a surprisingly welcoming sight. A growth of bone from the walls of the Sylo converged on the organ like scaffolding, intentionally molding the squishy organ into something that looked passably like a house. A thick layer of fatty white tissue overhung from the top like a roof, and there was even a little garden in front in which several variety of brightly colored molds and fungi grew. The walls were scored with scar tissue which gave the impression of brickwork, and a flowered wreath was hung above the fleshy flap which opened and closed in the front. Most welcome of all was the familiar old man sitting out front on a jutting piece of bone, his striped hat resting in his lap.

"George!" Noah exclaimed, rushing to his friend and throwing his arms around him as George stood to greet them. The gesture seemed to surprise them both, but it was such a relief to see a familiar face that he couldn't hold himself back.

"I've been expecting you," the old man replied warmly, "although I must admit I wasn't expecting Sam. I thought I warned you that the Netherworld was no place for the living."

"The living world is no place for the living, not with demons running around in it," Samantha said stubbornly. "I figure I'm just as safe here as I would be at home."

"That speaks more to your ignorance than it does to the danger, but I'm glad you're alright all the same. Ca'akan! Samantha's here. Get out here and say hello."

The flap in the house opened and a flash of purple sped out toward them. The lizard-like creature stumbled over itself with its rubbery legs. The demon's gelatinous body struggled to maintain its shape as it tried to stand up. Ripples of excitement cascaded down its body.

"Ca'akan! You've changed!" Samantha said. She moved to help the demon sort itself out, but George was quick to block her path.

"He's grown into a lava salamander. Don't touch! You'll burn yourself if you try to help him, and besides, he needs to learn to use his new body properly. Come in, come in, don't be shy. I know it's not what you're used to, but it's quite comfortable and I've got all the bile shunted off to feed the garden."

George waited until the fleshy flap collapsed before putting his foot on top of it to hold it down, gesturing for them to enter. Ca'akan scampered inside as soon as it could get its legs underneath it again, and Noah and Samantha followed it into the organ.

A kitchen table and chairs, made from what appeared to be real wood. Ca'akan tried to crawl onto one of the chairs, but George shooed him to the brick hearth where he lay his scalding body down upon the iron grate. There was a padded reading chair, piles of messily scrawled papers that may have come from the imps, and a crystal scry ball mounted on a pedestal in the corner. Thick rugs covered most of the spotted liver, and a series of gutters along the sides of the room caught the dribbling green bile to safely deposit it outside. A dense clutter of portraits were mounted upon the walls, and overall the place had a charmingly cozy feeling that was hardly recognizable as demonic guts at all.

George invited them to sit down, and while Samantha unpacked her turkey and mustard sandwiches she'd brought from home, he shared the news of the outside world. Noah had spent the last several months among the living, and despite the occasional scrying visits that Walter had been able to manage, he'd been largely isolated from the events of the spirit world.

Ever since the Trans Dimensional Department began banishing demons, the Netherworld has had a shortage of the black time opals the demons need to grow. George explained that the demonic incursions into the living world had initially been peaceful expeditions to try and serve the living instead, thus accruing time to bring back with them. Their attempt to form contracts with the living lead to the demons discovering how many people were existing without souls though, something which prevented them from forming the pacts at all.

The greater demons in the higher dimension were furious about the shortage of time being brought back to them, and in their anger they commanded the soulless to be slaughtered. At first it was difficult for the demons to find their way into the living world without being summoned, but a series of rifts were being opened throughout the world. Ordinarily these rifts would quickly collapse on their own, but they were being powered by a permanent energy source which kept the two worlds connected at these points.

"The Chainer batteries," Noah said. He in turn explained everything he knew to George, who had never heard of anything so horrible as perpetually killing and reviving a single soul in order to provide a constant flow of energy.

"It still doesn't make sense to me," Samantha said, counting out her remaining sandwiches and packing them into her backpack once more. "If The Matriarch is going to all this trouble to create an army of soulless people, why is she letting the demons in just to get them killed?"

"I don't think she cares if they're killed," Noah replied. "There must be so many of them if she's been at this for years. She's willing to sacrifice them."

"But why?"

"To get the Trans Dimensional Department involved," George Hampton said, scratching his bald head. "They see demons coming in and attacking people, and it forces them to fight the demons. I don't know what she's really after, but with the department and the demons and the living all fighting each other, she's certainly got everyone distracted."

George went on to explain that's where the Sylo came in. The demons are rarely coordinated enough to organize into a large school like this, but the greater demons have commanded them to prepare for war. That means learning about the living and the spirit world where they will be fighting, training for combat, and being grown in mass from lowly imps to all manner of destructive and powerful demons.

"It's going to keep getting exponentially worse from here," he said. "More opening rifts means more demons in the living world, which means more time being brought back to the Sylo, which means imps growing into more fearsome demons that spend more time in the living world. If this keeps up, the whole world might become overrun. And even if they only attack the soulless, there are enough of them that it will create chaos everywhere. Even the innocent will suffer in such violent times, or perhaps exclusively the innocent, if the soulless really can't feel anything at all."

"What if there was a way to put the souls back in the bodies though?" Noah asked. "If we could find where The Matriarch was hiding them and return the souls where they belong, then the demons wouldn't attack the living anymore. Then the department and the demons could reach a peace again, right?"

"It won't stop until the Soul Net is destroyed for good," George said. "You're right though. It would be much better to return the souls than to kill all the soulless."

"You'll help though, won't you?" Samantha pleaded. "You'll tell Mr. Mufflafo and the other teachers not to send the demons to attack people anymore."

"It's not up to them," George replied. "It's the Primes and the greater demons that you'll need to convince. The best thing you can do now is to pay attention in your classes and learn how to access the higher dimensions. What's going on is bigger than any of us, and it is too difficult to try and solve everything on our own. If we are patient, and if we trust each other to do our best, then I have faith that nature will sort itself out one way or another. How arrogant can we be, to believe that any one of us can truly disrupt the cosmic balance which has endured since the beginning of time?"

TIME DOES NOT EXIST in the Netherworld. Noah still couldn't make sense of what that was supposed to mean, but he had to admit that the longer he stayed here, the more it began to feel that way.

Nothing outside the Sylo changed from one moment to the next. No rising or setting sun punctuated the eternal stillness of the nether. No changing of the weather or the seasons. No light or darkness, no temperature or wind, no life and death. Noah tried to keep track of how many times he slept, but even this proved useless as he would always wakeup never quite rested, not knowing whether eight hours or ten minutes had passed.

Samantha kept track with the passage of her sandwiches until they ran out, at which point she had to rely upon eating whatever the raiding demons brought back with them from the living world. Despite not strictly needing food to survive, their increasingly frequent trips among the living caused some demons to begin adopting their habits. Hats in particular had become a sort of trophy among the imps as proof they had been to the living world and returned. No one had explained to them exactly what was a hat and what wasn't, however, and it became common to see imps wearing everything including towels, shoes, bowls, and anything else they could find upon their heads.

The classes themselves fell into four broad categories, led by the four teachers: George Hampton, Mr. Mufflafo, Sssalama, and a witch named Trebedara.

George's class was taught in his colorful moldy garden where the imps would gather, perching on every possible surface, including the roof of his little house. He would speak of the cosmic balance in which the living must die, and the demons must shepherd the spirits onward to the next life. When people at the Mortuary spoke of the role of demons, they always made it sound like they were there to serve and assist the spirits. The way George told it made the demons sound more like they were part of the same cycle as everyone else.

"There was once a time when all three moved in perfect harmony. The reason all roads from death pass through the Netherworld is because spirits would next become demons, and only then continue their journey into their next life. This only changed when the Trans Dimensional Department banned the transformation of demons into the living, and the knowledge was lost. From then on spirits went on directly to live again, and in doing so robbed the demons of their primary role in the cycle. After that demons could only grow and transform into other types of demons, which led to the formation of greater demons as ancient creatures continued to mutate, unable to start over and live again."

The lectures didn't have a set duration, and would rather go for as long as the imps could sit still. Invariably one of them would try to steal another's hat though, or they'd begin chasing one another, or some other distraction would arise. The imps would scatter and rush shrieking and chittering and giggling in every direction, and George would be forced to retreat inside his house to avoid being overrun by the wild creatures.

Mr. Mufflafo preferred to have his class among the branches on the very top of the towering Sylo where the imps could look out at the infinite nether. His class was much more technical, having to do with energy transfers and life-force dynamics. Noah remembered the term being used when he visited the department of energy, but he hadn't understood it properly until Mr. Mufflafo broke the terms down.

"The three principles are as follows," he said, using English so that Samantha could keep up. "The first is that souls must be planted to grow. Isolate them in a diamond and they are static, but plant them in a body, or a spirit, or a demon, and they will never stop becoming *deeper* until the body is destroyed. Then they must start again with as much of their old life as they can hold onto.

"The second principle is that energy is released when one phase passes to the next. The third law is that the energy of each type of phase has its own flavor, and the flavors do not mix. For example a spirit may exchange part of its life force using an aquamarine stone to another spirit, but he may not give that life force to a living human to extend his mortal life."

This explanation bothered Noah, but he couldn't figure out why until near the end of the class when the imps were beginning to swing wildly through the branches. The realization hit him all at once though, so suddenly that he couldn't help but interrupt the demon to blurt out:

"The second principle can't be true. I was there when some of the soulless were being killed. They don't have a soul to go from one phase to the next. I know energy was still being released though, because it was powering my mirror. So where did it come…"

His voice trailed off, drowned out by a high-pitched squeal. Two of the imps were wrestling nearby, and one of them was pinning the other. The one trapped on the ground had begun to chew on the other's foot in order to get free, which prompted another series of vicious squeaks.

"If the energy had to be coming from souls exchanging their body for a spiritual one…" Noah continued, thinking aloud as he went.

Mr. Mufflaflo didn't seem to be listening though. He was rolling along the branch the imps were fighting on. The squabbling imps were too distracted and didn't notice him coming until he had completely squashed the pair. The high-pitched squeaking doubled in intensity for a brief moment, but it was quickly muffled by the rolling layers of fat. Mr. Mufflafo rolled back the other way, heading back down the branch. Neither of the imps were anywhere to be seen.

Noah fell silent. Maybe it was best that Mr. Mufflafo hadn't heard him. He was out of place enough just being a spirit in the Netherworld, and it might be best not to draw too much attention to himself. Noah wasn't sure where those two imps had gone, but he was quite positive that he didn't want Mr. Mufflaflo to roll over him too.

"Collateral damage," Mr. Mufflafo answered at last. "You are correct that no energy would be released by the 'death' of the soulless ones. No more energy than a machine breaking down. Any energy that is released must have come from the death of living humans, also known as collateral damage."

"How could you?" Samantha scolded. "I thought you were better than that. That you were one of the good ones."

"I can smell your soul," Mr. Mufflafo said, steering to roll in their direction. "All demons can. We have no reason to kill a human... on purpose. Living flesh burns just as fast whether or not there is a soul inside. Falling buildings, the panic of fellow humans, or self-defense when there are no other options... You can't blame demons for being angry for how they have been treated. Just as there is good and evil in every soul, so are there demons who are not as gentle as I. There are those who love the fire that has comforted them more than the enemy who has oppressed them. Are you the one to say they are wrong for that?"

Noah clenched his mouth and turned away. Of course he sympathized with them, but how could that ever justify the suffering of the innocent? The misshapen demon loomed overhead, each discolored patch of skin and malformed facial feature in clear view.

"I'll say it. They're wrong," Samantha said in an emphatic rush of breath. "Those people weren't the ones who were treating you badly."

"She's right," Noah said, standing firm. "You can't hold them responsible for someone else's crimes."

The slow wheezing breath which escaped Mr. Mufflafo's folds came in short, halting bursts. It took a long, tense moment before Noah realized the demon might be laughing.

"Your soul is old, Chainer, but your mind is young. You have learned the lesson many times before, and when you are older and know the world more truly, you will come to accept it as truth. If you are one of us, then you will act like one. You will both accompany the demons next time they go through the rift, and you will bleed your anger dry."

Class ended without further incident when the restless imps proved too excited by the confrontation to settle down. Noah supposed he should be grateful that the situation didn't escalate, but he was still unhappy with how things played out. He couldn't imagine going to the living world and attacking other people, but he was also worried how his quest would be impacted if the demons decided he wasn't one of them after all.

Trebedara held her class on the other side of the Sylo. Noah and Samantha weren't sure where to go until they spotted a disorderly line of imps waiting at an opening in one of the broad stringy veins. Some manner of black liquid was flowing through the tube, but that didn't stop the imps leaping in headfirst to swoosh off as though riding a water slide. Noah would have preferred to circle round the outside of the demonic structure to look for an alternate route. He suspected Samantha didn't want to get in either, but she refused to admit anything that sounded like fear. She dove in with only the slightest hesitation, and that was enough to send Noah against his better judgement as well.

The black liquid felt like entering a scalding bath: hot enough to make him flinch, but not enough to do any real harm. The vein took them in a sharp corkscrewing pattern that sloshed back and forth before spitting them out into a dense receptive net of smaller tubules. The whole underside of the Sylo was a mess of stringy demonic filaments. The nether was crinkled and warped all around them where the folds of space converged. When one of the imps passed through an especially crinkled area, they appeared distorted as though viewed through a funhouse mirror.

"Gross, it's not coming out." Samantha was shaking herself, trying wring the black liquid from her hair which clung together as though doused in oil. "I can't believe I didn't pack shampoo or anything."

"You're looking more like a witch every day," Noah said, trying to suppress his laughter at her futile efforts.

"Eugh. Why didn't it stick to you? Being alive is the worst."

"This way, human girl. Step through the folded space," Trebedara said, materializing from a nearby crinkle like a paper doll folding before their eyes. Samantha took a step in the indicated direction before stopping to stare at Trebedara, fixated on her bizarre appearance.

"What's the matter? Never seen a naghog before, dear?" Trebedara asked.

The witch looked rather like a wild boar, if you could get past its four heads spaced evenly around its torso. All four heads had long, straight, blonde hair, which was made even more ridiculous as two of the heads proudly wore metal pasta-strainers. When she spoke, it was out of all four heads, the words slightly staggered to create a chorused effect.

"No ma'am," Samantha said, an uncustomary hush of reverence in her voice. "Are you really a witch?"

"Witches and demons have a long history of getting along. So what if I am? Will that make you do what you're told?"

Samantha rushed to step through the converging folds as she was instructed. As she passed through it, part of her seemed to flatten out into a pancake, puffing out again as she emerged on the other side. All of the black liquid squeezed out of her as though it was being scraped off by a paint wringer. Samantha's skin was red and scrubbed clean as she stepped away. She only had a moment to stare at herself in wonder before a press of imps converged on the fold from every direction, squealing and giggling as they did.

"You can thank the Sylo itself for folding the nether here. Anyone who is familiar with the shallow end will know that creases and pockets can be found throughout," the four heads said. "The more powerful the magic, the more the space will fold, until eventually it becomes so dense and complicated that it becomes like a maze connecting two dimensions. Creatures such as yourselves can learn to find their way through these higher dimensional spaces where the greater demons live."

Trebedara's class was all about the different dimensions of space. She said to think of it like you were standing at the bottom of a mountain. There could be a perfectly flat path that went all the way around the base of a mountain, and moving along that was like moving around within a single dimension. You could also work hard and climb a little higher to reach another dimension. That work was the energy put into creating a portal and going through it. The living world, the spirit world, and the shallow end of the Netherworld were all in their own dimensions, although they were so closely entangled that anyone with a bit of magic about them could reach over and interact with things in the other worlds.

"A witch is known for many things, but none perhaps as vital as navigating this mountain," Trebedara said. "Witches specialize in interacting with things from nearby dimensions. And if she is careful in her studies, if she is always listening for things no one else can hear and looking for things no one else can see, then there is no limit to how high the dimensional mountain she may climb. Until just like the great witch Bah-Rabba Kaba, she leaps off the mountain entirely to create her very own world. Her very own little slice of reality, decorated with her own colors that exist nowhere else. Though we cannot see them now, who is to say how many beings are up there on the mountain looking down at all that we do?"

"I can see things other people can't, but only with my right eye. Does that mean I'll only be half a witch?" Samantha asked.

"What makes one a witch has everything to do with how one sees the world, but nothing to do with their eyes. I don't know how the world looks inside your head, but it seems to me that a living girl wouldn't be in the nether if she could find what she was looking for at home."

"What if I don't know what I'm looking for?"

"Then you'll never stop looking, and to a witch, that's even better."

"Are the Prime demons at the top of the mountain?" Noah asked. "Can you teach us a spell that can send us there?"

"A spell? What is this nonsense about spells? The folds in the nether where the dimensions intermingle are what you're looking for. Magic isn't about learning some fancy words. It's about becoming the kind of person whose words are worth listening to."

Noah had never seen the imps sit still and listen for so long as when they were gathered around Trebedara. Samantha too had a look of rapturous fascination upon her face, an enchantment that remained unbroken until Trebedara said she was tired and had to lie down to rest. Fortunately they found a dry tube to bring them back to the main cavity of the Sylo, although Samantha still entered reluctantly, disappointed to leave.

"Being a witch seems a lot more complicated than I thought," Samantha conceded. "Do you think I'll ever figure it out?"

"I can't think of anyone who sees the world more differently than you," Noah told her honestly.

"You don't know the half of it," she replied, a sly grin upon her face.

"What do you mean? What else can you see?"

Samantha gave her best cackle, which reverberated hauntingly through the enclosed tube.

"Hey, that's pretty good. I can really believe that sound came from a raspy old woman with something nasty in mind."

"Thanks. I've been practicing."

The fourth and final teacher at the Sylo was the bat-like creature named Sssalama. Noah picked up from the chatter of imps that he was going to be teaching them to resist banishment, which didn't sound very useful to him as he didn't think spirits could be banished. He would have rather gone back to spend time with George, but Samantha insisted they try to keep an open mind.

The latest class was to be held within the beating heart at the very center of the Sylo. The internal structure was the size of a two-story building, and watching the trembling pulses run through it was grotesquely mesmerizing. It only beat once every minute or so, but when it did each chamber contracted powerfully with a sound like a gunshot. Sssalama was hanging upside-down from the thick aorta which throbbed with the black fluid which was being dispersed throughout the Sylo.

"Inside, inside, everyone in," Sssalama said. "Not all at once now, you have to time it out between the beats."

"Is it all wet and disgusting in there?" Samantha asked, running her fingers protectively through her dark hair.

"Goodness no," Sssalama said. "To think I would get my wings all slimed up so they couldn't fly anymore. No no, it's quite dry. Warm and dry, with a gentle breezes that smell like the ocean. There's even a little moonshine."

Noah wasn't sure that he believed him, but he followed the imps through the open vein into the first chamber. Halfway through he made a sudden stop. What was that whistling sound? Was it another kind of demon?

"Birdsong," Samantha whispered. "I think I really can smell the salt in the air."

"This isn't a part of the demon," Noah replied. "There's a portal inside."

"No blocking up the vein! Give a demon a heart attack, that's what you'll do."

A rough shove from behind sent Noah sprawling into the heart. He found himself inside a small opening surrounded by thick sheets of muscle. More imps were piling through the opening and crawling around his legs, so tightly packed that they were standing on each other's heads.

"All clear!" Sssalama's muffled voice shouted.

The walls closed in around them, threatening to crush Noah and all the imps together into a single point. There was a wall of pressure on every side and booming thunder in his ears. Then all at once there was light. Wind rushed across his face, and a full moon soared high overhead. Imps were scattering throughout the rocky shoreline, some already rushing into the crashing waves with unabated glee.

"No better way to learn than by doing," Sssalama's voice sounded like it was coming from a long way off. "We're going to gather some time in the living world. We're going to hunt the soulless ones."

DEATH OF THE UNLIVING

ALL THAT SEPARATED NOAH FROM THE NETHERWORLD WAS THE SPAN OF a single heartbeat. And though the heart may continue beating, no magic could let him linger upon the moment which first inspired it to dance. There was no portal behind him to return through, and each slow booming roll of the invisible heart pumped more imps into the living world. If they were being pushed through a rift, then it was only a one way trip.

"We can't participate in this," Samantha said firmly. She was leaning over and wagging her finger in an authoritarian fashion at the newly arriving imps. "Nobody deserves to be attacked, whether they have a soul or not. Do you understand?"

One of the imps was creeping up on the distracted one she was lecturing. The unsuspecting imp didn't notice until the other launched on top of it to viciously bite the top of its head. The two imps tumbled over one another, scattering the others. Some joined in the brawl, others, began digging into the cool moonlit sand, or scuttling off to investigate the nearby rocks and stick their heads between the cracks.

"You're right. Nobody deserves to be attacked." It was Sssalama who had suddenly materialized from the latest heartbeat. He looked sorely out of place crawling through the sand with his wing tips. "Fortunately the soulless are the nobodies we're looking for."

"That doesn't count! They've still got bodies. They can still bleed!" Samantha insisted.

"You might as well say a water faucet bleeds water. There's nothing in the soulless that can feel, and I will not permit you to mislead the imps with your unfounded sympathy. I am perfectly capable of teaching my own class, thank you anyway. Do not make us regret letting outsiders in."

Samantha crossed her arms and sat abruptly in the sand, hurtling downward as though she wished to crush whatever was below her. She glared at Noah with a look that said 'do something'. He shrugged helplessly and scrambled to get out of the way as yet more imps were pumped into the world through the thin black rip in reality.

"Gather round, gather round," Sssalama ordered languidly. He propped himself up on his wing tips, his great red eye swelling to the size of a soccer ball as it rotated in circles to survey the imps. "Though the girl's voice is shrill and needling, she does make an important point to keep in mind. We must not attack anyone until we've learned to sniff out their soul. I've already prepared a sample for us to practice on. Behold, an empty vessel."

The bat-like demon unfurled one wing the rest of the way to reveal a small child that tucked beneath one of them. He was even younger than Noah's grandson Lewis. Nothing about him indicated that he was soulless, except perhaps a lack of fear in his face. If anything, the child seemed bored by the inquisitive demons leering all around him.

"I can see the emptiness…" Samantha whispered. "I never used to be able to tell the difference, but there's no doubt about it. He doesn't have a soul."

"Your eye—the stone is still spreading. Half your cheek looks like it's made of marble," Noah replied.

Samantha gingerly touched her face, then shrugged. "Good. I want to be able to see more of what is deeply hidden."

"What happens when you drop a rock into a well?" Sssalama asked, cradling the child with his wing. "All you have to do is listen. You may hear a plop as it hits the water, or a thud as it hits the ground."

A leathery encasing blinked around Sssalama's great red eye. When it opened again there were sparks dancing around the bottom, gathering as though he was shedding a tear. When it became too bright it slipped free to drop down toward the child's face. Samantha pushed toward him, but Noah held her back with a hand upon her shoulder. The child looked up as the sparks splashed across its face, the light harmlessly dissipating into the air. The child didn't seem to notice, and soon he was glumly playing with the sand beneath him as though he was alone.

"Even hearing nothing will tell you something. Down down it goes, falling forever without a sound. So too may you probe the soul of the living, learning even from silence. All demons have an innate sense of the soul, an ability which has long been exploited by the spirits who wish to use our power as their own. There is no spell to learn; all you must do is reach out to your subject and center your awareness around the core of their being. When all is quiet, then there is nothing to stay your claw."

Sssalama raised the opposite wing as he spoke, and from the corner protruded a long, thin spike, unsheathing from the darkness as a cat's claw might. Noah turned away, unable to watch. A sharp intake of breath from the child—the chittering of imps growing louder by the second—then a high-pitched wail. Noah opened one of his eyes a sliver against his will, then all the way as he realized what had happened.

Samantha had leapt forward and seized the child away from the demon. She was cradling him protectively in her arms and backing away, but she couldn't make it far. The imps were pressing in around her, seizing her by the ankles and legs. Sssalama lurched toward her with his ungainly crawl through the sand.

"I won't let you!" Samantha shouted. "He still has a soul—it's just somewhere else right now. We can find it and we can bring it back—let go of me! Don't touch him!"

"This is what class is for," Sssalama hissed, dragging himself before her, "and this is a lesson you will not forget."

Noah tried to push his way in to help her, but there were too many imps all climbing over each other to get close. His vision was obscured for a moment, and another high-pitched wail from the child promised fresh horrors hidden from view.

"Lester? Is that you? Where are you?" An unfamiliar woman's voice responded to the cry. Desperate, fearful, strained and catching, as though the woman had been shouting for hours. "Hold on just a little longer, Lester. Mother's coming."

A ripple of confusion spread through the imps. Just for a moment —just long enough for them to turn their head toward Sssalama and chirp about what was going on. Just long enough for Noah to push his way through to Samantha. A moment later and they were breaking free of the circle of imps, both running toward the lone person on the moonlit beach.

A few seconds head start, that's all they managed before the startled imps began tearing through the sand after them.

"My baby! You've got my—" The woman's ragged voice cut short. She had caught sight of Noah and Samantha, and so too did she see the mass of scampering imps boil the darkness into a frenzy of motion.

"Catch that boy! Catch the soulless one!" Sssalama shrieked.

"Run! Get out of here!" Noah shouted to the woman, who had rallied admirably to rush toward them once more. Unfortunately that was the opposite direction she should have gone to avoid the imps.

"She can't hear spirits. Other way!" Samantha shouted. "We've got him. We've got Lester. He's not hurt. Just run!"

The mother wouldn't listen though. She kept coming toward them until Samantha was able to pass the child to her. She stared at the approaching demons, only to blink them away and turn back to the boy. The woman's eyes were stretched wide with anxious fright, and her hair was a frizzy tangle of humidity and exhaustion. Whether her boy had a soul or not was immaterial—the mother's emotion was too genuine to believe she didn't have a soul of her own. And that soul would be the one to suffer if anything happened to her child.

"What in the world..." the woman's voice trailed off, unable to tear her focus away from her boy long enough to properly register the demons.

"Not exactly." Samantha grabbed her by the hand to drag her farther along the beach. "They're only imps though. Are there more people nearby? Where can we get help?"

The woman nodded jerkily, still in shock. She kept trying to look over shoulder at the swarming imps, but Samantha ran ahead and kept hauling her along whenever she slowed.

"Up the stairs, this way," the woman blurted. "My car is parked on the side of the road up there. I've been searching all night, and..."

Her voice trailed off again as she turned to look behind. She stumbled in the thick sand, and the second it took her to regain her feet was a precious thing to lose. The electric light of a street lamp glowed from the direction they were headed, which gave an even clearer view of the imps springing at their heels. The humans hit the stairs leading from the beach first, and bounding several steps at a time were able to increase the distance a little more. A few extra seconds—that's all they needed to give her the time to get in the car and close the doors.

The final sprint through the parking lot gave them that edge. The imps were still clambering up the stairs when they slammed into the SUV at a dead run. Samantha and Noah tumbled into the backseat. The repeated click resounded as the woman kept making sure the doors were locked. She was trembling from head to foot, but that didn't stop her from starting the car.

One, two, steadying breaths. They were pulling into reverse, and the imps wouldn't be able to keep up. Panic was subsiding, but a sudden crashing thud on the roof made mockery of the momentary relief. The top of the car indented with the screech of twisting metal from the weight of the blow. Long, black, leathery wings draped down over the side windows. Sssalama had caught up with them.

"What are you doing? There's a demon on the roof. Step on it, lady!" Samantha shouted.

The woman made a croaking, whimpering sound as she slammed her foot down. The car veered sharply onto the street, prompting the ferocious blare of an unseen truck. An instinctive motion sent the car lurching back toward the side of the road. The demonic legion of swarming imps was apparently an insufficient excuse to spare the flash of a middle finger as the truck hurtled past.

The woman strove to navigate back to the road, but another terrible blow to the roof sent one of Sssalama's claws cleanly through the metal. His great red eye appeared at the opening, briefly narrowing on Noah and Samantha before turning toward the petrified woman in front.

"Please open the door, leave your child, and drive away," Sssalama said, the cleanly enunciated words at complete odds with his terrifying presence. "I can smell your soul. We have no business with you."

Down goes the foot, off shoots the car, exploding as if shot by a cannon. The wind howled through the hole in the roof. The woman cradled the child on her lap and hastily strapped in her seatbelt, instructing Samantha to do the same. The pounding resumed on the roof, the claw working around the twisted metal to widen the opening.

"Hold on tight!" the woman shouted.

She let the car accelerate to sixty miles an hour before she slammed on the breaks. The demon on the roof hurtled past the windshield to crash and roll on the asphalt ahead. Her plan worked in that respect, although unfortunately she wasn't aware of Noah's spirit in the backseat, and didn't account for how little resistance the car provided to him. By concentrating very hard he'd been able to remain in his seat during the acceleration, but the stop was so sudden that he went flying through the front seats, straight through the windshield.

"Keep driving!" Noah shouted. "Don't stop until there are more people around!"

The car began to accelerate again, but Samantha opened the door and rolled out before it got going too fast. The pressure of the wind slammed the door behind her.

"What is wrong with you?" Noah shouted. "They're going to kill you."

"I'm saving your ass, that's what. We're in this together. Hurry, before Sssalama gets up."

Their demonic instructor wasn't getting up anytime soon. He'd barely had time to raise his head from the ground before the car had started accelerating again. He was just beginning to spread his wings when the SUV crashed into him head on. The demon was dragged under the car as it rolled over him, prompting a nightmarish howl from the beast. The crumbled body was still on the street as the car sped into the night.

The imps had caught up meanwhile. A few separated themselves from the group to approach Sssalama cautiously. Others began a wide circle around Noah and Samantha, chittering hesitantly among themselves. Noah took a deep breath to steady himself despite not needing the air. He began walking toward their demonic instructor. Samantha grabbed hold of the back of his gray shirt.

"How about not? Let's get the hell out of here."

"We've got to help him," Noah said, pulling free. "The demons are still our allies, even if we don't agree about what to do with the soulless."

"We're not seriously going back to the Netherworld, are we? I don't think we'll be exactly welcome after this."

Noah didn't have an answer. He approached Sssalama anyway, unsure of what outcome he was even hoping for. What if he was dead? How were they supposed to get back to the Netherworld? Could demons even die? He'd only ever seen them banished before. The surrounding imps crowded closer as Noah laid a hand on one of the battered black wings. It flexed and stirred beneath his touch.

"I'm sorry, sir," Noah said, keeping his voice as low and calm as he could. "I didn't mean for this to happen. Maybe we can all go back to the Sylo together and talk about the soulless…"

"Boy," Sssalama rasped. The demon gingerly peeled its wings from the asphalt and wrapped them protectively around its body. "Human boy. You have forgotten what it means to be a demon. You are no longer one of us."

"That's not fair," Samantha interjected. "I'm the one who wouldn't let you kill the soulless child. Blame me if you want. Kick me out, I don't care. Noah needs to learn how to reach the Primes though. This isn't his fault."

"Girl. Human girl. You fancy yourself special just because your eye has been cut, but there is still so much you do not see. Either you're too stupid to recognize the soulless as abominations, or the gargoyle rot has already seeped into your brain. Either way someone as short sighted—someone with as little subtlety as you will never become a witch. Leave us—both of you. We have nothing more to gain from the others company."

Sssalama spread his wings to their full extent in a sudden, powerful motion. A cascade of clattering clicks signified the shattered bones in his wings snapping back to their proper locations. He was in the air again, rising amidst the clamoring cheers of the imps.

"You can't just go back to the nether and leave us here!" Noah shouted, his voice almost entirely drowned out from the uproar. "We don't even know where we are or how to get back home."

"We aren't going back to the nether." Sssalama's words were in demonic once more, punctuated by the heavy beat of his wings. "Not until we finish what we came here to do. Come my little ones, my lovelies. Onward to where the lifeless eyes of the city glare down on us. Smell out the empty vessels without a soul, and fill them with tooth and claw instead."

Sssalama soared into the sky, but his words were powerful and ferocious despite the distance. There was nothing Noah or Samantha could do to stop the flood of imps pouring into the street to follow their instructor.

"Well don't just stand there. Come on!" Samantha called, hustling to keep up with the trailing imps.

"Don't, Sam. Let them go. We can't stop them, and we'll only get ourselves killed if we try."

"Then let's try harder. Hurry up!"

The last thing Noah wanted to do was get in the middle of another city under attack. To hear the panic and the pain in the wind, to see the fire spreading from house to house, wild and indiscriminate in its fury. The only thing worse would be for Samantha to be in the middle of it by herself. Noah wished he'd never brought her along at all. There she was though, running alongside the demons who were out for blood. And there Noah was too, one hand clutching his jawbone necklace as it bounced against his chest while he ran after her.

The first houses were close. Imps were already scampering up fences and probing along windows, looking for a way in. Others plastered themselves to the walls, incessantly sniffing out the ones who would not survive the night. There was nothing Noah could do yet. He would have to wait for the first victims before he could animate the bodies and fight back. How could he hope to keep up with this many imps though? Surely they would descend on him as soon as he began to interfere.

Samantha's initial bluster was beginning to fade too. She slowed to a jog, then a walk, trailing the imps who converged on the sleeping houses, ignorant to the horrors creeping through their yards and peering into their windows. Samantha looked back pleadingly at Noah. The flush of frustration wracked her smooth skin. She picked up a stone and prepared as if to throw it. A few seconds passed before her arm came down again, the rock slipping from her trembling fingers.

"It isn't right," she said. "I wanted to believe in them, but they really are just evil."

"What's good to the living isn't the same as what's good for the dead, or the demon," Noah replied. "They're not evil, exactly, they're just..."

"Yes they are," Samantha declared emphatically . "It's not just the soulless who are going to suffer. You saw what happened when they attacked before. The fire, the grief, the crime. Nobody trusting each other. The innocent will suffer too. I don't care if the demons think differently than us. They're wrong. They're evil. And... and..."

The upstairs light turned on in a nearby house. Someone inside screamed.

"And you're going to make things right?"

"When I'm a witch, I will," Samantha insisted. "Until then, I guess we'll have to rely on them."

It took several seconds of searching the empty darkness before Noah realized what she was talking about. Samantha's keen eye had picked up on the slightest warmer shade of gray on an otherwise empty rooftop. An orange tie, dangling from a shadow. It shifted its weight to the other side, and a flash of white gloves glowed as they reflected beneath the street lamp.

"There's more of them all along that side of the street," Samantha said. "Down low, behind the bushes. More over there at the end of the street. I see one peeping over that brick wall. Do you think they were waiting for us?"

"I don't know. Should we warn the demons? Or help the people from the department?"

"Even if they're here to help the living, that doesn't make them the good guys. Don't forget they're the ones using the Soul Net…"

Noah and Samantha stared at each other in confusion. That was the only chance they had to do something, and they wasted it with too much thinking.

"Go! Teams Alpha, Beta, and Midnight Sparkles initiate flank," a gruff voice bellowed. It was Theodore Oswold himself, the prime minister of the department. He was dressed in pristine white, from his pants to his shirt to his vest to his coat. Golden buttons marched down the middle and a series of bright red medals were proudly pinned to the front. He looked like he was posing for a statue to be made of him, the way one fist was planted on his hip while the other jutted rigidly ahead.

"Move move move!" Erupted a second voice behind them, louder and more strained than a constipated drill sergeant. "Gamma, Delta, split up those grimy little monsters. I'm igniting the phase lock."

Noah turned to see a merman, looking entirely out of place with his fish tail coiled beneath him in the middle of the street. His white-gloved hand held a torch which cast sharp shadows across his rigidly angular face. Then the torch was falling from his hand, tumbling end over end amidst summersaulting shadows to land in a sticky, dark streak on the road.

The torch dimmed momentarily before the fire roared to life, shooting off in either direction. The wall of flames leapt several feet high and grew rapidly in length to form a large circle completely enclosing the arena. The circle remained unbroken, even where it had to go around trees, over obstacles, and even up the walls and over the roof of a house at one point. The rising sparks formed flashes of demonic symbols in the air, the billowing smoke folding into additional runes overhead. It almost looked as if they were standing inside a giant summoning circle.

The imps were terrified. The cohesive group exploded in all directions. Some cowered, pressing their face into the ground and covering their eyes with their stubby fingers. Others launched themselves haphazardly into trees, or smashed windows to scamper within. White-gloved figures leapt through the wall of fire from all directions. Long tridents formed an ever tightening circle, each overlapping with their neighbors range so perfectly that there was nothing to do but flee toward the center.

"Phase lock complete," shouted the strained voice. "Igniting the Chainer Battery."

"Clear to ignite," shouted Theodore's gruff voice from the other side.

A ripple pulsed through the air like the world had just hiccuped. Reality spent several seconds trying to clear its throat after that. A quick succession of pulses radiated through Noah, and as each one passed over him the world looked a little different than it had a moment before. Pulse—the fire was green. Pulse—it was already morning. Pulse—it was night again, but it was most certainly a different night because all the chaos had disappeared. Pulse. Pulse. Pulse. Everything was different. Pulse. Then everything was the same.

On the last pulse Noah felt the same sensation he had when the beating heart had summoned him into this world. All of a sudden he was back in the Netherworld, the Sylo's towering form in the near distance. The ring of fire had come with them though. The flames were searingly bright in the otherwise lightless nether. Noah and Samantha were still crowded with the imps into the center.

The two-dozen or more white-gloved department workers had accompanied them into the nether. They broke formation immediately, spacing themselves evenly in a 360 degree sphere around Noah and the cowering imps.

"Sylo confirmed. We're in the right location," shouted the strained voice. "Sir, watch out!"

A hideous screech exploded from the huddled imps which Sssalama had been concealing himself beneath. The dark wings spread and the great red eye swelled larger than ever as it bore into the prime minister. The nether swirled before that gaze like a draining whirlpool, condensing the stuff of the void into a deadly lance to accompany his charge.

Theodore Oswald raised an incredulous eyebrow. It was the face of a gourmet chef who was just discovering fast food for the first time. He didn't so much as take his hands out of his coat pockets as Sssalama bore down upon him. Noah fully expected the prime minister to have some trick up his sleeve, but he watched in shock as the swirling lance punctured straight through his belly and tore out the other side. Sssalama seemed equally taken aback by the success of his attack, and he left his lance and swooped away at the last moment before colliding with the man.

"Mr. Oswald!"

"Prime Minister!" several of the soldiers let out cries of alarm.

"I'm not blind, Lieutenant Greigex," Theodore Oswald replied quite calmly. He grasped the swirling lance protruding from his belly with both hands and pushed it deeper into himself, all the way until it popped out the other side. Noah could see the Sylo straight through the gaping hole in his mid-section. Theodore reached one of his own hands through the hole, gently patting a few dried and withered internal organs back into place where they remained.

The prime minister used both hands to reach inside his white coat that remained pristine without a drop of blood on it. He withdrew a pair of familiar glass objects with each hand: the Chainer Batteries. The wires within the glass casing pulsed as they siphoned the energy from the soul trapped at the center. Someone inside was being killed and brought back to life in a vicious and endless cycle. Was Elijah's soul in one of them? Noah didn't know he was using all that energy for, but he sensed he was about to find out.

A flick of the wrists sent the four Chainer Batteries spinning into the circle of fire. The flames turned blue and froze solid, each flickering and dancing spark locked in place. Then they began to grow—as tall as the prime minister, then twice his height, then soaring into an icy tower to rival the size of the Sylo in a matter of seconds. The glass hearts were embedded inside the wall on each side of them. They continued to beat within the walls, surging a fresh wave of crackling electricity into the structure which continued to grow.

"Let's burn these rats from their holes once and for all," Theodore Oswald growled. Then shouting, with flecks of spittle spraying down his clean-shaven face: "Do you hear me, demons? For too long you have tormented the living and the dead. From this point on, by decree of the Trans Dimensional Department, the shallow end of the Netherworld is home to you no longer. Back to the void with the lot of you, and good riddance."

"The Department has no authority over the nether!" Sssalama howled. He was circling overhead, now trapped within the tower of frozen fire, no doubt looking for an opportunity to dive in once more.

"The Department bloody well has authority over whatever I say it does," the gruff voice shot back. "We are the guardians of the sacred order. The custodian of souls, the protector of the living and the dead. We have been too generous for too long to tolerate such heartless monsters in our midst."

"Come on, we've got to get out of here," Noah said. "Not that way—down here. We can still get under the tower wall."

The terrified imps were pressing in on them from all sides, but Noah managed to make some space by spreading his arms and legs and making circles with them. Samantha did likewise, and together they pushed and prodded their way toward the bottom of the heap.

"Where are the other department heads?" Sssalama demanded. "They would never bless this violation."

"I am the Department!" the Prime Minister roared. "Soldiers, don't let this beast distract you from your battle stations. Greigex, take your men to the top of the mobile fortress and brace for impact. You must protect the tower until it's fully grown. They're coming."

Beat, beat, beat go the crystal hearts. The floor of the tower was growing as each wave of energy spread the static blue fire below them. Networks of electricity like arteries beneath the skin were continuing to branch throughout the structure. The walls were growing thicker, and several small turrets were separating from the main building. It wouldn't be long before they were sealed inside the growing fortress.

"Help is on the way," Sssalama hissed in the demonic tongue. "These arrogant mortals do not realize how foolish they are to follow us into our lair. Destroy them all."

The hatred in Sssalama's voice was so heavy that Noah didn't need to translate for Samantha. The low chittering amongst the imps prompted one of the white-gloved soldiers to thrust his trident into their midst. He might as well have stuck a pin into a balloon. The imps scattered in every direction at once, their mad rush surprising the guards and flooding past them. A few of the imps were intercepted by the sharp tridents and squealed in pain. They didn't dissipate as demons do when they were banished from the other worlds, and when they bled the dark liquid was suspended in the nether of the battlefield.

"Now is our chance. Go!" Noah shouted.

The tower floor was closing fast, but the guards were all too occupied trying to turn imps into shish-kebabs to notice the children. Noah and Samantha swam madly for the opening, bursting free from the tower just in time before the floor closed behind them. The blue walls were opaque, but they did little to muffle the snarling, squealing, and shouting from the battle within.

"It looks like it's almost finished growing," Noah said. "What's that at the top?"

Samantha turned upward and closed her green eye, staring with her inscrutable marble gaze. "A bell. It's a bell tower, and it looks like the Chainer Batteries are moving up the walls toward it."

"We can't stop here. We're still too close. Let's head for the..."

Noah's voice trailed off as he stared at the empty nether where the Sylo had been. He knew he had the right spot because the nether was still heavily scrunched and folded where the base had been, but the giant demon was gone. Samantha wasn't following Noah anyway though. She was still staring at the top of the growing blue fortress.

"They're coming," Samantha muttered, shivering. "Can you feel it?"

"Samantha get away from the tower. We're not safe here."

"We can't run from this," she mumbled, barely audible. "We can't ever get away from them."

"What are you talking about? What do you see?" But Noah was beginning to feel it too. The familiar prickle in the back of his mind, a soft static spreading through his body. "Soul Eaters... look, the Sylo is back!"

The ancient demon was returning, and it was returning fast. The tower came barreling in like a battering ram. It slammed head-on into the blue tower with an impact that caused a shockwave to rebound throughout the nether. The branching appendages at the top of the Sylo wrapped around the blue tower, constricting so powerfully that the blue-fire bent and shattered in places. Other branches lashed the walls like whips, or drilled into them to rip holes into the fortress. A burst of blue sparks exploded from the damaged walls, and toward these holes drifted the Soul Eaters like ghosts through the mist.

All the flaps in the Sylo were opened, and demons were pouring from within. Hissing, snarling, shrieking demons, with molten skin and morphing weapons and eyes of flame. The demons seemed hesitant to charge past the Soul Eaters though, and the rubbery gray beings floated in front of the advance. There had to be at least a dozen of them pressing themselves against the blue fortress, peering into the holes in the walls while they waited for the Sylo to break its way in.

"The spirits have trapped themselves inside. Are they all going to... lose their souls?" Samantha asked. "I mean, it's not like I'm that sympathetic toward them after they came barging in like this. But then again they did stop the demons from attacking people in the living world so... argh. Why can't there just be good guys and bad guys?"

"There are, they just happen to be the same people." George Hampton's voice startled the children. There had been so much going on that they hadn't noticed him until he was right beside them. The old man seemed more hunched than he had before, and the dense network of lines across his face seemed deeper and more wearied.

"One man's virtue is another man's sin," he added. "There was once a time when I thought the common soul that burned in each of us held us together more than any external difference could drive us apart. Maybe I'm too old for such fairytales anymore. Once you watch what is to come, perhaps you will stop believing too."

"Young people can have old ideas, but old people never seem to have young ideas," Samantha declared.

George Hampton chuckled. "And what young idea would you like to solve these irreconcilable differences with?"

"I don't know. But if we all just stopped this and talked, don't you think we could figure it out?"

"My dear that's a very old idea indeed. But perhaps when it is taken up by the next generation, an old idea can become young again. The Trans Dimensional Department has overplayed their hand, and they will pay the price for it today. I wouldn't be surprised if The Matriarch was behind this somehow, trying to supplant old Theodore for good. If his soul is eaten and everyone forgets him, it will be all too easy to imagine how the department will fall into her hands."

"Look at the bell," Noah said. "Something is happening at the top, but I can't tell what's going on from here."

"It's the Chainer Batteries," Samantha said. "They've made it all the way up the tower, and now they're in the bell."

"It's too little, too late, whatever it is," George Hampton said. "The Sylo isn't the only haven for demons in the shallow end. Demons have been massing here in preparation for greater advances into the living world. I knew Theodore was hot-headed, but I can't imagine what he was thinking coming here with such a small force."

"There he is now," Samantha said, her marble eye wide and unblinking. "The Prime Minister is next to the bell. One of the Soul Eaters is going right for him though. Can you see?"

Noah could just make out the gray form loping up the wall on all fours. They were too far away for the chilling aura to be much more than a prickle, but up close the Prime Minister must be about frozen stiff from the Soul Eater's presence. Its toothless mouth was gaping wider as it went, expanding impossibly to stretch the rubbery skin until the mouth took up the entire front portion of the demon's face. It didn't stop stretching though, continuing to open along the back of the head. Inside the mouth met the converging folds in the nether as space folded in on itself with maddening distortion. By the time the Soul Eater reached the top of the tower, there was nothing but mouth from one side of the head to the other.

"Don't look," George said.

The old man didn't turn away though, so neither did Noah or Samantha. Noah could already hear that terrible breaking sound of a destroyed soul echo in his mind from last year. He wished he wasn't here in the Netherworld. He wished he was back at the Mortuary, or hadn't gone at all, having never learned about demons or souls or an uncertain eternity. He wished he could hold his daughter again and tell her that she would always be safe, and to make believe that death wasn't as strange and horrifying as the vision playing before him now.

But he didn't hear the sound of a breaking soul at all. He heard the sound of a bell, high and pure and resonating with all of existence. And much to his surprise, that clear tone proved far more terrifying still.

TWISTING DIMENSIONS

THE NETHER BOILED. VIBRATIONS FROM THE BELL CASCADED OUTWARD from the top of the blue fortress. The Soul Eaters climbing the tower received the initial blast directly. First they hesitated, seeming perplexed. Then they began to tremble, pressing themselves flat and covering their heads with their fleshy grey hands.

Theodore Oswald struck the bell another mighty blow with his fist. Another, and another, each note lingering long after the bell was rung. This produced an amplifying effect which caused the nether to churn more violently by the moment. Another blow, and another, the prime minister hurling his entire body into each strike with a fervent vengeance.

It wasn't just the nether that was boiling anymore. It was the demons themselves. Their skin grew misshapen beneath the pressure as if thousands of bubbles underneath were trying to escape. Another blow, and another, and the bubbles really did begin to separate from the demons. They were shaking so violently that bits and pieces of them were flying off, disintegrating beneath the pressure. The whole top of the tower became inscrutable as thick clouds of black smoke flowed freely in all directions.

Noah, Samantha, and George were thankfully not affected in the same way, although the sound was growing so intense that they still had to clutch their hands over their ears.

"Dissipati Garder!" Theodore bellowed between blows. "You and your kind—are hereby banished—from all lands—where the living and dead may pass."

Nowhere was this power more apparent than the monstrous figure of the Sylo itself. Its branching appendages were still wrapped around the tower, so the more violently it shook, the more jarringly the entire fortress rattled. The massive demon hastened to free itself in an attempt to flee, its flaps opening and closing madly as black smoke poured from the openings. More dark clouds poured form inside the fortress, no doubt coming from Sssalama and the other trapped imps.

Theodore Oswald ceased the ringing to stand at the edge of his tower and survey his work. "The demon haunted clutches of the shallow end will be infested no longer! From today on I declare all roads from death will be reopened once more, and in the name of the Trans Dimensional Department I pledge never to rely upon demons to aid our passage back to life again."

His words were met by cheers from within the fortress. The other spirits must not have been affected by the bell either. It seems that all the energy from the Chainer Batteries had been directed exclusively toward banishing the demons.

"He couldn't have got all of them, could he?" Noah asked. "We can still stop this. If we can rescue the Chainer souls that are powering the bell, then the demons can still come back, can't they?"

"Maybe you're right. And then what?" Samantha asked. "You might as well try putting all the hornets back in a nest after you kicked it. They'll go right back to the living world, angrier than ever. And it might not just be the soulless they're after either."

"But we can't just give up on them!" Noah insisted. "We need the demons help, or we'll never destroy the Soul Net."

"You're both right, but we can't help anyone here," George Hampton said. "Watch the smoke. Where is it going?"

The Netherworld doesn't have an up or a down. It just has an onward and a forever. Noah assumed the smoke should have dispersed evenly, but it was clearly all billowing in the same direction: toward the densely folded and warped space which still existed beneath where the Sylo had dwelled.

"Where would a demon go if they're banished from the shallow end?" George asked, the familiar ring of an instructor back in his voice.

"To higher dimensional space. To where the Primes are!" Noah said at once.

"Exactly. And while the torrent of banished demons are passing through might be our best chance of making it too. A banished demon has essentially had their mass transformed into energy, and we should be able to ride that wave of energy up the dimensional mountain that is the Netherworld."

Noah didn't really follow what that meant, but George sounded confident about it and that was good enough for him.

"Yes of course I'm going," Samantha said.

"I didn't even ask—" Noah began.

"Good, because you shouldn't bother, because you couldn't stop me if you tried. Last one in is uglier than Mr. Mufflafo!"

Samantha swam hard toward the thickest cloud of smoke which continued to billow from the banishing Sylo.

"There's a fine line between courage and stupidity," George said, hastening to follow. "Although of course when we go up a dimension that line is likely to look more like a circle, and we'll be inside it."

"Can't you give us any better idea of where we're going? You aren't very encouraging, as far as teachers go."

"That's because I'm not your teacher any longer. My knowledge stops at the water's edge, so to speak. If we're going to continue in each other's company, then it would be best to think of one another as friends."

"I think I can do that."

"Did you hear that, Sam?" George called after her. "Noah said we were friends! Even though I stood there and watched him die. Isn't that nice?"

"Now that you mention it, I'm actually glad that gargoyle attacked me," Samantha replied decisively. "Otherwise I never would have known how much fun I was missing out on."

"Not to mention your marvelous marble eye. I wouldn't be surprised if we'll be needing that to make sense of the strange new world ahead."

The thick clouds of smoke provided perfect cover, and the companions were not pursued as they followed it toward the twisted space. Noah tried very hard not to think of all the demons that had been dissolved into the smoke around him. The harder he thought about not thinking about it, the harder he thought about it though. He became so preoccupied with wondering which greasy puff belonged to which part of which demon that he didn't even notice exactly when he passed over the horizon of warped space.

His first realization came after his foot landed on something rough and solid. The gel of the nether was still around him, but it seemed warmer than it had a moment ago. Warmer, wetter, and heavier, like he'd just stepped into a rain forest. It wasn't until the smoke began to clear when he recognized the extent of the transformation.

They were like trees. That was the word he'd have to use for them until he found a better one. They were at least as tall as trees anyway, although they were also purple and rubbery, possessing puffy white clouds of suspended gas in place of where their leaves should be. They grew out of the ground like trees—real, solid, earthy ground, albeit a ghastly shade of orange. It felt soft and welcoming on his bare feet though, so he hoped it really was soil and not some kind of supernatural waste product. The ground sloped gently downward on all sides, indicating they were on some sort of hill.

Now that there was a proper up and down again, the smoke was lifting away from them and dissipating into the open sky. And what a sky! It was as though all the stars were out on the darkest of nights, assuming all those stars were all many times closer and brighter than they were on earth. Entire spiraled galaxies each as bright as the moon littered the sky, not needing a sun for their radiance to illuminate the world into a permanent state of twilight.

Samantha jumped toward one of the low hanging white clouds and pulled some of it free. The cloud separated from the branches like cotton candy from the stick, and when she let it go it floated upward to return to its original space. She jumped again, swishing her hands through the columns of black smoke which billowed from the ground behind them.

"Why aren't the demons stopping?" she asked. "Shouldn't they turn back into demons here?"

"What should be and what shouldn't be are intuitions for a world we've left behind," George replied. "You would be better off focusing on what is, and what isn't, although even that may not be a reliable a guide here."

"How are we supposed to follow them now though?" Noah asked.

George shrugged and moved to run his hands along one of the purple trees. A small branch extended from the tree to pet his hand, feeling him as he did it.

"While I don't know anything about this world, we may still deduce some things from the world we've left behind. There we know a certain amount of power is required to banish a demon into a higher dimension. It then stands to reason that an even greater amount of power will banish a demon to several higher dimensions. They might be going all the way to the Primes at the top of the proverbial mountain now, although unless either of you know how to fly, they'll be leaving us behind this time."

"Do you think we're stuck here?" Samantha asked. She kicked one of the purple trees, dodging away just in time as one of the lower branches tried to swat her away.

"The deeper we go into the nether, the less we can be sure of anything. Yes it looks like we're stuck, but how can we be certain we're 'here'?"

"Were you ever married, George?" Samantha asked.

"Not in all my years, living or dying. Why?"

"That makes sense. Your wife never would never have let you get away with answers like that." Samantha kicked the tree again and waited for the branch to swing at her. She seized hold of it at the last moment, swinging herself into the lower branches as it recoiled. "I'm going to try and spot something more from the top."

"Be careful," Noah called, knowing it wouldn't do any good. If anything she was the kind of person to be less careful just because he said that. Inquisitive branches kept reaching down at her from higher up, giving her the opportunity to swiftly scale the tree with careless ease.

"Whoa, you've got to see this," Samantha called down. "The world looks way different from up here."

Noah clamored into the lower branches after her while George stayed at the bottom and stretched his back. "I have many fields of expertise to aid this journey, but tree climbing is not one of them," lamented the old man.

"I hope I never get old," Samantha said, sitting on a branch barely as wide as her arm to swing her feet below.

"At your rate, you never will."

Noah was still a layer of branches below Samantha, but he could already see what caught her eye. They weren't on the top of a hill like he first supposed. It was just that the world they found themselves on was so small that the slope was evident all the way around. Besides for this little orange sphere prickling with the strange purple trees, they were alone beneath the great glowing cosmos overhead.

"Do you see it?" Samantha asked eagerly. "Keep going all the way up and you'll have a better view."

Noah eyed the thinning branches mistrustfully as they swished around him. "We're on a tiny world. I get it. I can see it fine from here."

"Keep climbing. Don't worry, the branches are really strong."

Noah brushed aside some of the heavy cotton clouds which flowed around him and lifted himself into the top most branches. He inched along toward the edge where the clouds didn't obstruct his view. His eyes remained locked on the treacherous descent and the increasingly thin appendages supporting his weight, not looking up until he was out on the edge. Samantha was right—going a little farther changed everything.

"What do you see? Where is here?" George called from below.

"You sure you can't climb?" Noah called back. "You're going to want to see this for yourself."

"It's practically the only thing I'm positive of."

George's answer came from an unexpected source. The ground beneath them was shifting. The whole world was tilting, causing the trees to bend and the loose orange soil to stream in the opposite direction. George had to wrap his arms around a tree trunk to stay in place, while Noah and Samantha slipped through several of the thinner branches before larger ones below caught them and prevented them from falling farther.

"What's going on? What do you see?" George demanded.

"This world isn't like the earth—" Noah began, but he was at a loss for words.

"It's much smaller, for one," Samantha agreed. "And of course we don't have trees like this."

"It's moving, why is it moving?"

"Oh yes, that. Well you said so yourself, didn't you?" Samantha asked slyly. She was obviously enjoying herself, no doubt getting back at George for all his own evasive answers.

"I think it has something to do with the second lesson you wanted us to learn," Noah said, playing along. "If only I could remember what that was!"

"It's a demon. We're on a demon, of course we are," George replied, his voice a little fainter.

The angle of the ground had largely returned to normal, but that didn't mean they'd stopped moving. The whole world was steadily rising and falling, and by the movement of the surrounding cosmos, it was apparent they were all being carried in a particular direction. Exactly how fast they were going or where they would end up seemed more like questions of philosophy than anything reason could supply.

"And what does the demon look like?" George called.

"We can't really tell," Noah replied, inching out farther on the branch to peer through the clouds once more. "I think we're on the back of his head. There might be more of him, but it's too far away to see beyond that."

"Don't demons know about moisturizer?" Samantha asked. "If all that flaky orange soil is his skin, then he seriously needs to alter his routine."

"Does that make the purple trees his hair?" Noah asked. "Or maybe the demon *is* the purple trees, and he's just underground?"

"What kind of question is that? You might as well ask if the demons are the clouds."

"What good is a magical eye if you insist on only using your mouth?" George Hampton grumbled. "Don't guess, girl. *See.*"

Samantha took a deep breath and closed her green eye. The marble one didn't move or show any signs of life, but as Noah watched a tiny crack appeared on the top of her right cheek where her skin met the stone. A small patch of previously living skin was drying and losing color.

"Do you feel that, Sam?" Noah asked.

"Shh I'm trying to concentrate."

Her skin wasn't just losing color. It was turning to stone. Noah had grown accustomed to the marble being there, but he realized he'd never seen it larger than it was now. The stone was intermingling with the skin on least a quarter of her face, and bit by bit the skin was receding to leave nothing but that clean, white, static marble.

"The stone is still growing. Stop it, Sam. We can figure out what's going on another way. I think using your marble eye is what's causing the wound to spread."

"Fat chance. I'm not going back to being a normal girl, not even if I could. Witches are only witches if they can see things others cannot."

"You're going to end up being a statue of a witch if you don't stop. Is that what you want?"

"Shush already, I know what I'm doing. I think I've figured it out anyway." Samantha opened her left eye again and beamed. "We're riding on Pa-rook. He's a greater demon too, but much older than the Sylo was. You were right that we're on the back of his head—one of them anyway—but you're wrong about the trees. They're a different kind of creature entirely, although I haven't figured out what yet."

"How did you figure out the other stuff? There's no way your eye could have told you his name."

"Pa-rook is just the name I made up for him. And I'm going to call the purple trees Muma-lumas."

"Sure, okay. Why not."

"The Pa-rook produces the orange flakey stuff to nourish the Muma-lumas, and in return they protect the Pa-rook from the ravenous Wojan."

"I can't tell how much of this is real and how much you're making up."

"That's how it's supposed to be with witches. Things we make up become real, and things that are already real can be made up into something else. Is anyone else getting hungry?"

"So you're admitting it's all nonsense then," Noah said, his frustration rising. "Being trapped here is not a joke. Who knows what's going on back on the living world now that all the demons are gone. There might be armies of soulless ones, or zombies raised by the Trans Dimensional Department taking over for all we know. And if we're stuck here long enough, then the demons are going to find a way to strike back. Can you imagine what would happen if giant demons like this got loose at home?"

"I am being serious, thank-you-very-much," Samantha replied witheringly. "And if you don't want to listen, then that's your loss, because the Wojan has been gaining on us for a while now."

"The what-now?"

"The Wojan, remember? The thing the Muma-lumas are there to protect against? Keep looking, it should be close enough for you to see soon too."

Then Noah really did see it, although he wish he hadn't. He didn't have a word for the spindly legs which slipped between the stars, so he supposed Wojan was as good as any. It wasn't just a lack of names in his head though; there was a poverty of words which he possessed that could hope describe a creature so alien to his mortal senses.

The closest thing he could ascribe to the gradual appearance of the legs was watching the beginning of a drawing continue to draw itself into existence. Eight delicate legs were weaving amongst each other in a complicated dance, growing as they did so. One moment the legs seemed impossibly far away, like constellations in the sky, and the next they seemed as close as the neighboring tree, black and shiny with serrated spines along their length. The legs weren't just weaving themselves into existence either: gleaming black eyes suddenly shifted into being, a dark and glossy body swelling around them like an inflating balloon.

Noah blinked and rubbed his eyes. The way the legs moved through each other was almost hypnotizing to watch. The fluctuating distance made him feel like he was slowly becoming lucid while dreaming, with the remnants of a nightmare persisting with him between wakefulness and sleep.

"Wakeup Muma-lumas!" Samantha shouted. "Pa-rook is in trouble!"

"They were sleeping?" Noah asked.

"Yeah, but don't worry. They can hear me."

"Are you alright up there?" George called from the base of the Muma-luma tree. "You haven't gotten stuck, have you?"

"Wakeup, stupid trees!" Samantha shouted again, pounding the branch she sat on with her fists.

"Maybe they only speak demonic," Noah offered. He cupped his hands around his mouth and shouted the translation. "The Wojan is coming!"

The reaction was immediate. The orange soil streamed away from them, but this was no trick of higher dimensional space. The Muma-luma tree they sat on was surging out of the ground, soaring to a staggering height within seconds. It was all Noah and Samantha could do to wrap their arms around the branches and cling there for dear life. The reaction of their tree caused a chain reaction among the surrounding trees to shoot upward as well, which in turn caused their neighbors to rise. The wave rippled across the entire world, and soon the immense being of the Pa-rook was bristling with the grasping purple extremities.

The Wojan was not deterred from springing into action. All eight legs were now fully formed to launch it toward them like a hurtling black meteor. The blurred motion defied comprehension at first, but it soon became apparent that an after-image of the demon continued to persist at each point along its journey toward them. The Wojan's exact location became even harder to discern when the multitude of after-images began to spread their legs and alter their trajectory to land elsewhere in the Muma-luma forest. By the time the Wojan had settled on one of the white clouds, there were already hundreds of copies of it spreading all through the top boughs of the forest.

The tree Noah and Samantha were cowering in shook violently. One of the Wojan had settled right above them, and this was the first chance Noah was able to get a proper look at the demonic spider. The body was dry and wrinkled like an old prune, and the eyes were both above and below the body, a shriveled mass even smaller than the children. The legs were no thicker than Noah's arm, but they extended impossibly long and squirmed ceaselessly as if they each had a life of their own.

"Get down from there!" George shouted, barely audible in the distance. It was the last clear sound before a wall of noise assaulted their senses. The Muma-luma trees had begun to scream.

High-pitched, whistling, shrieking, throbbing sound, from all around them as far as could be heard. It was the sound of the soft white clouds being shredded to pieces by the turmoil of spider legs. The branches shot out to try and seize the bodies of the Wojan, but the agile creatures danced out of their reach while their incessantly probing legs sought a way past the defenses.

Noah and Samantha couldn't spare much attention for what was going on above them though, not with the demands of their descent through the agitated and swinging branches. A reflexive duck was all that kept their head on their shoulders at times, and often they'd have to simply cling to the trunk and wait for it to stop bucking before they could continue. Progress was difficult as all the lower branches were thrusting upward in their direction to prevent the spider legs from slipping past. Stopping or going back up was impossible though. The serrated spines on the spider legs bit deeply into the purple branches, and they'd have an even easier time slicing Noah or Samantha into deli meat.

Terror lends a powerful impetus, and despite these obstacles they might have made it all the way back down with a little luck. That chance never came, however, as three of the swinging legs dropped past them in a dive toward the orange ground. They were intercepted by the lower branches, which were quickly overwhelmed by the committed assault. Before the legs were forced to withdraw upward, the whole layer of lower branches had been reduced to stumps. There was nowhere remaining within reach for Noah and Samantha to continue their descent.

"Don't stop there!" George shouted. He was audible once more now that they'd made progress toward him, but he was still much too far to jump.

"We can't!" Samantha howled, clinging onto the trembling trunk with all her might.

"You've got to grab a branch from the next tree over. Get to one where the lower branches are intact and keep making your way down."

Easier said than done. There was at least a five foot gap before the outermost branches of the next Wuma-luma. Even if they could make the jump, they'd have to pass through the open air where the serrated legs danced before seizing a branch in motion that was likely to have moved by the time they got there.

"It's your only option," George insisted. "If you wait more branches will be cut. You have to do it now."

"Out of the question. It's insane," Samantha replied. She flinched as one of the swinging legs slashed the air in an arc less than a foot from where she clung.

"I'll go first," Noah said. "Once I'm there I might be able to hold one of the branches still and make it easier for you to grab."

"Noah don't. There's another way out of here, follow me."

Samantha bent her legs and jumped, grabbing hold of one of the higher branches to pull herself back upward again.

"What are you doing? We're even more vulnerable up there. Come on, we have to cross over."

"I see a better way! I *promise*."

"Samantha? Did you hear me?" George called more anxiously than ever.

"I heard you old man!" she shouted, persistent in her upward climb. "Come on, Noah. We need to get higher again."

There wasn't much higher they could get. By now most of the top most branches had been cleaved off to tumble around them. Soon Samantha would be as high as she could reach and would be forced to stop, dead ended. Noah thought he might be able to make the jump to the next tree over, but he couldn't leave her exposed and vulnerable like that in the open air. He was out of time to make a decision though. Frustrated and scared, each emotion feeding the other, he lifted a hand to the higher branches and pulled himself after Samantha.

"Now what are you going to do?" Noah shouted as Samantha reached the highest remaining handhold.

She stood unsteadily, her arms still wrapped around the trunk of the tree as the branch beneath her feet swished suspiciously back and forth.

"I'm following what's hidden and true, not what is clear and wrong," she said, an eager gleam in her green eye.

Noah looked away from her to focus on his grip as he hauled himself up to her level. His next glance met her at the very end of the branch, her hands pressed together in front of her as though in a silent prayer. Noah let go of the trunk to take several stumbling steps onto the branch after her. She looked back at him, smiled, and dove from that terrible height. She seemed suspended in the air for a moment before angling downward, arms outstretched as if she were merely diving into the water.

At first Noah thought she was still going to angle the dive to try and reach a neighboring tree, but she simply plummeted with no hint of resistance or panic. One of the spidery legs sliced the air behind her, but it was intercepted by the branch Noah stood on. He was already on unstable footing, and without the trunk to hold onto the sudden movement bucked him into the air. He flailed his hands where the branch had been a moment before, catching nothing but a few tattered scraps of insubstantial cloud. Then he too was falling, straight down with nothing but the ground rushing up to welcome him.

Samantha hit first, still rigidly vertical so that her hands made contact with the orange ground first. She vanished entirely in a puff of disturbed soil. Noah managed to stop flailing and straighten himself a bit before he impacted nearby. The force from his considerable height plunged him deep into the soft ground. Deep, and deeper, and then straight through, leaving the ground behind. Suddenly he was in the air again. Half a second more, and he slammed into a second ground, this one considerably harder and less yielding.

As it turned out, there had only been a thin layer of the orange soil, with an open tunnel below which he now found himself in. Long purple roots from the Muma-luma trees snaked around and burrowed through the walls. Small, toothy mouths at the end of these roots nibbled at the flaky soil all around them, producing an incessant chewing and gulping sound as they did. The only light came from the hole he punctured through, and it wasn't enough to illuminate anything more than the rough dirt road which extended in either direction along the tunnel.

Samantha was picking herself off the ground and dusting the orange soil from her long dress. A moment later, George Hampton came tumbling unceremoniously through Noah's hole to land on top of him. The two tumbled to the ground, knocking further clouds of loose soil into the air and further confusing everything. They were each exactly as alive as they started with though, and miraculously unharmed as the layer of soft soil had slowed their fall.

"See? I told you, didn't I? I so told you," Samantha was already saying. "I knew we had to get higher to punch through to the tunnel. You thought I was crazy though, didn't you? Didn't you? Admit it!"

"I still think you're crazy!" Noah grunted, trying to wave away the settling dust. "Do you think this tunnel was made by the roots? It seems too uniform for that."

"But how did you know it was there?" George asked.

"You have your secrets, old man, and I have mine."

"Secrets? Me? Why, I have been the pinnacle of truthfulness—an absolute paragon of clarity and openness. If you don't understand my truth, then I take no responsibility for that."

"It's got to have something to do with her eye," Noah said. "It seemed like she knew things about those demons that she couldn't have seen though, so I don't understand it either."

The conversation was interrupted as one of the spiny legs tore through the hole in the soil overhead. It clawed the air blindly for several seconds, forcing the companions to press themselves against the walls to avoid its reach. Then it was gone, withdrawn back upward to join the mad battle between the ravenous Wojan and the protective layer of Muma-luma trees.

"We can't stay here," George Hampton grumbled, readjusting his pin-striped hat. "I suppose our insightful princess will be knowing which way to go from here as well?"

"I am not. A princess. There's nothing special about popping out of a queen. A witch earns her respect, just like I'm doing now. Now both of you be quiet and let me concentrate."

There were a number of obstacles for concentrating as Samantha closed her green eye scanned the road on either side. She would have to tune out the shrieking clouds being pulled apart, as well as the clattering of broken branches as the trees bore the assault. She'd need to see through the darkness, and perhaps even around corners or through earthen walls as the tunnel wound its secret route. Most difficult of all to ignore though was the disembodied giggling which arose from the darkness to one side. Samantha opened her green eye at once, a keen eagerness about her flushed face.

"Well that makes things easier. We must be going that way," she said, indicating the direction from where the giggle slipped from the empty tunnel.

"Funny," George replied, "I would have thought just the opposite."

BAH-RABBA KABA

Soft giggling, snickering, chortling, filtering through the darkness. There was no pause in the sound where an orator might take breath. It sounded close, just beyond where the overhead light faded into shadow. There was just enough visibility to see how the tunnel meandered off to the side. If they continued down this path they would soon be lost in complete blackness though, unless the ravenous Wojan continued knocking holes in the roof, which was hardly a consolatory thought.

"Hello? Is there anybody there?" Samantha called.

"I don't suppose your eye can see down here, can it?" Noah asked hopefully.

"Sure can," Samantha replied cheerfully, striding off into the darkness. "It can only see one thing though, and that's the dark. I've still got my phone, but the battery has been dead for ages."

"That reminds me of a golden retriever I once had, made of real gold," George mused, disappearing into the blackness after her. "The jeweler Francisco Pintilo sold him to me, back on the island of Barbaros. He told me the dog could smell out where to find gold, but all he could smell was himself. Oh I never would have wasted so much time on things I didn't need if I knew how long I'd stay being dead."

The giggling sounded from the darkness again, no closer than it had the last time despite their advancement. Noah reflexively shivered as he trailed his hand along the wall.

"You haven't been dead long enough to learn a proper light spell though," Noah grumbled. "I'm sure they would have taught me one by now if I'd stayed in school."

"Of course I do. I know a dozen or more, every color you can imagine besides several you can't. But good luck casting a spell without any energy in the air. Remember that the second rule of life-force dynamics states that energy comes from phase transitions. It's hard enough working magic in the shallow end of the Netherworld, but here so far from the dance of life and death, there's no helping it."

"Do you mean that the Wojan weaving itself together and all the crazy things the demons do is done without any magic at all?" Samantha asked.

"Quite so. At least, not the same kind of magic as the undead use. It's part of the reason why someone on the outside can summon a demon, but a demon can't summon itself."

"Then how do they do it? The Sylo's heart pushed us through a rift, after all."

"Remember that demons only grow when they take time back from the other worlds, and time is a bit like magic. It changes things. It brings light, and darkness; life, and death. I wish I could tell you more, but to tell you the truth I hardly understand it myself."

"Stop—listen," Noah said. "The giggling is changing. It's getting deeper."

"Or are we getting deeper, and it's staying the same?" George replied.

"We are inside a demon though, aren't we? I mean, that's the only thing that's here, right?" Noah asked. "Do you think we'll start seeing organs and internal things again?"

"Trying to make sense of the world is an admirable thing for a student, living or dead," George said in a slightly condescending tone. "I don't think trying to make sense of this place is worth the bother though. I wouldn't be surprised if the demons are inside us, and that the outsides and the insides are switched. We might even be in a place where the befores happen after the afters."

An eerie green light permeated the darkness ahead. The way it shifted and pooled along the ground made it seem like a glowing mist.

"What about that? Does that surprise you?"

"Not in the least. I would have been more surprised if there wasn't anything here to surprise me," George replied with satisfaction.

The muffled sounds of the battle overhead gradually died as they entered the mist. The giggling was getting harder to hear too, although not because it had stopped. It was just growing too low to register, reduced to little more than a vibration which caused vibrating patterns in the mist. The quiet which remained was even more oppressive than the sound had been.

"We're doing this wrong," Samantha whispered with a seemingly mandatory hush that the quiet space demanded. "There's no point looking for a way out of a place that doesn't make any sense. I wasn't looking for the Wojan to show up, or for the Muma-lumas to defend against them. I was just imagining something that might have happened, and then it did. And when I dove into the ground, I was imagining the tunnel underneath. I thought that it was my eye giving me a premonition, but what if it was just my thinking that made it so?"

"How do you know you were the one imagining it, and that the thoughts didn't simply pop into your head from somewhere else?" George asked.

"How did I know I was the author of my own thoughts?" Samantha asked, slightly perturbed. "Well, right now I'm imagining a heaping pile of cheese and salami and crackers. I feel like I haven't eaten anything proper for ages."

The green mist had meanwhile been rising around them. It wasn't thick enough to obscure vision though, and instead provided valuable light. It illuminated the closed space, and the dead end of the tunnel just ahead. More significantly, it revealed a long wooden table that was prepared for them.

Four chairs, four silver goblets, and four clean plates were awaiting their arrival. There weren't any cheese or crackers, although the table was heavy with great wooden platters laden with food. A heaping serving of roast beef was still steaming as if it had been freshly cooked. Plums and peaches and strange golden fruits in the shape of doughnuts were piled into a small pyramid. A thick loaf of bread, heavy with seeds and grains, whipped butter, exotically striped vegetables with rice, and a chocolate cake interspersed with layers of rich cream.

"Even better!" Samantha exclaimed, rushing to the table to snatch one of the golden fruits.

"Wait—it might not be safe. You don't know where it came from," Noah warned.

"Easy for you to say, you're dead! And of course I know where it came from—it came from me!"

Samantha took a large bite from the golden fruit and grinned as the juices ran down her chin. "They're wonderful. I've never tasted anything like it."

George tentatively pulled a small corner from one of the loafs of bread and sniffed it. He placed it inside his mouth, and his eyes sparkled. "I can taste it too. Perhaps it has something to do with how demons can interact with both the living and the spirits. Go on, Noah, nothing to worry about."

Samantha had already begun piling food onto her plate with a wooden serving spoon. Noah approached with caution and sat down at the table. It had been so long since he'd eaten real food that he could hardly remember what it was like to taste. Still, there was something about the madness of this place that suggested any blessing was too good to be true.

"Why are there four seats?" he asked at last. "If your wish really did make this meal appear for us, then why wouldn't there be three?"

"Maybe it wasn't her wish," a soft, musical voice replied.

Samantha gagged on her food in surprise. Noah stood so fast that his chair tipped over backwards and hit the floor. One of the chairs was suddenly occupied, despite being empty an instant before. A woman with two long brown braids was sitting with her hands folded on the table. Her face was warm and pretty and flushed with youth, but her hands were withered and ancient, warped and twisted into arthritic claws. She wore a deep blue dress, so deep it was almost black, and a crown of dried flowers in her hair.

"Or maybe it was her wish, and I was what she wished for," the woman continued. "Please spare me all those trite questions about what is real and what is not. For as long as I've lived here, I would make no claims about the nature of this place."

Noah righted the upturned chair and sat down. When he looked up the woman was staring straight at him, and both of her eyes were milky white marble orbs, exactly as Samantha's had been before the stone had begun to spread across her cheek. It took several seconds before Noah was able to break away from that gaze, at which point he was shocked again to see George Hampton kneeling on the orange ground with his head bowed. The old man's whimsical nature seemed incompatible with the type of abject reverence he was displaying now.

"Thank you for your hospitality," George Hampton said, a slight tremor running through his voice that made him seem older than ever. He rose at last and sat down at the table with the others, although he never quite managed to make eye contact with the woman across from him. "We didn't mean to barge in or anything—we were only trying to follow the demons who were banished from the shallow nether. We never planned to end up in the house of the great Bah-Rabba Kaba."

"I've heard about you!" Samantha gasped. "You're a witch too, aren't you? Well I don't mean 'too' as if we're the same or anything. But I don't mean to say that I'm not a witch either, because I am, but no one has ever called me great." The rush of her words ceased as she took a deep, steadying breath. "At least not yet, anyway."

"It's so gratifying to see that you three children have been studying your history," the Bah-Rabba Kaba replied smoothly. "Although I daresay you'd know more about me if you'd been studying your prophesies instead, because what little I've done measures poorly against the weight of what is yet to come. Please eat, drink, make yourselves comfortable. It has been a long time since I've had the privilege of serving one of the Primes."

Those inscrutable marble eyes had shifted onto Noah once more. He self-consciously took a drink from the goblet, fumbling it between his hands. Something warm and sweet like a spiced cider ran down his throat, a half-forgotten sense that tasted like being alive again. He then wondered whether it was safe to drink anything offered from a witch and began to splutter. The woman smiled though, and her face seemed so kind and amiable that it was impossible to harbor an evil thought against her. Noah's eyes fell back to her withered hands though, a clear sign that she was not all that she appeared to be. Samantha meanwhile did not hesitate from diving into her plate of rice and vegetables with abandon.

"You're fearful. That's good," the witch continued. "Eat, eat, you will soon see that our desires are aligned. Allow me to share with you the reason for your visit, for though you know the destination of your journey, I sense you do not yet fully appreciate its purpose. I am not a demon here to trick you, nor one of the undead who understands only power and not its proper use. There is a beating heart in my chest and red blood in my veins. As one of the living I care deeply for the plight of my kind, even if I no longer dwell amongst them."

"Did you really build this whole world by yourself?" Noah asked. "That's what Trebedara, one of our teachers, said."

"Everyone builds their own world that is unique to them, whether they realize it or not. I just happen to live there. It isn't nearly as nice a place as it used to be, not since the unwelcome Wojan has moved in. You know all about it though, don't you?"

"Not really," Samantha said. "I expected to see them before I did, but I don't know why. And I still don't know what they are."

"What it is," Bah-Rabba Kaba corrected gently. "There is only one, though it is often found in many places at once. I thought you might be more familiar as you already discovered the calamity of its creation: the mighty web it spun that you call the Soul Net. You must understand that this was never intended to be a thing of evil. The Wojan is an ancient demon who has long spun its lattice between the dimensions of the nether. It preyed upon other demons who got lost between worlds, but it was so far removed from the living and the dead that it has never bothered them before. It was not until Mrs. Elanore Barrow, the one who calls herself Matriarch, chased Wojan from her home and corrupted its web. The Matriarch trapped the spider in my own world in order for her to steal the web and use it to harvest her power."

"There's a witch named Miss Thatcher where I'm from too. She doesn't like spiders either," Noah said. His words sounded so plain and ordinary besides the significant things Bah-Rabba Kaba was speaking of, but Noah was afraid to acknowledge these consequential matters without better understanding his own role in them. He cast a glance at the others for support. George Hampton hadn't touched the food yet, and his head was still hung as he stared down at his empty plate.

Samantha caught Noah's eye and raised her eyebrows. "I don't like spiders either," she said quickly. "Could be related. Maybe. I don't know. Hey, did you get attacked by a gargoyle too?"

"Ah, the eye. Yes my dear, we have both been cut by the same claw. I see there are many gaps in your awareness, so with your indulgence it would be best for me to start at the very beginning. The artificial life created by Master Noozwink is the abomination where all this story begins. You may remember him as the spirit who invented the Chainer Battery, although that is far from his only transgression against morality. Perhaps it was his nature to be a vile and bitter man, but no great harm came from it until he began to teach demonology at the Mortuary. And The Matriarch may have always been a jealous and greedy woman, but it was not until she met Noozwink that the two of them together delved into the forbidden art. Just as two soul mates might meet and forge something more glorious than either alone, so too can kindred spirits in wickedness bring out what was worst in each other.

"You see the gargoyles aren't like the zombies or ghouls, who are nothing more than flesh animated by their master. The gargoyles draw strength from the soul that is embedded deep within their breasts. That soul does not control the gargoyle as it would a living creature however, and it is nothing but a slave which gives power to its master. The Matriarch's power has been amplified greatly by the souls in her possession, and I can think of no power in this world or the next save for the Primes who can challenge her now. I do not know the full extent of the profane works those two created together, but I was not the only one horrified with the gargoyles that crept from the Mortuary.

"This was all long before your time, however, when the Elmond twins had spent two consecutive terms as Prime Ministers of the Department. A noble pair they were, both striving only for the truest harmony between all the worlds and their people. One or the other—whoever was in charge, I forget which—was outraged when he discovered what The Matriarch was up to. He would have gotten rid of her, would have shut down the whole school if he had to, if he'd only stayed in power just a little longer.

"The Matriarch must have understood that, because that is when she lent her support to the upstart Theodore Oswald. Together they vilified the demons that the Elmond twins were seeking to gain rights for. Their relentless campaign of hatred led to the infamous purges, a dark era in our time where many demons were ruthlessly banished and persecuted. Theodore Oswald granted permission for the use of gargoyles to protect the citizenry from the demons, and they have been in use ever since. My own eyes were cut out by one of the stone atrocities, and I fled to the depth of the nether where you find me now.

"This brings me now to the unfortunate truth about a gargoyle's wound. You must understand that the soul trapped inside the gargoyle is desperate for its freedom. When the gargoyle is in contact with someone, it is no surprise that sometimes that soul will try to escape. And with a wound as deep as mine or yours, there is enough damage for that soul to find a new home."

Samantha set her fork down in a slow, jerking fashion. "There's a... inside of me?"

"Two souls, as you have one of your own. It is the same with me.

No doubt your second soul has shown and told you things that you could not have known without it. Its fortune is intermingled with your own, and it wishes what is best for the both of you. Care must be taken though, and a balance must be reached, or its passions will conflict with your own. Give in to your eye too often and you will find yourself the one sitting in the back, watching as it lives your life without you. But do not shut it out completely, because it will show you things that will guide you on your road ahead."

Samantha pushed her plate away from her in an aggressive fashion. She ran her fingers along the extended stone which surrounded her eye. "I didn't know there was another mind trapped in there. I don't want it anymore. Take it out, please."

The witch lifted one of her gnarled hands and brushed the hair from Samantha's face. The girl winced as the old claw grazed her skin, but she did not turn away.

"Some hurts are too deep to take away, but do not fear. We are not unique in our suffering, and this does not have to be a curse to bear. All who are wounded by life are given the same choice: to either let their harm control them, or to learn to see the world through different eyes. Tell me, why do you want to become a witch?"

"Because I'm not like everyone else. Because my mother thinks that I'm not smart unless I care about the same things she cares about. Because my father is ashamed that I don't act like he thinks a girl is supposed to act. Even the other kids think there's something wrong with me, and maybe they're right. They're all stupid, and petty, and mean, and I wouldn't want to be like them even if I could. But if there really is something in me that's broken—if that's the real reason that I can't seem to get along with anyone—then I'd rather be a witch, because a witch doesn't have to hate herself for being who she is."

Samantha's face was flushed when she finished. She looked hurriedly down at her plate, pulling it back to her as though suddenly fascinated in the fatty ends of the roast beef that she'd rejected before.

Bah-Rabba Kaba nodded, satisfied by the answer. She turned her cold marble gaze on Noah, whose hands instinctively clutched his old jaw bone around his neck.

"What about you, Noah Tellaver? How does it feel to have been the Prime demon Zee Zee Balloo in a previous life? To know that great darkness has come at your hand, but so too persists the potential to do great good?"

"I don't like it either. I don't think who you've been has nearly as much to do with who you are as everyone else seems to think. It just makes people expect things from me, so much more than anything I have to give. But I'm here, aren't I? I'd rather be judged on how hard I'm trying now. When I come back to life someday, I'm going to be starting over fresh again, so the only thing that's going to matter is whether or not I get there and help others do the same."

"And you, George Hampton? You must have known what the demons were doing in the living world when you agreed to help them at the Sylo. Where do your true loyalties lie?"

The muscles in George's neck strained as he lifted his head as though he bore a great weight. He met the witch's eyes at last, and stared for several long seconds before he finally replied.

"I won't leave the children. Not so long as there's still work to be done. I lived a short life and have spent far more time being dead, but those few years were more precious to me than whatever eternity is yet to come. Knowing I've got the same soul as when I was alive is the only thing that's kept me going, and I'll always be on the side of the people who have souls—their own souls, mind you—even when they aren't always on each other's side."

"As the Trans Dimensional Department should have been. Would you become the Prime Minister and lead them now that Theodore has gone astray?"

"I'm no leader, never have and never will. But you can count on me to do the right thing, and if people want to follow that, then I can't say I'd be disappointed."

"Those who seek power to do good often find themselves more in love with the power than the good. Those who seek the good first will always find the power to do so, and they will keep no more than they need. Greed comes in more forms than a desire for possessions, and an obsession with power, or glory, or ego can overshadow the light of the brightest soul.

"It is not easy to find unity with those whose flesh and bones and brains and thoughts are so different from your own, but so long as you see through to the soul you all share, you will find your way. I will help you destroy the Soul Net, so long as you promise not to end your quest there. Not until you have united the Primes and discovered how to return all the souls to the bodies they belong to. Eat, eat, regain your strength. I will not have you leave my domain until you are ready for the road ahead."

Bah-Rabba Kaba would not explain how they were supposed to access the higher dimensions yet, and no amount of cleverly worded questions could convince her otherwise. She watched them finish the meal intently, insisting that they eat more until even Samantha had to refuse. The quantity of food remaining in the wooden bowls seemed no less than when they had started. The witch then sealed the bowls with a spell and packed them away into purple cloth sacks that Noah was sure hadn't been in the room a moment before. The coarse material seemed to be made from raw fibers of the Muma-luma trees.

"The magic wielded by the dead is weak this far from the living world," Bah-Rabba Kaba explained. "There is strength in this food that will do more than fortify your bodies though, and with this you will find the energy to do what must be done."

The green mist followed them down the tunnel and continued to provide light when Bah-Rabba Kaba was ready to lead them onward. The tunnel they passed through reminded Noah of a large gopher hole, except that every so often they passed through a fully furnished room. Past the dining room was a very comfortable living room, with a deeply cushioned sofa, a large brightly colored rug decorated with mystic runes, and many black and white pictures on the earthen wall. All of them were women, and Noah recognized one to be Miss Thatcher with her old imp dozing in her lap.

"They're all witches, aren't they? Are they your friends?" Samantha asked.

"These were taken at the last great coven," Bah-Rabba Kaba

replied, trailing her ancient hands along the frames. "That was back when the Elmond Twins were still around, the last time we all seemed to still get along."

"Why don't men ever become witches?"

"Some will become warlocks, but it's different and not as common. To be a witch you must accept that the magic you wield has been borrowed from nature and does not belong to you, and men tend to struggle with that."

"Whenever I hear something about what a witch is supposed to be, it's always so vague hard to follow. Isn't there something more concrete you could teach me?"

"There are spells, and curses, and potions, and those sort of things, but any common wizard can learn those. Things you can be taught aren't the type of things that witches need. No amount of knowledge can make you wise."

"How does one become wise then?" Samantha pressed.

"Wisdom is the introspection of knowing what is true for you, the empathy to understand what is true for me, and the discovery of what is true for both of us that neither realized before. I believe that you will be wise, Samantha dear. I believe you will be a witch one day. Don't diddle-dally all day though—you have rested long enough, and you must be off as the Wojan will return soon."

Through the white-tiled kitchen with toadstools growing on a mossy counter. Down the spiraled stairs lined with bookshelves, with titles like 'When Your Cat Gets Your Spellbook', and 'Clothing Optional: A Witch's Wardrobe'. The stairway went a good long ways, until presently Noah realized that he was going upstairs instead of down, despite not having changed directions in the slightest. This occupied a good deal of his thoughts until he realized they must have passed straight through the tiny world and were now climbing out the other side. This theory was proven correct when the witch opened a door at the end of the stairway and stepped out from the trunk of an especially broad Muma-luma tree.

"From here you will be entering the Road from Death, also known as the third dimension of the Netherworld. It is a place where the living, the spirits, and the nether are most closely intertwined. There you will find the Soul Net, although you need not fear it and will not become entangled so long as you still have your bodies."

"Do you know how we can destroy the net once we get there?" Noah asked, following her back onto the powdery orange surface.

"A witch will know what must be done when the time has come," Bah-Rabba Kaba replied cryptically. "So too will a witch know what price must be paid to make it happen. Now stand together—back to back, that's right. And you still have the food with you, good, good. Now take some of it out and sprinkle it on the ground around you in a circle."

Noah did so automatically, only thinking how strange a thing it was to do after he grabbed a fistful of rice. Samantha and George were doing likewise around him though, and he supposed the witch might have been using some of the energy in the food for her spell. The witch was meanwhile drawing a large circle around them by dragging one of her heels through the powdery earth. Red sparks were flowing out underneath her dress as she walked, pooling in the grooves to form a circle of light around them.

"I truly appreciate your help," George Hampton said, bowing once more. "We never would have been able to leave this place without you."

"A stroke of luck for both of us. Go on, throw the food about, the more the better," Bah-Rabba Kaba said. "Don't worry, you aren't going to run out. Eat some more if you like. Squelch it in your hands, rub it on your faces, whatever you like. The more there is, the easier it will smell you."

"What do you mean, smell us? Who will?" Noah asked. He had already gripped the food between his fingers and was in the process of smearing a bit onto his chin when he stopped.

"Didn't I tell you? I said we had to hurry because the Wojan would return soon. This time it will be able to find you easier, and it won't get distracted with the Muma-luma trees. There, you see? It's already coming now."

There in the sky, just over the tree line. The dancing legs of the giant spider knitting itself into existence. Noah jumped backward on impulse, but he rammed up against something searingly hot. The red sparks were rising in the circle, now forming a wall of heat that prevented escape.

"It's a stroke of luck indeed which brought you here. It is no simple spell to banish one to the Road from Death where the three worlds meet. If it was, then I would have banished that horrible Wojan the instant it set foot in my garden. Now that I have the living and the dead together though, along with the demon spider, I have the trinity I needed to send you all away together. Stay close now, the spell won't begin until the demon is in the circle with you."

"Wait—won't it eat us?" Noah asked tensely.

"I certainly hope not," Bah-Rabba Kaba replied, smiling sweetly. "But do try to look on the bright side. At least it won't be bothering me anymore."

"How could you?" Samantha demanded. She tried to step forward, but the intense wall of heat was too much for her to even approach. "We trusted you! *You* said you believed in me."

"I do believe in you, dear, and now you have a chance to prove me right. Brace yourselves, dears, he's coming."

The gigantic spiders began to drop from the sky one after another. Their long legs trailed behind like the tails of comets. Bah-Rabba Kaba was speaking in an unrecognizable language, each word mirrored in the dance of red sparks. The ghost of each syllable hung in the air long after it was spoken to form a mounting crescendo as the spell reached completion.

"Do not be afraid," the witch's words floated through the spell somehow, despite her mouth being entirely occupied with the incantation. "A witch will know the right price to pay."

There was no running, no hiding, no defending themselves. Noah cowered to the ground beside Samantha while George Hampton stood protectively over them. The old man was conjuring some spell of his own. All at once a set of gigantic rib bones sprouted around them to shield the trio on all sides. An instant later and the bones rattled from the impact of the massive spiders crashing down on top of them. The black legs wove through the protective ribs and completely blocked out the light of the surrounding stars.

Blackness, and then the jolting sensation of falling. The three of them reached out for each other in the darkness. The encompassing rattling of bones indicated that their shield and the spiders were falling will them. Further confirmation came as the sound shifted to a brittle, snapping sound as the spider tore itself through their defenses.

Whatever blessings or horrors were to be found in the Road from Death, there was no denying that the spiders would be there on top of them when they arrived.

THE SOUL NET

The sensation of falling and the darkness evaporated in the same instant. Gone were the orange soil and the purple trees, gone the endless cosmos in the sky overhead. The companions weren't the only ones startled by the sudden shift either, because gone too were the tangle of spiked legs which had encompassed them a moment before. The streaking black blurs of the Wojan could be seen on all sides as the giant spiders scattered across the surreal new landscape. There was no doubt that they had entered another world.

The soft light of a sleeping city now engulfed the travelers as far as they could see in any direction. There was no mistaking this place for the living world though, as the city was utterly infested with thick black cords, gently pulsing with a white glow. Every lamp post, every street, and every house were thickly entangled with the strands of the Soul Net. A silent car rolled down the street beside them, passing directly through the webs without the slightest interaction.

The moving car appeared strange for another reason. A blur was maintained about its motion which left an after-image behind where the car had been a moment before, as well as a preceding shadow where the car was about to be next. Noah stared as the car slowed to a stop at the end of the street, causing the blur to stop as the before and after images coalesced into one. The shadow of the car then turned ahead at least a second or two before the rest of the car turned to follow it.

"Look at those two men coming down the steps of that old house," Samantha said, pointing at the pair huddled together in silent conversation. They were wearing large coats turned up around the neck. There wasn't enough light to see their faces, but it was clear what Samantha was referring to. There was a translucence about their edges that was distinct from their surroundings, likely marking them as spirits. They too walked straight through the web without seeming to notice its presence, and they were similarly oblivious to the shadow before and after each motion which lingered in the air.

"It's happening for me too," Noah said, waving his hand through the air with a blur of motion. His hand came in contact with one of the black strands which spanned the street. The web grew brighter at the point of contact, and Noah jerked away from it. "I can't go through it though. It feels gummy and sticky."

"The Road from Death," George Hampton said, turning in a slow and shambling circle. "I wasn't sure if I'd ever see this place. And even if I did, I was sure I wouldn't remember it because I'd be born again not long after. And yet we must have all been here before, or else we never would have lived at all. Careful girl, what are you doing?"

Samantha had begun to wave to the two men across the street, but neither of them looked in their direction. "I don't think they see us," Samantha said. "I thought they might see me because I was still alive, but I guess they're not really here. Or maybe we're not really here, in which case, where are we?"

"I'm more worried about where the Wojan is," the old man replied, scratching the back of his head. "That thing can really move."

The shifting of a cloud overhead brought a flood of pale light into the scene which continued growing brighter by the second. The emerging moon was gigantic: at least four times the size it ought to have been. And with that light sent a fresh sparkle through the air like a sunrise glistening on freshly fallen snow. A tranquil moment of serene beauty was slowly replaced by a deep, gripping dread.

"They're souls," Noah said. "Thousands of them, trapped in the web."

Samantha approached one of the black strands and stretched to reach for one of the low hanging gemstones. Even standing on her tip-toes she couldn't quite reach.

"Leave them," George instructed. "There are too many to take with us. We need to stay focused on finding our way deeper into the Netherworld."

Samantha ignored him and jumped, falling short of the glowing soul. She leapt again and managed to get her fingers around it. She was left dangling in the air for a moment as the red gemstone remained fixed to the web, but she kept tugging at it until the soul slowly peeled free and she was able to drop once more.

"At least this one is safe. You don't know what it's like being in there, alone and helpless."

"And you do?" George asked, a hint of suspicion in his voice. "What has that eye of yours been telling you?"

A sly grin spread across Samantha's face. She turned away to stare at the red stone in her hand.

"Try holding it up to the light," Noah said, remembering what he had done when he held Salice's soul in his first year.

She did so with a sharp intake of breath as the moonlight caught the stone. "There's an old woman sitting inside a small stone room. Hello in there, can you hear me?" Samantha held the stone to her eye for several seconds before her hand dropped, a sour disappointment on her face. "She wouldn't look at me. She was just sitting there on the floor, rocking back and forth. Can you imagine how awful it must be for them? All alone, trapped between life and death without a way out at either end…" Samantha's voice trailed off, and she shivered.

The black strand of the web had continued to vibrate after the soul had been removed. The amplitude of the wave wasn't decreasing over time either. No, it was actually increasing, and the frequency too— faster and faster until it filled the air with a low hum. Somewhere else farther along the crossing street another strand began to vibrate as well, this one making a slightly higher pitched sound. More notes were joining in to produce a pleasant harmony. A slow, plodding, rhythmic melody filtered through the sound, these notes fading to silence more naturally as though one guitar string was being plucked at a time.

"Put the soul back," George Hampton said quite firmly.

"No thank you. She'll just be used to power a gargoyle or a battery." Samantha clutched the stone protectively against her chest. "I'm not going to leave her."

"I've learned better than to argue with you," George said. "It's a good thing Bah-Rabba Kaba's food means that I don't have to." He wrapped his fingers around his bone ring and began to mutter something.

"Noah! Tell him to stop it!" Samantha howled.

The music meanwhile was changing subtly in the background. The low hum was growing higher pitched, and the pace of the plodding melody was picking up in tempo.

"You should do what he says," Noah said. "We can't let ourselves get distracted. Saving one won't do any good if we can't destroy the whole net."

"It'll do good for her, won't it? And I'm not the one getting distracted, you are. Don't forget that it's probably going to be me and my eye that finds a way out of this place."

George wasn't having it though. His hand with the bone ring suddenly detached, and using his other hand he hurled the thing at Samantha. She tried to slap the hand out of the air, but the grasping fingers latched onto her own and held on. The severed hand then leapt onto her other fist which was closed over the gemstone and began wrestling her fingers loose.

"You're only making this harder on yourself," George grunted. "Let go already! You don't know who could be listening."

"Sam, look out!" Noah cried. "George, leave her be. It's coming back!"

The distracted girl hadn't noticed the dark streak which sped across the web toward them. She didn't look away from George's detached hand until the shadow had already blocked out the light of the moon. Three of the Wojan descended from the web toward them. The music reached a frenetic pitch in the same instant, each note steadily merging into an omnipresent piercing tone of alarm. George began to mutter a new spell, but it was too late.

A rush of black legs converged on each of them. Their mobility through the air made it impossible to escape. The long legs reached toward Noah, seeming to grow as they stretched, the blur of their speed and morphing shape mixing hypnotically with the blur of the after images. Then came the brief and terrifying instant where Noah could see the pre-image of the legs seize him in the future, despite not yet feeling the jagged spines clamping around his waist.

Darkness returned as the black legs swarmed in from every direction. Silence as the ringing alarm grew muffled. The tension of a fragile second as Noah anticipated the spines breaking his skin, and the prolonged suspense of waiting for that moment which never came. Noah first wondered whether time had stopped, which seemed at least somewhat plausible in this sort of place, before deciding that the Wojan was simply holding him without attacking. A sliver of light through the legs revealed that the spines had relaxed lengthwise along the hard black appendages so they would not pierce him. As inexplicable as it seemed, the demonic spider had simply wrapped around his body in a gentle, almost cradling way.

"Silence," rasped the voice all around him, and Noah knew it must be coming from the spider. The word was spoken in the demonic tongue though, so Noah echoed it softly to the others.

"And don't struggle. He doesn't want to hurt us," Noah added as loudly as he dared.

"Silence," repeated the spider. "She approaches."

Noah was growing more accustomed to the darkness inside the spider's legs, and he was able to see more with the sliver of light which snuck through to him. He saw the spinning yellow sparks that he'd come to associate with an opening portal. Then came the hem of a midnight blue dress studded with stars, and he knew who must have arrived.

The Matriarch stepped from the portal. Her eyes darted suspiciously from side to side. Behind her, Noah caught a glimpse of the heavy iron doors and the spiral stairway of the Mortuary. There came a flash of longing to be back there, back with his friends, fantasizing about his next life, surrounded by the hope and excitement of the other students that had long since been denied to him. Did Walter ever get the attention of the woman he used to love? Was Jamie still trying to work with Brandon, even after he had betrayed them last semester? Had the minds of the other students been completely poisoned against the demons, or was there still hope for a resolution after the war?

The Matriarch left the iron door open behind her, and a constant spray of sparks kept the portal open. She continued to scrutinize her surroundings, at times looking directly through where Noah and the others were concealed by the Wojan. She started walking toward them, and Noah thought they had been spotted for sure. He remained frozen though, and as The Matriarch approached it became apparent that her attention was fixed on the Soul Net beside them. She reached out a hand and stroked the empty place where Samantha had taken the stone. The strand resonated at her touch, responding with a low hum like a purring cat happy to see its human.

Her back was turned, but it didn't obstruct the clarity of her measured words. "Don't steal from me, Noah Tellaver."

Noah stiffened. The legs around him constricted a little tighter, and even the sliver of light he'd been spying through was extinguished. He could still hear the shuffle of her feet though. It sounded like she was turning toward him.

"Do you hear me, boy?"

The shouted words pummeled him. Her voice was raw and angry and loud, projected to carry a good distance. As frightening as it sounded, at least it indicated that she still didn't know where he was. The soft hush in her following words was much more disconcerting.

"Ungrateful brat. I took you in and sheltered you. I could have turned you into a battery, you know. I could have sent the gargoyles back to your house and taken your family for myself. There's so much good that I could have done with those uncommon souls, but I showed you mercy. There aren't many old souls like us. I thought you understood that we were better than the rest of them, that we didn't have to play by their rules. But now…"

Footsteps, moving away. Why did she keep talking, if she really couldn't see him? Noah was thankful he didn't have to hold his breath.

"Do you know how lonely it can be in the company of the soulless? To see them smile and hear them laugh, and to know there is nothing inside to reflect that happiness? I would have told you about the net. I would have blessed you with its power, and one day you could have ruled over the dead after I had returned to life."

The sizzle of sparks, and the sound of iron grating on iron.

"Your friend Elijah told me who you really are. Don't you realize how much we need each other, Zee Zee Balloo? Why won't you show yourself? No matter, it's all a game to me. You will find your way back when you have remembered yourself."

The echoing clang of the door as it shuts, and then silence. The pale light began to sneak through once more, then all at once the spider lifted from him and dragged itself up into the net above his head. Noah looked around, panicking momentarily when he couldn't see the others. Legs began to peel themselves out of nothingness, stitching themselves into existence until two more of the spiders were lifting themselves from where George and Samantha had been concealed on the ground. These demons pulled themselves away from the ground, joining the third spider in the net. No—they weren't joining it all—they were overlapping with one another. And then all at once there was only one Wojan, with the slight blur before and after its motion as the only indicator that there were ever more than one.

"Thanks for not eating us," Samantha said to it, standing and brushing herself down.

"She knew I was here. How did she know?" Noah blurted out to no one in particular. "And if she did know, why did she let us go? And if she didn't know, then why was she talking to me?"

"Silence," rasped the Wojan with at least three voices at once. "The Lady has eyes beyond her head. She listens to what she cannot hear. We are not safe here—follow me."

There was a blur of future motion as the spider's legs moved ahead of the body, and another blur as the after-image lingered and then hurried to catchup. The Wojan used the thick black strands of the Soul Net to shimmy down the street. Samantha began to follow as soon as Noah had translated the demonic words, but Noah held back with George who seemed mistrustful of every step.

"Do not touch the souls," the Wojan continued from above once they had reached the end of the street. "The Matriarch can feel it as surely as you brushed against her skin."

Noah translated for the others, prompting George to add: "Reckless girl. This isn't a game. You can't keep doing things on your own before without letting the rest of us think about it."

"Just because it's serious doesn't mean it isn't a game," Samantha countered. "We can't beat The Matriarch if we're too afraid to play. You hate her too, don't you Wojan? She stole your net and trapped you in another world, and you want to get revenge. We can help you get it if you want to play with us."

The spider stopped, hanging idly by one of the thick strands. The others stopped below her. Faint footsteps behind them—a man with slumped shoulders with a hoodie concealing his face walked obliviously toward them. He passed straight through Noah and Samantha without noticing, although he did give an involuntary shiver which ran from head to toe.

"Yes, we will play together," Wojan rasped. "You have brought me back to my web, and I am thankful. Tell me though, is it true what the evil woman said? Are you truly Zee Zee Balloo?"

"I think so. I saw a Rasmacht in a mirror of my past, and that is what he told me. I don't know for sure that it's the truth though, or what it means if it is."

"What would happen if The Matriarch gets caught in your web?" Samantha asked. "Would her soul become trapped too?"

The Wojan stroked the web tenderly with its front legs. There seemed a certain slow sadness in its motion, as though caressing a loved one who lays on their deathbed.

"Yes, I hate her. I hate her as the fire hates the water, as the moon hates the sun. Where one is the other cannot, and nothing is sacred while she remains. For her the prison is not good enough; her soul must be consumed. I knew this day would come when the Prime Demons rose again. We will know if you are truly Zee Zee Balloo when we call your brothers to drain her dry."

"Are you talking about summoning the Soul Eaters?" Noah asked, the words scratching his throat. "I thought that once too, before I looked in to the mirror of ancestry and it told me the Rasmacht wouldn't do any good. It said we had to sacrifice a soul just to summon it."

Wojan spread its two front legs to gesture at the surrounding web. "We have no shortage of souls to spend. We shall pluck the souls like fruit from the vine. The Matriarch will return, and the Soul Eaters will be waiting for her."

Samantha crossed her arms and flushed slightly in anger, but surprisingly she bit her tongue and said nothing.

"Unacceptable," George Hampton said firmly. "Souls are not ours to spend, even if it means releasing the others. If you can help us continue our journey to find the other Primes, then together we can be rid of her without such a sacrifice."

"At least one soul is mine to spend," Samantha cut in.

"Don't—" Noah began.

"Oh shush. If having a soul is so important, then I should be the only one deciding what to do with it."

"You don't understand. You don't *have* a soul. You *are* a soul. If your soul is eaten then there won't be any you left. There will have never been any you at all."

"Of course I understand, you silly ancient-demon-who-thought-he-was-an-old-man-but-looks-like-a-boy. But I'm already sharing this body with another soul, the one in my eye. A body doesn't need two souls. A body needs one soul, feeling proud that it did the right thing."

"Why not just sacrifice the soul in your eye instead? Then you could have your body back."

"Absolutely not," George said. "It doesn't matter which one is getting eaten, sacrificing a soul will always be wrong. And have you forgotten about how many lives will lose a piece of themselves when The Matriarch is written out of them? We can't stop until we've found the other Primes."

"Souls will be destroyed, whether it is by your hand or another," Wojan replied. "Typical human shortsightedness, to let idleness shield themselves from guilt. There is nothing out there to judge you for summoning the Rasmacht, yet there are many that will be thankful."

Samantha withdrew the red soul stone that she had plucked from the web and was staring at it. The Wojan lowered itself from a strand of web until it was right behind her, whispering into her ear.

"Tell the girl to give me a soul—any soul will do. It won't matter to the Soul Eater once he has swallowed it down. Why stop at one when there are so many though? The more you feed them, the more will come, and the better the chance to bring The Matriarch down."

Noah translated reluctantly, pierced by the scrutiny of Samantha's inscrutable gaze. George Hampton took Noah and Samantha underneath the elbow and began to lead them away from Wojan. "We've heard quite enough from you," George called over his shoulder. "If you can help us reach the higher dimensions where the greater demons live, then we will be in your debt. No souls will be given as payment though, not to you, not to anyone."

"Predictable, but disappointing. Very well, I shall do it myself."

Noah almost finished translating what it said before he realized what the words meant. Too late his voice twisted into alarm. The long legs moved like lightning, snatching the red soul from Samantha's fingers. She leapt after the spider which was already launching itself back into the air. It looked like Samantha wouldn't be nearly fast enough, but the before-image of her movement caught hold of the after-image of the spider. This resulted in the last image of Wojan being pulled cleanly away from the rest of them, so that suddenly there were two spiders again. Only one of them held the soul though, and he was safely out of reach.

"Stop that! Give it back!" she shouted, releasing the second spider and flinging it away from her with disgust.

"Why? It's not yours. I'd pluck a new one and let you have that, but that would send another alarm and The Matriarch would come back before we were ready. This is really the most practical choice."

"George, stop him!" Samantha cried.

The old man was already gripping his finger-bone ring and was muttering under his breath. He let his hand slip and shook his head a moment later. "It's too late. The Soul Eater is already here."

"Without a summoning circle? How?" Noah looked wildly about him in all directions before looking up. That's when he noticed how round the web overhead really was. It's when he saw the red sparks sizzling out of the circle to fall around them like searing rain. Already he could feel the cold spreading throughout his body as though his veins had turned to ice. A rubbery grey limb pulled itself free from the spider, with several more flopping after it. They twisted and turned in on themselves as though there were no bones at all, until the appendages found sufficient grip to pull the Rasmacht loose.

"Hello, old friend," the Wojan said. "Something for your trouble." It extended its front leg and offered the glowing soul to the newly summoned demon. Rubbery hands reached out to it, its featureless face cocking to the side to marvel at the gift.

"You have to stop it!" Samantha begged, wrapping herself around George's arm. "I saw the woman inside that stone! She hasn't done anything to deserve this!"

"The Rasmacht is already here, don't you get it?" Wojan snapped back, his voice unusually harsh. "It isn't going to leave again before it has been fed."

They watched in horror as the toothless mouth gaped in anticipation, stretching wider and wider until both halves approached each other at the back of its head. The air around the mouth warped and folded into a twisted mass of darkness. But it was so much more horrible than darkness, because that place was somewhere further than light could ever reach. It was the place before the beginning of the universe, and the place which remained after it had gone.

Even as the soul slipped into this timeless warp, Noah could feel his memory of the soul growing hazy. He wasn't sure whether Samantha had ever picked the soul at all, or whether he had only imagined it. The numbing cold in his mind only made it that much harder to think. Then the mouth was closing, and Noah couldn't remember what the Rasmacht had even eaten in the first place. He didn't need the memory to understand what was happening though, and he didn't need the icy cold to feel so heavy, and weary, and sad.

"That's what you came for, isn't it?" Wojan cooed, stroking the side of the Soul Eater's head with one of its long spindly legs. "I've often wondered how marvelous a soul would taste... but no. I have not the body to digest it, nor the mind to trust myself if I had. You would like another though, wouldn't you old friend?"

The Rasmacht drew away from the Wojan's caress. It lifted its face and appeared to be sniffing the air, although with no nose or eyes it was impossible to tell how it was able to locate anything. Noah imagined it must be sensing the world as he did when he was in the shallow part of the Netherworld. Then he remembered that Zee Zee Balloo was one of the Soul Eaters, forcing him to wonder how many souls he himself must have consumed amid the shadows of a forgotten life.

"No, not up there. Focus on me," Wojan continued. There was a blur of motion as the two spider bodies merged together. The Rasmacht dropped to all fours and began to work its way toward the Soul Net where more souls were embedded, but the Wojan blocked its path.

"The soul I have brought you here for hasn't arrived yet, but she will be coming soon. It's a very old soul, a very special one, and it will taste like nothing you've ever had before."

Noah shifted uncomfortably from one foot to the next, casting a glance at the others. George was standing behind Samantha, his hands on her shoulders in preparation to prevent whatever impulsive thing she did next. Samantha was standing as still as a statue though. All the color had drained from her face so that it was hard to tell exactly where the skin and the marble met. The right side of her face seemed more dominated by the stone than ever though. As he watched, her marble eye rolled toward him in its socket, and a second later the rest of her noticed him as well.

"Are you okay with this?" Noah asked. He didn't know what to do if she said no, and it wouldn't be any easier if she said yes. Noah had been preparing for this moment for over a year, but now that it was here he wished for any excuse to push it away.

"We don't have to be okay with it," she replied sadly. "This isn't about us, after all."

Noah had the unnerving realization that she wasn't including him in her plural response. It felt more like he had interrupted a quiet conversation between her and the soul in her eye. There was no chance to explore the thought further, however, as the Wojan had already plucked a new soul from the web. The black strands began to hum in alarm, slowly building in intensity as they had before.

"She will be suspicious, but she will come. You must help by distracting her until I can catch her in my net, and then the Soul Eater will finish the job."

"She's already expecting me," Noah agreed. "I'll be waiting when her portal opens."

"We all will," George replied stoutly. "This is not your fight alone."

"Hide yourselves," Wojan replied, scurrying higher into its net. The demon carelessly dropped the new soul it had plucked as it went, although Noah was able to catch the falling stone. "The more she sees, the more on guard she will be. Quickly now, she's coming."

A circle of spinning yellow sparks was already manifesting itself into the air. George caught hold of Samantha's arm and pulled her away, the two of them stepping around the corner of a nearby house. The Wojan's extendable legs dropped down around the Rasmacht and lifted it into the net above, concealing the Soul Eater with its body. The Wojan covered the rubbery creature so throughly that even the numbing chill of its presence faded from awareness.

Noah understood now why The Matriarch hadn't seen them

before; once the Wojan was wrapped around the Soul Eater they both appeared to vanish. He stood alone in front of the spinning disk as it enlarged before him. Would she know something was wrong? Was it even her that would come through the portal, or would a flight of gargoyles or harpies or something too horrendous to imagine come charging through, ready for a fight?

Noah braced himself, holding onto the soul stone that set off the second alarm with both hands. It was warm to the touch, yielding in a living way. He hadn't remembered Salice's stone feeling like this, but then again he had been trapped as a spirit. The thing he was holding was something trapped between life and death, and seemed to Noah more like a softly glowing egg than anything else.

"Come out, come out, wherever you are."

The Matriarch's voice could be heard before she could be seen. Noah positioned himself directly in front of the portal and waited, his hands folded over the soul stone in front of him. Even after all this time being dead, it felt strange to be as anxious as he was without the feeling of a beating heart in his breast. As surely as he once lived for his family, Noah felt that this was the moment he had died for, and he was ready.

"I'm not hiding," Noah replied. "Not anymore."

"I thought it was you. I knew you'd return to me."

The flash of the midnight-blue dress, and there she was. The sparks continued to radiate through the air behind her for several seconds, illuminating her in a soft bright halo that looked almost divine. Each grey curl on her head was perfectly formed, each star in her dress twinkling with a warmth not found in her voice. It was easy to see how someone could be fooled into trusting such a confident and stately woman. Even standing before her now, with that kind and patient smile on her face, it was hard not to believe she didn't have the sincerest of intentions. Such lies can only be sold with the currency of hope.

"What did you mean that I could have ruled over the dead when you came back to life?" Noah asked straight away. He knew it would be pointless for the others to attack while the portal was still open behind her. He'd need to stall.

"Don't play coy with me. What else could it mean for you to be my apprentice? I never planned to stay dead forever."

"You're just in charge of the school though. You don't rule anything."

"Come now, you know better than that."

"You made Elizabeth your apprentice first, and you just got rid of her."

"What, the rabbit? You didn't seriously think something like that could command respect, did you?"

The portal hadn't begun to shrink yet. Did she realize what was going on? Was she leaving an escape route open on purpose? Or perhaps she was preparing to seize him and drag him back to school with her. All he could think was to buy more time.

"I'm sorry I left. I just wanted to stop the attack on my home, and I couldn't figure out how to get back. I miss my friends, and my professors, and my classes."

"Why did you leave, Zee Zee? Why did you really?"

Noah stiffened. There was no use lying to her. She was too clever for that, and it would only raise her suspicions and defenses.

"I know who I am," he answered, slow and solemn. "The Prime Demons are supposed to be together."

"You're right, of course you are. Such a clever boy, it is no wonder that I have chosen you."

"You're going to help me find them?" he asked in surprise.

"Of course I will. Who am I to stand between you and the will of the universe?"

"What do you mean, 'will of the universe?'" He pretended to be intrigued, but the words sounded repulsive from her mouth. If she cared a damn about the will of the universe, she wouldn't be working so hard to interrupt the cosmic balance of life and death. Was she simply trying to trick him into following her?

If she wouldn't close the portal, then Noah would have to lead her away. He took a few staggered steps away from her. It wasn't hard to pretend to be afraid when the real feeling was so close beneath the surface.

"You want to capture my soul. You want the Primes for yourself."

"Oh phooey." The Matriarch waved her hand dismissively, stepping after him. "It's not like I've had any shortage of chances to do that if I'd wished. I only meant to say that power exists to be used, and it doesn't help anybody to lock something so precious in higher dimensional space. That's where you're headed, isn't it? You can show me the way, and I can help you summon them back to the living world. Just imagine the good we could do when the demons learn what it means to serve again."

"No..." Noah continued backing away. "I don't know how to find them, and the Primes are too dangerous to bring back even if I did. Please don't come any closer. This is all so confusing."

She seemed hesitant to stray any farther from her portal until he said *'don't come any closer'.* There was something predatory about the way she picked up speed after that, like a shark that had just smelled blood in the water. Noah shielded the red soul stone protectively in his arms during his retreat.

"You're coming back with me, one way or the other. Let's not make this any harder than it has to be."

"I can't go back now. I've come so far already..."

"We'll find them together. You, me, Borrowrath and Momslavi, all helping each other. You must know by now how much energy it requires to push your way into higher dimensions. You'll never make it without my help, not without my batteries which produce all the energy we could ever need. Won't that make things so much easier than doing it alone? Stop running away from me!"

"Go!" George shouted, leaping out from behind the corner. Samantha was there, hurling both of George's detached hands toward The Matriarch.

At the same instant the Soul Net overhead dropped directly onto The Matriarch's head. Right behind the net came the Rasmacht, a numbing wave freezing everything before it. The mouth was already gaping wide, distorting space as it warped the air toward The Matriarch's head. She didn't look like an evil tyrant in that moment. She looked like a frightened old woman, staring at the approaching onslaught with the shock of disbelief.

"Hurry, hurry! Don't let her speak!" The Wojan howled. "Don't stop until you've eaten her soul!"

DEMON FOOD

DEATH USED TO SEEM LIKE THE MOST FRIGHTENING THING IN THE world. How innocent and naive that seems for the spirits who have already passed to the other side. That existential fear is not erased by death, however, as even the immortal soul needs to be protected from harm. The idea of losing one's soul is more terrible by far than simply closing your eyes for the last time. It's the idea that you've never closed your eyes at all, that there never were any eyes to close. It's the fear that all you've ever loved are no more aware of your existence than the characters in a movie are aware of their audience. That all you've ever fought for, all you've ever suffered for, all good and evil and pain and joy were nothing but a dream within a dream. The waking world has shed you from it, and life goes on without a tear.

Wrapped from head to foot in the thick black web, The Matriarch was poised on the edge of that timeless fate. One of George Hampton's detached hands was clasped over her mouth to prevent her from casting spells, while the other hand held down the net around her feet. The long legs of the demonic spider were a blur of motion as they wrapped ever more strands around the old woman, pinning her arms against her side. And ever the Soul Eater descended, its gaping lips wide enough to fit the Matriarch's entire head inside.

It didn't feel like victory. It felt like an execution without a trial. Frozen by the Soul Eater, deep into the netherworld, somewhere outside of time and space where no law existed beside that of the strong over the weak. Nothing could make this victory taste more sour than when they heard the muffled laughter escape The Matriarch's mouth. There was no chance to make sense of this through the numbing cold, not before the Rasmacht made its final lunge through an opening in the web. The thick distortion of space blended the Soul Eater with The Matriarch. Then it was through her entirely, emerging on her other side. The laughter was louder than ever.

"Ow, let go, you old hag!" George Hampton grunted.

The Matriarch had bitten one of the fingers covering her mouth. She bared her pearly teeth and chomped down harder, cleanly severing the finger and causing the rest of the hand to drop away. The Rasmacht was lunging up at her again, but once more it passed directly through her without success.

"Ish tht it?" The Matriarch spat the finger from her mouth, further smearing her lipstick to compliment the wild look in her eyes. "You were going to destroy my soul? That was your plan?"

"What's going on?" Noah demanded of Wojan. "You said this was going to work!"

The spider retreated immediately, bounding back into the higher strands spanning the top of a street lamp to a nearby roof.

"There's nothing to eat," Samantha said in a somber voice. "She doesn't have a soul."

Uninhibited, The Matriarch stretched both hands above her head and began to wriggle through an opening in the web. George Hampton's second hand snatched hold of her ankle, but a swift incantation from her caused the hand to burst into flames. George swore violently as he rushed to retrieve it, smothering the flames in his untucked button-down shirt.

The Rasmacht was midway through turning back for a third dive when The Matriarch seized it by the loose skin on the back of its neck. Grey fingers snatched at her face, narrowly missing the diamond in her eye socket. She shook the Rasmacht violently, yellow sparks pouring out from under the sleeve of her dress. They swirled around the demon, each circling several times before deciding where to dive into the gray rubbery skin. Within seconds the Rasmacht was dissolving into thick clouds of black smoke.

"Stupid girl, of course I have a soul," The Matriarch said. She freed herself from the remainder of the web and hurled it to the ground, turning sharply on Samantha. The Matriarch was temporarily taken aback to see the living girl, but the momentum of her rage kept her going. "You really think I'm the evil one, don't you? You self-righteous, ignorant, hypocritical brats. You don't like what I'm doing with souls, so you destroy a soul just to get at me. Can't you see that you're only proving my course is just? You with your soul, him with his, me with mine, all of us fighting because our souls all want different things. An endless cycle of being born and fighting and suffering and dying, only to come back and do it again. I can change all of that forever, and you, Zee Zee Balloo—you can help me do it."

"You're absolutely batty," Noah shot back.

"We won't let you keep taking souls for yourself." George Hampton pushed his way protectively in front of Noah, both of his hands now securely back on his wrists.

"You wouldn't think so if you thought clearly, but that's more proof for what needs to be done." The Matriarch was calming down considerably, although there was still a feverish light in her eyes. She wiped her smeared lipstick away with the back of her hand. "I'm giving more than I've ever taken away. I may stop souls from entering new bodies, but my own soul burns in the heart of all my children. Imagine a world where all living things share a single soul, a single mind, my mind. Where the living and dying of individuals matters no more than losing a few hairs from my head, always regrown without the despair of death. Where the lessons one of us learns are learned by all, an eternal knowledge which never has to retrace its own footsteps. Where everyone shares the same hopes, and dreams, and a kindness for each other as deep as the love one feels for themselves. Do you know how much I'd give to live in such a world? To *be* such a world?"

Noah could imagine such a world, but it wasn't nearly as beautiful as how she described it. To him it sounded like a world of slaves, where one mind controlled the rest and all the souls but one were trapped in stones. An eternity of giving power to a world they would never be part of. It wasn't some distant future either—if the Soul Eater couldn't get at her soul now, then it must be because she had already spread herself between all the soulless ones. The burden of giving speech to such a horrible thought was too much to bear, and Noah remained in silence.

"Everything. I'd give everything to live like that," The Matriarch hissed. Light was bleeding from the sky without a discernible reason. Contrasts grew sharper, the street lights grew dimmer, and a blanket of shadows was settling over the land. "And you will help me, Zee Zee Balloo. The souls of the three Primes are exactly what I need to finish the job."

The Matriarch began to chant in an unfamiliar language, dark and guttural in a way that didn't seem possible from her human mouth. All of the light which had been draining from the sky poured into her right eye, or at least the diamond in place of where her eye had been a moment before. Noah was transfixed by the piercing light. He couldn't turn away or even blink as it continued to grow brighter, until soon everything else was smothered into silhouettes and that light was all there was.

Noah instinctively put up his hands to try and block the light, which worked for a second. A second where the rest of the world reformed around him, a second to look around and see George and Samantha rushing to his aid. A second to see a focused beam of white-hot energy spiraling from The Matriarch's eye toward him, blocked by the object he still held in his hands. With horror, Noah realized that he was shielding himself using the red soul stone that he still clutched. Then that second was over, and the soul in his hands shattered into a thousand pieces.

It wasn't the stone that had broken into pieces though—it was everything around the stone. Houses ripped loose and spun through space, leaving great rifts of emptiness between them. The road peeled up from the ground like a carpet being rolled up, and below it there was nothing forever. Trees were dissolving as their leaves shot out in every direction at once, and parked cars were splitting down the middle to drift in separate directions. The sky itself was stretching, growing wider and wider and thinner and thinner until all at once it ripped to pieces like shredded cloth.

"This is your chance." The distinctive hiss could only have come from Wojan. Exactly where the spider was in this maelstrom of a disintegrating world was impossible to say, but his voice was clear enough. "I'm using the energy from the shattered soul to propel you further into the nether. Don't stop until you've reached the red gates. You must tell Borowrath and Momslavi what you've learned. Do not hide your true self, and walk proudly through the depths of the netherworld. The demons are your allies, and we will never let this abomination come to pass."

"Where did you go?" roared The Matriarch's distant voice, growing fainter with each word. "You cannot hide from me, boy! There is no world beyond my reach."

The piece of pavement that Noah, Samantha, and George were standing on remained under their feet while the rest of the world dissolved around them. A nearby streetlight on the sidewalk remained as well, casting its feeble rays into the infinite darkness on all sides. It seemed to Noah that he could walk a few steps in any direction, but no farther lest he tumble off the edge of the sidewalk to plunge endlessly into the unknown. Slowly, gradually, a new world began to resolve itself around him as though it had been there all along and his eyes were simply adjusting to the dark.

"The land of greater demons," Samantha said, a hushed awe in her voice. "All of them are…" Her words softened to silence, overpowered by the rising noise around them. Hot, heavy gusts of air like breath carried with it a thousand distant voices. Harsh, discordant voices, each endlessly repeating their own strange mantra in a timeless chant that seems to have begun long before they arrived, and will continue long after they were gone.

"That was my intuition as well. Do you suppose that makes me a witch too?" George Hampton replied. His tone had a forced nonchalance which could not disguise his own apprehension toward this new world.

Noah had seen all shapes and sizes of demons before. He didn't think anything could surprise him after attending classes amid the organs of the massive Sylo. Even seeing a demon the size of a tower did little to prepare him for the sight of an entire city. Structures of skin and bone with great eyes on top. Palaces whose pillars were clawed legs, ponderously dragging the gargantuan things about. Great plains filled with houses, domes, spires, and all manner of infernal architecture beyond mortal possibility, chaotic in their presentation but uniform in their unmistakable demonic life.

The only thing that looked familiar was the dense network of meandering streets, until these too began to slither and rearrange themselves amidst the feet of the massive demons. The chorus of chanted mantras emanated from the most massive and stately demons clustered around the city center. There the tallest towers huddled together, their tapered and slender heads bent together at the tops as though in quiet conversation. Orange and intricate tattoos covered every inch of these demons, reminding Noah of the tattooed skin Elijah had carried with him.

"Even human cities aren't this big," Samantha said. "Look over there at the far end. Those things that look like mountains. They're moving this way."

"Eyes, eyes everywhere," Noah muttered. "How can anyone live like that?"

"Maybe they don't like it either. Maybe that's why they're always trying to get out," George said.

"They seem really overcrowded," Noah added. "I can't see a spare inch that isn't wiggling or hopping or swarming with something."

"No surprise there," George answered. "All the demons were banished here from the shallow end, remember. Not to mention all the bans on summoning demons back in the spirit world. They've probably never had so many all here at once before."

Even the sky couldn't be said to be open when giant flocks of misshapen beings beat, swam, and lurched through the air. The sky itself was a dull, red color, a perpetual sunset which had grown weary of its faded glory. The single monstrous red sun—at least three times the size of the living world but only half as bright—was often blocked by the passage of a demonic flight which projected twisted shadows over the land. The sun also appeared much closer than it ought to, as evidenced by the single ladder made from bones which stretched from the heart of the city all the way up to the fiery orb.

"There are doors in the sun," Samantha said, following Noah's gaze. "Red doors. I think that's where Wojan intended us to go."

Noah took a step toward the end of the sidewalk. A hand on his shoulder—George was holding him back, staring tensely off to the left. The long scaled street had reared up to watch them like a snake poised to strike. Nearby houses slowly turned in order to stare at them with whatever eyes they had available. Even the rooftops of these structures grew littered by flighted demons which had landed to inspect these strange intruders.

Noah went through the motions of a deep breath. "We've already come this far, no point in holding back." Then in a louder, more confident voice, he called out to the surrounding onlookers in the demonic tongue. "Friends, allies, I come as one of you. We are here to speak on behalf of the living and the spirits who still wish for unity with the demons. The name of this body is Noah Tellaver, but you have once known me as the Prime Zee Zee Balloo. Please take us to see Borowrath the Unsplendid and Momslavi Lapis."

None of the demons moved for several seconds after he finished speaking. Then all at once, like a stone thrown amidst birds, the flighted demons took off and scattered into the air. The cumbersome houses slowly shifted away once more, and the great serpent nestled back into the earth to form a street again.

"I guess they weren't impressed. I can't say I blame them," Samantha quipped.

"What do you know. You don't even speak demonic," Noah replied bitterly.

"That's what *you* think," she replied haughtily. Then after a moment's skepticism, she added: "Okay fine, you're right, I don't. But

I do know you're still a fleshy little meat bag trying to sound all high and mighty next to giant monsters that could rip you limb from limb without a second thought."

"Fair point."

"Noah Tellaver. I've been wondering when you'd turn up."

It turns out that not all the demons had dispersed. There sitting on the open street, no longer concealed by the rearing serpent, sat the familiar form of Visoloth. The demonic dog cocked its head to the side, apparently enjoying the surprise its appearance elicited.

"How did you find us so quickly?"

"The same way I found you in the shallow end of the nether. Come, there isn't any time to waste."

The dog turned and began to trot down the winding street. Noah was hesitant to step off the concrete onto the back of the giant serpent, passing through the city where the houses leered down on him from either side. Of course Samantha wasn't going to wait though, and he wasn't about to let her go alone. The serpent reared slightly in annoyance as he stepped on it, causing a sharp downward incline which had him jogging before he knew it.

"Stay close, and don't draw so much attention to yourself," Visoloth said over his shoulder. "Soul Eaters, Shawsheen Strikers, Undulating Fematoads, and far worse might be listening."

"It's okay, I'm here to help," Noah said. "We're all working toward the same goal of getting rid of The Matriarch and her Soul Net."

"Is that the goal of all humans and spirits too?"

"Well, no, not all of them, but…"

"Then don't be stupid enough to say all demons think the same either. Some believe that humans have selfishly dominated the living world for too long. Others wouldn't mind destroying the Trans Dimensional Department and regulating the passage of souls ourselves. I myself am still sympathetic to killing all the soulless ones before The Matriarch is able to start doing damage with them."

"We found out that they aren't completely soulless after all. They're just all sharing the same one: The Matriarch's soul."

Visoloth stopped abruptly, allowing the others to catch up with him. He shook his head vigorously as though trying to knock the thought loose from his head. "Doesn't matter, they still must be destroyed. My point is that you can't think of us as monolithic in thought. Watch out, don't step in the Moolang Spool."

Visoloth deftly avoided what had first appeared as a puddle of orange goop on the side of the street. Now that they were paying attention, it was clear that the puddle was slowly oozing against the inclination of gravity, and that hundreds of tiny hands with thousands of needly fingers underneath dragging it along.

"As if I'd step in that nasty goop, even if it wasn't a demon," Samantha said, hastening to add. "Oops, sorry sir, no offense." The orange puddle folded itself upright like an omelet, gesturing angrily at Samantha with all its little hands.

"We haven't been idle here while you were training in the shallow end," Visoloth said. "Not for a thousand years have the Prime demons walked the mortal world, and there have been many rituals and preparations all throughout the city of Wallom. You have witnessed evidence for this already though, both with the chanting of the greater demons and the construction of the ladder which rises to the doors of Almorada. When the three Primes finally emerge, you will see how quickly the war will shift."

"If this is to become a war then we've already lost," Noah said. "We can still avoid the worst of the fighting if we're successful in our plan. And we don't need all the demons to agree so long as we get the other Primes on our side."

"You are so sure that the Primes will not prefer the path of slaughter?" Visoloth asked. "There is old magic at work that you could not possibly understand."

"We're the ones who don't understand?" Samantha asked as soon as Noah translated. "You didn't even notice Zee Zee Balloo was standing right beside you until he revealed himself to Noah. Or rather Noah revealed it to himself. Or Zee Zee... oh you get what I'm talking about. Visoloth's talking nonsense, pretending he knows more than he does."

"Samantha, please," Noah murmured. "We're here to work with the demons, so let's try to be respectful."

"Do you trust everything you're told?" she replied curtly. "Ever since I've been to the Netherworld, I've listened to demons lecturing me like I'm a child and they know all the secrets of the universe, but you know what? I think they're just making it up as they go along. The Matriarch tricked the demons into fighting the department and getting themselves banished. She tricked the Wojan and stole his net. Now the whole city is going through all this trouble to get the Prime demons, not seeming to notice or care when one of them is already here. How do we know they'll even recognize Momslavi or Borrowrath when they see them if they've been locked away for so long?"

Visoloth stopped at a crossroads, his tentacles tasting the air. They were forced to wait for a procession of hollow, curved demons like monstrous bowls with faces to crawl along the street on their hooked talons. Each was overflowing with dried herbs, flowers, glittering stones, waxen candles, and other unfamiliar ingredients. The sheer quantity and complexity of the ritual in store must be staggering in proportions. While they waited, Visoloth turned his narrow yellow eyes on Samantha, scrutinizing every inch of her as she continued.

"The real reason The Matriarch has been beating us is that she's learned to turn us against each other. She turned the spirits against the demons, and the demons against the living. I don't believe demons are really so alien from us that they don't understand what killing the soulless does to the rest of us. When people are afraid, they don't trust anything to keep them safe, not even each other. Not even themselves. Watching us all go after each other like this makes me understand what The Matriarch is trying to do. She thinks the only way for us all not to fight is for everyone to share the same soul, but that's the mistake that's going to bring her down. We need to be doing the thing she expects the least: we need to trust each other."

Visoloth turned forward once more to lead them across the street. The greater demons who served as structures were getting more massive as they continued, and soaring walls of fur and scales and mottled flesh blocked out much of the light from the sky.

"And what would you have us trust, human child?"

"That you need to work with the spirits and the living. If Noah and I start teaching the living how to summon demons, then we can undo the banishments. It will also prove that the demons and the living can coexist, which will help the spirits accept the demons again. We can expose The Matriarch for the evil meddler she really is, and turn everybody else against her. Of course, this will only work if the demons don't attack the soulless once they're summoned though."

"We'd just have to put that agreement in the contract," Noah said, growing excited by the idea. "If it's in writing, then any demon that tried to attack the soulless would be instantly banished. It will be a lot easier getting the humans to feel safe again if they know that part."

"Did you come up with that idea yourself?" George Hampton said, adding a low whistle. "Or was that your little friend?"

"Sometimes it's hard to tell," Samantha said, smirking sheepishly. "We do so get along."

"A worthy ambition for any of us," Visoloth conceded. "As you have already seen with your first announcement, the demons will not be easily swayed from their intent. The summoning ritual to open the doors of Almorda will continue, but there is sill much work to be done. But how do you plan on getting to the living world in the first place?"

Noah translated, prompting George to brighten up and smile. "I know just the trick. Demons aren't the only beings that can be summoned, you know. Anything can be summoned from the Netherworld, it's just that there isn't usually anything to be found except demons. We'll need to find a way to scry the living world though, so I can instruct our own summoning."

"Such marvelous creatures, humans are," Visoloth replied. "To see the hope on the other side of struggle is surely their greatest gift. I shall take you to a place where you will find what you seek, and the demons you bring out amongst the living will bless you for this opportunity. I look forward to the day this battle is finally over, and I may plant my soul amidst such auspicious roots, to live again as a human child."

Visoloth turned away from the busy streets with their procession of marching demons. He turned away from the towering walls of greater demons, choosing a small winding path that skirted the monstrous heart of the city. This new road was tiled with emerald green scales, and it had the added benefit of slithering in the same direction they wished to go like a moving sidewalk to hasten their journey.

"I know a place where you can communicate with the living," Visoloth continued. "A secret place. A quiet place, so quiet that one may hear their own thoughts as though they were spoken aloud. Most demons do not go near it for fear of what may be uncovered beneath the shroud, but I trust my present company does not suffer such faint of heart."

Noah and Samantha shared a private glance, both evidently uncomfortable with the idea but unwilling to admit it out loud. None of them seemed more disconcerted than George Hampton, however, whose wrinkled face was furrowed deeply. As soon as he noticed the attention he was receiving, he changed sharply though, causing all his wrinkles to shift into a deliberate, rather waxen smile.

"Excellent, ideal, absolutely superb," the old man said. Then realizing again that he may have gone too far, he dropped the smile to add in a more solemn voice: "Well there's no use beating around the bush then. The people I mean to contact are my brother and sister, and we haven't always been on the best of terms. In fact my brother is the one who killed me, while my sister helped cover it up. They're not bad people—not deep down. It's just that they might take some convincing is all."

"Killed you on purpose? Like a murder?" Samantha asked with unabashed fascination.

"How long have you been dead for anyway?" Noah added. "Your siblings must be ancient by now."

"They're actually younger than this old body of mine. You see, we were all very young when I died. Now that I think about it, that could be why I've always been eager to spend my time away after death. I never had the chance to grow old while I was alive, so the price of growing older with every purchase seemed more like an added benefit than a cost. I'm sure there is a lesson in there somewhere—something about youth being more valuable than wealth, as nothing accrued in life is more valuable than the time lost to get it..."

"You're not going to ramble your way out of answering that easily," Samantha interjected. "Why did your brother kill you?"

George Hampton sighed and scratched the back of his head as though trying to remember. Visoloth continued to lead them until they'd reached near the head of the serpent, which looked more like a leech than a snake as it was dominated by spiral rows of hooked fangs. The demon dog seemed to be instructing the street where to go.

"There's a troubled story there, one you won't get out of me even if some of my thoughts slip out by accident. It's enough to know that my brother discovered that I could see into the spirit world and became convinced that I was possessed by a demon. My brother thought it was his responsibility to be rid of me, while my sister to her credit learned to commune with spirits to say she was sorry. Our relations have improved somewhat since my death, but I would be misleading you if I pretended it will be easy to convince them to side with the demons now. If we're going to have any hope of repairing relations between the demons and the living though, we cannot shy away from such suspicious minds who will be turned against us from the start."

"They're going to love me then," Noah said dryly. "I guess we'll need to keep my demonic past a secret."

George Hampton shook his head, staring resolutely at the path ahead. "The prejudiced will always believe in lies to justify their mistrust. We cannot go to them pretending to be anything other than who we are. We have all taken different routes to get to become ourselves, but none of those paths have detracted from the souls we carried with us. All souls deserve acceptance and love. If we can believe that, then we should also believe all souls are capable of acceptance and love."

The emerald street had completely exited the demonic city and was now winding through barren red sand dunes. Occasionally a tentacle or a claw emerged from the sand on one side or the other, or they would pass the gargantuan imprints where some creature had recently traveled. Other times the ground itself would shift like a living thing, and entire sand dunes would pick themselves up to wander away. These reminded Noah of the flaky orange soil where the Bah-Rabba Kaba lived, and that although it wasn't always apparent at first glance, nearly everything in the Netherworld really was a demon.

"Look how the sand is stirring in the wind," Samantha said in a hushed voice. "And listen. Do you hear it moving?"

Noah shook his head. "Not really. Why?" He hadn't intended to whisper, but his own voice sounded muffled to him.

"We're approaching the quiet place," Visoloth said, sounding as though from a long way off despite being only a few steps ahead. "We must travel on foot from here."

The serpent beneath them responded immediately with a sudden stop. The many-toothed mouth shifted along the body, sliding as easily as a boat slips along the surface of the water. Noah and the others had to leap off the demon's back and into the sand to avoid the mouth passing directly under them. Soon the mouth had traveled all the way to the other end, at which point the serpent reversed direction and began slithering back toward the city of Wallom.

"Travel where? There's just sand and sand and more sand in every direction," Samantha said.

"Still yourself girl, and listen," Visoloth instructed. Noah translated, earning an additional fierce glare from the demon dog. "We cannot bring sound with us where we go."

Noah hurriedly translated the last part as well, avoiding Visoloth's gaze as he did. The group of them then waited, not knowing what to expect as the sand blew silently across them. Little sounds they'd grown accustomed to like the shuffling of fabric, or the distant chanting from the city, had now been completely extinguished. Samantha put a hand to her chest, feeling for a heartbeat that she could no longer hear. Nothing but silence, nothing but nothing, and then:

This must be what it feels like to be dead.

Noah was about to reprimand Samantha for speaking when he realized her mouth hadn't moved. She realized it too—her green eye was stretched wide in alarm.

I wonder if they'll even remember me. That thought came from George, who smiled in embarrassment and recognition.

Silence. Stillness. Patience. Visoloth began to dig with his front paws in the sand. *The humans are blessed in their ignorance of what is to come.* Visoloth stopped digging abruptly as that thought was involuntarily released into the air. He then seemed to shrug his shoulders and returned to digging.

I hope nothing really embarrassing comes out, like what I was going through when I was trying to stop my wife from leaving. Noah winced as his own thought slipped free into the empty air. Samantha slapped a hand over her mouth to avoid making a sound, but Noah could tell she was grinning.

The sand was stirring beneath them, swirling with an invisible current like water rotating the drain. Visoloth moved and began to dig in the center of the vortex instead. His thoughts were clear and focused, almost as though the demon was willing himself to only think that which he wished to share.

The black pool waits in the heart of silence. You will be able to contact the living from there.

No translation was necessary. They weren't hearing the words so much as experiencing the thoughts, that intent which rose in their minds as clearly as Noah thought it himself. They watched as the sand in the center of the spiral tumbled away into empty darkness, a steadily widening hole which endlessly ate the falling sand.

I don't want to go in there. Please don't make me. Please, Sam, I'm scared. Noah couldn't tell who was thinking that one. There wasn't any familiar inflection or tone which could be attributed to any of them. George and Noah both turned rapidly trying to discern the source, until they realized Samantha was the only one who didn't seem surprised. She pointed a finger at her marble eye.

There was no further chance to explore this mystery though as the ground beneath them gave way all at once. Without a sound they tumbled through the raining sand, although a chorus of surprised thoughts rebounded through each of their heads. There were so many surprised voices all racing round each other that it felt like a panic attack trying to sort them out. Even after they landed on something soft and yielding, it took a good while before the clatter of thoughts settled down enough to make sense of their new surroundings.

It's beautiful.

It was impossible to tell who thought that first, because they all must have been feeling the same thing.

It's terrifying.

An equally true thought resonated just as loud.

THE SUMMONING

IN THE DARK AND QUIET BENEATH THE RED SAND DUNES OF THE DEMON city of Wallom stretched a sleeping jungle of spectacular flowers. The center of each flower contained a central column where the pollen might be found in an ordinary flower, although the wet gloss and sinuous movements might be better attributed to an inquisitive tongue. They had landed on the broad expanse of one such blossom whose colossal red petals spread at least a dozen feet in every direction. Similar flowers blanketed the ground, climbing on twisted vine over subterranean hills and valleys for as far as their dim overhead light could reveal.

The garden of Wallom does not grow on light, but on sound. If it were not for these flowers, you would have been deafened by the clamor of the cosmos before you've taken your first step on this world.

How is that supposed to help us reach the living?

That must have been Samantha. Noah was starting to grow accustomed to hearing the other's thoughts in his head, although the most difficult part to overcome was the baseline anxiety and dread which seemed to be emanating from Samantha's marble eye. Raw emotion more primal than words were leaking from it, mixing with Noah's own feelings and leaving him on edge.

The red desert is made from its pollen, Visoloth continued. *The plant forms connections with outer worlds to disperse its seed, colonizing barren lands for the demons to occupy. Proper targeting should allow a connection with your living world, which will at least allow communication, even if it will not be stable enough for you to transverse directly.*

The demon dog dropped off the voluptuously silken petal to the hard stone beneath in perfect silence. He bent the thick vines beneath this way and that, adjusting the angle of the flower as though aiming a satellite dish.

Get out... get out... get out...

The words were deep and subtle, like the unconscious mind clinging to the repressed memory of a nightmare that the conscious mind refuses to acknowledge. Noah shivered and tried to empty his mind, which was an impossible feat with this many thoughts freely flowing between them.

How are we supposed to communicate with the living if we can't make any sound?

Your thoughts are their thoughts, although they will be faint and distorted from such a distance. It will be easier for you to be heard if you reach out to them when their own mind is quiet, although even then your thoughts will seem surreal and mysterious for them.

Get out... of my body. I want it to myself. I deserve a body of my own.

That had to have been Samantha's eye again. She didn't seem to pay it much notice though. Could she have been hearing such thoughts from the other soul for so long that she learned to tune them out?

George Hampton's tone flavored the next words. *If you meant dreams, you could have just said so. Do you really think the humans can learn something as complicated as a summoning from a dream? No wonder no one likes demons... oops, sorry, but you know what I mean.*

Let the flower taste you. It will find your relatives more easily if it has a reference.

No worse than living in the Sylo's liver... George Hampton slid down the silken petal toward the flickering tongue in the center. He reached out with a tentative hand, allowing the tongue to wind its way through his fingers and wrap around his wrist.

I know you all can hear me. I'm not stupid. Why won't anyone help me?

Noah looked at Samantha, who intentionally turned her back on the rest of them.

Sam? Are you okay in there? Noah thought, unsure how to broach the subject.

It really is beautiful down here. I can't believe I brought my phone without any way to charge it. I should have taken a camera instead.

I have a name, you know. It's Alley. I'm Alley. For all your talk about souls, you'd think you'd have a little more empathy for mine.

Don't mind her, thought Samantha. *She's just been bitter ever since the Rasmacht didn't eat my soul like she wanted.*

Calm your minds, I can hardly hear myself think—from Visoloth. He tilted the flower slightly to the right, then to the left, then back to the right. *I might have found them.*

Lot of good that does me. I'm glad you can all hear me, because if you really care about your friend you'll help her find me a body. Or don't be surprised when I take this one for myself.

I'm not your hostage. You're lucky to be out of that gargoyle—from Samantha.

Don't worry, Alley, we're going to help everyone get their own body—from Noah.

What if my brother isn't even alive anymore? What if my sister thinks I'm just a nightmare?—from George.

Stop. Thinking!—from Visoloth.

A sliver of time without sound, without thought, completely at peace. Then clear as a flame on a dark night, a blast full of undisguised resentment and anger flared out:

I'll kill her. It's your own fault if you don't believe me. I've already taken half of her face, and it won't take long before I reach her brain. I can make her heart stop, or forget how to breathe. And good luck ever coming back to life with blockheads like you running the show.

Samantha couldn't disguise her distress any longer. Her fists were clenched into little balls, her arms straight and tense and locked, her jaw working through a silent scream. The part of it that was a thought still came through, feeling like part of your brain was screaming while the rest was pretending everything was fine.

Don't hurt her, Noah pleaded, hoping the sincerity and urgency he felt echoed through the others as surely as the scream had torn through him. *Please. I promise to help you find a body of your own. We're doing the best that we can, but this is all too big for us. We're not trying to hurt anyone, but everyone is hurting and it shouldn't be up to us to make it all better. I'm hurting, and I wish someone who has lived more lives or understands more truly or has more power can swoop in and take away the responsibility, but they don't. Everyone who should know better is as lost and scared and sad as I am. So please, just be patient, and one day we'll figure out how to make it all right. And if we can't, then don't blame us for it, because none of us chose these paths that our souls must follow.*

Silence, deep and pure, or brooding and foreboding, or empty and uncaring, or all at once, there was no way to know. And though no words were articulated in any of their minds in that moment, there remained a sense of shared empathy where each forgot exactly what it was like to be themselves, and remembered a little of what it was like just to be. Whether that existence was a triumph or a torment both seemed equally plausible in the ocean of emotions that were shared between them.

I want to go home.

It could not be said that the thought came from any one of them, because the sensation was experienced by all.

I've found them. Peter Hampton and Chrissy Dekon, Visoloth interrupted. *Chrissy is still awake, but Peter is asleep and preparing to dream. Are you ready to join him?*

I'm ready, George Hampton replied, his trepidation a wave on the ocean between them. *Peter? Can you hear me? It's your brother George. I know it's been a while since you've heard from me, but it's very important you remember this when you wake up...*

PETER HAMPTON WAS BEGINNING to grow bald, and the baseball cap he wore to cover it up looked rather ridiculous with his professional, if slightly shabby, suit. He'd been meaning to get a new suit, but he told himself he'd wait for the next special occasion, and that was over five years ago. Peter kept a regular schedule to make sure he always had time to stop for coffee before going to his job at the bank, and he always left fifteen minutes early to help beat some of the traffic on the way home. He loved his wife Margaret, his two children Elaine and Alex, and his three-legged dog Bilbo very much. He would do anything for his family, but this was the first time in his life he had ever been asked to summon something from the Netherworld.

As prophets and poets have long testified, there are dreams that come in every man's life that cannot be ignored. There are nights so black that the possibility of morning is forgotten, and from them births a longing that aches so deep that it cannot be healed by a shower and a coffee on the other side. Perhaps the reason the dream lingered so insidiously in Peter's mind was that it reminded him of his brother. That secret of his childhood had no place in the world he understood himself to belong now, however, and Peter did his best to keep those dark and repressed memories locked below where casual awareness could stumble across them.

The fact of the matter was that Peter had plenty of practice burying such thoughts which threatened the stability of day to day life. There was once a time when he could even see the shades of the dead, but a lifetime of deliberate disbelief had robbed them of their potency. If the conversation ever slipped into the supernatural, Peter would adamantly deny the possibility of demons, to such an extent that he half-believed his own claims. His brother George really had fallen to his own death when they were children. The idea that he had pushed his brother to his death to kill the demon inside was as ludicrous as a fleet of invading space aliens, or that the Kraken had simply been sleeping ever since the invention of better cameras.

"Are you still awake, sweetie? Is something wrong?" Margaret asked him the next night.

Peter lay on his back, his fingers clutching the sheet harder than he'd realized. It was the same dream as the night before, with a circle of blood dribbled around his clean kitchen floor. Something was coming out of that circle, something that didn't belong anywhere outside of a nightmare. Peter's eyes were still open, boring into the still ceiling fan above him which had never looked quite so much like a grasping claw.

"Just a bad dream, dear."

"Do you want to talk about it?"

"Go back to sleep. I can hardly remember it myself."

Willing yourself to forget something is never as easy as it sounds though. The harder Peter tried to forget, the more he thought about the dream, and the more he dreaded it coming again. By the third night he was tossing and turning for hours before he fell asleep. There was the circle of blood again, so clear and vivid that he could make out each individual symbol scrawled into the blood. His children were there too, sitting back to back in the circle. A lucid thought pierced the haze to wonder why he was summoning his children before he realized his mistake. Whatever he was really summoning was coming out of his children, as if the shadows from their own dreams were birthing directly from their minds.

Peter wasn't the only one who was having trouble sleeping. Alex and Elaine were so bleary eyed and sluggish that they both missed the bus to high school. Margaret had already left to work, and it was up to Peter to rush them out the door and drop them off before he too was late.

"It's not my fault," Alex whined, flinging his school pack into the back seat. "I was having such a horrible dream that it didn't even feel like I was sleeping."

"Me too! That's why I'm late," Elaine piped up.

"Why are you always copying me?" her older brother complained. "Get your own excuse!"

The two fell into bickering in the back, and Peter didn't interrupt them. He decided that the less he knew about their dreams, the less he'd think about his own. That strategy backfired spectacularly though, and for the rest of the day Peter couldn't stop wondering if perhaps his children had the same dream he'd been having. The more he tried to convince himself that was impossible, the more terrible it seemed if it were true.

"Is that your third bottle of beer?" Margaret asked that night over dinner. "You never drink more than two."

"I thought it would help me sleep," Peter confessed. "I thought I'd go to bed early so I'd be well rested when meeting Hoffman from corporate. Did I tell you he wanted to put me in charge of the new hires?"

"Why did you invite Aunt Chrissy over then?" Alex asked, peering out the window in an apparent effort to ignore his sister who was trying to show him her notebook.

"I never invited—"

A short burst of knocks on the door, rapid and authoritative. Peter had only risen halfway out of his chair when the front door flew back against its hinges. He winced at the familiar: "Hello, hello lovelies. Who wants to come give Aunt Chrissy a hug?"

Alex remained nonchalant in his seat while Elaine jumped up to greet the broad woman with the long, chemically platinum hair. Peter groaned, put off by the idea of having to entertain his sister. The dismay only lasted for a moment though, until his eyes landed on the open notebook his daughter had left on the table. Peter stared at the crude sketch of the bloody circle that haunted his dreams. The warm buzz of alcohol was no longer a relief, serving only to blur the already thinning line between reality and that which lies on the other side.

"Oh good, you already know why I'm here. That's such a relief, because I spent the whole way over trying to think of how to tell you."

Peter traced his sister's gaze to the open notebook and his heart sank a little more. He had a sudden urge to stop time, knowing full well this could be the last moment before dreams stopped being dreams.

"Hey! That looks familiar," Alex said, noticing the notebook for the first time.

"See? I told you, but you wouldn't listen. It's the same circle you were talking about, isn't it?"

"Yeah, I even recognize that loopy spiral thing at the bottom. Wow, you got it almost exactly."

"I told you! I told you! And that's you and me, sitting in the middle."

"What are you all talking about?" Margaret asked, the sweetness in her voice brittle as thin ice.

"Hello Chrissy, what a pleasant surprise," Peter interrupted. "Is there an occasion we can thank for this interruption?"

"Oh don't play dumb with me, Peter—you know you always win that game. It's George, you know it's him."

"Who is George?" Margaret asked. "I do love games, but I'm beginning to feel left out of this one."

"George. George Hampton, Peter's brother. Has he never told you about him? Goodness me, how long have you two been married? Almost twenty years—you'd think it would have come out by now."

"He's never told us!" Elaine squealed.

"That's right," Aunt Chrissy said, putting down her glittering bedazzled purse on an empty chair and joining them at the table. "And he's coming to visit us after all this time. Isn't that nice?"

Peter had gone quite pale by this point. He went to the fridge to retrieve a fourth bottle of beer, more to have something to do with his body than out of any real desire to drink. Then again he didn't have to talk while he was drinking, and if he drank enough then maybe he'd wake up and this would turn out to be part of the dream too.

"Peter? Is there something you'd like to tell me?" Margaret prodded.

"No, not really," he answered honestly between gulps.

"Alex—Elaine—I'm going to need both of your help with this. Peter, if you really aren't comfortable, then you and Margaret can go out for a movie this evening and let me help out with the kids. We'll be all finished by the time you get back."

"You're not thinking of really... in my kitchen? No, absolutely not, out of the question."

"Ewww gross!" Elaine exclaimed. "Why do you have a chicken, Aunt Chrissy? Is it alive?"

The sleepy three-legged mutt Bilbo had arrived on the scene and had begun to ferociously sniff Aunt Chrissy's purse.

"Don't be silly, of course it's dead. Who goes around with a live chicken in their purse? Oh don't give me that look, Peter. You're perfectly free to participate or not; I don't see how this is going to be a problem for you."

"You don't see how summoning a demon in my kitchen is a problem!?" If those words weren't spoken in anger, he might have had a chance to stop himself from saying them at all. It was too late now though, and the moment of silence which followed only magnified the weight of his words.

"Yes. Absolutely yes," Alex said, grinning from ear to ear. "You did say demon, right?"

"Can we each have one, or do we have to share?" Elaine asked innocently.

"You should have stopped at two beers," Margaret said testily. "I'm sorry, Chrissy, but this really isn't a good night."

"See, now look what you've done? You've gotten your poor wife all worried over nothing," Aunt Chrissy said, laying a reassuring hand on Margaret's arm and causing her to flinch. "George isn't a demon at all. I mean, sure, maybe he used to be, but who hasn't in the big scheme of things? The point is that he's been human for a good long while. He is dead, however, and apparently needs us to summon him because he's gotten stuck in the demon world. Also, do you happen to have any thyme in the cupboard?"

"I'll—I'll have to go check," Margaret managed, eager for any excuse to pull away from the woman. She passed Peter on his way back from the fridge and seized him by the arm. "I've always known your sister wasn't right in the head. Ever since she started hanging out with those dreadful—what's she call them—her *coven*! You have to do something!"

"Why me?"

"What do you mean *'why you?'* Who else? She's your sister and clearly needs help!"

"Is this exactly how you remember the circle going?" Aunt Chrissy asked, leaning over the notebook with Elaine. "I thought I remembered it being more symmetrical. This looks more like a goose egg."

"It definitely had a top and the bottom. In my dream it looked bigger at the bottom," Alex said, leaning in from the other side.

"Do you really mean to say that all of you have been having the same dream?" Margaret asked. She clutched the bottle of thyme to her chest protectively as though it was a knife needed for self-defense. She watched her children and Aunt Chrissy nod before rounding on her husband. "You too? With the same circle and everything?"

Several competing emotions flashed across Peter's face as they all struggled for the microphone. "It was only a dream, dear," emerged at last, spoken in such an unsteady voice that it could not hope to calm her down.

"What do you mean George is 'dead'?" Margaret tried again.

"Oh dear, now I understand why you're confused," Chrissy replied cheerfully. "It's just that he doesn't have a physical body anymore. He's a spirit, so you probably won't even be able to see him."

"That doesn't make it better," Margaret replied adamantly.

"It doesn't make it worse," Peter said, half-apologetic. Margaret glared daggers at him.

"So... it's just... all sort of a game then..." Margaret said, nodding as though to encourage the others to nod along with her.

Chrissy opened her mouth to reply, freezing in an 'O' shape as she caught Peter's eyes. "That's right, dear. It's all a game. For the children. How hilarious that you thought this was all real."

Margaret visibly melted in relief as her shoulders softened. She set the thyme down on the table, casting a suspicious glance at the dead chicken peeking out of Chrissy's purse. Bilbo was sitting rigidly to attention beneath the table, waiting for someone to include him in the game.

"Alright then... if it's just a game. Just make sure you clean everything when you're finished. Honey, can I have a word with you upstairs?"

"Um, actually I think it might be better if I supervise down here.

Make sure things don't get out of hand. But I'll be up as soon as the game is over and tell you all about it."

"I'm sure you will. It was nice seeing you again, Chrissy." Up the stairs Margaret went, taking them two at a time.

"High school, huh?" Aunt Chrissy said, leaning back to admire the children. "And this is the first time you've ever summoned something from the Netherworld? Peter, you should be ashamed of yourself."

"Of course I am. All the time. Isn't everyone?" Peter replied, looking down at his beer. "Alright, let's get this over with. Alex, why don't you grab the chicken, and Elaine, we're going to need a bowl for its blood. Not one of the china ones, please."

Elaine didn't like looking at the blood on the tile floor, and she refused to sit inside the circle. She figured she already did her job by drawing the runes from her dream, and she was happy just to watch and keep Bilbo from interfering.

Alex didn't mind at all. He thought the blood was cool, and said he would be getting a better grade in his art class if they let him paint with it instead. Peter told his son never to say that during school, or out of school, or just to be safe, to never say it again.

Peter volunteered to sit in the circle so his children wouldn't have to. He hadn't wanted to, but the action allowed him to focus on his pride for being such a brave and protective father. It helped him not focus on his meeting with corporate tomorrow, and the fact that they were about to summon his dead brother's spirit tonight.

Aunt Chrissy reviewed the circle at the end, correcting a few of the symbols and distributing leaves, berries, and herbs strategically throughout. Elaine found some old birthday candles in one of the drawers, which they lit and placed around the circle. Alex jumped up to turn off the lights, and they all stood and admired the glistening blood beneath the flickering flames.

"Are you sure the spell requires birthday candles?" Peter asked sarcastically.

"Not specifically, but it does look better with lights off, now doesn't it? If you're going to play, you have to be a good sport,"

Chrissy scolded him. "Go on, take your seat in the middle. One spirit won't take more than five minutes, tops."

Peter obliged by entering the circle, grumbling as he did so to make sure his children knew their aunt wasn't really the boss of him. Elaine and Alex both seemed too excited to let his resistance get them down.

"How come you never told us about uncle George?" Elaine asked her father.

"Is it because he's weird like Aunt Chrissy?" Alex volunteered.

"Well excuse me for wanting to let the dead rest in peace," Peter sniffed. "Really Chrissy, I'm sure the dreams would have gone away on their own without all this nonsense. And what will we do if we can't get rid of him once we've brought him back?"

"Family picnics, I imagine," Aunt Chrissy replied amiably. "All you've got to do is sit very still in the center where the lines of blood converge. Try your best not to move at all, especially when his spirit starts to pull itself free from your body."

"How will we know it's happening if we can't see the spirit?" Elaine asked. She was sitting quite close to the circle now as Bilbo had continued scooting forward. Her fascination with the ceremony was apparently overwhelming her distaste for the chicken blood.

"Don't worry, I'll let you know. George will still be able to hear you, and I'll be the medium that tells you everything he's saying." Aunt Chrissy then pulled a small black notebook from her purse, flipped open to where a pressed wildflower was being used as a bookmark, and began to chant unfamiliar words in a low sing-song voice.

"This was in my dream too!" Elaine exclaimed. "I'd forgotten all about it though. How do you think she remembers it all so well?"

"This isn't her first spirit," Peter replied morosely. "You can't imagine how many problems George and she caused when we were all children before the incident."

Alex and Elaine gasped simultaneously, staring at their father with wide fearful eyes.

"Oh don't give me that look. You already know he's dead, otherwise what would be the point in summoning his spirit?"

"Stop talking! You're supposed to be staying still!" Chrissy snapped. She'd stopped chanting and was now staring at her brother with the same wild-eyed intensity. Peter didn't think he could get more uneasy than he already was, but every passing second competed with the last for that achievement. An itching, burning sensation was growing on the back of Peter's head, and he didn't have to be well versed in spirits to know that he shouldn't be able to physically feel them. The alarm on the faces of the onlookers perpetuated the feeling that something was going terribly wrong.

Slowly, as calmly as he could, Peter lifted a hand to feel what was going on behind his head. His fingers brushed up against warm, living skin. It wasn't his. He didn't have to see it to clearly visualize the creature pulling its way out of his head.

Bilbo started barking and Elaine screamed. Alex jumped to his feet, knocking over the wooden chair he sat on in the process. Even Aunt Chrissy seemed dumbstruck by what she was seeing, but she still cut through the commotion with an authoritative command.

"It's very important that you don't move, Peter. She's getting out just fine on her own, so please be patient."

"She? What do you mean, she? What did we summon? What is coming out of me?"

"A girl!" Elaine nearly shouted. "There's a girl about my age dressed all in black! Where is she coming from?"

"And a spirit too. A boy, wearing grey without any shoes on. And there's George Hampton! George, you never told me you were bringing company!"

A fresh scream rattled them all to their bones. Margaret began to descend the stairs to see what all the fuss was about just in time to see the top half of a teenage girl pulling herself out of her husband's body. Their skin appeared fused together at the point of contact, although it didn't take long before the girl had completely pulled herself free and the pair had separated into two unique bodies.

"Three nights!" Samantha declared. "You've been dreaming about summoning us for three whole nights before you got around to it! I know I should be thankful and all, but what if we were being crushed or eaten and needed your help? We could have been dinner for demons, thanks all the same."

"Did you say demons?" Margaret gasped. She was as white as a ghost and had to cling onto the banister with both hands to avoid toppling down the stairs.

"I absolutely did. You are all related to George, aren't you? Didn't your dreams give you time to prepare for having demons in your house? Oh hello there, who is a good boy?" Bilbo had stopped barking and was wagging in excitement at the visitor. "I see you've already got a dog, so a demon won't seem like that much trouble."

"They're only mortal, Sam. You can't expect everyone to take their dreams as seriously as you do," Noah said. He and George had now fully emerged from Peter's body as well, although no one was paying them as much attention, as they were invisible to most of the Hampton family.

"You're right, you're right, I've been unfair." Samantha sighed. "Let's start over. Hello my name is Samantha. I'm not a demon; I'm just an ordinary girl who happens to be sharing her face with a dead soul. I trust you already know George—yes he's still dead—and that over there is Noah, also dead. Used to be a demon, trying to make friends with his old demon pals again."

"How do you do?" Peter asked meekly, looking to his wife for support. Margaret hurried down the remaining steps to stand protectively in front of her two children, neither of which looked like they needed protection at all. Alex and Elaine were completely enthralled by what they had just witnessed and didn't appear afraid in the least.

"Just peachy, thank you," Samantha replied with a curtsy, "but I must confess our work has just begun. Now who wants to learn how they can summon demons to save the world?"

"Can we, mom?" Alex asked eagerly.

"We promise to clean up any messes they make," Elaine added hopefully.

"Ask your father," Margaret replied weakly.

"Oh Peter, yes let's," Aunt Chrissy coaxed. "What better way to make it up to George than showing we don't look down on him for being different than us. You can't carry a secret like that with you until your grave and not expect it to you weigh you down. You can fight it like you did when we were kids, you can run from it like you did your whole life, or we can all work together and be a family again."

"Please please please please can I have a demon?" Alex needled.

"Okay okay, we can summon one. One! And remember what you promised about cleaning up after it."

"Peter!" Margaret bellowed.

"What? You told them to ask me!"

"Oh we're going to need a lot more than one," Samantha said. Then in response to Peter's uneasy cough, she hastily added: "But once you see how well the first one behaves under a strict contract, I'm sure you won't mind the others. They're so eager to get out of the Netherworld that I'm sure they'll be on their best behavior. Noah, you'll be in charge of the contracts, okay?"

"I'm already on it," Noah replied, accepting the notebook which Elaine handed to him.

"And this Noah is... one of the dead spirits that I can't see?" Peter asked uncertainly.

"That's right. Although he used to be a Prime demon in a previous life, which helped him remember the demonic language for the contracts. As you can see, we're really trying to be as upfront and honest about everything we can."

"And Prime demons are..."

"One of the three original demons that are either responsible for the balance of the universe, or an apocalypse that destroys it, or maybe both. Depending on who you ask."

"I... see... well alright then," Peter said, who didn't really see at all and was sure it would not be alright if he did. "And you said my brother is here? Right now, in this room?"

"All is well, old friend," George Hampton said, smiling and bobbing despite being invisible to his brother. "I harbor no ill will for your role in sending me down this path."

"That's right," Aunt Chrissy confirmed. "He says he forgives you too. Oh I'm so glad we could all get together again like this. Do you think we should call mom and let her know that we're all here getting along?"

"I tried to visit her in the mirror once," George replied. "Scared her half to death, the poor thing. No, people will have enough to get used to with all the demons, let's not push them to accept spirits at the same time."

"Then we all agree," Samantha declared decisively. "We'll only summon a few to start—one to start, just one for Alex and one for Elaine, so two—so we can prove how polite they can be. Then once people see how useful demons are, everyone will be clamoring for one of their own. Before you know it humans and demons will be friends, and we won't let anyone pit us against each other ever again. We might want to do this outside though, just in case the carpet and curtains catch fire."

AN IMP FOR EVERYONE

THERE WAS SNOW OUTSIDE IN THE QUIET TOWN THAT NOAH AND THE others found themselves within. Samantha stared at the white ground in disbelief, having trouble coming to terms with the fact that months had passed since they first entered the Netherworld. Noah knew exactly how she felt. Despite spending his whole life in the living world, it seemed surreal and alien to him now. To walk on solid ground beneath the dark blue sky, with familiar scents and sounds and all those lonely souls obliviously going about their lives.

Standing here, it was hard to believe that countless people woke up every morning, went to work, and even kissed their families without a soul inside to guide them. The very existence of other worlds, populated by monstrous beings and ancient rites seemed preposterous. The thought that every man, woman, child, and stray cat alike might spend their few short years on earth only to become trapped in a stone, sending the rest of time reflecting on the brief life they had lived. Or worse to have their life force harnessed to power a gargoyle or battery—too horrible to even imagine.

"What would the world be like, if everyone shared the same soul?" Noah asked Samantha. He wasn't sure if he really wanted a reply, or whether he just couldn't bear the burden of that thought alone.

"It might be peaceful, but man would it be boring," Samantha replied. "I've been thinking a lot about what the Bah-Rabba Kabaa said about wisdom, and how it has to do with finding a greater truth that rises above the conflict of two lesser truths. As bad as conflict seems, I think some degree of it is necessary for people to grow. A single soul for the whole world might not even be that peaceful. If I was the only one in the world, I might just end up tearing my own hair out for the pointlessness of it all. Self-destruction would be even worse than people fighting each other, because how could anyone ever grow from that?"

George Hampton offered brief instructions for summoning the first imps, but Noah felt like he already knew what he was doing after his apprenticeship with the demonology professor Salice. Alex and Elaine were ecstatic about their new imps, which in turn were overjoyed to be released into the living world once more. Alex returned from the garage with one of Bilbo's leashes for his imp, but the demon decided that was firmly below his dignity and promised once more to behave if it could be free. Likewise Elaine wanted nothing more than to dress her imp up in some of her old pajamas, a suggestion which was met with less resistance as the imp suspiciously tolerated the garments.

Noah explained thoroughly that the imps were only permitted to be here if they didn't attack anyone or cause too much trouble. Not even the Soulless ones were to be bothered. The imps reluctantly agreed, on the condition that they wouldn't be asked to serve anyone who didn't have a soul. Fortunately Peter and his family were all fully human, and this wouldn't cause any immediate problems.

It was late into the night by the time the first pair of imps were summoned and instructed. Aunt Chrissy had continued to supervise while Peter and Margaret had gone to bed, and the children were clearly exhausted despite their excitement. The imps were instructed to clean up the mess, but when one of them tried to pull down the curtains to wipe the floor, it became clear they would require continued supervision.

"Are we sure this is going to work out?" Samantha asked in exasperation as she pulled one of the imps from the couch where he'd been hiding from Bilbo. "We're going to need to summon a lot of demons if this is going to work, and they won't all be little imps either. We can't keep an eye on all of them at once, so we're going to have to start trusting humans more and more with their own demons. We all know how reckless humans can be."

"You *are* human. You don't get to talk about humans like some sort of exotic animal," Noah protested.

"Hmph. You know that doesn't count, because I'm more of a witch than anything else. All I'm saying is that the demons are going to become plenty noticeable plenty fast. I don't know how we're going to stop the Trans Dimensional Department from noticing what we're up to before we've summoned enough to make a difference."

"I knew there was something special about you, girl," Aunt Chrissy exclaimed. "A witch, you should have said so earlier!"

"Well it's not like I have a certificate or anything," Samantha replied.

"Hardly important. I never received one myself, and neither has anyone else in my coven," Aunt Chrissy said, her eyes glittering with pleasure. "Being a witch isn't about what other people think about you though…"

"It's about what you think about yourself," Samantha cut in with satisfaction. "Of course you're a witch—who else would have a dead chicken in their purse just in case? How many of you are there? Will the others help us against the department?"

"I don't know much about the department, and I must confess I'm not exactly a senior member of the organization," Aunt Chrissy replied. "I can't make any promises on their behalf, except that my sisters will sure to be interested in anyone who has been sightseeing in the Netherworld. Especially such a self-confident, driven young lady such as yourself."

"I'll stay here to keep an eye on the freshly summoned imps," George Hampton volunteered. "Peter and I have some catching up to do anyway. I think the barrier in his mind is already coming down, and he'll be able to even see me before long. I'll admit I was a bit trepidatious in returning home, but I'm so pleased and proud to see how accepting you've become of the supernatural since we were children. I couldn't have asked for a better welcome."

The word "coven" conjured all sorts of mystical imagery: witches on broomsticks beneath the gleaming moon, secret gardens to grow occult ingredients, magical potions and powerful enchantments. Samantha could hardly contain her excitement, bouncing from one foot to the other as Aunt Chrissy led them down the dark driveway to where her car was parked on the street. Noah thought it might be better for him to walk to avoid being hurled through the car in the event of a sudden stop, but Aunt Chrissy promised to drive carefully and Samantha offered to hold him in place.

The first bit of glamour died when Aunt Chrissy began alerting the other witches via texts. The feeling was exasperated by the amount of emojis she managed to fit into every sentence.

"I don't suppose you have a crystal ball?" Noah asked as he climbed into the backseat.

"'Course I do," Chrissy replied without looking up from her phone. "Just has a crack on it, that's all. And a bit of dust. It's just so hard to check your email and get games on a crystal ball. What, don't give me that look. I know that look, my nephew gives it to me every year when I give him a basket of toadstools for Christmas. I never made any claims about my skill in witchcraft, only that I was part of a club that was devoted to that sort of thing."

"A club?" Samantha asked, crestfallen.

"A coven. I meant a coven, absolutely," Aunt Chrissy declared, distracted by her phone. "Give me some credit; I summoned you, didn't I?"

"As long as someone has a working scrying crystal that I can use to contact Mr. Wolf and Walter," Noah replied. "We're going to need their help too, and you can't text the dead."

Aunt Chrissy looked out the window as though pondering this thought for several seconds before turning back to her phone. She put it down shortly after and started the car.

"Mrs. Velleur will have one for sure," Aunt Chrissy replied. "She's the leader of the group—I mean coven—and you ought not to cross her as she has a bit of a dark side. Also don't comment on the fact she is our leader, as Miss Bailey and Miss Toofin can be rather touchy about the very idea of any form of social hierarchy. Then there's Willow and her boyfriend, who isn't really invited to the coven but sometimes shows up with pastries from his bakery. Oh you're going to love them, I just know it. I do so want to learn about your journey, but don't spoil it for me yet. I want you to tell everything to all my sisters, then I'm sure they'll want to help as much as they possibly can."

"Your coven meets in a diner?" Samantha asked in a deflated voice as they entered.

"Not all the time," Aunt Chrissy replied defensively. "Anyway, it's after midnight, and not everywhere is open. Besides you look half starved to death, you poor dear. Yoohoo girls! I've got visitors!"

The word "coven" would not have been the first to come to mind to anyone watching Miss Toofin eating baked beans out of a can with a spoon. Miss Bailey was drinking coffee out of a plastic skull and looked like she had been woken up several days too early. Willow was a pale faced, pretty young woman wearing a thick coat and mittens, looking ridiculous in the warm room. In fact the only one that properly looked like a witch was Mrs. Velleur, from the grim expression on her severely angled face, down her tightly buttoned black wool dress, all the way to her tall black boots with their wide silver buckles. Samantha seemed primarily interested in her.

"Remember what George Hampton said about telling the truth," Noah softly reminded Samantha. "We're going to need to trust them if there's ever a chance of them trusting us. Don't be afraid to tell them anything."

And that's exactly what they did. At first Noah thought he would only hit the main points before quickly getting to the task at hand, but more and more was drawn out of him. The women were all so warm and curious and comforting, except perhaps Mrs. Velleur who barely said a word or changed her rigid, sharp expression. All of them could see Noah except for Miss Toofin, who had to keep whispering back and forth with the ample Miss Bailey to keep up. Samantha kept ordering dishes one after the other, talking between mouthfuls until the full arc of their journey was complete.

"... so we're going to need help summoning the demons back from the depths of the Netherworld where they've been banished," Noah concluded. "Do you think you can help us prove that demons and the living can get along?"

"Will the demons obey their contracts?" Mrs. Velleur enunciated precisely.

"Of course they will," Samantha said. "And Noah is completely fluent in demonic, so he can specify exactly what rules they should follow. Then we figure once everyone starts seeing how useful demons are, they're all going to want one."

"But will all the humans obey? I see you're counting on more than just having demons do what they're told. Your plan also requires that all the people who have demons aren't going to start turning them on each other. What is it about human nature which leads you to this conclusion?"

Noah and Samantha exchanged an uncomfortable glance under Mrs. Velleur's scrutiny.

"We'll cover that in the contract too," Noah answered. "We'll make it so any demon that tries to attack another human or demon or soulless or... no, we'll just ban any kind of violence at all. And if they do, the magic in the contract will send them straight back to the Netherworld."

"And what if a demon is ordered to steal something for the owner? Or give a car a flat tire. Or they're put to work in a factory, and all the people working there lose their jobs."

"Well, um..."

"There is no end to the creativity of humans in their capacity to make each other miserable. There's a reason demons have not been common in the living world for such a long time. Trouble follows them, whether they are morally responsible or not. I'm sorry, but putting that much power indiscriminately into the hands of even well intentioned people seems neither prudent nor wise."

The other witches hung their heads in disappointment at Mrs. Velleur's words, but none of them pushed back against her.

"Trouble is already here, Mrs. Velleur, whether you like it or not," Noah replied quietly. "It isn't a matter of whether or not I trust every single person. I trust people as a whole more than I trust The Matriarch or the Trans Dimensional Department. I trust an uncertain future more than I trust certain despair. If you believe what I've told you about her plan, then you must help us stop her through any means necessary."

Mrs. Velleur's eyes were locked on Noah while she reached down to retrieve a cigarette from her purse. She placed it unlit into her mouth, whereupon it immediately began to smolder and leak pale pink smoke. A deep inhale, and all the other witches seemed to be holding their breath until the smoke was released and she spoke again.

"No," Mrs. Velleur said at last, taking another long drag on her cigarette.

"They aren't wrong, Velleur," Willow said sharply, earning herself a puff of pink smoke in the face as the older witch turned her direction.

"Mrs. Velleur, be reasonable," Aunt Chrissy pleaded. "They've come straight from the Netherworld! They've seen and know all sorts of things that even we—"

"No, no, we're afraid not. While we sympathize with your desire to do good, you are all too rash and impatient. It is so easy to get caught up in the motion of the waves that one loses sight of the ocean. There is good reason not to trust the department, but these political cycles will come and go, and there will be new challenges that also seem like the end of the world, and so on and so on—"

"Fine then, who needs you?" Samantha shot back.

Mrs. Velleur was so surprised at being interrupted that the cigarette fell from her open mouth onto the table.

"We'll do it without you, and Miss Toofin, and Miss Bailey, and Willow, and Aunt Chrissy—they're all going to help us, because they don't need anyone's permission to do what they know is right. Isn't that true, ladies? Witches don't let anyone tell them what to do."

"But aren't you telling us what to do now?" Miss Bailey voiced hesitantly. "How is that any different?"

"No, I'm not," Samantha replied stubbornly. "I'm showing you the right thing to do, and letting you choose it for yourself."

"Rude, nasty girl," Mrs. Velleur scoffed. "What do you know about summoning demons? You won't find another witch with half the power I have. You can't summon an army of demons without me, and you won't have my help. The answer is no."

"Bah-Rabba Kaba is going to help us," Samantha shot back, "and she's twice the witch you'll ever be. We're going to scry her, and the teachers at Noah's Mortuary, and the demonic instructors from the Sylo, and we're all going to work together because that's what good witches do. Good witches see broken pieces and know how to make them whole again. They don't just look at them and cry about how they're supposed to be broken."

A ferocious glare passed between Samantha and Velleur that surely would have sizzled anything unfortunate enough to pass between them. The girl then added in a softer voice: "But first I think I'd like to call my mother and tell her not to worry about me, because she who faces her destiny has nothing to fear from friends or foe. Thank you for the pancakes all the same. They were fluffy and warm and delicious, and I'll pay you back once I've finished saving the world."

For the first time Mrs. Velleur smiled. She reached within the thick folds of her clothing and withdrew a crystal ball a little smaller than Samantha's head. Without a word she rolled it across the table for the girl to catch. A moment later, and a cell phone was slapped onto the table and slid across as well.

Samantha snatched the cell phone, and for a moment seemed torn between it and the crystal ball. With a deep breath she placed the crystal aside and began to dial a number on the phone. As she lifted it to her ear, Miss Toofin could be heard whispering to Mrs. Velleur: "You've got to respect a girl who calls her mother before saving the world."

"I respect anyone who I can learn from," Mrs. Velleur obliged. "I believe she has earned all of our respect in that regard."

"Mom? ... Yeah, it's me... No I can't come home yet, but I wanted to let you know that I miss you. And I love you. And to ask if you'd like to have a demon do my chores until I get back."

NOAH AND SAMANTHA retired to Peter and Margaret Hampton's house to rest, although the first shafts of silver light were already lancing the horizon by the time they arrived. Weariness hung thick about them, and Noah privately dreaded the additional cleaning that might need to be done in wake of the imps they'd already summoned. The place was extraordinarily tidy, however, with one of the imps cleaning the windows while the other pulled weeds from the flower beds where George Hampton was dozing.

The old man was smiling to himself in his sleep, all the obstacles of their journey having slid off him without a trace. Noah supposed that he himself might wear such an expression one day when he was with his family once more. His grandson would be simply happy to see him, unburdened by the knowledge of Noah's perilous journey and without judgement for the mistakes he made along the way. Someday life would go on like it was always supposed to, and Noah would be part of that life. He may himself forget everything he had been through, just as he had forgotten all the trials of the lives he'd lived before, but that would be alright so long as he could appreciate each new life for the miracle that it was.

The process of bringing demons into the living world fell into three broad phases: gathering allies, connecting with humans, and the summoning itself. Of course there was also the fourth step of bringing back time to the depths of the Netherworld where it could be used to open the doors of Almorda, but there was already enough going wrong with the first steps to worry about that for now.

They were surprised and gratified when the scrying task was aided by Velleur, who admittedly seemed more interested in meeting Bah-

Rabba Kaba than she did in the plan actually succeeding. Each time the crystal ball pierced the nebulous nether, the old witch chanted mystical words that Samantha was swift to emulate. Together they expanded their vision into a myriad of alien worlds that looked nothing like the orange soil of Bah-Rabba Kaba's home. After a dozen or more attempts, it became clear that the higher dimensional space of the Netherworld was so enormous that contact would be more challenging than anticipated. Velleur remained intent upon her task though, and she was left to continue searching while Noah and Samantha pursued the more manageable task of contacting the school.

Willow scrounged up a second scry ball—cracked and cloudy though it may be—although she was so proud of her possession that Noah wouldn't think to let her know. Noah only had a rudimentary idea of scrying magic, but George Hampton helped narrow the location until they were able to make out Mr. Wolf's tower. Noah figured Wolf's loyalty was firmly rooted in his own self-interest, which the spirit doubtlessly thought remained with the headmistress of the school. They inched their way along the blurry hills, but soon their vision became so distorted that George gave up in frustration. He said there must be an enchantment over the Mortuary to prevent scrying, and that if they were going to contact the teachers they would have to find another way.

A morning filled with hope had been dampened by the two failures, but the severity of their task and the resolve they brought against it would not be dissuaded. Unable to connect with their spiritual allies, Noah and the others would have to introduce the humans to the demons on their own. Noah suggested that Alex and Elaine could introduce their friends to the imps, who would doubtlessly all become jealous and want one of their own. George frowned on this idea, however, thinking that a bunch of children with demons would surely get into too much trouble and draw too much attention to themselves before they'd summoned a sufficient quantity.

Samantha had a better idea. She argued the best people to receive demons first would be those who are mature and responsible. People who don't get out much, people who are isolated and lonely, people who need all the help they can get.

"No, you don't really mean—" Noah protested.

"Exactly. Just think about it. Who would benefit more from having their own demon than the elderly? And once they've grown attached to them, what right minded person is going to force old people to get rid of their cherished pets and helpers?"

The witches Toofin and Bailey thought it was a marvelous idea and volunteered to help at once. As luck would have it, Miss Toofin was a nurse who frequently traveled to patient's homes to administer care. Samantha and George accompanied her to perform the summonings while Noah remained at the Hampton's house to copy as many contracts as his trembling fingers would allow. After a few practice drafts, he produced one that meticulously forbid as many ways of harming people as possible. There was no going back now—just as the prophetic nature of the Prime demons foretold, the beginning of either salvation or apocalypse was at hand.

This stage of the plan was a roaring success. The companionship and utility of the demons proved an irresistible gift, and word was beginning to spread through the older community. Once they finished providing demons for people who lived in their own homes, they moved onto group retirement facilities where the demons were as much appreciated by the healthcare workers as they were by the elderly. The orange, goopy Moolang Spool was a particular favorite, as the pressure of its skin had the miraculous ability to mend damaged bones, arthritic hands, and all sorts of internal ills that could not otherwise be addressed without surgery. It wasn't long before hospitals all over the state were submitting requests to have their own demons in residence.

The resistance to the demons was lighter than Noah had dared to hope. The little monsters were so thankful for being summoned that they readily obeyed to their contracts, and for now none of them even wanted to test the bounds of what they could get away with. They were so stupendously useful—from heating homes, to generating electricity, to manual labor. The opposition to demons only lasted until the offended party was able to obtain a demon of their own. Sludge-like demons were more than happy to take on the foulest work in the sewers, while Gobblers consumed trash and garbage without any problems besides the occasional noxious belch.

It turns out that a large part of the appeal to demons was for them to do the jobs that people were unable or unwilling to do. Demons could perform difficult jobs under short durations, immediately releasing them and allowing them to return to the nether with the power of a completed contract. This allowed a rotating shift of demons to bring back a constant stream of time back to the Netherworld, thus aiding the great ritual. It was difficult to calculate exactly how much time was required to open the doors of Almorda, but their operation was expanding as quickly as Noah could copy out the contracts, and they were sure to make real progress if they were allowed to continue uninterrupted.

Less than a week passed before the sighting of the first gargoyle. Samantha was the one to spot it, or perhaps it was the soul in her eye, it was so hard to tell. She traced the path of the gargoyle swooping a low arc over the town before it hastened off in the direction of the Mortuary. Samantha tried to bring it down with a pair of Shawsheen Strikers, but their contracts were so stringent that there was no room to instigate violence of any kind. She explained all of this to Noah in the evening after she had returned from a full day of summoning.

"It's only a matter of time now before the department shows up," Samantha explained in frustration. "You should have left a clause about it being okay to attack the kind of spirits that are going to try and stop us."

"No, you were right to forbid violence," George countered, drifting through Miss Toofin's car and joining Noah in the garden. In a matter of days the imps had transformed the wilted flower beds into a thriving nursery. Thick, fresh soil was bursting with dozens of fledgling plants, including a few exotic polk-a-dot ones that Noah was sure hadn't come from this world.

"Having the moral high ground is real nice until you get hit," Samantha grumbled. "Mrs. Velleur still hasn't found Bah-Rabba Kaba, and we won't have anyone fighting for us when the department comes. We're all going to get banished back to the Netherworld, and all this work will have been for nothing."

"It's even worse than that." Noah sighed. "The demons can be banished, but we won't be. And this time we don't have any way to follow them, so we might even be captured. We might be put in a soul stone, or sent off to The Matriarch to do what she likes with us. Maybe we should quit now before it's too late."

"We've come too far to stop," George Hampton replied with a knowing smile. "The demons and the living are already getting along better than I thought possible. Keep up the summoning: I have a plan to deal with old Theodore if he ever dares to show his face around here."

Try as they might, the others couldn't get a straight answer out of George regarding his plan, but they trusted him to act when the time was right. Until then it was up to Noah and Samantha to make sure the demons were so thoroughly fused with society as to be absolutely integral to the living.

"We can ship them," Samantha volunteered.

"What, like in a box? In the mail?" Noah asked, skeptical.

"Why not? Can't you tell how happy they are to be summoned from the Netherworld? Being in a box isn't nearly as difficult as going through one of those dimensional rifts, or some of the nasty places they live in over there. Besides, they'll be harder to banish if we spread them out more."

So their operation expanded again. Miss Toofin and Bailey initially treated Witchcraft more as a cultural icon than a communion with nature, but now they were embracing the occult and were more than eager to help any way they could. The demand for demons was now too great to be supplied without more assistance, and these fledgling witches were the perfect acolytes to learn the art of summoning. Willow and Aunt Chrissy refused to be left out either, and between the lot of them they were bringing in nearly a hundred demons every day.

It wasn't long before it was more common to see a flock of imps than a flock of pigeons drifting through the park. New gardens were sprouting up everywhere with alien plants thriving in the native soil, and the streets had never been so clean with bounding gobblers diving on every stray piece of trash. From transportation, to growing food, to earning money, it seemed that so long as demons lived to serve the humans they would never go without. There were more gargoyle sightings, but for some reason they never stuck around long, and soon they were ignored completely.

Everything seemed too good to be true until all of a sudden it wasn't. The popularity of the demons had grown consistently so long as they were viewed as a universal good, but as their numbers continued to increase, so too did the evidence of the silent divide within the community. The demons refused to serve nearly half the people in town, a fact that was growing harder to ignore with every passing day. Noah wasn't sure how the word leaked out, but suddenly everyone seemed to know: if someone wanted a demon but didn't have one, it was probably because they didn't have a soul to serve. For the first time it became possible to identify who had a soul and who didn't, and things would never be the same.

The same day that realization began to spread, more rumors began to fly. A young woman had been killed on her way to class at the local community college. Her dress was torn in a dozen places, and burns and tooth marks covered her body. The girl did not have a demon of her own, and by all accounts had never wanted one.

The reaction from the town was immediate, visceral, and utterly divided. To those who didn't have demons, this was proof that these monsters were a threat and a menace to society. To those who had learned to depend on the demons, it was equally clear that the soulless were the ones who did not belong.

Two more bodies were found that night, ripped and maimed almost beyond recognition. They clearly appeared to be demon attacks, although Noah maintained that was impossible as the contracts would immediately banish any demon which tried to violate them. The evidence of their eyes could not be disputed though, which quickly led them to a deeply unsettling answer.

They weren't the only ones summoning demons anymore. Someone else was writing contracts too, and these contracts permitted, if not encouraged, their demons to kill. If they didn't put a stop to this soon, then it was only a matter of time before the whole town devolved into violence.

THE LIVING AND THE DAMNED

THE WINTER AIR IS SUPPOSED TO SMELL CLEAN AND COLD AND PURE. The occasional foul odor is expected from a town of any size, but the flavor which now tainted everything was more than can be explained by the distant blood of the victims. It was the smell of fear which pervaded every house, wafting down every street, reflected on every face. These outsiders that were welcomed into the town were no longer to be trusted, and no one knew where the next attack would be.

No one except Mrs. Velleur, that is, the stern witch who had been staring into her crystal ball so long that she'd forgotten how to blink. Her eyes radiated weariness as they peeled away from their crystal to bore through Noah and Samantha as though the children were hardly there.

"You'd better not say I told you so," Samantha snapped, breaking the chilly tension in the air. "It wasn't one of our demons who attacked someone, and you know it. What's going on isn't our fault."

"Then I will tell you so, and so it will be," Mrs. Velleur replied. "I'm not interested in bickering over the past, not when the future is so much more interesting. I have spoken with the Bah-Rabba Kaba, and she can remember what is yet to come."

Samantha shifted uneasily from one foot to the other. George Hampton placed a comforting hand on her shoulder to steady her. Behind them Peter, Margaret, and Aunt Chrissy had their backs to the wall of their living room. Their two children clutched their imps to their chest with their dog Bilbo dozing between them, unwilling to relinquish their demons despite the looming threat which hung over them all.

"Is she coming to help us?" Samantha asked hopefully.

Mrs. Velleur ran her fingers over the crystal in a practiced motion. Noah and Samantha crowded closer to peer into the swirling depths, but to their disappointment the elder witch did not resolve into view. Rather there was the body of a young man lying on a park bench, draped in the shadows of the night. A long and bloody line ran from his neck to his hip, seeming so deep that he might split in two and fall away at any moment. Noah glanced out the window, noting that the sun had not yet set.

"He isn't dead yet, is he?" Noah guessed. "We can still save him?"

The stern witch furrowed her brow and said nothing.

"I recognize that park. It's Beaver's Glen, on the other side of town," Margaret said in a small voice. "It's the demons that are doing this, isn't it? Just like the ones the children have."

Elaine's imp clucked angrily, and she held onto it even tighter. "Our imps would never do something like that. You can still stop the bad ones though, can't you?"

"The Bah-Rabba Kaba has seen this," Mrs. Velleur replied, a tremor in her voice. "The man will die. The only question is whether he will be the last or not."

"Who says he has to die?" Samantha asked. "The sun hasn't even set yet."

"We should hurry," Aunt Chrissy agreed. "I can drive."

"I want to go too," Alex said defiantly. "People will never be okay with our demons unless we get rid of the bad ones."

"Absolutely not," their mother said. "Do you want the same thing to happen to you? This is much too dangerous for children."

"What about Samantha? Why does she get to go?"

"I'm not a child," Samantha huffed, already halfway to the door. "I turned fifteen while I was in the Netherworld, and I count as twice that because I'm a witch. What are we waiting for, let's go!"

"The man will die," Mrs. Velleur repeated, stopping Samantha in her tracks. "Do not waste your time on the dead—present company excluded, of course. Look into the crystal: it is the killer that we must find."

There was a growing light inside the crystal ball. The clouds overhead reversed their direction, and the sky blazed bright from the sun which rose from the west. The mortal wound closed in the man's chest, and a dark blur rippled across the orb. A crackling arc of electricity rose out of the crystal before vanishing in a spray of sparks. The image froze on a sleek, glistening bird with beady black eyes and feathers that ended in electrical discharge.

"A Shawsheen Striker will kill him at sunset," Mrs. Velleur said. More blazing current ran through the crystal ball, and in another wave of sparks the image violently dissipated into the air. "The Bah-Rabba Kaba can see no more from her home in the Netherworld, and it is up to us to find the source of these foul summonings and put a stop to them."

"Why doesn't the Bah-Rabba Kaba come here then? Couldn't we summon her?" Noah asked.

"Not against her will, not with an army could you force the elder from her home," Mrs. Velleur replied. "Trust a witch to know where she belongs, just as you trust yourselves to know what must be done. I will keep watch from here and aid you as I'm able, with vision into this world and the next. May the fate awaiting you be kinder to you than it was to the man you seek, and may your mind be at peace knowing his blood is not on your hands."

Aunt Chrissy volunteered to drive George, Samantha, and Noah to the Beaver's Glen park. The streets were quieter than usual, with more demons than living ambling about their tasks. It was that smell of fear in the air, the tension in the atmosphere that voiced the unspoken dread of what they helped come to pass. What if they had been wrong? What if demons and the living were just too different to ever coexist? Noah watched the setting sun as they drove, trying to remember exactly what height it was at the moment the man was killed. Was he already dead? Was it happening right now? Did it even matter?

"There, over those trees—close to the horizon. Did you see that?" Samantha asked. She was sitting in the backseat with Noah, holding onto his arm to keep him flying through the car during a sudden stop.

"Electricity," Noah replied, nodding. "The Shawsheen Striker."

"I'm on it," Aunt Chrissy confirmed, pulling to the right. "I don't know how I'm supposed to keep up with it though."

"Cut across the park!" George insisted.

"What, on the grass? It'll make such a mess!"

"Just do it!"

The car took another sharp turn, then a lurch as it bucked over the sidewalk. Samantha gripped Noah and George by the arm to keep them from flying out of the car. The electricity moved like lightning through the trees, each time pausing to rest a few seconds before launching off again. The car churned the grass to mud beneath the tires as it tore after the escaping demon.

"Oh no. Please no," Aunt Chrissy said. "Not the flower beds."

"Flowers can be replanted, grass can be regrown," George countered sharply. "Don't let it get away."

Aunt Chrissy moaned as if in physical pain as the car thundered over the alien vegetation that the demons had planted in the park. Ordinary flowers wouldn't have had much of a say in this decision, but these plants pulled their roots from the ground and dove out of the way. The demonic bird paused to rest again. They were gaining ground. George Hampton had already detached his right hand and opened a window, preparing to hurl it at the bird. He might have caught it too if the car hadn't made a ghastly crunching sound as it ground to a halt.

"Did we hit something? What happened?" Aunt Chrissy cried.

"No, something hit us," Noah said, his head passing through the floor to peer below. "Some of the plants have grabbed hold of us. Stomp the pedal!"

The car roared in complaint as the tires spun, digging a deeper hole into the mud. Alien vines were snaking their way up the side of the car, intertwining with the metal underneath.

"Drat darn it all to hell," Aunt Chrissy shouted.

Samantha opened the door and leapt out before the vines had a chance to pin them inside. "Look, the Striker has stopped! We can still catch it!"

Just as she spoke, the electricity spun through the air once more, although this time it wasn't dashing through the trees. The lightning lanced down to the ground to illuminate a dark figure with green stringy hair they hadn't noticed before. The demonic bird landed on his forearm, its light radiating onto the face of the figure.

"Meep Warlington?" Noah said, tumbling through the car door after Samantha.

"Who?"

"He's the minister of energy at the trans dimensional department, but he never trusted The Matriarch. I have no idea what he's doing here."

"Noah Tellaver?" Meep Warlington called, just as surprised as they were. He lifted a white-gloved hand to his eyes to peer into the gathering dark. "Is that you?"

The confusion on Meep's face only lasted a moment before he seemed to realize they were pursuing him. He turned to flee, but the delay had already cost him. One of George's hands went flying past Noah's face, clawing its way through the air until it seized hold of Meep by his bright orange tie. Long green hair flailed above Meep's head as he struggled to shake it off, but his violent motions succeeded in nothing but shaking the Shawsheen Striker from his wrist. The lightning bird shot off through the air once more to settle in the trees overhead.

"Dissipati!" Aunt Chrissy shouted. The word traveled through the air as a visible blue wave which overtook the bird, dissolving it into a thick cloud of black smoke.

Meep Warlington began to run. A violent tug on his tie from the disembodied hand sent him spinning to the grass. By the time he'd risen to his knees, Noah and Samantha had already reached him, diving to knock him back to the ground.

"I give up! I surrender! Don't hurt me!" Meep wailed, struggling in vain as George and Aunt Chrissy swiftly came to reinforce.

"What are you doing here? Does The Matriarch know where you are?" Noah demanded.

Meep recovered his wits, his dark eyes glinting with cunning as he scrutinized his assailants and calculated his next move. "I could ask you the same thing. Shouldn't you be in school?"

The two glared at each other suspiciously as Aunt Chrissy caught up with the others. "Mrs. Velleur was right. We're too late," she sighed. "Over there under that big elm tree—the poor man is already dead."

"What I do on official business from the department is of no concern of yours, nosy woman."

Meep tried to stand with an indignant huff, but Samantha put a knee to his chest and forced him back to the ground. He turned his attention on her, and especially toward the hard marble which consumed nearly half her face.

"Is that a... did you survive a gargoyle attack? And it left its power source behind, quite fascinating."

"Her name is Alley, and she isn't a power source. She's a soul, and she has more right to her own body than you do," Samantha replied defiantly. "If you don't explain yourself, I'm going to kick your soul out, lock it in a stone, and grind it to dust. I'm a witch, you know. I can do it if I want."

Meep furrowed his brow, then smiled to display the full range of his grotesquely bent and yellowed teeth. "Very well, go ahead. Although I can't imagine she'll enjoy being in this nasty old corpse better than the body of a little girl which—by the looks of it—she's very close to taking for herself."

Samantha sat back on the grass, fuming at her bluff being called. Or perhaps his comment hit closer to home than she wanted to admit —was that a hint of fear in the girl's ordinarily stoic face?

"We worked together with the dwellers to stop a demon attack before. I don't understand why you're working with them now. If you're honest with me though, I will be honest with you. I know what The Matriarch's plan is, and I know that we both stand to lose if she wins."

"I'm not working with them, I'm using them—the vile monsters. There's a difference," Meep grunted. He was able to sit upright now that Samantha had backed off. Meep moved with excessive caution, casting a distrustful eye on George and Aunt Chrissy to his sides. "You're a clever boy though, it's no wonder The Matriarch chose you as her apprentice. The honest truth is that my mission has nothing to do with the old bat. You see there's an election coming up for prime minister of the department…"

Meep's voice trailed off, as though that explained everything that needed to be known. Confronted with their looks of confusion, he sighed and continued: "Well of course Theodore scored some substantial points by banishing all the demons from the shallow nether, so imagine our surprise when one of my gargoyles spotted the little beasties turning up again here. Worse yet, they were even getting along with people! Can you imagine how bad that looks for a war hero trying to capitalize on his victory?"

"So your mission had nothing to do with The Matriarch?" George Hampton asked suspiciously. His disembodied hand had released its captive and was now crawling its way down his chest, checking his pockets as it went. Meep snatched desperately for the inside of his vest, but the probing fingers darted in first, emerging a moment later twirling a gleaming red stone between their digits. "And I suppose she didn't give you this either?"

"Ah, well, technically no…" Meep said, twisting his lips into an insincere smile. "It might have been a gift for Theodore, and he might have thought I'd find it useful, but in any case there was certainly no scheming going on."

"What is it?" Samantha asked. "That's not a Chainer Battery, is it?"

"No, it's an ordinary soul stone," George Hampton said, retrieving it as his free hand scurried back to him. "One that I believe Noah will be familiar with."

Noah frowned and took the stone, holding it up to the light of the silver moon which had just begun to emerge from the tangled trees obscuring the horizon. A shiver of shock and recognition ran down his spine.

"I've never been very good at summoning demons, truth be told," Meep replied weakly. "They don't seem to like me very much. That's why I was given this tool to help get the job done. You don't have to make it weird or anything."

"Hello boy." Faint as a whisper spoken into the wind.

"It's Salice," Noah said breathlessly. "My demonology teacher in the first year—the one who showed me the Soul Net in the first place."

"The one who wanted to sacrifice your family to summon the Soul Eater," George Hampton reminded sternly. "Do not be too careless around that devil."

"He who fears the prisoner fears his conscience and nothing more," Salice's faint words dispersed through the air. "I see you've failed to bring down The Matriarch, the same as I."

"I was only using it to write the contracts," Meep Warlington admitted. "Now that I've *misplaced* the stone, I'll have to return to Theodore and tell him I cannot continue though. Head hung low and tail between my legs, metaphorically speaking. Such is life, such is death, I suppose I'll be going then…"

"Not so fast," Samantha shoved the minister roughly back into the grass. "A soul isn't an object to be used. And don't think we forgot those contracts you needed help on were for killing people. You aren't getting away that easy."

Meep Warlington sighed and stretched his hands behind his head to rest upon. "I could have been a graceful Angelfish by now, riding free in the ocean currents. Lingering here for power has been one of the worst decisions of my death."

"Are you alright in there?" Noah asked Salice. "You're not in pain or anything, are you?"

"I would trade this for the most excruciating pain, only to feel again. Locked in here, no light or darkness, no body or touch, not living or dying. Just waiting for nothing, forever and ever…"

"Ahh!" Samantha yelped, clutching her marbled face with both hands.

"What's happening? Are you okay?" George asked.

"She wants a body of her own too," Samantha said, grimacing. "Alley no, not yet!"

It was all the distraction Meep needed. A thousand tiny legs like those of a centipede stealthily emerged from his back, and without having to stand upright he shot off across the grass. George took a bound after him, but another cry from Samantha sent him spinning around again. The girl's breathing was coming in short, ragged gasps, and she doubled over in agony.

"Wait until we've found the Primes, and you can have my body!" Samantha spluttered. "I promise, Alley, please be patient."

All at once her breathing slowed. She straightened up, wiping a cold sweat from her forehead. "Don't give me that look—stop Meep! He's getting away!"

But it was too late. The circle of sparks was already radiating through the air, and before they could even begin to close the distance, Meep was already slipping through the portal he'd conjured. "Freeing the Primes, are you? Theodore won't be so disappointed in me after all!" And so cackling Meep slipped into the portal, disappearing in a flash of light.

"Drat, shit, damn it all to hell!" Samantha cursed, pulling on her hair hard enough for a fistful of strands to wrench free of her head. "I shouldn't have said that!"

"Goodness, don't blame yourself, you poor girl," Aunt Chrissy cooed. "We got rid of the beastly man, that's what matters. He won't be summoning any more demons to terrorize the town."

"No, don't you see?" Samantha growled. "The Department is onto us now. They're going to try and stop the doors of Almorda from opening! He's going to ruin everything, and we don't even know how to get back to the Netherworld to stop them!"

"Are you so sure about that?" the feeble words drifted through the night air. "Tell me all that you've learned since I have been imprisoned. If your path is true, then know there is no crevice of the demon haunted world too deep for me to penetrate."

"Can we risk trusting him?" George asked Noah skeptically.

"Can we risk not?" Noah replied. Then to the stone: "First tell us what you know of the Primes, and what freeing them means to you. Why did you never mention them while I was your apprentice? What were you trying to hide?"

"My job was to teach you what is, not what might be. The Primes are to demons what gods are to man, both believed and forgotten, feared and loved, salvation and destruction. First year students have enough to worry about without such a sword hanging over their heads, inescapable in life and death and in between."

"I'm not a child anymore. You can tell me anything."

"We are all children next to the Primes. I cannot tell you much of their appearance as they have taken as many different shapes through the years as stars burn in the sky. I can only tell you what the world looks like when one of them has dominion over the others, for each of them heralds the coming of a new age. When Momslavi Lapis rises to power the oceans rule the land, and great beasts are known to rise from their hidden chambers beneath the sea. Borrowrath the Unsplendid gives rise to the monsters of the mind, unleashing within us that which our sanity pleads us hide. And Zee Zee Balloo is perhaps the most mysterious of them all, with knowledge of the end of time, ushering a twilight where the last soul will splutter out. You see why it is useless to discuss such matters in one's schooling. The speculation on such mythology is beyond the scope of our wildest imagination. It is their constant struggle against one another which has hitherto kept such terrors at bay."

"And if they're all released and reunited? What if they're all getting along?"

The deepening darkness in the quiet park seemed like it could be such a time at the end of the world. Samantha knelt enraptured before the stone, while George and Aunt Chrissy paced a little further back in silent agitation.

"It's funny," Salice mused, his weak voice riddled with cracks. "I had thought since I've left my body behind I would be beyond such mortal perturbations as this veil of fear. You truly wish to bring such a time to pass?"

"Zee Zee Balloo wishes it, yes. He is the one who told me what must be done to stop The Matriarch, and I fear the future she promises more than any you've described. The Prime lives on in me. Whether it is fate or choice that guides me down this path, I do not know. I will do whatever is in my power to stop her though, if only you will help us return to the deepest part of the Netherworld where the other Primes are waiting."

"Zee Zee Balloo… I knew there was something special about you boy, from the moment you stepped up to the weighing ceremony. I too have witnessed the vile future The Matriarch is building. Listen closely to my instructions, and I will tell you how to return."

"The other Witches and I will keep bringing demons into the world while you're gone," Aunt Chrissy said. "I must confess all this business about bringing time back and the end of the world are beyond me, but I know truth seekers and good doers when I see them. I can only imagine the weight of such an awful burden, but I know that pure hearts like yours will do right by the rest of us."

"Thank you, dear sister," George replied. "I will stay to help you with your work. I've reached the limit of my understanding as well, but at least here I know I'll be able to continue to do good."

"You can't leave us now," Samantha said. "We never could have come so far without you."

"You'll need all the time you can get to open those doors—and besides, the witches will need help if old Theodore and the department tries to interfere with us again. Trust yourselves as I trust you, and you will see this mission through to the end."

"You should stay as well, Samantha," Noah said. "Bringing you to the Netherworld once was risky enough, but I know what I'm supposed to do now, and I don't need you to put yourself in danger for my sake again. I'm the only one who needs to go through those doors."

"Nonsense, you're helpless without me," Samantha replied stiffly.

"Alley and I can see things you can't, and even if it turns out that I'm completely useless, then at least you'll have a friend when you need one most."

"You would have made a fine student," Salice whispered, "and perhaps will one day when the Mortuary is run by better hands. It is settled then—I will take the two children to the heart of darkness where the Primes will be reunited at last. I will need you to collect some ingredients though, and one of you will need to write down the following words to say during the ceremony…"

DESPITE HIS LACK OF BODY, Professor Salice had lost none of his insight into the demon world. Most of his theoretical discussions with Mrs. Velleur and the Bah-Rabba Kaba went far beyond Noah's understanding, and phrases like "dimensional tunneling" and "inside-out space" were rapidly bandied back and forth. The one thing that was clear is that the passage to the depths of the Netherworld would be one of the most subtle and complicated ceremonies they had ever witnessed, and Noah was sure they could never have accomplished it without Salice's help.

When the preparations were finally complete the sun was beginning to set once more on the following day. Noah and Samantha stood rigidly to attention as they followed the intricate instructions, performing dozens of half-turns, hand symbols, and dance steps along the spiraled pattern drawn into the earth. A slight slip or miscommunication inevitably led to Salice sternly whispering "Again", and back they'd go to the beginning once more.

Noah and Samantha were well aware that a small misplacement in the ceremony could lead them to a demonic rift in a forgotten place from which they might never return. They did not complain, no matter how many times this process was repeated. The repetition of the practiced movements and the soft hiss of Salice's voice soon lulled them into a sort of trance. Noah became so intent upon the position as he traced out each pattern that he lost track of time and his surroundings, until presently he became aware that he was no longer on earth without any memory of having left.

Suddenly there was chanting, felt as much as heard as heavy gusts of warm breath washed over their bodies and the ground shook beneath their feet. Salice's ceremony had been so precise as to bring them to the very heart of the demon city of Wallom where the soaring greater demons reared above them on all sides. The sunset that had graced the sky before their departure had spread until the entire dome above them was the color of deep blood. The hue was even richer than their last visit, pulsing more powerfully than ever from the two red doors high in the air.

"I do not need eyes to feel we have arrived," Professor Salice purred with satisfaction, his stone still clutched in Noah's hand.

"It's busier than it was before," Samantha said, turning in a slow circle to take in her surroundings. Indeed there was a long line of lesser demons crowding the streets, waiting their turn to deposit offerings of black opals within the heads of those massive bowl-shaped demons they had witnessed on their previous venture. "Alley says she recognizes some of them," Samantha added. "These are the demons returning from their work in the living world."

"They're bringing back the time they earned from their service," Noah replied. "I thought our ceremony was complicated, but this one hasn't taken a break the whole time we were gone. They must be exhausted. How much longer do you think we have to wait?"

"The doors of Almorda have not been opened in my lifetime," Salice said, "but we do not need to know the details of their summoning to know the end is near. Do you not recognize the words, boy?"

Noah concentrated on the chanting all around them, so deep and rhythmic that it threatened to lull him back into a timeless trance. It was hard to discern individual words from the ocean of noise, but gradually he filtered out a few recognizable syllables.

"Numbers. There is a countdown woven through the chant," Noah confirmed. "Some of the others are counting up though, and others are bouncing around all over the place. I can't make any sense of it."

"Focus, apprentice," Salice replied, savoring the word as though in pride. "Unweave the strands and tell me what they say."

Noah closed his eyes and furrowed his brow. "They're counting the stars. And the planets, and the souls that live on them. They're counting off the angles of the interlocking shapes in their circle, and a hundred other things. But there is only one set of numbers that are going down." He opened his eyes again, staring up at the great red doors. "They aren't going to open, no matter how long we wait. I'm going to have to open them myself."

"Noah, wait—where are you going?" Samantha asked, rushing to keep up with him.

"Don't worry, I've learned better by now to try and go anywhere without you. The countdown won't finish until we climb the ladder."

"How do you know?"

"I don't know. I remember—Zee Zee Balloo remembers."

With those cryptic words Noah pressed himself into the ranks of demons waiting their turn to deliver their offerings. This caused quite a commotion amongst them, and many monstrous forms reared and screamed at the boy in their unearthly tongues. It seemed that the demons were about to descend upon him, but Noah did not falter or turn away. It was a long tentacle that seized him first, one that had lashed down from the incredible height from one of the greater demons participating in the ceremony. Samantha hesitated only for a moment before offering herself to the demon, and soon she was snatched up as well and carried high into the air.

The dizzying speed of their capture was cut short so suddenly that Noah was glad he no longer had a mortal stomach to rebel against the motion. The tentacles unwrapped from around their waists, depositing them at the very base of the ladder in the midsts of the three most colossal demons of the entire city, right at the heart of the ongoing ceremony. It was difficult to distinguish these greater demons apart from their size, as each of them was so chaotically assembled with misshapen limbs, jutting bones, scales and teeth and eyes and other bulges best left unmentioned. It was impossible to tell exactly where their faces were—if they had faces at all— but it was clear that their attention was fixed upon Noah by the curvature of their long and corrupted bodies.

If there was any doubt about their focus, it was dispelled when the three colossal beings ceased their chanting from each of their numerous mouths. Next the surrounding greater demons fell silent, and then the ring after that, the silence cascading as a wave which rapidly spread across the whole city. The last demonic syllables hung reverberating in the air long after their final utterances had ceased, until these too were replaced by the preternatural stillness. Noah smiled to see Samantha slap a hand over her mouth, understanding implicitly that she was bursting with so many questions that it was all she could do not to interrupt the quiet. But nothing lasts forever, even here at the end of all worlds where time does not exist as it does among the living. Even this stillness was interrupted by a trio of booms, like earthquakes converging on them from every direction at once.

The bodies of the three colossal demons had slouched into the earth around them, like towers collapsing beneath their own weight. Those demons with discernible legs were bending to kneel, and those with heads bent them as though in prayer. Serpents pressed themselves flat, flying demons landed upon the shoulders of other giants, and at the center of it all Noah remained standing, more out of shock than any deliberate defiance. The shockwave of reverence sped across the city as surely as the silence had. Then the colossal demons were chanting again, and all the city rose in a chorus of song which returned more fervently than ever.

Noah tucked Salice's soul stone into his pocket and grasped hold of the ladder of bones, eager to climb above the deafening clamor as quickly as he could. He paused only long enough to make sure Samantha was climbing behind him before speeding upward with all his might. He could not escape the noise though, which rose in feverish intensity the higher he climbed into the air. Noah tried not to think about the nature of the brittle bones beneath his fingers, nor imagine what would happen if they snapped from the pressure and caused him to slip and tumble back into the sea of demons far below.

The light emanating from the two red doors grew more intense the higher he climbed. When he was about halfway up, it was too bright to even keep his eyes open. From there he was forced to continue blindly, never knowing how much farther there was to go. The light piercing his eyelids soon became so bright that it felt like his eyes were still open. It seemed to him that it would feel no different if he was climbing directly into the sun instead.

Hand over hand, Noah climbed so high that he left his fears behind. All the worries and doubts of the journey were replaced by the calm inevitability of what was to come. When at last his fingers closed over the empty air, he knew he must have reached the end of the ladder. Still unable to open his eyes, he reached forward as far as he could without being able to feel the doors he knew should be there. After several moments of blind groping, he realized that the doors must already be open.

There was nothing left but to step off the ladder and hope not to plummet the terrible height he already climbed. Despite the distance, the cacophony below continued as frenzied as ever. It occurred to him that Salice could be shouting words of warning in his feeble voice, and Noah would be deaf to him. A moment of panic seized him as he teetered on the top of the ladder, promising unimaginable horrors waiting for him on the other side of those doors. Noah was overwhelmed with a compulsion to lean backward and topple directly from the ladder, accepting any fate besides that which now seemed inescapable. The feeling did not subside until he felt a hand upon his ankle, when he knew Samantha had completed the same journey as him without succumbing to its trials.

Noah stepped from the top of the ladder and the light extinguished at once. The roaring sound gone, the heat quenched. And with it the only man Noah had ever known himself to be was gone: a mask that had been worn so long that he'd forgotten who lay underneath. The Prime demon had returned home, ready at last to meet his brothers.

DOORS OF ALMORDA

BEYOND THE VEIL OF LIFE, BEYOND THE CHAOTIC NETHER, OUTSIDE OF time and space where no mortal has ever gone before, Noah was possessed by the feeling of returning home. He found himself standing on a grey stepping stone only barely wide enough for him to balance on. Another step would have sent him into an empty blackness, perhaps falling forever amidst the distant stars which glimmered around him in every direction as far as he could see. Behind him he could clearly see the open red doors with the red sky on the other side. The light which poured out of them didn't seem nearly so overwhelming anymore, although Noah had the strange sensation that it was his eyes that had changed, and not the intensity.

"Wait, Samantha, there isn't room—"

But of course she couldn't hear, not with the roaring chanting blasting her on the other side. There was another stone ahead of Noah though, to which he leapt just in time before Samantha stepped through the doors into the space he'd been occupying. A long line of stepping stones suspended in the night sky ahead, each about four feet apart. It was an uncomfortable leap with such a terrifying emptiness below, but perhaps this path had never been intended for humans to take. Samantha stood on the first stone for a long moment, her marble eye swiveling independently in its socket as she gazed around her in awe.

"Well at least I can still breathe here," she said at last.

"Oh right. I forgot you still do that. Can Alley see anything else beyond the stones and the stars?"

"They aren't stars. They're doors. Round ones, blue ones, cabinet doors, basement doors, thousands and thousands of doors going..." She shrugged her slender shoulders, looking quite small and lost in front of such an immense background. "I don't know where they go, but they're all open, and that's where the light is coming from."

"After all this work to open these doors? Where are the Primes? Do you think they've already escaped?"

Samantha shrugged again. "Only one way to find out. Keep moving, or I'm going to knock you off."

She wasn't kidding either. She was already crouched, about to leap when Noah jumped onto the next stone in front of him just in time. There was a reason she was in a hurry too—the marble had spread again, all the way across half of her mouth, down her chin, with splotches of it embedded into the skin of her neck.

There was no knowing when Alley would try to take control again or what trouble The Matriarch and the department were up to in their absence. Delaying was not an option. From one stone to the next, the pair skipped towards an uncertain future. Samantha with her keen sight was the first to discern their destination.

"There's an island among the stars. It's got a little grass on it, and an old withered tree, and that's about it. No, wait—there are a few chairs or something. Three of them—I think they're thrones."

"Maybe that's where the Primes are supposed to sit."

"Maybe, but I don't see anyone or anything. It's not a big island, there shouldn't be anywhere to hide except behind the tree."

Soon it came into vision just as she'd described. 'Thrones' wouldn't have been the word Noah would have used though. Three massive skulls resolved themselves from the darkness, each missing their upper jaw to provide a natural place to sit on the lower one. Each was unique with a variety of long tusks, elongated bone, and unfamiliar shapes that would have made it clear they didn't belong to a human even if they weren't such an impressive size. As they got closer, Noah was able to see that every inch of the bone was intricately engraved with demonic symbols and geometric runes.

The light from the red doors had all but disappeared into the background of stars by the time they arrived at the island. Nothing stirred as they landed on the grass with a final grateful leap. Samantha fell to her knees in exhaustion, panting to catch her breath while Noah's whole body felt thinner and more insubstantial than he'd ever remembered before. He noted large, clawed footprints in the grass as he advanced on the three skulls, bending to read the symbols to the best of his ability.

"Life and death are each other's shadows, cast by the light of eternity," he read aloud. "I recognize those words—they're carved into the stone at the Mortuary."

"The Matriarch has been here before."

The voice made Noah jump. He'd been so distracted by this new world that he'd forgotten that Salice was still in his pocket.

"That's bad, isn't it? Could she have already taken the other two Primes? Why aren't they here?"

"I don't know, but I doubt it. Even she would be hard pressed to capture two Primes, and those words have been carved above The Mortuary doors for as long as I can remember. It is clearly no coincidence that the three thrones were intended for the Primes though. I suggest you take your rightful place, Zee Zee Balloo."

Noah shuddered. "Don't call me that. I don't like it. And I don't want to sit in that nasty skull."

"Come on, they're actually pretty cool. Here, I'll go first." Samantha leapt up on one of the peripheral thrones, swinging her legs through the giant teeth of the lower jaw. "See? Nothing to be afraid of."

Noah put his hands reluctantly on the central skull. It's not that he was afraid—quite the opposite, actually. Like metal drawn toward a magnet, he felt a visceral compulsion to take his place in this particular seat. It was exactly this inexplicable allure that gave him pause though. He hadn't been honest when he called the skull nasty either; Noah found a beautiful familiarity about the chair as though he had just been reunited with one of his most treasured possessions. He lifted himself from the ground and swung his legs into place just as Samantha had done, taking his seat to look out at the sea of endless stars.

The reaction was instantaneous. A booming crash like a distant thunderbolt reverberated through the eternal space. Then another—and another—faster and faster, coming from every direction at once as the innumerable blasts merged into a single audible assault. Samantha was shouting something, but she had to keep repeating herself before her words managed to slip through the incessant wall of noise.

"The... doors... are... all... closing."

That's when he noticed it wasn't just the noise. The stars were snuffing out one by one. The rational part of Noah's mind understood this as the light behind the doors being obscured as they closed. As he could not actually see the doors though, this produced the visual effect that the entire heavens were being extinguished, an abhorrent illusion which could not be dispelled no matter how hard he tried to convince himself otherwise.

This must be what the end of the world felt like. He'd often wondered about what an apocalypse might really mean, ever since he heard the first legends of the Primes. Now in the growing darkness each thundering crash was more terrifying than the last. It was only too easy to imagine being on earth and feeling the terror all around him as the real stars disappeared one by one, casting the world into an unending night. Could this be happening for them right now? Would it be all his fault?

The light grew fainter and fainter over what felt like a few minutes, until at last the final doors crashed shut sending everything into perfect darkness. The violent clash was still ringing in Noah's ears when a new voice reverberated through the empty space.

"Welcome back, Zee Zee Balloo." The words echoed with countless tones and textures as though thousands of different voices were speaking in practical unison, with only the tiniest fraction of a second between them to produce a hauntingly echoed effect. "We've been waiting for you."

The voices were coming from the empty throne on Noah's other side. Or maybe it wasn't empty anymore—the perfect darkness was so complete that Noah couldn't even see his nose on the end of his face. He winced as a sudden bright white light punctured the emptiness to illuminate Samantha. The presence on Noah's other side hissed with displeasure at the intrusive light, and Noah almost laughed to realize it was the flash light coming from the back of Samantha's cell phone. His body was too tense for a sound like laughter to escape though. He held himself stiff and still as Samantha's trembling fingers slowly turned the flashlight—first on Noah, then on the third throne where the voices had spoken from.

The light reflected from a thousand stones that had not been there before the darkness fell. A creature in the shape of an unnaturally tall man now occupied the space. The glittering gems were embedded in every inch of his skin and face, leaving no room for any clothing or distinguishing feature of his own. As the sharp light passed over the stones it revealed the shadow of creatures within, just as Salice's stone revealed his shadow when it was held up to the light. The identity of the underlying creature may be obscured, but it appeared that every one of the stones contained a living soul.

"Kill the light! Kill the light!" whispered a thousand simultaneous voices. The sounds combined into a single powerful scream. An electric discharge like lightning tore from the creature's hand, surging into Samantha's cell phone and blasting it from her fingers. When the electricity dissipated the darkness was complete once more, their single source of light destroyed.

"I would have turned it off if you gave me a second. You didn't have to break my phone," Samantha grumbled.

"What blasphemy brings a living girl to sit upon the Prime's throne?" roared the thousand whispers.

"She's my guest. Don't hurt her," Noah cut in quickly. "Which of the Primes are you? Borrowrath or Momslavi?"

A sound like a rolling avalanche—the chuckling from a thousand throats.

"We keep the sanctuary while our masters are away. You may call us Neera. Though we must seem divine to mortal eyes, we are not worthy of the title of Prime. There have been no Primes on the throne for a long, long time. Until now."

Noah vehemently wished the light hadn't been destroyed. A side-effect of Neera's many compounded voices was that it was difficult to place exactly where they were all coming from. Was the creature still sitting in the throne, or was it creeping closer? It had called him master, yet Noah felt utterly helpless to the creature's power.

"Thank you for your service, Neera. Now tell me where the other Primes have gone." Noah said, trying his best to project an authority he didn't feel.

"You seek an answer that only you can give. The Primes know where to find their brethren."

"If I knew where they were I wouldn't have come here looking for them. If I'm your master, then my command is for you to find them for me."

There it was again—the hail storm of snickering laughter. The sound sent shivers down Noah's spine.

"Our master is blinded by his mortal coil. He must shed his mask of spiritual flesh before he remembers himself. Do not worry, master, we shall free your soul from the prison of this boy."

Flashes of light punctured the darkness, and Noah wondered why he'd ever wanted that in the first place. Neera had risen from his throne and arcs of electricity were discharging between his many stones, dancing across his body to concentrate into a single fist. Strobed flashes brought the creature toward Noah in lurching bursts. All the mysteries collapsed into a single point of keen understanding: if Noah came in contact with that force, it would be the end of him.

"Wait—don't touch him!" Samantha cried.

"Zee Zee Balloo will not forgive you!" Salice cut in sharply. "Your master does not want this!"

"You're wrong, Professor," Noah said. "This is exactly what he wants—it's the reason he led me here. I have to die again for the Prime to be reborn."

These words surprised Neera even more than they did Noah's companions. The demon paused before Noah, the electricity still coursing across its body.

"Your grace of understanding has exceeded our expectations. We ask forgiveness for our hasty judgement—it is no curiosity that the Prime's soul would choose a vessel such as you."

"Noah, you can't," Samantha begged. "What about your daughter? Or your grandson? You came all this way for them, and if you throw yourself away like this… There won't be anyone left to watch over them and keep them safe. You might think you're being noble right now, but you're not. Giving up this easily is nothing but selfishness."

"I'm not giving up." The careful poise in Noah's tone finally broke, and the voice he heard sounded like nothing more than a scared little boy. "When I'm gone—when the Primes have found each other again, they'll put a stop to The Matriarch. They'll destroy the Soul Net and send all the souls back to their bodies, or find new ones when they're free to live again. Please Sam, don't make this harder than it has to be. It was fate that brought me here."

"Fate is bullshit." Samantha sounded like she was close to tears.

"It's not. I wouldn't have come this far if I wasn't ready to give everything for this. If only… if I could just ask one thing…"

"You may make your request," the voluminous chorus replied.

"Could I see them again?" Why was there a knot in his throat? Why did it make him so angry that it was so hard to speak? "Mandy and Lewis. I don't have to visit them. I don't even have to talk to them. I just want to know they're alright before I… Just once. Just to say goodbye."

The electricity running across the demon spluttered and subdued. The darkness endured for longer between each arc of lighting, and then it was gone, replaced by a soft blue glow from the center of each of Neera's stones.

"We can find the mortals you seek. Place your hand upon our chest, and think of them for the last time."

So Noah did, and the thoughts came in a torrent. A lifetime of watching Mandy grow and play and discover the world. Of each fleeting joy and sorrow, each seeming the most important thing in the world until the next adventure took hold. Of Mandy becoming more distant as she grew older, and the pride Noah felt when she needed him again. Of Lewis being born, and all the innocence of childhood that seemed forever lost rekindled by the ever strengthening bond between Noah and the both of them.

Noah poured all these thoughts into the demon, and the blue light in the creature's face shifted to reflect them. Each stone became the facet of a larger image, and suddenly there was Mandy's face—young and pure and smiling like she hadn't since her husband's death. She was sitting on the floor with Lewis racing around her, laughing with pleasure as her boy sped faster and faster in circles. Too fast for the boy to control—he tumbled over one of his mother's outstretched legs, but Mandy caught him and swept him up in her arms and held him close.

All too soon the image shattered as the blue light faded, replaced by a soft red glow. Neera pulled away from Noah's hand. Suddenly—stiffly—the demon turned and began to walk away.

"Is that it? I said I'm ready! Where are you going?"

"To collect the other Primes," the demon said without turning.

"What are you talking about? You said you didn't know where they were."

"We didn't. Until you showed us."

"What? What? Hey wait!"

"Noah, they're the other Primes!" Samantha exclaimed. "Mandy and Lewis—all three of you! You all came back to life as a family."

"No wonder The Matriarch was able to accumulate so much power unopposed," Salice mused faintly. "She waited to act until all three of the Primes had forgotten themselves in their new life."

Neera's long strides were picking up speed. A single red star reignited in the distance, illuminating the demon as he bounded down the stepping stones. Noah took a few staggered steps after it, faltering to a stumble at the futility of keeping pace.

"They weren't part of the deal!" Noah shouted. "You can't have them!"

The pressure of a wordless scream built in Noah's chest, tearing out his throat in an unrepressable wave of rage and frustration.

Neera had already reached the red doors, that pinprick of light in the distance. He must have, because with the sound of a thunder crack the light vanished again. The darkness was complete once more—they were trapped here. Trapped and helpless while the demon sped to kill Noah's family. After all he'd been through to keep them safe, it had all been for nothing.

"Noah, don't—we'll stop him," Samantha said. He felt her warmth approach him from behind in the darkness, but it brought no comfort to his tormented spirit.

"No we won't. You were right before. I'm so selfish. I never should have asked to see them again. This is all my fault."

The pressure was building in Noah's chest again, but he turned all his anger toward pushing it back down. It didn't work—the sound that came out was more like a strangled sob this time.

"Their sacrifice won't be in vain," Salice said thoughtfully. "The Primes will still be reunited."

"I don't care! They'll be killed, they'll forget me. They'll forget each other—I'll forget them. It would have been better if none of us had ever lived at all. What good is saving the world if I can't save my own daughter?"

"That's why fate is such garbage," Samantha said. "It wants us to accept the unacceptable, and give up before it's too late. A witch doesn't believe in any fate she doesn't create herself. I wasn't about to let myself get stuck in the Netherworld again, so I made plans with the other witches to try and re-summon us every few hours. The summoning isn't a compulsion, so I figured we could just turn it down until we were ready to go back."

"Elegant, simple, innovative," Salice mused. "An excellent plan."

"A few hours isn't good enough!" Noah cut in. "Mandy and Lewis don't have a few hours! And who knows what a few hours on the outside even means in here!"

"What are you yelling at me for? I'm the only one who even made an escape plan."

"Well it's not a very good plan if we don't have a way of contacting to let them know when to summon us."

"Then go sit on your throne for the rest of time for all I care! I didn't even have to be here—ah! Alley, no!" The last words were sharp and shrill and filled with pain.

"What's going on? Are you okay?"

"It doesn't count as finding the Primes until we've reunited with them!" Samantha shouted. "Stop it Alley! Stop it! Please!"

The fear in the girl's voice did more to ground Noah than her shouting ever could. A wave of guilt crashed over him upon the realization of how much Samantha was really going through just to help him. How could he be this selfish over and over again without even realizing it?

There was no chance to apologize or even begin to make things right though. A familiar tug at his spirit felt just the way it had when the witches were summoning him the first time. The darkness cracked in a thousand places, and clean, pure sunlight began to filter through. He embraced the feeling and let it guide him away from this nightmare. The world around them was beginning to resolve from the void as though everything was being created before their eyes.

Walls swelled up from the ground around him, and Noah was surprised to see that they weren't returning to Peter's house. The shining white tiles, the stainless steel, the wide glass windows—this was Mandy's house, with George Hampton sitting in the bloody circle to host the summoning. A moment later and Mrs. Velleur's chanting voice filtered into existence. She was performing the ritual while staring into the crystal ball clutched in an outstretched hand.

"Please, please, please!" Samantha begged. The desperation in her voice was harder than ever to endure. The other witches at the back of the living room came into focus as they rushed around Samantha with alarm and concern.

"The secondary soul is taking over the host," Salice explained quickly. "We need a new body for the second soul, or it is likely that one or the other will not survive."

"Take mine then," Noah offered at once, staggering out of the summoning circle. "I have to lose my body soon anyway for the soul of Zee Zee Balloo to be restored."

"Nonsense," George Hampton said, brow furrowed. "Half the city is made of soulless ones, empty vessels ready to be filled."

"Those souls are still out there, and they'll want to get back to their own body. If you know how, then take mine and make it quick. We don't have a moment to lose."

"Your body won't do any good," Mrs. Velleur snapped. "Sit down, shut up, and let us handle things from here."

"What are we even doing here? How did you get to my daughter's house?"

Mrs. Velleur then explained how they had watched Noah and Samantha through the crystal, and that they knew to come here at once as soon as they learned the truth about his family. Samantha held her head and groaned in pain while Willow, Miss Toofin, and Miss Bailey anxiously fretted around her.

"Where are Mandy and Lewis now?" Noah asked.

"Lewis is at school, Mandy has gone to pick him up," Aunt Chrissy replied. "She wouldn't let us in, so we had to wait until she left to perform the summoning here."

"Can't imagine why," Mrs. Velleur added dryly, looking around at the bloody circle. "Willow, sponges, mop—let's get this cleaned up."

"And you just let her leave? Neera could already have her!" Noah erupted.

"If you calmed down long enough to think, you'd know that he wouldn't be able to escape the nether until he was summoned," Mrs. Velleur said. "I have no doubt a demon as powerful as that can possess or manipulate a mortal into summoning him, but that will still take time. In the meanwhile, we must get you and your family together and find a way to awaken the Primes with the least possible collateral damage."

"Like killing us all, you mean," Noah said.

Mrs. Velleur forced a smile. A fresh gasp of pain from Samantha caused the older witch to turn away from Noah.

"There are two clear options remaining for the girl," Mrs. Velleur continued. "Either she will destroy the soul and reclaim her body, or she will be destroyed and it will take over. As noble as it was for Noah to offer his own body, Samantha and Alley's souls are so intertwined that an attempted separation would likely destroy them both. The pair of them have thought together with one mind and felt together with one body for so long that they are the only ones who can settle this now."

Samantha sat suddenly and rigidly upright. The living half of her face was flush with sweat, while dozens of hairline cracks had appeared on the marble side. A nasally voice quite unlike her own slipped from her parched lips.

"Samantha has only ever seen from my eye what I allowed her to see. I can see the demon now. I know where he is, what he's doing, when he'll be here. Would you like me to tell you?" A shuddering spasm passed over Samantha's body.

"There's another way," Samantha gasped in her old voice. "The Bah-Rabba Kaba shared her body with two souls as well. We can learn to live together."

"Give me the body. I want it—you promised me!"

Noah found it deeply unsettling to watch Samantha's lips continuously move while different voices alternated from her mouth. He looked pleadingly to Mrs. Velleur, who was staring once more into her crystal ball.

"The great witch's spirit did indeed endure such a thing, but you are just a child," Mrs. Velleur said. "You are untrained in our ways, and Alley has already made her intent clear. Lowering your defenses against her to further mix your souls would mean your certain death."

"I can do it," Samantha said in her own voice, now hardened with resolution. "We can do it, although I'm not sure how to—" the voice shifted back to Alley's—"I'll kill her. She promised me—she lied to me—I'll kill her!"

"No, I trust her. I want to let her in," from Samantha again.

"You can't seriously trust her after what she's saying," Noah said, bewildered.

"I do, with all my heart," Samantha replied. "A witch knows that wars cannot be ended until you've learned to trust your enemies as you would your friends. I'm going to put myself in her power, and she's not going to harm me. Just tell me what I need to do."

"You're insane. You're going to get yourself killed!" Noah protested. Mrs. Velleur was smiling though, and that made Noah angrier than ever. "You aren't seriously going to let her do this to herself, are you?"

"You don't *let* a witch do anything," Samantha and Mrs. Velleur scolded in almost perfect unison.

Mrs. Velleur's smile deepened, and she added, "I hesitated at first too, but I have seen the courage in her conviction and doubt the girl no longer. You must trust her too, or if you can't, then at least trust that she trusts herself and know that is enough."

The clouds in Mrs. Velleur's crystal ball swirled while she spoke, and now the Bah-Rabba Kaba's youthful face appeared in the glass.

"I have been expecting this moment," the great witch said. "Listen carefully—you will only have once chance to do this right. If you are ever going to survive becoming whole, you must first find the wall in your mind. On one side are the familiar thoughts, pleasant memories, and a model of yourself as you wish yourself to be. On the other side lies suppressed emotions, secret shames, and unforgivable regrets. This is a forbidden place that we keep locked so tightly that it is difficult to even acknowledge its existence until a nightmare finds a crack to seep through. It is this wall that you must destroy if you're to let your other in, and these nightmares that you must let out to play in your secret garden. Have you found your wall?"

"Yes," whispered Samantha. Her eyes were closed in concentration, and beads of sweat dampened her long dark hair. Alley's voice came next, adding, "I'm breaking through, whether she lets me in or not."

"A nightmare loses no potency upon waking," Bah-Rabba Kaba continued. "Burying it behind the wall does not destroy an evil thought, but rather plants it in the darkness which is the only place it may grow. And grow it will, corrupting other dreams and thoughts and memories until they have become so tainted that they too must be locked away. So the beast does feed, and so the wall grows higher, and broader. Until one day the wall has grown so big that you find it serves no longer to keep the darkness out, but rather to keep the light imprisoned within. The day has come when the wall is suffocating the dwindling part of you that you aren't afraid to call yourself. Are you afraid of such a day?"

"Yes." The simple word struggled to make its way out of Samantha's knotted throat.

"It is good to be afraid. That fear is proof that the dam is breaking. Do not run from the fear, do not put up new walls to keep it at bay. Find it, face it. Rip and tear at the hole to widen the flow—the fear that comes will be an ocean, and now is your last chance to learn to swim."

Samantha was breathing heavily now, gulping and panting in irregular gasps. Willow was unable to continue watching, and she buried her face in her hands. It was just as uncomfortable for Noah, but he refused to rob her the dignity of her suffering by turning away.

"A witch shall not fear fear, shall not hate hatred, shall not suffer suffering. You are a witch if I've ever seen one, your own master from this day until forever ends. A witch shall face her adversary head on, and if she is to be struck down, she will go looking her enemy in the eye. She will lay her own soul bare and naked for all to see, and force those who would slay her to bare their soul to her. You are strong and you are wise, and your friends and enemies will know it the same. You are brave and you are pure, and your foe cannot strike you without striking those qualities from themselves. One soul to another, with another, is another, forever and ever. The wall is broken—you and your enemy are one."

Samantha's head jerked backward with a final gasp as she flung herself to the floor. One or more of the witches screamed in alarm, but Noah couldn't tear his eyes away from his friend. She was lying very still, shaking no longer, not even breathing for the longest time. Then the strangest, most unexpected sound burst from her like a bird taking flight: a brittle, cracking, cackling sound. She was laughing, and in that moment Noah knew it was neither her nor Alley that he was hearing, but both of them combined. He must have been the first to realize this though, as George and the other witches still looked as anxious and terrified as can be.

"We see him!" Samantha exclaimed suddenly, the laughter dying as swiftly as it appeared. She sat bolt upright, her damp hair swinging wildly about her face. "Neera has completed his own summoning. He's in the living world."

From fear, to grief, to celebration, back to fear, the emotions in the room were strained to their breaking point. It was all too much for Miss Bailey, who rocked backward to collapse on her ample frame. Mrs. Velleur's had a tense face and wringing hands, while George Hampton had begun to anxiously pace again. Samantha was the only one of the lot who was smiling, but there was light in her eye and a bounce in her step as she rose to her feet that brought hope to all who saw her.

"He's coming this way, but we still have a little time," she added. "Don't worry—we know exactly how to safely release the Primes before he arrives."

UNION OF THE PRIMES

"Of course I'm glad she survived, but that doesn't mean the ordeal hasn't rattled her mind," Mrs. Velleur snapped.

"I don't see how it will end well. I'm sorry, I just don't," George Hampton grumbled.

"Don't worry dear, we'll come up with something. You need your rest," Aunt Chrissy pleaded. "Noah, you must know better than anyone how foolish her plan is. Can't you talk some sense into her?"

"I think it's an amazing idea," Noah replied, grinning despite their fluster. "And you know it will surprise the Trans Dimensional Department."

"The Matriarch won't have anticipated it either," Salice conceded faintly.

"Because it's stupid, that's why," Mrs. Velleur huffed indignantly. "I simply won't scry Theodore Oswald and ask for his help. He's the establishment embodiment of everything that's wrong with spiritual society."

"Wars cannot be ended until you've learned to trust your enemies," Samantha replied, prompting an uncontrollable twitch below Mrs. Velleur's eye.

"Please don't be bitter, Mrs. Velleur," Willow said. "Just because the Bah-Rabba Kaba found a new favorite witch…"

"Oh please." Mrs. Velleur snorted. "Do I look intimidated by some upstart young thing? And why haven't you finished cleaning up the summoning circle? Mandy is going to be returning home with Lewis any moment now."

"My turn with the crystal then," Samantha said, snatching away the orb from under Mrs. Velleur's nose. The older witch began to splutter protests, but Samantha didn't give her the chance. "Just think about it. Theodore can't possibly refuse to come, not when he knows we're looking for the Primes and we tell him they're here. The first time Noah and I saw Neera, we thought he was a Prime, and someone as headstrong as the Minister won't think twice before going into battle. We also know The Matriarch has her minions planted all over the Department, and she'll be sure to get the same message."

"So you want Theodore and The Matriarch to battle with Neera…" George Hampton said slowly.

"That's right. And while they're fighting him for us, we'll have time to release the real Primes. I understand now that the Prime souls are walled off from Noah and his family just the same way I had a wall within me. I know I can help them all break through to access their power without anyone having to be killed."

"Then all three of the Primes will be released together, and they'll be able to destroy The Matriarch who showed up to fight Neera!" Noah exclaimed.

"How do you turn this thing on, anyway?" Samantha asked, shaking the crystal. Mrs. Velleur smirked and reached to take the orb back, but Samantha pulled it away again, saying: "Oh never mind, I got it."

"Even you never figured out how to scry without being taught," Willow called across the room.

"Floors, now!" Mrs. Velleur barked. "And hurry, I already hear the car in the driveway."

"And how exactly did we decide to explain to Mandy that we all broke into her house while she was gone?" Aunt Chrissy asked innocently.

Like most groups of witches, these women had an opinion on practically everything. This happened to be one of the rare exceptions where everyone was waiting for someone else to speak first, but no one did. The sudden silence of the group made the rumble of the opening garage door abundantly clear.

Keys in the door—the witches seemed to have found a way in without unlocking it. The squeaking swing of the hinges. The crash of a bag of groceries hitting the floor, and then Mandy screamed.

"It's not so bad!" Willow shouted in distress. "I've got almost all the blood out!"

"Papa!" Lewis shouted from behind. The child shoved past his stunned mother to rush into the room, oblivious to the gaping witches as he barreled forward to embrace Noah. A slight pressure like a heavy mist was felt as his grandson sailed through him to the other side. "Mama look! Papa's home!"

All things considered, Mandy took the surprise much better than anyone expected. Her incredulity was rapidly replaced by a droll acceptance that reminded Noah of Mandy's late husband Barnes, who didn't seem to even mind when The Matriarch sacrificed him last year. After the initial shock Mandy didn't scream or curse, but allowed Samantha to quietly lead her by the hand and sit her down on the sofa to explain everything the best she could. Mandy nodded along, subdued and quiet as she listened. She never gave any indication that she could see Noah, and despite his relief at being with her again, he was disappointed not to see any of the life and fire that he always remembered her having as a child. She just seemed tired, and sad, although Noah supposed that was understandable in such wearisome times as these.

Noah was vaguely aware of Samantha sitting in the kitchen with the crystal ball, with Theodore's graveled voice floating somewhere in the periphery. There was a hint of discourse between the witches and George Hampton, perhaps something to do with preparing for Neera's arrival, but it seemed so far away and inconsequential that it might as well have been coming from a television show in the background.

All that existed was Mandy sitting on the couch and Lewis showing off his train set on the floor. Prime demons the both of them, living their unwitting lives oblivious to the cosmic dance which brought them to this point, or the hand of fate guiding them to destinies they couldn't begin to fathom. And somewhere caught in the middle flared these fragile mortal lives, inconsequential in the grand scheme, and yet important enough for all the masters of the universe to trade their knowledge and power for one more chance to play. And who was to say they were wrong to do so, when all the wonders Noah experienced after death were but a shadow of the simple life he'd lived with his daughter?

"Of course I see him." Those words from Mandy grounded Noah's flying thoughts. She was looking right at Noah for the first time, not through him as she'd always done before. "So what? He's dead, so why should I care?"

Those words brought great agitation to the gathered witches, but Noah didn't stay long enough to watch it play out. He stood rigidly and drifted away, floating as gently as the night which fell around the little house. He didn't have any destination in mind—anywhere seemed as good as everywhere else. There weren't any thoughts in his head, no disappointment in his heart. He passed straight through the wall to stand alone in the yard, watching the fading light through eyes that had forgotten the difference between ugliness and beauty in all they saw.

Death—not spirits, not demons, not the passage between, but true honest nothingness where no happiness or hurt traveled with him. Death where there was no him to travel at all—a real honest death would not be such an evil in a world where such words could escape his daughter's lips. Noah watched the leaves and the grass stir beneath an unfelt breeze as time slipped by unheeded. It was a good thing, he decided at last, when thoughts no longer burned too brightly to be examined in his mind. It was actually a good thing that she did not love him anymore. She was lucky that she wouldn't be bringing anything so painful as love with her into whatever life she passed into next. It would hurt less this way when the final act played out, he told himself, if not for him, then at least for her.

That ending was upon them now. Neera had arrived. Noah could feel him in the stillness and hear him amid the silent houses. He could see him in the fading light, and smell him in the acrid air—the stench of a demon like lightning before it tears its way into a world it does not belong. Then all at once there was light again, a second sunset which flared back to life after the first had trailed into grey tendrils in the sky. A house went up in flames in the near distance. Then a second—then a third—spitting ravenous sparks to devour the empty sky. Each burning house burst on its own accord, the consecutive lights forming the shape of a massive circle around them with Mandy's home directly in the center.

There weren't any lights on in the houses before they caught fire, nor people fleeing the destructive halo. The place had been cursed and dying since the demons first attacked, and Noah noticed how truly empty the neighborhood had become since his ventures in the Netherworld. It seems that Mandy had been the last one to remain in this neighborhood which would prove to be their final battleground.

Searing yellow sparks spun unnaturally from the fire as portals began to open all around him. White gloved hands gripping tridents came marching through in pairs, an endless procession of spirits caught in a struggle that they had no power to end. The smoky air churned with the beating of stony wings as flights of gargoyles plummeted from unseen heights. Theodore Oswald had taken Samantha's warning seriously after all, and he was ready for battle. That was just as well, because now the thousand voices of another messenger were being carried by these winds of war.

"Tonight the Primes are united," hissed those thousand voices. "No man, nor spirit, nor demon shall resist their awakening."

"There he is, Theodore!" Samantha's voice cut through, so clear and small and unafraid amid the mounting din. "The union of the Primes, just like I told you! He's inside the circle, this is your chance!"

Noah craned his neck to spot Neera amid the billowing smoke. A hand on the back of his shirt yanked him away before he managed to locate the demon, physically dragging him back into the house.

"What the hell are you doing out here?" Samantha scolded. "Lewis and Mandy are ready—let's go!"

Noah tried in vain to shrug off her grip, as implacable as stone. "What's the point? I don't care about forgetting this life anymore. Mandy has already forgotten me. Let's just give Neera what he wants."

"Shame on you, giving up so easily. If the Primes are here and you are not, then what makes you think they'll do what you want and save anyone at all? You have to care or they won't—all the power in the world won't do any good without someone in there who gives a damn."

Samantha shoved Noah through the door and onto the floor where Mandy and Lewis were already sitting. His grandson was losing patience and trying to crawl away to look out the window, but Willow was sitting beside him trying to coax him in place.

"The department will slow Neera down at the very least," Mrs. Velleur said, snapping the curtains back into place and turning away. "It is time for the walls within you to come down."

Mandy nodded vaguely. Noah had trouble looking at her, and she certainly wasn't paying any attention to him as he sat beside her on the carpet. Aunt Chrissy seized hold of Mandy's hand and thrust it into Noah's grasp while Willow joined Lewis's hands with Noah and Mandy to complete the circle. Their grip was loose and insubstantial between Noah's fingers, but there was also a hint of warmth that seemed the realest thing there was.

"There's nothing to be afraid of," Samantha said reassuringly.

"'Course not," Noah managed weakly. "Just the end of us, and the end of the world, and everything in between."

"Other than that, I mean."

Noah smiled, despite himself. He gripped the hands of his family a little tighter and felt the pressure increase as their fingers overlapped.

"Nothing on the other side of that wall is half as bad as the wall itself," Samantha said. "Are you ready?"

"I've been ready." The words welled up unbidden in Noah's mind, slipping from his mouth in a high whistling tone quite alien to him. Zee Zee Balloo was right below the surface, now more than ever.

A blinding light flooded through the closed curtains, swiftly followed by a tremulous thunderclap which exploded nearby. There was screaming—more horrible for how brief it was, dissipating as quickly as the light.

"What's going on out there?" Noah asked.

"What's going on in there? Focus." Mrs. Velleur demanded.

Noah felt the ghost of a squeeze from Lewis's hand. He closed his eyes and tried not to imagine the deadly battle waging just out of sight. He thought back to the Bah-Rabba Kaba's words, effortlessly conjuring the image of a mighty wall in his mind. At first he pictured it as impenetrable slabs of stone, but without meaning to, the image morphed into a single seamless shine. He recognized it as the mirror of ancestry at once, its infinite expanse flooded by the shadows of the long history of his soul.

"The department is holding strong. Concentrate," echoed Samantha's voice, sounding as though it came down a distant pipe. Indeed all the sounds from the outside world were more imaginary than the alien voice which spoke from Noah's own lips.

"You have done well to find us again, Noah, and have earned your rest. We have no further need of you," the high voice with the English accent said.

"I'm ready to rest," Noah admitted. "What will you do if I let you take control?"

"We will start over again. That is what the Primes are for. Borrowrath the Unsplendid will bring a fire that will turn the land to ash. Momslavi Lapis will unleash the oceans and wash the fire away. And we—and I—will plant the souls to grow into whatever world will grow next. That is the way it has always been, and the way it will always be."

"And nothing will be saved?"

There were cracks running through the wall already, but they were not of his creation. A dull pounding like the beginning of a headache coursed through his mind, and with every pulse new cracks were forming in the wall. The shadows on the other side grew clearer—the grey featureless flesh of the Soul Eaters pressing, probing, desperate to be free.

"No memories of the lives we've led?" Noah pressed urgently.

"Nothing."

"No works of art, no books, no laws or governments or—"

"Nothing, nothing, nothing. And then something new. Not better, or worse, just different."

"We aren't all bad, you know. There are things we've learned, wisdom from the witches, and mistakes that ought not to be repeated again. Things that are worth holding onto."

A shimmering shard of the wall in Noah's mind shattered and spun away. A searing line of agony followed its wake as though a hot knife was cutting him from the inside out. Grey fingers slid through the hole in the wall, grasping the jagged edges, letting it cut into their skin without concern. An illusory pressure gripped Noah's hands, fainter than ever before. They were losing their battles too—he didn't know how he knew, but he was sure of it. If he was going to break after all this time, then what hope did his family have who were thrust into this war against their will?

"There is nothing to be gained from resisting me," Zee Zee Balloo growled, suddenly ferocious. No—it had always been wild, always been angry—Noah just hadn't realized it because of how distant the presence had been. But now the wall was coming down, and there was no hiding from it anymore. The Prime wasn't speaking of the end of the world with indifference or inevitability—the demon would relish the destruction that was to come.

Distant screams from the battle outside graced the edge of Noah's awareness, but what were they compared to the untold suffering of the apocalypse that was to come? Every second lost was another second closer to the end—the wall was shattering in a thousand places. There were no more chances but one. If Noah didn't act now, there wouldn't be any Noah left to act, not ever again.

"I won't try to keep you out," Noah said.

"You couldn't if you tried."

"I'm not trying. I want the wall to come down, but before I go, I'm going to ask you one question. The most important question in the world."

"You wish to know where the Primes came from? The fate of the first souls? The last words spoken at the end of time?"

"You never told me why you have an English accent."

Zee Zee Balloo laughed. The Soul Eaters on the other side of the wall gnashed their wide mouths as they laughed in uncanny unison. It wasn't a pretty sound.

"You want to know that? All the secrets of the universe, and you want to know why I speak with an accent?"

"I think it's very important for me to know. And it's alright if you don't tell me, because I think I know the answer. I think that I'm not the first time you've been human. I think that in one of those lives, somewhere long ago, there was something you wanted to hold onto. And because I know you better than you give me credit for, I want to guess another thing: not only were you English in that one life so long ago, but you found yourself in love and never forgot what that was like."

The headache was pounding more powerfully than ever—a migraine which ricocheted through Noah's entire body. But that pain gave Noah hope, because he felt that Zee Zee Balloo was doing everything in its power to distract Noah and keep him from saying what he was about to say. It wasn't going to work.

"You fell in love, and every life since you've never let that go. You held onto your accent because it was the only thing reminding you of what it was like to be who you were. As much as you pretend you want to wipe it all clean and start again, you chose to live again one more time. You chose to leave all your power behind and be born as me, just so you could have one last chance to remember what it was like to love. And even now with so many things going wrong, even when that love isn't being returned even hurts to hold onto sometimes, you aren't ready to let that feeling go. I know because that's how I feel in my soul, in our soul, the one we share."

The sounds that the Prime forced from Noah's lips could not said to be words anymore. Hissing, gurgling, choking—and Noah knew why too. Zee Zee Balloo was trying to stop Noah from talking, stop him from thinking what he knew to be true. One word at a time, each a labor against the war inside him, Noah forced the demon to listen to what he had to say.

"You brought Borrowrath and Momslavi Lapis with you to become your family. You pretend to be above everyone and everything, but you wanted nothing more than to be part of it all. You don't need to tell me, because I know it's so. The great Prime, the last demon at the end of the time, not brave enough to face even one lifetime alone. But I'm not judging you, because I am you. I'm the same way, and it's okay. Because here we are alone together, realizing what that means at last. It's okay because I'm going to be the one to tear down the wall, and so long as we're together, neither of us ever has to be alone again."

Noah didn't run from the hurt that was pouring through the cracks in the wall. He let it fill his awareness, drowning out his senses and tossing him from across its waves. Noah didn't run because he knew the only reason it could hurt so bad was because the life he was defending mattered so much. All that pain flowing into him was his greatest strength, and as soon as he stopped trying to hide from it, he realized it was the weapon he could use to bring the rest of the wall down.

Assaulted from both sides, the barrier could not stand. In an explosion that felt like waking from a nightmare and falling asleep to escape one all at once, the whole wall shattered in an endless cascade of glittering shards. The Soul Eaters were pouring through into his mind, and they were him. Every horror and harm they'd ever done, every world they destroyed or gave birth to, all of it was intermingled with every life he'd ever lived and every love he'd ever felt. In that moment he was alive as much as he was dead, as in grief as he was in joy, knowing one could not exist without the other. Life and death were each other's shadows, neither better or worse, first or last, but each giving meaning to the other.

Noah opened his—their eyes—to the burning house around him.

The screams and the roar of battle flooded his ears once more. There were demons all about them now, and it seemed that Neera must have opened a full rift rather than merely compel his own summoning. They were fighting viciously against the spirits and the soulless humans who marched past the window in perfect unison. Anyone who saw this and only this would be tempted to believe The Matriarch was right—that it was the diversity of souls which doomed them to a life of unending struggle against one another.

Somewhere beyond the violence, Noah felt all the countless souls who desperately plunged along the narrow path of their existence. They were each alone in their heads, blind to the long string of lives which brought them to where they are. They were blind to tapestry of all the other souls which were woven to form the image of their world.

He thought of how easy it was to fall into the mistake of believing all one sees is all there is, and how easy it was to think that the world would be better off without him. It was hard to see the beauty in each individual point, each individual thread, each different color which clashed and tangled with those around it. If only they could pull back like he had done, they would see the full pattern which could not exist without the many individual colors and flavors that demons, spirits, and the living uniquely possessed.

The Prime's power flooded through Noah's body like fire through his veins. Mandy and Lewis rose to their feet on either side of him, ready to put an end to all the foolishness that brought them to this point. There was nothing left to fear, and nothing that could stop them now—

"Mandy, look out!" Samantha shouted, pointing at an empty patch of wall beside the front door.

Mandy turned to watch the flames licking their way through the broken windows. Samantha must have been referring to the danger on the other side of the wall though, because a moment later and a searing white light burst through the barrier to send burning shards of plaster and wood in all directions. It was The Matriarch, now wearing her fiery red dress as she forced her way through the devastation. Both her hands were clasped around a pulsing crystal heart—one of the Chainer Batteries which was the source of the powerful white beam. Her diamond eyes burned with an intense anger which was reflected in the contortions of her face.

"Neera is a distraction!" she bellowed over her shoulder. "The Primes are in here!" She lifted the crystal heart to shoulder level, pointing it at Noah and his family as though aiming a gun.

"Take cover!" Noah shouted.

He snatched Lewis from the floor and took several large bounds to the right before noticing that Mandy hadn't moved. She didn't so much as lift her arms or make the slightest effort to defend herself, and merely stood gawking at The Matriarch as the light swelled within the crystal. Had she lost her internal battle against Momslavi Lapis? Did she care that little about being alive?

"Let's see how well you oppose me when there are only two Primes left," The Matriarch snarled.

Noah safely deposited Lewis with the coven of witches who were all cowering in the corner of the room. He was headed back for Mandy now, but she still hadn't prepared in the least. In fact she was walking directly toward The Matriarch, as easy and open a target as could be desired. Noah could feel Zee Zee Balloo's unnatural speed pushing him forward, and if he could just reach her in time—

The light exploded from the Chainer Battery and poured into Mandy's chest. The intensity of the blast didn't dim in the least as it punctured straight through her body and tore out the other side. Noah's daughter crumbled to the ground without so much as a whimper. Noah froze in his tracks, staring at the mortal wound without comprehending what he saw. The union of the Primes was broken, but that seemed trivial next to the immensity of watching the life fade from his daughter's eyes. The battle was over before it had even begun.

"Who is next?" The Matriarch cackled. "Don't be shy, you'll all get your turn. I have plenty of bodies already and don't need to preserve yours."

"Snap out of it!" Samantha shouted. "Ignore Mandy—she's fine. You've got to fight back, Noah!"

"Fine?" Noah asked, rushing to kneel beside the empty shell where his daughter had been. "This is fine to you?!"

"There isn't a spirit coming out. There was no soul inside her body. The Matriarch had it the whole time." The unfamiliar voice was coming from Lewis. It sounded so alien to him, dark and strained as though it was resisting the urge to yell. The tone softened as he continued speaking though, and Noah was sure that both the demon and the boy had learned to coexist together. "Momslavi Lapis persists within The Matriarch's right eye."

"When? How?" Noah stumbled over his racing thoughts. How could he never have noticed that his daughter didn't have a soul? Was that why she had been so cold to him for so long? How long, exactly? "Since you were born," Noah said, thinking furiously out loud. "She changed when you were born. And I thought she didn't love me anymore…"

"What nonsense is this?" The Matriarch scoffed. "I think I would have noticed if I already had one of the Primes. I collected this Chainer soul when…" Her jaw went slack, alarm etching itself into the wrinkles around her eyes.

"When I was coming back to life," Lewis spoke in childlike voice that sounded more like his own. "I was the last of the three Primes to be reborn when I became entangled in your net along the way. That's when Mandy came to you and offered her own soul in exchange, if you would just let me live my life and be free."

The Matriarch's eyes narrowed. "She could talk to spirits. She was a Chainer. Of course I'd want her soul."

"She was more than a Chainer," Lewis said, striding toward the old woman who took a hesitant step back. "We both were so much more, but you were so intent upon your greed that you didn't even notice the Primes right beneath your nose."

Noah was advancing on The Matriarch now too. There was a subtle shadow beneath the diamond surface in The Matriarch's eye. That's where Mandy really was. The fear in the old woman's face was more apparent than ever as the realization fully dawned on her. If Noah and Lewis reached The Matriarch, then the three Prime demons really would be together at last.

The Matriarch turned her battery toward Lewis and the light began to swell within her battery once more. A flash of orange sparks burst from the diamond in her right eye and disrupted her though, causing the old woman to howl and clutch her face in pain.

"Don't come any closer. Stay away from me!" The Matriarch shrieked. "Theodore! Where are you Theodore? The Primes are in here!"

"Coming, my lady!" bellowed the reply.

The Matriarch was almost cornered with Noah and Lewis closing in on her fast. Theodore Oswald barged through the hole in the wall a moment later, his once pristine white suit now thickly soiled with streaks of blood and soot. A long, naked sword glistened in one hand with another Chainer Battery in his other. The frenzy of battle shone on his face, although some of the flush faded the moment he surveyed the scene.

"You don't mean these children, do you? The great Matriarch, cowering from one of her students and a baby who has barely learned to walk?"

"Kill them! Destroy their souls! Everything that threatens your rule—everything you hate burns within their breasts!" The Matriarch spat. More orange sparks were sizzling from her eye, seemingly driving her mad from the pain.

Theodore's eyes narrowed to slits as he leveled his sword against the advancing children. "They don't look like demons," he said, hesitating.

"Theodore, dear, remember me?" Samantha said. "I'm the one who called you here. I told you that you'd never remain head of the department if you didn't come, and here you are."

"Why are there so many children on my battlefield?" Theodore asked, more unsettled than ever.

"It doesn't matter. Kill them! Kill them!" The Matriarch shrieked.

Theodore Oswald looked about self-consciously, noticing his

soldiers outside watching him through the window. "Such a victory would not rally the department behind me. This is not the deed I wish to be known for."

"You can't scare people into supporting you forever," Samantha said. "The three Primes are together now, and they're going to put a stop to this war. The Matriarch needs your help because she can't win alone, and she won't be in charge of the Mortuary after this. If you aren't careful, you're going to have a whole generation of spirits learning about every soul you ever hurt, and every lie you ever told. You can't decide how the war will end, but you still have a chance right now to decide whether you want to be on the winning side or not.

"There are already humans and demons working together and prospering not far from here. The witches are going to keep summoning them, and you're going to make more enemies than friends if you keep attacking them. All the souls you bullied into not walking the Road from Death are going to resent you when they realize you stopped them for nothing. And most importantly of all, all the souls that The Matriarch trapped are going to be released. And they'll be free to decide for themselves whether they want the department to be run by an ally of The Matriarch who imprisoned them, or by the hero who finally stood up to her and set them free."

Theodore's sword had been slowly slipping toward the ground while Samantha spoke. He now lifted it once more, turning his narrowed eyes on The Matriarch. "She's the one who told me humans and demons could never get along. I'm not the one you should blame."

"Demons are bad enough," The Matriarch snarled, "but they're no worse than spirits who have betrayed me. I never planned for you to remain until the next election anyway, so now is as good a time as any to be rid of you."

The Matriarch lifted the pulsing crystal heart in her hands once more, this time aiming the light directly at Theodore. The Prime demon in her eye did not intervene in the same way as when it was protecting Noah and Lewis. There was nothing to stop the beam from lancing out, slicing through the air toward the startled minister. He half-raised his sword to defend himself, but he was far too slow to intercept the speeding light. It would take the power of a Prime demon to defend against such a blast, which is exactly what happened when Noah hurled himself in its path.

Lewis acted just as swiftly, snatching hold of one of Noah's hands and grasping The Matriarch by the ankle with the other. Light flowed freely between them, creating an impenetrable barrier which deflected The Matriarch's attack. Her beam froze in midair between them, and for a moment it seemed uncertain who the target of the energy would be. The Matriarch was straining with all her might, draining so much energy from the crystal heart that it beat at a frantic pace. It seemed she might be able to redirect the energy into Noah, but at the last instant the diamond in her right eye exploded outward to roll onto the ground.

The Matriarch scrambled onto her hands and knees after the diamond. The instant she stopped directing the energy, though, the blast turned back toward her. The light poured into her body, transforming her into an incandescent explosion. Noah saw the stark contrast as all her bones became visible beneath the skin, and watched as each one shattered simultaneously. By the time the light cleared, there was nothing left of The Matriarch except her diamond eye that never belonged to her at all.

"There isn't even a spirit left," Samantha said in wonder. "She must have spread herself so thin that there was nothing left inside."

"Why would you protect me? Are you a demon, or are you not?" Theodore asked. He was cowering on the ground, still shielding his eyes from where the brilliant light had been.

"Yes, I'm one of the Prime demons," Noah replied, offering a hand to help the man stand. "I didn't help you because I was a demon though, I helped you because you have a soul. Same as every spirit, every living being, and yes, every demon too. No war between souls must endure so long as no soul is at war with itself."

Their voices were drowned out by a tremendous howl outside. Noah rushed to the window to see the soulless ones collapsing to the ground where they stood. Without the Matriarch they were nothing more than corpses, ready and waiting to be refilled with their proper souls once more.

"I've made a terrible mistake," Theodore Oswald sighed, tumbling onto the ground as surely as the soulless had. "I wasn't trying to hurt anyone, I swear. I only wanted to protect my people. And now..."

"And now your job is more important than ever," Noah said, "now that you've realized that your people include everyone, even the ones who look nothing like you. Do you think you're still up for the job?"

A grim smile made its way onto the man's stern face. "If you're up to yours. Set the souls free, I will leave my fate in their hands."

THE THREE PRIME souls had found each other, and at last they remembered each other as they did themselves. No wall between worlds was a barrier to their power, and it was no hardship for them to pass through the Netherworld to the Road from Death. There the Soul Net had already begun to decay without The Matriarch's magic, and the soul stones were dropping from the air like ripe fruit falling from the tree. The Wojan was there to assist them in gathering all the souls. Samantha and the other witches were there to spread the word that it was only thanks to the demons that souls were able to pass back to life once more. Together they would be instrumental in summoning the demons from the nether and integrating them back among the living and the spirits where they belong.

From then on The Mortuary and all the other schools of the dead would not fail to teach how important demons were to the balance of life and death. The vacancy of headmaster for the Mortuary would now be filled with Professor Salice, whose keen understanding of demonology would ensure such prejudices would not be repeated again. No longer would it be considered profane for the spirits to be reborn as demons. Nor would it be looked down upon for demons to join the living, as Visoloth would be the first of many to do under the instruction of the Primes.

As for the Primes themselves, the spiritologists have a number of competing theories as to their ultimate fate. Some say that they have split again, with Lewis continuing his life as a human, Noah transforming into a demon, and the soul of Mandy persisting in the spirit world so that the balance would always be maintained. Those who knew them best prefer to think that they are together, their completed work allowing them to begin a new life with all these troubles left behind.

No matter how many lives makeup the journey of a soul, there is always a little something that is preserved from one to the other. Maybe it's an accent, maybe a recurring dream, maybe an inexplicable attraction. Maybe it's even a book, whose unlikely journey follows a soul, and as if by chance finds its way into their hands again and again. And like one life speaking to another, in the right hands such a book might remind someone of who they used to be, and ever so subtly, guide them into who they will become.

PUBLISHER'S NOTE

Please remember to
honestly rate the book on Amazon or Goodreads!

It's the best way to support me as an author and help new readers discover my work.

WHAT ARE YOU AFRAID OF?

Join the Haunted House Book Club
For more free books and stories.

TobiasWade.Com

ABOUT THE AUTHOR

Former neuroscience researcher, born again novelist. During my studies, it struck me as odd that I could learn so much about behavior without understanding the intricacies of human nature. I realized that I learned more about what it means to be human from reading stories than I ever had from my text books, and I was inspired to write.

I spent several years selling scripts in Los Angeles, but was ultimately frustrated with my lack of control over my projects. A general stubbornness and unwillingness to compromise my creative pursuits led me to starting my own publishing house to do things my own way.

I now work full time as a novelist and publisher with Haunted House Publishing.

Made in the USA
Coppell, TX
23 February 2020